Lili St. Germain is a *USA Today* best-selling author who writes books featuring vengeful anti-heroes and compelling villains. Her books have sold over a million copies worldwide

Aside from writing, her other loves in life include her gorgeous husband and two beautiful children, good coffee, travelling, binge-watching Tarantino movies, and reading spy thriller novels. She loves to read almost as much as she loves to write.

CORRUPTED KINGDOM

LILI st. GERMAIN

HarperCollins*Publishers*

HarperCollinsPublishers
Australia • Brazil • Canada • France • Germany • Holland • India
Italy • Japan • Mexico • New Zealand • Poland • Spain • Sweden
Switzerland • United Kingdom • United States of America

HarperCollins acknowledges the Traditional Custodians
of the land upon which we live and work, and pays respect
to Elders past and present.

First published on Gadigal Country in Australia in 2015
This edition published in 2023
by HarperCollins*Publishers* Australia Pty Limited
ABN 36 009 913 517
harpercollins.com.au

Cartel copyright © Lili St. Germain 2015
Kingpin copyright © Lili St. Germain 2016
Empire copyright © Lili St. Germain 2017
This collection *Corrupted Kingdom* copyright © Lili St. Germain 2023

The right of Lili St. Germain to be identified as the author of this work has been
asserted by her in accordance with the *Copyright Amendment(Moral Rights) Act 2000*.

This work is copyright. Apart from any use as permitted under the *Copyright Act 1968*,
no part may be reproduced, copied, scanned, stored in a retrieval system, recorded,
or transmitted, in any form or by any means, without the prior written permission
of the publisher.

A catalogue record for this book is available from the National Library of Australia.

ISBN 978 1 4607 6525 8 (paperback)
ISBN 978 1 4607 1709 7 (ebook)

Cover design by Michelle Zaiter, HarperCollins Design Studio
Cover images: Roses by Biel Morro/Unsplash; all other images by istockphoto.com.
Typesetting in Sabon LT Std by HarperCollins Design Studio
Printed and bound in Australia by McPherson's Printing Group

CORRUPTED KINGDOM

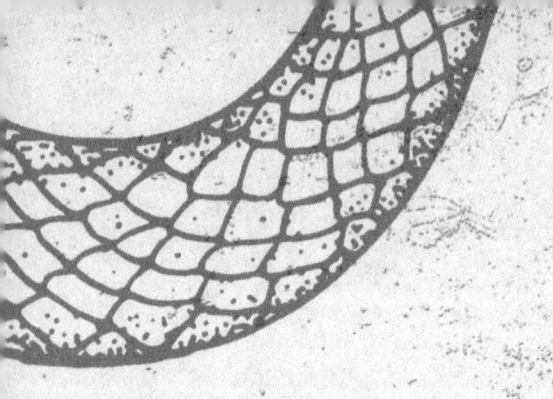

PART 1
CARTEL

Our fate lies in the hands of the things we love, and sometimes the things we love are the things that lead us to the destruction of ourselves.

R.M. DRAKE

PROLOGUE
MARIANA

Of all the things in life, love is the most confusing. The most all-consuming. The reason we breathe, the light in our darkness.

At sixteen, love devastated me, his perfect button nose and sweet-baby smell overwhelming as my father took him from my arms and into the night. At nineteen, love saved me, a dangerous man with a heart that was determined to own mine. At twenty-nine love almost freed me ... but in the end, love broke me.

I wish I could tell you that things ended differently — but I'd be lying. I don't know if he regrets what he did, or if he's happy, but it doesn't matter, really.

It doesn't change the fact that the man who loved me ended up being the same man who would destroy me.

CHAPTER ONE

EMILIO

BOGOTA, COLOMBIA, DECEMBER 1998

The fucker owed him money.

Emilio Ross paced across the verandah that flanked his brother's house. Beneath him, the city of Bogota sprawled herself out in a dazzling array of lights, a city peppered with skyscrapers and lush green mountains that rose up in the distance like a protective shroud.

It was beautiful, and he couldn't wait to fucking leave.

'How much?' Emilio asked, sucking on his cigar and letting the smoke leave his mouth with a humph.

Julian, his younger brother, uncrossed his legs and set his snifter of brandy down beside him. 'Thirty.'

Emilio's fists tightened around his own brandy balloon, a hairline crack appearing in the delicate glass. 'Thirty?'

'It was a large shipment, boss.'

Julian always called him boss when they spoke business.

Emilio stuck his cigar between his teeth and attempted to channel a sense of calm. He was the kingpin of the Il Sangue Cartel, the goddamn owner of the coke empire that ran from the depths of Colombia all the way across the gulf, its tendrils reaching into northern California and beyond.

He was Italian mafioso — *la famiglia* — and when he made up his mind, axes fell, and heads rolled. Whether the thugs and mobsters he hired lived or died meant nothing to a man like Emilio Ross.

But family — ah, yes, family was different. There was an unspoken rule between the cartels of South America.

Hands off the family. After all, *Il Sangue* was Italian for 'the blood', and blood was thicker than water in the cartel. It meant something. *Il Sangue è sacra. Famiglia è sacra*. Those were the words he lived by.

If you crossed the cartel, you got a bullet, simple as that. But your family, your wife and your kids, would go unharmed. At your funeral, a cartel lackey would deliver your wife a couple of hundred bucks to get by on, maybe more if you'd been a long-time employee, and you'd have taken your last breath knowing that at least your family would be okay after you were dead and buried.

But thirty grand worth of coke was a big fuck-up. A royally big fuck-up. Because the thirty grand it cost to produce, package and ship Colombia's finest white powder would turn into half a million dollars of pure profit by the time it hit the streets of Los Angeles and was divvied up among the small-time dealers and suppliers.

Five hundred thousand dollars in potential profit, and Marco Rodriguez had driven the goddamn truck right into the open arms of the American Drug Enforcement Administration. Emilio's coke was in lockdown in some government warehouse, the dealers of Los Angeles were screaming for more product to fill the void, and Emilio was down half a million big ones.

He cast Julian an irritated look. Julian stopped chewing on the ice cube in his mouth and let it sit on his tongue.

'Can we get into the DEA warehouse?' Emilio asked, already knowing the answer.

Julian shook his head, swallowing his ice. 'Nope.'

Emilio nodded in resignation. 'Then, you know what we need to do.'

'Pay Marco a visit?'

Even the mention of the fucker's name made Emilio want to smash his fists into the man until his eyeballs burst and his teeth shattered.

'Pay Marco a visit,' Emilio echoed his younger brother. 'And his family,' he added. 'He has children, no? A wife?'

He was going to teach this fucker a lesson. A big lesson. And then he was going to shoot him and let him bleed out as punishment.

'Three children,' Julian said warily. 'One wife.'

'Good,' Emilio said. 'Tonight, then. We'll pay them a little visit they won't soon forget.'

Julian looked troubled.

'You know what they say about extraordinary times?' Emilio mused, puffing on his cigar again. 'They call for extraordinary measures.'

'You want me to fuck the family up?' Julian asked.

'No,' Emilio replied, smiling so his lips stretched wide, baring his teeth. 'Leave that to me.'

CHAPTER TWO

MARIANA

BANG.

Este and I were watching fireworks in the clear night sky when the first shot rang out.

Gunshots weren't that uncommon in Villanueva, the town where I lived. Besides, it was almost impossible to hear a gunshot amid the chaos of the fireworks that marked *Día de las Velitas*, the Celebration of Little Lights that marked the beginning of the Christmas season.

Now, when I say we were watching the fireworks, what I mean is, he had me pinned against the wall of a back alley, my dress gathered around my hips as we made fireworks of our own.

Yeah. We were totally going to get caught at any moment, but damn, did that man make me want to do things I'd never do with anyone else. His lips on mine, the sweet taste of anise and rum mixing in our mouths as we moved in a steady rhythm. I moaned into his mouth as he did something with his hips that really hit the spot. A bed would have been a little more comfortable, but despite me being nineteen my father had forbidden me from bringing my boyfriend back to the house. My father hated my boyfriend.

It just made me love Este more.

BANG.

I cocked my head to the side for a moment, unsure of what I'd heard.

BANG. BANG.

My heart sank as I pushed Este away from me. I knew what gunshots sounded like, and somehow, this time, I knew the bullets carried my name on them. Este looked confused, but he could obviously see the terror on my face. Instead of protesting, he tucked himself back into his jeans and buttoned up, as I panted and pulled my black sundress down to cover my thighs.

'Baby,' I whispered urgently, 'someone is shooting close by, do you hear?' At nineteen, I shouldn't have known what gunshots sounded like, let alone been intimately acquainted with them, but I was no ordinary girl. I had been born into a life of terror and violence. Images of my father suddenly sprang forth in my mind, and my heart rate rose considerably. My father was a complicated man with a complicated life, and when I heard gunshots, it was usually because of something he had done, or something he was punishing someone else for doing.

Este ran a hand through his dark hair, curled at the ends from the humidity, as he bent to pick up the paper lantern at his feet. The candle inside flickered at the sudden movement before settling down again to a steady, even flame. I grabbed my own lantern from the ground beside me and stepped out from the darkness and relative privacy offered by a large air-conditioning unit, peering cautiously down the alleyway. The city street beyond was crowded with people focused on the bright sparks of colour that lit up the night sky.

Este pulled me closer and smiled tightly, his hazel eyes gleaming in the flickers of dim candlelight as he addressed me in Spanish. '*No te preocupes, amor. Probablemente es solo un idiota disparando al cielo.*' Don't worry, my love. It's probably just some idiot shooting into the sky.

So long as none of the bullets rain down on us, I silently prayed.

'Este!' I chastised. 'In English! Remember?'

Rolling his eyes, his easy smile soothed me, and the tension was momentarily broken. 'Baby, you don't finish university for another three years. We have plenty of time to practise the American language.' He said each word in English slowly and deliberately, the words rolling off the edge of his bowed lips. Anyone could tell that it wasn't his native tongue. Esteban hadn't had the privilege of attending an American school like I had. Esteban hadn't had the privilege of attending any school once he turned fifteen and had to support his family by going to work. And so, his English was faltering and his Colombian accent thick; unlike me, whose accent was merely a lilt, an intonation that I could turn off completely if required.

I shook my head defiantly. 'We're going to get there sooner,' I said. 'You're going to get this scholarship, you'll see.' In my head I indulged in my fantasy briefly. I saw the beach, and a pier, and felt sand beneath my feet. I could almost taste the freedom that America offered people like me. Away from the suspicious eyes and the brutal reach of the ruthless cartels, and the meddling of my troubled father.

BANG. BANG. BANG.

My gaze cut to Este's, and any casual hope was extinguished.

BANG. BANG. BANG. BANG.

I bristled, looking over my shoulder. The shots were getting louder.

Closer.

'We should go,' Este said slowly, his eyes locked onto the street.

Although alarmed, I'd been holding onto the hope that the loud pops were just drunk people shooting at nothing.

When the screaming started, my heart sank. Suddenly, I couldn't breathe properly.

A trio of heavily armed men burst through the crowd at the open end of the alley and I almost fell over. They looked both fierce and bored, if that were possible. Dressed entirely in black, shirts and heavy-duty cargo pants, they held impressive-looking guns. None of the men looked Colombian. In fact, I would have guessed European, with their olive colouring. More specifically, I would have guessed Italian, because somewhere in my brain the puzzle pieces were snapping together.

My knees went weak for a moment; I choked on a breath.

I recognised them.

'We have to get out of here,' I said, turning and tugging on Este's wrist. A shot rang out, much too close to me this time, and suddenly Esteban's weight was dragging me down, down, down to the ground. I struggled to see what was going on in the darkness. Este's lantern had fallen, the flame snuffed out, and I held up my own paper lantern to see. I choked as I watched a red stain blossoming on his chest, swiftly soaking through his bright blue t-shirt.

'Este!' I screamed, on my knees beside him. I took my hands and pressed them to his chest, trying to stem the flow of blood that rose and bubbled over his sides, gushing onto the slick cobblestones below us.

The shot had probably killed him instantly. That was the rational part of my mind, making an observation, and I pushed it away, horrified. No. He wasn't dead. He couldn't be dead!

Numbness swept through my chest. His glazed eyes remained open and unseeing, and an odd pallor swallowed up any colour from his bronze skin. Fuck. What could I do? How could I fix him?

Anger surged through me as I whirled around to face the bastard who had planted a bullet in the man I'd called my lover for four years. The one.

They'd killed him.

I fought a violent urge to throw up.

We were so close to getting out of this life, away from Colombia, away from my father. So fucking close.

Not close enough.

Shaking, I rose to my feet and balled my hands into fists. 'You shot him!' I screamed, my throat aching from the sudden exertion. My rage gave me false bravado as I rattled off a string of obscenities, some in Spanish and some in English, at the three men. They remained largely impassive as they aimed their guns at my chest.

This couldn't be happening. I locked eyes with the middle shooter and glowered up at him.

'Come on, tough guy!' I yelled, pressing my chest against the barrel of his assault rifle. 'You gonna shoot me, too? Go ahead, pull that fucking trigger, *cholo*. What the hell are you waiting for?'

For a moment I thought he might, until he raised the butt of his rifle and brought it down onto my skull with a loud crack. Stars swam in my vision and I crumpled to the floor like a rag doll.

Everything faded around me in slow motion as I melted, unwillingly, into an abyss that was made up only of darkness and agonising pain.

They'd killed him.

And nothing would ever be the same again.

CHAPTER THREE
EMILIO

He was lighting a cigarette when the unconscious girl landed on the seat next to him with a thud.

'Sorry, boss,' Carlos called as her head flopped onto Emilio's shoulder.

Emilio glared at Carlos and shoved Marco's older daughter off him. Her forehead hit the window opposite his with a loud thunk before she settled in the corner between the window and back seat.

He puffed on his cigar as he surveyed her. She was pretty enough. Long, coffee-coloured hair fell across her face, partially shielding it from his view. He already knew what colour her closed eyes were. The twin irises were the exact hue of cerulean blue as the ocean beside his childhood house in Italy. It was the single feature that had stood out to him when he first met her as a small girl, back when Marco was a lot more capable and a lot less drunk.

Her hands were bound in front of her with rope, and the calm void of unconsciousness softened her features, making her look younger than he knew she was.

Nineteen. And she wasn't going to see her twentieth birthday.

He reached over impulsively, moving the hair off her face with the back of his hand. He narrowed his eyes, taking her in. Full lips. That bronze skin the Colombian girls wore so well. She wasn't his type, but he had to admit to himself that she was pretty.

He made his left hand into the shape of a gun and pressed it against her temple. Taking a drag of his cigarette, he blew a cloud of smoke in her face as he simulated blowing her brains out with a tip of his wrist.

It was almost a shame he was going to ruin that pretty face with a bullet.

CHAPTER FOUR
MARIANA

When I awoke, red, crushing pain greeted me. I squeezed my eyes shut again, desperate to get back to that place where the darkness sat in my limbs, cool and comforting. But there was no peace to be found.

I was moving. Rattling around in the back seat of what looked to be an expensive car, travelling at some speed down a bumpy road. My hands were bound in front of me with thick rope that looked like it belonged on a boat or wharf, not on a girl's wrists.

I could tell the car was expensive even before I opened my eyes. The smell of artificial air freshener invaded my nose as I felt soft, supple leather at my back and underneath my thighs.

People like me didn't travel in cars with leather seats, unless they were cracked and rough, the kind of frayed, hard leather that dug into your skin and made you wish you could afford to buy a car-seat cover to save your back and ass.

I sat up, just in time to glimpse a large apartment block the locals referred to as *La Casucha Hacienda* passing by the window. The Slum Estate spanned several blocks of crumbling high-rise apartments joined by courtyards, and littered with used syringes, broken glass, and local thugs who liked to hurl abuse at anyone who dared walk past. It was a place most didn't venture near, but when your family was a part of the cartel, you ended up knowing half the people who lived in *La Cas* on a first-name basis. My heart rose and then crashed as I recognised the familiar route.

They were taking me home.

I'd been upright maybe three seconds before a hand closed around my loose ponytail and dragged me down, the side of my face coming to rest in a man's lap. What felt like expensive material brushed my face and I smelled tobacco and peppermint among the designer fabric. Whatever thick weave these pants were made of didn't feel like the scratchy, cheap suits my father wore. And my father didn't even use aftershave — he probably just slapped straight tequila on his cheeks after he shaved.

Terrified, and not expecting the sudden movement, I fought as hard as I could — which wasn't very hard with the way I was positioned and my hands useless in front of me. Still, I gave it my best, turning my head and sinking my teeth into the leg of whoever was holding my head painfully close to their crotch. I gagged on the taste of dry cotton as fingernails dug into the back of my neck.

'Fuck!' the man roared, wrenching me back from his leg. A hand pushed my face forcefully away, so that I landed on the other side of the back seat, the back of my head slamming into the window.

I brought the back of my hand up to my face and tried to wipe some of the cotton lint out of my mouth. As I did, I glanced over at the man who would become my damnation.

I knew straight away who I was with, and the reality of my hopelessness began to sink in to my gut, hot and prickling. Emilio Ross, infamous kingpin of South America's most powerful drug cartel, the Il Sangue Cartel, and my father's long-time employer. With his dark eyes and pointed European nose, he reminded me of a wolf. *And I was the goddamn lamb.* Well, this lamb was going to put up a fight, even if it killed me.

'Guess I won't be putting my dick in your mouth without a gun to your head,' he observed in English, goading me. He was probably in his late fifties, and my stomach turned at the thought of anything of his anywhere near my mouth. His eyes were dark brown with tiny flecks of amber in them, amber that reminded me of fire. *Asshole.*

'Sounds like fun,' I responded in Spanish, sarcasm so thick it almost dripped from my lips. 'I wonder if you can pull the trigger before I bite your dick off?'

My mama always said it would be my mouth that got me into trouble. And my mama was always right.

The fire-eyed man laughed.

'It's been a long time, Mariana,' Emilio Ross said casually, his voice deep and loud. 'I haven't seen you since you were a small girl.'

I still remembered the last time we'd spoken. I couldn't have been more than eight, and he was visiting my father. I had scurried away to my room after being forced by my father to say hello. The fact that Emilio remembered the fleeting visit troubled me greatly.

'Not long enough, obviously,' I said to him, still speaking in Spanish.

He drew his brows together, smiling. I *amused* him. 'Do you speak English, *puta?*'

'I speak Fuck You,' I replied, in perfect English.

He chuckled. 'You're not like your father,' he said, his gaze moving from my eyes lower, lingering on my lips and breasts before flicking back to my face. A smirk grew on his mouth like a jagged crack in his face.

'No,' I replied flatly, still in English. 'I'm not.' After a year at an American boarding school and two more in a stateside university, English came to me just as quickly as my native Spanish tongue.

'You must know that your father owes me a lot of money, *puta?*' There he was, calling me a bitch again. I suspected it was because he only knew a few Spanish swear words.

'Oh, yeah?' My nerves started to rattle and fray, and my mind along with them. *Papa and his stupid, selfish gambling.*

I was pretty smart, good with numbers, and I'd been doing some creative accounting with my father's finances for years, but there was no denying that he owed a lot of people a lot of money.

My father's casual attitude towards the entire situation made my blood boil. It was fine to risk your life when you were single and unencumbered, but he had a wife and three children to think about. It didn't seem to mean anything to him, though. He kept gambling and taking money from loan sharks until there was nothing left to lose. When he stopped being able to pay the bookmakers back, things had gotten really ugly.

They had started on his fingers. Three months ago, he lost an index finger, and two months ago, a middle finger. It was only a matter of time before they collected the rest. That's when my brother, Pablo, had been shot in the thigh. Then my younger sister had been followed home by men we knew, men who had grown tired of issuing threats and decided to collect their outstanding debts in the form of my sister's frightened pleadings. They didn't rape her, but the threat was clear — they could, and they *would*, if my father didn't front up the cash he owed. That was three weeks ago, and after my mother called me in hysterics I had left the relative safety of my stateside university to come home. To try to help my father claw back some control before we were all killed and hung off a freeway overpass as a reminder never to cross the cartel. Since I'd come home I'd been trying desperately to funnel some funds through accounts I had purposely hidden from my father for this eventuality, and pay off the most bloodthirsty of the people he owed.

Evidently, I was too late. Emilio Ross could tear us all apart if he wanted to.

I slumped in my seat, all the fight fleeing my body. I stared straight ahead at the back of the black leather seat in front of me, and set my jaw squarely.

'You're surprised?' Emilio asked.

I shook my head from side to side; I was not surprised. I battled to keep the anger from my face, the disgust, but failed. Rage burned in my blood, but not for the man who sat beside me. No, the rage inside me was reserved exclusively for my father. The man who was meant to protect me, the man who had promised to keep me safe when I was a little girl. The man who drank more than he should and laid his fists into me, into all of us, when it got too much. They say every little girl wants to marry her father, but I wanted mine to vanish.

He was an idiot. A selfish fucking fool. And now I was going to pay for his sins.

'Are you going to kill me?' I asked calmly, as if we were talking about who had won the soccer game on the weekend.

He replied just as casually.

'Yes, of course.' He frowned. 'It's nothing personal against you, *cholita*.' Tough girl, he had called me. I bit my lip and nodded, the sadness in my chest locked tightly away. I refused to show weakness in front of anyone, least of all the man who was probably about to end my existence.

Esteban. His face floated into my mind and I clamped down the thought. Flecks of his blood still clung to my bare knees. It didn't matter now; none of it mattered.

'How much does he owe you?' I blurted out. 'Are you sure he can't work the debt off?'

Emilio's eyebrows rose, and I heard the driver cough awkwardly up front. I wondered what kind of punishment I'd earned for daring to question the notorious drug lord.

'Tell me,' Emilio asked slowly. Taunting me. 'What he can do for me that will be worth five hundred thousand dollars.'

Oh.

I returned my attention to the back of the headrest in front of me.

'It's a lot of pesos, *cholita*,' Emilio said, reaching his hand over to squeeze mine. His sympathy was a ruse, nothing more than a macabre gesture to invoke desperation.

'No shit,' I muttered, the feel of his oily palm on my hand was nauseating. 'It's a lot of pesos.'

I looked down at my bound hands, startled as they shook violently. It wasn't fear; a lifetime of being a drug trafficker's daughter had numbed me to many terrors, real and imagined.

It was anger.

I was well-acquainted with anger. My mother called me feisty. My father preferred terms like 'ungrateful' and 'whore'. I figured that he was just pissed that when he drank too much and laid his fists into me, I didn't freeze like the rest of them. I fought back. I gave as good as I got, and I'd put my heavily drunk father on his ass more times than I wanted to remember. Yes, I was angry. I carried my anger with me beneath my skin, and I had for many years.

Emilio didn't know that. He probably thought I was just scared.

Anger, though, would be much more useful if I were to try and overpower him, to somehow catch him off guard.

'Where are we going?' I asked softly, trying to appear more scared and defenceless than I actually was. I was petite, five foot two, and I had nothing to fight with except my teeth and a pair of bound hands.

'Home,' Emilio answered, apparently not annoyed by my direct questioning. It surprised me that he was so chatty, to the point of being flippant, when he was about to slaughter me and my entire family.

'Maybe I could —'

Emilio held his palm up. 'No. There is nothing you can do, *cholita*. I will kill your father slowly, but I promise you, the rest of your family will die quick and painless. I have no feud with you.'

I nodded, hardly believing my ears. What was I supposed to say? *Thanks for killing me quickly? Thanks for not raping me in front of my father? Thanks for not disembowelling me while my mother cries on the sidelines?*

A glint of silver at the driver's hip caught my eye as we passed under a bright series of streetlights and I blinked, trying to decide what it was.

Yes. It was a pistol, silver and sleek. My hands were tied in front of me, and if I could just distract Emilio long enough to grab the gun, I could shoot them both and hope that the car didn't crash too violently.

It was worth the risk. We had just made a sharp turn into the road that marked the small town I lived in, and we were less than ten minutes from my house.

Less than ten minutes from death.

But Emilio was shrewd, and as I glanced sidelong at him, I could see that he had already anticipated my plan.

'Don't,' he said, shaking his head. 'I can make your death very painful, *cholita*. I can take that very gun and rape your mother with it. *While you watch*. Would you like that?'

Damn it! He could hurt my father if he wanted to and I'd say the bastard deserved it, but my mother? No. I would not let my mother suffer for me.

'No,' I replied sadly, deflated. 'I would not.'

'Well then,' Emilio said. 'Let's just get there in one piece, shall we? Who knows what could happen once we get there. Maybe your father has finally won the lottery.' He laughed, unfolding a newspaper and turning to the business section.

The seconds dragged on painfully as terror bloomed thick and fierce in my chest. It curled around my heart like vine tendrils, squeezing until I thought I was having a heart attack.

Focus. Get him to feel sorry for you. Do something! The voice inside my head screamed at me to take some kind of action. Get him onside. What did men like Emilio Ross want as currency?

Money, of course. I had none of that. Drugs? I didn't have any of those, either.

Sex?

I shuddered inwardly at the thought of offering my body to the man who was about to execute my entire family. I wasn't sexually inhibited — I'd started experimenting when I was way too young and now that I was back home, Este and I had been pretty adventurous in the bedroom. And the car. And back up against an alley wall before the fireworks only a few hours before.

Este. I pictured the way his eyes had blanked out after he was shot. How he was there with me one moment, and dead on the ground the very next, leaving me alone and adrift in this madness.

It made me want to die with him. But I wasn't dead. I was here, with this horrid man, and I needed to find a way to survive his wrath before he reached over and snapped my neck.

Yeah. He looked entirely capable of that.

I glanced down at his lap and reached out my bound hands tentatively, licking my lips. 'Surely there's some way I can change your mind. I could —'

He just glared at me, a scathing stare that made me wither inside. He didn't even need to say no.

I averted my eyes and settled back into the leather seat, donning my resisting-bitch face. I might've been terrified inside, but I'd be damned if I would show him.

'You bitches are all the same,' he said stonily. 'You think you've got a golden pussy, *cholita*? You think I don't have access to pretty Colombian *chocho*?' He grinned. 'You think if I wanted *yours*, that I'd wait for you to offer? No. If I wanted to fuck you, you'd be on your back screaming my name. If I wanted you to suck my dick? You'd be choking on it right now. If I wanted to kill you in this car? You'd be dead already.'

I stopped myself from reeling off a snappy comeback.

And his last comment made me wonder. How many people *had* he killed? How much blood was on his hands?

As I wiped my own bloody palms on my dress again, I decided I didn't really want to know.

The unsealed road closer to my family's home was corrugated and rough, hundreds of small stones flicking out and flying back at the expensive car, creating a constant metallic dinging noise. Good. I hoped it scraped the paint off the car and made it look like shit.

Ten minutes could have been ten years, the way it was dragging on. My palms were sweaty and I continued to rub them nervously on my black sundress.

'You're a long way from Italy,' I said finally, my curiosity getting the better of me. 'Colombia? Really?'

He chuckled, returning to his newspaper. 'I like the humidity.'

'I bet it helps the coca plants grow nice and tall,' I replied, suddenly irritated at his casual manner.

'Yes,' he answered slowly, not moving his eyes from the newspaper. 'The coca plants that paid for your private schooling, *cholita*. The coca plants your father gambled with. *My* coca plants, *cholita*.'

I opened my mouth to talk again.

'Stop,' he said. 'Stop talking. I'm sick of listening to your voice.'

I closed my mouth and looked outside. We were pulling into my driveway.

Arriving at my death.

CHAPTER FIVE

MARIANA

A black stretch Mercedes pulled in behind us, reminding me of a funeral heass, and I watched nervously as the three men from the shooting climbed out and made their way over to the car we were in. One of the men who had shot Esteban approached my door, and I nervously twisted the black onyx ring that wrapped around my middle finger. *This can't end well*. I thought of fighting for a brief moment, until he jammed the muzzle of a revolver under my chin and pulled me from the car.

'Please,' I implored Emilio. I hated begging. I'd begged for only one thing in my life, and it hadn't made a damn lick of difference to the way things turned out. In my eyes, begging was for the weak. But my primitive survival instincts were kicking me in the ribs like painful steel-capped boots. I didn't want to be executed on my knees and dumped into a hole in the dirt.

I didn't want to die, and so I begged.

Emilio just smiled. His canine teeth showed when his lips drew back, making him look like he was going to devour me.

Maybe he was.

The man who had wrenched me from the car shoved me in front of him. 'Walk,' he said gruffly, in Spanish.

I fought to retain my balance, skittering up the steps to my front door. I didn't want to fall in front of these men. I was already humiliated enough, and falling would only make me an easy target for their boots.

I stared up at the house I had grown up in. Maybe I was looking at it for the last time. *Oh, Jesus. This is happening. They're actually going to kill us.*

The house was nothing special, a limestone-rendered villa that blended into the hill just like the rest of the houses that surrounded it. A sea of middle-class families, a little better off than those in the slums, but not by much. With the money my father had made over the years in trading powders and people, he could have purchased a house on millionaire's row by now; had it not been for his crushing compulsion to gamble it all away every night.

If he had been smarter with his money — if he had done what I had told him years ago — he'd be able to pay off his stupid debt to this deplorable cartel kingpin, and my family wouldn't have to die.

On the crumbling mosaic-tiled steps that my mother had always nagged my father to repair, I made a vow to myself. I vowed that before my father got his bullet between the eyes, I was going to make him understand just how stupid and reckless he had been with our lives.

Seconds later, I was being pushed into the house. The house was like a cool balm after the hot summer night outside. I glanced down at the orange tiles that lined the floor and remembered how, as children, we would all lay on them on the hottest days, our bare bellies sucking every iota of coolness from their porous depths.

And now our blood would flood those porous tiles, staining them forever.

'Keep going,' the man behind me muttered, shoving the barrel of his pistol deeper into my neck. I winced at the pain, walking a little faster lest his trigger finger get itchy.

I rounded the hallway and saw my mother sitting slumped at the dining table, sobbing as she clutched my sister to her side. Karina was only ten months younger than me, and so two months of each year we were the same age. We had always been a fiery duo, two sides of the same coin in a constant struggle to be the one in charge. We fought more than we ever got along, but I loved her deeply. And seeing the panic in her glazed eyes as she tried to comfort my mother broke my goddamn heart. A man I hadn't seen before stood behind them, looking bored, clad in black military fatigues and aiming a Beretta sub-machine gun at my sister's head.

'Ana,' my mother gasped when she glimpsed me. She pushed on her heels, obviously intending to stand and rush to me, but large hands dug into her shoulders and thrust her back down into her seat.

I choked on everything I wanted to say right then, but couldn't.

Emilio appeared in front of me, blocking the view of my mother and sister.

'Take her in there with the boys,' he instructed, and terror gripped me as I wondered which boys I was being taken to. I stayed rooted to the spot despite the guy behind me pushing between my shoulder blades with the tip of his gun. I wasn't about to make it any easier for them to take me to boys who would pin me down and hurt me.

Emilio smiled, a fake gold tooth catching the light from the old brass chandelier that hung above the dining table. '*Cholita*,' he mocked, smiling at me. 'Don't you want to say goodbye to your father?'

Oh. Those boys. My father and brother.

I shivered despite the hot Villanueva night, refusing to acknowledge his question, but following him into the kitchen. My heart sank even lower as I saw my brother and father kneeling side by side in front of the refrigerator, a guy in front of them also holding a Beretta sub-machine gun. My brother's face was cut up and covered in his own blood, and he had thick packing tape stuck over his mouth. I guessed by the way he swayed unsteadily that he'd put up a fight. And lost.

Another guy stood in the corner, slightly removed, wearing a pressed grey suit and studying his fingernails. My skin prickled as I turned my attention back to the thug who had his gun casually pointed at the male half of my family, as if it were just another day at the office. I was used to seeing AKs slung over the shoulders of mercenaries and guards, not these sub-machine guns.

Still, it made sense. Emilio was Italian, mafioso, and obviously proud of it.

I tore my attention away from the gun and back to my father and brother. Pablo was a year older than me, and we'd always been close. He had always been less fiery than my sister and me, much more mellow, and his laidback temperament meant that we got along most of the time.

'Papa?' I choked. Revulsion and despair engulfed me as I looked upon the man who had raised me. Physically, he was everything Emilio Ross was not — balding, overweight, a sheen of sweat coating his brow as he knelt in one of the cheap suits he wore like a uniform. He'd been on his way out, judging by his slicked-back hair and the fact he was still wearing a suit this late at night.

Emilio's men had probably arrived just as he was getting antsy and about to go out and spend whatever cash he had on a losing bet. His biggest weakness was cards, poker, more specifically, but he'd been known to bet on anything and everything. He almost never won any money, and if he did, he just lost it all again. The house always won. *Our* house always lost.

Emilio nodded at the guard in front of my father and brother and the guy responded without missing a beat, aiming his Beretta expertly between my father's eyes.

'Wait!' I cried, and the thug flicked me a look of derision before returning his attention to my father. I watched in horror as he applied a few pounds of pressure to the trigger, millimetres away from letting the clip loose into my papa's head.

'Emilio,' my father said nervously, pressing his meaty palms together in a desperate prayer, 'please believe me when I tell you I was ambushed by those motherfuckers. They were tipped off!'

I sucked in a breath, watching Emilio as he stared my father down. 'You lost us a lot of money, Marco. A *lot* of money. And you were *drunk*. You understand?'

'I know,' my father blubbered, still holding his hands together in prayer. I doubted that Emilio Ross was going to take pity on him because he was begging. 'I swear, Emilio, I swear I will repay you. Everything of mine is yours. Take my house, take it all.'

Emilio's mouth turned down at the edges as if he'd just sipped sour milk. He glanced around at the peeling wallpaper, the dented fridge, and then, he looked at me.

'I'll take her,' he said, his eyes lighting up as he pointed at me.

My stomach dropped. *He'll do what?*

My father's eyes grew wide. 'No, please. Anything, Emilio, but not my family. Please, sir, not my family.'

Sadness washed over me as I listened to my father beg for my life. I might have been mad at him, and he might have been a shitty father, but he didn't deserve to die on his knees, execution style. It would be like ripping the last piece of his dignity away and grinding it into the dirt he'd be buried in. But it seemed those were his only two options — die in the dirt, or let Emilio take me away and do God only knew what with me.

'Then I kill you all now,' Emilio said, nodding at the guy with his gun to my father's head.

'Wait!' I demanded shrilly, reaching out and closing my bound hands around Emilio's arm. 'Take me. I'll do whatever you want. Just please don't kill them.' The words tasted like ash in my mouth as I observed the look in this man's eyes. Soulless. *He was enjoying this.*

'Your father has disrespected me greatly,' Emilio said, shaking my hand off like it was a dead cockroach. 'Whether I take you or not, *cholita*, he must pay the price for his mistakes.'

'Please,' I begged. 'Please just take me and let them go.' My heart leapt as a spark of *something* appeared in Emilio's eyes and he raised his hand to the guard, who lowered his gun slightly and took his finger from the trigger.

'You could kill him,' I pressed on. 'He probably deserves it, for what he's done. But wouldn't it be so much better to let him live? For him to know, every day for the rest of his life, that his transgressions were paid for with the life of his daughter? For him to suffer, knowing it was all his fault?'

I was angry, but I could not watch my father — my whole family — be executed in front of me.

A small glimmer of hope wrapped itself around my chest and contracted painfully; Emilio was listening.

'Wouldn't it be more satisfying,' I continued, 'to destroy him completely, instead of just putting a bullet in his head? Isn't that too kind a retaliation? Your cartel is named Il Sangue. What is more important to any man than blood, the blood of his family?'

Emilio's lip curled.

'If it doesn't work out, you can still kill us all,' I pleaded. '*Please.* My mother and my brother and sister don't deserve to die because of my father's mistakes.'

'No, baby,' my father said urgently. 'Better for them to kill me than put their hands on you. You don't deserve that.'

I narrowed my eyes as I took in his stricken expression, softened by booze. I could tell he was struggling to keep up with things since he was half drunk, and that realisation lit my veins on fire as anger burst inside my chest. 'That's not an option,' I snapped. 'They either kill us all,' I flicked my gaze to Emilio, 'or this man is smart enough to realise how much more money he could make from me.' I swallowed the last of my lingering fear and stood straighter.

'I'll clean your house, I'll smuggle your drugs, I'll suck your dick, I'll do your books. I'll fuck your sons and I'll lick your boots if that's what it takes. Just *please*,' there was that horrible word again, 'please don't kill them.'

'Mariana!' my father yelled. 'Stop this talk!'

Emilio frowned, completely ignoring my father. 'I prefer blondes.'

I fought the urge to roll my eyes as I tried not to imagine just *what* this dirty old man preferred doing with blondes.

'For you,' I said sweetly, 'I'd wear a wig.'

That made him chuckle. 'I like this one,' he said to my father, jerking his thumb towards me.

'Your girl is a real *cholita*. Wonder how tough she'll be when my boys take turns fucking her in her fleshy Colombian ass.'

My father lunged at him, but didn't get very far, the guard smacking the bridge of his nose with the barrel of the gun.

'Well, this has certainly been an interesting turn of events. *Cholita*, I admire your loyalty to your family. It is something your father clearly lacks.' He glared at my father. 'So, although your life will never recompense me for the street value of my cocaine, it will more than cover the production cost. I can recoup my initial loss and make an example of you at the same time, Marco.'

The wolf looked positively excited.

'I told you!' my father yelled. 'I have thirty thousand American dollars for you! I'll wipe my debt clean and kill those DEA fuckers who interrupted the transfer!'

My heart sank. Thirty thousand dollars. A little under four hundred thousand pesos. It was nothing. It was *everything*. It was what I was worth in this cruel world.

Emilio tutted, waving his long, bony finger in the air in front of my father's face. 'Thirty thousand was the production cost. Do you know how much money you've lost me? That was half a million big ones on the streets, *bandito*. Half. A. Million. *Dollars*.'

He raised his hand in a fist, smashing it down into my father's nose. Another girl might cry out, struggle to get to her father, maybe mop the blood from his face and kiss his temple.

But I was not that girl. I was a girl with a rage inside me. Este. *Oh, God*. I clutched at the small crucifix that hung around my neck and said a silent prayer for Esteban's soul.

I pushed down the urge to cry. My mother's muffled sobs reached me from the next room as I drew a solemn, burning breath into my lungs and tried to stop the room from spinning.

'You are giving yourself to me, yes?' Emilio asked, clenching and unclenching the fist he'd just hurtled into my father's face.

I nodded. *Oh, fuck. What am I doing?*

'Words, *cholita*. A nod means nothing in my world.'

'Yes,' I said defiantly, head high, chin stuck out stubbornly.

'For how long?' He was testing me.

The breath hitched in my throat. 'For as long as you spare my family.'

He nodded, and began to pace in the several feet of bare floor that separated my father and me.

'And you submit to do anything I tell you?'

This time it was harder. 'Yes ... Wait,' I added falteringly. *Oh, God*. 'Do you promise not to kill me?'

It was a silly question to ask a man who didn't deal in promises but in bloodshed and human lives, but I had to ask anyway. I couldn't bear the thought of offering up my life, only for it to be taken away at his hand. I didn't want to hope for nothing.

Emilio rubbed his chin thoughtfully. 'I can promise you that if you obey me at all times, you won't die by my hand,' he said. 'But I can't promise you that you won't beg me to kill you anyway.'

His words cut to my very core, and that was precisely the effect he had been aiming for.

I bit my lip, then cursed myself for showing a reaction. Emilio waited patiently, his eyes only for me as my father bled before us.

'What'll it be, *cholita*?' he asked me. 'There's no shame in changing your mind. A bullet would be much less painful.'

'I am yours,' I conceded finally, my voice quiet but firm. 'Do with me what you will.'

Just then, a pathetically inadequate digital rendition of Mozart rose, buzzing, from somewhere on Emilio's person, and I frowned in confusion. He reached a hand into his suit jacket and withdrew a cellphone. '*Pronto*,' he answered in Italian, and before he had finished saying the word, a loud voice started screeching on the other end.

Emilio placed his hand over the receiver and gestured to the guy in the suit, the one who'd been admiring his own fingernails as we spoke of life and death, the one who I'd forgotten was even there.

He was actually going to answer a call while we were in the middle of talking about my *life*. Emilio didn't even look at me, just strode into the next room, speaking a steady stream of Italian that I couldn't decipher.

The man in the corner spoke up. The Suit, I decided to call him. I looked at him properly now. He was tall and wiry, with intense sapphire-coloured eyes, a mop of shaggy brown hair and an imposing stature. In another context he might have been attractive; but there was something in his eyes that troubled me. I watched them closely and noticed they never stayed still. Every tiny mood change and thought was expressed through those crazy ice-blue eyes, the subtle shifts in his neck muscles, and the way his long fingers fidgeted with his middle suit button.

Buttoned. Unbuttoned. Buttoned. Unbuttoned. The guy couldn't stay still, and when I heard him sniff again, I guessed why.

He'd been sampling the goods.

'If he let it go to voicemail every time he got a call in the middle of shooting someone,' the Suit said, 'well, he'd have a lot of fucking voicemails.' He tilted his head as he spoke, just adding to the psychotic vibe he was giving off. His accent was distinctly American.

I threw him a disgusted look before returning my gaze to my father.

I'm sorry, he mouthed, and I fought the urge to roll my eyes. It was a bit late for sorry, and he just looked pathetic trying to apologise while he was on his knees at gunpoint. I shook my head minutely and stared at the ceiling instead, making sure to keep the Suit in my peripheral vision at all times. No way was I turning my back on that crazy-looking bastard.

Emilio returned to the room, tucking his cellphone into his suit as he walked with purpose. 'Time to go,' he barked.

'Can I at least pack some things?' I asked, my brain screaming at me to stall what was happening. *What the goddamn was happening?* Este was probably still lying dead in the alleyway, and my entire life was disintegrating in front of my very eyes.

And the worst part was, I wasn't even surprised. I'd been waiting for this moment since the day I found out what my father really did.

Emilio almost laughed. 'This isn't a holiday, *bambina*. You are not a person any longer, do you understand? You just became a piece of property. *My property.*'

Panic bubbled within me. 'Your property is going to be cold at night without her coat,' I said stubbornly. 'Please —'

'No,' Emilio said. 'Don't make me shoot you all, *cholita*. You *will* obey me.'

My head was spinning, and for a moment my vision blurred.

'Can I at least say goodbye?'

'No.' He snapped his fingers, gesturing to me, and the Suit pushed off from the wall he was leaning against, approaching me. *No!*

Out of the corner of my eye I saw the Suit smile. It was so small I barely caught it at all, but it was there. My hands began to shake.

'Enjoying the show?' I shot, before I could stop myself.

He laughed, feigning amusement, but the tightly bunched muscles in his neck told a different story. 'You're riding with me on the way back,' he said, his weird eyes going even wider. 'So yes, I *am* enjoying this.'

The smile vanished from his face, replaced by a scowl, as he pushed past me, deliberately knocking me. *Motherfucker.* The guy who'd been watching guard over my brother and father was suddenly beside me. 'Walk,' he said, pushing the tip of his gun into my ribs. I recoiled from the gun, hurrying quickly behind Emilio and the Suit.

'I'll be okay, Mama,' I called out in a shaky voice that teetered on hysteria.

I didn't look at my mother as I left the house I had grown up in. The house where I had spent almost my entire life. I couldn't look her in the eye, because if I did, I would have reneged on the deal, ran to her, and let her hold me in her arms as bullets ripped us all apart.

I looked at the floor instead, and tried feverishly to ignore her sobbing, the protests of my sister, the muttered swearing of my father. I pushed it all away, focusing only on the bright tiles on the floor.

The Suit appeared in front of me, looking excited as he held a black piece of hessian material in his hands.

A bag. And I knew exactly where he was going to put it.

'We're going to have so much fun,' he said, grinning.

My hurt blossomed into a steadily increasing rage as he seemed to feast upon my family's misery. I longed to strike out, to channel my rage physically with a fist to his face, pushing my nails into his eyes until I heard two meaty pops, but I pushed it down, delayed it. Later. Use it later. Instead, I hung my head, and waited as the black bag went over my face. The world turned dark as the thick material covered my eyes, and I struggled to contain my rising panic as ropes at the bottom of the bag were pulled tight around my neck, making it hard to breathe. A firm prod to my back with the gun, and I walked from the only home I had ever known, the last sounds to reach my ears being my mother screaming my name, and my father cursing the cartel.

CHAPTER SIX

MARIANA

It was entirely disconcerting to be wearing a hood over my head in the back of a car, with no idea where I was going. Even worse, I wasn't sure who was with me. I guessed the Suit was in the car, but I couldn't be sure who else was in there. My legs stretched out in front of me without end, suggesting we were in some kind of a limousine. The car drove for what seemed like hours before anyone spoke.

'Excited?' the Suit asked, sarcasm dripping from his words. I jerked upright at the sudden noise, muffled as it was through the bag on my head. He was somewhere in front of me. We had to be in a limousine. I imagined the fuck-you grin he was sporting, and pushed away thoughts of launching out of my seat and flying at him. I wasn't even entirely sure if he was sitting opposite me or further away. And even though I was regretting my rash move to offer myself up, I still didn't want a bullet in my head.

So instead of biting back at him I remained silent, chewing on my lip to try and distract myself.

'Not in a talking mood, huh?' he attempted casually. I chewed harder, not wanting to give him anything.

Cold fingers touched my bare knee and I jumped. He chuckled, but kept his hand there, squeezing my leg.

'You've got a pretty face, Ana,' he said, and my name from his mouth sounded wrong. But not as wrong as what he said next.

'I liked watching you come before,' he whispered, squeezing my knee hard for effect.

'What?' I replied sharply, playing right into his game. *Damn.*

'In the alleyway,' he drawled, dragging his hand higher up my leg. I clenched my thighs together as tight as I could to stop him from going any higher. I remembered how Este had pushed me up against the wall behind a shop selling tacky tourist souvenirs and fucked me — made *love* to me — hard and fast, the fireworks in that alley as bright as the fireworks in the night sky. Tears burned at my eyes as I realised that it had only been a few hours ago that he had been alive, warm as his arms held me tightly, and now he was dead.

'You weren't there,' I scoffed, my eyes burning, my heart thudding wildly. 'You were already at the house when I arrived.'

He chuckled, a sound that made the hairs on my bare arms prickle uncomfortably. 'I left once I saw your little boyfriend bleed out on the ground,' he taunted. 'So, yeah. I saw you in the alley with your skirt up around your head. They have rooms you can rent by the hour, you know?'

His words were razor sharp, laden with derision, and it bewildered me. This guy didn't even know me! Why did he seem so offended by my sexual proclivities?

More to the point, why was he getting under my skin so badly?

'You were spying on us?' I asked in disbelief, as embarrassment and indignation flushed my face. For the first time, I was thankful I was wearing the black bag on my head and that he couldn't see me blush.

'You weren't exactly hard to spot,' he said, placing a hand on each of my knees and wrenching them apart as I cried out in horror. 'You're obviously up for a good time.'

I didn't care what the rules were meant to be, if I was meant to comply now that I was 'property' and let this guy have his way with me. My hands weren't tied anymore and I pushed that bastard's creepy hands away as hard as I could, raking my fingernails along his flesh for effect.

His entire body tensed up and I cringed in my seat, waiting for a blow that never came.

'Stop.' A voice cut through the tension. Emilio.

'I'm going to kill you, you little whore,' the Suit spat.

'Stop!' Emilio's voice rang out again, filling the car.

Relief flooded through my limbs as I realised he was in the car. It was swiftly followed by confusion and then shame, that I was happy my new owner and likely murderer was present.

'The little slut made me bleed,' the Suit protested, and I heard Emilio tut.

'You should have been more careful, Murphy.'

Murphy? A stupid name for an asshole of a man.

I sniffed, placing my palms on my thighs, tugging my dress down to cover as much skin as possible.

'You crying under that bag, sweetheart?' Murphy mocked me. 'Because where we're going, tears are weakness. Those boys'll tear you apart, and I'll watch the show.'

'Fuck you,' I said bitterly, the material muffling my voice as I slouched back in my seat.

'Oh, no,' he drawled, and I could picture the smirk on his lips. 'You'll be screaming, they'll be fucking you, and *I'll* bring the popcorn.'

I had never felt so alone in my life, and shit was going to get a whole lot worse before it got any better.

***

The drive ground on for what seemed like days. Weeks. *Years.* I was desperately thirsty, but didn't dare ask for any water. Didn't dare ask for anything. Every time I relaxed, felt myself drifting on a daydream of numbed shock, I would remind myself who I was in the car with. That knowledge would cause me to sit upright, as my heart rate skyrocketed and fresh sweat formed a slick on my palms. I was tired, and terrified, and I desperately needed to pee.

When the car finally did come to an abrupt halt, I wasn't prepared for the sudden braking. I was thrown forward, and I gasped as I caught myself on my hands and knees on the carpeted floor.

Murphy laughed, and I felt his long, ice-cold fingers at my neck as he undid the rope that secured the bag over my head. When he pulled it off I winced, his arrogant face the first thing that swam into my vision.

I realised I was on all fours, my face way too close to his lap. I scrambled backwards into my seat just as my door was opened. A hand closed around my upper arm and tugged. 'Out.' I fought the urge to scream and stepped out of the limo, jumping as the door was slammed loudly behind me.

'Nunio!' Emilio said sharply. 'It's not a fucking *chingalera*, so why are you treating it like one?'

Nunio looked ruefully at Emilio, who had just told him not to treat the car like a piece of shit. 'Sorry, boss,' he said, tugging me along. I looked up at the tall building we were in front of, the cars parked in a large, opulent circular driveway.

'You live here?' I asked Emilio.

He looked at me like I was an idiot. 'This is a hotel,' he said, and gestured at the big red and gold sign hanging above the double glass doors. 'I thought you were smart, *cholita.*'

I chose not to answer that as I was marched into the hotel between Nunio and Murphy, Emilio leading our odd-looking entourage. I looked behind me, wondering if I could make a run for it, but I was met by the glares of the three guys from the house as they stood guard at the entrance. *Fabulous.*

The plush hotel foyer was completely deserted as we made our way through, my bright blue Havaianas making a dull thwack each time I lifted my foot and then put it back down on the marble floor. I clenched my fists, trying to stave off the urge to let go and pee all over the shiny floor. Still, if it hit Murphy's feet, that would be a plus.

I smiled to myself, imagining that scenario as Emilio punched a button for the elevator. I got a firm push into the elevator when it arrived, and I stumbled to stop myself from falling flat on my face.

'What the fuck are you smiling at?' Murphy asked.

Emilio looked peeved. 'Murphy,' he said, as the doors slid shut, 'give it a rest.'

'I want to know what the little Colombian *chocho* thinks is so funny.'

Did he just call me a cunt? He did. Asshole.

Emilio sighed, massaging his temples. 'And I want some peace and quiet, so shut the fuck up. I only let you come along because you said you'd stay out of it.'

Murphy rolled his freaky blue eyes as the doors opened smoothly. I fought the urge to flinch as their hands were on me again and I was herded out into a carpeted hallway.

'I said I'd stay out of it when I thought we were going to off them,' he said. 'I didn't even get to play with her sexy sister.'

Emilio stopped and turned so sharply, I collided with his chest. He wore a look of annoyance like it was an old friend.

'Come on,' Murphy wheedled, as Nunio swiped a card against the door we were crowded in front of. 'Can't I at least stick my dick in her mouth? Look at those lips, Emilio.'

'Look at these teeth,' I added, as Nunio shoved me inside. If Murphy thought any part of him was going to get anywhere near my mouth, he was in for a rude shock.

Emilio pointed to an overstuffed leather couch that looked over the city. 'Sit down,' he said, in a tone that didn't inspire me to argue.

'Can I use the bathroom first?' I asked, hating that I had to ask permission for such a basic thing.

Emilio waved his hand, and I took that to mean yes. I walked down the hallway of the lavish suite, in the general direction he had gestured. I spotted the bathroom and practically ran inside. I might have been about to begin the worst possible part of my life so far, but at least I'd spare myself the indignation of pissing my pants in front of these bastards.

As I turned to close the door, I nearly did pee my pants. Murphy was standing in the doorway, the bright light in the bathroom bouncing off his weird eyes and making him look like a complete psychopath. He grinned, opening his mouth to speak, but I slammed the door as fast and as hard as I could, snapping the lock into place.

'Bitch!' I heard on the other side of the door.

'Go away!' I yelled. I rushed to the toilet, threw the lid open, wrenched my panties down, and sighed at the blissful relief that followed.

Once I'd finished, I washed my shaking hands with some strong-smelling hand soap. I dried my hands on an expensive-looking towel, white and fluffy, nervously going through the motions as I distastefully surveyed the opulence of a room designed exclusively for washing and eliminating bodily waste. A room that looked more expensive than my entire house back in Villanueva.

A man who had enough money to spend on hotel rooms like this shouldn't miss five hundred thousand dollars, let alone thirty thousand dollars. It made me want to scream.

Este. I pushed him out of my mind right then, because thinking about him was going to send me over the edge so fast I wouldn't be able to come back.

I'm sorry, Este, baby. I love you so much. I'm going to make these bastards pay for what they did to you. I'm going to make them suffer.

I smiled, catching a glimpse of myself in the large gold-framed mirror that hung above the basin. Yes. I would be the faithful servant, the piece of property, the slave girl. I would bide my time. Keep my sorrow locked tightly away. Push thoughts of my loved ones to the farthest recesses of my mind.

I would be an obedient little *chocho*. And once I gained their trust, even if it took me the rest of my life, I would find a way to make these fuckers pay.

CHAPTER SEVEN

MARIANA

I left the bathroom quickly — I knew that if I let myself get comfortable in there, one of them would have to break the door down to get me out.

Daydreams of violence filled my every thought as I made my way back to the main area of the opulent apartment. It was late — most of the lights in the hills were out, meaning most people were tucked up in bed in their houses. While I, in stark contrast, was trying to survive my first hours as Emilio's possession. That knowledge made my skin itch. The primitive part of my brain screamed at me to run away, to fling the door open and run out into the street. To find a safe place and lock myself away so nobody could ever find me.

But I didn't. I held my head high and forced myself to breathe evenly, knowing that these men were like dogs — they could sniff out fear better than anyone.

Emilio stood at the window, which was actually the entire fourth wall of the apartment. Though his hands were in his pockets and he was facing away from me, his presence was overwhelming.

'Eat something,' he said, without turning around. I guessed he could see me in the reflection of the glass. I looked around, my eyes landing on a platter of tamales and empanadas and a bottle of *aji* hot sauce.

I was a stress eater. Trauma made me hungry. My mouth watered as I tried to walk casually over to the counter, when really I wanted to run as fast as I could and see how many pieces of food I could fit into my mouth at once.

I spotted a stack of white paper napkins and took one, loading it up with two tamales and an empanada. I bit into one of the banana leaf-wrapped tamales, every tastebud in my mouth lighting up at the delicious chicken and spices encased in sweet fried cornmeal. Bliss.

Well, bliss for a starving girl who'd just signed her life over to the man who'd had her lover shot and her father by the balls. Relative bliss, I suppose.

I played with the heart-shaped locket around my neck absent-mindedly. It hung on a gold chain, along with the small crucifix my mother had given me at my Confirmation when I was a small girl. Panic burst in my chest as I thought of the contents of the locket ... because it suddenly occurred to me that Emilio didn't know about my son.

Luis was three years old. Este and I had been stupid when we were younger, and hadn't used protection when we'd first started screwing like rabbits at every opportunity. And, well ... I was pregnant in less than a month, and had a little boy who I named Luis, after Esteban's late father.

But I hadn't been allowed to keep my baby, and all I had was a letter once a year with an updated photograph to let me know how he was going. The most recent photo was tucked into my locket, and the thought of Emilio finding it and using Luis against me made me turn cold inside.

I looked at Emilio. He appeared to be deep in thought, and I used the moment to open the locket and dig out the small photo. I screwed it up in my fist, devastated that I hadn't thought of it in the bathroom where I could have had one last peek, but I had to be strong now, and this was the smart thing to do.

I would never tell them about Luis.

I edged over to the rubbish bin that sat in a small recess between the refrigerator and the wall, tossing the photo in and giving the bin a kick to make sure the photo tumbled down underneath the plastic water bottles and balled-up napkins that already sat in there.

Shaken, and with an entirely new sense of loss, I stepped back over to the counter and looked at Emilio. He hadn't budged. *Thank God for small favours.*

I devoured several more empanadas, then helped myself to a glass of water in the kitchen. After I'd had my fill of food and water, I stood at the kitchen counter, nervously folding napkins into different shapes. A butterfly. A star. By the time I'd finished fashioning a pistol from two napkins folded together, Emilio was watching with barely concealed interest.

'You are an odd girl,' he said, eyeing me intently. 'Who taught you to do that?'

My boyfriend. The one who you had killed.

I remembered the day he had taught me — I was sixteen years old, in the throes of a protracted labour, and the judgmental bitches who called themselves nurses refused to give me any pain relief. To teach me a lesson. I'd already learned my lesson when my father told me I couldn't keep the baby, but those bitches still took their pleasure in watching me writhe as my small frame was swamped with contractions.

Este had held my hand as I screamed, and in the moments between contractions, he showed me how to fold just about anything out of paper napkins. By the time I started pushing, I'd learned how to fold swans, stars and all kinds of animals.

And guns, because, you know, we were the children of mobsters.

'My boyfriend,' I answered. 'Your men murdered him.'

Emilio slid the napkin gun closer to him and picked it up, his lips quirking slightly as if he was amused by my haphazard paper weapons.

'Do you know how I came to be the most powerful man on the west coast?' he asked me, setting the paper gun down on the counter between us. 'How I wrestled power from my enemies to become the fucking kingpin of the cocaine trade?'

'By controlling those below you?' I guessed, keeping my voice monotone. 'By holding their daughters hostage?'

He chuckled. 'You are a smart girl, even if you do think people live in hotels.'

We stood there like that for a few moments, both of us apparently deep in thought. It was odd; I wasn't afraid of him the way I thought I ought to be. I was hesitant, yes, but as much as it disgusted me, I understood. My father had let him down, in an industry where you do *not* let your boss down.

'So my father,' I said casually, playing with the edge of a napkin. 'He really screwed up, didn't he?'

Emilio nodded, his dark eyes betraying nothing if he was annoyed at my questioning.

'Why did you stop that man from raping me?' I asked, cringing inwardly at the way my question came out.

Emilio's lip curled up, and I could tell he was amused. 'Did you want him to rape you, *cholita*?'

'No!' I said quickly. 'No, no, no. I was just wondering. Why you protected me when you could have let him at me. Why you were nice to me.'

He grinned, and I fought the urge to back away, sensing that I had stirred something within him. Oh, shit. He leaned across the counter and tucked a stray hair behind my ear, letting his hand linger for a moment that was entirely too long and uncomfortable.

'I didn't let him rape you because you do not belong to him. You belong to me, *cholita*, and I will use you as I see fit. For now, I want you untouched, clean and beautiful.'

For now? Something inside me died as I wondered what those seemingly benign words meant coming from a man like Emilio Ross.

'What are you going to do with me?' I whispered.

I shivered as he replied. 'I'm going to recoup at least some of my losses.'

I can't promise you that you won't beg me to kill you anyway.

I couldn't pretend to be strong a moment longer. My knees became shaky and I had to grab onto the counter to stop myself from sliding to the floor in a heap.

'Open your mouth,' Emilio said, a glass of water and a round white pill materialising in his hand as if by magic.

I hesitated, earning me a slap across the face that had me flying halfway across the kitchen, my ears ringing in its wake. He slammed the glass of water on the counter, staring me down.

'I would have punched you,' he said, rounding the counter and crouching in front of me, 'but I want you to look pretty for me.'

He squeezed my jaw, forcing my mouth open, and dropped the pill into the back of my mouth. Then he pressed my mouth shut, clamping his thick fingers over my mouth and nose.

'Swallow,' he said. I tried to wrench my head away, but he was strong. I couldn't budge an inch in his vice-like grip. I swallowed, the dry pill almost catching in my throat as I tried not to cough.

'Good girl,' he said, releasing me. 'The first night is always the hardest.'

'The first night of what?' I croaked.

He must have seen the terror in my eyes. 'The first night of the rest of your life,' he said, offering me his hand. 'You're not a college student anymore, *cholita*. You're not somebody's daughter. You're not somebody's little girlfriend. You're somebody's *possession*. You're nothing. You're *mine*.'

***

Not long after, I tossed and turned in stiff hotel sheets, trapped between sleep and terror. The pill Emilio had given me must have been a sleeping tablet, because I was groggy, but I refused to sleep in case that other asshole came in and tried something on me. My door was locked from the outside. A man had been standing guard when I entered the room, and I had no doubt he was still out there, keeping tabs on me. The windows were high and barred, completely different from the living room's windows, which would have been pretty easy to break and jump out of.

The room was devoid of artwork, devoid of anything. There was one small wardrobe, completely empty save for a bare rack that I'm sure nothing had ever hung from. A small double bed with white sheets, white comforter. White pillows that were too high and stiff with feathers. Beige walls.

It was like being in solitary confinement, only worse, because that was still safer than what was outside my door.

My eyes were closed and my body painfully heavy, but I still couldn't sleep. It was like someone had locked me inside my immobile body and left me to try and survive. The sleeping tablet gnawed at the edges of my consciousness, promising relief if I just let myself slide into a deep, black sleep, but I knew better. I knew that I was not safe in the room.

It felt like hours had passed, but it was still dark outside — I could see a tiny sliver of sky through the high, heavily fortified window.

I eyed the open wardrobe again with interest. *Yes*, I thought. I gathered up the stuffy pillows and the white comforter and rolled out of the bed, crawling over to the wardrobe and closing myself in. At least in here, I would be able to hear someone enter the room in the dark. A pillow behind my head, I half-laid, half-leaned against the back wall of the wardrobe and fell into a drugged, numb void.

CHAPTER EIGHT

MARIANA

The room may have been escape-proof, but it definitely wasn't soundproof. I awoke in the dark, momentarily confused. I sat in pitch blackness, a hard wall at my back and a blanket twisted around my legs. I smelled old blood and wondered if it was mine.

Am I dead? Did somebody bury me?

The events of the previous night came crashing back into my mind. I sucked in a deep breath as the image of Este's bloodied corpse hit me like a punch to the stomach.

And then, the rest of the night's events came hurtling back, unrelenting, even as my drugged brain struggled to catch up. Emilio. The drive. The creepy dude in the suit. *You're mine.*

If I'd had anything left inside me, I would have burst into tears, but I couldn't let go. I was too tightly wound, my heart thudding loudly in my ears and my hands shaking as foreign sounds reached me through the wardrobe door.

Cars on the city streets below. Horns blaring. A truck's reversing siren, loud and obstinate at what felt like a ridiculously early hour.

A knock on the bedroom door, followed by the door opening, had me scrambling to stand up. As it was, the wardrobe had a shelf about four feet from the ground, and I only succeeded in slamming my head against it. 'Ow,' I muttered, reaching out for something to hold onto. I steadied myself on the wardrobe door just as it was wrenched open, and I spilled out onto the person on the other side.

Murphy grinned as he took in my dishevelled appearance and my sleeping quarters.

'You look like shit,' he said. I narrowed my eyes, flicking them up and down his outfit as I disentangled myself from him. He wasn't wearing a suit anymore. He looked like a garish tourist who belonged in Florida or somewhere similarly tropical, sporting tweed shorts and a bright blue shirt printed with palm trees. The loafers on his feet looked cheap and nasty, a complete contrast to the expensive leather shoes he had been wearing last night.

'You look like Hawaii threw up on you,' I retorted, rubbing sleep from my eye. I looked down at myself, barefoot, still wearing my black sundress and Este's blood all over me.

Murphy stepped back, his smile still wide and freakish, and gestured to the door. 'Time for breakfast.'

I eyed him warily as I side-stepped him, walking as quickly as I could to stay out of his reach. I'd take Emilio and his violence over this freak and his wandering hands any time.

I entered the main living area again, expecting to see cereal or perhaps some fast food on the small round dining table, but what greeted me instead made my stomach flip.

Emilio sat on the far side of the table, sipping an espresso from a tiny cup as he read the paper. He was studying the stocks this time, and I wanted to ask if I was allowed to fix a coffee for myself, but I was too distracted by the plate that lay between us.

'Sit,' he said, without looking up.

I sat across from him, trying to suck my stomach in to suppress the loud growling noise it was making. I was so hungry I'd eat anything.

Except what was currently in front of me.

'You don't seriously expect me to do *that*?' I asked, barely concealing the horrified tone in my voice.

He swallowed, annoyance showing in his cocked brow. 'Did I say you could speak?'

I looked down at the table, trying to cover my rage. What I really wanted to do was stand up, throw the table on its side and scream 'FUCK YOU!', but I knew if I did that, he'd punish me. Probably by letting Murphy put his hand up my dress.

I stared at the table for a few moments, as Emilio returned to his paper. When he didn't speak again, I let my gaze wander higher, eyeing off the bottle of olive oil and the plate stacked high beside it.

Surely he wasn't going to make me do *that*?

He folded the paper up leisurely, placing it on the table as he drained the last of his coffee.

'Right,' he said. 'Good morning, Ana. I trust you slept well?'

'Like the dead,' I replied, without missing a beat.

'No doubt. We need you looking fresh and well-rested. You've got a long day ahead of you.'

'She looks like shit,' Murphy said again, making me prickle in annoyance. 'They're going to stop her in customs looking like that.'

Just fuck off, I wanted to say, but instead I bit my tongue and ignored him.

Customs. So it was what I had suspected.

'I'm a drug mule?' I asked Emilio in disbelief. 'That was fast. What if I go to the police in the airport?'

Emilio chuckled. 'I own the police,' he said, his gaze shifting momentarily to Murphy before returning to me. I choked on that inference as I whirled around to face Weird Eyes. 'You're a *cop*?'

He glanced at Emilio, for once not engaging with me. I guessed that he hadn't wanted me to know that.

'Murphy here is a Federal Air Marshal,' Emilio said, his amusement evident as he rolled one of the rubber-coated pellets on the plate between his fingers. 'He helps us get our product from A to B.'

'You're a *drug-trafficking cop*?' I asked Murphy, who continued to give me nothing.

'The drugs are an attractive part of the package,' Emilio teased, dragging out my torture. 'But he specialises in moving *other* possessions of mine.'

Oh.

'I bet he does,' I said sharply, imagining Murphy taking full advantage of the women he trafficked from one country to another. It was enough to make me want to stab them both more than I already did.

'Can I at least eat something first?' I asked, eyeing the pellets nervously. There had to be at least thirty of the fuckers, gleaming smugly at me from their spot on the table.

'No,' Emilio said. 'If you eat, your metabolism will start working. No food until you're on American soil.'

'If you shit these out on the plane ride,' Murphy added behind me, 'you'll have to rinse them off and swallow them again. We wouldn't want that, would we?'

My skin crawled at the thought.

Emilio laughed, gesturing at me as he addressed his associate. 'She's Marco's daughter and she's never been a mule? I don't believe it.'

I eyed the pellets again, each about the size of my thumb, tightly wrapped in plastic. I might not have acted as a drug mule before, but I wasn't stupid — I knew what would happen. And I wasn't as worried about them going in as I was about them coming back out again. *Ouch.*

'The plane leaves in three hours,' Emilio said. 'In the meantime, Murphy, I suggest you go and buy *cholita* some fresh clothes and that shit women put on their face to get rid of the bags under their eyes.'

'Concealer,' I said. 'It's called concealer.'

Murphy whistled as he left the apartment, for once not arguing. I jumped in my seat as the door slammed loudly, and sat on my hands to stop myself from fidgeting.

I stared down at the plate in front of me, at the reality that greeted me. Plastic-wrapped pellets full of pure cocaine.

'What if one of them bursts inside me?' I asked Emilio, who was arranging a passport and papers in front of him.

'You die,' he said casually, as if I had asked him what would happen if it rained today. 'You die, and I get very angry, and I cut you open to get the rest of my coke out.'

I shivered despite the warmth, imagining my lifeless body in a bathtub, dead and gutted. I imagined my blood sprayed on the walls as faceless men pushed their hands inside me and removed bloodied plastic pellets full of Colombia's finest white powder.

'They won't burst,' he said, setting the papers to one side and fixing his beady eyes on me once more. 'I am a professional. I wrap my product properly. They will only burst if you don't get them out quickly enough, if your stomach acid eats them away.'

My stomach roiled. I was thinking there was probably a lot of fucking acid in there right now. I wanted to throw up and I hadn't even begun.

As if reading my thoughts, Emilio unscrewed the bottle of olive oil and took one of the pellets from the plate, balancing it in his palm. He added a swig of olive oil to his slightly cupped hand and worked the oil over the pellet until it was coated in the slick substance.

'Open wide,' he said, standing and leaning over the table. I swallowed, keeping my mouth firmly closed.

'I will rape your mother and kill your father,' he said, pressing the pellet to my lips. 'Or you can swallow a few tiny little packages for me.'

A tear burned in my right eye and I blinked it away hurriedly, opening my mouth to allow the pellet inside. The strong smell of the olive oil hit my nostrils and I fought the urge to pull away.

'Wider,' Emilio instructed, forcing the pellet past my lips and teeth. My eyes bulged and my throat protested as his finger pushed the pellet all the way to the back of my tongue, aggravating the sensitive gag reflex.

I jerked away in one sharp movement, gagging and choking as I chased the slick pellet around my throat with my fingers. I couldn't get hold of it, it was too slippery, and finally I just dropped my head forward and let it fall out into my shaking hands.

'I can't,' I said, panicking. 'Please, I'll do something else. I won't run away. *I'll be good.*'

The words tumbling from my mouth were completely foreign to my ears and I felt hot shame rise in my face as I heard myself beg.

Emilio slapped the table loudly, circling around and grabbing hold of my jaw. I whimpered as he squeezed.

'Look at me,' he commanded. And me, being the obedient slave, did what I was told. I met his dark brown eyes and saw my worst nightmares within them.

'This is a test,' he said, gripping my chin. 'You think I would let you out of my sight without some kind of insurance policy? I know you will stay with me, *cholita*, when you've a belly full of drugs and a United States Air Marshal by your side. Do not forget the deal you struck with me last night. Do you want your family to die?'

He released my chin, pushing me roughly as he stepped back. I looked at the pellets and gagged again, not as loudly this time but enough that I thought I might throw up.

Emilio returned to his seat across from me, breathing heavily, and I could tell he was trying his hardest not to fly off the handle and beat me to a bloody pulp. Not because it would make him feel bad, but because he wanted me to look pretty.

I took a deep breath in turn, let my shoulders drop, and tried to calm myself. 'I'm sorry,' I said, recalling his threat about my parents. 'I'll try again.'

His lip curled up into a sneer and he simply gestured to the plate.

I bobbed my head, tentatively picking up one of the pellets in one hand and the olive oil in the other. Taking a deep breath, I repeated what I had watched Emilio do with the olive oil in his palm.

Without giving myself time to think, I slid the pellet as far as I could to the back of my throat and swallowed forcefully.

Shit!

The pellet lodged painfully in my throat for an agonising moment, and for a brief second I thought it would remain there. Thankfully, it eventually went down, and I swear I could feel it travel all the way to the depths of my stomach and settle on the bottom like a brick dropped in a fish tank.

I smiled, hitting myself lightly on the chest. 'I did it!' I was pleased, until I remembered where I was, who I was with, and how many pellets were left on the plate in front of me.

Oh, Christ.

Emilio looked amused as I stared in horror at the rest of the plate.

'I don't think they're all going to fit inside me,' I told him.

He chuckled. 'Of course they will. I've fit twice that amount inside girls half your age.' *Half my age?* Visions of nine-year-old girls swallowing these pellets made my heart contract painfully.

'You're trying too hard,' he said. 'It's just like taking a tablet. Or sucking a cock. I'm sure you've had a cock in your mouth before.'

I almost fired a retort at him until I remembered I actually had had one of those in my mouth the night before, in the alleyway, before Este and I had moved onto other things.

'Speaking from your own cock sucking experience?' I finally managed.

Without pause, Emilio stood and reached across the table, backhanding me across the face with a ferocity that had seemingly come out of nowhere.

I cringed, holding a palm up to my stinging cheek. When I pulled it away, a small amount of my blood marked my palm. I glanced at his hand, seeing a large gold ring adorning his ring finger. *Great.*

I was too shocked to say anything. I just pressed my palm back to my cheek and watched Emilio, my mouth slightly open.

'I wasn't always this rich,' he said, twisting his ring back to the correct position on his finger. 'I was a smuggler before I was a kingpin, tough girl. I built this business up from the ground level.'

'Your parents must be so proud,' I muttered, one hand on my stomach as it growled in hunger. *Don't eat through the pellet, stomach acid, please don't eat through the pellet.*

'My parents are dead,' he replied without a trace of sadness. I cowered, expecting another slap for speaking out of turn. I had to stop mouthing off or it would be the end for me. 'They were slaughtered by a rival mafia family in Italy when I was just a boy. My father was not as smart as me. Kind of like you and your father. We're more alike than you realise, *cholita*.'

'How lovely,' I replied.

'Quit stalling and get the rest into you,' he said, pushing the plate closer to me. 'We leave for the airport in one hour.'

My heart sank as I faced the impossible task in front of me.

He's not lying. He'll kill your entire family if you don't do what he says.

I pulled the plate closer and continued.

***

Nineteen pellets. One for every year of my life. That's how many I'd been able to swallow over the course of an hour, before my stomach refused to take any more. I still wasn't entirely sure if the nineteenth had made it all the way down, or if it was still lodged in the bottom of my throat. I felt fuller than I'd ever felt before, fuller than I felt after the biggest *El Día de las Velitas* dinner of *buñuelos* and rum.

Emilio watched my face carefully, as I clutched my stomach and fought the urge to throw up. I really didn't want to be sick. I was pretty sure the pellets wouldn't make their way up as easily as they'd gone down, not that they went down very easily. Still, I could imagine them getting stuck, banked up in my throat, bursting, killing me. No, I definitely did *not* want that.

'That's enough,' he said, pulling the plate back to his side of the table. He handed me a passport and the stack of papers he'd been fidgeting with. 'Memorise these details. You will be flying with my associate today. I expect you to stay quiet and act normally. Accept a meal on the flight, but do not eat anything. Sip water, but not a lot. When you get to the other end, further instructions will await you.'

My head spun as I looked at the photo in the passport. The girl looked nothing like me. 'How is anyone going to believe this is me? The guards at the airport will laugh in my face.'

Emilio shrugged. 'I own the guards. I own the airport. I own everyone. This is merely for show. It would look odd if you walked right through without a passport, *cholita*.'

I opened my mouth to protest. Murphy strode in right on cue, tossing a full plastic shopping bag at me. I glanced down into the bag to see a jumble of reds and blacks, gaudy lace and polyester.

Great. He was going to dress me up like a hooker. That didn't bode well.

'The girl did good,' Murphy said, seeming genuinely impressed with the almost-empty plate on the table.

'Just like sucking dick, right?' I said to him. 'Looks like it'd come naturally to you.'

He flashed me a wicked grin. 'Your words, not mine,' he said, laughing.

He sobered immediately as Emilio cleared his throat.

'How many, boss?'

'Nineteen,' Emilio answered. 'One for every year of her pathetic little life. Right, *cholita*?'

I chose not to respond.

'Right,' Murphy said, rubbing his hands together. 'Let's go on vacation, little lady.'

I rolled my eyes, and he laughed.

CHAPTER NINE
MARIANA

The travel arrangements were nauseating — more nauseating than the fact that I had nineteen plastic-wrapped pellets full of pure cocaine powder in my stomach. According to my passport, I was Maria Reyes, wife of Danny Reyes, also known as Murphy. We were checked in express and I was acutely aware of the heat Murphy was packing underneath his gaudy Hawaiian shirt. I was mortified at the outfit he'd picked for me — a black skin-tight dress that hugged me in all the right (or wrong) places with a plunging neckline that stopped barely above my navel. That was only a slight exaggeration. He ever so graciously let me pack a grey zip-up hoodie in my carry-on bag (again, purchased by him, tacky and cheap) and I hugged that jacket tightly around myself as we took to the skies.

It didn't erase the cold terror that was growing in the pit of my stomach, though. With each moment that passed, as we got closer to our destination, thoughts of what Murphy might do to me once we were on land and alone plagued me. I talked a brave talk, and I snapped back at these men in conversation, but I already knew Murphy was bigger than me, stronger than me, and if he wanted to pin me down and force himself on me, I'd be pretty fucking useless to stop him without some kind of a weapon.

Oh, how I longed for a weapon.

The plane ride was bumpy at first, as we flew through storm clouds that were common in the tropics. I was used to flying back and forth from my stateside college a few times a year, but I still hated flying. Hated not being in control. This time, however, I lifted up the window shade and watched jagged streaks of lightning spark between clouds, thinking I was safer up here than I would be once we landed. After the pilot managed to divert the plane from the bad weather, we levelled out and the air hostesses started rolling food trolleys down both aisles.

'No thank you,' I said sharply as the air hostess tried to hand me a tray. She was distracted and continued to push it in my face, so I pushed it back towards her. 'I'm not hungry,' I said, louder this time.

The air hostess looked affronted, and was about to withdraw the foil-wrapped tray when a hand shot across mine and grabbed hold of it.

'She's watching her weight,' Murphy said to the air hostess, charming her with his fake smile and candy-sweet tone. 'I keep telling her she's beautiful just the way she is, but she keeps on with these silly diets.' He shook his head for effect and took the tray from the air hostess.

The air hostess moved on and I felt a hand grip the back of my neck.

I tried to wrench my head away, but Murphy was surprisingly strong. With his other hand, he unlatched my tray table and let it fall into my lap, pushing my meal in front of me.

I recoiled as he brought his mouth close to my ear. 'Take the foil off,' he said, his nails digging into the soft skin on my neck. 'Move the food around, put some in your mouth, and spit it back into your napkin.'

He pulled at my neck, forcing me to meet his gaze.

'No,' I replied. I knew I should just do what he said, but I'd always been the stubborn, hot-headed girl who hated being told what to do. This was all I had — a small chance to defy him, to defy someone. A tiny choice that I could make in a reality where I was no longer in control of *anything*.

His jaw tightened. 'You know air marshals carry guns, don't you, Ana?' he threatened.

I returned my gaze to the TV screen in front of me and feigned indifference.

'Go fuck yourself in the ass with your gun,' I hissed.

He leaned back and away, as far as he could, which wasn't very far in the cramped confines of economy. 'You're not afraid of me, are you?'

Of course I'm afraid of you. I could feel his eyes burning into the side of my face as I pushed my food to the side. 'Nope,' I said boldly.

Murphy took the meal from my tray and held it in his hand.

'You should go to the bathroom while you have a chance,' he said pointedly.

I was confused. 'Emilio said —'

'It's a nine-hour flight,' Murphy said in a low voice. 'If someone noticed you hadn't used the bathroom once in that whole time they would think it very strange.'

I saw the opportunity for a few minutes alone and latched my tray table up. Murphy sat to the side, letting me pass. I slid past him, trying my best not to touch against him any more than I had to. I might have told him I wasn't afraid of him, but truthfully, I was terrified.

I was just good at hiding that from him. I'd always had an excellent poker face.

Must have gotten that from my mother.

I hurried down the narrow aisle without looking back. I wished Este was here with me and suddenly I was overwhelmed with visions of him. It was getting harder and harder to push my terror down, to stop myself from having a complete meltdown. I'd told myself that I was only allowed to break down and sob when I was alone. The closest bathroom stall was vacant and I stepped in, closing the door with a small sigh of relief. I caught sight of myself in the mirror and immediately wished I hadn't; I looked awful. Rather than covering up the black circles under my eyes, Murphy's dodgy concealer job had actually intensified my exhausted appearance.

My eyes were bloodshot, and cheap mascara clumped my black eyelashes together in haphazard sections.

I turned the tap on, cupping water and bringing it to my mouth. Small sips, Emilio had said. I let myself swallow a little water and spat the rest down the sink with great reluctance. As I straightened again, I stuck my tongue out. It no longer looked pink and smooth; instead, it had angry red indentations scalloped around the edges. I'd been clenching my teeth so tightly since the moment I had seen Emilio's men in the alley, it was a wonder my teeth hadn't started to crack under the pressure.

My head began to spin as the events of the last day came crashing back into me again.

I closed the toilet seat lid and sat down, dissolving into hot, salty tears before my ass had even hit the seat. What the hell was happening? In less than twenty-four hours I'd gone from college student, girlfriend and daughter to a drug mule and a fucking hostage 35,000 feet in the air.

I thought for the first time about what this meant for my baby boy. My Luis.

In my mind, my fingers traced his perfect rosebud lips and dark eyelashes as he stared back at me with my mother's eyes, a brighter blue than my own.

I started to sob loudly, pressing my hands over my mouth to try and suppress the noise.

I almost had a heart attack when a loud rap sounded at the door. 'I won't be long!' I called to whoever was out there, jumping to my feet. The knocking continued. 'Go away!' I yelled.

Suddenly, the door burst open and the tiny space was filled with *him*.

'I thought you might do this,' he said, slamming the door shut behind him so I was trapped.

I jerked backwards just as Murphy's hand closed around a handful of my hair. I let him pull me towards him, not enjoying the prospect of losing part of my scalp in an aeroplane toilet.

'Get out!' I protested loudly.

'No,' he replied. 'You've been in here long enough, sweetheart.'

'I'll scream,' I threatened, glancing at the door behind him. 'I'll scream so loud, people will think I'm being murdered. The hostesses will help me.'

'Who do you think let me in here?' he taunted, his bright blue eyes wild with excitement and anger. 'I'm a fucking air marshal, sweetheart. Remember?'

'Fuck you,' I spat, pushing his chest with my hands.

That pissed him off. He clenched his jaw, then reached out and slammed my head into the wall. I was too distracted by the pain in my temple to stop him from wrapping his arm around my throat. His chokehold was tight, leaving only a tiny opening in my windpipe to sip at the air.

The room spun. 'I can't breathe,' I rasped, clawing at his arm. In the mirror, I saw the crazy look in his eyes and my stomach lurched. His nostrils flared as he breathed heavily, one arm around my neck, the opposite hand pulling my hair, forcing me to meet his gaze in the mirror. And what I saw there terrified me beyond belief. This man could actually kill me right now, in this toilet stall on a fucking aeroplane.

'I think you misunderstand the situation you're in,' he said through gritted teeth. Black dots started to swim in my vision. *Don't pass out.* If I passed out, who knew what he would do to me. The thought of what he was capable of made me shudder.

'I'm in charge here, do you understand? If I decide you're a risk, I will shoot you in your pretty little face before you can argue with me about it. And all of this will have been for nothing. I'll go back to Colombia and I'll kill every single person you've ever met.'

His eyes flashed as he delivered the final sentence.

'Including your son.'

I'd gone limp in his chokehold, but the mention of Luis sent me into a frenzied struggle. I kicked at the counter in front of me, driving us back into the wall behind Murphy. He was jolted enough that his hold on me loosened minutely, and I took the chance to tilt my head down and open my mouth, biting as hard as I could into the meaty bit of skin below his wrist.

'Bitch!' he yelled, pulling his arm away. I whirled around and lashed out with my fist, getting him in the nose with a satisfying crunch and a burst of blood. I thanked my lucky stars that I'd chosen to swing with my left hand, the black onyx ring my grandmother had given me entirely responsible for the damage to Murphy's face.

My hand throbbed from the impact. I shook it, trying to ease the pain a little, and stared at my knuckles. The skin had split and was bleeding over my index finger.

Without warning, a hand wrapped around my face, pushing me back into the mirror. The back of my head hit it with a dull thunk, and something cold pressed into my forehead.

A gun.

I scrambled to get a hold on the counter behind me, looking up past the gun between my eyes at an enraged Murphy. He looked as bad as I felt, or possibly worse, wiping his bloodied nose with the back of his hand as he stared me down. I cowered, silently willing his finger away from the trigger.

'You can't shoot a gun on a plane,' I whispered, closing my eyes. Fresh tears tracked their way down my cheeks and dripped onto my chest.

'Yes, I can,' he murmured. 'I know just where to shoot you so there's no exit wound.'

He was an air marshal. Of course he knew how to shoot a gun on a plane without risking the rest of the passengers by puncturing the hull with a mis-aimed trajectory.

'Open your eyes,' he demanded.

I did, but I immediately regretted it. In his free hand he held the crumpled picture of a sweet baby boy, the picture I'd taken from my locket and hidden in the rubbish bin.

Blank face. *Blank* face. I tried to convey confusion. 'What is that? Is that a baby?' I shifted my eyes to his face. He wasn't buying.

'Oh, Mariana,' he hissed, pressing the gun into my forehead so hard I cried out. 'I know all your secrets, sweetheart, and all your lies. Luis, right?'

He knew his name. If he knew his name, he knew everything.

'*No*,' I moaned, feeling my face shift into sorrow and terror as I reached out for the photo. He snatched it away and shook his head.

'Mine now,' he said, pocketing the photo.

'He's not my son,' I lied.

Murphy sneered. 'Of course he is. Little Luis. You think I didn't do my research last night after you went to sleep, *Annie*? I have access to every single thing about you. Hospital records, adoption papers ...'

FUCK!

I took a shuddering breath inwards. 'Did you tell Emilio?' I asked in a small voice.

'No. But I will. Unless you start fucking *behaving*.'

Oh, God. 'What do you want?' I asked in a voice that sounded far calmer than the fear and rage swirling within me.

'Nothing, yet. For now, do as you're told. If I tell you to visit the bathroom, visit the fucking bathroom. If I tell you to take the food tray? Take. The. Fucking. Food. Tray. If I tell you to do *anything* —' he paused for effect, pressing the gun deeper into the flesh between my eyes, '— you *do* it.' His eyes flared wider, and I flinched.

I nodded, letting my shoulders sag under the weight of my defeat.

'Good girl,' he said, letting the gun fall and patting me on the head, as if I were a goddamn dog. He lifted my chin so we were eye to eye. 'You're brave, I'll give you that. You're not like the other girls. But in this world, you're going to have to start being smarter, or somebody is going to snuff you out.'

***

The rest of the flight ground on so slowly, I started to feel like I was going insane; that maybe I had actually been shot in the bathroom stall, and this was hell, and I was stuck here forever.

But eventually, after a stopover in Mexico City and another five hours of hellish turbulence, we arrived at San Diego airport. I had remained largely mute for the rest of the first flight and the second flight, only responding if questioned by Murphy or a flight attendant. Inside me, nineteen capsules full of cocaine churned along with my rising panic. Murphy knew. He knew about my son, and he was using the knowledge of Luis's existence against me.

He had found my Achilles heel.

The power he held over me, in a crinkled-up photograph from the locket around my neck, meant he could ask me to do almost anything, and I'd have to do as he wished.

At San Diego airport we walked past a sign, 'Welcome to the United States of America', and my heart contracted painfully as I remembered my conversation with Este only the night before, moments before he was shot. How he had been so sure we would make it together. Start a new life, away from my father and the cartel.

It made me wish I'd died with him.

I walked as slowly as I could through customs, but they didn't give me a second glance. I dragged my feet as we made our way to the parking lot, lagging well behind Murphy. He seemed confident that I wouldn't run — he barely turned around to check I was still behind him. But eventually we arrived at a sleek black BMW, and I was ordered inside while Murphy packed the luggage in the trunk.

'Don't worry,' he said, as he slid into the driver's seat. He slipped on a pair of aviators and gave my thigh a squeeze. 'I'll play nice if you do.'

I didn't answer him. Instead, I pressed my forehead to the window and swallowed back my grief as the place of my dreams became the place of nightmares.

**

As soon as we reached the motel, I rushed to the bathroom. I'd started experiencing intense cramps, and I needed to get the pellets out of me before they ruptured.

Murphy laughed as he settled into a recliner.

'What's so funny?' I demanded.

He shrugged. 'Oh, nothing.'

I was about to close the bathroom door, but then something occurred to me. Feeling the blood rise in my cheeks, I turned back towards Murphy, who had cracked a beer. I had no idea where he'd gotten it from.

'Don't I need a ...'

He raised his eyebrows mockingly, tilting his head. 'A ...?'

Bastard. 'A strainer, or a bowl or something,' I said through gritted teeth.

He sniggered, taking a swig of his Corona. 'Flush 'em,' he said.

I must have looked stunned, because he burst out laughing. 'Your face!' he said, spitting some of his beer out as he laughed.

I shifted uncomfortably. 'I have nineteen pellets of cocaine in my stomach, and you want me to flush them down the toilet? Emilio will kill me! *What* is so funny?'

Murphy settled down enough to take a breath between all the laughing.

'Cornflour,' he said, wiping a tear from his cheek as he rocked back in his chair.

My stomach growled as if on cue. 'Cornflour?' I repeated dumbly.

'You just smuggled in about fifteen pesos worth of pure cornflour. You could sell it and buy yourself a taco.' His face said he thought he was hilarious.

I clenched my jaw. 'I don't believe you. Get Emilio on the phone. I want to hear him say it himself.'

His mouth returned to a sneer, but he got his phone out, and dialled.

'Boss,' he said. 'We're at the motel. The little girl doesn't want to flush the junk.'

Emilio said something on the other end that I couldn't catch, and Murphy tossed it to me. I caught it, surprising myself, and put it to my ear.

'Yes?' I said, keeping my voice monotone.

'You have my permission to get rid of the pellets,' Emilio said smoothly. 'You are not required to keep them for me.'

Anger flashed inside me and I tamped down the desire to start smashing things. I made my free hand into a fist and squeezed it as hard as I could.

'Why?' I managed to utter.

There was a brief silence on the other end. 'It was a test,' Emilio said. 'Congratulations. You passed.'

CHAPTER TEN

MARIANA

Several agonising hours later, with all of the pellets somewhere in the greater San Diego sewer system, I heard the beginnings of an angry buzz.

Motorcycles?

I swallowed the French fry I'd been chewing on and glanced at Murphy, who was sitting across from me, watching me with those weird blue eyes.

The buzz turned to a steady growl that threatened to shake the room.

I don't know how I knew it was them. It just made sense.

'Gypsy Brothers,' I whispered.

That got Murphy's attention. 'Oh, you know them, do you?'

I glared at him. 'I know of them.' If you knew of Il Sangue, it was kind of impossible not to know about the Gypsy Brothers motorcycle club. The two went hand in hand. Like clouds and rain.

Like blood and death.

Murphy's grin grew wide as he observed my horrified face. He took one last swig of his beer and slammed it on the table in front of me, his eyes never leaving mine.

'I would have been so much nicer to you than them.' He shrugged. 'They're gonna rip you apart.'

The collective buzz reached its peak. I drew the curtain back and glanced outside to the shitty parking lot, my heart hammering in my chest as I saw about fifteen bikers pull up on Harley Davidsons and dismount. They looked strictly business as most of them stayed close to their bikes, a few at the front of the pack approaching our motel room.

They looked fierce, but I'd grown up with fierce.

No, they looked *terrifying*.

Even though the bikes were silent, their buzz continued to resonate in my head. Panic grabbed my throat and squeezed. *Just breathe*, I told myself. *Breathe*.

Three hard raps hit the door to the motel room, and I jumped out of my seat. So far I'd been able to hold it together, but now, with this fresh hell outside the door, I was breaking apart.

I dropped the curtain and turned back in time to see Murphy opening the door. Three men in full leathers and open-face helmets strode in like they owned the place. Hell, they probably did. They sported identical patches on their leather vests, tapered triangles that rounded at the corners in black and white threads. I glanced at one of the patches nervously, mentally cataloguing the wings that framed a sword, a ribbon furling across the bottom with 'Gypsy Brothers' embroidered in block letters.

The one who was clearly in charge — the one with the bright red and black patch that said 'VP' underneath the Gypsy Brothers ribbon — knocked Murphy with his shoulder on his way past. Murphy clenched his jaw and stepped back. I smiled a little, my fear momentarily forgotten as I realised Murphy was shitting-his-pants scared of these guys. I wondered if they'd ripped *him* apart before, and his warning was from personal experience.

The VP was as terrifying as he was handsome. He looked to be around thirty, maybe a little older, the few fine lines around his eyes and slight peppering of grey through the front of his hair only adding to his raw appeal. He wore three-day-old stubble like it was his bitch, his deep brown eyes so dark, they blended almost seamlessly with his black pupils. VP — vice-president? The way he carried himself made me wonder who could possibly preside over somebody like him. I must have been staring for a moment too long. I caught the glint in his eye as he stared right back at me, the raw power in his eyes almost like a jolt to my system. His wide, sensual lips tugged up at one side in amusement.

'Thought you said she was a screamer,' he said to Murphy, never taking his eyes from me. 'She looks more like a crazy one to me.' When he spoke, his voice was like gravel. It was so deep, each of his words reverberated in my chest. It was the kind of throaty sound that would either terrify or reassure.

I wondered which one it would do to me.

My small smile turned to a look of derision as I glared at Murphy. 'A screamer?'

'More of a moaner,' Murphy said stiffly, like a geek trying to fit in with the popular guys.

'Too bad you'll never know,' I shot back at him. He narrowed his freakish blue eyes at me, and my skin crawled.

'Shut your mouth,' Murphy said, but the biker in front of me seemed utterly absorbed in what I was saying. His mouth twitched at the side again, and he rubbed his stubbled chin with his fingers.

'What's your name, sweetheart?' he asked, a wolfish grin spreading across his face.

I resisted the strange impulse to smile along with him. *Just because he's smiling doesn't mean he's a nice guy.*

'Go fuck yourself,' I replied. *Go fuck yourself* seemed to be my go-to response when cornered by strange men.

'Huh,' he said, something I couldn't decipher coming alight in his eyes. Anger? Excitement? Whatever it was, it thrilled down my spine even as it scared the crap out of me. 'I don't blame you for being shy,' he said, jerking a thumb at Murphy. 'I wouldn't want to spend one more minute with him than I had to, either.'

I shot Murphy a fuck-you smile, and to my surprise, he grinned.

'Oh, honey,' he said, shaking his head. 'Good luck.' He walked to the door, picking up his duffel bag on the way. 'You're gonna need it.'

'Wait,' the VP said, addressing Murphy but still not taking his eyes from mine.

Murphy stopped stiffly in the doorway, his gaze fixed firmly on his car outside.

'Did you touch her?'

Murphy chuckled. 'Sure. A little. I didn't sample the merchandise though, if that's what you're asking.'

I glanced down to see the biker's fist clench tightly.

'Did he hurt you?' he asked, his gaze intense enough to make the tiny fine hairs on the back of my neck prickle.

I shook my head slowly, unable to form words under the pressure of his black eyes.

'Get the fuck out of here,' he said to Murphy. Murphy was out of the door and shutting himself in the car before anyone else could stop him. Asshole.

'You two, wait for us outside.'

Without hesitation, the two other bikers hauled out of the room, slamming the door in their wake.

And then, it was just me and the VP who thought I looked crazy.

'My name's Dornan,' the biker said.

Dornan? My blood turned to ice in my veins as I realised who he was. Dornan Ross. I'd never laid eyes on him, but the chatter among the families of my father's business associates had painted a picture of cruelty and bloodshed that was just as bad, if not worse, than Emilio's lethal reputation.

'Emilio's son Dornan?' I asked, hoping desperately that I was wrong.

He gave a short nod. *Great.*

'Seems an awfully big party to greet one little girl, Dornan,' I said, looking outside to the assembly of bikers. I desperately wanted to change the subject before he asked me my name. Before he asked me anything about myself. Because he was so suave, I was afraid I'd spill all my secrets before he'd even asked me. 'You afraid I'll do something?'

He dropped his gaze only to check me out. I felt naked under his eyes as he let them roam slowly over every part of me.

'Are you afraid you'll do something?' he asked. He still looked amused. Beneath my latent fascination with him, I felt the vague stirrings of irritation at his casual nature. I was a piece of property, for shit's sake. And he was talking to me like he was about to hit on me in a bar and buy me a goddamn strawberry daiquiri.

'You do this a lot?' I asked abruptly.

He took a step closer. I took a step back. It was timed so well, it was almost as if we were dancing some sort of macabre waltz.

He laughed when we moved in unison.

'Depends,' he replied, 'on what *this* is.'

'Pick up pretty girls for your daddy?' I shot back.

Something passed over his face for a moment and settled in his eyes. Something hard. And then, I blinked, and it was gone again.

'Sure,' he said, and his voice had changed somehow. Become more reserved, more guarded. Damn. The only person who'd shown me the tiniest bit of normality, and I had just alienated him. As usual, I was running off at the mouth before I thought about what I was actually saying.

'None as pretty as you, though,' he added. My gut twisted painfully at his words. *I want you to look pretty.* His father's words came back to haunt me.

He was silent for a beat. And then, 'I didn't catch your name.'

I weighed my decision for a few moments before deciding he'd find out as soon as he spoke to his father, anyway.

'Mariana,' I said softly. 'People call me Ana.'

'*Ana,*' he said, smiling. 'Welcome to the United States. The land of the free and the home of the brave.'

'Really?' I asked dubiously. 'You're quoting "The Star-Spangled Banner" to the girl who your father owns like a slave?'

'For now,' he replied.

'For now, what?' I asked, confused. 'You going to start quoting Backstreet Boys next?'

His grin was maddening and thrilling all at once. 'For now, my father owns you. But my father isn't here,' he said, gesturing with his open palms around the motel room. 'It's just me and you. And I *like* you. You're feisty. I think I might just keep you for myself.'

I swallowed thickly at what that could mean.

***

Outside, the bikers were getting restless. It was hot, and I could see beads of sweat glistening on Dornan's forehead and cheeks. 'Straight home, boys,' he ordered, making a twirling motion with his index finger. Within seconds the air was filled with the deafening noise of over a dozen Harleys gunning it down the road.

Dornan handed me a black helmet and I lifted it onto my head without arguing. It was weird, but I was so relieved to be away from Murphy, and so far from Emilio, that I was willing to do whatever Dornan said. Which made no sense at all because his reputation preceded him. He was a bad motherfucker, as bad as they came, and he was merciless. I had heard stories of the things he'd done, the ways he had killed people. His trademark was decapitation: cutting off the heads of the people who'd pissed him off and sending them to whoever needed to be sent a message.

I really hoped I wouldn't piss him off.

The inside of the helmet was blacked out, so I started to push the visor up with my hand.

'Leave it down,' he cautioned, grabbing my wrist as my world was engulfed by darkness. 'You try to open it while I'm riding, and I will pull over and hit you until your eyes swell shut. You hear me?'

I nodded, causing the too-large helmet to rattle around on my head, and he let my hand drop.

'Hold on, little lady,' he said, guiding me onto the back of a bike. 'We ride fast.'

A nervous thrill ran through me as he slipped onto the bike seat in front of me, reaching behind and curling his fingers around the backs of my knees. I yelped as he pulled, wedging me firmly against his leather-covered back.

He wasn't lying. As the last of the motorcycles tore out of the lot, we joined them, the drone so loud it felt like my teeth were coming loose.

I hung on to the man in front of me as tightly as I could, wanting to cry as I dug my nails into his washboard abs.

I didn't know if I was driving to my actual death, but part of me was dying as the wind tore at my loose hair and froze my neck.

I might just keep you for myself.

His words tore at the very fabric of my existence as I turned them over and over in my mind.

CHAPTER ELEVEN
DORNAN

She was pretty, but he'd seen pretty. Dornan Ross, vice-president of the Gypsy Brothers motorcycle club, had seen hundreds of pretty girls, broken and abused, usually by someone else but occasionally by him. As soon as the little minx had opened her mouth, his dick had twitched in his jeans at the thought of all the deplorable things he could do to her. She had sass, and spunk, and something else that he couldn't quite figure out.

She's a survivor. The phrase jumped into his head. She wasn't like the girls they typically had under these circumstances.

Women in the Gypsy Brothers world were divided firmly into three camps: Old ladies, who were wives or partners of the bikers and not to be shared around. Usually, they weren't welcome at the club, but occasionally they wheedled their way in. Then there were party girls, who were usually young and fucking stupid, and would pretty much let you stick it anywhere you wanted. Dornan had his favourites, the ones he used and abused, and he didn't feel guilty about it one little bit, because they chose to stay. They each got their pay-off in some way — drugs, protection, the thrill of danger. Sometimes they left the club, and other times, if they were found to have divulged club information — hell, even if they had *seen* something potentially incriminating — they were taken up to the roof of the clubhouse and given a bullet. Quick, efficient, and more often than not, nobody even reported them as missing, let alone actually *missed* them.

Yeah, it was a pretty bleak way to handle things, but the smart ones stayed alive because they knew what would happen if they stepped out of line.

Which made Dornan consider the third group of women who were frequently around the club compound.

The transients. The ones who didn't belong there. The ones who made him slightly uncomfortable, the ones his father insisted on dealing in.

The slaves.

Human trafficking was a nicer term for what they were doing with those girls, but not by much. Typically the girls were an in-and-out job, a truck or a boat or a carload that needed to go from point A to point B; usually teenage girls from out of state or, less frequently, from overseas. Sometimes, the girls would beg him to help them, and it broke his fucking heart every time he turned a blind eye to what his father was doing.

But he still did it, and so he was an asshole. He accepted that. It was part of who he was.

John Portland didn't like it. He was Dornan's best friend and the president of the Gypsy Brothers, and he abhorred the practice of taking these young girls and forcing them into a life of prostitution or drug smuggling. He wanted to fucking save everyone all the time. Dornan often had to remind him that his role as president was largely symbolic; he was not the one in charge.

It hadn't always been that way. The club had been just that — a club. Not a gang. Not organised crime. Just riding, free as birds, setting up camp and sleeping under the stars. They'd both ditched school in favour of seeing the world, riding their Triumphs across the USA, along Route 66 and beyond.

It had been John who suggested the name Gypsy Brothers. They'd jokingly tossed a coin and declared the winner the president, the loser VP. John had called heads, and the coin landed heads up. They'd cut lines into the flesh of their palms with a pocketknife and sealed the deal with a handshake marked in blood. Blood Brothers. Gypsy Brothers who travelled the roads, and had each other's backs.

And then everything had gone to shit. They'd returned home to LA to find Dornan's girlfriend, Lucy, pregnant with his baby, John's younger sister needing cancer treatment that he couldn't afford, and Dornan's mafioso father finally having caught up to his wayward son.

It was a complete clusterfuck. John's sister wasn't even eighteen, yet she was riddled with cancer. Full of cancer and no insurance meant one thing: John needed money, a lot of money, and fast.

It had seemed straightforward at the time. A road trip, a simple swap. Drugs for cash. But once Emilio had them under his thumb, it happened time and time again. The Gypsy Brothers club expanded to deal with the mounting work Emilio was throwing at them. Dornan liked to claim it was his family obligation, but really, he knew he couldn't argue. His father was a stone-cold killer from old-school *Italia*, and Dornan had always known that he would be called to the darkness one day. He'd felt that familiar violence bubble under his skin more than once.

He just didn't realise his best friend would end up as deep in the blood of innocents as him.

Lucy had crafted the Gypsy Brothers patches and the leather cut-off jackets that John and Dornan wore with pride. Lucy loved to fucking sew, especially when she was eight months pregnant and could barely move. It drove Dornan insane; every time he walked around the house barefoot he'd step on a goddamn sewing pin, sticking precariously out of the carpet. That had been before everything really went to shit, though. Once things got crazy and she was washing blood and pieces of brain matter out of her husband's clothes on a semi-regular basis, she'd stopped sewing.

It had started in the simplest, most innocent of ways; two friends, drinking beers by an open fire, shooting the shit and talking about how their lives might turn out. Things had been good then. Simple. Fun.

And now ... now, the Gypsy Brothers dealt in the darkest of sins. They stole lives and they ended them, and they did a damn fine job of both. Dornan sometimes wondered how things would have turned out if he had just kept riding, had never returned home, had never accepted his father's offer of cash to help John's sister in return for their souls.

The saddest thing of all was that she died anyway.

She died and Lucy ended up divorcing his ass, two kids and one affair later. So Dornan rarely thought about the old days. Rarely thought about the way he and John had signed their lives away, because, in the end, it had all been for nothing.

***

It wasn't that difficult to ride with a raging hard-on — unless the reason for that hard-on was seated behind you, her delicious warmth pressed up against the small of your back with her legs draped over your bike.

Dornan figured he must've had a guardian angel for the ride from San Diego, because there was no blood left in his head to help him think straight. It was all directed into his lap, dangerously close to the girl's small hands as she clung to him. At one point, when they reached open road and opened up their bikes, she held onto him so hard, her nails were gouging through his leather cut and t-shirt and into the firm flesh of his torso. He didn't say anything, though.

He enjoyed the pain.

Just before Tijuana, the boys broke up into several smaller groups to avoid attention. The bright lights of the San Ysidro border crossing that straddled Mexico and the United States marked the almost-there point, and Dornan was glad for that. He loved being on the bike, but there was shit to do to sort out this coke shortage, plus his dick wasn't showing any signs of calming down.

He revved his engine and made the turn into the road that led to his father's compound, and with one hand he reached behind and pulled the girl closer to him, so her heat was jammed up tight against his back. He thought he felt her gasp, and that only excited him more.

From what his father had said, this girl was going to be staying with them for a *very* long time. It made him fucking ashamed that he was looking forward to her captivity.

CHAPTER TWELVE

MARIANA

The ride had been hellish. With no reference to time or indication of how far we had left to travel, I had had no choice but to hold on to Dornan or let go and smash myself to pieces on the highway behind the bikes. Not being able to see anything was the worst part, and it made me feel ill, but I couldn't be sick in the narrow confines of the helmet. I doubted they'd stop to let me clean myself if I threw up, so I clenched my teeth and swallowed down my nausea for what seemed like hours.

And then, finally, the bikes slowed to a stop. Dornan patted my hand and someone else hooked their hands under my arms, pulling me off the bike. I stood on legs that threatened to dissolve underneath me, supporting myself against the bike with one shaking arm. I was sore, I was tired, and the only thing I'd eaten since I had arrived in the States — a greasy burger and fries — sat in my stomach like a rock that wanted to come back up.

My hands itched to pull up the visor, but I didn't touch it. A cool chill settled on my skin and I guessed that it must have been evening wherever we were.

'C'mon,' Dornan said, taking my wrist and guiding me up a flight of stairs, into what I assumed was some kind of building, and back down another flight of stairs. My stomach flipped nervously as I wondered where we were going and what was about to happen.

What *did* happen to slave girls, anyway?

Was he going to beat me? Force himself on me? The shock of Este's death and the past twenty-four hours were still clinging to my consciousness and making me act in a kind of weird, detached way that was completely foreign to me. I was normally feisty, determined and demanding. Not a meek, quiet girl who let herself be blindfolded and led into the pits of hell.

Este. I *ached* to weep for him, to unleash my anger with fists to the walls, to smash my knuckles into something until they bled. I wanted to hurt something, or someone. I wanted to hurt my father. But he wasn't here, so maybe I could hurt Dornan, instead. A door slammed and the helmet was finally removed.

'You didn't tell me you were taking me to the Hilton,' I drawled, turning my head to take in the small room we were in. Dornan set the suitcase Murphy had purchased and filled with clothes in my size on the ground. I guessed one of the other bikers had brought it. 'I gotta take a piss,' he said, turning to leave the room.

'Nice,' I replied, my eyes burning under the single bare bulb that hung from the ceiling. 'Thanks for the information overload.'

He smiled, one hand on the door knob.

'Wait,' I said, sounding much too desperate for my liking.

He stopped, but didn't turn around.

'Will you ... will you come back?' I didn't want to be with him, but I wanted to be alone even less. And I figured I was going to be here a good long while, so I'd better start off on the right foot with Dornan before Murphy reappeared or Emilio decided I was better off dead.

There was something about Dornan, something different. I was afraid of him, but not in the same way that I was afraid of Emilio or Murphy. It was a different fear.

How silly I was. I should have feared him the most, because he would be the one to destroy me in the end.

But I *was* silly, and foolish, and grieving. I didn't want to be alone.

'Do you want me to come back?' he asked.

I did. But why? Because I liked him? No. I hated him and everything he stood for.

But I was afraid. Of the dark. Of the quiet. Of the possibility that once he left the room and slammed the door shut behind him, I'd be forgotten, clawing at the walls for days and weeks until my throat stopped being able to scream and I lay down and died. What if they just left me here to rot?

'Yes,' I whispered.

He let his hand drop from the door handle and turned slowly, meeting my eyes with what could only be described as a predatory gaze. He had something on me, even if it was as insignificant as my terror of being alone, and he *knew* it. He trailed his eyes down to my chest, over my waist and down to my feet, before repeating the journey in reverse.

I stood rooted to the spot as he dragged a pack of Marlboros from his pocket and lit up, drawing in a long, apparently satisfying breath. He took two steps, bridging the gap between us as he offered me the cigarette, blowing smoke in my face.

He grinned, rolling the cigarette between two fingers in front of my face.

'You know,' he said slyly, 'I'm not here to save you, Ana.'

Devastation squeezed at my chest as I accepted the cigarette, my skin burning where it touched his. *Nobody can save me now.*

Placing the cigarette to my lips, I took a long, steady drag and blew a cloud of smoke right back at him.

'That's okay, *Papi*,' I replied, tapping ash onto the ground as unexpected spikes of something ran down my spine in a shiver. 'I'm not here to be saved.'

He took the cigarette back, smiling at me in the dark.

CHAPTER THIRTEEN
DORNAN

He didn't care that he was married, or that she was his captive. When she stuck his cigarette between her lips and inhaled, it took every ounce of Dornan's willpower not to press her up against the wall and suck the smoke right out of her mouth as he devoured her. Instead, he settled for studying every inch of her with his ravenous eyes, as she spoke in that sexy little accent and slow-blinked those big eyes at him.

And *she had asked him to come back*. His dick was practically trying to jump out of his pants and into her, and he bit the inside of his cheek to distract himself.

He found himself dreaming up scenarios to extend his father's business trip in Bogota, ways to have this girl to himself for a few days instead of just a few more hours. He wanted to touch her. He wanted to run his hands down those smooth brown arms that'd been wrapped around him for almost an hour, and he wanted to brush his fingertips against those lush rosebud lips that made the difference between her being pretty and being beautiful.

Beautiful. He realised it had been forever since he'd thought a woman beautiful. He'd seen plenty of pretty girls, plenty of sexy women. But truly *beautiful* women were few and far between in his world. It was too violent, too bloody, too masochistic for beautiful women to survive, and so they somehow knew to stay away.

But she had offered herself to his father, a willing captive, in exchange for the safety of her parents and siblings. It impressed him. It intrigued the hell out of him. Dornan respected his father, but if the right person came along and wanted to take Emilio out, Dornan would probably load the bullets into the gun and hand it to them himself.

Yeah, he had issues. Didn't everyone, though? He saw the haunted look in this girl's eyes and knew that it was unintentional. She thought she was being cocky, a smartass, and for the most part that was what he saw. But there was something else in her gaze, in those big, almond-shaped eyes that begged him to stay with her.

Sadness. Wisdom. She was older than her nineteen years, much older. He wondered about the things she had seen that would make her like that, and he vowed to keep her close until he knew all of her precious secrets.

But for now? For now, he was going to take a piss before he exploded. Then, he was going to take a long, hot shower and beat one out. He was going to close his eyes and imagine that it was her pink lips at the end of his dick as he took the edge off. He needed to get her out of his goddamn brain for two minutes so he could focus on business.

And the business was particularly demanding of his focus today. Ana's father had lost a shitload of cocaine to the DEA, and Emilio's carefully supplied network was screaming for product that they didn't have. The coke trade that was the foundation for everything Emilio and Dornan did was a beast, and the beast was screaming to be fed.

Despite Ana's request, he didn't go back into the room immediately after using the bathroom down the hall. Instead, he made the somewhat reluctant pilgrimage upstairs to the kitchen, from where his mother had been banished in anticipation of a heated meeting with some of the Cartel's main players. His uncle Julian was sitting at the long oak dining table, next to Emilio, who was at the head of the table. Of course. The old man took every chance he could get to assert his position of power, and remind everyone else they were beneath him.

Dornan found it both annoying and fascinating.

'You just get in?' Dornan asked, confused.

He nodded a greeting at Julian as he watched his father stab a cherry tomato and devour it.

Dornan thought of what he'd just done. He had picked the girl up with a contingent of his men because Emilio had told him he'd be away for a few more days, and couldn't do it himself. And now here he was, in the kitchen, sitting at the dining table eating fucking tomato salad and arugula.

Emilio shrugged, chewing on a mouthful of food.

'Where is everyone?' Dornan asked, more than a little irritated.

His father shrugged again, and Dornan bit down on his tongue until he tasted blood. His fucking father was infuriating.

Dornan turned and left the room, not bothering to look back. He'd learned over the years that it was so much easier to walk away from his father. Every other motherfucker who annoyed him had to answer to him, but Daddy dearest was sadly off limits. After all, Emilio was the man who ensured their shady world kept turning.

Dornan left the kitchen, letting the heavy door close behind him as he stalked across the foyer. Tall double doors with brass handles reached up in front of him, and he grabbed both handles at the same time, flinging them open onto the verandah that flanked the front of the house.

A sea of motorcycles greeted him, but no Gypsy Brothers to accompany them. What the fuck? A dozen guys in leathers weren't easy to miss. He looked to his left, noticing two cars had been pulled out of the three-car garage and parked in front of the closed doors. Bingo.

He covered the distance between the house and garage quickly, throwing open the single service door to the garage that sat right next to the first of three tilt-doors. The smell of sex immediately invaded his nostrils, entirely unwelcome since it wasn't him who was taking part in the act.

The garage was massive. It was slightly insulting that Emilio chose to banish any of Dornan's crew to the garage instead of letting them into the house, but right now Dornan couldn't fault his father. He raised his eyebrows as he saw one of the young Mexican women who cleaned for his father, completely naked on the hood of his mother's Mercedes. The poor woman would have a heart attack if she saw how her car was being corrupted. The chick on the hood, the girl who dusted his mother's blinds and washed their fucking towels, had her legs spread wide and one of his guys was mouth-fucking her. She moaned loudly, throwing her head back as she said something unintelligible in Spanish. She looked like she was having a fine time.

Dornan stepped closer and cleared his throat, the woman's body shuddering at the same time as she opened her eyes, the shock on her face almost comedic. She slammed a hand over her mouth and locked eyes with Dornan, stifling a loud moan as she came.

Her cheeks went bright red and she looked down at the Gypsy Brother between her legs, trying to bat him away with her free hand. Apparently Viper was too far into what he was doing to even realise his boss was standing behind him. He stood up, not paying attention to the chick's expression as she covered her face in shame, pulling her hips closer to him and slamming himself into her.

'Vipe,' Dornan said pointedly.

Viper jumped so high in the air he almost took the chick off the hood of the car.

'Fuck!' he yelled in surprise, falling on top of the car's hood and making the woman scream as he no doubt gave her his all.

'Vipe,' Dornan repeated, starting to get angry. 'What the fuck are you doing?'

Viper pushed himself up on the hood of the car so he wasn't crushing the woman, a sheepish look on his face. 'I was waitin' for you, D,' he said, continuing to thrust.

Dornan sighed. 'You've got two minutes to get out of that woman and into the kitchen. You can fuck the help after we've sorted this coke situation.'

'I figured you'd be banging that one we just picked up,' Vipe said.

Dornan chose not to answer. 'You get your jizz on my mother's car, I'll cut your nuts off myself.'

He left Viper to his business and stalked back into the house. There was only one other place his boys would be. He burst back into the front doors, taking a sharp right down the hallway until he reached a door at the end. He threw the door open and what he saw made him want to laugh until he cried.

His mother had insisted on having her sitting room made big enough to accommodate their large extended family. It was an impressive room, all high ceilings and wing-backed brown leather chairs nestled between overstuffed sofas. His mother sat in her own custom recliner, an espresso balanced expertly between her thumb and forefinger.

That wasn't the strange part. The strange part was the twelve Gypsy Brothers sitting around awkwardly sipping on coffees.

'Ma,' Dornan chided. 'What the hell are you doin' back here with this lot?' His mother, a short, blonde woman in her fifties, raised one manicured eyebrow as she extended a slender arm to her mouth and sipped her coffee.

'The boys have been filling me in on your latest endeavours,' she said, her Queens accent as strong as it had ever been, even though she'd been in San Diego for the better part of thirty-five years. 'Seems your father's gotten himself into a dire situation.'

Dornan balled his fists angrily, glaring at the brothers. 'Everybody,' he said, deadly calm. 'Get the fuck out of this room and into the kitchen. Now.'

Most of them appeared grateful as they dumped their cups on the coffee table and high-tailed it out of the room in a stampede of leather and heavy footsteps. Once the last Gypsy Brother had vacated the room, Dornan turned to face his mother. She made no move to stand as her son towered over her.

'You know,' she said, glancing down into her coffee, 'I used to take you and your brother to the park when you were little. You liked the swings the best. When it was time to go home, you'd scream and beg me to stay.'

Dornan softened slightly; he never could stay angry at his mother, even though she did have a nasty habit of sticking her nose in where it didn't belong. He already had Emilio breathing down his neck with every step he took. He didn't need his mother keeping tabs on the club as well.

'I'd pick you up in my arms and carry you away. You were probably only three or four.' Her blue eyes sparkled as she reminisced. 'You used to yell, "Help! Mommy, help me!"'

Dornan's mouth twitched up at the memory.

'You looked nothing like me,' she said, some of the joy having leaked out of her voice. 'You were all your father. Still are.'

Something inside Dornan's chest buzzed painfully as he crouched down in front of his mother.

'Ma,' he said gently, trying to catch her gaze.

Her blue eyes filled with water as she finally made eye contact with him.

'Not like your brother,' she whispered. 'He was just like me. Just like me.'

Dornan recalled a small boy with blonde hair and blue eyes. A boy who never got old enough to leave high school before he was gunned down on his way from school as retribution for something Dornan couldn't even remember anymore. A casualty of the war that never seemed to end.

'Ma,' he repeated softly, taking her free hand and squeezing it between his own palms.

'I worry about you,' she said plainly, her eyes still glassy. 'You're all I've got left.'

Such a display of emotion was rare from his mother; she almost always maintained a ruthless calm that served her well. Her reputation was that of a woman to be feared, a cartel queen who has earned her right alongside the king. But here, now, Dornan saw the fear inside his mother's eyes, and that fear pulled at him.

'You don't need to worry,' Dornan said, giving her hand one last squeeze before he placed it back in her lap.

He stood and turned to leave, her final words like a knife in his chest.

'That's what your brother said,' she murmured.

***

His mother's vulnerability had rattled him. Still, there was business to attend to, so Dornan did what he was best at: pushing away everything else and focusing on the task at hand. He'd become adept at compartmentalising things after Raph had died. If he didn't push the dark things down into the abyss inside him, he'd be eaten alive by rage.

In the kitchen, things were finally happening. Emilio still presided over the head of the table, Julian by his side. Dornan's men sat and stood around a spot beside Emilio that was obviously meant for him. Dornan glanced at the empty seat beside his father before taking a spot at the opposite end of the table, directly opposite his father.

'What'd I miss?' Dornan asked, folding his arms across the Gypsy Brothers crest that adorned the leather cut he wore.

His father turned his eyes up to acknowledge him before returning to the map in front of him. 'Los Angeles,' he said briskly. 'Who else do we know who supplies?'

Dornan frowned. 'That's the thing about a monopoly,' he answered. 'Nobody else supplies, Pop. We're it.'

Emilio didn't look impressed.

'We've got a shipment of meth coming, right?'

Emilio continued to stare at his son, a small shrug of his shoulder the only indication he had heard the question.

'We push that,' Dornan suggested. 'Discounted until we can get our coke situation covered.'

Emilio grunted. His indifference infuriated Dornan.

'We done here?' Dornan asked. 'These boys can accompany the shipment personally this time. It's due tonight, is it not?'

'Midnight,' Emilio answered. 'At the dock.'

Dornan nodded. When no one moved, he threw his hands up.

'Everyone get that? Nine o'clock at the dock.' He glanced at his watch, seeing they still had a few hours to kill. 'Leave now. Go get something to eat. I'll see you boys out there.'

Viper, who'd been silent until this point, suddenly spoke up. 'You're not coming with us, D?'

Dornan shook his head, avoiding his father's amused stare. 'I said, I'll meet you there. Get out of here, all of you.'

They filed out of the room, the heavy kitchen door slamming after them. Dornan pressed his palms flat on the table and studied his father.

'Was there something else?' Emilio asked, looking up from the papers in front of him.

Dornan shook his head, pressing off the table with his hands and leaving the room.

But he'd lied. There was something else. Her name was Mariana.

And she'd asked him to come back.

***

Dornan didn't enter her room once he was downstairs. Instead, he stood outside the door, pressing his eye to the peephole that showed a fish-eye view of the small room. Yeah, he was a fucking pervert. It didn't bother him. She was a grown woman, and she had asked him to come back.

For a while, she paced, probably waiting for him to return. He bore the time patiently, dismissing the hunger in his stomach after a full day on the road. Once he went upstairs, he'd be on the phone and screaming at the rest of the guys to try and get some product out onto the street. So he took his time, and he watched the girl pace in her tiny room.

Three paces, turn, three paces. She did this over and over again, and he imagined for a moment that she was doing it for him. But she seemed oblivious to his peeping, her stride getting quicker, her face turning from carefully controlled detachment to an anxious rage. She stopped at the far end of the room, her back to him, and struck out at the wall in front of her. She kicked it a couple of times too, but most of her energy seemed intent on using her fists to smash the fucking wall to smithereens. It wasn't as if she was trying to escape — the wall was solid limestone, anyone could see that.

No, the little Colombian girl that made his cock ache was mad. Ropeable. Absolutely fucking *enraged*.

He watched her a little longer, a vague sense of concern pressing at him as he saw the blood dripping from her knuckles. She stopped hitting the wall, but she didn't stop hurting herself. She marched over to the suitcase he'd left inside the door, opened it and spilled the contents onto the ground. Selecting a small round compact from the pile of clothes and make-up, she opened it and threw it at the ground. The mirror shattered into several pieces, and he watched with interest as she knelt down and selected one of the larger pieces.

He assumed she was going to hide it, use it as a weapon for when he re-entered the room, but what she did next surprised the hell out of him. She took the piece of mirrored glass in her hand, sat on the narrow bed that took up one corner of the room, and held out her wrist.

Is she going to ...?

She was. She dragged the sharp tip of the glass down the inside of her wrist, and fresh blood sprang forth. The sight excited him — yeah, he was a sick motherfucker. He enjoyed the sight of blood. He wanted to burst into the room, kneel in front of her, and lick the deep cut in her arm from end to end.

As long as she didn't stab him in the neck while he did it.

Make sure she isn't marked.

His father's words came back to taunt him, and it gave him the perfect excuse to interrupt her psychotic attempt at self-mutilation.

Make sure she is untouched.

Well, that one was a little more difficult, but he'd do his best to make sure he at least didn't leave bruises on her if he found himself unable to resist. He'd never raped a woman, but he'd never needed to — they usually found his enthusiasm a turn-on more than anything. He might have coerced or blackmailed, but he'd never straight-up held a woman down and driven himself inside her against her will.

Yet.

He liked to think he never would, but he was his father's son. The darkness that flowed through his veins disgusted him, but trying to resist it had only ever made things worse. When he tried to control the darkness inside him it didn't abate, but stored up in increments, until it inevitably bubbled up like poison, rendering his violence uncontrollable. He'd killed people over trivial matters when he let things get too pent up, so he figured it was better to destroy the people who were the source of his rage in the first place. Even as he justified the blood on his hands to himself, he knew that he was a bad man. Hopefully, though, he wasn't the worst.

Make sure she isn't marked.

Dornan groaned as he opened the door and saw Ana sitting on the bed, sobbing incoherently as she bled all over herself.

'What are you doing?' he asked her as he closed the door behind him. He expected her to try and hide the glass, or run from him, or attack him. He expected something. What he didn't expect was for her to continue what she was doing, dragging the sharp glass down her arm as if he wasn't there, as she muttered and shook and wept.

'Hey!' he said, a little louder this time. He crossed the room in two quick steps and grabbed hold of the hand that held the offending weapon, squeezing hard until she was forced to drop it. The glass fell to the ground, breaking into two bloodied, uneven shards.

'Seven years bad luck,' he said flippantly, looking from the glass to her glazed eyes. He felt relief when she glared at him, the daze seemingly broken.

'Are you kidding me?' she growled. 'I think I've got a lifetime of bad luck ahead of me, don't you?'

He kicked the glass away and sat beside her on the bed, close enough that his jeans brushed her blood-smeared thigh. 'What did you do that for?' he asked, genuinely curious.

She shot him a look so scathing, it made him want to shrink back — only, he was Dornan fucking Ross, and he shrank back from nobody, not even his own father.

'I know you were watching me,' she replied, and it made him smile.

'I like watching you,' he said, shocked by his own honesty. 'Does that bother you?'

She continued to stare boldly at him. 'Your father's men killed my boyfriend last night,' she said, making a choking noise at the back of her throat.

There it was. Her anguish. Her struggle. Her *why*.

'I'm sorry,' he said, noticing how the blood was still pouring from her wrist. She'd cut deeper than he'd first thought. 'May I?' he gestured towards her wrist and she shrugged, which he took as an invitation. He gathered his grip around the underside of her wrist and cradled it up to the light, gently inspecting the cut.

'Are you trying to kill yourself?' he asked, probing at the wound with his fingers to determine its depth, all the while biting down on the tip of his tongue to stop it from darting out and licking up her blood.

'Of course not,' she retorted, pulling her hand away. But Dornan didn't release his grip on her, and they stared each other down in a silent battle of eyes and wills.

'Don't you ever want to hurt yourself because you can't hurt the person who fucked everything up?'

Her words were frank and revealing, making him ponder them. Every time he smashed his own fists into a boxing bag, or a whore, or another Gypsy Brother, he relished the pain, and welcomed the relief that spilling his own blood offered.

'Let me guess,' Dornan said, rubbing his thumb along her cut as she watched in silence. 'My father?'

She snapped her gaze back to him, a sadness bursting forth from her that made him drop her wrist and stand up, lest that sadness infect him in some way.

'Yes,' she said brokenly. 'Your father. And mine.'

He didn't take his eyes from her until he remembered the blood, and looked down to see it coating his palms.

'You like blood, don't you?' she asked suddenly. 'Other people would recoil at the sight of it, but not you. You wear it like an old outfit. It suits you.'

Anyone else would have been embarrassed to admit it, but not Dornan. He traded in lives and in blood, so why shouldn't he like it? And in this case, she had spilled it of her own volition, which made him all the more excited.

'I like *your* blood,' he replied, smiling wolfishly. 'I like it very much.'

CHAPTER FOURTEEN
MARIANA

To say I was embarrassed would be an understatement.

I was *mortified*.

When Dornan didn't come back, I'd assumed I was on my own for the night. And, truth be told, I was terrified. I eyed the bed at first, thinking that I could maybe get a little sleep, but the thought of being woken with a knife at my neck or a gun in my mouth made me determined to stay awake.

So I paced. I always paced when I was nervous, or impatient. This time, however, I was pacing almost entirely to keep myself from passing out and waking up to an even worse situation.

My stomach cramped into a twisted, painful knot, and for some reason it made me think of Luis.

I will never see him again.

The thought stabbed at my insides with such ferocity, it doubled me over with grief. I clung to the limestone wall, bits flaking off and coating my palms with a powdery chalk.

Was I dying? It felt like I was dying. As far as my sweet boy would know, his mother would have vanished.

He would never know all the nights I had cried for him, clung to him while he was still in my womb, wishing for us both that he could just stay in there forever so he didn't have to leave me.

And now I had left him. Because my father had fucked up again.

I had paid for his sins with my life. And it sickened me.

I didn't even realise I had struck the wall at first. There was a burst of pain in my fist that lanced through my arm, the shock registering in my neck and head. My ears rang. It hurt. It felt *good*.

So I did it again.

And again.

And again.

Until my hands were covered in blood and my knuckles were a pulp of red, broken skin.

The blood calmed me a little, I'm not sure why. It was the same reason I'd hidden a razor blade in my mattress at boarding school and traced thin cuts into my thighs while my roommates slept, blissfully unaware. Back then, the blood that sprang from my skin had made my sadness tangible. It had distracted me from the fact that my baby was thousands of miles away, on another continent, and everybody was acting like he didn't exist. It had soothed the tears that dripped silently from my face onto my thighs, mixing with my blood. It had made me strong.

I suddenly craved that feeling again. Punching the wall had brought a temporary relief, but it waned quickly, and I wanted more. I knew Murphy had packed a small round mirror in with the cosmetics he'd bought for me — I had been forced to sit still while he painted my face with blush and lip gloss before we boarded our first flight. I knew there was glass in there that I could break and drag along my flesh; glass that would bring me some of that sweet relief I was craving.

So when Dornan had walked in, I didn't even see him at first. Honestly, I was so hysterical by that point, I'd kind of forgotten where I was or what was happening. Hence the self-mutilation. I needed to come back down to earth.

And come back to earth I did when I finally saw him.

My own father had caught me cutting myself in the bathroom once. I was on summer vacation, and he wouldn't let me out of the house to see Este in case I got knocked up again. It hurt my heart to be so close to the boy I loved, yet so far away. I had sobbed and raged, but my father responded by giving me the beating of my life and telling me to fuck off. It was the only time he'd ever hit me when he was sober, and it had hurt all the more because of that fact.

So I had gotten the razor out. And as the first blood had emerged from my thigh, my father had walked into the bathroom without knocking.

He never said a word to me. Never asked why. He just looked at me in disgust, turned on his heel, and slammed the door shut.

So, naturally, I expected Dornan Ross to do the same. But he wasn't an ordinary man. Somehow I already knew this from our brief interaction earlier. He didn't avert his eyes or stay away from me.

He came closer. He touched me where I bled. I watched him lick his lips unconsciously as he studied my handiwork.

It should have made me afraid of him, but what did I have to lose? I'd already lost everything.

I couldn't help myself. When he had got up to leave me, I couldn't bear the thought of being alone again with my despair. When he told me he liked my blood, and his eyes had gleamed with a hunger unlike anything I'd ever seen, *I knew*.

He was a dangerous man. And he liked me. *Liked my blood*. If I could get him on my side — maybe, just maybe, I could get myself out of this mess.

He said he liked my blood, but he left me anyway. I thought he wasn't coming back, until he returned a few moments later with a first-aid kit.

I sat on the edge of the bed and let him play doctor. It was jarring, the way he picked my hand up like it was made of glass and examined it, the skin on his fingers rough but his touch gentle. For a six-foot tall, muscled, tattooed biker in leathers, his touch was surprisingly tender.

'You've done this before,' he said, glancing at the faint lines that marred my thighs. I didn't answer him, tugging my dress down again to cover the scars.

'I'm not suicidal,' I said suddenly. And why should it matter if I was? But for some reason I wanted him to know. I needed him to understand.

'Darlin',' he said, as he dragged a sterile wipe over my bloody arm. 'Nobody would blame you if you were suicidal. You're pretty fucked right now.'

I diverted my eyes to the floor.

'What's going to happen to me?' I blurted out suddenly. His hands stilled, but he didn't speak. I raised my eyes to his in question, and what I saw there made my stomach lurch.

'Do you want me to lie to you,' he asked, continuing to wrap the bandage around my arm, 'or do you want me to tell the truth?'

I pondered that.

'Lie,' I said softly. I would ask him for the truth in a moment, but I was curious to see what he came up with.

'Lie,' he repeated, studying the wall behind me as he appeared deep in thought. 'Well, I'd say you're going to be taken upstairs and given a reprieve. You'll be allowed to walk out of those front gates, and go on your merry way home. And this is all just temporary.'

Temporary. Huh.

'And the truth?'

He smiled. 'I thought you'd never ask.' He finished with the bandage and let my arm drop softly in my lap. The smile left his face and that glimmer in his eyes faded.

'You'll be stuck down here until Emilio decides what he wants to do with you. And you'll do it. Or he'll put a bullet in that pretty little head of yours, and bury you where nobody will ever find you.'

'Oh,' I said, that sinking feeling in my stomach coming back.

'What do you think he'll want me to do?' I asked.

He paused and my heart leapt into my throat as I anticipated what he might say. *You'll have to fuck strange men. You'll have to suck their dicks. You'll have to let them hurt you. You'll be punished if you do, and punished more if you don't.* Or even the simple, *Welcome to hell.*

But he didn't say any of that. Instead, he picked up the first-aid kit and stood, gazing down at me.

'Come on,' he said. 'You know what's going to happen. You're a smart girl. You don't need me to spell it out for you.'

My heart broke. He was right. I knew exactly what was going to happen. I was going to be used and abused, until there was nothing left.

CHAPTER FIFTEEN
MARIANA

When Dornan left, promising to return with something for me to eat, I didn't anticipate him returning ten seconds later with his father in tow.

I could tell that Emilio was annoyed, but I had no idea why. I'd done as I was told. Flown thousands of miles with his psychotic employee. Ridden on the back of his son's bike, effectively blindfolded. Gone to my dungeon like a good little girl.

And then I remembered the blood.

'What the *fuck* is this?' Emilio asked, after he'd burst past his son. Dornan said nothing as Emilio snatched up my arm, tearing at the bandage. He glared at his son. 'I specifically said not to mark her. Did you do this?'

Dornan remained blank. 'No,' he said. As soon as Emilio turned back to me that glint of amusement sprang forth in Dornan's eye.

'Who did this to you, girl?' Emilio demanded. 'I'll skin their fucking hide.'

His concern was odd and I was terrified of telling him that I had cut myself.

'She fell off the bike,' Dornan broke in unexpectedly. 'Fainted. It's lucky she didn't hurt herself any worse. I don't think that fucker gave her anything to eat the whole time he had her.'

Emilio ground his teeth around the toothpick that was jammed between his lips, muttering obscenities in Italian. 'Fucking Murphy,' he said.

He shook his head, hands on his hips. He looked like the damn Godfather in his tailored suit. 'Have you checked her out yet?' he asked Dornan, with such a casual tone it made my skin crawl.

'Checked me out?' I repeated.

Emilio threw me a look of derision before looking back to his son.

Dornan shook his head. 'I was busy cleaning her up. I know you hate mess.' His jaw clenched as he spoke, and it was obvious to me that he didn't like the power his father wielded over him.

Interesting.

'What do you mean?' I asked, louder this time. 'What does he mean?'

'Shut up, bitch,' Emilio said, clearly annoyed that I was speaking.

'Whatever, old man,' I replied.

He paused, turning slowly.

'What did you say?'

'I said, *whatever*,' I repeated. 'I might have offered myself up as a trade for my family's lives. Doesn't mean I need to *enjoy* it.'

He chuckled, the rage still evident in the way his neck tensed. 'You'd be a sick little whore if you did enjoy it here.'

'You're an asshole,' I answered.

I was rewarded with a punch to the jaw. Seemed his rage overrode his desire not to mark me. It fucking hurt, too, propelling me backwards. I fell against the bed in a pile of limbs, covering my face with my hands.

'Wait,' I said, panting a little. 'So you get to call me bitch and whore, but I don't get to call you what I want? That's hardly fair.'

His smile vanished and he spat the toothpick out, stalking towards me.

'Life isn't fair,' he said emphatically. 'If life were fair, your stupid father wouldn't have LOST MY FUCKING COCAINE!'

His tone terrified me, and I couldn't help but close my eyes as Emilio's spittle landed on my cheek.

My reaction seemed to calm the beast, to satisfy him. He sucked in a breath and let his shoulders drop, as if composing himself.

'My name is Emilio,' he breathed, his gold tooth glinting in the harsh light of the bare bulb above us. 'But you will call me *Master*.'

Before I could protest or cry or make some smartass joke, before I could even decide how to react, he reached around and grabbed the back of my neck, pulling me from the bed and slamming me forcefully to the ground. The damp concrete knocked the air from my lungs, and I gasped.

Crack!

He kicked me in the ribs, forcefully enough for me to hear a snap as something broke. White-hot pain sang in my bones, reaching a brutal climax when my nerves relayed the searing message to my brain.

I thought I'd be braver. I thought I'd be able to take his torment, his violence, and smile at him with blood-smeared teeth. But I wasn't brave. I was scared.

I broke.

I opened my mouth, and screamed.

He left the room after that. I curled into an awkward ball, not too tight, because my ribs were screaming in agony, but as tight as I could, because it was freezing in the room.

Time stretched out, as my stomach rumbled and my ribs protested their pain.

Hunger. Pain. Sadness. Despair. They all threw a party inside me, and all I wanted was for them to go away, to give me some peace for a few brief moments. *All I wanted was for the pain to go away.*

I recoiled as I saw a boot appear in my vision.

'Hey,' the voice that belonged to the boot soothed. Dornan. 'It's okay. I'll save my beating for tomorrow.'

I frowned, looking up at him as he knelt beside me; he was smiling and I couldn't tell if he was joking or not.

'I think my ribs are broken,' I wheezed.

He nodded. 'Probably. I heard something snap.'

I moaned, trying to roll over. I eventually managed to get to my knees, and he helped me to my feet like I was as light as a feather.

I sat on the edge of the bed gingerly, trying not to move anything. Each time I took in a breath, white-hot pain radiated from a spot underneath my heart. He broke my ribs! Beneath the fog of pain, I was furious. Wasn't taking me from my family enough? Wasn't killing my boyfriend enough? Wasn't forcing me to swallow those fake cocaine capsules *enough*?

Of course it wasn't enough. He would keep hitting, keep hurting, keep taunting, until I stopped responding. He was a power-hungry psychopath. He did a *magnificent* job of playing the bastard. He didn't care if I suffered; in fact, my suffering was essential to him.

I chastised myself for being so receptive to Dornan. He was the enemy. It was like a really shitty version of good cop / bad cop, and I had fallen for it hook, line and sinker.

'I'll get you something to eat,' Dornan said. 'I'll be right back.'

I looked at him with all of the disgust I could muster.

'Don't bother,' I said mechanically, no emotion in my tone. He was Emilio's son, not my friend, and though he'd bandaged me up, and said he liked my blood, it would be the last of my blood he would get to touch without a fight.

I wasn't falling for his bullshit act. He was a Gypsy Brother. They might own me now, but it didn't mean I had to like it. Like *him*.

Dornan raised an eyebrow. 'Lost your appetite? Yeah, he does that to me, too.'

I didn't respond, and eventually he took the hint, and left.

CHAPTER SIXTEEN

MARIANA

I fell into a broken sleep shortly after Dornan left me alone with my broken ribs and rumbling stomach. I was so worn out, so beyond thought, that I no longer cared if someone murdered me in my sleep. I just needed to pass out for a couple of hours and regroup. But nightmares of my mother's crying face taunted me, making me twist and turn, my ribs protesting with white-hot pain every time I did so.

Morning came eventually, and with it, a fragile sense of calm. The hum in my ribs was still high, but it had settled down from its original peak.

Este. I couldn't bear to think of him, the way his eyes had glazed over as his life had ebbed away, his blood dripping into the cracks of the cobblestoned street beneath him and leaving an empty void.

I sat up with a start as something banged on the other side of the door. 'Christ,' I muttered, as the sudden movement shifted my ribs painfully. It hurt so much, it took my breath away. Dornan stood in the doorway, a troubling look on his face. It looked somewhere between amusement and cool detachment, the smile of his mouth saying one thing but the fact that it didn't reach his eyes saying another.

'Here to check me out?' I asked sarcastically.

His smile blossomed into a wide grin. He thought I was funny?

'I'm so glad my questions entertain you,' I said, getting to my feet. 'Can I please go to the bathroom now?'

I was ready to burst. It'd been a long time between visits.

'Sure,' he said, opening the door wider and stepping to the side. I looked up, startled, and this time he did laugh at me.

'There are armed guards all the way down the hall,' he said. 'So yeah, I'm letting you take a piss. You've got five minutes.'

I glared at him, my bladder winning the battle between running and staying put. As I sidled past him, our hands brushed together, and I recoiled at the sudden spark that seemed to ignite between our skin.

He's the enemy.

It bothered me that I even had to remind myself of that fact.

He was right. There was a guard near the bathroom, holding one of the same sub-machine guns as the ones my father and brother had had pointed at their heads. Berettas. I was going to end up with a urinary tract infection pretty soon, unless I was granted a toilet break more than once every twelve hours.

I contemplated asking to take a shower as I gazed longingly at the small, screenless cubicle beside the vanity.

'Hurry up,' Dornan called from my room, and I sighed, trudging back.

I froze when I saw what he had in his hand.

Years ago, my highly paranoid father had insisted on having all of us microchipped, in case we went missing. In case we were abducted, to be more accurate. Some schemer had spun him a story about the microchips having GPS capabilities, but he had been lying. They were the same chips people put into their pets in case they went missing, so that if someone found them, they could scan the chip, return the pet to its owner and everyone could live happily ever after.

Or, in our case, so that our bodies could be identified.

I snapped from my thoughts back to the scene in front of me — Dornan, standing in the middle of the small room in his full biker garb, holding a microchip scanner in his hand.

Shit.

I feigned indifference, walking slowly into the room and trying to look anywhere but at what he was holding. The small scar in my unharmed wrist throbbed painfully, threatening to burst and spill all of my secrets.

Dornan watched me enter the room with amusement, licking his lips as he took me in from head to toe.

'What's this?' I asked, picking up on the vibe that something was different about today. Different from his friendly manner of yesterday, when he'd liked my blood and bandaged me up.

'Clothes off,' he said.

I choked. So this was really happening. My skin burned at the thought of being separated from my dress.

'Why?' I asked.

He waved the scanner in his hand. 'A little bird told me you've got treasure hidden somewhere. I want to go treasure hunting.'

Asshole.

'What are you talking about?' I stalled.

He took a step towards me, erasing the space between us. I tried to back up and ended up with the backs of my calves pressed against the bed frame.

'I think you know what I'm talking about,' he said. 'If you tell me where it is, you can keep your dress on.'

I glared at him.

'Or maybe you want to take it off for me?'

'Go fuck yourself,' I muttered.

He tensed momentarily. 'Dress off it is. Hurry up. Or I'll kick your ribs until the rest of them are broken, too.'

I scowled at him, but I started to lift my dress up, praying that the chip was redundant and that his scanner wouldn't pick it up. I was terrified of him finding the chip and having a reason to cut me. I might have hurt myself sometimes and relished the pain, but it was about emotion, about the control I sought to wield over those emotions.

Just because I sometimes enjoyed cutting into my own flesh didn't make me want someone else cutting into it.

Just because I was becoming accustomed to being in pain didn't mean I enjoyed it.

My eyes watered as fresh pain spiked in my chest. I gasped and dropped the hem of my dress.

'I can't,' I said, clutching my side.

He rolled his eyes and set the scanner down on the small pine table that stood next to my bed.

I didn't fight when he reached out and slid the thin strap of my dress over my shoulder and down my arm, then repeated the action with the other side. He gave a solid tug, and I looked away as my lace-covered breasts emerged from the dress, popping out dramatically as the tight material slid down and over my waist. He whistled in appreciation, and my cheeks burned in response.

'You could just tell me where it is,' he said, chuckling. 'Then I wouldn't have to do this.'

I stared at the floor. Screw him. Although it killed me to be so exposed, I refused to give him the satisfaction of my complicity. If he wanted to find a microchip underneath my skin he could damn well go searching for it.

The dress pooled at my feet and I cringed at the sudden exposure. I was well aware of how I looked in the very revealing, plunging, boosting and altogether ridiculous black lace underwear that Murphy had insisted on buying when he stocked my suitcase for our fake-cation.

Dornan took a step back and grinned. 'I didn't pick you for a lingerie model,' he said appreciatively.

I snapped my gaze up to his, furious. 'It was that asshole Murphy,' I spat. 'He said if I didn't wear this —'

Oh.

Dornan frowned. 'If you didn't wear this, what?'

I searched my mind for a suitable lie, something that didn't involve the knowledge of my son.

'He said he'd make me regret it,' I said, technically not lying.

'Huh,' he said. 'Well, now that I know he chose these, I'd like to rip them off you and burn them.'

My face burned, never mind my clothes. I had never in my life felt more exposed.

'Please don't,' I replied sharply.

'For now, you can keep 'em. Arms out, little lady.'

I rolled my eyes and held my arms straight out in front of me.

'Let the treasure hunting begin,' he said gleefully, taking one of my arms and wrapping his fingers around my wrist. I glanced at the scanner, lying silently on the table, but thought better of mentioning it.

As Dornan's fingers skated smoothly over my skin, I fought the urge to shudder violently. My flesh rose in goosebumps and I curled my toes to stop from squirming.

His touch was feather-light. It wasn't a search — it was a caress. As he locked his gaze on me and continued to poke at the skin around my bandaged wrist, I realised he didn't really give a shit about any microchip.

And I didn't really give a shit that I was standing in front of the son of the man who owned me, in gaudy lace underwear, being felt up by him.

I should have cared, though. I should have been disgusted.

What was wrong with me? *He shouldn't have been making me feel like this.*

It was the loneliness, I decided. I was only feeling the way I was around him — flushed, unable to keep still, with an itch that wanted to be scratched by him — because I was so terribly lonely.

I rationalised things in my head. It was okay. I was confused. And him touching me didn't change the way I felt — because as soon as I got my chance, I would kill him.

I acted bored as his grip tightened on my forearm. He placed his thumb and forefinger over a thin, hard rod embedded under my skin.

'What's this?' he asked.

'Contraceptive implant,' I replied quickly, immediately regretting uttering those words.

His eyes lit up at that as his gaze travelled across my chest and wandered down to the most private of places. I was clothed and covered in the right places, but in front of him, I felt completely naked. The feeling was unnerving and delicious all at once, which only confused me further.

So he's sexy as hell. It doesn't matter. He's the enemy.

'It doesn't matter anyway,' I added hastily. 'I've got a nasty case of the clap. Better not rape me or your *pico* might fall off.' I thrust my chin out as I used the Spanish term for 'small dick', smirking at the Gypsy Brother as his warm hands continued to roam every bit of bare flesh on my arms.

Dornan laughed at my admission, a throaty noise full of gravel and insolence that made me increasingly unsteady on my feet.

'I'm not going to rape you,' he replied, amusement dancing in his dark eyes. 'And you don't have the clap. So don't use that one on me.'

I rolled my eyes at him as he continued his probing of my flesh with his rough hands. I spied a gold wedding band on his finger, something that hadn't been there yesterday — I was certain, because I'd specifically looked for one. 'What does your wife think of what you're doing?' I asked sharply.

Dornan snickered. 'My wife is a cunt,' he replied, without missing a beat.

Dornan placed his fingers in the space just below the crook of my elbow, then slowly walked his fingers down towards my wrist. He smiled smugly.

Shit.

'Bingo,' he said, pressing the pad of his thumb against the tiny microchip all the Rodriguez children had been given several years ago. An ineffective insurance policy in case we were ever taken.

My eyes filled with saltwater and anger as my heart sank. I didn't enjoy suffering, and I knew what was about to come next.

It was going to hurt.

Sucking on his bottom lip, Dornan seemed to enjoy my reaction to his discovery. He didn't tear his eyes from mine as he reached into his pocket and withdrew a slim, sheathed switchblade, flicking it open with a casual precision that suggested he had done it countless times before.

My eyes widened slightly as the blade snicked open. I didn't dare move as he balanced the knife in his open palm, hovering in the space between us.

'You want to cut it out, or should I?' he asked.

And in that fraction of time, I saw my way out.

Before he could blink, I snatched the knife out of his hand and, without hesitating, leapt forward, plunging the blade into the meaty section of his left shoulder.

He swore and staggered back. As he moved, I used every ounce of energy I still possessed to wrench the blade free. I wasn't about to give up the only weapon I'd managed to grab hold of during my captivity.

I took a step back and widened my stance, shifting my weight to the balls of my feet and raising onto my tiptoes, ready to move swiftly.

'That was unnecessary,' Dornan growled, touching a finger to his bleeding shoulder before pressing it to his mouth, tasting his own blood.

I tried to fight the urge to lick my lips as I revelled in the satisfaction of spilling his blood. I couldn't help myself and my tongue darted out over my lips as I tasted the blood in the air between us.

Apparently unconcerned, Dornan held his palm out in front of me. 'Give me the knife,' he said, wiggling his fingers for effect. I just smiled at him, ready to lunge forward, waiting for the right moment to attack. *As if I'd give it back*.

Dornan shrugged and reached into the waistband of his jeans. Before I could blink, the cold, smooth barrel of a gun was wedged firmly underneath my chin, forcing my head back at an uncomfortable angle.

Damn it!

'Ever heard the expression, "Don't bring a knife to a gun fight?"' Dornan asked, clearly happy to once again have the upper hand. I let the knife go, wincing as it clattered to the ground beside my bare feet. Dornan kept the gun trained on me as he knelt to pick up the knife, then stuffed the gun back into his waistband.

With rough fingers he seized my arm once more, hovering the bloodied blade over the spot where my useless microchip was implanted.

'Sweetheart,' he said, grinning widely. 'This is gonna hurt.'

He wasn't gentle as he brought the blade down across my flesh.

CHAPTER SEVENTEEN
DORNAN

Dornan headed for his room upstairs, once he'd bandaged the girl's bleeding wrist and chained her to the wall, tightening her shackles until she whimpered. She wanted to stab him? He would show her how quickly he could make her existence agony. But also, he kind of loved that she had reacted that way. Grabbing a blade, sinking it into his flesh, licking those beautiful lips of hers when she thought he wasn't looking. It made him imagine the fight she'd give if he were to pin her down, force her arms over her head, and fuck her tight little body.

His cock throbbed painfully at the thought of her. He needed release. But he would be damned if he'd let her know what kind of effect she was having on him.

The fire she was lighting through his veins.

He entered the room his father set aside for him during such visits and slammed the door shut behind him. Stalking to his bathroom, he began shedding clothes in his wake.

He made the water as hot as possible, wanting to burn her touch from his skin, to wash away her blood, syrupy and sticky as it congealed and dried on his hands.

But at the same time, he didn't want to wash it away. He wanted to savour it. To bathe in it. To sink himself into her until she begged him for release of her own.

His hand stirred to his engorged cock, where he squeezed hard. The water washed some of the blood from his hand and it dribbled down onto his cock. He squeezed again, mesmerised. Her blood. His dick. *Yes*.

He briefly considered returning downstairs. He'd be careful, and maybe, just maybe, she'd lie still to protect her broken ribs.

But he didn't want her to lie still.

He wanted her to thrash and writhe. He wanted her to fight back even as she gave in to him. Because she was so damn good at fighting back. She seemed to enjoy it.

Jesus. What was happening to him? He was careful and controlled, measured. The volatility that lived inside him was a beast that he'd learned to leash a long time ago, and now he was going crazy over one girl?

No.

He let go of himself and grabbed the bar of soap, scrubbing his hands until they were close to bleeding. He would erase every trace of her.

But sure enough, after his skin was raw and clean, his cock was still rock solid, and in desperate need of some attention.

'Jesus *fucking* Christ,' he muttered, shutting the water off. He wrapped a towel around his waist and wrenched the bathroom door open.

He wasn't alone. Interesting.

'Bella,' he growled. He wasn't in the mood for any shit. 'What the fuck are you doing here?'

His accountant and occasional piece of ass sat in an overstuffed armchair in the darkest corner of the room, a devious glint in her eyes. She uncrossed her legs and rose to her feet, and it seemed almost as if she were materialising out of thin air. Her dark brown hair was pulled into an immaculate chignon at the nape of her neck, heavy eyeliner accentuated her blue eyes. She was pale, like a porcelain doll, but Dornan knew if he threw her, she wouldn't break.

He looked down at her hand, a glass of Scotch clutched loosely in perfectly manicured fingers. He looked at her vacant blue eyes and clenched his jaw tightly. Not even 10 a.m. and she was halfway to drunk. No wonder their businesses were losing money. She used to be so reliable. This morning drinking was new. And it annoyed the ever-living shit out of Dornan.

She didn't speak, just raised her perfectly groomed eyebrows in question.

'Come here,' he said, taking her elbow.

'Baby!' she protested, trying to pull away. 'Your father wants a meeting with us. Can't this wait?'

'Don't fucking question me, woman,' he spat, wrenching the glass from her hand and slamming it down on a sideboard. Amber-coloured liquid sloshed onto the timber and he shook his wet hand, irritated.

Bella knew better than to keep going, and she shut up. Dornan dragged her over to the bed and pushed her down roughly. As she righted herself, he stepped over and slammed the door, locking it for effect. He didn't really care if anyone came in and saw what was about to happen, but he wanted Bella to know that she was not welcome to leave until he was done with her. She got off on that shit.

'I missed you, baby,' she said, slightly slurring her words as he stalked over to the bed. He pulled her to the edge and let the towel around his waist drop to the ground. Bella's eyes went round as a dick was shoved at her face, and Dornan felt a glimmer of satisfaction at the power he wielded over his pretty, but slightly unhinged employee.

Mariana. Tough Girl. He needed to get her out of his mind.

'Open your mouth,' he said, taking his dick and pressing it against her lips.

Bella drew back, smiling. 'This is how we said goodbye. Isn't it my turn?' She thrust her hips up at him. 'I'm bare for you, baby.'

'Bella!' he roared. He was not in the mood to go on a pussy expedition. Not with Bella, anyway.

She snapped her watery eyes to his and seemed to realise he wasn't fucking around. Her smile turned to a lustful gaze, and without hesitation, she moved her face closer again and opened her mouth enough just to let the tip of his painfully hard cock graze past her teeth.

Impatience peaked inside Dornan's chest. She should have known better than to tease him.

'I said open your mouth, not brush your teeth with my dick.' He grabbed her shoulder and dug his fingers in hard, making her moan around his cock as she opened her mouth a little more.

'Open wider,' he instructed her. 'Take it all.' He gripped the sides of her head and wrenched up, forcing his hips forward so that she gagged violently.

But it still wasn't enough. He withdrew suddenly, letting his cock bounce out of her mouth. He patted her absent-mindedly on the head as she retched and giggled, her throat probably rubbed raw by his need. Not that he cared. The rougher he was, the faster she got off.

Theirs was a strange arrangement.

'On your back,' he said. 'Hurry up.'

Just want to tear her apart.

When she didn't move immediately, he grabbed a handful of her dark hair and yanked. She moaned. 'Alright, alright!'

He pushed her onto her back and crawled on top of her. With his taut muscles and measured movements, he was the perfect predator, but he didn't want this insipid bitch who was panting beneath him to be his prey.

He wanted *Mariana*. Beneath him, writhing and begging for his touch, his name on her lips, as he fucked her raw.

Bella was wearing a tight pencil skirt, the ones that normally drove him crazy with desire. Half the pleasure was in the thrill of the chase; in trying to hitch it up far enough to spread her legs and get access to what was beneath that see-through lace thong. He was a man who enjoyed a challenge.

'What the hell has gotten into you?' she asked, desire in her heavy lidded eyes. That made him laugh. She must have thought him mad — and she hadn't even seen the blood on his hands that had started all of this enraged excitement in the first place.

Ana has gotten into me. And I need to get her out.

He ripped Bella's cornflower blue silk blouse open, sending buttons flying everywhere. Below, her pale flesh and small tits underwhelmed him. What he really wanted was to see that light bronze skin and heaving rack that he'd just feasted his eyes upon in the basement.

Bella just wasn't doing it for him.

He leaned down and took her nipple into his mouth anyway, the feeling of her in his mouth completely disappointing. She hitched her skirt up higher and took his hand, guiding it between her legs.

He laughed and smacked her hand away. In that moment, he didn't care about *her* pleasure. In that moment, she existed for *his* pleasure.

He wrenched her legs apart, pushing them as wide as they would go, and pushed her panties to the side, positioning himself at her entrance. She was already wet for him. Yeah, she liked this shit; the rougher he was, the more excited she got. They suited each other just fine.

He drove into her as hard as he could, enjoying the way her breath caught in her throat and how her eyes seemed to almost pop under the pressure of him inside her. As he set a steady rhythm, it felt good, but something wasn't right. Apart from the obvious — she wasn't the woman he was eager to fuck the life out of right now.

Her hands found his and suddenly she was guiding them to her neck. 'Choke me, baby.'

He indulged her; as his large palms pressed around her throat, she started to thrust her hips up harder to match his rough strokes.

No matter what he did to this woman, it didn't faze her. The more brutal he was, the faster she got off, and the more she wanted to go again five minutes later. She was unique. She was insatiable. But right now, she was dull.

He pushed harder. But still, it wasn't enough.

Then he saw the pillow beside Bella's head. He leaned over her pale body and took the pillow, pressing it over her face before she could protest. Better.

She struggled beneath the pillow, but her strength was no match for his, and the pillow muffled her yells. Soon, she stopped struggling, and as he drove harder inside her, her yells turned to lust-filled — albeit muffled — moans. He pressed down on the pillow, not enough to render her unconscious, but enough to make her head spin in circles while he pretended she was somebody else.

Yes. That was much, much better. He picked up his pace, thrusting into her relentlessly, spurred on by Bella's wildly enthusiastic response and the image of Mariana's smooth bronze skin.

As she clenched tighter around him, Dornan lost it, shuddering violently as he came.

He withdrew, cleaning himself off with the towel as Bella rearranged her skirt and attempted to re-button her ruined shirt with the few buttons that still held onto the material.

He should have been satisfied, but he wasn't. He needed more. He needed *her*.

'That was fucking amazing,' Bella said, stretching out on the bed. 'You must have missed me, baby.'

He looked to the ceiling and bit his tongue; he hadn't missed the insolent bitch *one single bit*.

'Aren't you late for a fuckin' meeting?' he asked, glaring at her. She pressed her lips together and kissed the air that separated them. 'I love you too, baby,' she cooed, sashaying out of the room with her ruined shirt clutched tight around her.

He shook his head. She was insane.

Thank fuck he wasn't alone in that regard.

CHAPTER EIGHTEEN

MARIANA

I stared vacantly at the bandages on my wrists, and beside them, the shackles that pinned me to the wall. It struck me as hilarious that I now had deep cuts to both of my arms, especially when Emilio had asked his son to ensure I wasn't marked. Why, I still wasn't sure. I didn't really care at this point. I was just tired and hungry and sore from being chained to the wall for so long. And I wanted to go home.

What a ridiculous thought. I was never going home.

The delirium was brought on by my hunger, I decided. Hunger and blood loss. I eyed my suitcase, wondering if there was something I could eat in there. Not that it mattered, since I was fastened to the wall. I wasn't even indignant at the way Dornan had restrained me.

I mean, I had stabbed him.

I catalogued my diet over the past several days. I'd been told not to eat anything on my flights, convinced that I was a drug mule with cocaine pellets in my stomach. So, apart from the greasy burger and fries Murphy had so graciously bestowed upon me before cutting me loose with the Gypsy Brothers, I'd not had anything to eat in days.

And then, as if by magic, Dornan was standing in my doorway with a bowl of soup and a plate of bread.

My eyes practically bulged out of my head when I saw the goodies he was holding. I should have known they'd come at a price.

Everything always did.

CHAPTER NINETEEN

DORNAN

The girl looked terrible when he got back to the room. Her bronze skin had a sickly pallor that he was hoping to fix by feeding her up. He cursed himself as he realised she hadn't been given a drop of water to drink in the whole time she'd been there.

He dumped the soup and bread on the small wooden table and left, returning with a glass of water. After removing the heavy cuffs from their bolt in the wall, but leaving them on her wrists, he handed her the glass of water. She thanked him as she took it with shaking hands, but she didn't meet his eyes this time, fixing her gaze in the distance as she emptied the glass.

Odd.

She was a feisty little thing. Maybe she just needed something to eat before she started up the banter with him again. He loved the way she spoke, her slight accent, which gave him a pant-busting crush on her, the way she licked her lips when she was unsure, but, most of all, he enjoyed the attitude behind her words. He liked all of it. And, much to his chagrin, fucking the life out of Bella hadn't tempered his desire for Mariana at all — if anything, it had inflamed it.

Perhaps he was just using her as a distraction from the work he needed to do upstairs. From the mess that the cartel was involved in. From the reality that even he couldn't bear to face. Rival suppliers. Rival biker clubs. Nothing mattered when the white powder flowed freely, but now, because of her stupid father, their precious white snow was sitting in a processing plant owned by the DEA in New Mexico, and Dornan and Emilio were fresh out of product.

'Sit,' he said, gesturing to the bed. She obeyed without any of her usual snark. Maybe she had broken already. *She stabbed you*, he reminded himself. No, the girl was definitely not broken. The girl was on fire inside. She was just dormant in this moment, probably from lack of sustenance.

He dragged the small wooden table in front of her. 'Eat.'

She didn't hesitate, diving in with gusto. Tearing bread, dipping it into the soup his mother made so well, bringing it to her lush lips. Chew, swallow, repeat.

'How are you doing?' he asked. And then immediately cursed himself. *She's a fucking prisoner. She stabbed me.*

Something tugged up at the corner of her mouth for just a second, and he exhaled, amused. She was laughing at him. She was so different to the typical girl they saw here, he wasn't sure whether he wanted to fuck her, or shoot her in the head and be finished with it all.

'How's your shoulder?' she asked, meeting his gaze for the first time. Her eyes burned with an intensity he had never seen in a woman before. She wasn't afraid of him, he realised. That troubled him. Why wasn't she afraid? Because she was hiding something?

Or because she had nothing left to lose?

'My shoulder is great,' he said, leaning against the wall across from where she sat. 'Never better.'

And he meant it. She had made him bleed … and it wasn't a bad thing. It still throbbed from time to time, but the blade was sharp and she'd missed anything major.

'I'll have to try harder next time,' she said between bites.

Huh. It was one thing that he liked her feisty, but he didn't want her to think she had power over him. Threats were for him to make. He would have to show her that he was the one in control.

'This isn't a fairytale,' Dornan said wryly, as he watched her bring the soup-soaked bread to her mouth.

She paused with the bread in her hand, looking around the room in mock surprise. 'You mean, we're not Beauty and the *fucking* Beast?'

He laughed.

'Well, you're certainly beautiful,' he said.

'And you're definitely a beast,' she countered, pushing her empty bowl away and resting back on the bed.

'But there's no happy ever after for you,' Dornan added, his eyes trailing over the chains to reach the cuffs that were now permanent bracelets on her wrists.

'No,' she said evenly, matching his intense gaze. 'Not for any of us. Not in this world.'

'It probably doesn't make a damn bit of difference to you,' Dornan said, 'but I'm sorry that this is happening to you. Sounds like your dad fucked up majorly.'

What on earth had prompted him to say that? He was going fucking soft.

'It's okay,' she said quietly, looking at the wall. 'It was bound to happen one day.'

'He have a tendency to fuck things up?' Dornan asked, his interest suddenly aroused. He didn't give a shit about her dad, but he wanted to learn more about her. About her life. What did she dream about at night? Or were her nights filled with nightmares, like his were?

He had never cared before. He loved his children, would lay down his life for them. He loved his first wife in some way, and his second. He had a fierce love for his own mother. But he had never been obsessed with what made them tick, what drove them in life, the things that haunted them. Everybody else he had ever known had been taken at face value.

So to feel this obsession for the thoughts of the girl in front of him? It terrified him. And Dornan Ross did not enjoy being scared. Especially not of dirty, insignificant things like feelings. Feelings and emotions made a man weak. Better not to feel them at all.

She let out the breath she'd been holding and glanced at him. The brave mask she wore slipped a little, and he saw the exhausted girl underneath all the sarcasm and witty retorts.

'My father is a complicated man,' she said quietly.

When she didn't elaborate, Dornan nodded. 'Seems we have that in common. Complicated old men. They all have their own ... anomalies.'

Mariana huffed. 'Anomalies.'

Dornan rubbed his stubbled jaw as he watched her. 'You know,' he said, 'when you first got here, something about you struck me as odd.'

Her lip curled up minutely. 'Just the one thing?'

He matched her small smile with one of his own. 'You were so ... accepting of what was happening. Almost like ... you were expecting it.'

He saw her stiffen slightly and sit up straighter on the bed. She seemed to be contemplating whether to share more with him. Dornan studied her, not making a sound. People always wanted to fill silence, and if you waited long enough, they'd rush forth to do it in your absence.

'It should have happened years ago,' she said quietly, massaging her wrists where the cuffs dug in. 'I've been pretty good at holding off the debt collectors.'

Dornan's curiosity was piqued. 'With your pretty face?' he guessed.

Jesus Christ. He might as well give her the knife back and let her carve out his heart.

'With creative accounting,' she said. 'Take some from here, tack it onto there, and when that stops working, the cheque's always in the mail.' Her eyes bored into him. 'Of course, it's much more complex than that.'

Dornan sat back and studied her with newfound appreciation. Beautiful *and* clever. A rare — and dangerous — combination in the cartel.

'Interesting,' he said. 'Very interesting.'

She didn't look interested; she looked positively despondent.

'What's going to happen to me?' she asked him again, and that steely look in her eyes was clouded over with worry. Just for a second, and then he could almost see the way she pushed her panic down and composed herself again. The ice queen. He saw right through her act, good as it was. She must have practised that indifferent stare for years, it was so automatic. He wondered what had happened to her that she needed to hide her feelings away so well.

'I told you,' he said. 'Drug mule, maybe. Your English is good enough. But you'd be a flight risk with that pesky family of yours.'

She opened her mouth to argue, but he put up a palm to stop her. She closed her mouth, and again, that surprised him.

She really wanted to know what came next. And he didn't have the heart to tell her.

'You've got a pretty face, Ana. I'm sorry that you do. I wish you didn't.'

Her eyes grew wider.

'If it were up to me? I'd put you to work in one of our finest gentlemen's clubs.'

Only, I wouldn't. I'd keep you all for myself. But of course, he couldn't tell her that.

She huffed. 'A whorehouse.'

He nodded. 'Yup.'

Her shoulders sagged. 'When?'

'I imagine very soon.'

He saw the thought cross her mind, it was so obvious.

'Maybe you could —'

He pushed off the wall and took two long strides, his fingers coming to rest against her mouth as he cut her off mid-sentence. Sadness bloomed in her eyes, then, watery and dull. And resignation. The resignation to one's fate was always the thing that got to him the most. He preferred it when they still had fight left in them, because fight meant hope.

Once upon a time, he'd wanted to save them all. These days, he was numb to it. But now, with this inexplicable woman sitting in front of him, he almost wavered. The temptation to take her away, to save her, overwhelmed him momentarily. Had she seen? Had she caught sight of the fleeting devastation on his face before he managed to wipe it away again?

'I can't,' he said plainly, to himself as much as to her. 'Remember? This isn't a fairytale. I'm not your hero, Ana. Nobody is. *Nobody is coming to save you.*'

He stopped talking, but didn't take his fingers from her mouth. Something disturbing stirred in his belly for the girl.

He already knew he wasn't going to save her. He didn't want to *want* to save her. He wanted to forget her. She'd be used, and hurt, and she'd be dead within five years. He knew this with certainty. Girls who were traded in this world never lasted long before it destroyed them, and the Gypsy Brothers had the blackest touch of all.

She blinked her huge eyes, and tears fell from them, running down her cheeks and hitting his hand. He lifted his hand off her lips and brushed more tears from her cheeks with his fingers.

He wanted to tell her she shouldn't cry. That crying implied weakness. But, as the saltwater leaving her body burned on his hand, he said nothing. Because the minute he left the room, he was going to press his tongue to every one of her tears that had fallen onto his skin and taste how sweet they were himself.

CHAPTER TWENTY

MARIANA

I was so annoyed that I'd cried in front of him. I'd cried *on* him, right into his hand. I was so *angry* with myself. Before he left, he didn't take the cuffs from my wrists, but he didn't shackle me back to the wall, either. The manacles were heavy, and I rested them in my lap as I sat on the bed.

I had seen a look on his face. Had I imagined it? Just before he had told me that he couldn't help me. It was a look that said he wanted to, and I sat with my whirling thoughts, the stunned disbelief and helplessness seeping into every one of my pores until I was trembling with the futility of it all.

I was going to be a whore.

I was never getting away.

And I couldn't decide which one was worse.

My breath quickened as I imagined strangers' hands pressing me down, hurting me, taking everything from me until I was an empty shell.

I was so confused, so achingly numb. But the numbness was punctuated with fear, random moments of panic that would suddenly slice through me unbidden. He had answered the question of what was going to happen to me, and been smart enough to realise what I was trying to do before I even really realised myself. Making pretty eyes at him and trying to get him to help me. I could tell that he liked me. But I couldn't figure out how to make that *like* into something that could save me from the hell that was imminent.

A couple of hours after he'd so graciously fed and watered me, Dornan was back, this time with Emilio. I flinched as soon as I saw the insipid kingpin, my ribs reminding me not to piss him off. I didn't move from my spot on the bed when they entered, just watched and waited.

I was expecting something nasty, but when he asked me the first question, I definitely wasn't prepared.

'Are you a virgin?' Emilio asked casually.

A virgin? I opened my mouth and laughed, a genuine laugh that started in my belly and spread through the room, unwelcome. I stopped abruptly when the vibration rocked my ribs, gasping and holding my side. I looked past Emilio to see Dornan's mouth twitching up at the side.

Bang! Before I knew it, Emilio had stepped closer and struck my cheek. I tasted blood.

I cleared my throat. 'I'm sorry,' I said in an acid tone. 'I figured you were *joking*.'

Emilio grinned.

'We'll just have a look, shall we?'

I rolled my eyes, but fear crept into my bones and glued my thighs tightly shut. 'I assure you, I haven't been a virgin in a long time.'

Emilio snapped his fingers and Dornan stepped forward.

'I want you to find out if she's a virgin or not,' he said, his condescending expression fucking infuriating.

'I already told you, I'm not,' I snapped, narrowing my eyes at him.

He was going to turn me into a prostitute. Images of a never-ending line of faceless men, with bad breath and sweaty palms, grated at my nerves.

Panic bubbled up inside me, replacing the calm I'd worked so hard to maintain.

Don't ever show fear.

Emilio grinned, his gold tooth glinting. 'Have fun,' he said, slapping his son on the shoulder. 'And take an inventory while you're there. But don't mark the little bitch. We've already lost enough time from her unfortunate fall.' He made rabbit ears with his fingers as he said the word 'fall', and I cringed.

He was almost at the door when he thought of something. 'Check if her tits are real,' he said casually to his son, as rage burned inside me.

Dornan watched as his father left the room, slamming the door in his wake.

And then slowly swivelled his head back to me.

I surveyed him with quiet determination, suddenly calmer without Emilio present. Safer. It didn't make sense, yet it did. Because Emilio demanded that I call him Master, and he broke my ribs, and Dornan didn't really seem to care what I called him.

'*Papi*,' I said flatly. I licked my lips before I could catch myself, a nervous habit that I often displayed when unsure. *Damn it! Stop it. He probably already knows exactly what you look like when you're scared. He watched you cry like a blubbering baby this morning.*

Dornan laughed, and I could have sworn my chains rattled at the low, booming noise that reverberated every fibre in my being.

'Doesn't that mean daddy?' Dornan asked, his face relaxed and his stance casual, unlike yesterday, when I'd seen him tightly wound.

The time he'd smiled as my blood poured from my wrist and onto the floor.

I smiled back, despite myself. Despite the situation. *Try to get him on your side*. 'It's a friendly term. Casual.'

He pursed his lips. 'So do you want me to be your friend,' his lips quirked up into a sneer, 'or your daddy?'

My cheeks burned at his question as I trained my eyes on his, refusing to let them dart lower. Screw trying to get him on my side. The way he asked the question while he stared at my chest — it was pretty obvious what he was getting at.

'How about neither?' I replied condescendingly. 'How about you're just an asshole?'

He chuckled. And that made me mad.

'You're afraid of him,' I blurted out. 'Your father. I see the way you talk to him.'

Dornan's eyes flashed darker, his eyebrows bunching together. He clenched his jaw, and I imagined the teeth inside grinding down on each other.

He reached out and fingered my cuffs. I stood and drew a sharp intake of air. I hadn't even noticed him get that close, he was so beguiling. Sleek, like a panther. And just as deadly.

I didn't want to be sitting down when he pounced. He looked like he wanted to rip me to pieces.

'I'm not afraid of anyone,' Dornan growled, his tone measured, his fingers light as a feather on my wrist.

Liar.

'But you, on the other hand …' he trailed off, his impressive six-foot physique overwhelming my five foot two. I craned my neck to look up at him as he drew closer still.

He was beautiful. He was *terrifying*.

'What about me?' I asked, my voice wavering slightly.

'That's the thing,' he replied quietly, a low rumble that threatened to break me apart. 'I can't figure out if you're more scared of me, or of yourself.'

I glared at him. I felt utterly naked. He saw inside me, and I hated it. I bit the inside of my cheek to stop myself from speaking further.

It was too easy to speak to him, to share my secrets, like falling into an abyss. I enjoyed talking to him, enjoyed being around him, and that revelation was disturbing.

His fingers caressed my arm, landing on my bandaged wound. 'How's your wrist?' he murmured, his voice smoky.

'Empty,' I said truthfully. Emptied of blood and hope.

He continued to caress my arm, his fingers burning into my skin. I had an irrational thought that maybe he would still help me — maybe he would save me.

It killed me that I wanted him to.

'My father doesn't believe you'll behave,' he said, and a thrill of fear brushed along my spine.

I shrugged. 'Do you?'

He grinned, letting my wrist fall as both his hands travelled up my arms and across my collarbone, where they rested for a moment before drifting down further.

I drew in a sharp gasp as he palmed my breasts. I still hadn't had the chance to shower, and as he squeezed my nipples, I felt the nauseating burn of Este's blood where it stained my skin.

'What are you doing?' I gasped, trying to wriggle away, only succeeding in creating a friction between his fingers and my nipples that made a blush creep up my neck. *Este. These people killed Esteban. Do not think of him as anything but a coward and a murderer.* 'What do you want with me?'

'I'm sorry about your boyfriend,' Dornan said, seeming to read my mind. 'And I assure you, darlin', the only thing I want from you right now is to know whether these beautiful titties are real or not.' He gave one last squeeze for emphasis, something glinting in his eye. Amusement. I amused him, chained up like this, hurt and broken and *owned*.

'You don't have to enjoy it so much,' I spat, turning my head to look away from him.

His hands continued to skate across my skin, and just as it had thrilled me when he was searching for the thin microchip hidden under my flesh, my body responded again to his touch. *This is so wrong*, I thought. Shame burned at my cheeks as gooseflesh sprang up on the skin at my collarbone where his hand had come to rest. His grip was loose, but dominating at the same time. So why did I want him to keep his hand exactly where it was?

I had stopped struggling. I realised I had been holding my breath, and I let it all out at once, gulping in new air. Not fresh air. It was the same air I'd been trapped inside since I'd arrived.

Our eyes met again, and his face softened minutely. It was a glimpse past his usual fierce expression, not that I terribly minded his fierceness, and that was the whole problem. I liked his fierce far too much. He was the polar opposite of Este, who had always been gentle and loving and kind.

I despised Dornan Ross in that moment, because I wanted nothing more than for him to take his other hand and put that on me, too. Pick me up and take me somewhere, anywhere, far away from here.

I was pinning my hopes on the wrong man. He'd already said he wouldn't — couldn't — save me from my fate.

I tamped down my arousal with every fibre of my being, and called upon the other feeling that flowed through me like poison in my veins. My greatest fear of what was going to happen to me made my hands shake with anger.

'Taking inventory to sell me?' I asked bitterly, my eyes defiant as he looked back into my fiery gaze. I had finally voiced the fear that had been gnawing at my edges for hours. *Slave. Slave. Slave.*

I expected him to laugh, as he and his father did whenever I said something like that. Instead, his grave reaction terrified me.

I wanted him to say no. I needed him to say no.

But what he said instead, one tiny word, was enough to shatter my world.

'*Yes*,' he answered, without missing a beat.

CHAPTER TWENTY-ONE

DORNAN

He didn't want his father to sell her.

It was business, plain and simple, but the rage that burned inside him at the thought of what happened to girls who were sold ... it physically pained him. His father had told him from the very beginning the fate he had chosen for Mariana, but that was when she had been just another girl. A commodity. A product.

Now he had tasted her blood. Her tears. And she was *oh so fuckin' sweet*. Not sweet in temperament — the girl was a spitfire. But the way her life blood tasted took his breath away.

He paced in the corridor outside her room. A guard near the bathroom studied his sub-machine gun to avoid Dornan's gaze.

He couldn't stop what was going to happen. He knew that. And so, he vowed to get on with things upstairs. To forget about the girl. To leave her to the fate she had volunteered for.

Upstairs, club members were mobilising, heading back to LA. He knew his father was up there working hard to try to stem the damage from the cocaine loss. People were baying for Gypsy blood. It made Dornan want to go and blow the DEA's fucking headquarters sky high.

He was dragging his feet because of the damn girl. He should have been back in LA already, getting the rest of the club into motion. John would be fine without him, but he wanted to be a part of the action. He needed to know what was going on. His father, more specifically, needed him to be the eyes and ears for the cartel's interests. People had a way of being saved when John was left to his own devices.

His father summoned him with a hearty yell from above. He climbed the stairs a little faster than he would have liked, fantasising about caving the old man's head in and taking control of the empire himself. After all, he was the one who did the dirty work. The one who got the blood on his hands, snatched the girls from the pickup points, made the drops to the suppliers. His father just sat behind his desk and yelled orders while he got his cock sucked by his very blonde, very young secretary. But even as Dornan fantasised about Emilio's comeuppance, he knew what he really wanted was just for his father to tell him he was proud of him. He was pathetic.

'Pop,' Dornan drawled.

As if to reinforce his thoughts, the little blonde hurried past him, her skirt ruffled and her bright red fuck-me lipstick smeared across one cheek. Dornan made no move to step aside, crowding her with his broad shoulders as she squeezed past.

'Be nice,' Emilio said sharply. 'Don't think I've forgotten about what you did to Margie.'

Dornan snickered as he remembered Margie moaning beneath him. He hadn't done anything to her that she hadn't wanted. The girl was practically begging for it.

'I wonder how Margie's going?' Dornan said, sitting down across from his father. Small talk. It was what they did before getting to the business side of things.

'Going nowhere with a bullet in her head,' Emilio said dismissively.

Dornan raised an eyebrow, genuinely surprised. 'I thought she was your favourite?'

'She was talking to the boys in blue.'

Dornan balled his fists angrily. You couldn't trust anyone in this business. He shook his head in disdain.

'In that case,' he said, 'I hope you made it slow.'

Emilio grinned, and Dornan couldn't help but glance at his gold tooth. He hated it, always had. As a small boy, it had freaked him out, and the feeling hadn't abated as he grew. He imagined the tooth sparkling as his father ate someone's flesh from their bones. He was a sadistic motherfucker.

'Oh, yes,' Emilio said, clearly revelling in his trip down a blood-soaked memory lane. 'I fucked her with the gun first. One of those .45s. It was a big *bastardo*. She didn't like that at all.'

Dornan chuckled, knowing it was the expected reaction, but inside he felt disgust. Not surprise, though. He'd stopped being surprised by his father's abhorrent antics a long time ago.

'So,' Emilio said briskly, and Dornan knew what would come next. 'Business.'

Bingo. Predictable old bastard. He was only sixty but life had been hard on him, and the wrinkles around his eyes told of some of that hardness. Some of that struggle.

'I've managed to rustle up some product to get us through.'

'Not from that fuck Murphy,' Dornan said, before he could bite his tongue.

Anger flashed in his father's cold eyes. 'He's a crazy motherfucker, Dornan, but he has something that I need. That *we* need.'

Dornan fought to maintain some semblance of calm.

'I need your boys to go and get it.'

Dornan wanted to roll his eyes so badly, it hurt. *Of course you do.* The old man always fucking needed *something*.

'When and where?' Dornan asked.

Emilio began to recite times and addresses, as Dornan struggled to pay attention. A thought of the girl flashed in his head. Would she still be here when he returned? He waited patiently, committing to memory everything his father recited. He bore the conversation with outward patience, the girl's eyes filling up every facet of his being inside.

Finally, Emilio got to the end of his spiel, surveying his son with cold precision. Dornan dreaded that look. It was like his father saw right through him. And invariably, he *did*.

'Ask me what you're going to ask me,' Emilio said bluntly.

Dornan shrugged. 'I wasn't going to ask you anything.'

Emilio's look of indifference morphed almost immediately. '*Figlio mio*,' he drawled, as his grin rapidly expanded. *My son.* 'I know your thoughts before you do. You want to know what will happen to the girl.'

Mother. Fucker.

'What girl?' Dornan challenged, feigning disinterest. 'The blonde who just left her lipstick all over your *cazzo*?'

Emilio stood, still with that maddening look on his face, signalling that their meeting was over.

'I'd let you play with the little Colombian,' he said as Dornan approached the door, 'but I need to be brutal. I need to make an example of her.'

The image of five headless bodies his father had made examples of when he draped them across the top of the San Ysidro border crossing only months before twisted at Dornan's gut. The girl was too good for that. Even if Dornan did want to hurt her — it wasn't like that. He enjoyed a little bloodletting, sure, and a healthy dose of intimidation, but not the stark brutality his father favoured.

'Have you considered using her other talents?' Dornan asked casually. *Don't let him see. Don't let him know.*

Emilio narrowed his eyes, but his expression was light, playful even. Dornan had seen his father stab a man in the face with an icepick while he was in this kind of carefree mood.

'Other talents?' Emilio echoed. 'Does she have a golden pussy? A mouth that sucks better than a vacuum cleaner? A third tit somewhere?'

Dornan huffed out a small laugh. 'She's a book cooker. A bean counter.'

Emilio shrugged. 'And?'

Dornan wanted to shake the old man. 'And she's probably better than fucking Bella at getting our accounts in order.'

Emilio waved a hand dismissively. 'She's too young. What does she know about hiding money and sending it offshore?'

Dornan raised one eyebrow and stood. 'She's Marco's daughter. Someone's been covering his ass for years. I'm pretty sure it was her.'

Emilio laughed. 'She needs to be an example — a graphic one.'

Fucking bastard! Dornan wanted to leap across the desk and smash his fists into his father until the old man was obliterated from existence. His fist twitched at the fantasy.

'Well, her chip's out now,' Dornan said, referring to the microchip he'd removed from her arm. 'Go for your life.'

As he slammed the door behind him, he thought he heard his father laugh.

He couldn't wait until the old fuck was out of the picture.

CHAPTER TWENTY-TWO
DORNAN

Dornan headed out to the front driveway, where his bike stood alone. The rest of the Gypsy Brothers had already returned to the clubhouse ahead of him. He'd have a busy few days organising the distribution of the new coke. Only, now that he knew it involved that fuck Murphy, he was more worried about it than ever.

'John,' Dornan barked down the line.

The connection wasn't the best, but they made do.

'You need to get back here,' John said.

Dornan didn't like being told what to do, but there was an urgency in his friend's voice that suggested panic.

'Everything okay, brother?'

There was a deep sigh. 'Caroline's in the fucking hospital.'

He left off the word *again*, but his tone implied it. Dornan sucked in a breath. This was getting ridiculous.

'She gonna be okay?'

'Sure,' John said dryly. 'If I can keep her in there.'

Dornan pinched the bridge of his nose. John's old lady was starting to become a real pain in the ass with her liking of the white powder. Not coke. She favoured heroin, and it was interfering in club business.

'Sequester her,' Dornan said wearily. 'Forty-eight-hour psychiatric hold.'

There was a stunned silence. 'She's my wife,' John protested.

Dornan looked longingly back at the door that led to the basement, and to his dark desire imprisoned below. How he'd love to blow off business and go down there with her. Take her away from this place, even. Show her a good time. She looked like she could use a good steak dinner.

'You want to save her from herself?' Dornan asked, not waiting for an answer. 'Psych hold, my friend. She'll be dead inside a year if you don't shut this shit down.'

John didn't answer.

'I'll see you in four hours,' Dornan said. 'Get it sorted, John. Is Julie at home?'

'She's with Celia,' John said stiffly. 'She's fine.'

She's at *your* house with *your* wife, was what John meant. It was still a rare bone of contention between the two best friends, even though Juliette was six years old now. John had been in Sing Sing Penitentiary when his daughter was born, addicted to heroin and having withdrawals so bad Dornan had come dangerously close to murdering Caroline himself for her selfish stupidity. Because while John rotted in jail for twelve months for something Dornan had done, Caroline had been shooting up and sucking the dick of every Gypsy Brother with loose morals and a baggie of smack to give her in return. As payment for his sins, Dornan and his second wife, Celia, had played mommy and daddy to a baby that never stopped fucking crying.

He hadn't really minded, though he'd briefly contemplated throwing her out of the window a couple of times on those really long, loud nights where she'd just scream and scream. On those nights, he and Celia would take turns soothing the poor kid, stripping her down to a diaper and resting her on their bare chests. She still cried, but it seemed to help a little. He'd never done anything like that when his sons were babies, but the guilt that ate him alive every night over John being in prison seemed to ease somewhat when he gave the baby girl some comfort.

Every time he looked at her, it reminded him of that time. It reminded him that Caroline's idiocy had almost killed a bright little girl.

But she was safe now. She was at his house, with his wife and sons.

Celia had a shotgun and a pistol, not to mention his burly teenage sons, and she knew damn well how to shut shit down.

'You still there?' John asked down the line, and Dornan realised he'd been off somewhere else.

'Yeah,' he said, still looking at the house that held the girl prisoner.

'I'll see you in four hours,' Dornan repeated. 'In the meantime, sort your fucking wife out.'

He ended the call, taking a cigarette from his pocket and lighting it.

He took one drag, frowned, and crushed the cigarette under his boot heel.

It didn't taste the same without Ana.

He climbed onto the bike and started it with great reluctance. Would she even be here when he got back? Emilio had said she'd be with them a long time, but she was kind of unpredictable, and unpredictable women were fucking dangerous to have around. Less than twenty-four hours into her stint and she had stabbed him. His fingers went to the tender flesh he'd sewn back together, and that foreign ache in his gut intensified. *I want her.*

He sighed as he fastened his open-face helmet. He'd much prefer it if she was coming with him, her breasts pressed against his back as he took her away to a place of his own.

One final glance, and he steeled himself, kicked up the stand, and tore out into the warm San Diego sunshine, homeward bound.

CHAPTER TWENTY-THREE
MARIANA

They were going to sell me.

No matter how many times I turned those words around in my mind, rearranged them, dissected them and put them back together, my fate remained the same.

They were going to *sell* me. I'd grown up in Colombia, kidnapping capital of South America for a brief period of time in the nineties, until the Mexicans caught on that ransom kidnappings were an easy way to make money.

Dornan hadn't returned to my room for a while. It was hard to keep track of hours and days when there was no natural light. An hour could be a minute, could be a day. But then, it didn't matter, did it? Every minute that passed was just a minute closer to whatever fresh hell they'd decided to throw me into.

I spent so long on my own without interruption that when the door finally did burst open, I felt an odd sense of relief. Being stuck in limbo was excruciating.

My heart sank as I saw the man in the doorway wasn't who I'd expected.

'Oh. It's you,' I said.

Murphy strolled into the room, his hands in his pants pockets. The suit he wore this time was dark grey and impeccably pressed. It didn't look cheap.

'Who were you expecting, Annie?'

My skin crawled as he got closer. My father called me Annie. Nobody else got to call me by that name.

'Hey, asshole,' I greeted him. 'Come to take me on another vacation?'

He snickered. 'You wish. Follow me.'

When I didn't move to follow him, he turned on the ball of his black leather loafer and grinned, reaching into the breast pocket of his suit. I knew what he was going to show me before he'd even removed the small crumpled square.

He had me over a goddamn barrel, and he knew it.

'Stop,' I said sharply, putting up a hand. 'I'll come.'

He laughed. 'Usually they tell me to keep going when they come.'

'You're so immature,' I muttered, shaking my head as I followed him down the hallway and to something worse than I had ever imagined.

At the other end of the hallway, past the bathroom I was allowed to stop off and use, stood a large, blank room. It looked like it had once been a garage, but now it was an open space, sunlight streaming in from thin rectangular windows that flanked one side. The ceiling seemed very high, in stark contrast to the small room I'd been in. It reminded me of the way the sun had streamed in through the stained-glass windows of our church, back when Papa had still insisted on us attending.

'Over here,' Murphy said, pointing into the middle of the room, and that was the moment my heart froze in my throat.

What the —

I backed away, towards the door. 'I'm not getting on there,' I said, looking at the bed with stainless-steel stirrups. A trolley with scalpels, and other sharp instruments that promised blood and pain, stood beside it. *Holy Jesus, what was he going to do to me? Were they going to harvest my goddamn kidneys?*

'Relaaaaaaax,' Murphy coaxed coldly, his bony fingers encircling the back of my neck and pulling me along with him.

'Wait!' I pleaded. He paused momentarily, surprising me.

I burned with shame as fresh tears fell from my eyes. I didn't cry! I wasn't weak! What was happening to me? I was so angry with myself for crumbling at the moment when my strength was most crucial.

'Please,' the words bubbled from me as my cheeks heated with shame. 'Please just tell me what's going to happen.'

His face softened minutely, as did the grip on the back of my neck.

'Nobody's going to kill you,' he said, pushing me towards the bed.

I put my hands out to stop from falling onto it.

'It's a medical check. Get your pretty panties off and get on the bed.'

A medical check. That required stirrups? *Jesus Christ.*

I turned my back to the bed so I was facing him again, and sucked in a deep breath. He must have seen the hesitation on my face, because he rolled his eyes and reached into his breast pocket, his eyebrows raised.

That goddamn photo would be the death of me. I held up a palm and then hitched my dress up, reaching underneath and tugging my panties down. My heart sank as I thought of all the things he could potentially ask me to do, holding that photo of my baby boy as ransom.

All the things I'd say yes to, to protect my son.

I kicked off the panties and went to grab them from the floor. 'Leave them there,' he said. 'Get on the bed.'

I scowled, but I left the panties on the floor and shimmied up onto the bed. It was so high, it was like it had been made for giants. I leaned against the back of the bed, which was in a sitting position, but didn't put my legs in the stirrups.

My pulse quickened in my chest as Murphy bent down and collected the black lace panties he had purchased for me. He brought them up to his nose and breathed in deeply, before pocketing the panties. That wicked glint was back in his freakish blue eyes as he circled around to the end of the bed and stood between the stirrups.

I was about to tell him how lovely he'd look wearing my panties when he yanked each of my ankles forward and draped them over the stirrups. The move was so violent, so unexpected, that I barely had time to make sure my dress was covering between my legs, let alone try to kick him in the face.

I panicked as he deftly fastened a velcro loop around each ankle and pulled tight, trapping me.

He smiled victoriously, pinning me to the bed with his eyes. Jesus, he'd make a great serial killer in one of those cheap slasher movies my fellow students at the American boarding school enjoyed watching. I'd never been able to understand why they enjoyed those ridiculous films so much. Didn't they know enough horrors existed in the real world?

But, I guess horrors didn't exist in their worlds the way they did in mine.

Emilio entered the room, his pace brisk and business-like. Another guy followed behind him, wearing a pair of surgical gloves, and my heart sank.

I surveyed both of them with open revulsion, which Emilio greeted with a fuck-you smile and a wink. A wink? Was he *trying* to be funny?

'She good?' he asked Murphy.

Without warning, Murphy reached under my dress and stuck his finger right up inside me. I squealed a little louder than I'd like to admit and desperately tried to shimmy up the bed, away from his touch.

'Tight,' he said, slowly taking his hand away. I stared at the ceiling, more embarrassed than I had ever been in my life, as he wiped his finger on the hem of my dress.

Emilio cocked his head to the side, a look of surprise on his face. 'Virgin?'

Murphy shook his head. 'Just tight.'

Emilio gestured for Murphy to step aside. As Murphy stepped back, the guy who'd entered behind Emilio, a Mexican man who looked to be in his mid-thirties, rolled a stool over and perched himself right between my open legs.

God. Could it get any worse?

'Right, *cholita*,' Emilio said, placing a hand on one of my knees. I looked at it like it was a dead cockroach, but he didn't move it away. I winced as the doctor at the foot of my bed of horrors rummaged for something on the table of torture instruments.

'Time to make sure you aren't carrying any nasty diseases. Or secret pregnancies. We've had both of those come through these doors before.'

Murphy's mouth twitched at the mention of secret pregnancies, and I glowered at him.

'Do you have to make it so ... uncivilised?' I asked through gritted teeth.

Emilio squeezed my knee with the same affection one might squeeze their daughter's knee, and I suppressed the urge to leap up and kill him with my bare hands. Mostly because that wouldn't have worked and I'd have earned a black eye for my efforts.

'Of course,' he said, and in that moment I realised just how much pleasure he took in my misery. Feasting on my sorrow lit him up from within. I blinked to stop tears from welling up in my eyes, and he tutted at me.

'*Cholita*. Come on!' he chided. 'Did you really think I'd put you to work as a maid? Washing dishes, scrubbing floors? You need to suffer so your father suffers.'

'My father can't see if I'm suffering or not,' I retorted. 'He's in Colombia.'

Murphy shifted on his feet, an amused look passing over his face. I groaned. 'Unless someone is telling him?' I glared at Murphy.

'Enough!' Emilio demanded. 'Murphy, tell the little bitch what comes next and when the auction is. And put some shit on her cuts to make them fade faster.'

He strode out of the room without turning back, his words slicing into my soul. What comes next. *Auction.*

Murphy popped a stick of gum in his mouth and started chewing loudly. As he snapped the gum between his teeth, I smelled the sickly sweet tang of fake strawberries in the air.

I tore my eyes from Murphy as the guy between my legs shoved something up and inside me that felt like a big, hard plastic dick. 'What the fuck?' I yelled.

The doctor looked to Murphy with raised eyebrows, pausing momentarily.

'It's a speculum,' Murphy said in disbelief, from his spot right next to the bed. 'I'm sure your dead boyfriend's dick was bigger than that. Quit complaining.'

Your dead boyfriend. That slammed into me like a freight train and knocked the wind from my lungs. Before I even knew what I was doing, I'd balled my fist up and swung as hard as I could.

Murphy wasn't taken off guard this time, like he had been when I'd scratched his face in the car on the way to Emilio's hotel. He parried the blow easily, grabbing hold of both of my wrists and slamming me back onto the bed.

'You see that scalpel over there,' he snarled, lifting his chin towards the tray the doctor had been fiddling with. 'If you don't stay still, I will take it and I will put it where the sun don't shine. Do you want to be fucked with the sharp end, sweetie? *I* am the one in charge here. Not you.'

'Fuck you,' I spat. 'You think you've got power? You've got nothing. Untie me and then see if you can stop me from kicking your ass.'

He rolled his eyes. 'I'm not letting you up off this bed until you've got a full check and a pretty, tight, bare pussy.'

'You're making my pussy pretty so you can sell me off to some pervert who'll keep me chained in his basement? What a powerful man you are.'

'The customer is always right.' Murphy grinned. 'And the customer wants bare pussy.'

I rolled my eyes. 'So, most of the girls you sell are actual virgins? You'd have to get them pretty young to ensure that, right?'

He let go of one of my wrists and slapped me across the face. I relished the pain as my cheek stung.

'Let's hurry this along,' Murphy told the doctor. Emilio re-entered my line of sight, and I was even more mortified.

I struggled against Murphy's grip and the restraints on my ankles, but it was no use. I couldn't budge, spread-eagled in the stirrups, my most intimate of places centimetres from the unspeaking doctor's face.

I shivered in revulsion when Emilio leaned over my leg and trailed his index finger up my thigh, sinking it into me without any warning. It hurt — I wasn't exactly wet, after being finger-fucked by Murphy. It's not like the experience had been a turn-on, after all.

He withdrew his finger and laughed, a deep boom that rattled my chest.

'I should make you tighter,' he taunted me. 'I should punish you for being disobedient. Sew you up so tight, you're a virgin again.' The bastard made his thumb and index finger into a circle, then watched my face intently as he curled his fingers tighter until the circle was tiny.

Sew me up? Down there? No way.

Out of the corner of my eye, I saw the doctor start to thread a needle with thin, translucent thread.

Jesus Christ. He couldn't possibly —

'Wait!' I yelled. Suddenly I was breathing so fast, I was probably in danger of passing out. 'I'll do whatever you want.'

Emilio tipped his head to the side, grinning. He loved my fear, I could tell. Men like him lived on the fright of subservient humans.

He snapped his fingers and the guy between my thighs handed over the needle. Emilio's mouth twitched as he brought it up to my eye, his other hand fisting my hair to stop me from shrinking away. Beads of sweat gathered at my temples as the tiny, sharp needle got closer and closer to my eye, so close that the tip of it blurred completely.

'Whatever I want?' Emilio asked.

'Yes,' I panted. 'Please, I'm sorry. Anything.'

Emilio grinned, withdrawing the needle. I gasped as I watched it fall neatly into the breast pocket of his suit, such a tiny scrap of metal, but a violent threat to keep me toeing the line.

'Remember this when you talk out of turn,' he said. 'Remember what you are to me. What I am to you.'

I bit back angry tears. He owned me for life. The present I could somehow handle, but my future? It was almost too much to bear.

The guy between my legs scooted closer, his movements hesitant and slow.

Hurry up, I wanted to urge, but I refused to show any more weakness in front of these men. Instead, I laid back and braced myself for the pain.

And found his eyes, piercing into mine.

Not Emilio's.

Murphy's.

In the shadows, his blue eyes gleamed with amusement. And something else.

Satisfaction.

'I'll leave you to it, doc,' Emilio said, walking out into the hallway. A second later, he ducked his head back in and called out to Murphy, 'You coming?'

'If it's all the same to you, boss,' Murphy said, grinning, 'I think I'd rather watch.'

Emilio chuckled and disappeared.

My mind hurtled back in time, remembering a scene almost exactly like this. I was sixteen years old, and I'd just pushed my baby boy out into the cruel world that would insist he be taken from me. I had been allowed to hold him, the nurses laying him on my chest for a few precious minutes before he was whisked away. I had looked longingly into a set of perfect, dark blue eyes that stared into my own; a piece of my own soul made physical and brought into the world.

Now, pinned to the bed by crazy Murphy, I looked into a different pair of blue eyes. But there was nothing loving or soft in these eyes. There was just a dominance that fed on my terror.

Hot wax was applied to my delicate skin, and then the burning began. Burning, and pain. It was hot. Much too hot. And as I looked at Murphy, I could tell they'd made it too hot on purpose. It felt like I had fire stuck to my skin.

'You can cry if you want,' Murphy said, his mouth forming a devious smirk. 'They all do.'

I didn't want to. But I did. I cried.

As my tears fell faster, his grin widened.

I hated him.

CHAPTER TWENTY-FOUR

DORNAN

He was sitting behind his office desk when she sidled in.

Dornan whistled. 'Caroline,' he greeted John's wife. 'Looking good.'

What he meant was, she looked clean. She'd had forty-eight hours to detox the junk out of her system, and he damn well hoped it had made a difference. But he saw the desperation in her puffy green eyes, and his gut clenched unpleasantly.

'Fucking hospital,' she seethed. 'Can you believe they kept me in psych for two fucking days?'

She sat her skinny ass on the edge of his desk, right next to him, flipping her auburn hair over her shoulder. Dornan was amused. Caroline was young, twenty-five, and she was the epitome of a club whore. She belonged firmly in party girl territory, but he guessed she'd seen her meal ticket in John and taken it.

'I wonder why you're in here,' Dornan asked, lifting his boots up onto the desk and crossing his ankles.

'I just wanted to say hello.' Caroline shrugged.

Dornan pursed his lips to stop from laughing. 'Hello, Caroline,' he said lightly. 'Where's your daughter?'

Her shoulders slumped and the light in her eyes all but bled away. 'With Celia,' she said softly.

Of course she was. In an instant his amusement at her predictability turned into pure apathy.

'With Celia,' Dornan repeated, dangerously calm. 'And I guess you're on your way to go pick her up, aren't you? Take her home, cook her a real meal. Read her a fuckin' book?'

He taunted her because if he couldn't voice his frustration he would start hitting her with his fists. And he had to remember that she was John's wife. *Don't do it, don't do it.*

Caroline hovered nervously at the edge of the desk. 'Go home, Car,' Dornan said sharply. 'Go be a fucking mother to that girl for one single night.'

She still didn't move, and he saw the unanswered desire in her eyes. Not for him, hell no. They'd fucked once before — back when John was in prison and Dornan was drunk — but he had nothing in him for her. She reeked desperation like cheap perfume.

'I'm strung out, D,' she begged. 'Please. The doctor said I should wean off slowly. I just need a little —'

'There it is,' Dornan said sarcastically. He'd been waiting for her to ask for some smack. What she really wanted. Her begging was like clockwork.

Dornan dropped his feet back to the floor with a solid thud, standing with emphasis so that he was towering over the junkie his best friend had had the misfortune of marrying.

'I'm sick of your shit, Caroline. I'm cutting you off. Get the fuck out of my face before I hurt you.'

Amusement rose inside him as he watched her panic. She was about to lose her shit right in front of him, and he kind of wished he had the time to let her. She deserved to beg a little, maybe even grovel.

'You can't do this,' she stammered, trying to stay rooted to the spot as he dragged her towards the doorway by her arm. 'I'll tell John what you did to me while he was in prison!'

Dornan stopped dead in his tracks and dropped her arm like it was covered in shit.

'If you're referring to the time I woke up on your couch to see you'd climbed your dirty snatch up onto my dick, please tell him. I'm sure he'd love that.'

Anger and frustration rolled off her in waves, mixed in with the faintly sweet odour that seemed unique to junkies coming down. That anxious, desperate sweat smell. Like fruit before it turns and starts to rot. The edge. She was on the edge.

'I'll tell him you forced me,' she threatened.

That tipped *him* over the edge. He grabbed a chunk of her greasy auburn hair and tugged, pulling her face to his.

'Just fuckin' try it,' he hissed through gritted teeth. 'I dare you.'

The fight went out of her, and she became limp in his grip. Junkies were all the same. He'd had to deal with enough of them in his line of work. He pushed her out of the doorway and slammed the door shut before he started laying punches into that stupid face of hers.

Fucking bitch.

CHAPTER TWENTY-FIVE

MARIANA

Three days passed. Three days of pacing the room, of scratching the wounds on my wrists that were only just now beginning to heal. Three days of three meals a day, delivered by Murphy himself. Three days of pure and utter hell.

Three days, and no sign of Dornan.

I should have known he wouldn't help me.

And then, in an instant, everything began happening too quickly. Murphy handed me a towel and pointed to the door.

'Go shower,' he ordered. 'Wash your fucking hair. It looks like greasy old spaghetti.'

I glared at him, but I also really wanted a shower. I hadn't bathed in days, and I was completely and utterly worn out.

Freshly showered, I edged back into the room wearing a towel and new underwear. I sidled past Murphy, dreading what he might decide to do with me now that I was clean and half-naked in front of him.

But what he did surprised me. He handed me a folded black piece of clothing, and as I shook it open with one hand, my knees gave way.

It was a dress. Innocent enough, a simple silk number with no sleeves that would reach to the floor on my frame.

But it wasn't the dress that worried me. It was the *why*.

'No,' I said, dropping the dress at my damp feet and scurrying back. 'No, no, no.'

I jumped as a woman appeared at the door. She looked a few years older than me, but immaculate, like a porcelain doll. Huge blue eyes were the main feature of her pale face, her thin lips fashioned into a scowl. Her glossy brown hair was slicked back into a bun and she wore a black shift dress that looked expensive. She was like a beanpole, so thin her cheekbones jutted out, her elbows and knees angular. Maybe she was a prisoner, too.

When she spoke, however, I realised she was definitely not a prisoner. 'She's chubby,' the woman snapped, her ice-blue eyes raking up and down me. I still had my towel on, but I felt exposed under her withering glare. I backed away towards the bed. Her accent was hard to pin down, but I was guessing New York. And she was definitely Italian. Oh, Jesus, was this Dornan's wife? Was this the one he had been talking about? If so, I completely understood the 'My wife is a cunt' comment. I couldn't think of a better word to sum this woman up.

'I'm practically obese compared to you,' I agreed, just as snappily. 'Who are you?'

'Shhh, Bella,' Murphy said with a small smile. 'You're just jealous of her rack.'

Bella. Definitely Italian. But it was the wrong name for her. She was pretty, regal, but she was certainly not beautiful.

She huffed, feigning disinterest as she addressed Murphy. 'I don't have all day,' she said, holding up a small red bag in her palm. A make-up bag. 'And I'm going to need a while with this one.'

They were either getting me ready to sell, or getting ready to induct me into the whorehouse hall of fame. Neither sounded appealing. I clenched my jaw, moving as far as I could into the corner of the room. *Dornan, where the hell are you?* I doubted he would be able to do anything to stop Emilio from selling me, but for some reason I still wanted him to be there. Clearly, I had issues.

Murphy surveyed me from the doorway, then slammed the door shut.

'Put the dress on,' he said.

'What's happening?' I demanded, clutching the towel to my chest.

He stepped forward, the expression on his face grave. It suddenly struck me as odd that this time, for the first time since I had met him in my father's house, there was no sexual innuendo, no inappropriate touching and no threats. He was sombre, and that was more terrifying than I could have ever anticipated.

'You're nervous,' I said incredulously. I looked at his hand, seeing a slight tremble there. 'Why are you nervous?'

The unflappable bastard had had his cage rattled. But by who, and why?

'Put the dress on, honey,' he said shortly. 'Or I'll take you out there naked, and trust me, you do *not* want that. You'll be eaten alive.'

Bella laughed dryly behind him.

'What do you care?' I muttered, but I turned my back to him and hurriedly threw the dress over my head, letting my towel drop at the same time. I didn't like the idea of being eaten alive naked, whether it was a real threat or not.

Somehow, I knew that things were about to change. I'd sensed it as soon as Murphy had walked into the room.

Are you going to sell me?

Yes.

YES. Dornan's reply rose in my throat like bile, and I swallowed anxiously.

I panicked while I was smoothing the dress down. I panicked as Murphy sat me on the edge of the bed.

I panicked while the skinny bitch chewed gum and carefully applied make-up to my skin. I panicked as she used a blow-dryer to dry my hair. It was a silent scream that tore at my insides, threatening to bubble up and spill from my lips unbidden.

Never show fear. The mantra that I had chanted in my head, over and over, since I had offered myself to Emilio. But my resolve was wearing thin, and my fear was breaking me open, shining through the cracks like a million dying stars in the night sky. People would see through those cracks, and they would know. They would see my fear and they would enjoy it.

I didn't fight Murphy or his bitch offsider Bella because I knew what was held over me. I could practically see the crumpled photograph of Luis in Murphy's breast pocket, right over the spot where his dead black heart would sit.

I didn't fight, because I knew it would be futile. This was the part where they would take bids on my life.

'Stand up,' Murphy ordered, after Bella had finished applying a truckload of mascara to my eyelashes. 'Give daddy a twirl.'

I didn't twirl. He could go fuck himself.

Murphy stood to the side a little as Bella tossed the make-up bag on the bed and left the room, slamming the door behind her.

My eyes still on the door, I jumped as Murphy grasped my chin in his long fingers.

'I'd buy you,' he said.

I took all the rage and the hate that had been sitting inside my chest for the past few days, and channelled it into my knee. I smiled sweetly as I brought it up into his balls, hitting my target with force and precision.

I grinned as he doubled over in front of me.

'*Baby*,' I said in his ear, 'you couldn't afford me.'

CHAPTER TWENTY-SIX
DORNAN

He could feel his father's eyes on him; could feel the rage inside Emilio, burning two holes in his face.

The girl was going to be auctioned off, and the sadness that spread through Dornan's chest at that fact was deeply unsettling. He'd spent mere moments with her.

But he had tasted her tears.

Tasted her blood.

And he couldn't bear what would come next.

He briefly considered bidding himself, but he didn't have fifty grand. He might have a rich father, but Dornan was rich in assets, not cash. He had six sons, for shit's sake. Six sons who ate him out of house and home.

'You do not want to sell her,' Dornan said, jabbing his finger in the direction of the basement.

'Of course I do, *figlio*. And I want her owner to be the most brutal motherfucker. I want to send Marco pictures that will make him wish he was dead.'

Dornan's fingers tightened around his tumbler. Scotch on the rocks, to ease his fraying nerves. That little whore Bella had always been good at two things — sucking dick, and relaying gossip to him. So when she'd called a few hours ago and told Dornan there was an auction tonight, he had jumped on his bike before he'd even hung up. He'd sped as fast as his bike and the traffic would allow, weaving dangerously between cars and trucks on the busy stretch of highway that ran from Venice Beach, LA, all the way down to the ends of San Diego where the US touched Mexico.

'Pop, I've spoken to people,' Dornan protested. His trigger finger was itchy, and he had an impulsive desire to rip his gun from its holster and shoot his father in the face. He had a tendency to be volatile when cornered. 'I've been speaking to Marco's business associates.'

Emilio looked up sharply from where he was studying a handwritten list of names. 'You what?'

'It was a coincidence,' Dornan continued, the lie as easy as the truth.

He had inherited his silver tongue from his father, and so it was much harder to sway him. But it was worth a try. He couldn't let Ana go; he hadn't thought of anything except her for the past few days. He'd tried to fuck her out of his system, then resorted to booze and drugs, but nothing worked.

He wanted her, and he was going to find a way to get her.

Emilio stood up and rounded the desk, standing over Dornan. 'You want to defy me, son? For a girl? A fucking Colombian whore?'

He did. He really, really did.

'Gino says she's been doing the books for Marco for years. Two or three. Says she's pretty fucking good at taking dirty money to the laundromat and cleaning it up.'

Emilio took a step back, his indignation fading slightly.

'Go on,' he said.

'Apparently our Marco has been quite the gambler. He owes a lot of bookmakers a lot of money.'

Emilio threw his hands up in exasperation. 'You're telling me things I already know. Get to the point.'

'She was using Gino's workshop as a front. Funnelling a lot of illegal money through, holding off the bookies by laundering their money for them.'

Emilio looked bored. 'The point,' he urged, clicking his fingers.

'I think Bella is in over her head,' Dornan said. 'The burlesque club in Venice is bleeding money, and she's too fucking dumb to figure it out. I say we put this girl to work, see if she can do better.'

Emilio didn't seem overly keen, but then, he wasn't ordering Dornan from his office, so it wasn't all bad. He circled back to his side of the desk and uncapped a decanter of whiskey.

'If it doesn't work, I'll shoot her myself,' Dornan offered.

Emilio rubbed his fake tooth with the pad of his finger, like he did sometimes when he was thinking.

'Gino's shop woulda been small fry,' he said.

'Millions, Pop,' Dornan corrected his father. '*Millions*.'

'I've already invited sixteen fucking people to this auction,' Emilio snapped. 'Could you not have come to me with this yesterday?'

Dornan scoffed. 'I very much doubt she's the only girl you have at your disposal.'

Emilio grinned. By saving Mariana, Dornan knew he was only condemning someone else. He wondered if she was older. No, probably younger. Probably a girl who'd been promised a better life and herded into a shipping container, then driven to her doom. Dornan's gut turned to ice. *Forget about it. Focus.*

He couldn't save them all, and he *needed* Mariana.

'And you're going to vouch for this little bitch?' Emilio's eyes were beady, alight with something all of a sudden. Anger? No. He was amused.

Dornan sat back in his chair, surveying his father.

'Sure,' he said. 'She's just one little Colombian bitch; what's the worst she could do?'

Emilio raised his eyebrows. 'You know better than to assume that, boy.'

'I'll keep her under lock and key. I'll make sure she's watched by the brothers.'

Emilio grinned. 'Just watched?'

Dornan laughed. 'Of course not.' *Nobody else will fucking touch her.* But Emilio didn't have to know that.

He could see his father was teetering on the edge of a decision.

'If she's an issue, we deal with it. There's nothing to say we can't sell her again in a month. But in the meantime? She might be able to actually repay some of Marco's debt.'

Emilio chewed on his lip. 'Fuck it,' he said, raising his glass in Dornan's direction. 'Take the little *chocho*. Work her. Make sure she experiences a full Gypsy Brothers welcome. And Dornan?'

He needed to get away from his father so he could smile. He needed to smile or his face was going to fucking break.

'Yeah,' he said, casual as anything.

'I want photographs,' Emilio said, taking a mouthful of whiskey and making a hissing sound as he swallowed. 'I want to show that fucking Marco her blood. Her suffering. And I'll be needing proof that this actually works. Otherwise, it's a bullet for her.'

Dornan snickered. 'As you wish, boss.'

Emilio launched out of his chair and gave his son a fatherly slap on the cheek as he left the room. 'Lock up when you're done,' he called, and then he was gone.

Dornan waited a beat, keeping his breath even and measured.

He couldn't believe it.

He grinned as he stood up, shoving his fists into his jean pockets to ease their shaking.

Emilio had bought the story, and Mariana was going to be *his*.

CHAPTER TWENTY-SEVEN

MARIANA

Murphy had recovered from his knee in the balls enough to slap me. I knew he really wanted to smash his fist into my face, judging by the way his fingers twitched by his side, but he couldn't very well mark me just before I was about to be sold, could he?

'I should kick you in the cunt for that,' he said.

I didn't reply, too busy laughing instead. The door burst open and I was still smiling as I spun around in my pretty black dress. The smile died on my face as I saw him.

'You,' I whispered.

Dornan Ross leaned against the door frame, the smile on his face almost contagious in its intensity.

'You're dismissed,' Dornan said to Murphy, never once taking his eyes from mine. Something burned between us; something powerful. Something that frightened me, because I liked it. I liked *him*. And I didn't want to.

'You're interrupting,' Murphy replied, grabbing my elbow. 'This one's up first, apparently.'

I drew in a sharp breath as I watched Dornan's face transform from a smile to something terrifying. He took his gun out faster than I could blink — man, he was a quick draw — and aimed it at Murphy.

'I said, you're dismissed,' Dornan replied, flashing the fakest cheesy grin I'd ever seen.

Murphy looked from me to Dornan and back again. My heart was hammering in my chest now, because he was here, and he had a gun to Murphy. Was this really happening? Was he here to help me? Surely not. He was the son of Emilio Ross.

'So you convinced him, huh?' Murphy said bitterly. 'What a fucking waste of my time.' He turned on me. 'Should've just shot you when I had the chance, huh?'

I tried to pull my arm away, but his fingers were like a death grip, my skin underneath each one turning white.

'What'd you tell him, huh?' Murphy demanded, shaking me as he addressed Dornan. 'What lie did you come up with this time, *D*?'

Dornan cocked the hammer on his gun. In the quiet, the metallic sound echoed off the walls.

'Mind your own business,' Dornan ground out. 'Or I'll decorate the wall with your fucking skull.'

Murphy scowled, letting go of me and storming out. Dornan kicked the door shut behind him, and it slammed forcefully in his wake.

'Feel free to breathe now,' Dornan said, holstering his gun. I realised I'd been holding my breath, and I let it out in a loud whoosh.

We studied each other across the room. Something passed between us ... something that made me want to cry, because his father was about to sell me. The same father whose men had killed my boyfriend, the love of my life.

Part of me demanded that I look away. That I break this stare, stop whatever was happening between us.

'You didn't come back,' I said quietly. And now, it was too late. Maybe it had always been too late.

He smiled. 'Been busy.'

I nodded.

'You look pretty,' he said, his voice a little strained.

And I suddenly remembered why. *Damn.*

'Apparently, I'm for sale. Murphy says he'd buy me,' I said numbly. 'What about you? Would you buy me, Dornan?'

His smile returned. I didn't flinch as he stepped towards me. He leaned down, his lips at my ear. The next words that came from his mouth would define my very existence.

'Baby,' he whispered, '*I already did.*'

CHAPTER TWENTY-EIGHT
DORNAN

In the back of his mind, during the three days since he'd last seen Mariana, he'd been turning over a plan of what life might look like if he were fortunate enough to stop his father from selling the girl. He'd been holding onto an apartment in Santa Monica, a bachelor pad he'd won in a double-or-nothing game of poker five years ago, for a situation just like this. He'd managed to keep the apartment a secret from almost everyone, especially Celia, and he fucking loved it. It was a place of refuge, the calm away from whatever was brewing at the clubhouse or his own house. Even Bella didn't know it existed — it was much more preferable to throw her over a table at the clubhouse when they did the dirty.

The last few days he had subjected the club whores to things he had never done before. He had hurt them, made them bleed, and he had liked it. But it had barely scratched the itch that was his desire for the curvy Colombian woman. If anything, it had made the itch worse. Impossible to scratch.

A tiny part of him was a little disturbed by the dark ideas that assaulted him on an hourly basis. He was slipping, losing control over his own thoughts, and he knew she was going to haunt his every waking moment until he could drive himself into that soft, wet spot between her legs.

He had this perverse fantasy that once she was with him he would be able to enact all the wicked fantasies he'd been imagining. He'd be able to stretch her out, restrain her limbs until they ached, and fuck her until she begged him to stop.

Not that he would.

He saw the power he could wield over her, and part of him lusted for it.

He didn't let her pack any of her things — he didn't want her wearing the cheap, gaudy shit Murphy had loaded her up with. He would buy plainer clothes, blacks and blues that would go beautifully with her light caramel skin. And with her black and blue bruises, if she didn't obey him.

He was kind of hoping she wouldn't obey him. Because he didn't just want to hurt her. No, that would be too brutal.

He wanted to hurt her, and for her to enjoy the pain, and then he wanted to soothe her, over and over again.

Then again, maybe she would be a terrible prisoner. Maybe he would end up fucking her and killing her, dumping her body in the ocean, weighted with concrete. It was a possibility he'd prepared himself for. He'd never raped a woman, but he'd killed one. Several, in fact. And he had steeled himself for the potential shit storm that might be unleashed when he brought Mariana into his unforgiving world.

The ride to his Santa Monica apartment was exhilarating, an emotion that he rarely felt anymore. At any moment, he expected to see his father's sleek Mercedes fly past, cut him off, and demand the girl be returned to the tiny little room underneath Emilio's lavish compound. He'd ridden fast for that very reason, fast and hard, and he'd fantasised about Ana while her slender fingers curled around his waist, gripping him tightly.

So now, shut safely inside the confines of his apartment, they stood across from each other in the long, white tiled entrance hall.

She looked around the hallway, uncertain. 'I can stay here?'

He tilted his head. 'My father wants you to suffer. He let me take you because I bought you to be a club whore.'

'A club whore?' She raised her eyes to his, her hands were shaking. 'Is that what you said to Emilio to stop the auction? That you would *buy* me for your club?'

He chuckled. 'I didn't buy you with money, doll. I bought you with a promise.' He dipped his head so his lips were right beside her ear, speaking in a whisper. 'A promise that I would make you suffer.'

Her eyes widened, and the devious pleasure he felt reached all the way to his cock and squeezed painfully. 'I told my father I would take you to the clubhouse and let the boys use and abuse every inch of that pretty Colombian skin. Fuck you in every hole you've got. Make you bleed.'

She whimpered.

'But here's the thing,' he said darkly, pulling back and down slightly so they were eye to eye. 'We're not at the clubhouse. Because I don't want to share you.'

She swallowed, not moving. He caged her against the wall with his tattooed arms, the bright colours in stark contrast to her bare, bronze arms.

He saw the way she looked at him. He hadn't imagined it. And the spark that passed between them ... He *knew* that she would be his if he just played things right. If he made it seem like she had a choice.

He wanted her to choose him more than he'd ever wanted anything.

He tucked a stray hair behind her ear.

'It's your choice, Ana,' he said. 'I won't make you do anything you don't want to do.'

She didn't say a thing.

'What'll it be?' he asked finally. He half expected her to rebel, tell him to take her to the clubhouse and let them destroy her, just so she'd have the satisfaction of saying no to him.

But he'd seen the desperation in her eyes the moment he mentioned the Gypsy Brothers clubhouse. He'd figured out her true fears. She didn't want to be a club whore, a shell that got used up and tossed aside once it was ruined.

'Do you promise?' she asked softly.

'Promise what, baby?' His tone was conversational.

'Promise that if I stay with you, you'll protect me from them?'

He brushed a thumb against her lips and grinned. 'I promise if you stay here with me, and you do as you're told, I'll protect you from the whole world.'

Tears formed in her eyes. Not enough to spill over to her cheeks when she blinked, just enough to make a thin, watery film over the dark blue.

She trembled. 'Thank you.'

It made him feel like the biggest asshole in the entire world. He was taking advantage of this girl for his own sick purposes, giving her a choice between two different versions of hell. And she was thanking him?

'Don't thank me,' he said gruffly. 'Just don't let me down by trying to run away. I don't do second chances.'

She nodded, the relief on her face palpable. Goddamn it, couldn't she be a little less grateful?

'You'll have to do some other shit too,' he said. 'Accounts and things. I told Emilio what you did for your father. The money laundering.'

Her face fell. He could tell she was upset he had divulged her secret.

'It was the only way,' he clarified. 'Your skill set is in much higher demand than a club whore's. You have a job, and your job helped get you out of being sold.'

She nodded. He'd never seen her this quiet. She seemed ... shocked.

'So ...' she began.

He raised his eyebrows in anticipation. 'Mmm?'

'So my job is to do accounts and pretend to be a whore,' she said. 'What's your job? What do you actually do?'

Dornan snorted. 'I'm a consultant.'

She smiled. There it was. A little of that fire came back into her eyes, made his heart do something weird inside his chest. 'Oh, really?' she teased. 'Can I have your business card?'

He braced his clenched fists against the wall. Without a second thought, Dornan dipped his head lower and swooped on her lips, pressing his mouth to hers like it held the air he needed to breathe. He felt her stiffen momentarily, but he didn't pull back. He waited one beat, two, and it was like something broke inside her. She melted against the wall, opening her velvety lips wider and meeting his tongue with hers. Her small hands wrapped around the back of his head as she kissed him with the same wild ferocity he had started with. They explored each other's mouths, and held each other tight.

It didn't make sense. She didn't belong in his world. She was much too beautiful, and beautiful things always ended up broken with him. But here, alone, nobody knew. Nobody saw. It was just them.

Dornan eventually pulled away with great reluctance; one more second of a kiss like that and he'd be tearing her clothes off and pinning her to the wall with his achingly hard cock. He didn't want to scare the shit out of her, not when they'd been in the apartment all of five minutes.

He gave her a devilish smile as he took a step back and drank her in. Dark blue eyes that watched him intently, heavy lidded after that kiss. Her lips slightly apart, cheeks flushed, her long coffee-coloured tresses mussed up from his big hands.

'What was that?' she asked, her voice a little strained.

'My business card,' he replied. 'You can get me there any time.'

He liked the way she blushed when he said things like that.

She smiled at him, and his chest swelled.

Yeah. He had fucking saved her.

And now, she belonged to him.

CHAPTER TWENTY-NINE

MARIANA

Power.

For days I had had no power. I had had nothing.

And now, *he* had come back. He had taken me out of that hellhole, set me on the back of his bike and brought me here.

He had saved me.

We'd been on the road two, maybe three hours. Still wearing the blacked-out helmet that rendered me blind, I was completely unaware of where we were heading. I clung to Dornan like he was the shore and I was drowning, and with every moment we travelled further from Emilio's compound, I felt like I could breathe a little easier.

Which was stupid, really. Because for all I knew, Dornan could've been taking me out into the wilderness to shoot me and bury the evidence.

I considered letting go of Dornan's leather vest so I would fly off the back of the bike, through the air, until the hard, unforgiving asphalt broke my body and claimed me.

But something stopped me. I hung on for dear life, for hours, until I felt the bike slow and then come to a stop. I heard the ocean, or at least I thought I did.

'Open your visor,' Dornan said.

I hesitated for a moment, sure I had heard him wrong.

'It's okay,' he added. 'Open it. Look around.'

I flipped the blackened visor up, cold air rushing into the helmet. My eyes watered for a moment, unaccustomed to the wind.

We were in front of a beach. It was the middle of the night and the streets around us were empty, the line of stores and restaurants on one side completely deserted.

'Where are we?' I breathed.

'Los Angeles,' he said. He gunned the bike and rode off again, as I rested the side of my helmeted head on his back and watched the coastline pass us by.

After a while he made me shut the visor again and we rode for a while longer until the bike stopped again and he helped me dismount. Once we were inside the apartment he took the helmet off and for a moment I thought things might be okay, but then he had said the words 'club whore'.

Hearing those two words slammed the door shut on the faint hope I'd had since we'd left the compound. Hope that he might let me go. Hope that it might all be some insane nightmare that I could wake up from.

But it was real.

Club.

Whore.

I'd trembled, remembering the way Murphy had held me down as I was waxed. A useless, painful gesture for an auction that didn't happen. But it was still there, my reddened skin now smooth and hairless, and itching like crazy, a reminder that whoever decided to hold me down and rape me first would be able to see what they'd fashioned me into. A fuck-me doll. A piece of merchandise.

I couldn't bear the thought of what they would do to me. Faceless men dressed in leather who would press themselves onto me so I couldn't breathe, who would make sure that whatever they did hurt me so that I screamed.

But then he offered me a choice.

And, among all my fear, he had leaned down and kissed me.

And I had kissed him back.

But it was more than just a kiss.

He had taken me away from that horrible place, away from the auction and brought me here.

Dornan, surprisingly, was the one to break the moment. I saw the moon hanging low in the full-length window at the other end of the hallway we were standing in. And something else — something large and round glittered in the distance. A ferris wheel lit up in the night.

'What is that?' I murmured, craning my neck to see. Dornan started down the hallway, gesturing for me to follow. I didn't move for a moment, watching him stride away with purpose. His leather cut hugged his solid shoulders, the white t-shirt underneath offering a peek at the tattoos that adorned his arms. His dark hair was shorter than it had been the last time I'd seen him just days ago, and I wondered if he'd cut it for me. Of course not. That would be ridiculous.

Though, this entire situation was ridiculous.

I followed him, passing a bedroom on one side, a living room on the other. At the end of the hallway the apartment opened up, a kitchen and breakfast bar on the right. The left side of the apartment housed a small leather sofa and a glass dining table with chairs tucked neatly beneath it. But the real view, the one that had made me divert my gaze from the delicious-looking man in front of me, was outside.

Dornan seemed to read my thoughts, opening the glass sliding door and stepping out onto a balcony big enough to hold a table, two chairs and him, with room left over. We were on the second storey, and beneath us the ocean lapped at the shoreline lazily. I stepped out behind him, greeted by fresh salty air that stuck to my skin in tiny droplets of moisture.

The apartment itself was nothing fancy, but to a girl who'd been cooped up in a cell for the better part of a week, it was beautiful.

'Is this where you live?' I breathed, coming to stand beside him at the edge of the balcony.

My question seemed to amuse him. He took his eyes from the water to look at me.

'No,' he replied, 'it's where you live, now.'

Instinctively, as I had always done before, I put my hand to my chest, searching for my locket. Damn. The events of the past week slammed into me, and I gripped the balcony when my knees turned to liquid. It was only a moment, but he noticed.

'You all right?' he asked, and his concern killed me. I nodded, my hand still resting over the bare space where my locket used to sit; where my well-worn photo of Luis had rested. Gone. All of it, gone.

I kept swallowing, trying to clear the lump in my throat, but it wouldn't go away. My grief consumed me like wildfire, tears spilling from my eyes as I stared at the water below. I thought of climbing up on the railing and stepping off, landing on the sidewalk that ran along the beach. I raised myself up on tiptoes to get a good look underneath me. Not high enough. I'd probably break bones, but I doubted I would die.

Don't be an idiot, I chastised myself. I couldn't kill myself.

'What was his name?' Dornan asked. 'Your boyfriend.'

I swiped my hand across my face, wiping away the tears that clung to my skin.

'Este,' I said, my stomach twisting violently at the mention of him. 'Esteban.'

Dornan nodded. 'It's probably not worth much, but I'm sorry for what happened to him.' His hand pressed into the small of my back, and I felt a little less alone.

'I can't close my eyes without seeing his face,' I confessed. I felt guilty that I was even talking to him about Este, when it had been his father's men who had gunned him down in the first place. 'It was so unnecessary, you know? They didn't need to shoot him. They didn't need to hurt him at all. He was just in the way, so they killed him.'

I was disgusted with myself. Este had bled to death before me only a week ago, and now I was kissing a strange man in a darkened hallway?

'And now I'm here with you and I just … kissed you, and he's probably still laying in a morgue somewhere in the cold.' I cried. I cried so hard, I could barely breathe, picturing my dead lover zipped into a bodybag and stacked in a fridge. He didn't deserve that. Nobody did. He had been killed because he loved me.

'Don't feel bad,' Dornan said. 'I kissed you darlin', remember? He's not gonna haunt you for that.'

I thought about that for a few moments. Maybe he was right.

'Nobody'd blame you for trying to survive. It's the smart thing to do.'

'Is that all it was?' I asked. 'Just the smart thing to do?'

It hadn't felt smart, the way I had responded to him. The way I had been disappointed when he'd pulled away.

'For you, maybe,' he said, that amused glint back in his eye. 'For me … I think that was the opposite of smart.'

'So why'd you do it then?' I asked boldly.

He laughed, the sound light and innocent, in complete contrast to his fierce demeanour. It floated away on the waves as the tide pulled out from the shore, and all too soon, it was quiet again.

He turned to me, his head cocked to the side slightly. 'I have no idea,' he said. He reached out, running his fingers along my arm. 'You're cold.'

I leaned into his touch for a fraction of a second, but guilt and revulsion tore me apart again. It was exhausting, this see-saw of emotions.

'Isn't your wife waiting for you?' I asked, shrugging my arm away.

His smile vanished. He let his hand fall away from me slowly. 'I doubt it,' he said. 'She knows better by now.'

He gestured for me to step back inside, locking the door with a key as I moved past him into the apartment.

He looked down at the long black dress I was still wearing. My auction costume.

'I'm gonna burn that fucking dress the next time I'm here,' he said vehemently.

He turned to leave.

'Wait,' I said, suddenly terrified at the thought of being alone. 'When are you coming back?'

He scooped up his helmet and walked down the hallway to the keypad by the door, punching in a combination of numbers. 'When my wife lets me out of the house,' he threw over his shoulder, slamming the door shut behind him.

And then, just like that, he was gone, my lips still burning from where he had kissed me. I held my fingers to my mouth, and felt them tremble.

CHAPTER THIRTY

DORNAN

Goddamn it. God fucking damn it! She had him wrapped around her little finger, and he was panting like a fuckin' dog in heat around her.

Better to put some distance between them for now, let her start to appreciate the situation for what it was. The situation where he'd hauled her ass out of Dodge and planted her in some sweet digs after having known her just a matter of days.

Despite what he'd said, he wasn't going home. Celia had been giving him the shits lately, probably had her damn period, and he steered clear of her when that happened. Besides, the woman wasn't stupid. She knew what Dornan was like. He liked to think they had an unspoken understanding. She got to live in the nice house and spend his money, and he got to go out and do whatever the fuck he wanted, whatever pretty little opportunities the Gypsy Brotherhood brought to him.

He rode fast again, but not too fast. This close to LA, he didn't want to pick up any undue attention. He had the local sheriff in his top pocket, but it never hurt to play along and act like a law-abiding citizen to keep things flowing smoothly.

When he parked his bike and entered the Gypsy Brothers clubhouse, it was after midnight. It'd been a long day, a tedious day of hostage negotiations, and he really wanted something to take the pain away.

There was music playing, and he walked down the hallway and into the main area of the clubhouse with the swagger of a man who owned the place. He wanted to forget about Mariana Rodriguez for a couple of hours. The stress of her existence, of having vouched for her with his father, was wearing at his nerves. The distinct possibility that she might make him look like a fool burrowed into his thoughts and remained there, taunting him. He needed a distraction, and fast.

Jimmy and Viper were drinking at the bar. John wasn't there, but that wasn't a surprise — he was hardly ever there. The club was more of a burden to him these days. And with his junkie wife, Dornan could understand why. It was like owning a bar and being married to an alcoholic. The last thing Caroline needed to be around was a place like this, full of booze and drugs and fucking.

Dornan, on the other hand ... well, he fitted in just fine.

He slid onto a stool and slapped the bar in front of him. The chick behind the counter was new, and completely naked, save for a bottle-opener she wore on a piece of twine around her neck. She looked young, but legal. That was important in a club with a reputation like theirs. They might've had the local cops in their pocket, but it didn't stop the fucking narcos from turning the place upside down on a semi-regular basis, looking for drugs and underage girls.

The girl handed him a beer and told him her name, which he promptly forgot. They all looked the same, and he had to wonder who the fuck was doing the hiring around here. Blonde, young, with perky tits.

'You look like hell,' Jimmy said, clinking beers with Dornan before taking a swig. 'Let Destiny here take your mind off it.' Jimmy pointed over the bar at a second girl who was stacking beer bottles into a fridge. Unlike the first blonde, she still had her panties on. It was the only way he could tell them apart.

'Destiny? What kind of a name is Destiny?'

The girl stood up, kicking the fridge shut with her stiletto. So, she had shoes on, too. They looked good on her. Dornan glanced down at his lap. Nothing. Not even a stir. What the hell was wrong with him?

'The VP,' Destiny drawled, biting her lip sexily. 'I've heard about you.'

Dornan winked at her, taking a sip of beer. He was Dornan Ross, son of Emilio. Son of Il Sangue. Of course she had heard about him. Everybody had always heard about him by the time he'd first laid eyes on them, and that was a major part of his problem. His reputation, real or otherwise, preceded him to such an extent that he hardly bothered correcting people anymore. Let them think what they wanted. He didn't have time to care.

He was daydreaming again, and while he was, the chick had rounded the bar and come to stand beside him.

'I heard it was your birthday,' she said, licking her lips suggestively and looking down at his lap. 'Viper said I should give you a present.'

'Oh, did he, now?' Dornan asked, smacking Viper over the head with his hand. Viper had earned his nickname due to his penchant for biting every woman he screwed. Dornan noticed bruised bite-marks on Destiny's shoulder and his dick went even softer, if that was possible. If Viper had been biting and fucking this girl, Dornan sure as hell didn't want her.

'I'll tell you what I want,' Dornan said, fishing his cigarettes out and lighting up. 'I want you to lay on that pool table,' he gestured with the end of his cigarette, 'and stay there.'

She smiled, her tits bouncing as she practically skipped over to the table. Dornan withdrew the small plastic package he'd taken from the apartment while Mariana hadn't been looking. Last thing he needed was for her to find his coke stash and OD before he got back to her.

Destiny was already laying on the pool table, her breasts up in the air and her red thong barely covering anything. Dornan grinned as he tapped a fat line of white powder just above each of her tight pink nipples, setting the bag aside to roll up a greenback.

'Happy birthday,' Destiny said, as he leaned over and snorted the blow off her tit. A jackhammer smacked right into his brain. Yes. It felt good to be this powerful. He smiled as the coke bubbled pleasantly into his bloodstream, masking the exhaustion and the uncertainty. Now, he felt good.

He leaned down and licked the remainder of the powder off her tit, letting his tongue linger longer than it needed to.

Life was good at the top.

CHAPTER THIRTY-ONE

MARIANA

I expected him to come back. I wandered around the empty apartment, too scared to shower or sleep in case someone else — Emilio, Murphy, a Gypsy Brother — decided to pay me a visit. I found the refrigerator and pantry fully stocked and decided to fix myself a sandwich to eat. The television set worked, so I turned that on and watched infomercials, still curled up in my auction dress.

I don't know when I dozed off, but when I woke up, it was light, and from the sofa in the living room I could see the front door swinging open. The click of the lock disengaging must have been what woke me — in my dream, Emilio was holding a gun to my head, and the click had been him cocking it. Crazy. I peered around the corner cautiously, watching as a tattooed arm came around the door and placed a bag on the floor. The door shut again, the lock engaging, and footsteps retreated.

'Wait,' I pleaded, rushing to the door. I recognised the tattoo. It was Dornan, and he'd left me — a bag full of clothes?

I heard a bike roar to life and tear out of the parking lot. He was gone, and I hadn't even seen his face.

The day passed slowly. I changed into a shirt and cut-off denim shorts that I'd found in the bag he had left inside the door. Night came, and still no Dornan. There was plenty of food in the kitchen. I wasn't about to starve to death. But I was starving for human contact. I watched as much TV as I could stand, and watched the sliver of ocean that I could glimpse from inside the apartment. He'd locked the balcony door and taken the key, probably after seeing the way I had been gazing down at the pavement below.

I wondered if he'd ever come back. And, strangely enough, in the quiet nights that seemed to stretch out for eternity, random thoughts of Dornan would make their way into my head, burrow in and stay there. I still wasn't sure if they were welcome or not. His eyes, the way they appeared dark brown until you got up close and saw the little flecks of amber in them. His lips. The way he smiled. His hands on my bleeding wrist.

One night turned into two, into five, into twelve, and he still hadn't come back. Part of me was furious. The other part of me was terrified. What if he never came back? Sure, I could try breaking a window, but I was more worried about what would happen afterwards. Even if I managed to escape, he would just hunt me down. They wouldn't let me live if I broke our deal, not a chance. I imagined my dead body rotting in a stormwater drain, or maybe dissolving in a barrel full of acid. Maybe they'd string me up over the freeway overpass.

I couldn't escape, and I couldn't bear to stay. I had nothing.

I had nothing but Dornan Ross in this sorry world, but even he was gone.

Every day, I waited. And still, he didn't return.

CHAPTER THIRTY-TWO
DORNAN

'Where the hell have you been?' Mariana yelled, hugging her arms around herself in the cold night. He'd intended to come back the afternoon after he'd dropped off the clothes for her, but the DEA had pounced on yet another of Emilio's shipments, and this time the cartel couldn't even blame Marco. The DEA were monitoring Il Sangue and their associates closer than ever. The cartel had learned from last time, and had been splitting shipments up, bringing them over every day, sometimes several runs in a day. The seizure wouldn't affect business, but it seemed there was a mole in their operation, and it was Dornan's job to find it and cut its head off.

He'd spent all week in Mexico interrogating the team, eventually coming up with the traitor. Juan had been with them for years, but his service came to an abrupt halt when Dornan planted a slug between his eyes. You couldn't trust anyone these days.

He hadn't seen his kids in a week. Celia was bitching about him always being away. And now tough girl was standing in front of him, her eyes red-rimmed as she glowered at him from the kitchen.

Oh, and he'd just been shot.

Her angry stance softened when she saw his blood dripping onto the floor beneath him. 'Shit,' she muttered. She rushed to him, looking for the wound. He gave her a smile that was probably a grimace as he stumbled over to the kitchen table and collapsed into a chair.

'What happened to you?' she asked, as he peeled his blood-soaked black t-shirt off with great difficulty. He threw his shirt on the ground. 'Vodka.'

'Vodka happened to you?'

He was about to snap at her, but she was already reaching for the bottle he kept on top of the fridge. Through the red haze of pain he saw that it was a lot less full than it had been when he had left her.

She unscrewed it and handed it to him. He took a gulp, welcoming the burn in his throat and chest that took away just a little of the pain in his shoulder. Goddamn it, that bastard from the Deviants Motorcycle Club had come out of nowhere. He thought he had squared away shit with their prez months ago. Seemed they were more than a little upset about their coke supply drying up in the wake of Marco's epic fuck-up.

He was about to bark at her, tell her to get the first-aid kit, but she was already onto it. The red container with the white cross sat open onto the table beside him, and Ana was rifling through. She held up a pair of tweezers, applied some rubbing alcohol on the ends, and then she was practically sitting in his lap, digging around his blood-soaked arm.

'I can't see with all the blood,' she said quietly. 'I need to get a better look.'

He shook his head, snatching the tweezers from her hand and thrusting them into his arm. The feeling of the metal inside his wound made him want to throw up. It was an entirely odd sensation, and he didn't have the focus to go on a bullet hunt in his own gunshot wound.

'Somebody shot you?' she asked, her voice full of concern. 'I can't imagine anyone finding fault with you.'

He was irritated by that, until he looked at her and saw she was smiling. She was a sarcastic bitch, but she was funny, and that took his mind off the pain a little. With his free hand he reached over and grabbed the vodka, taking another long gulp and enjoying another burn as it worked down to his belly. He slammed the bottle down and reprised his bullet hunt in the torn gore that used to be his upper arm.

Jesus. He couldn't find the bullet, but he could feel that motherfucker burning inside him, hotter and hotter. The pressure was intense.

'You should just leave it in there and sew right over the top,' Mariana said. 'Doctors leave bullets in people all the time.'

He would have yelled at her if he'd had the energy, but right now he just needed to dig around some more, and — yes! There it was. He squeezed the tweezers around the hard piece of steel in his arm and yanked.

The bullet came out in one piece, albeit a bloody one. Dornan dumped the tweezers and bullet on the table in a pool of his blood, at the same time feeling pressure on his arm.

She was there, above him, pressing a towel to his wound. 'Let me guess,' she said. 'They started it?'

He shook his head, chuckling despite his pain. Damn, she was a pain in the ass, and he'd missed the shit out of her.

'Someone called Marco started it, I think.'

Her face fell. Damn. That had been the wrong thing to say.

'My father wouldn't shoot you,' she said, backing away with the bloody towel still in her hand. He snatched the towel away from her and pressed it to his arm, trying to backtrack.

'You don't understand —'

'Was he there?' she asked gravely. 'Did you shoot him?'

'Mariana!' Dornan said sharply. 'It wasn't him, okay? It was some fucker from another club who got shitty because your pop lost our coke.'

She was perfectly still. 'So he's okay?'

'Yes! Goddamn it, why would I shoot your father? Why would he shoot me?'

She raised one eyebrow. 'I can think of a few reasons.'

He clenched his jaw, felt his teeth grind along each other. 'Yeah, well,' he said, rummaging in the first-aid box for the sewing kit he kept for occasions like this one. 'It is what it is, right?'

He located the sewing kit and struggled to open it with one hand. Mariana stepped forward again, reaching down and snatching it up.

'Allow me,' she said. 'Finally, sewing class has a purpose.'

He watched as she disinfected a sewing needle and threaded it. Bringing it up to his arm, she motioned for him to move the blood-soaked towel from his wound.

She smiled as she brought the tip of the needle down to his arm.

'Sweetheart,' she said wickedly, echoing the words he had used when he'd cut out her microchip. 'This is gonna hurt.'

He tensed as she began to work on him. Damn, it hurt, but wasn't that the point? He'd come here specifically after getting the bullet, instead of going home to Celia or to the clubhouse.

Blood and pain, it was what had brought them together.

What would keep them together.

And he liked it.

***

After she had finished stitching and spread a huge bandage across his arm, they went out on the balcony. The wind was fierce, but she insisted on standing at the edge and taking in huge breaths, He didn't try to stop her. She'd been cooped up in the apartment for days, weeks, and she was probably going stir crazy.

Dornan stood beside her, his good arm brushing against hers. She jumped a little, but didn't move away.

Did she — had she moved closer? Or was that his imagination? He couldn't decide. He'd drunk a fair amount of vodka in a short space of time, and although he wasn't drunk, he couldn't call himself sober, either.

He still held the vodka bottle in his hand, and she took it from him with a tight smile. He leaned back a little, watching the way her graceful neck stretched out as she took a gulp, and then shivered.

'I started to think you weren't coming back,' she mused, her eyes locked on the dark water below them.

As if he could stay away from her. She was like a magnet drawing him in, a magnet that was impossible to leave the more time he spent in her presence.

He grabbed her shoulder and spun her towards him, her hair flying every which way in the breeze. 'I will always come back,' he said gruffly. She nodded, licking her lips and passing him the vodka. He had to let go of her arm to take the bottle back with his good arm, and something about that saddened him. Everything was better when he was touching her.

'I thought I was going mad,' she said, bringing her fingers to her lips. 'I could have sworn you kissed me before you left. But now, I can't remember if it was real or if I imagined it.'

His belly tightened as her cheeks flushed. She was getting pale, gaunt. She looked like she hadn't eaten properly since he'd left. She was still grieving her boyfriend, her old life, but he didn't like the dark circles under her eyes and the way she seemed defeated. He set the vodka down on the lip of the balcony railing and cupped her chin with his hand. She didn't move, didn't speak, just looked up at him with those huge, dark blue eyes.

'You been eatin'?' he asked. 'Sleepin'? 'Cause you look pretty fuckin' skinny to me.' He ran a finger underneath her eye, where a dark hollow had formed.

She didn't answer.

'What's going on?' he asked, and his voice demanded an answer.

Her eyes were wet and glossy in the moonlight. 'I guess I'm just ... sad.'

He sighed, looking out to the choppy waves below them. Not a soul was outside; even the ferris wheel on the beach below was dark tonight.

'Christ, Ana, I didn't bring you here so you'd be fuckin' *sad*.'

'Why did you bring me here?' she whispered. Her long hair fanned around her in the wind. She looked like a goddamn angel of death, standing in front of him with her big, sad eyes and her trembling lips.

He ground his teeth together, searching for the answer. How could he tell her when he didn't even know himself why he had chosen her? Why she was different from the rest of them? Why she deserved to be saved while others were condemned to hell?

'I don't know,' he finally answered.

'You have to give me something!' she snapped, her eyes wild. 'I'm like a fucking prisoner here. Talk to me,' she implored, softer now. 'Tell me something. *Anything*.'

He balled his fists up, the gunshot wound in his arm throbbing when he did so.

'I'll tell you something,' he ground out. 'I've seen girls like you. I've seen them sold. I've seen them killed. Sold and fucking slaughtered, like they were cattle. I knew what they'd do to you. And I couldn't live with myself if I didn't try and stop it.'

'Oh,' she said. She seemed surprised by his sudden admission. And so was he.

'I gotta go,' he said abruptly.

She scowled and stepped back, looking at the floor.

'Great,' she mumbled. 'See you in two weeks.'

'Jesus, Ana,' he said. 'What do you want from me?'

'It doesn't matter,' she said. Shaking her head, she snatched up the vodka bottle and stepped inside, making her way up the hallway towards the bedroom that sat just off the front door.

Women. They were impossible to decipher. And this one was driving him insane. He followed her, grabbing her elbow and pushing her against the wall beside the bedroom door.

They stared off for a moment. Dornan reached down and tried to take the vodka bottle, but Ana's fingers were wrapped around it tightly. In the end, he had to use his other hand to prise each finger off and take the bottle from her that way.

'Go to bed,' he barked, pointing into the bedroom.

He turned to walk away, stopped by the lightest of touches on his hand.

She gazed up at him, a peculiar look in her eyes skipping across the space between them. His eyes dipped down to her chest. She was breathing quickly, and as he watched the rise and fall of her breasts under that thin cotton top, he realised he was breathing faster, too.

He took in the swell of her chest, imagined the light brown nipples underneath pebbling between his fingers. The heat that was pouring off her was a sweet, seductive scent that threatened to overpower everything inside him, every last bit of thinly coiled resolve.

She licked her lips, but this time he didn't think she was nervous. No, this time she licked her lips with *hunger* as she stared at his mouth.

He placed his hands on either side of her head, the vodka bottle still hanging from his right hand.

'Go to bed,' he said.

Her mouth twitched, the ghost of a smile appearing and then disappearing, replaced by wanton need.

'I'm not tired,' she whispered.

Goddamn this girl.

Her cheeks flushed, her chest still moving rapidly, she reached up with one tentative hand. When he didn't stop her, she ran it through his short, dark brown hair, taking hold of his head.

Explosive.

That was the only word that came to him as her lips crashed into his, a fiery embrace that both thrilled and deeply unsettled him.

He was completely surprised by the aggression in her kiss, the way she threatened to devour him if he let her. Her delicate fists closed around tufts of his hair and gripped him with an urgency that was almost violent. *Almost.* Together, they skated the thin line between pleasure and pain, between necessity and madness.

Finally, when he couldn't take much more before he ground her into the wall and fucked her until she screamed, he pulled away. Finger by finger, he unfurled her grip from his hair, pressing her arms to her sides. When she went to reach for him again he shook his head, reaching down and wrapping one hand around her pretty throat. The vodka bottle rested by his side in his spare hand.

His grip on her throat wasn't hard enough to be painful. Just a gesture. *Stay still.*

She seemed to understand. She pressed her palms to the wall behind her, watching him, waiting.

Restraint, Dornan. Restraint.

With great reluctance, he stepped away until he was backed up on the opposite wall of the hallway. He needed to create space between them. He needed her to understand that she didn't have to do anything like this, at least not yet. He wasn't an animal.

Well, okay, he was. His straining cock confirmed it. But still. He had a conscience.

'Go to bed,' he said, for the third time. His voice was deeper this time, more commanding than ever. It said: *Don't fucking disobey me.*

Amusement flitted across her features. She tiptoed across the divide that separated them and placed a gentle hand in the centre of his bare chest. His heart was pumping as if he'd just run a marathon, and it made her smile.

'Aren't you going to kiss me goodnight?' she asked.

She took his hand and teased one finger away from the rest. He watched with fascination and disbelief as she put his index finger to her lips and sucked it into her hot, wet mouth. He felt her tongue swirl around the tip, saw the invitation in her eyes, and his resolve exploded into a million pieces along with the vodka bottle as it slipped out of his grip, smashing onto the tiles at his feet.

He was going to pay for this.

But it would be worth it.

CHAPTER THIRTY-THREE

MARIANA

He had told me to go to bed, and instead, I had crossed the void that existed between us, a symbolic space he'd constructed when he took two steps back and leaned on the opposite wall. He had said he would let me choose, and I was choosing him. Not because I loved him — Jesus, I wasn't sure I even *liked* him — but because I saw my out, and I grabbed that out with two hands as I dragged his lips to mine. It didn't have to be about love. It could just be sex, and he could rid me of this problem.

This loneliness, this aching void inside me. He could get rid of that for me.

And maybe, just maybe, I could make him feel something for me in the process. Yes. Get him wrapped around my finger so tight, he'd do anything for me. I wasn't stupid — I knew I was a pretty girl, and the tension that sizzled between us was larger than either of us.

I'd felt the switch inside him flip, in the way he grabbed my arms and squeezed them almost to the point of pain. His mouth on mine tasted too good for me to believe he was my enemy, but therein lay part of the thrill, I suppose. Beating him at his own game. Owning him so he didn't just own me.

He'd picked me up with two impossibly strong arms, carrying me into the master bedroom as we continued to kiss each other with a fire that threatened to destroy us both. He was already naked from the waist up, and I wanted to join him sooner rather than later. I dragged my tank top over my head and let it fall to the floor.

When he leaned me against the bed and unbuttoned the top of my denim shorts, I wasn't prepared. Before I could catch up, he snaked his hand down the front of my pants and thrust two fingers inside my wet heat.

I moaned. It was loud, desperate.

His eyes flew open and he dropped me like I was on fire. I landed on my back on a soft bed, with Dornan above me, my legs trapped in the space between his thighs as he stood over me.

'Are you okay?'

'Yeah,' I said breathlessly, inexplicably embarrassed.

He leaned back slightly. 'You sure you wanna do this?'

I swallowed. He looked affronted.

'Get dressed,' he said, picking my tank top up and throwing it at me.

I caught the top and threw it back at him, just as hard.

'Scared?' It was a challenge.

'Of hurting you? Yeah,' he said darkly.

I moved forward so I was kneeling on the edge of the bed.

'I'm sure,' I said.

Before he could move away, I kissed him again. If I could just make him feel something for me, maybe he'd protect me. Este was dead. And I was dying inside, a ghost girl trapped alone in a world Dornan had created for me.

He held the cure to my suffering.

I pulled him down again, kissing him with more urgency this time.

'Fuckin' Christ, woman,' he said in between hard, furious kisses that scratched my delicate skin with stubble and made me wet with excitement.

He broke the kiss and pushed me forcefully away. I landed on my elbows and ass, thankful that I had a mattress to break my fall. For a moment, I figured that he would leave me again, unsatisfied and scared, alone in the dark with my nightmares.

But then he grabbed my ankles and pulled me down the bed towards him, and in that moment I *knew*.

I had him. I had him in the palm of my hand.

'Get your fucking panties off before I rip them off,' he growled, and I quickly obliged, hiking them down my thighs and kicking them off my feet onto the floor.

I took in a terrified, excited breath as he grabbed my ankles again and ripped them apart, forcing my legs as wide as they would go.

'You better scream real fuckin' loud if you want me to stop,' he breathed, lowering his mouth to my leg and kissing a trail up the inside of my thigh. 'Because unless you scream, I *ain't* gonna stop.'

I gasped, rocking my hips involuntarily as his tongue brushed ever so lightly across my sensitive bundle of nerves. I jerked as he gently pushed one finger inside me and moaned against my pussy. 'Fuck, you are so wet,' he groaned, as he fucked me with his finger and his tongue. It felt so damn good, it was worth the blood rising to my cheeks at his mention of how wet I was. I shouldn't have been so turned on in that moment, and yet, *I was*.

Somehow, I knew he was going to make me scream, but I wasn't going to let him stop until he was well and truly done with me. I writhed beneath him as he used his tongue to drive me to the brink of insanity, bringing me close to the edge.

My boyfriend was dead. I was a slave. And the man whose head was between my legs was, by association, responsible for my boyfriend getting shot.

All of these thoughts coursed through my mind as my knees began to tremble violently and I crested towards the precipice, gripping the sheets below me as if I were about to fall. Inside, I knew that once we did this, the last remnants of who I used to be would be washed away with blood and tears.

I snapped back to the present moment as Dornan added a second finger, moving quickly but gently. I ran a hand through his silky hair, pulling him closer to me as I cried out.

Just as I was getting close, as that white-hot pleasure threatened to blanket me and steal my breath, he stopped. Stone cold fucking *stopped*. Withdrew his fingers, took his mouth away from the spot he'd been sucking on so perfectly, and stood up.

I made a small sound of annoyance at the back of my throat, hoisting myself to my elbows and opening my eyes to get a better idea of what was going on. I heard a zip being opened and the rustle of clothing, and as my eyes were still adjusting to the dark, his figure loomed over me. I still couldn't see him properly, could only make out his outline, and my brain struggled to catch up.

Before I knew what he was doing, before I had the chance to brace myself, I felt him position himself at my entrance. I sucked in a breath as he slammed himself inside me, the feeling something I cannot fully describe. Fireworks and fury. The violent end to a violent beginning.

He groaned.

I screamed.

He stopped where he was, still full and almost uncomfortable inside me, as I struggled to catch my breath.

My whole body continued to tremble, with grief and pleasure and the overwhelming finality of it all.

I had just invited the enemy inside my body, into my *soul*. In that moment, I wanted to die. I was so ashamed.

Because, even through the haze of sorrow, *I liked it*.

My eyes adjusted to the dark, finally, and all I could see were two dark brown eyes, so dark I could barely distinguish the pupils from the irises. Black eyes, like the devil. I had just given my soul to the devil.

'Are you all right?' he asked, and I heard genuine concern in his voice. Odd. He was my enemy and yet he touched me like he was my lover. I couldn't reconcile the two.

Tears formed in my eyes and I struggled to find my voice.

'Yes.'

'You screamed.'

'I know.'

'Do you want me to stop?'

Did I want him to stop?

It terrified me that I didn't want him to.

I'd been alone for so long. Mourning Este, mourning our son. Mourning *myself*. Everything was stark and cold in this harsh new world, and I needed someone to be with me the way Dornan was with me.

I already knew he wasn't a good man. I'd suspected that from the first moment I saw him. They say you can tell by a man's eyes if he's killed a person, and Dornan's eyes held the souls of many. I saw them sometimes, dancing around the murky black as he contemplated his next victim.

I made no excuses for him. I didn't love him.

But I needed him.

I didn't want to be raped by strange bikers, one after another. I didn't want them to hold me down while they filled me with themselves. I wanted to be safe.

I wanted to be with Dornan.

He had saved me.

I wrapped my ankles around him and locked them behind his back.

'No,' I said finally. 'Don't stop.'

He grinned, started to move again, and the pleasure intensified. I gulped at the air, fisting my hands into the sheets beneath me, as a fire began in my womb.

Every stroke was *excruciating*. Excruciating because it was so fucking good. We fit together like we were the last two pieces of a forgotten puzzle.

Physically, we were made for each other.

But as my nerves began to sizzle and fray, the friction almost unbearable, Dornan reached between us and pressed his thumb to my sensitive bundle of nerves, and I flew over the side of that precipice I'd been coasting, into the dark night.

My orgasm ripped through me, and it was as painful as it was sweet. I felt myself squeeze around his cock as he continued to pound into me, almost hurting me, over and over, until I stopped shaking and let go of the sheets, panting to catch my breath.

I whimpered as he pulled out of me, the sudden emptiness more painful than the fullness of having him there. I throbbed and ached. It was the best kind of ache, an ache that said we were something other than strangers in the dark now.

Dornan stood beside the bed, still fully erect in front of me.

'Get up,' he said. I didn't hesitate. I knew what he wanted, because I wanted it, too. I rolled over to my front and raised myself on hands and knees, crawling towards him.

He held the base of his cock in one hand, and fisted my hair roughly with the other.

My family might have been shocked by my behaviour, but in that moment, I was somebody else.

Somebody who did whatever it took to ensure she survived.

I like your blood.

I opened my mouth and darted my tongue out, licking the very tip of his cock. I tasted myself and his salty arousal as I swirled my tongue around and took the tip into my mouth.

I like it very much.

Blood and violence and fucking and pain. This was what my life was reduced to. This was the person I had to be if I had any chance at surviving this hell.

I clamped down my gag reflex as I took him deeper into my throat, as deep as I could. He sighed in appreciation, a deep rumble that seemed to come directly from his chest and wrap around me like vine tendrils. He'd already been close, I could tell when I put my lips on him and he pulsed between them.

A couple more strokes, and he went rock hard, pinching my shoulder as hard as he could. The universal sign for *I'm about to blow my load in your mouth.* Last chance to turn back.

I didn't. I relaxed my tongue and waited to feel the first pulse jet against the back of my throat, and it didn't take long. I waited until he was done, and swallowed it all down. I wasn't about to spit and disappoint him. I was committed to the final, warm spurt as it slid down my throat.

He pulled himself from my mouth and I took the opportunity to massage my aching jaw. My small mouth and his impressive appendage didn't really match, but, in a disturbing way, I was insanely proud of myself for what I'd just done.

Almost as if it had been a test, and I had passed.

'Did it hurt?' he asked me, in the stillness that came after.

'No,' I replied.

He paused for a beat.

'Did you like it?'

I felt my cheeks pool with blood as I nodded in the dark.

CHAPTER THIRTY-FOUR
DORNAN

When she came, he'd almost exploded. He couldn't believe it. He'd stopped himself once he had his fingers inside her, snapped to his senses by the sound that had come from her mouth.

She was sad. He saw it in the hollow of her cheeks; he heard it in the guttural wail she had let out when he touched her. He had stopped, fully prepared to leave, even if the blue balls might kill him. He refused to make her sadder.

But she hadn't wanted to be alone.

She had wanted to be with him. Wanted to be beneath him. Wanted to be *around* him.

He'd barely been able to hold back, but he was damn glad that he had. Because the way she finished him, took it all and swallowed and looked at him for approval afterwards — it made him feel like the motherfucking king.

Rationally, he knew that she was fucking him because it was in her best interests. It was about survival.

But she had *liked* it. He knew it even before she'd said it. He felt it in the way she locked her ankles around him and pulled him deep inside her. In the way her lips sought out his; in the tight little sobs that escaped her mouth as he fucked her into oblivion. Yeah, she was definitely using him, but at least she seemed to get off on it almost as much as he did.

It made him uneasy about what he was going to do next. The drive. The devastation that would ensue. But he reminded himself that it was necessary. One of his men, Jimmy, was already in place. He had another one, Viper, trailing Mariana's father and brother.

He knew exactly where they were going. After all, he'd told them where she was.

He watched the steady rise and fall of Ana's chest as she lay sleeping in his bed. He had had the sense to cuff her wrists to the headboard before he'd drifted off to sleep, so there was no chance of her spoiling his plans. He didn't think she would, especially after the way she'd responded to him, surrendered to him, but he could never be too sure. He never trusted women. They always ended up letting you down in the end.

She stretched in bed lazily, and as she did, the cuffs around her wrists clinked against the bed head.

Her eyes flew open and she gasped, realising she was chained up. Dornan leaned against the bedroom's door frame, sipping coffee, black and strong. He felt himself grow hard again just at the sight of her, spread out deliciously in front of him like a goddamn buffet, but he wouldn't try to fuck her again this morning. As much as his dick was trying to protest, the girl had to be sore after last night's marathon.

She looked from the cuffs above her head, down to her naked form, and finally to him.

'Good morning,' he said. 'You hungry?'

She nodded. He set the coffee down and undid her cuffs, one by one, probably letting his hands linger a little too long on her delicate wrists as he did so.

Breakfast was bacon and scrambled eggs with chilli sauce, and a side of strong coffee. She wrinkled her nose up in distaste, reaching across and sliding her coffee cup closer. He'd contemplated making her eat breakfast naked, but at the last moment let her have one of those hotel dressing gowns he'd somehow ended up with. It was white and fluffy, with little flowers sewn into the hem. Against Ana's creamy caramel skin it looked positively divine. It covered her breasts but showed the definition of her nipples.

'What is that?' she asked, holding her coffee to her chest as she surveyed his sauce-slathered eggs dubiously.

He laughed. 'Mongrel's breakfast.'

'Which is?'

He chewed his eggs and swallowed. 'A little *huevos rancheros*, some Italian coffee, and good ol' American bacon.'

She studied him as he continued to devour his food.

'You're kind of a mongrel, aren't you?' she asked.

He grinned. 'Am I?'

'I mean, your family is Italian, you're American, and you like to hang out with a lot of Colombians.'

'And I grew up on the border of Mexico,' he added, shovelling the last piece of bacon into his mouth. 'In the house where you were being kept.'

Her face paled three shades lighter right in front of him. 'You grew up in that place?'

He swallowed and pushed his plate away. 'Yeah. I fuckin' hated it. Still do.'

Neither of them spoke for a while.

'Who lives here?' she asked finally.

'Sometimes me, sometimes nobody,' he said. Despite what was about to happen, he was feeling awfully chipper this morning. Probably because every time he looked at her lips, it reminded him of the night before.

She was very good at being bad. He appreciated a woman who was both resourceful and devious. Often they were one or the other, but to have both was simply delicious.

'Where else do you live?'

He saw right through her feigned casual manner.

'That's for me to know,' he snapped, standing abruptly and circling the counter, tossing his empty plate into the sink.

'I'm sorry,' she said quickly. 'I just meant … will I stay here? Or will I go somewhere else?'

He softened slightly. 'That depends.'

She cocked one eyebrow. 'On whether I please you?' Her words sounded submissive but there was a glint to her eye that turned him on.

'It's not hard to keep me happy,' he said gruffly, trying to restrain his desire. 'Just don't try to escape. It's that simple.'

She nodded, a faint smile on her lips.

'Eat something,' he ordered, pointing to the pantry. 'If you don't want my breakfast, get some goddamn cereal or something. I don't want you starving yourself.'

He smiled as she stared at her coffee. 'What are you thinking?'

She rolled her eyes. 'I'm thinking of ways to ask you questions that won't piss you off.'

He laughed.

'I just screwed your brains halfway back to Colombia last night. I think we're past being polite.'

She blushed.

'Just ask me what you're gonna ask me. If I don't want to tell you, I won't.'

She nodded slowly, and he could practically see the cogs turning over in her mind.

She finally cleared her throat. 'Am I safe here?' she asked. 'I mean, will anyone else ever —' She tilted her head towards the bedroom.

'No,' he said abruptly, cutting her off. 'The only person who gets to touch you is *me*.'

'Your father would disagree,' she said quietly.

He slammed his fist on the counter. 'He's not fuckin' here, is he? I brought you here to keep you from him. Besides,' he struggled not to explode with anger in front of her, 'he's too busy with all the other girls.'

Her head snapped up. 'The other girls?'

'No more questions,' he growled. 'You need to get dressed. And eat something or I'll make you eat me when I get back. And trust me, baby, you're gonna need a full stomach for the drive we're about to take.'

He slapped the pantry with one hand as he left the kitchen, walking down the hallway towards the front door.

'Wait!' she pleaded. 'What if there's a fire? How will I get out?'

He turned slowly, swivelling on his heels. '*If there's a fire, in the forty minutes I'll be gone, then it was really fuckin' nice knowing you.*'

He slammed the door behind him and shook his head in amazement.

Little bitch was almost too smart. She might have given him her body last night, but he saw the fear in her eyes, the hate. She would be dangerous for a long time to come.

CHAPTER THIRTY-FIVE
MARIANA

I sat on the floor in front of the washing machine and watched as the white sheets tumbled around and around, hot suds rinsing away the evidence of everything we'd done the night before. Not that it mattered. I could wash the sheets, hell, I could burn them, and it wouldn't erase the invisible marks he'd left on my skin.

After Dornan had left, I'd cleaned up the table, disposing of the bloody bandages and the bullet that he had torn from his arm. Then, I'd had a shower and shampooed my hair until it squeaked between my fingers. Finally, I had stripped the sheets from the bed.

What I really wanted to do was go to the front door and scream and pound my fists until someone helped me out. I was starting to feel increasingly uneasy about my situation, especially in the wake of throwing myself at Dornan last night.

Este had been dead less than a month, and I'd gone and done that.

But I didn't pound on the door, or scream for help, or any of the other dramatic scenarios I'd imagined. I found some bread in the freezer and fixed myself some toast, buttered thickly, and made another coffee. Then, partly to stop myself from anxiously pacing the front hall, I took my toast and coffee and sat on the floor in front of the washing machine.

It was an odd spot — I could have sat on the couch, or at the breakfast bar, even on the bed — but I'd chosen to sit in this small room and breathe in the artificial scent of sunshine, thanks to the fabric softener I'd located and added.

Sunshine. How I wanted some of that, for real. While I chewed on my toast, I tried to picture living here long-term. It made me think of the enormous risk Dornan had taken in bringing me here, somehow convincing Emilio not to sell me at auction, and although I doubted he would ever say anything about it, the fact that he seemed to give a fuck about what happened to me made a strange warmth crawl up my stomach and into my chest. Beyond the obvious physical attraction we had, the big bad biker seemed to genuinely care about me in his own fucked-up way.

I was still trying to figure out my thoughts when I heard the front door slam.

Damn.

I was meant to be ready to leave. He'd said that before he left. Shit! I scrabbled to my feet, forgetting about the sheets and the scent of fabric softener.

I dumped my plate and mug on the breakfast bar just in time to see Dornan standing in the hallway.

He dropped his helmet to the ground beside his feet, and I jumped when it crashed on the white porcelain tiles.

He stalked towards me. He looked angry.

'I'm sorry,' I said. Jesus. Since when had I become a submissive girl? What was I apologising for, anyway?

I was tired, I realised. So bone-achingly *tired*, and I didn't want him to get angry and leave me alone again for weeks.

'I was washing the sheets,' I said quickly. 'I'll get dressed now.'

His expression morphed, that infuriating grin appearing on his mouth again. He didn't say anything else, so I took that as permission to get dressed. I headed for the bedroom, giving him a wide berth.

Not that it mattered. It seemed that no matter how far apart we were, Dornan would always find a way to reach for me. He took a step forward and shot his hand out, curling his grip around my arm.

I didn't struggle. I stood where I was, halfway between the kitchen and bedroom, his fingers digging deep into my skin.

'Look at me,' he commanded.

Slowly, I turned my gaze to meet his.

His eyes raked over me, like he knew he already had me.

And he did. His father might technically hold the deed over my life, but after last night, there was no mistaking who was in charge of me.

Dornan Ross.

I wanted to shiver, but I refused to let him see what he was doing to me.

He dropped his grip from my arm and stepped in front of me, reaching for the tie around my waist that knotted my robe shut. He pulled one end quickly, and the robe fell open. I gasped. I was completely naked underneath, and goosebumps broke out on every inch of my exposed skin, despite the Californian heat.

I started to close the thick material, but he slapped my hands away, pressing me backwards until my back hit the wall. It was pretty much the same place I'd stood last night when I'd pounced on him; tried to get him on my side.

He trailed one finger along my shoulder. With his other hand, he gripped the base of my throat. It wasn't tight, but it was uncomfortable enough to relay the message. He was calling the shots.

'You washed the sheets.' It was a statement. I didn't dare move.

I nodded.

'Why?'

What did he mean, why?

'Because they were dirty,' I said hurriedly, frowning in confusion.

He appeared to think about that for a moment before releasing his grip and taking a step back.

'Get dressed,' he said. 'You've got one minute. *Go.*'

I stumbled to the bedroom, fully aware that if I wasn't dressed in one minute, he'd make me leave the house in my birthday suit. I dragged a denim skirt and panties from the closet and threw them on, followed by a bra and a black scoop-neck tank that clung to my breasts. There had been no pants in the bag of clothes he had left me a couple of weeks ago. I didn't miss the significance of that.

I heard the click of fingers, and knew I'd narrowly escaped an outing in my underwear.

I quickly tried to grab a pair of shoes, but he was already there, blocking my way.

'No shoes,' he said. 'Shoes make it that much easier to think about running.'

I gave a small nod to say I understood.

'Where are we going?' I asked dully, looking at the floor.

He took my hand and looked at me sidelong as he guided me to the front door.

'You'll see.' The threat in his words was unmistakable.

CHAPTER THIRTY-SIX
DORNAN

The road was rough — the sealed asphalt had gone as far as the main tourist drive of Joshua Tree National Park, but beyond, the corrugations were more rustic. He drove and drove, Mariana fidgeting beside him.

Finally, she spoke.

'Can I have some water?' she asked softly.

'No,' he replied. 'Nothing until we leave.' He didn't want her to try and run from him. No shoes and no water made her even more helpless than she already was.

'I'm thirsty,' she protested.

He glared across at her, one hand going down to his belt. 'There's only one thing in this car that's going in your mouth,' he threatened. 'Your choice, darlin'.'

She closed her mouth and slumped back in her seat, staring out of the side window.

Thought so. He put his hand back on the wheel. Damn, being a bastard came a little too easy to him sometimes. He almost delighted in her suffering.

'Are you bringing me out here to kill me?' she asked a few moments later.

He raised his eyebrows. 'No.'

'Seems an awfully convenient place to bury a body,' she continued.

He snorted. 'If I wanted to kill you, I wouldn't waste my time driving to a national fucking park, baby.'

She nodded, apparently satisfied.

A few minutes later, they pulled up onto the shoulder of a narrow, dirt track.

'Out,' Dornan said.

She eyed him warily. 'I don't have shoes.'

He grinned. 'I know.'

He got out and circled around, opening her door for her. Fuck, he was such a gentleman. The irony made him chuckle.

She stepped out, walking tentatively over rocks and scrubby groundcover weeds, until she reached the back of the car.

'Stay there,' he said. He popped the trunk, taking out a sniper rifle that would make GI Joe's eyes water. It had cost the Brothers a pretty penny, and Dornan guarded it like a precious diamond. He'd killed a couple of guys with it, blew them to pieces actually. He wasn't a long-range marksman, but she didn't know that.

He slung the rifle over his shoulder and gestured up the hill in front of them. 'We're going up there,' he said. 'If you dawdle, I'll tie you to a fuckin' tree and let the ants feast on those pretty bare feet.'

She gave him a blank stare before falling into step beside him.

The terrain was harsh, unforgiving. He saw the way she winced as the sharp rocks in the limestone trail cut at the soft soles of her feet.

'Almost there,' he said. She gave a small smile of appreciation. Wait. Why the fuck was he comforting her? Because they'd fucked the night before?

When she crested the hill and he gave her a set of binoculars, she wouldn't be smiling in appreciation anymore. She'd be bawling her fucking eyes out in despair.

He couldn't figure out if the annoying buzz in his stomach was excitement or dread.

He was about to destroy the girl who already thought she'd lost everything.

CHAPTER THIRTY-SEVEN

MARIANA

My feet were bleeding and blistered. We'd finally reached the peak of the trail, which was washed out in some places, and completely gone in others. Still, Dornan seemed to know where he was going, as he pressed on.

But the bastard was wearing hiking boots. He had water. I'd resorted to licking the sweat from my palms whenever I thought he wasn't looking.

'That won't work,' he said, as I pressed my palm to my mouth again. 'Too much salt. You're only making yourself thirstier.'

I glared at him, stopping where I stood.

He stopped a few paces ahead of me and turned sharply, sending rocks skittering from beneath the soles of his heavy boots.

'You really want to test me?' he asked. 'You don't know what I'm capable of.'

I blinked back tears. My top was clinging to my back, drenched in sweat. Flies buzzed around my face, trying to extract the last bit of moisture from the corners of my eyes and mouth. I swatted at them, but they were relentless.

'Please,' I pleaded. 'My feet are bleeding.'

He pointed to a spot about a hundred metres up. 'Just a little further. Then you can sit.' He grinned. 'I'll even give you some water.'

He winked at me and pressed on, widening the distance between us. I hesitated a moment, taking a chance to get a breath and look around. This wasn't the family hiking trail, oh no. We'd passed several signs that warned we were trespassing on private property, and to turn back. Dornan had ignored every one of them.

My hesitation evaporated as I took in the hot desert around us, punctuated by mountains and a salty marsh. The terrain was unforgiving.

If I ran, I'd die. Even if I managed to evade Dornan, the desert would swiftly claim me.

Now his refusal to give me water made sense. I was dependent on him, even out here. Of course, I wouldn't run.

I started walking again, pushing my hands on my knees to try and get some traction with each heavy, sharp step that tore open fresh skin on the soles of my feet.

Finally, I reached the top of the impressive hillside, panting as I stood beside Dornan.

He took a long sip from his canteen. 'Want some water?'

'Yes, please,' I said.

He nodded, gesturing to a rock beside him. 'Sit.'

I did, grateful to have the weight off my poor abused feet.

He crouched in front of me, the grin on his face annoying the fuck out of me.

'*What* is so funny?' I asked, a little more sharply than I should have.

Darkness snapped back into his eyes again and I flinched.

'I'm going to show you something,' he said, his voice completely serious now. A charge of electricity sizzled and burst as it flared between us.

It was like the air suddenly became thicker, more humid, and if he touched me, I'd burst into flames.

'Okay,' I said, my thirst driving me insane.

'You're not allowed to run,' he warned. 'If you run, I'll shoot you. Do you understand?'

I nodded.

'What I'm about to show you,' he continued, 'will seem like cruelty. It will make you feel like you want to die. But you're not going to die, Ana.'

My hands began to shake as I took in a dry, hot gulp of desert air.

'Are you sure I want to see it?' I whispered.

He nodded. 'You'll thank me, one day.'

'Water first,' he said. Delight sprang forth inside me.

I smiled like a good little slave. 'Thank you,' I said, and I meant it. I was so fucking thankful that he was finally letting me have something to drink.

Still crouched in front of me, eye to eye, he took the canteen from a loop on his belt and unscrewed it. He smiled slightly as he pressed the stainless steel canteen to his lips, taking a mouthful.

Taunting me?

He set the canteen at his feet, and I frowned in confusion. His smile remained, wolfish and self-assured, and I realised he hadn't swallowed. He gestured with one crooked finger for me to come closer.

Oh.

I leaned forward. In that moment, I couldn't have given two shits that he wanted to give me the water from his own mouth. Ordinarily, the power play would have annoyed me no end. But now, all I saw was an opportunity to slake my unending thirst.

He pressed his lips to mine, raising himself slightly so he was above me. Then he opened his mouth and let the cold water inside flow into my mouth.

It was divine. It was bliss. It was exactly what I needed.

As I swallowed the last drop of water, his hand reached around the back of my head. I tested his hold gently; I wouldn't be able to pull away if I tried.

Our mouths had been simply touching before, a bridge to pour the water from one vessel to another. But the water was gone now, and I jolted as I felt his tongue against mine.

It was cold, still fresh with the moisture from the water. Without thinking, I pressed my lips against his harder, tilted my head, and caressed his tongue with my own. I would have eaten him alive if I thought it would quench my thirst.

I felt his lips twitch, and I knew he was smiling. Bastard. I tried to pull away but he anticipated my move, opening his mouth wider, and kissed me with a violence that was as terrifying as it was exciting.

I stopped resisting. I melted into his possessive embrace.

I was already going to live and die with this man.

I might as well enjoy it.

CHAPTER THIRTY-EIGHT

MARIANA

He was the one who broke the kiss, surprisingly. His face was serious again, and that made me nervous.

'Is everything okay?' I asked as he pulled me to my feet.

He gave me a long sidewards look, a look that held something impermeable just beneath the surface. Something I could almost, but not quite reach out and touch.

The uncertainty made me dizzy.

He stood before me and placed a hand on each of my shoulders.

'Don't hate me,' he said gruffly. 'What I'm about to show you ... It's mercy, baby. It's better this way.'

My stomach lurched. He squeezed my shoulders and then let me go, unclipping a small pair of binoculars from his belt and pressing them into my palm.

I took a step back, my heels hitting the rock I'd just been sitting on. 'I-I don't want to look,' I stuttered, trying to give the binoculars back. He just pushed my hands away. 'You don't want to see your father?' he asked. 'Your brother?'

I looked at him for a beat as those words sank in. He wasn't lying.

I whipped those binoculars to my eyes and scanned the flat desert below us, seeing nothing but scrub and salty marsh broken up by the occasional boulder.

A hand covered mine, and Dornan tilted me the right way.

Two people came into view, grainy at first, but as my eyes adjusted, I choked. My father was walking along a trail, carrying something small and round in front of him — a compass, perhaps? Behind him, Pablo followed, two shovels resting across the back of his broad shoulders.

'What are they doing?' I whispered. 'Do they know I'm here?'

Dornan tutted. 'Watch.'

I took my eyes from the binoculars and glanced at Dornan for a moment. He wasn't paying any attention to my two family members; he was watching my every expression with a severity that suggested he was waiting for me to react to something.

My stomach dipped uncomfortably again.

'Are you going to shoot them?' I asked quietly, staring at the sniper rifle hanging from his shoulder.

He ran his fingers through my hair, starting at the crown of my skull and combing them all the way through to my split ends, patting my back to finish the comforting gesture.

'I won't shoot them,' he said. 'Unless you attract their attention. You know what that means, don't you? No screaming, baby. No shouting. And definitely no running away.'

I nodded in understanding, bringing the binoculars back up to my eyes.

An odd sensation of impending doom began to blossom inside me as I found my brother in the round viewing panes again. While we'd been talking, he had started to dig. For what, I wasn't sure, but a terrifying suspicion was starting to form in my mind.

A body. They were digging for a body.

Suddenly, my brother struck something. He dropped his shovel and dropped to his knees, shifting dirt with his hands. My father joined him, the two hefting dirt and clay with their hands as fast as they could.

'Ana,' Dornan said beside me. I tore my eyes from the sight in front of me to look at him in horror.

'What are they digging up?'

He didn't reply, instead pointing to his rifle. 'I'm looking through the scope to get a better visual,' he warned me, bringing the gun up to his shoulder. 'I'm not going to shoot.'

My mouth opened and a strangled cry came out. Tears burned at my eyes.

'Okay?' Dornan demanded. I nodded.

'Don't lose your shit yet,' he said, peering through his scope. 'This is for your own good.'

I didn't see how that could be possible, but there was nothing I could do anyway, so I returned to my binoculars.

A hand. There was a hand sticking out of the dirt. As my brother shifted, I saw a foot, and then a flash of black material clinging to dull bronze thighs.

I choked, looking to Dornan for answers. 'Please,' I begged. 'Please don't tell me that's my sister. Please.'

I was sobbing now, racking sobs that carried through my chest. Had I done something wrong? Was this my punishment?

Dornan lowered the rifle, letting it fall around his shoulder by the strap, and circled his arms around my waist. He leaned down, tucking his face into the hollow space between my cheek and shoulder.

'It's not your sister,' he said, and that was the moment I knew. I lowered the binoculars, staring at my bare hand. My black onyx ring, the one I'd been wearing when I was taken, had been removed the night Murphy readied me for the auction.

I cried harder as Dornan confirmed my suspicions.

'It's you,' he whispered, holding me so tightly, I could barely breathe.

My father screamed then, so loud that I heard it clearly despite the considerable distance between us.

'But it's not me,' I said desperately, through the tears. 'They'll see my face!'

Dornan gripped me harder as I began to struggle in earnest against his burly arms.

'Look again.'

He gripped my hands, bringing the binoculars back up to my eyes.

'Wait,' I said, wiping my eyes against my shoulder, getting rid of the tears.

I swallowed, steeled myself, and peered into the binoculars once more. They wouldn't know that the body wasn't me.

It didn't have a head.

I froze, unable to tear my eyes away from the headless corpse they'd dragged from her shallow grave. She wore my black dress and my grandmother's black onyx ring, but she wasn't me. I wondered whether she was already dead when Dornan found her, if he'd simply taken advantage of the situation, or if she had died purely for this grotesque little freak show Dornan had staged.

I drew in a sharp breath as my brother knotted a handkerchief around his nose and mouth before taking a large hunting knife in his hand.

The microchip. Of course.

He started to cut into the unyielding flesh of the corpse. It looked slippery, tough, and I winced as he had to stop several times to collect himself.

He did it, though. He sliced into that rotting skin and pressed his fingers into the flesh. The dead corpse didn't bleed like a live person would.

My brother pulled something out and handed it to my father. It was the microchip. My father wailed and dropped to his knees.

'They think you're dead,' Dornan breathed in my ear.

No shit, hombre.

'I don't want to watch anymore,' I said. 'Please, why are you doing this?'

'Wait,' Dornan breathed. I did what I was told, and I waited.

I didn't have to wait long before a third person entered my highly magnified field of view.

No.

'Stop,' I pleaded, but Dornan pressed the binoculars closer to my eyes, the pressure on my eye sockets enough to make my eyes water.

I drew back from the binoculars violently as I caught a glimpse of her face.

Holy. Fuck.

It was my sister. She was crying and screaming as she saw what she thought was my dead body, and I watched in horror as she leaned over and vomited next to the rotting corpse. Seeing her distraught reaction made me snap.

I began to struggle with every bit of strength I had, elbows flying. I pitched my head forward, which Dornan obviously wasn't expecting, and snapped it back, crying out in pain as the back of my head slammed against his face. I heard a sickening crunch and wondered if I'd broken his nose.

'Stop,' he said firmly, as something warm and wet dropped onto my shoulder. I had made his nose bleed. But I didn't care. I continued to struggle, even as he wrapped one hand around my face, pinching my nose shut and sealing off my mouth at the same time with his death grip.

I immediately tried to get a breath in and failed, sucking at the airless vacuum Dornan had created.

'Calm down,' Dornan murmured in my ear, his blood continuing to trickle onto my shoulder. But I was possessed by grief, in the most ironic way. I had grieved my family, and now they would grieve me, and none of us had actually died.

Dornan's mouth was warm at my ear, his words sounding further and further away as I struggled for breath.

'Listen, baby,' he whispered in that smoke and gravel voice. 'They will mourn you. They will grieve you. And they will stop trying to get you back.'

I fought for air, but none came. The world started to spin, the only constant and clear thing in my universe the haunting voice in my ear.

'You're free, now,' he murmured. 'They will let you go.'

I reached my hands out desperately, wanting to touch my loved ones, even though I knew they stood hundreds of metres away. They couldn't believe this farce, surely? It wasn't me. Her arms were shorter than mine, her skin was lighter. I was alive! I was right here.

The sun pounded overhead, blinding me with its ferocity, and I continued to reach out, until my arms grew too heavy. They fell to my sides as I drooped in Dornan's unrelenting embrace, and the world burst from yellow to black.

CHAPTER THIRTY-NINE

MARIANA

Dornan must have carried me the entire way back down the trail and hefted me into the back seat. I awoke to my head hitting the window behind me.

I tried to back up as he crawled on top of me, his fingers like vices on each of my thighs.

I screamed, and he slapped me across the face so hard I tasted blood. Rage poured off me in waves, and if I clenched my jaw any harder I was going to shatter every tooth in my mouth.

Well, fuck. I couldn't beat him and he was too strong for me to even try. The struggle left my limbs as I let myself melt into the car seat below me, wanting to die. I'd just witnessed my family unearth my corpse, or what they thought was my corpse, so why press on? Why hope that life would ever be any different?

'If it makes any difference,' Dornan said quietly, 'I am very sorry that this happened to you, Ana.'

I sobbed, then, because there was nothing else for me to do. I opened my mouth and sucked in deep lungfuls of air, my head whirling, as my body shook with my despair.

'I don't want your pity,' I spat, my eyes flooding with more tears.

And then, softer, 'You took away their last hope. Why did you do that?'

He gazed down at me, and he was terrifying. He caressed the side of my face with a dominance that said he wasn't ever going to let me go.

'Let me tell you a story about hope,' he said through gritted teeth. 'I loved a girl once. She was beautiful, and funny, and smart.' He swallowed angrily. 'One day, she just fucking vanished. Gone. I looked but I never found her. I looked for eight fucking years.'

'And don't you hope that she's alive?' I asked.

He laughed mirthlessly, rolling his eyes before bringing them back to pin me down. Fury and grief radiated from him, mixing with my own anger and sadness.

We were a sorry pair.

'I wish she was fucking dead,' he growled. 'Hope is a piece of shit that gives you nothing, you understand? Hope is a useless fucking emotion.'

I lashed out furiously with my fists. He caught them easily before I'd even connected with his face.

'It's not up to you!' I screamed. 'You're not God! It's not your right to decide!'

He didn't seem angered by my outburst, though. He lowered his face to mine and kissed my cheek, my mouth, my neck and my collarbone — everywhere the tears had touched.

'Why do you think I showed you?' he whispered in between kisses that were growing more and more urgent.

I laughed like a crazy woman, my eyes so puffy I was only seeing half of the world. 'To torture me. To make me cry.'

He grabbed my chin, forcing me to look at him. I stared into his eyes with hatred.

'I did it to make you understand what's happening.'

'Oh really,' I asked, less hateful this time. 'What's happening here?'

He stopped kissing me for a moment and lifted himself so his face hovered above mine.

'A show of good faith,' he murmured, one finger tracing my lips. 'Something to hope for.'

'You just said hope was a useless emotion. And besides, I have nothing left to hope for.'

'But you do,' he countered, his hand palming my breast. He was already hard as steel against my thigh, but now he pressed against me with more urgency.

He dipped his lips to mine and kissed me gently; a contradiction for such a man. He was testing me, I realised. Seeing if I'd kiss him back.

And I so badly wanted to kiss him back. I wanted to melt into him until all of the pain and horror was a distant memory.

I opened my mouth wider, inviting him in. I had nothing left in this world anymore, nothing except pain and loneliness. Pain and loneliness and *him*. He pushed my legs further apart, until they were as wide as they could go in the small confines of the back seat. Unconsciously, my hand went to his belt and unbuckled the clasp, popping the top button of his jeans and slowly sliding his zipper down. He reared his head back and stared at me, panting, as I wrapped my hand around him and squeezed.

What am I doing? I screamed at myself.

I don't want to be alone, I answered myself. *I cannot bear to be alone. He has to want me. He has to come to love me. And then he will protect me from the rest of them. I am a ghost. Without him, I am nothing.*

'What do I have left to hope for?' I asked, as he pulled my panties aside and dipped his finger into me, making me shiver. 'That you'll let me go?'

He shifted above me. He pushed my hand away and reached into his jeans. His cock bounced out, and he held it between us, his eyes questioning me. I nodded minutely, kissing him deeply once more, giving him permission. *Yes.*

I drew in a sharp breath as he gripped himself and pushed into me, tenderness and pleasure merging into one. I moaned at the feeling of fullness, from being stretched slowly as he continued to push himself deeper.

'No,' he said, pushing my top up around my neck and pulling my bra down to expose my breasts. 'I'm never letting you go.'

Grief and pleasure overwhelmed me as he began to rock his hips back and forth, sliding in and out with a pressure that was as devastating as it was utterly pleasurable.

More tears tracked down the sides of my face as he continued to fuck me. It was raw, it was primal and it was the only thing I had left in this sorry world.

He stroked my sensitive nub and my legs jerked open wider in response.

I wanted to cry. I wanted to scream. Everything inside me was on edge, and in that moment, my body betrayed me. Rationally, I wanted to push him away, but instead, I drew him closer. Deeper.

He was nothing. He was everything. He was the only thing I had.

'You hate me?' he asked, his voice strained, his pace unrelenting.

'Yes!' I cried. 'I fucking hate you!'

He grinned. 'One day, you'll love me. I promise.'

I was afraid that he was right.

CHAPTER FORTY
MARIANA

I burned with shame as Dornan drove home. I had just willingly had sex — again — with the man who was holding me captive. Had sucked his dick and let him inside me twice now, and it was so goddamn confusing.

And my family thought that I was *dead*.

'Are you thinking about them?' Dornan asked suddenly, interrupting my thoughts.

'No,' I answered. 'I was thinking about you.'

He frowned for a moment, then glanced at me before looking back to the road ahead. It was almost dusk, and the sun had moved low and grown golden-orange in the Californian sky.

'Thinking of how much you hate me?' he asked seriously.

I shook my head. 'No.'

He didn't ask me anything else after that.

Back outside the apartment, I stared at the car door. I wanted to open it, but I couldn't figure out how.

I'm in shock. The thought came from nowhere, struck me as odd, and I dismissed it.

Dornan understood. He helped me out of the car and supported me as we walked as one up the stairs to his apartment. To my apartment? It didn't sound right. But this was where he had brought me, and this was where he wanted me to be.

Once inside, he ran me a bath. Undressed me, with slow fingers that took the opportunity to slide against my flesh, dropping my clothes on the stark bathroom tiles until I was naked before him. I didn't push his hands away. He might be a monster, but this was a good touch. I would rather he caress me than kick me.

I would rather he fuck me than kill me.

He held my hand as I stepped into the deep bathtub and sank into the water. It was bliss. He'd filled the tub with a fragrant lotion of some kind, something that smelled of sandalwood and orange, but not the kind that bubbled.

I knew why.

Bubbles would obscure the view.

I laid back in the tub, my feet burning as water rushed into every crack and crevice caused by the rough terrain I'd had to walk on barefoot. I pressed them against the far end of the tub, hoping the pressure might ease the pain a little.

I slumped down in the tub, took a breath, and let myself slip under the water. Surfacing a moment later, I rubbed drops of water from my eyes and smoothed my hair back.

'Better?' he asked me from his spot on the edge.

I nodded.

He left the room, returning a moment later with a glass of amber-coloured liquid.

He sat on the edge again and held the tumbler out to me. I took it wordlessly, tossing it back. It burned on the way down, but I no longer cared.

I no longer cared about anything.

Dornan pulled a pack of cigarettes from his top pocket and lit up, taking a deep breath. I stared at the tip of the cigarette, hypnotised by the way it burned bright, leaving grey ash in the wake of fire.

Dornan must have noticed I was transfixed on his cigarette, because he took one more drag and offered it to me. I took it. Why the hell not? I'd never been much of a smoker, other than a few stolen moments as an experimenting teenager, but I already had a death sentence. Maybe a little lung cancer would get me out of this shitty world a fraction quicker.

I closed my eyes, letting my arm hang loosely over the side of the tub. Every now and then, I'd take a drag or a sip of whiskey, but mostly, I just lay there and prayed the warm water would wash away my terrible sins.

There were so many. So many sins. I should have tried harder to yell. To scream. Just one scream could have gotten their attention. Hell, for all I knew the car that passed ours while we were screwing in the back seat *was* Karina and Pablo and my father.

A lump formed in my throat that all the cigarettes in the world wouldn't be able to burn away. The whiskey dulled it slightly but didn't take it away for more than a second.

Something brushed against my cheek and I opened my eyes to see Dornan stroking my face.

I began to weep as I remembered how I had pulled him deeper. Harder. How I had kissed his mouth with a passion and a desperation I'd never experienced before. The way he'd made me tighten around him, despite the horror I'd just witnessed.

'What are you thinking now?' he asked. His tone held no malice, only casual interest.

'I'm thinking about what a bad person I am,' I said despondently. I took another drag of the cigarette and tilted my head back, blowing a cloud of smoke above me. It resembled how I felt: as if a grey cloud hung above my head, colouring everything in darkness.

'Why?' he pressed. 'Because they're alive, and they think you're dead?'

I looked at the ceiling, tapping ash into the water where I heard it sizzle faintly.

'Because I'm alive, and my boyfriend is dead,' I whispered. 'And even though your people killed him, I'm still somehow drawn to you.'

He nodded. 'Did you love him?'

I stiffened, looking at him worriedly. Did I say yes? Did I say no? He'd warned me not to lie to him. I weighed up the cost of a lie over the cost of the truth. And finally, I just held my hands up in confusion.

'I don't know what you want me to say. If I say I don't, I'm lying. If I say I do, will you hurt me?'

He smiled and shook his head. 'I won't hurt you. Tell me about him. Tell me how you met.'

I eyed him cautiously. 'Okay,' I said slowly. As I told him the story of Este and I, I remembered to leave out the details of my accidental pregnancy. Of our son. I would hold that card close to my heart until it was prised from my cold, dead hands.

Or until Murphy voiced it for me. The reality that he knew about Luis, and that he could use it against me at any moment, was terrifying.

After I'd finished, I realised I had gotten rather carried away with telling the story. I must have been talking for fifteen minutes or more. Dornan hadn't interrupted, other than to get more whiskey and light fresh cigarettes for both of us. So, by the time I was finished, I was exhausted, tipsy, and my throat felt numb from all the nicotine.

'I'm sorry,' I said again. 'I don't want to make you mad.'

'I enjoyed your story very much,' he said, in that deep, throaty way of his.

Tears filled my eyes and a strange ache took up residence in my chest, as I looked up at this frightening, beautiful man who ruled my entire existence. 'Why?' I asked.

'Because,' he said, tucking wet hair behind my ear, 'you loved him. I like hearing the way you speak of him. It's ... tender.'

That couldn't be it, though. He was far more diabolical than that.

'And?' I pressed him.

'And,' he said, leaning down so his face was inches from mine. 'One day, you're going to speak about me like that.'

I didn't respond.

I didn't know what the hell to say to that.

Afterwards, when I was wrinkled to prune status and the water had turned cold, he hoisted me out of the tub and wrapped me in a fluffy white towel, carrying me to the bedroom.

He laid me down and pressed himself into my back, his body hugging around mine like a protective cocoon. It was comforting, in the strangest way.

'Why did you save me?' I asked him in the dark.

I heard the breath hitch in his throat. 'You know why.'

I shuffled around so I was facing him and put a tentative hand out, searching in the darkness until I found his cheek. I brushed my thumb along his jaw, enjoying the way his stubble tickled my hand.

'But why me?' I pressed. 'Why not some other girl?'

'You're different,' he said. 'You're not afraid of me.'

I drew breath sharply. 'Yes, I am,' I whispered. My lips trembled as those words slipped out. Of course I was afraid of him.

He ran a hand over my shoulder, down to my waist, then back up to the skin and bone that shielded my heart. He left his hand there. The weight of it felt oddly reassuring. 'There's something here,' he finally murmured. 'Something that's on fire.'

So he felt it, too. It wasn't just me.

'So you don't go saving every girl your father takes possession of?'

He chuckled. 'No. You're definitely the first and last.'

Something about that resonated with me deeply. Impulsively, I leaned forward and kissed him on the forehead.

'Thank you,' I whispered. God, I was so confused. Part of me was screaming in protest — why was I thanking Emilio's son? His men killed Este.

But Dornan had saved me. He had stopped me from being auctioned like a head of cattle or a piece of furniture; stopped me from enduring even more horrific punishments.

'You know,' I said, resting a hand on his chest, 'I don't really know anything about you.'

He laughed. 'I'm an open book. What do you wanna know?'

I bit my lip as I thought. 'How long have you been married?' I asked. Might as well get the worst question out of the way first.

He stiffened momentarily. 'Too fucking long,' he said. 'Marriage is overrated. I know. I've done it twice.'

'Twice!' I pushed his chest lightly.

'I have six kids,' he said quietly. 'All boys.'

My heart leapt into my mouth. He was a father. I hadn't realised that.

'And you're here with me?' I asked. 'Shouldn't you be with them?'

His gripped my wrist tightly. Maybe I'd asked the wrong question, pried too deeply.

'I'll go home to them,' he said, 'soon. Right now, I'm here with you.'

'What are their names?' I asked, as I thought of my own son. Maybe I could tell him. Maybe it would be all right.

'Chad's the oldest,' Dornan said quietly, his expression softening. Pride. It wrapped itself around his features and clung tight as he rattled off another five names. A proud father.

Este would never be a proud father because he was dead.

I suddenly felt awful. If Este could see what I'd become ...

'Does your wife know you sleep with other women?' I asked.

Another chuckle. 'I've never asked her. But yeah, I'm pretty fuckin' sure she knows.'

I opened my mouth to ask another question but he pressed a finger to my lips.

'My turn,' he said. 'Tell me something about you, Ana.'

I squirmed. 'I just spent forever telling you all about me in the bath.'

'No you didn't. You told me all about Esteban. You told me nothing of you. What you think. What you feel in here,' he took his finger from my lips and tapped it against my chest.

His question affected me more than I could've anticipated. I swallowed, tears forming at the corners of my eyes.

'My dad is a disaster,' I said, almost fondly. 'He used to get drunk and think he was Muhammad Ali or something. Only, he'd hit me and my brother and sister and my mama.'

Dornan moved his hand to my arm and squeezed tightly. 'What did he do to you?' he asked, and I heard the thinly veiled rage in his voice.

I laughed. 'What did I do to him, you mean? He was such a clumsy drunk. I broke his nose once. He never could finish what he started.'

Dornan's grip loosened, and I heard him release his breath. 'He sounds like an asshole.'

'Yeah,' I said. 'It could be worse.'

'How?' Dornan asked.

Without thinking, I replied, 'He could be *your* father.'

Dornan breathed out. 'Pretty and smart. What else is in that pretty head? Something you've never told anyone before. Anything.'

I thought about that for a moment, mentally cataloguing all of my dark secrets before selecting one of the more ambiguous ones. A safer one.

'Sometimes I'm so lonely,' I whispered, and I *was*. 'Sometimes, I'm so lonely, it hurts.'

He wrapped his big arms around me and drew me into his chest, almost crushing me with the intensity of his embrace.

We lay there like that for a long time, while my head whirred and tilted painfully. I was dizzy with it all.

'What was her name?' I whispered. 'The girl — the girl you loved? The one who disappeared?'

He tensed, letting out a sigh. 'No. You don't get to ask me *that*.'

CHAPTER FORTY-ONE
MARIANA

The next day was a Monday, and it marked a change in my life.

I woke naked and alone, to the sounds of the coffee machine and the smell of bacon.

'It's a big day today,' Dornan told me, as I slid onto a seat at the breakfast bar.

I cocked an eyebrow. My eyes still felt puffy from all the crying I'd done the night before, and I was beginning to wonder if I was going crazy. It wasn't right to feel attached to my captor.

'Work, baby. You didn't think spreading your legs was going to pay off your debt, did you?'

The words affronted me. Of course I hadn't thought that.

He winked at me as he jammed thick slices of bread into the toaster. He was having a dig at me. 'Time to show us those laundering skills.'

***

I'd assumed we would be going to the biker headquarters, or compound, or clubhouse. Whatever they called it. I couldn't keep the terms straight in my head. I needed another coffee just to get through the day without collapsing in a grief-induced coma.

Pablo. Karina. My parents. Este. *Este.*

They filled my every thought, plagued my mind, until I found myself actually shaking my head from side to side to try and rid myself of their ghosts.

Thinking about them wouldn't help me. I had to act like they didn't exist.

Our destination wasn't the Gypsy Brothers clubhouse, but a burlesque club.

I'd referred to it as a strip joint, but Dornan assured me it was more upmarket than that. The girls wore glitter-encrusted circles pasted onto their nipples and performed routines that didn't involve humping a pole. Somehow that made it different, though I wasn't entirely sure how.

I was ushered into a small, windowless room on the second floor of the club and almost choked when I saw who was waiting for us.

'Good morning, *cholita*,' Emilio greeted me. His smile looked more like a grimace, especially with his gold tooth glinting under the fluorescent office light, and I had to fight to compose myself. What I wanted to do was scream and run away, but that would only earn me a beating, or quite possibly a bullet.

'Sounds like you had quite the weekend,' Emilio said, playing with a toothpick between his teeth.

Was he talking to me? I wasn't sure. I stared at the ground and tried to appear docile. I was kind of hungover, and no amount of concealer had been able to cover up the after effects of last night's tears.

'Answer him.' Dornan snapped his fingers in front of my face. I jumped at the foreign tone in his voice, and focused on not shrinking away.

'Tell him how you were used and abused,' Dornan said jovially, 'by one Gypsy Brother after another.'

Oh. He was lying for me.

Wait. *He* was lying for *me*?

Emilio snickered, turning away to pick up his briefcase from the ground. As he did, I glared at Dornan. A question in my eyes that I knew he understood.

We didn't even need to speak. He had lied to his father to protect me.

Was this some kind of test? An elaborate ruse to catch me out?

Dornan turned and grabbed a stack of manila folders from the desk, thrusting them at me. 'Here,' he said.

'Uhhh ... thank you?' I replied, taking the large pile of haphazard papers and cardboard.

I looked around the room, wondering where I should sit.

Dornan pointed to a small table in the corner. 'Set up over there,' he said.

I started to walk towards the desk, stopping when Emilio addressed me.

'You've become very compliant in just a few weeks, Ana,' he said appreciatively. 'Seems like the Gypsy Brothers have fucked the fight out of you.'

I was about to open my mouth and reply when Dornan beat me to it.

'I've been reminding her about her poor dead boyfriend,' he said, trailing his fingers through my hair and giving a hard jerk on the ends.

A chill swept over me and I stumbled as he pulled at my hair. The folders in my arms went flying, landing in a mess all over the floor.

'I'm sorry,' I stammered, getting to my knees and collecting papers. Emilio stepped on one that I was about to grab.

'Skirt up,' he said. 'We need something to look at while you clean up your mess.'

Gritting my teeth, I let go of the papers and sat up on my knees, hiking my pencil skirt up above my hips so it sat bunched around my waist. Cool air rushed around my ass and I felt my cheeks burn in embarrassment. I had been expressly ordered not to wear panties this morning. Now, I knew why.

So I could be humiliated.

I continued to collect the papers as quickly as I could, feeling two sets of black eyes staring at my ass.

After I'd rearranged the stack of documents I went to stand up.

'Wait,' Emilio said.

I stayed where I was, not game enough to look at him.

Dornan cleared his throat but said nothing.

'Face to the floor,' Emilio ordered, walking around behind me. 'Hands by your sides.'

I did what I was told. I didn't want him to kick me between the legs. I didn't want to make him angry at me when I was this vulnerable in front of him.

I pressed my forehead to the musty carpet, hoping I wouldn't catch herpes from it. I ground my teeth as I felt a hand grab each of my ass cheeks and spread them apart.

I choked a little on a cry. I was still tender down there. My eyes watered as fingers touched and probed, like I was being prepared for a fucking pap smear.

'Have you been a good girl, *cholita*?' Emilio asked, as he pressed his fingers against me.

I whimpered at his touch. It wasn't like Dornan's. It didn't make me want to move closer.

It made me want to die.

'Yes,' I replied, fresh tears stinging my eyes.

He patted my left ass cheek, a strange gesture, then pulled my skirt down so I was covered again.

'That's good to hear,' he said. 'You may get up now.'

I felt Dornan's eyes on me as I stood and pulled my skirt back down to cover myself. But I couldn't look at him. Instead, I stared at the floor as anger and disgust burned between my legs and in twin pools of flame on my cheeks.

You're nothing. You're mine.

Dornan might have taken me away from his father's cruel grip, but there was no mistaking the fact that Emilio still owned me.

***

Two hours later, and I was wading knee deep in shit. In corruption and double-accounting that was cleverly disguised, but not cleverly enough for a girl who specialised in it. I'd been doing it in my father's business ventures for years, managing to scrabble money from people who thought they owed it to us when they actually didn't. The accounts were a mess, but the same, seemingly innocuous deductions were taking place twice over and then over again.

'Find anything useful?' Emilio asked.

I snapped my gaze to him. I hadn't even been aware he was in the room. I fought the rising terror in my throat as I remembered what a spiteful, strong-willed girl I had been the night I met him.

I didn't know where she was anymore. I craved her, but I knew if she showed her face too many times, I'd end up dead.

Submission it was, then. Even the word tasted like a lie.

He must have seen the apprehension in my face because he pulled up a chair and sat across from me.

'Tell me,' he demanded.

I swallowed. 'Please don't kick me in the ribs for telling you,' I said, handing him a piece of paper I'd used to tally all of the dodgy figures I'd found so far. 'But someone is stealing from you.'

He appeared calm. But something about his expression told me I'd surprised him.

'This much?' he asked, pointing to the figure at the bottom of the page.

I nodded. 'Yes, sir. I'm only halfway through the stack, so it could go higher.'

I called him 'sir' because I refused to call him 'master'. I hoped that he wouldn't notice.

Something flashed in his eyes. He was *pissed*. His annoyance made me want to laugh hysterically. But I clamped that down.

I refused to let myself become the target of his rage.

Another thought occurred to me, too late to make a difference.

Whoever had been in charge of the accounts was probably going to die, very soon and likely very painfully.

I had just handed Emilio the death sentence of someone who I didn't even know.

It had been a test. It was always a test and, this time, I had passed.

But who would die as a result?

CHAPTER FORTY-TWO

DORNAN

'How long's she been gone for?' Dornan asked, sipping on his black coffee. He'd added a little Scotch to it this morning. It had been an eventful weekend, to say the least.

John paced in front of him in the burlesque club's small communal kitchen that served both the dancers and the guys behind the scenes. John worked here most days on the business side of things. It was an unspoken agreement that John spent as little time as possible in the clubhouse, while actually fulfilling the role of club president.

He was a lackey, and he knew it.

But here, in this dance club, he was in his element. He always seemed a little less stressed when he was here, and not because the dancers gave good head. No. John was a loyal man, and Dornan knew he'd never strayed from Caroline.

That undying loyalty of John's had made it even harder for Dornan when he'd woken up that night all those years ago, half drunk, to find Caroline naked and bouncing on his dick. He'd thrown her straight off, threatened to bash her to death, but she had just laughed. Crazy bitch.

He was fairly certain John knew nothing about it, but either way, he still felt like shit every time he spoke to his friend. Some lines just weren't to be crossed, and unwittingly, he had crossed that one.

'A week,' John said.

'Divorce her,' Dornan suggested.

John balled his fists. 'If I divorce her she could take Juliette and run,' he said gravely. 'She threatens it every time we have a goddamn fight. She's unpredictable. At least this way, I give her a little money, she goes crazy, but she always comes back.'

Dornan crossed his ankles and nodded to show he was listening. 'Except when she doesn't come back,' he pointed out.

If it had been anyone else, Jimmy or Viper or any other motherfucker in the club, he would have told them to grow some balls and harden the fuck up.

But it was John. His best friend. They were like brothers.

Dornan wondered if now might be a good time to mention he had cut Caroline off, nixed her supply. He hadn't really known how to break it to John, since he wasn't entirely sure John knew he had been giving her a pinch here and there.

John stopped pacing and punched the doorway. Dornan didn't try to stop him.

Sometimes, a man just needed to get his demons out.

'I just wish ...' John said, his fist still pressed against the door he'd just assaulted.

'You just wish?' Dornan asked. He knew what John wished. He wished that he'd never met Dornan. He wished he'd never had the brilliant idea to be Gypsy Brothers. One dream — to ride the highways and live like transients, brothers in arms — had been shattered the moment they'd agreed to work for Il Sangue.

John took a deep breath and let his fist fall to his side.

'I just wish she would come home,' he said finally.

But they both knew that was not what he'd really been about to say.

Dornan's father entered the room, quietly, like a snake. The old bastard was always ready to strike, to slither in and manipulate any situation to his own benefit. The fact he'd put his hands on Ana earlier disgusted Dornan. *Mine. She's mine.* Despite that, Dornan both admired and detested his father. And he had long suspected that John simply hated Emilio.

'What's the deal?' Dornan asked, standing as his father entered the space. John turned from his spot at the wall, nodding at Emilio in greeting. Respect was on the top of the list for the ruthless kingpin, and everybody fell into line or died at his hand.

'John.' Emilio nodded, acknowledging the boy who'd grown to a man beside his own son. 'Can we have a moment?'

John nodded. 'Yeah. Sure.' He slid past Emilio, making his way to the office.

'Does he know she's in there?' Emilio asked his son.

Dornan shrugged. 'He will now.'

Dornan took a sip of coffee and stared out of the small window to the bleak, overcast day outside. Theirs was a stunning view of the pea-gravel parking lot that lay behind the back of the club. *Living the dream.* At least at the Gypsy Brothers clubhouse, if you went up to the roof, you had unrestricted views of the Venice Beach coastline.

No wonder he didn't spend much time here. He always felt trapped, like a rat in a cage, spinning in his wheel as he went around and around. He didn't know how John could stand being here all the damn time.

'Find anything of interest?' Dornan asked his father.

Emilio's look was so furious it actually made Dornan take a step back. 'Whoa, Pop,' he protested, holding his hands up in surrender. 'I don't know what she did, but I swear, it wasn't me.'

He was trying to make light of the situation, but Emilio wasn't smiling. 'Which whore are you talking about?' his father asked him.

'I don't know,' Dornan replied slowly. 'Why don't you just go ahead and tell me what's on your mind?'

Wordlessly, Emilio handed Dornan a piece of paper. He scanned down. There were a lot of numbers in columns, the same number often repeated twice in a row, and they all added up at the bottom to a hefty amount.

'This is how much she's going to save us?' Dornan asked his father. He whistled. 'That's a pretty sum of money. She'll be debt-free in a couple of years at that rate.'

Emilio snatched the paper back, his eyebrows quaking together in an expression Dornan knew and feared.

He drained the last of his coffee and was about to swallow it when his father replied.

'This is how much that other *cunt* has siphoned out of our accounts.'

Dornan choked on the coffee mid-swallow. Slamming his mug down on the counter, he hit himself on the chest as he coughed and spluttered.

As he was catching his breath, Dornan held out a hand, gesturing for the piece of paper again. Emilio relinquished it, and Dornan read the figure at the bottom of the page with a sinking feeling in his gut. *Oh, Bella, you stupid, stupid girl.*

'Are you sure?' he asked.

Emilio's eyes burned with a rage that would not be contained until he'd tasted the accountant's blood himself. Dornan didn't need to hear his father say the words. He saw her fate in his black eyes.

'Where is she?' Dornan asked.

'On her way,' Emilio replied. 'If you see her, make sure you grab the thieving bitch and let me know.'

'Will do, Pop,' Dornan answered, as his father stalked out of the room.

Fuck. He knew the club had been losing money, but he assumed generous waitresses overfilling drinks and stealing twenties from the register had been to blame. But Bella? He couldn't believe it.

'Jesus Christ,' he murmured, shaking his head. The bitch hadn't exactly been discreet. He'd wondered a few times at how she could afford the diamonds that she wore, but she'd assured him she had a great eye for costume jewellery, and that she was adorned in cubic zirconia.

But this ... this. It made sense. They'd found the hole in their finances, and it was in the most unlikely place of all.

He felt a small pang of nostalgia; Bella gave an excellent blow job.

At least he had Mariana now.

CHAPTER FORTY-THREE
MARIANA

Somewhere in the back of my mind, I had been wondering what kind of a man could be president of the Gypsy Brothers. The way Dornan acted, the way he moved, the fact that he was the son of the leader of the Il Sangue Cartel — all of these things told me he should have been in charge, not somebody else.

Until the day the *actual* president stormed into the office, and I understood why.

He was roughly the same height as Dornan, about six foot, with a shock of blond hair that looked like it belonged in a shampoo commercial. It was messy and unkempt, but I bet he copped shit for it from the other Gypsy

Brothers anyway. He wasn't as stocky as Dornan, but just as muscled and well-defined. He looked like a surfer trapped in biker's clothing, or maybe a sheep dressed in wolf's clothing, come to think of it. He was tanned, and I guessed he got to see the sun a lot more than I did.

He looked stressed, his jaw clenched tightly.

'Who are you?' he asked, coming to a stop in front of the desk I was working at. I looked up with uncertainty, and more than a little attitude.

'Who are *you*?' I echoed, placing the emphasis on the last word.

He scowled, his hazel eyes flashing in annoyance as he pointed to the prez patch that adorned his leather vest.

'I'm the boss,' he said, staring me down. 'Who are you?'

My eyes darted to the door and back to him. I was starting to feel more than a little apprehensive about being stuck in this room, alone, with a Gypsy Brother. And a man who ruled over a club with such a ferocious reputation surely couldn't be a good man, right?

'What are you?' He pressed. 'An assistant? A friend of Emilio's? What?'

Maybe he saw the panic in my eyes, I don't know. Whatever it was, his expression softened a little; perhaps he could tell I was nervous, and that I was trying to word my response carefully.

'I'm Ana,' I said, giving him a small smile. 'And I'm not sure what I am.'

CHAPTER FORTY-FOUR

DORNAN

There were two dead girls at his clubhouse when he arrived there later that night.

He'd taken Mariana back to the apartment, and though he'd wanted to stay with her, his life was full of obligations, like a goddamn juggling act. Everything always up in the air, and if he didn't finely choreograph every minute of the day, it would all come crashing down on him.

He'd arrived at the clubhouse to find a black Pontiac sitting in the large garage that housed their motorcycles, the car's windows splattered in blood, two female bodies slumped in the back seat. The stench of congealing blood filled his nostrils. When he'd said he liked blood, he did not mean like this.

Holding a rag to his nose to stifle the smell, he ripped out his cellphone and called his father. The phone rang and rang.

'*Figlio*,' Emilio answered after ten rings.

'Pop,' Dornan responded, tightly wound and ready to blow. 'Missing something?'

Emilio chortled. 'A favour, if you will, son. Get some of your boys to clean it out and get rid of the bitches.'

Dornan pocketed the rag and rubbed his chin, glancing again into the back seat of the car. His stomach roiled as he saw a fly crawl over one of the girl's open mouths.

'Weren't these girls meant to be auctioned?' Dornan asked, shaking his head. Fucking Emilio, always laying his dirty jobs on the club.

'They were indeed,' Emilio responded.

'And?'

'And, they were sick. They were no longer useful.'

No wonder the car stank. It was ninety degrees out and the dead girls had been in the car for a day already.

'Right,' Dornan said, ending the call.

He rounded up a couple of Brothers, who complained loudly but soon got to wrapping the bodies in plastic and organising for the car to be dismantled and scrapped. Dornan watched it all from the sidelines in detached horror.

It could have been her. That could have been Mariana in the back of that car, her brains blown out over the seat.

It was much, much too close for comfort.

CHAPTER FORTY-FIVE

MARIANA

Dornan got back to the apartment late. I'd stayed up, drinking strong coffee, on the small chance he was returning.

Yeah. I was pathetic.

But his presence was so fleeting, so addictive, that I would do anything to make sure I didn't miss him. My ears were attuned to his footsteps, my skin to his touch. We were the dirtiest, most forbidden secret of them all.

And I loved it.

Desperation and loneliness fed the overwhelming desire inside me.

He took care of me. Made sure I ate, made sure I slept. Made my existence vastly less painful when he was in it.

He was a bad man, the worst there was.

But my heart, that treacherous thing inside my chest that sped up whenever he was around?

It wanted to betray me.

I was falling in love with a monster.

And somehow, in this new life of mine, where the old rules didn't count and power was measured in blood and bullets?

I didn't care.

Sex. It was the only thing that made me feel, the only thing that broke up my otherwise sad and lonely existence. And yet, I hated it every time he made me come. Hated *myself*. In the moment, I'd cry out in exquisite agony, as he fucked me or licked me or fingered me to the point of no return. But then afterwards, after he'd come inside me — it always had to be in me or on me somehow, marking me as *his* — we'd lie side by side, catching our breath, and guilt and despair would tear my soul apart piece by broken piece.

I heard the beeps of someone pressing the pin code into the keypad outside, and then a click as the front door lock disengaged. A slight creak and the door opened; another, and it closed, revealing the man who had come to consume my every thought.

I leaned forward against the kitchen counter. The travel magazine in front of me was all but forgotten as I watched my dark lover approach.

He dropped his helmet on the tiles, just like he always did. It bounced once and rolled into the corner, forgotten, as Dornan Ross moved down the dimly lit hallway towards me. He moved like a predator, that possessive lust in his black eyes that had once been a glimmer, now a forest fire that threatened to consume us both. He was drenched from the rain that had been falling all evening, a rain that still wasn't taking the heat away. It made me feel like I was back in sticky, humid Colombia.

He was wearing new clothes. A tight black tee that hugged his defined arms, black jeans and his leather cut. Dressed all in black, he looked like the sexiest motherfucking Grim Reaper I could imagine.

He grinned as he approached me. I started to turn, to greet him, but his hands wrapped around my waist, pulling my ass firmly into his erection. Butterflies swirled in my stomach as he lifted up the bottom of my black silk nightgown, gathering the material in his hands until my panties and lower back were exposed. He squeezed his hands around my hips, rocking his hardness against me, only our clothes separating our bodies.

He reached one hand around to the front of my panties and dipped his fingers in. I shuddered as soon as his fingers brushed against me, it was so powerful.

'I got back as quickly as I could,' he murmured in my ear as he continued to graze his fingers along my wetness. I was breathing fast, panting under his touch. I wanted more. I wanted it all.

'You're so wet,' he whispered.

There was something very wrong with me. Something dark had blossomed inside me, spreading like a cancer that obliterated everything else within. In the moments when his hands were rough against my skin, as he bent me to his own desires, I existed because of him. I existed *only* for him.

'Do you want me?' he asked. I nodded.

He fisted one hand in my hair and yanked; not enough to hurt, but enough to make me take notice. 'Say it,' he demanded.

'Yes,' I whispered, writhing against him. 'Yes, I want you.'

Palms flat on the counter, I couldn't see what was happening. I could only feel as my panties were yanked down to my ankles, a knee between my legs forcing them wider apart.

Then he pushed inside me, the friction and the pressure enough to make me gasp. My nightgown still up around my waist, he dug his fingers into my skin hard enough to leave bruises as he began to move inside me. He was rough, he was fast, and it was exactly what I needed.

'Fuck!' I cried, as he slid deeper inside me. It felt like each stroke erased a part of me and replaced it with something new. Something dark.

Pressure had already been building inside of me, and I felt my legs drop away as the most powerful orgasm I'd ever experienced rocked through my body. I opened my mouth, letting out a guttural moan as he held me up and stopped me from falling.

'That was fuckin' amazing,' I heard him say, through the haze. I dropped my forehead onto the counter, utterly exhausted, my whole body still tingling with aftershocks. He continued to thrust behind me, and I heard an unmistakable groan, followed by his strong body curled around mine.

We both struggled to catch our breath.

'That,' I panted, '*was* fucking amazing.'

He pulled out of me and laughed, spinning me around so I was facing him.

'What's so funny?' I asked, crossing my legs to stop his salty fluids from running down them and onto the floor.

He kissed my forehead, an oddly intimate thing for him to do. 'You never used to say the word fuck so much,' he said teasingly. 'Look what I've done to you.'

I felt bold. 'You never used to smile so much,' I countered. 'Look at what I've done to you.'

Dornan just shook his head and kept on smiling.

***

In the shower, after Dornan had bent me over the kitchen counter and fucked me senseless, he pressed the top of my arm until he found the small rod that was embedded just under the surface.

'How long is this good for?' he asked me, stroking my skin with his warm fingers as water and the scent of sandalwood surrounded us.

'Two more years,' I said, without thinking.

'We'll have to make sure we get you a new one then,' he replied, moving it underneath my skin. 'I think I've got enough kids, don't you?' He was teasing, but I froze as his words sank in.

Two years. I'd been in the apartment for mere weeks, and I couldn't imagine two more years of this strange and terrifying existence. I had to get out. *I was never getting out.*

It was too much to bear. Instead, I focused on Dornan's fingers as they travelled down my naked stomach and began to rub my sensitive nub again. It might have been devastating each time I let him touch me, but it was equally a welcome relief from the dark thoughts that plagued my mind. And the lighter ones, too. The ones that terrified me the most. When Dornan wasn't there, I missed him. Longed for his touch. Craved his company. And for a girl who had watched her boyfriend bleed to death in front of her, it wasn't acceptable to feel those things.

I tried to push down the feelings that blossomed inside me. I was determined not to let myself get sucked into the fantasy of having a man save me from his horrid father, from a life as a slave. But my heart had a life of its own, and it wandered happily even as I tried to rein it back.

He was all I had. Those five words played on a constant loop in my mind.

During the moments in between, I cried. A lot. No amount of concealer could cover up the suitcases that had taken up permanent residence underneath my eyes. In those still moments when I was alone, I often thought of my family. I thought of my little boy, even though the mere memory of him was enough to drive me to madness. How my arms ached to hold him in them. I recalled the crumpled photograph in Murphy's pocket and felt sick that he held that piece of my soul with him.

The next morning, I woke up alone. Loneliness and melancholy spiked in my chest, and I wondered how I would get to the office. There was a keypad that I didn't know the code to, and if there was a fire in the apartment I actually would be burned to death. Dornan almost never gave me notice of plans, he just randomly showed up. I let myself sleep in an extra five minutes before I took a shower and dressed in work clothes.

This time, I wore panties. Emilio wasn't getting his dirty hands near my pussy again. I had a sudden violent daydream of murdering him with a stapler as I started the coffee machine in the kitchen.

The day before, I'd worked hard to clean up the books, and what I found was very dirty indeed. Someone had made a small fortune by siphoning funds from the burlesque club and several other businesses that were fronts for the Il Sangue Cartel and for the Gypsy Brothers. I was still a little confused about the dynamic between the two, to be honest. There was no clear line delineating where one finished and the other began. Although there was no denying that Emilio was in charge of everyone. Owned everyone, with secrets and lies and threats. It sickened me. How much power, how much money and dominance, did one man actually need? And when did that need become a greed that obliterated everything in its path?

I feared he'd crossed that line a long time ago.

Soon, it was 8 a.m., and I was ready. Dressed in a sleeveless black shift dress that reached to my knees and zipped up at the back. I'd managed to get the zip three-quarters of the way up and I figured I'd ask Dornan to zip it the rest of the way up. I was standing at the breakfast bar, drinking coffee and looking at a box of Cheerios with disdain. I'd completely lost my appetite in the last few weeks.

There was a knock at the door, and without thinking, I walked towards it. It was only when I got to the door and put my hand on the handle that I realised I couldn't open it. I didn't have a bloody code.

It didn't seem to matter, though. The person on the other side hit the keypad in a series of muted beeps, and I heard the lock disengage. I didn't move. I assumed it would be Dornan.

Big. Fucking. Mistake.

Before I could slam the door shut, Murphy was inside, pushing me down the hallway with a strength I had no hope of beating. His smile was cocky and full of excitement.

'Good *morning*,' he proclaimed loudly, stalking me with methodical precision as I backed down the hallway. The kitchen. There were knives in the kitchen.

'What are you doing here?' I asked, trying to make sure I didn't trip and fall on my ass. 'How'd you even know I was here?'

'I'm picking you up for work, *sweetie*,' he drawled, with a saccharine sweetness that made me want to puke in my mouth. His eyes were brighter than ever this morning, his demeanour terrifying. 'And I know everything, remember?'

'Where's Dornan?' I asked, almost at the kitchen counter. Almost at the knife block. I glanced behind me. Just a few more steps —

I'd looked away for less than a second, and he'd used my inattention to pounce, grabbing my wrists and throwing me up against the counter with a ferocity that frightened me. I braced myself on the lip of the sink behind me and struggled to think of how I could get out of this. *Jesus!* I was so stupid. It could have been anyone standing out there! Someone coming to hurt me. Someone coming to kill me. Somebody coming to rape me. Murphy, who looked like he wanted to do all three.

'Your big bad biker got called away,' he said, his voice dripping with mockery. He might have been dying to fuck me, but he hated me, I realised. Hated me because I wouldn't willingly give him what he wanted.

'Emilio will expect me,' I blurted out.

He crowded over me, forcing my top half to bend backwards uncomfortably until the back of my head was almost dipping into the cloudy dishwater I'd used to wash up earlier.

'He's with the big bad biker,' he said, shrugging his shoulders as he grinned wickedly.

No. NO. If he was telling the truth, I was alone. With him. In an apartment I couldn't get out of.

And nobody was coming to save me.

CHAPTER FORTY-SIX
EMILIO

He'd beaten Bella almost to death, but the bitch was stubborn. She was still protesting her innocence, even after Emilio had had Mariana's figures checked and double-checked by his associates. The girl had done well. She'd picked up in three hours what Emilio had been trying to figure out for months: where his money was going. And there had been a lot of fucking money going.

He stood above the thieving little cunt, watching her bleed from her latest wound, a jagged slice in her forehead that was dripping blood into her eyes.

He'd already sliced a pretty patchwork of designs over her naked form, but she was strong-willed. She still hadn't broken down. The little bitch blinked rapidly, her eyelashes fluttering as blood pooled under her eyes. She was a brunette, but her pretty brown locks were almost entirely red now, coated in her own blood.

'Tell me why,' Emilio asked, holding the knife close to her eyeball, so close the metal was almost scratching at the white of her eye.

She gulped, trying to pull back, but her head was locked tight in his other hand, his fist gripping a handful of hair at the base of her skull.

'Why does anyone steal?' she'd answered him finally, after a day of torture and starvation. A day of being fed nothing but cock and straight liquor and being beaten black and blue. In a sick way, he admired her ability to hold out. 'Because I wanted pretty things. Because I wanted a better life.'

The bitch was strong.

Bitch was a thief, too. He reminded himself of that when he was cutting into her skin while she screamed. She had been diabolical, manipulative, and all the diamonds in the world couldn't save her now.

That gave him pause. Yes. She could choke on her own greed. He wanted to watch her struggle as she fought to breathe, as sharp, precious rocks crowded her airway. It would be a fitting death, and afterwards he would cut her open and extract the jewels, and hope to recoup at least some of the funds she'd channelled into fake accounts over the two years she'd been cooking their books.

But she hadn't quite suffered enough yet.

'If you let me go, I'll tell you where the money is,' she pleaded.

He grinned.

'If you tell me where the money is, I'll let you go.'

The last shred of hope died in her eyes. Emilio Ross didn't let people go once they'd crossed him, no matter how slight their mis-step. Bella had witnessed enough deaths in the few short years she'd worked for them to understand her fate.

He sauntered over to the small table he'd had Jimmy drag into the dank little room. On it were a variety of makeshift torture devices, but there was one that he hadn't used yet, but wanted to. The bite gag. He smiled, selected the crude device from the pile, and set the long butcher's knife down.

He approached Bella, who was hanging from the ceiling naked, secured by her wrists, covered in blood and blooming bruises that had painted her skin various shades of black and blue and purple. Emilio noticed new bruises where he'd dug his fingers into her tits. Her pink nipples were hard from the cold and he pinched one, making her groan painfully. She was only a few colours short of a fucking rainbow, he surmised as he released her nipple and used both hands to wrap the contraption around her face.

She attempted to whip her head from side to side, but screamed as soon as she did. Emilio smiled, taking the opportunity to shove the rubber gag bit into her mouth and press it into her cheeks, forcing her mouth open into a perfect O. One clip at the back, and it was secured. Now, if she tried to bite down, she'd bite through her own cheeks before anything else.

He smiled as fear replaced the dazed look on her face.

'I knew you'd be hard to break,' Emilio said, sticking his finger into the perfect open hole that went all the way down to her throat. She gagged as he hit the back of her throat, and he withdrew before she vomited. He didn't want her stomach contents anywhere near him.

'You know what happens next, don't you, Bella?'

She screamed. It sounded strange with her mouth prised open in such a fashion, but it still made his chest puff out with pride.

She had tried to steal his power when she stole his money, and now he would show her who was truly in control.

There was a short rap at the door, and then Jimmy and Viper were there. Two of the sickest fucks he'd ever met, and that was saying a lot. Viper was holding a bottle of bourbon and a hose, and they both looked ready for anything. That was the thing with these fucking bikers. At first, he'd been horrified that his son had decided to form his own motorcycle club, but the things they could do, the depravity these men nursed within their own souls — it was very handy, indeed. It made Il Sangue more than just a cartel. They owned the entire west coast, from San Francisco deep down into South America. In short, they were untouchable.

Emilio backed away from Bella with a wry smile. 'Go for it, boys.'

As he closed the door behind him, Emilio heard an unmistakable gagging noise and figured the boys would give the bitch exactly what she deserved.

Nobody thieved from Emilio Ross and lived to enjoy it.

CHAPTER FORTY-SEVEN

MARIANA

Murphy pressed against me, trapping me against the counter as he grinned like a son of a bitch.

'What do you want?' I snapped.

His shit-eating grin said 'fuck you' as clearly as if he'd spoken the words. My back was screaming as he bent me backwards, using his body weight to trap me as he pinned my wrists to my sides. He was hard against my hip, and I wanted to be sick, knowing exactly what he wanted already.

'I want to know if you're a moaner ...' he drawled, 'or a screamer.'

I gathered all of my strength, every bit of my anger and sadness, and directed it into my forehead. Then, praying that I wouldn't pass out from the impact, I drove my head forward and barrelled my forehead into his mouth. He let go of me and staggered back, and I straightened, holding my forehead in one hand as it buzzed angrily.

He took a handkerchief from his top suit pocket and dabbed at the blood that was coming from his split lip. Huh. I'd gotten so used to Dornan's fascination with blood, I'd forgotten other people didn't appreciate it so much. The thought that I'd hurt Murphy made me smile.

He didn't seem to like that.

'Come here,' he ordered, tucking the bloodied handkerchief away. 'You can try and fight me all you want, but I've got all day, honey.'

He had that glint in his eye, and I didn't trust him one inch. But Dornan was gone, and Emilio with him, and I was backed into a corner with nothing to protect myself. Not even shoes on my feet to kick him with.

Murphy reached into his pocket again and withdrew the photo of Luis. 'You don't want the boss to find out about this, right?'

My heart sank.

'No.'

'Well,' he said, 'let's make a deal.'

I swallowed, my eyes fixed on the photo. 'I'm listening.'

He smirked. 'You do whatever I want for today, and I'll give this back to you and pretend like I never saw it.'

I chewed on the inside of my lip and looked between his crazy blue eyes and the photo. My baby. I missed him more than anything. It frightened me that I'd already started to forget little things, like the exact shape of his face and whether his hair in the photo had been dark brown or completely black. I felt shame at such things, and wondered if my mind was simply blocking out things that were too painful for me to deal with.

'How do I know you'll keep your end of the bargain?' I whispered.

He sneered, and the shift in his expression made his lip weep fresh blood. 'Here's the thing,' he said, crowding me against the counter so that I was trapped once more. He tucked a hair behind my ear and the gesture revolted me. 'Either way, I'm getting what I want. So you can either cooperate,' he pulled my hair, exposing my neck, 'or you can fight. Both would be a lot of fun for me.' He snaked out his tongue and licked my neck, making me shudder.

'Do we have a deal?'

My shoulders slumped. He had the photo that I desperately wanted, and I had nothing to lose except my mind. I couldn't let Dornan and Emilio know about the son Este and I shared. Luis deserved better than that. I wouldn't pile my sins on him the way my father had piled his on me.

Did it really matter? This was my existence now. Owned by powerful men, used and abused until I would become a rotting, hollow shell. It was exactly as I'd expected when I'd signed on, but somehow, the reality was still shocking enough to take my breath away. I couldn't give in.

'No,' I said blankly.

I would never say yes to a man like Murphy.

But as he grabbed something behind me and held it to my throat, I stilled. A knife. He had a knife at my throat.

'Then I guess we do this the hard way,' he sneered.

'You want to rape me on the kitchen floor?' I asked, throwing him a look of disbelief.

He tutted. 'We'll start in the kitchen,' he said, 'but honey, we've got an entire apartment to work with here.'

I swallowed down my disgust and eyed the sharp butcher's knife in his hand, the one I'd been silly enough to think I had a chance of using on him.

He flashed a wide smile and pointed to his pants. 'Well then,' he said, tipping his head to one side and fixing those weird blue eyes on me, 'I suggest you get on the floor and get naked.'

I gritted my teeth and stared as he squeezed his cock through his pants, then started to stroke it slowly, as much as the material would allow. He didn't take his eyes from mine the entire time.

He looked at me in mock despair, using his free hand to gesture down to his hard-on. 'Well, come on,' he said. 'I don't think it's going to suck itself, Annie.'

My skin crawled as he used that name again. Swallowing back tears and screams, I took one tiny step back.

'I'm not putting my mouth anywhere near that,' I said emphatically. He grinned, placing a hand on my chest, between my breasts.

'You think you're too good for me, you little Mexican bitch?'

I looked at the ceiling momentarily, trying to bite my tongue. 'Colombia,' I said, taking a deep breath.

'What?' he responded, running a hand over my breasts.

My veins began to sizzle as anger poured through them. I stared at him, so fucking angry at Emilio, at Dornan, at my father. Because of them, I was here, trying to save myself from a man I despised. I pictured my father at a blackjack table, gambling away my future, and it made me want to put a gun to his head and pull the trigger myself.

'I said, I'm from Colombia,' I repeated, louder and more pissed off this time. Murphy stopped stroking my breasts and turned his full attention to my face.

'My apologies,' he said gleefully, not apologetic at all. 'But time's a wasting, and this photo seems to be burning a hole in my pocket, so I suggest you *lay down now*.'

I set my jaw stubbornly and shook my head. He looked angry, suddenly pressing the knife to my throat again, hard enough that I felt my skin break apart. I stayed as still as possible, imagining what would happen if he slipped and I drowned to death in a pool of my own blood.

Once I was still, he circled around me slowly, pressing himself into my back as he hiked my dress up roughly with his free hand. The other still held the knife at my throat, the little serrations on the blade pulled at my skin every time I shivered.

I squeezed my eyes shut as he reached between my legs and pushed my panties aside roughly, sliding his bare hand over me. Shame and rage rose hot and red in my cheeks as he chuckled. 'Looks like you're already ready for me,' he exclaimed.

Motherfucker.

Before he could pull me closer, I balled my hand into a fist and brought it up over my shoulder, slamming it into the side of Murphy's smug face. His head snapped back and to the side, and I gritted my teeth, ducking down and away before he had a chance to draw the blade across my neck.

It had been a daring move, but I couldn't just stand there while he violated me.

He looked pissed, bringing the knife up as if to stab me in the face. I drew my own throbbing fist back again and waited, my expression a silent challenge.

Before I could swing, he feinted to the left, before changing direction and coming at me like a freight train. As he tackled me we fell together, landing hard on the tiles. Stars swam in my vision and I groaned, reaching up to see if my throbbing head was bleeding.

Murphy's blue eyes glimmered as he hovered above me, taunting me silently as I was pinned by his weight.

'I knew you'd like this,' he said, pinching my nipple through thin cotton. 'All this banter. All this tension. It's fun.' He widened his eyes for effect when he said 'fun', drawing his fist back and slamming it into my cheek. My eyes watered and the side of my face throbbed. *What a fucking life*, I thought. *I'm finally here in the goddamn land of the free.*

But I was not free. I was just a possession. Not even a treasured one.

'You have to rape me because you know I'd never choose someone like you,' I said, keenly aware that his hardness was still pressed up against my stomach. 'And that kills you inside, you pathetic bastard.'

His smile was instantly replaced by a look of utter scorn. He was about to reply when I spied something out of the corner of my eye. He'd emptied his pants pockets onto the counter when he'd first arrived and taunted me with the photograph, but I'd been too busy keeping him in my line of sight to look at what he'd put on the counter besides the photo. But now, I saw. And it terrified me.

A syringe. It was capped and half-full with something clear. *Oh, Jesus*, I thought as he thrust his hips, dry humping me through the thin cotton that separated us. *This is going to happen. This man is going to rape me.*

'You were going to drug me?' I whispered shakily.

I was about to say something more when a fist caught me hard on the mouth, stunning me. I brought my hand up to my face and my fingers came away wet and red. I slowly turned my gaze to Murphy's.

He tutted, grabbing my wrists and squeezing until I thought they would snap in two. 'Shut up and lie still,' he said.

Screw that. I wasn't lying still. I struggled and fought as he continued to pin me down; my strength no match for his.

'You're a firecracker,' Murphy hissed, choking me with one hand as he rolled one of my nipples between his thumb and forefinger with the other. The knife now lay beside his knee, out of my immediate reach. 'And right now I'm going to fu—'

He was cut off by the front door crashing open. His eyes grew wide for a brief second and when I tried to push him away, he held my hips tightly.

'Where do you think you're going?' he asked me, ignoring whoever was standing at the door.

'Let me go,' I whispered urgently, turning my head to see who had arrived.

Dornan wasn't alone. I didn't know whether to be relieved, or horrified. I was a little of both.

'Gypsy Brothers,' Murphy said, as he forced his thumb into my mouth. My eyes watered as I looked to John and Dornan with a pleading stare.

Dornan's eyes locked with mine, that unmistakable current passing between us once more. He looked like he was ready to beat Murphy to death with his bare hands. 'Motherfucker!' he roared, charging towards us.

'Uh-uh,' Murphy tutted, grabbing my chin and forcing me to look at him. The knife was back in his hand, back at my throat. I hadn't even seen him pick it up.

'It's rude to interrupt, guys,' Murphy drawled, seemingly delighted at the disgust written all over my face. 'You should probably wait outside. I don't want to slip and cut her pretty little head off by accident.'

'Let go of her,' John ordered, one hand behind his back. He was going for his gun, I realised. *Jesus Christ*. I hoped he was a good aim.

A vein was pulsing in Dornan's forehead. *He was going to explode*.

'I'm not raping her,' Murphy said, looking to me. 'Tell him. Tell him how much you want it.'

'Go fuck yourself,' I said through gritted teeth.

'Tell him who you want to be with,' he said, reaching with one hand for the photograph that sat above him on the counter. Fuck! If he took that back, he'd hold it over me and do something worse next time.

'Let go of her,' John said. Murphy sneered at him, still gripping me tightly, and then his smile vanished as John aimed his gun at Murphy's head.

'You don't want me to ask a third time,' John warned. Murphy dropped my wrist and the knife, and held his hands in the air in surrender. 'John,' he hastened, 'you don't want to shoot a federal marshal. We were just having some fun. It's not my fault the girl's crazy.'

'Get up,' John ordered. Before Murphy was even on his feet, Dornan had him in a chokehold, dragging him into the living room.

I shuddered as a strong arm scooped me up and set me on shaky feet. I pulled my dress down, humiliated and sickened.

John crossed his arms and leaned against the counter. He looked impressively scary in his full leathers. He rocked the prez patch on the back of his leather cut, and the gun he held so casually in one of his hands, with two intertwined snakes engraved down the silver barrel, looked different from the rest I'd seen.

'What's the photo of, sweetheart,' he asked me. I froze, opening my mouth to speak, but no words came out. My son. *My son.*

John saw that I was having some kind of emotional seizure and looked over to the living room, where Dornan was beating the shit out of Murphy. He looked like he was going to kill him. Without missing a beat, Dornan drew his gun and cocked it. Inside the apartment, the sound of the metal click was as foreboding as it was terrifying.

'D,' John said slowly.

Dornan pressed the tip of his gun to Murphy's forehead and applied pressure to the trigger.

'Did he hurt you, Ana?' Dornan asked, his voice dangerously calm. 'Did he rape you?'

'Yes,' I said. 'No. He punched me. He didn't get to — I mean, you guys stopped him before ... *that*.'

'D, do not shoot that motherfucker,' John urged. 'I want to, you want to, we all want him dead. But killing a cop is gonna rain down a whole world of trouble on us. Think, brother.'

Dornan flexed his jaw angrily, every muscle in his body poised and ready to destroy the worthless piece of shit in front of him. And, scarily enough, part of me wanted him to shoot Murphy in the face.

John approached Dornan, his hand out. 'Give me your gun,' he said.

Dornan turned and looked at John as if to say, are you fucking kidding me? He raised his gun above Murphy's head, bringing it down onto his skull with such force that he was knocked out cold. John huffed, crossing his arms over his chest.

'Tie him up,' John said. 'I'll get Viper to pick his sorry ass up.'

John came back to stand by me, his eyes landing on the photograph. I snatched it up in my hand and curled my fist tightly shut, glancing over at Dornan, who was lost in a world of his own as he threw rope around Murphy's limbs and pulled tight.

When John looked at me, his eyes were kind. He suddenly seemed so different from anyone else I'd encountered since the night I'd left my father's house. His smile was genuine, and it reached all the way up to his hazel eyes.

'Are you all right?' he asked. He glanced at Dornan, who was dragging Murphy out the front door by his bound feet. A moment later, I heard him yelling instructions at someone over the phone.

I nodded at John, swallowing again. I'd suddenly become a mute.

He took my balled fist gently and brought it up in between us, softly unfurling my fingers one by one. He took the photograph from me as if it were a precious thing and studied it.

'Is this your baby?' he asked quietly.

I dissolved. I put my hands to my mouth to stifle a scream, as tears rained down my face. I couldn't stop shaking my head. I couldn't stop crying.

John looked sympathetic. He held the photo out to me and I took it quickly, gratefully. He waited patiently as I wiped my cheeks and took a few deep breaths in an effort to calm myself.

'Is this going to be a problem?' he asked.

I shook my head. 'No problem. I swear.'

'You'd better find a better hiding spot for that,' he said, pointing to the photo.

I nodded, looking around. I couldn't find anywhere. John plucked it from my hand and shoved it in his top pocket, just as Dornan re-entered the room.

I could tell Dornan wanted to crush me in his embrace, judging by the way he held his arms, the way his fists were balled up tight. But he couldn't; we were a secret so forbidden, he couldn't even embrace me in front of his best friend.

And now that friend held an even darker secret in his pocket. A piece of my past. *My son.*

CHAPTER FORTY-EIGHT

MARIANA

John and Dornan had let me compose myself and then driven me to the Gypsy Brothers clubhouse, an impressive compound in the heart of Los Angeles. Six-foot fences topped with razor wire blocked the view from outside. The place looked like a goddamn prison, and I was terrified that once I went in, I might not get back out.

Suddenly, my little apartment on the beach seemed like the best thing that had ever happened to me.

John and Dornan walked me up to a small bedroom and left me alone, with the door locked from the outside.

I sat on a double bed that smelled like old sweat and sex and stared at the phone on the nightstand.

Mama. Papa. Karina. Pablo. Luis. Este.

I recited their names to the pounding of my heart.

I stared at the phone. I'd overheard Dornan saying that all of the burlesque club's numbers were unlisted. Untraceable.

Would it be the same here?

Could I risk it?

I dialled the number I had learned off by heart as a young girl. My heart pounded and I watched the door as the line rang with agonising slowness. One ring. Two rings. I was about to chicken out and hang up when a female voice answered.

It was Mama. I clapped a hand over my mouth, tears springing to my eyes. I muffled a sob as she repeated the same greeting, probably thinking she was about to be connected to a call centre.

The door swung open. Fuck! Dornan rushed at me as I slammed the phone down and jumped to my feet, backing as far away as I could get.

His face was full of barely controlled rage. 'Who was that?' he ground out.

I hit the wall behind me. 'I didn't say anything,' I stammered. 'I swear, Dornan —'

He rounded the bed and grabbed at me, even as I foolishly tried to push him away.

'WHO WAS IT?' he roared, two hands going around my neck and squeezing.

I panicked, scratching at his hands with my fingernails. He didn't budge an inch.

'Was it your father?' he asked through tightly gritted teeth.

I couldn't talk, because he was strangling me to death, so I just nodded as best I could.

He loosened his grip and looked away from me for a moment, appearing to be in thought. He nodded finally, licking his lips.

He pressed me against the wall, his entire body covering me like a heavy blanket, and he shook me roughly.

'I fucking told you, Ana,' he breathed in my ear. 'I warned you about contacting anyone. And you chose to disobey me? After *everything*?'

I was trying to apologise, but his hands were still around my neck. I wheezed and bucked as tears rolled down my cheeks.

He nodded again, as if affirming a thought to himself. 'I'll show you what happens to people who disobey, shall I? Your first and final warning, baby.'

He released me and I fell to the floor, a crumpled heap of arms and legs that had no strength anymore. I managed to push myself up to my hands and knees as I hacked up a lung. My throat felt raw, bruised. I'd have a nice handprint there in the morning, no doubt. Add that to the hickey Murphy had branded me with, and I was a freaking sideshow of bruises and abuse.

I coughed and spluttered, screaming hoassly as a hand grabbed a fistful of my hair and pulled upwards. 'Get up,' he roared. I scrambled to my feet, stumbling blindly as he led me out of the room. My heart was beating so fast I thought I was about to pass out, but there was no time for that. I was being led deeper into the clubhouse, past men dressed in leather who averted their eyes when they saw their VP dragging a girl who was probably about to be slaughtered.

I sobbed as he continued to drag me. Down stairs and up hallways, until it seemed like we were going in circles. We were in the basement, judging by the lack of windows. Dornan stopped at a door, his hand resting on the knob as his other hand continued to pull at my hair.

'Remember,' he said, his voice low, 'when people lie to us, we kill them. But if you betray me, Ana, I won't just kill you fast. I'll make it last for days, you hear me?'

I nodded. 'Please,' I whispered, 'let's just go. I promise I won't do it again.' Somehow I knew there was something awful beyond that door, and it was something that wouldn't be able to be unseen.

Dornan appeared to calm down momentarily. I heard a scream on the other side of the door — a woman's scream. Whoever was in there was in pain.

He seemed to think twice, the woman's scream apparently shaking him out of his stupor.

'Promise me,' he said gruffly, shaking me by my hair.

'I promise. I swear! I was just scared after what Murphy tried to do, and I slipped. Dornan, I'm sorry.'

He breathed heavily as the woman behind the door continued to wail. I cried, pressing my hands to my ears to try and drown her out. 'Please,' I begged. 'Please, Dornan.'

The woman let out a bloodcurdling scream and Dornan snapped back to reality.

He started dragging me back down the way we'd just come, back towards people and the safety of the clubhouse. The safety. It sounded ludicrous, yet I knew it was much more preferable to be up there with those bikers than down in the basement being tortured. *Thank God.*

He dragged me back to the bedroom and shut the door, pushing me onto the bed.

'Stay here,' he barked. He went to leave, then turned back, yanking the phone cord from the wall and taking the phone with him.

As the door slammed behind him, I began to sob heavily. Soon I was hysterical. But the last thing I needed was to attract any more attention.

I slid off the bed and crawled underneath, lying on my side among years of dust and other, nastier things. I pressed my face into my knees as I drew them up to my chest. I would hide here. I would hide here and cry and maybe nobody would ever find me.

I could only hope.

CHAPTER FORTY-NINE
DORNAN

Bella was a mess. Literally. Someone had punched a couple of nails into her forehead, reducing her to a mumbling zombie. Her eyes couldn't focus, and her blood was everywhere. Thank fuck he'd come to his senses before he'd opened the door and shown Ana. It was something she would never be able to get past. If she had seen Bella in this state, it would have ruined her.

Dornan shook his head. Whoever the fuck had done this was an evil, twisted son of a bitch. Even he couldn't do *this* shit, and he was pretty fucked up. This had all the markings of his father. The man was as dead inside as this girl was about to be all over.

He drew his gun from his belt and shot her twice, in the heart. She died immediately, and for that, he was glad.

CHAPTER FIFTY
MARIANA

When Dornan came back, he was calmer, and he'd removed his shirt. I was still hiding underneath the bed. The first thing he did after locking the door behind him was push the bed to the side and crouch in front of me.

'Come on,' he said, offering me a hand.

I trembled at the sight of him. At the touch of his hand, I cringed.

'I'm not asking,' he said.

'What did you do?' I whispered.

He tugged my arm, and reluctantly I uncurled myself, letting him pull me to my feet.

He had ignored my question. But I'd heard two faint pops, and somehow, I knew they'd come from him.

'Did you shoot someone?' I asked. 'Are you going to kill me?'

He set his jaw as he glanced between the door and me, his hands coming to rest possessively on my shoulders.

'I put her out of her misery,' he said. 'She was too far gone. Do you understand?'

I nodded. Honestly, I didn't have a clue what he was talking about.

But then — I remembered the papers at the burlesque club, and I choked.

'The accountant?' I asked, hearing the pitiful desperation in my voice. 'It was her, wasn't it? Oh, *God*. Oh my God.'

I broke away from him and started to pace nervously. The accountant who had cooked the books had died a horrible death.

'She died because of me,' I said, raking my hands through my hair. 'I didn't mean for her to die!'

Dornan's hands shot out and grabbed me, pulling me to his chest in a crushing embrace. I couldn't decide if he was trying to comfort me or just trap me.

'I need to throw up,' I said dully. He immediately let go of me, and I made it to the rubbish bin just in time to decide I didn't need to be sick, after all.

I might have held some hope before, but the woman's last death scream had wiped hope clean away, and replaced it with nothing but fear and despair.

I stood, and Dornan handed me a glass of water. I drank it all, and he took the glass from me again.

He held my shoulders as I stared up at him, I saw that animalistic look in his eyes that usually meant one thing. Oh, Jesus. I couldn't. Not now. I burst into tears, shaking my head frantically as I pushed him away.

'I just want to hold you,' he said. He pressed my arms to my sides as he crushed me once more, an embrace that took away my breath and left me gasping. He kissed me on the top of my head, and I shivered at the intimacy. *He doesn't want to fuck me*, I realised with a start, suddenly understanding that I'd misread that fierceness in his eyes. He wanted to comfort me. I pressed my face into him, breathing in the leather and salt air smell that seemed to cling to him. His arms were so strong, his embrace so tender, that it almost brought me to tears.

After a moment, he released me, tipping my chin up with his finger so I had to meet his gaze.

'You're so pale,' he said, cupping my jaw in his hand. 'You're wasting away, Ana.'

I swallowed back the rock in my throat, a couple of tears welling out of my eye and splashing down onto my cheek.

He's trying to protect me from this monstrous world.

That singular thought spun around and around in my head, like some grotesque merry-go-round, gaudy flashing lights in shades of bloody red. I leaned into him as he brushed his thumb against my cheek. It confused the hell out of me that he would risk everything to protect me. It made me uncomfortable, because *I liked it.*

'You never let me go outside,' I whispered, nestling my face into his grasp. I was sad. I was so very, very sad. And I *was* pale, he was right. No sun and a life spent wallowing in the artificial world he had constructed for me meant my bronzed, sun-kissed skin had dulled to a sickly white pallor.

I was trapped. Forever. Within a world that dealt in lives and in blood. I was sinking deeper and deeper into an abyss that was claiming me, one drop of blood at a time. One day soon I was going to drown in all that blood.

He kissed me, and I hesitated a moment too long. Stupid girl. His grip on my neck tightened, becoming painful. I pleaded for him to let go with my eyes, but he didn't waver.

'Tell me what you're thinking right now,' he commanded. I was too afraid to lie. I was too afraid, in that moment, of the possibility that he was already reading my thoughts.

He loosened his grip enough for me to take in a small breath and whisper my response.

'I'm scared,' I said, tears slipping down my face.

'Mmm-hmm,' he said, pressing me to the wall, trailing rough, forceful kisses up my neck. Pressing his lips through the salty tears and onto my skin. Marking me. Because I was his.

'What else?' he asked, between kisses. His breath was hot on my cold skin, and I shivered violently.

I choked. 'Don't make me say it,' I pleaded, utterly broken. I thought again about the dead accountant downstairs and wanted to be sick.

'What else?' he repeated, squeezing my neck again.

'I think I love you,' I whispered, bursting into tears. I didn't know if I meant it. God, I was so close to the brink of insanity, I could feel the imaginary straitjacket being laced up at my back. But the things I felt for this man, the way he made my heart beat furiously, the thrill he sent through me whenever his fingers brushed against my skin — there was no denying the things we provoked in each other.

He smiled. A delighted look that held my entire existence within it. Because I was his. And there was nothing I could do about it. I tensed as he gripped the back of my head, relaxing when I realised he was only bringing my face to his shoulder. A gesture that was meant to be comforting.

'Of course you do,' he said, running his thumb along my lower lip. At that moment, there was a sharp rap on the door. I recoiled as I heard Emilio's voice.

Dornan stepped away from me as Emilio unlocked the door, letting it swing open.

'Am I interrupting?' he asked, one eyebrow cocked as he looked from Dornan to me and back again.

Dornan shoved me hard enough that I hit the wall. 'Absolutely,' he said. 'Can't a man get his cock sucked in private around here?'

I fixed my face into a blank stare — my favourite expression around Emilio, it seemed — and sat back down on the edge of the bed. My cheeks burned as I waited for Emilio to hurry up and leave the room and put me out of my gut-wrenching anxiety.

'You shot the lying bitch?' Emilio asked Dornan, obviously referring to the accountant.

Dornan nodded, gesturing to the blood that was spattered over his skin. 'Yeah, Pop,' he said. 'And now I'm gonna take a fuckin' shower.'

He left the room, brushing past Emilio, who didn't budge from where he stood in front of me. I didn't dare look up at him, but the weight of his stare burned into my skin.

'*Cholita*,' he said finally. I pressed my palms flat on the bed on either side of me to stop them from shaking.

'Yes, sir,' I responded, meeting his cold black eyes.

He studied me for a long moment, while I pictured him as a rat. The long nose and the way he spoke reminded me of a rodent.

'Are they treating you well in casa Gypsy Brother?' He pursed his lips together as he studied me some more.

Fear prickled on my skin as I remembered all of the stories Dornan had made me memorise.

'Please,' I begged Emilio. 'I don't want to upset any of them —'

He cocked his head to the side, putting up a hand to silence me. 'Never mind about them,' he said. 'The only person you need to worry about upsetting is me.'

I nodded, licking my lips. 'I, uh, well ... a lot of them like to do ... strange things. Things I haven't ever seen before.' I was lying out loud. I'd never even seen the inside of the clubhouse until today.

He grinned like a Cheshire cat. 'Oh?'

'They take turns,' I said. A total, outrageous lie. Would he buy it?

'Do they hurt you?' he asked, his eyes suddenly lit up like Christmas trees. He was probably going to find a blonde and get her to relieve him after he'd listened to my imaginary tales of sexual deviance and submission at the hands of his employees. I tucked a stray hair behind my ear, thanking the sweet Lord in heaven that I'd been born a brunette.

'Yes,' I whispered.

His mouth stretched impossibly wide, baring his teeth. He looked like he could tear me limb from limb with those teeth. Especially the fake one. I fought the urge to shudder in disgust.

'Good,' he said. 'Some time, I'll have to call your father and tell him all about it.' I looked up in confusion as he beamed down at me. 'Oh, no,' he said, 'that's right. They think you're dead.'

Motherfucker.

'I assume you know what happened to our last accountant?' he asked casually.

It took me a moment to catch up with the change of topic. Oh, yeah. The girl downstairs who had been screaming so loud I could still hear the noise reverberating in my ears. The girl who was dead now, thanks to Dornan.

'Yes, sir,' I said again.

'Let that be a warning,' Emilio said, turning and walking to the door. 'Let that be a lesson in what not to do, and you'll go far.'

He closed the door behind him. As soon as he was gone I heaved a sigh of relief, slumping further down onto the bed.

This is way too precarious, I thought to myself. *This existence is actually terrifying.*

In that moment, I longed for Dornan. He'd know what to say. He always had the words — or the touch — to take that choking loneliness away.

CHAPTER FIFTY-ONE

DORNAN

It killed him to walk out of that room and leave her with his father. She was good with the books, so good that Emilio would hopefully consider her valuable and keep her around. In the meantime, though, it was going to be up to Dornan to keep her out of harm's way, while at the same time not alerting his father to how he felt about the girl.

I think I love you.

Her words ran through his head, over and over again, filling him with fear, with wild rage. When he reached the small bathroom he locked himself in, shedding bloody clothes on the floor.

Fuck, how he wanted her to be here with him. If she were here, he'd throw her up against these tiles, wrap her legs around his waist, and drive into her until he was feeling good again. Because around her, all he felt was arousal and fear, fear that she would be taken from him, fear that he'd lose the best thing that had ever happened to him.

Dornan turned the water on and stepped into the shower, that familiar rage at his father duelling with his constant need for approval from the man. *Blood is thicker than water*, he told himself. *The family comes before the girl.*

But even as he repeated those words to himself, he knew he didn't really mean them. He craved his father's approval; but his heart didn't know that. The things he felt for Mariana, he'd never felt before for anyone. It was a dangerous proposition, to be falling in love with a woman who was owned by the cartel. At any moment, Emilio could decide to move her, or just kill her, and there was not a thing Dornan could do about it.

The last woman he'd truly loved wasn't even owned by the cartel, and she'd still been taken from him. Eight years, and nothing. Her memory taunted him as he thought of Mariana, as he wondered if their fates would be the same.

He roared, lashing out with his fists. He connected with hard tile, his knuckles blossoming with pain as they smashed into the unforgiving wall, the pain bringing him some strange sort of calm, some clarity among the chaos that raged within him. He might not be able to fully control what happened to Mariana, but he had to at least try. After all, he'd kept Emilio away from John all these years, kept him from killing the man who had too much of a conscience, in Emilio's words, to be a part of their world, much less be in control of the Gypsy Brothers. *Yes*, Dornan decided, *he could do this*. He would do it, for her, because she'd been terrified when she had let those words fall from trembling lips — *I think I love you* — and he couldn't bear the thought that she would fall in love with a man like himself, only to be punished with a bullet to the head.

He bore the afternoon patiently, not daring to go back to the bedroom and seek her out. When it came time to leave, he entered the bedroom to find her still sitting on the edge of the bed, staring at her hands. When she saw him, the relief on her face was palpable. It almost broke his black heart when she looked at him like that — when she was so fucking happy that her monstrous hero had returned.

They didn't speak. He led her downstairs, into the garage, and jerked his thumb at the bike. His heart thumped wildly as she climbed on behind him.

When they got back to the apartment, he acted casually. After all these years, he still didn't know if he was paranoid, or if his father's eyes really did follow him everywhere he went. As soon as the front door closed behind them, he pointed to the bathroom. 'Get in the shower,' he ordered. 'Now.'

For once, she didn't argue. Maybe she had heard the desperation in his voice. The fear. He followed her, like a lion stalking its prey, slow and methodical.

She undressed quickly, turning on the water and standing under the spray. Waiting for him. His cock stirred at the sight of her naked body, the way her full breasts practically begged him to grab them, the slight wave in her dark brown hair that reminded him of the times he'd wound it around his fist and pulled.

He undressed, stepping in beside her, relieved that they could finally speak somewhere safe.

He pressed her against the wall and lowered his mouth to her ear.

'That was too close today,' he murmured. 'Too close.'

She nodded feverishly at his words.

'If my father finds out about us, Ana, he'll kill you. You know that, right?'

Another emphatic nod. Dornan drew back so he could take in her face.

'I would die if anything bad happened to you,' he said firmly, and her eyes widened slightly at his admission. 'We have to be more careful, you understand?'

'Yeah,' she said, biting her lip. 'Yeah, I understand.'

I think I love you. Her words came back to haunt him.

'And darlin'?' he added. She raised her eyebrows in response.

He grinned, resting one hand in the hollow of her throat as he caged her against the wall.

'I think I fuckin' love you, too.' He pressed his lips to her forehead, knowing that with his own admission, he had probably damned them both to hell.

He drew back to see her reaction, laughing when he saw the smirk on her face.

'I don't know if I believe you,' she said playfully, running a finger down his arm. 'I think you should show me.'

His grin grew so wide, he thought his face might break.

'You are gonna be the death of me,' he growled, grabbing her and picking her up effortlessly. He pinned her to the wall, spreading wet kisses down her neck.

'Oh, God,' she moaned underneath his touch, 'I can think of worse ways to die.'

PART 2
KINGPIN

*Loving me will not be easy.
It will be war. You will
hold the gun and I will hand
you the bullets. So breathe,
and embrace the beauty of
the massacre that lies ahead.*

R.M. DRAKE

PROLOGUE

MARIANA

2007

I watched from where I sat, grief beating inside my chest as Dornan placed a cupcake with a single candle on the table in front of me. A tear formed in my right eye, blurring my vision and the pink frosted cupcake warped momentarily. But I would not cry. I would not break down. Because it had been too long, and I struggled to remember my life in Colombia before this. I only knew that it had been happier, freer. Mostly, I remembered being less afraid.

I blinked the tear away, making sure none of it made its way onto my cheek. Dornan saw it anyway.

'Happy birthday, baby,' he said, his voice low and husky in the quiet, still night.

My eyes filled again at the tenderness in his tone. Someone else would miss it under the rough exterior, the 'fuck you' attitude, the way he held himself.

But I heard. I saw. I *knew*.

'Aren't you going to blow out the candle?' he pressed, his rough hand caressing my cheek as he stood behind me. I nodded, swallowing thickly. I took a breath, pursed my lips and blew across the flame. It flickered at first. I hadn't leaned in close enough. I took another breath, blew a steady stream of air at the flame, and extinguished it.

'Did you make a wish?' Dornan asked me, his hand squeezing my shoulder. I turned to meet his gaze. I thought of a boy with tiny, chubby hands and bright blue eyes. Wondered what *he* wished for when he blew out his candles. Did he wish for me, like I wished for him? He would have been twelve that year. *Twelve*.

Nine years spent together with this man, and he still didn't know about the son I gave up before we met.

I nodded. I smiled. I pushed all other thoughts away.

Dornan smiled back at me, his dark brown eyes lighting up. He knelt beside me on the ground, and I turned in my seat, opening my legs so the insides of my thighs rested on either side of him. I cupped his face in my hands, pulled him closer and pressed my lips to his forehead. His skin was warm. He always ran hotter than me, like a furnace. As I gazed down into his eyes, I felt my heart jump, like it always did when I was with him.

I was twenty-eight years old.
We were in love.
And it was the saddest fucking thing in the world.

CHAPTER ONE

MARIANA

**2007
NINE YEARS GONE**

Five days a week, I dressed in smart business clothes. I ate breakfast and painted my face, like countless other women. I was an accountant – well, technically, I was a bookkeeper, because I had had to leave college before I could complete my degree. At the office – a tiny, cramped room in the back of a run-down strip club off La Cienega – I drank coffee and spoke to nobody and worked my ass off. Then I was driven home – the home *he* had chosen for me. Some nights, my lover escorted me to the door, opened it for me, and spent the evening worshipping my body in ways I'd never imagined possible before meeting him. He was rough, he was dominating, and he made me feel safe even with a hand wrapped around my throat, cutting off my air supply just long enough to make my head spin. I liked the way he drove me to the peak, how he dangled me over the edge and then pulled me back up just before I fell.

Dornan Ross might have been a brutal man, but to me he was shelter. Even when he hurt me, he made it feel like love. Because at least if he was hurting me, he was there. I'd become addicted to him and had stayed that way for nine years. I was either alone, or I was with very bad people like Emilio Ross, or I was with him. But mostly I was alone. So I took everything he gave me, and I took it with a smile.

If you and I passed each other on the street, you'd think I was just like all the other girls, getting through each day as best as I could.

But nothing about my life was normal. I was not just a girl who went to work and went home and cooked dinner and had sex. If you passed me on the street, you'd probably miss the biker who walked five steps behind me, the 'roommate' I'd been given who was actually my keeper for all those hours when Dornan wasn't around. You'd miss the handprints around my neck, hidden by long hair and scarves, marks left by brutal love that I looked at in the mirror and delicately touched in the safety of my bathroom, to remember what it felt like to be alive, to be on the brink of coming and passing out at the same time.

If you knocked on my door and I was alone, you'd think I wasn't there. You'd never imagine I was pressed against the other side of the door, listening to your every move, begging silently for you to go away but wanting you to stay at the same time.

You'd never guess what I really was, because that reality was too dark, too painful for any normal person to entertain.

I was a slave.

Nine years ago, I'd made a deal with the devil. Emilio Ross, Kingpin of the Il Sangue drug cartel, had been seconds away from slaughtering my entire family for a debt my father owed him. Perhaps foolishly, I'd offered myself up in return for my family's safety. As long as I stayed with the cartel and worked off my father's massive debt, they'd be safe in Colombia.

My money laundering had paid off the original debt a long time ago, at least by my count, but Emilio had since made it clear that the deal didn't have an expiration date. He owned me.

I had been prized property of the Il Sangue Cartel for nine years, and there was one thing that I knew for certain.

I was never getting out alive. Truth be told, I'm not even sure I wanted to get out. The part of me that craved my son's embrace, *she* wanted to get out. The mother inside my soul desperately craved the feeling of holding my child in my arms. Years before I'd become entangled with the cartel, I had given birth in secret. Teenage pregnancy was worse than murder in my family, and I'd been forced to give my son up hours after I pushed him into this cruel world. My father had forged my signature on adoption papers, and I never saw my son again.

Maybe when we met again, it wouldn't be in this nightmare. Maybe he'd hold me just as tightly as I wanted – needed – to hold him. Maybe, more likely, I'd never see him again. Because of the sins of my father, I'd never see my precious boy again, and that thought was harder to fathom than knowing I was a prisoner of Il Sangue. I'd happily die if it meant I could spend just one day with Luis. But I couldn't sacrifice my entire family for my selfish needs.

Besides, I didn't even know if Luis' adoptive parents would let me near him. I had no legal recompense to the child I'd carried in my womb for nine months, the child who was half me and half Esteban, my boyfriend who'd been murdered in front of me by Emilio's men.

But by far the most compelling reason to stay away from Luis was that he was probably better off without me. I hadn't believed my father when he had told me that, as he pried my fingers loose and took my only child from me, but over the years his words had played on my mind. *He's better off without you.* It didn't matter that I was screwing the vice-president of the Gypsy Brothers, or that we were in love. None of it mattered, because if I went to my boy, my lover would probably be the one who'd plant a bullet in my back before I even got to touch Luis.

Dornan was an enigma, a combination of brutality and tenderness, wrapped up in one man. The only son of my 'owner', Il Sangue kingpin Emilio, Dornan had been the one who'd saved me from being sold into sexual slavery. Emilio had intended to reclaim the money my father owed by selling me as a whore in one of his slave auctions, but Dornan had convinced him that I was more valuable as a money launderer in the cartel business. I'd proved him right very quickly, and we'd fallen for each other even faster.

Everyone in my immediate family thought that I was dead – they thought that Emilio's men had killed me on the night they shot up my family's home – and somehow that made it simpler to disconnect from my old existence. Dornan thought it'd be easier that way – for them, because they'd be able to stop searching, and for me, because I'd be free from the soul-crushing guilt of knowing they were looking for me while I was hiding in plain sight with the Gypsy Brothers in Los Angeles. I never had a choice in the matter. The man I was falling in love with dragged me up a rocky mountain, kissed me and then made me watch as my brother and father dug up a headless corpse they'd been led to believe was me.

And I still fell in love with him. I'm smart, but maybe I'm also really, really stupid. Because I truly did love Dornan Ross, with every part of my dark soul. I needed him like I needed air to breathe. I came alive whenever he was around me. My light to his dark, a delicate balance of pleasure and pain.

We were like a match made in heaven.

Wait. That's wrong.

We were a match made in *hell*.

CHAPTER TWO

MARIANA

1999
SIX MONTHS GONE

Every cartel needs someone who can make their dirty money clean, and I was the best damn money launderer on the West Coast.

Six months after I'd arrived in Los Angeles, John Portland – president of the Gypsy Brothers Motorcycle Club and Dornan's best friend – paid me a visit. I'm not sure why he chose that particular day, or why he'd waited months to voice his suspicions about who and what I really was. Maybe he'd wanted to bide his time, watch me, make sure he wasn't raising any suspicions by visiting me at home, away from the strip club and the Gypsy Brothers clubhouse where we frequently crossed paths.

We shared the same small office at the clubhouse but John was hardly ever there. I suppose presiding over a one-percenter biker gang like the Gypsy Brothers wasn't really a job you could do from behind a desk. But he was always around, delivering big crumpled bundles of cash for me to clean and launder, picking up packages that were probably full of drugs or guns, monitoring the front business that allowed us to channel money obtained illegally through a legal avenue – peepshows and lap dances. The reality was the strip club (or 'burlesque club', as they somewhat euphemistically called it) ran at a loss, and the majority of the clientele were Gypsy Brothers, who came in for free blow jobs and beer in between their club business. The dollar bills floating around this club were usually reserved for snorting coke, not stuffing in strippers' panties.

I'd learned much about John Portland in the six months since Emilio had parked me in the back office of the VaVa Voom strip club with a pile of blood-smeared hundred dollar bills and a boxy old computer that whirred whenever it overheated. Tidbits of information that I had filed away for the future, just in case.

John had a wife who liked to shoot drugs into her arm to make her forget she was a biker's wife, a daughter who was the light in his world, and a club full of Gypsy Brothers he was responsible for leading. He was covered in tattoos, mostly over his muscled arms and up his neck, the only part not covered was his face. The club tattoo that stretched across his tanned back was the largest, and I'd seen it only once, when he'd been stabbed in the stomach by a rival gang member and he stitched his wound in front of me. Yeah, John Portland was a bad ass. His blue eyes, ringed with hazel flecks, were framed by dark blonde hair, and he alternated between clean-shaven and a full beard. With the tattoos and the bike, it didn't really take away from the tough exterior when he shaved the beard off. He still looked like he could kill you with his bare hands.

I'd learned some other things about him. He was kind. He was thoughtful. He liked to surf. When he smiled, his whole being lit up. He almost never smiled, though, instead wearing a constant hard-set expression that was halfway between a grimace and a frown. Most of all, I'd learned that he was trapped here, just like me. He might not have realised it – hell, maybe he did – but he was as much a pawn in the Il Sangue Cartel as I was ... maybe even more.

Six months in and John Portland knew nothing about me besides the fact that I carried a photograph of a small baby around with me. Christopher Murphy, a federal air marshal and Emilio's long-term link to bribing the American government, had stolen it from me and used it to try and extort sex and compliance from me in exchange for his silence. Until John arrived. He had never spoken of the photo again after he wrestled it from Murphy and silently returned it to me months later, and for that I was eternally grateful.

But John knew, and I didn't know what he would do with my secret. I'd vowed early on to give him nothing else – not one more shred of incriminating evidence that he could potentially use against me. Whenever he asked anything about me or my family I would find a way to change the subject, to deflect his questioning, to respond with something vague and non-committal. I was very, very careful with my past, with the way I interacted with people. One word answers. Blank stares. Outright ignorance. The strippers who frequented the hallways didn't call me The Ice Queen for nothing. Sometimes, if they were particularly bitter, The Ice Cunt. But I'd only heard that once, from a girl called Mindy. After Dornan threatened to knock all her teeth out and set her up as the permanent blow-job station in the corner of the club, she didn't say it again. After that, none of the girls had really spoken to me, let alone bothered me. The only person who ever spoke to me outside of the holy trinity – Dornan, Emilio and Murphy – was John.

But for all of my one-word answers, blank stares and outright ignorance, it felt like John Portland could lower my guard without me even noticing, until it was too late and I'd revealed parts of myself better left in the dark.

I don't think he knew what I really was – a prisoner – or maybe he just didn't want to admit it to himself – until he came to see me at the apartment one day. Dornan was in Mexico on Gypsy Brothers business, and I needed to be checked on, obviously. John knocked on the door. I waited for him to punch in the code and come in, but he didn't.

'Mariana!' he yelled, kicking the bottom of the door. 'I've got my hands full, can you let me in?'

I panicked.

I still wasn't trusted with the code to my own apartment. Other select people could get in, but I couldn't get out. Dornan said it was for my own protection.

And it had worked fine. Until John.

'Uh, just key in the code and come in,' I replied, rooted to my spot on the couch.

He yelled a few more times, but I couldn't move. I was paralysed with fear. I knew he suspected something wasn't right, from the first moment he'd laid his baby blue eyes on me and demanded to know who I was, and what the hell I was doing in his office. He wasn't an idiot.

Eventually, he punched in the code himself. The front door to my apartment swung open and there he was, his helmet in his hand and a question on his face. I got up and hurried to the door, as if I'd been about to open it.

'Can I get a hand here?' he asked.

Barefoot, I stepped out onto the landing with him. There was nothing there.

'I thought you said your hands were full,' I said, looking around.

Before I could stop him, John grabbed the door handle and pulled it shut.

'Oops,' he said. 'Can you open it back up for me?'

I gave him a blank look, but inside my stomach was twisting into knots. *Oh God, he knows, he knows about me. He knows I'm not normal. He knows I'm trapped in here.*

'Sure,' I replied. I stared at the keypad, tried to think of a number Dornan would use. His birthday? I punched that in and tried the door. Nothing.

I looked at John, who had one eyebrow raised. He was dressed in black from head to foot, his leather cut and jeans hugging his body as he towered over me, black steel-capped boots encasing his feet. His dark blonde hair hung in front of his eyes, adding a smudge of boyish charm juxtaposed against his ferocity.

I shrugged. 'This thing's temperamental,' I said. 'I swear it hates me.'

I tried another couple of combinations. Of course, they didn't work.

'Forget your own birthday?' He rolled his eyes, shouldering me out of the way and stabbing at the keypad with his index finger until the door gave a small metallic click.

He'd tricked me. *And how the hell did he know when my birthday was?*

Furious, I shoved the door open and tried to slam it behind me. John wedged his boot in the door before it could close. I tried to push his boot out of the way using the door, but he was much stronger than me.

'I can stay here all day,' he said. Finally, I moved back, letting him into the apartment.

He closed the door behind him and strode past me, down the hallway and into the dining room, which faced the ocean and had its own small balcony.

'It's hot today,' he said. 'Why don't you have this door open?'

I shrugged. 'I'm home alone. It feels safer with everything closed. How do you know when my birthday is?' *How did he know anything about me?*

'Bullshit,' he said. 'I bet if I try this door right now, it'll open, won't it?'

'Of course it'll open,' I responded, panic building inside me. 'It's just a door.'

He made a point of opening and closing the balcony door, then passed me again, going back to the keypad at the front door. There was one inside and one outside, and he armed the inside one with quick fingers.

He crossed the apartment again and tried the balcony door.

It wouldn't budge.

John turned to me slowly, his eyes practically bugging out of his head.

'They keep you here,' he said slowly. 'They keep you here like a fucking prisoner. Don't they?'

Fuck. What if he spoke to Dornan about this? What if he spoke to Emilio?

I pressed my teeth together in my mouth and tried not to scream.

He rushed towards me, and for a moment I had the uncanny thought that he was going to grab me by the throat and toss me against the wall. Conditioning, I suppose. Living in the middle of a fucking drug cartel with people like Emilio Ross and Christopher Murphy always hovering on the edges of your existence could do that.

But he didn't grab my throat. He grabbed my shoulder with one hand, his touch gentle, and the other hand trailed along my chin, forcing my head up so we were eye to eye.

'Don't they?' he repeated, much quieter this time. His eyes were full of anguish, and something else I couldn't quite fathom.

'What do you want from me?' I whispered, turning my head away.

He cupped my cheek with his hand, his other palm starting to burn as it gripped my shoulder.

'You don't need to lie to me,' he said, and something in his words snapped me back to reality. I did need to lie to him – to him and to everyone else in the world if my family was going to be safe. My sacrifice, my complicity, my ownership at the hands of Emilio Ross and the Il Sangue Cartel meant that I had to lie every time I opened my fucking mouth, lest I find a gun jammed down my throat for my transgressions.

'I'm not a prisoner,' I snapped, levelling my gaze at him again as the mask slipped back over my soul. 'I'm forgetful.'

His eyes were like twin fires, his grip on my shoulder getting even tighter. 'You're hurting me,' I said, wrenching my shoulder away and stepping back.

He turned and left, and the cocky bastard didn't set the lock when he slammed the door behind him.

Was he giving me a chance to escape?

Or was he testing my loyalty?

Emilio had found countless ways to test my loyalty ever since I'd been painfully initiated into the Il Sangue Cartel, and by default, the Gypsy Brothers.

I didn't leave. I didn't take my chance to escape.

No, I re-programmed the lock myself (now that I knew the code) and sat on my couch, drinking vodka instead. You could say that I was weak, that I was suffering from Stockholm syndrome, that I was the worst kind of victim because I refused to help myself when the opportunity arose.

And I'd say *fuck that*. I'd made a deal with Emilio Ross, and at least four lives – my mother, my father, my sister and my brother – hung in the balance every single time I made a decision. Five, if you counted Luis. Oh, and then there was the small fact of my own life. That hung in the balance every single day, and everything always felt so goddamn *temporary*.

So I didn't leave. I sat, and I waited.

John came back an hour later with a box. Plain, brown cardboard packaging.

'What is this?' Did I even want to know?

He took a knife from the rack and made a slit down the side of the packaging, pulling out a cellphone. I eyed the small black phone dubiously, pulling my own cellphone from my pocket.

'For you,' he said. 'A burner phone. Nothing to identify you. Nothing to trace back to you. Nobody listening to you. But you have to keep it hidden, okay?'

'I have a phone,' I said.

John's eyes flicked to me, soft and with the hint of a smile. 'Your phone,' he said, 'is bugged. But you knew that already, right?'

I looked around the apartment nervously. Last thing I needed was for Emilio or someone else to overhear this conversation and decide I was getting too dangerous to keep around.

'How do I know you haven't bugged *this* phone?'

He smiled. 'You just saw me open the packaging. Plus, you should know by now that I don't have time to eavesdrop on your calls. I've got too much other shit to do.'

I had been standing stiff beside him; I felt the tension melt from me piece by piece as he held out the phone.

'You can trust me,' he said softly. 'I'm not like them. I'm not like Emilio.'

I nodded, looking away, salt tears burning my cheeks at the weight of his kindness.

'Mariana,' he whispered. He put his finger underneath my chin again and tilted it up, so I had no choice but to meet his cerulean gaze.

'What?' I asked.

'If you change your mind – if you decide one day you need to leave – you tell me. And I'll help you, okay? I'll make sure they can't find you. Dornan's my friend – my best friend. But he's also Emilio's son, and there are things he cannot control.'

I burst into tears, covering my face with my hands. I'd been *theirs* for six months by then, six months where the only visitor I got was Dornan, and the only person I spoke to every day was myself, in the mirror, talking myself out of doing something crazy like killing myself. And I loved Dornan. But I hated my life.

'You don't understand,' I said finally. 'He loves me. He *saved* me.'

John looked at me sadly, the smile fading from his face.

'You call *this* saved?'

***

Two weeks later, Dornan showed up with Guillermo. A Gypsy Brother. Dornan figured out I'd been operating the locks without him. It was only to get out onto the balcony, to smell the salt air rolling in from the waves below, a welcome refuge from my gilded cage. I had the code now, but I'd never try to run. I wasn't an idiot. I didn't dare try to leave, not even for a moment. And then I couldn't have, even if I'd wanted to, because somebody suddenly decided that I needed a full-time bodyguard. Dornan might have loved me, but he didn't trust me – he didn't trust anyone.

'It's for your own protection,' he said. 'I know you want to go outside.'

Because I had begged him to go outside. To shop for groceries, to feel the wet sand beneath my feet, to breathe in the fresh air on my balcony.

I got my wish.

I got to go outside, whenever I wanted, Guillermo Reyes always by my side or five steps behind.

It was easier, I decided soon afterwards, to be alone and locked up in a glass tower than to have someone watching my every move.

I realised much too late that things are almost never as bad as you think they are, and just when you think you've got everything figured out, everything will change again.

I wanted to go outside. I wanted to stop feeling so alone.

I got my wish.

I was never allowed to be alone again.

CHAPTER THREE

MARIANA

2007
NINE YEARS GONE

Sunday.

A sacred day. The one day a week when I was guaranteed time with Dornan.

I just had to jump through a few hoops first.

He'd been late to pick me up, which wasn't a surprise. Still, I didn't like it. I hovered inside the entry to the apartment – I still didn't feel right calling it *my* apartment, even though I'd spent almost a decade trapped between its walls – and paced nervously. My black patent stilettos clicked on the tiles as I walked back and forth, wanting to wait outside in the fresh air and open space, but knowing Dornan wouldn't be happy to find me out there. Because, according to him, I was something to be protected. Something to be hidden away.

I was about to fix another coffee when I heard boots thunking on the concrete stairwell, getting louder as he approached. It felt silly that even after all these years, he made my stomach buzz nervously just by showing up. I hadn't seen him in weeks, since he'd been away and then he was tied up with his wife and kids, but today was *ours*. At least, this afternoon was ours. Once we'd served our purposes to other people, we could serve each other.

There was a snort from the man sitting at the kitchen counter. 'Your master is here, bitch.'

I narrowed my eyes at Guillermo, my excitement fading.

He laughed, slapping his leg with a hand covered in gang tattoos. Guillermo was now a constant in my life. He was my unofficial bodyguard, babysitter and someone who watched over me when Dornan wasn't around. He lived in my apartment, ate my food, drank my good coffee and annoyed the living shit out of me every minute of the day. Don't get me wrong – he wasn't a bad person, or at least no worse than any other small-time gangster-slash-biker.

However, he was in my apartment. It was technically Dornan's, owned by some dummy corporation on paper, won in a poker game years before I'd arrived and now a convenient hideout for me. And, sadly, Guillermo. He was in my apartment, and I very much did not want him to be here, because Dornan had arrived.

'Jealous?' I asked, smiling sweetly as I slammed two coffee cups down in front of me.

Guillermo, Latino and thirty-something, was attractive in an unkempt, rugged sort of way, but he wasn't my type. One of Dornan's thugs, he was also a fully patched member of the Gypsy Brothers and a skilled drug trafficker. He knew everything about me. Almost everything. He knew as much as Dornan and Emilio. As far as I could tell, Murphy was still the only one who knew for sure the details about my son.

'Nah,' Guillermo answered. 'Just thinking should I get my earplugs before you two start fucking like dogs in here.'

I scowled. 'You could always *leave*,' I suggested helpfully. 'Don't you have something to do? Somewhere to be?'

'Yeah,' he replied stonily. 'At the clubhouse. Church is about to start, and if you make me late—'

'I hardly think they'll notice if you're there or not,' I interrupted. 'You're not the president or anything.'

He laugh-snorted, shaking his head. 'Your man ain't the prez, either, cholita.'

I looked around the apartment, as if he were talking to somebody else. 'Since when do you call me cholita? That's Emilio's thing.'

He shrugged lazily. 'Whatever. Don't make me late.'

I glared at Guillermo. He glared back, until his face broke, and he started to laugh. I tried to remain stony-faced, but something about the way Guillermo laughed was contagious. I might have wanted my own space, but his sense of humour was a lifeboat in my lonely existence. I'd never tell anyone that, though.

The front door opened, and I turned eagerly. *Dornan*. He stood in the doorway, his silhouette illuminated by the bright sun outside. He was dressed in dark blue jeans and a black T-shirt that hugged his defined chest, a black leather jacket over the top. He dropped his helmet on the ground and it landed with force on the hard floor, before rolling into the corner, forgotten. His dark eyes gleamed with anticipation.

'You're late,' I said, but I was grinning like an idiot. Guillermo dragged a cigarette out and lit it, breathing a cloud of smoke in my face.

'Guillermo,' Dornan growled in warning.

'I'll see you later,' Guillermo said to me. '*Woof*.' He sauntered past Dornan, who looked on in amusement.

As soon as the door slammed shut, Dornan turned to me. 'What was that about?'

I shrugged. 'Just Guillermo being his charming self.'

Dornan smirked, almost barrelling into me as he closed the space between us. Impulsively, I jumped and wrapped my legs around him, our mouths locked together in a dance we'd rehearsed plenty of times before. It seemed we were always being reunited after long stretches apart, even though I saw him all the time, even though he lived in Venice Beach, only a few miles from the apartment in Santa Monica. But at the strip club there were always people, always Emilio hovering, or Murphy, or John giving us disapproving glances. Plus, Dornan spent most of his days at the Gypsy Brothers clubhouse, which was only a few blocks from the strip club, but we weren't exactly the kind of couple that did lunch. No, he was usually mopping up blood or burning evidence from the sounds of it, and I was usually trying not to flip out and lose my shit if Emilio decided he was going to show up and ruin my afternoon with his wandering hands and outlandish demands.

Dornan pressed me up against the hallway wall, his mouth devouring mine.

'I missed you,' I said, something catching in my throat as I spoke.

He must have heard that waver in my voice, because he stopped kissing me, pulled back to look at me. 'Everything alright?' he asked quietly, his low voice vibrating in my chest.

I nodded. I hadn't seen him since the night we'd celebrated my twenty-eighth birthday together, in this very apartment, with a lone candle and an impossible wish murmured as I cut my cupcake in half.

He frowned, like he wanted to press me further.

'We'll be late,' I whispered, tracing the outline of his mouth with my index finger. His stubble scratched at my skin, but it was a welcome feeling, familiar.

Dornan groaned, setting me on my feet on the floor. 'Are those the shoes I bought you?' he asked, taking a step back and whistling. 'Goddamn, they look even better than I thought they would.'

I gave him a wicked smile, stepping out of the apartment in my brand new black patent heels. 'I'll wear them for you later.'

His hand closed around my wrist and he pulled me back inside, slamming the front door and shoving me against it. His fingers curled around my arms with pressure that bordered on pain, pressure that would probably leave bruises. My stilettos screeched on the tiles, and I laughed. 'We'll be late ...' I warned him again, shivering as he pressed me into the door and began to kiss a trail from my neck down to my breasts. He bit each nipple through the material of my dress, pain and pleasure merging deliciously as one, stopping only to tug my dress up around my hips and kick my legs wider with an insistent foot.

He dropped to his knees, and I watched in anticipation, pressed against the door. Dornan's stubble against the insides of my thighs was fucking torturous, brushing so close to my pussy I wanted to scream.

'Wider,' he demanded, taking hold of my right leg and hooking it over his shoulder. The moment he tugged my panties to one side and his greedy mouth descended on my clit, I yelled, 'Oh, *fuck*!'

He chuckled against my sensitive flesh, sending vibrations through me that made me shudder involuntarily.

'Your father is going to kill us,' I gasped, rocking my hips against his face.

Suddenly, the tongue disappeared. He stopped. I made a small sound of surprise in the back of my throat, opening my eyes to see what he was doing. He lifted his head long enough to glare at me. 'Don't ever mention my father when I've got my mouth on your pussy again, you hear me?'

He put his mouth on me again, and I whimpered as I heard Guillermo's motorcycle start downstairs. 'Don't stop,' I whispered, threading my fingers into Dornan's hair as his tongue did dirty, delicious things to me. My legs started to shake under the pressure of trying to hold myself upright on one stiletto while being tongue-fucked against a door. Just as I started to get close, he took his mouth away and stood upright, yanking his jeans down and palming his cock. 'I've been thinking about fucking you against this door for weeks,' he ground out, putting his hands on my bare ass and lifting me so that his cock was pressed against my wetness.

I wrapped my arms around his neck, crying out when he thrust into me in one rough stroke. 'Don't wear panties to this meeting,' he said against my neck. 'I want to feel your pussy on my back when we ride.'

Oh, I wanted that, too. I barely went on the back of a bike these days because I barely left my apartment, but when it was just Dornan and me flying down the highway, it almost felt like we were free, just the two of us. And the thought of being naked against him, rubbing against the leather of his cut while his Harley sent vibrations through the both of us – it was almost enough to make me come on the spot. He thrust into me slowly, forcefully.

'I want you to come,' he demanded, gathering my hair in one fist and pulling hard enough to force my head back. 'You're going to touch yourself. You're going to come with your mouth around my cock.' And just like that, just as he'd gotten me close again, he pulled out of me without warning.

My mouth watered at this suggestion. There was something so completely carnal about coming with your lips wrapped around a cock, your moans being muffled by someone fucking your mouth. He let go of my hair and I fell to my knees, opening my mouth and teasing the head of his cock with my tongue. I tasted myself on him. 'Make yourself come,' he groaned, bucking his hips until his cock hit the back of my throat. 'I'm about to explode.'

I reached into my lace panties and started making shallow circles around my clit. I was soaked from my own wetness and Dornan's tongue, and my finger slipped a few times before I found a rhythm. It didn't take long. Already perilously close, I crested that wave, moaning loudly around Dornan's cock as I orgasmed.

'Oh, fuck,' he whispered. 'That looks so fucking good.'

He thrust against the back of my throat one last time, coming across my tongue and down my throat as he cupped my face in his hands.

Guillermo was waiting on his bike when we finally made it downstairs, his engine purring loudly, helmet secured. He was ready to go. He took in my slightly dishevelled appearance and made a tsk-tsk noise.

'You two are like fucking animals,' he said, shaking his head in mock disapproval.

Dornan, who'd killed other men for saying less, laughed as he started his own bike. I fastened my own helmet under my chin and straddled the seat behind Dornan as delicately as I could, using my hands and the hem of my dress to shield the fact that I wasn't wearing any panties.

Dornan tore out of the parking lot and I had to hold on tight to make sure I didn't fall off the back of the bike. The man liked to go fast.

Seeing Dornan had sated me, but the closer we got to the clubhouse, the more anxious I became. It was always the same fucking shit with these people, and after nine years I was growing weary of it all. I wondered how much longer Emilio planned to keep me around.

I wondered if he'd ever decide that I'd paid my father's debt and was free to leave.

Ha. When hell froze over, I'm sure. I knew deep down that he never had any intention of letting me leave.

CHAPTER FOUR

MARIANA

Ten minutes later, we were pulling up at the Gypsy Brothers clubhouse. One of the young prospects manning the entrance waved us in, and Dornan steered his bike through the razorwire-topped gates, parking in the lot.

I climbed off the bike, smoothing my black dress down. I'd already checked my make-up in the mirror and made sure my cleavage was on display. See, I didn't want any attention, but more than that, I needed it. I needed to appear non-threatening. When I'd first started work in the cartel, processing accounts and siphoning money offshore for Emilio and his counterparts, I'd dressed plainly to avoid roving eyes. I thought it was the best course of action, to blend in, to be invisible. But I'd quickly learned that the prettier I looked, the less suspicious people were of me. It was a lesson I'd learned from my predecessor, Bella. She'd been the cartel's chief accountant before me, and she'd ended up in landfill somewhere, a bullet in her head and a swathe of stolen cash to her name. Collateral damage, Dornan had called it.

I had vowed not to meet the same fate.

She wasn't all that good at embezzling – creating fake receipts and paying ghost vendors twice. When Emilio had tasked me with investigating the shoddy paper trail Bella had left in her dim-witted wake, I'd encountered a mess the cartel should have noticed a lot earlier.

I was much smarter with the way I stole from them.

Technically, it wasn't even stealing; it was keeping my options open. Because although I loved Dornan, there was still the ever-present possibility that one day my existence would become too much of a liability and I'd be snuffed out. So I kept my own collateral in the form of offshore accounts. Nobody ever needed to know that I was a required co-signatory on most of them, not unless it came down to a situation where my life was at stake and I needed a bargaining chip. It wasn't even about the money. It was about being smart, about realising my gig with the Il Sangue Cartel and their offshoot branch, the Gypsy Brothers MC, could be terminated at any moment. Because although Dornan had shepherded me away from his father and Il Sangue, the reality was that the Gypsy Brothers weren't exactly any safer.

The Gypsy Brothers weren't even a one-percenter club.

They were worse. They were the one percent of the one percent, a toxic wasteland that chewed up and spat out everything they touched.

They'd chewed me up nine years ago, when I was taken from my family.

I was still waiting for them to spit me out: kill me, sell me, *destroy* me.

In the office, I sat in my chair, rigid, as Emilio circled around behind me. I flinched minutely as he sifted his hands through my long ponytail, tugging lightly on the ends.

His touch – his very presence – was nauseating.

Across from me, Christopher Murphy, one-time federal air marshal and now a top-ranking DEA agent, was smirking as he held my gaze with his cold blue eyes. In another person's skull that hue might have been beautiful, but in his, it was freakish. He'd barely changed in nine years – tall and built like a weed, with shaggy brown hair he'd cut a little shorter and an imposing stature. Someone, somewhere, found him attractive enough to date, because he'd backed off from all the eye-fucking he'd been giving me since we met. Not me, though. I couldn't get past the fact that he was a total fucking psychopath.

'The figures are up this week,' Emilio murmured, tracing light fingers across my shoulders and down each of my bare arms. I swallowed thickly, not daring to move, not daring to recoil from his touch. I'd done that once, back in the early days, pulled away when he reached out. That earned me two black eyes, a face full of cuts and a bruised ego, since he'd beaten me to a bloody pulp while Murphy sat and watched with a cruel smile. And then probably went home and jerked off to the image, knowing him. Sick fuck.

I never knew exactly where Il Sangue's money came from, and I kind of preferred it that way. I knew they dealt in coke and weapons, but I didn't see the particular transactions, didn't know what was what. A hundred grand here, twenty grand there. Sometimes it came in as cash. Sometimes as numbers on a statement, deposited into the bank accounts of any number of front businesses the cartel controlled. I didn't like the cash. Often it was marked with cocaine, or blood. Sometimes both. I didn't enjoy peeling apart and drying what was, quite literally, blood money. The smell always reminded me of death.

Mostly I just did my part, funnelled the majority of Emilio's funds out of the United States and into offshore accounts. Kept my mouth shut and my head down. I managed Murphy's money as well, made sure it didn't look suspicious when he was living a caviar lifestyle on a government agent's salary. Needless to say, Murphy had some very generous fictitious relatives.

I hated that part more than anything, the fact that I was enabling the two people I despised the most in the world to live lives of affluence and grandeur. I spent many an afternoon daydreaming about making their cash disappear and burning their houses down.

It was better than the alternative. Better than being dead in the ground. Most of the time.

Moments like this, I wasn't so sure.

'You're doing an excellent job, Mariana,' Emilio murmured, placing his hands on my breasts and squeezing them. It hurt, so much that my eyes watered and I had to bite down on my tongue to keep from crying out, but I didn't move. Fighting was futile. Besides, it would be over soon. It would be over, and then I could be with Dornan again. And everything would be okay until the next week, when we'd go through this all over again.

'Thank you,' I replied, my gaze matching Murphy's, my gut twisting with impatience. Hurry, I wanted to say. Just get this over with so I can wash my hands of the fucking filth you two make me feel.

'Alright,' Emilio said, taking his hands away and motioning for me to move. 'Get up. We'll keep going now.'

'See you next week, Annie,' Murphy crowed as I passed him on my way out.

The first time Murphy had called me Annie, nine years ago, he'd been trying to hold me down and rape me on my dining room floor. The only reason he hadn't succeeded was thanks to John and Dornan arriving at my apartment unexpectedly and kicking the living shit out of him. Dornan had almost killed Murphy, would have if John hadn't stopped him.

I swallowed down my disgust and eyed the sharp butcher's knife in Murphy's hand, the one I'd been silly enough to think I had a chance of using on him that day.

He flashed a wide smile and pointed to his pants. 'Well then,' he said, tipping his head to one side and fixing those weird blue eyes on me, 'I suggest you get on the floor and get naked.'

I gritted my teeth and stared as he squeezed his cock through his pants, then started to stroke it slowly, as much as the material would allow. He didn't take his eyes from mine the entire time.

He looked at me in mock despair, using his free hand to gesture down to his hard-on. 'Well, come on,' he said. 'I don't think it's going to suck itself, Annie.'

My skin crawled as I was thrown headfirst into the memory of him on top of me, his insistent hands grabbing at my thighs, his gaze pinning me along with his arms that he'd used to cage me in. *Annie.* His mouth curled up a little on one side. I knew he was thinking about the exact same thing as me, only he was clearly enjoying the memory. He wrinkled his nose up and smiled, winking.

Rage and nausea bubbled up in my stomach, but I swallowed them down. I didn't bother replying. It wouldn't make a difference, it never had.

I'd already used my daily dose of polite on Emilio, and nobody ever seemed to care if I was nice to Murphy or not. So he didn't even get my wasted breath on a snarky comeback or a meaningless goodbye.

CHAPTER FIVE

MARIANA

Sunday afternoons were like rituals. Dornan would talk business with his men – sometimes I heard shouting, sometimes laughter – and then he'd finish, find me in the rabbit warren of rooms that made up the Gypsy Brothers HQ, take me home and fuck the life out of me.

I had my own responsibilities to attend to while the Gypsy Brothers convened in the great room at the front of the clubhouse. While they spoke business and made plans, I was tasked with a meeting of my own.

With Emilio. And Murphy.

Every single Sunday.

But now that meeting was over, and I had another hundred and sixty-seven hours before I had to endure it again. Seven whole days before I had to endure Emilio's touch and Murphy's roving eyes. Today had been tame. Some weeks, the things Emilio did to me ... He'd never actually held me down and raped me, but it had gotten close a few times. Who knew if the old bastard could still even get it up? Maybe that was the only saving grace that had stopped him from raping me. Or, like he said, maybe he just preferred blondes. Who knew? I wasn't exactly dwelling on if or when he'd consummate our owner/slave relationship. Mostly, he just liked to threaten to hurt me. It was all part of his sick, twisted mind-fuckery.

I wandered down the long hallway that ran through the centre of the Gypsy Brothers clubhouse. It always made me nervous, being alone in there. Although Dornan was a formidable VP, and would no doubt kick the living shit out of anyone who dared touch me, it still didn't feel right, being in this place. It was obvious the warehouse conversion was for men, and men only – no women graced its hallways, except the club whores. And me. Walking into the place was like disappearing down a dark hole, a hole that smelled like beer and gasoline. The slivers of sunlight that did manage to get in were framed by barred windows that you'd never be able to escape through in a fire.

I made a sharp right at an intersection in the hallway, turning into the large communal kitchen and dining area. The Gypsy Brothers had many, many members, and they demanded to be fed and watered and liquored to keep them tough and at the ready. The place was deserted, a sign that the club meeting hadn't finished yet. I crossed the room briskly, my heels making sharp clicks on the polished concrete floor, threading through tables and chairs as I made my way to the fire escape. That was our place to convene, Dornan and I. Our safe haven, if only for a couple of hours.

'Hey,' a voice called out to me. I stopped in my tracks and turned slowly, looking for the source.

Caroline Portland, John's wife, sat at one of the tables that was partially hidden from view by a half-wall. I hadn't seen her when I entered the room, but I could see her now, and what a sight she was. Her hair stringy and dishevelled, she was wearing jeans and a checked shirt that swam on her emaciated figure. I hadn't seen her in months, had counted myself lucky to avoid the displeasure of crossing her path, and now here she was in all her junkie glory.

I smiled thinly at her, but didn't offer a response.

'Where the fuck you think you're going?' she slurred, leaning her head in her hands as she slumped over the table. I was about to turn and walk away when I saw her teenage daughter walk out of the kitchen, a glass of water and some graham crackers in her hands.

Juliette didn't notice me as she walked towards her mother. An image of my own father danced before my eyes as I watched the young girl try to rouse her mother from something that she was obviously in too deep to shake off.

'Mom,' she said softly, setting the water down in front of Caroline. But Caroline ignored her. She could hardly focus, her eyes were rolling around in her head so violently.

'Mom!' More forcefully this time. Caroline's eyes fluttered shut completely and she sagged forward on the table.

The girl looked around, noticed me for the first time. 'Do you know where my dad is?' she asked quietly.

Something stabbed painfully in my chest. She was only a little older than my son, and I wondered if he would be taller than her, if he had his father's dimples when he smiled.

I nodded. 'I'll get him.'

Walking towards the front of the clubhouse, I veered into the hallway and back out, a set of double doors in front of me not the only barrier to finding John. There were two club prospects eyeing me like I had an AK-47 in my hands and a belt full of ammo. Great.

'Nobody goes in until they're finished,' the older of the two said. He must've been eighteen at most, his hand on the gun at his hip.

'Get out of my way,' I said, my voice saccharine sweet, 'unless you want Dornan to shoot you in the face.'

'You a Gypsy Brother?'

I stared down the younger one, his eyes squinting at me as he tried to appear larger than me. Which he was, easily, but for some reason he hunched when he stood. I, on the other hand, did not. I stood ramrod straight, looking him directly in the eye. I was the furthest thing from a Gypsy Brother. 'Do I look like a Gypsy Brother to you, boy? *Move*.'

It worked. They both parted, looking at the ground as I opened the double doors and entered the sacred space reserved only for Gypsy Brothers.

Sixteen pairs of eyes turned towards me as I looked past Dornan's inquiring frown to John, sitting at the head of the long table, and waited to be addressed. Nobody spoke. John raised his eyebrows as if to say, *What do you want?*

'You're needed,' I said to John. 'Family business.'

Fifteen pairs of eyes averted as John stood, following me out of the room. I ignored the prospects as they closed the doors after us and resumed their spots. I'm fairly sure they were only there to keep them out of trouble. I mean, if someone really wanted to get through those doors, a couple of punk kids with revolvers tucked into their pants wasn't going to stop much.

'Is it Juliette?' John asked, matching my stride as he followed me down the hallway.

We reached the kitchen/dining area and I stopped. I didn't need to explain. It was all clear as day: his daughter, growing more frantic as she shook her mother, the puddle of vomit beside Caroline's head on the table making a nauseating *dripdripdrip* as it cut a path from the tabletop onto the ground. *Idiot*. She had a husband, a child, a career and a life, and she did this so regularly, it was no longer shocking to see her almost at death's door. Usually the kid wasn't a part of it, though. That irritated me. If I had Luis, he'd never have to do anything like that for me. I would love him and take care of him and make him happy.

The fact that Caroline Portland eschewed her freedom while I fought for every minute of mine made me want to grab her by the hair and grind her face into the vomit.

'You want me to call an ambulance?' I asked John flatly, watching the scene unfold in front of me. Some might say that I had no empathy, but if it had been anyone else dying in front of me like Caroline was right now, I would have reacted differently. The problem was I'd seen it all before, and whether she lived or died was irrelevant to me. In fact, if she died it would only make life less difficult.

It's funny how nine years in hell hardens you.

John was shaking Caroline when I felt a hand at my elbow. I whirled around, expecting to see Murphy's freakish blue eyes staring back at me, but I softened when I saw Dornan.

'What'd I miss out here?' he asked, raking a hand through his dark hair, peppered with grey. He'd let it grow just long enough to have that perpetual mussed-up look, and it definitely suited him.

'The usual.' I spoke quietly enough so that John wouldn't hear me. The poor bastard had it hard enough being married to that opiate-soaked waste of space, without hearing us pass judgement.

I don't know why I hated her so fervently. Maybe because, even then, I sensed something about John. I saw his kindness, the very thing she rejected, and I seethed with jealousy at their beautiful child. Mostly because mine existed as nothing more than a worn photograph and an image in my head that faded more each day. Sometimes I couldn't remember what he looked like without looking at the photograph, and that frightened me.

But this whore had everything I would never have, everything I had always wanted, and she chose to space out on heroin every fucking day.

Yeah, that's why I hated her.

'Time for the cold water?' I interjected. I'd had the delight of pouring water on the bitch to wake her up more than once.

John shook his head. 'I'm taking her to the hospital. Her pulse is barely there.'

I turned to Dornan to tell him to help, but he was already stepping forward, car keys in hand, as John took Caroline in his arms. He looked back at me.

'Can you …?' He jerked his head in his daughter's direction.

I nodded. 'Yeah, of course. Go. I'll take her back to my place.' I didn't much care if Caroline met her maker, but I didn't want John to suffer. We'd worked together for the better part of nine years. I spent more time with him than I did with anyone. I knew he was a good man. I knew he still carried my secret with him, and I believed he'd never divulged it, not even to Dornan, his best friend and VP. It's funny – John hadn't asked me about that crumpled baby photo he'd found in my apartment once in nine years. He'd never asked if the baby was my son. And I'd never volunteered the information. I'd already perfected a lie in case he did ask. I'd tell him, and anyone else that asked, that the baby was my brother. And if Murphy got involved and spilled the truth – that I had a son, who was now somewhere in Colombia with adoptive parents – well, I'd burn that bridge down if I ever arrived at its edge.

Dornan didn't look at me again as he left, following after John. I knew he'd be disappointed. Angry. He hated Caroline at least as much as I did, and probably more.

I thought of the prospects again, their cocky little grins and know-it-all attitude. 'Come on,' I said to Juliette. 'We'll let the new boys clean up this mess.'

Juliette looked tired. 'I should clean it up. My mom will get mad.'

I will pound your mother's face into a fucking wall if she gets mad at you for not cleaning up her vomit. That's what I wanted to say, but

I refrained. 'Nonsense,' I said, extending my hand. 'Those boys need to prove their worth.'

Almost as if on cue, bikers started to pour into the room. They all looked at me openly as they passed, but no one said a word. They wouldn't dare. I felt itchy all of a sudden, needed to leave before Emilio and Murphy came out of their own meeting and noticed I was still around. Murphy had a bad habit of trying to corner me, and I'd developed a sixth sense around his impending approach.

Several of the bikers greeted Juliette. Most of them had known the girl all her life, saw her as one of their own. But she was coming up to fifteen, and she was a beautiful girl. I'd seen girls who looked younger than her around this clubhouse. I wasn't stupid. I closed the space between the girl and myself. 'Come on,' I said to her, putting a hand on her shoulder.

Two young Gypsy Brothers appeared in front of me, blocking our path to the door. I looked between the young men with thinly veiled disgust. Dornan's two oldest sons, Chad and Donny, seemed to find Juliette the way ... well, the way Murphy seemed to find me.

'Move,' I said. Saying 'excuse me' didn't do any good in a place like this.

Chad, the older and burlier asshole of the two, folded his arms across his chest and leered at me.

'What's the hurry?' he said, reaching out and dusting imaginary lint from my shoulder. Chad's eyes slid down to my chest. And stayed there. He licked his lips, making a suggestive sound in the back of his throat.

'The accountant,' he said, chuckling. I noticed Donny, the younger, weedier brother, edging closer to Juliette. 'Seems like we need to get you to more parties, sweetheart.'

Parties were when they all got their dicks wet with whoever they pleased. Probably in this very room. I wrinkled my nose up in distaste.

'What are you, twenty? I think I'm a little old for you, kiddo,' I said, taking Juliette's arm firmly in my grip as I spotted Murphy enter the room to my left.

Fuck. I was surrounded by idiots. Horny, moronic idiots.

At least I knew I could handle Murphy. I pulled Juliette in the opposite direction, making a beeline for the DEA agent who I despised with a passion. I didn't even look back at Chad and Donny as we made our way out of the room and into the hallway.

'Need a ride?' Murphy asked, falling into step beside me so I was flanked on one side by him, and Juliette on the other. The girl didn't speak, and I had to wonder if she was doing okay. Something struck me as odd. How did they get here? I looked down at Juliette's balled fist to see a set of keys peeking out from her grip.

'Did your mom drive here?' I asked her, knowing I wasn't going to like the answer.

'No,' Juliette said. She didn't elaborate, and I didn't press her. I already knew. She was fourteen, and *she drove her fucking mother here*, through busy LA traffic, because Caroline had taken too much heroin. Again.

I stopped short in the hallway, deciding I didn't need Murphy to drive us, after all. Sweet baby Jesus, that was a relief. The price of a favour from that motherfucker was always way too high.

I wondered, briefly, where Guillermo had gotten to. He'd probably hightailed it to the strip club to get a piece of ass on his one afternoon off, since Dornan and I usually spent Sunday afternoons alone at the apartment.

'Emilio was looking for you,' I addressed Murphy, a blatant lie. 'We'll wait out front.'

Murphy stopped beside me, his mouth curled up into an unimpressed smirk.

'Liar,' he murmured, his eyes flicking from me to Juliette, and then back again.

I smiled sweetly. 'Wouldn't want to be wrong, and keep him waiting, would you?'

Murphy muttered a stream of expletives as he left us, and I started walking briskly towards the front doors of the compound-esque building, Juliette right beside me.

'Which car?' I asked her, once we were past the guys on the door. She pointed to a silver Caprice that had seen better days. I held out my hand for the keys. 'Come on,' I said, aiming for upbeat and probably failing miserably. 'Let's blow this joint.'

Juliette smiled at me, dropping the keys into my hand.

CHAPTER SIX

MARIANA

John and Dornan arrived at my apartment a couple of hours later. Both had bloodshot eyes, which I suspected were for very different reasons. As soon as John walked in, his daughter ran to him, her blonde hair streaming behind her as she rushed to the front door and hugged her father tightly.

I retreated into the kitchen, still in earshot, but I busied myself making coffee. I didn't want to interrupt their moment. Juliette had sat on my couch for the past two hours, mute, resisting all of my attempts to coax something out of her until I gave up and let her be.

I heard steps approaching and poured steamed milk into two espresso-filled cups, setting the jug down and turning when I felt a hand on my elbow. I was expecting Dornan. My smile was a secret just for him, but as I turned, I saw John instead.

My smile dropped. All of a sudden I didn't know what to say. So I went for the first thing off the top of my head.

'Is Caroline okay?' I asked.

John threw me a sceptical look. 'Do you care?'

Nope, not at all. 'Of course I care. I care for you. I care for your daughter. She's spoken five words to me in two hours, John.' I almost added in the part about her driving the car to the clubhouse, but I bit my tongue. The last thing I wanted to do was get the girl in trouble.

He looked over his shoulder. I shifted slightly to the right so I could see the front door. Dornan was talking in hushed tones to Juliette, and she was smiling.

I don't know what it was about seeing them like that, but something stabbed painfully inside my chest. He was a good man, underneath all the bravado and the leather. He had made Juliette smile in moments, whereas I couldn't even elicit a single one from her in two hours, not since she'd handed me the car keys back at the clubhouse. But with Dornan she beamed. Under that gruff exterior, he had the capacity to put you at ease ... but only if he wanted to. It was clear he loved Juliette, and I remembered him telling me stories about how he'd been there when she was born, how he'd brought her home from the hospital afterwards and he and his wife had looked after her as their own, since John was in prison and Caroline went MIA soon after the cord had been cut.

'You know she drove the car to the clubhouse,' I said quietly, changing my mind. He needed to know this shit. I wished he'd just leave his wife, or that she'd finally get it right and take enough heroin to die and release him from their hellish marriage. Yeah. I wasn't a very nice person, wishing people dead, but she didn't give me any reason to wish differently.

John turned back to me, his mouth set in a hard line. He raked his hand through his hair, staring at the floor.

'Caroline ...' John shook his head, meeting my gaze again with his magnetic blue eyes. Intense, like Murphy's, but nothing alike. John's were clear and bright, and trusting. Compassionate. Kind. They were like windows to his soul, turned down ever so slightly at the edges, the stress making them look older than his forty-odd years.

I liked his eyes. They reassured me.

'Caroline used to be well,' John continued. 'She was never like this.'

You've been saying that for nine years, I wanted to say to him. But instead I said nothing.

'Where is she?' I asked.

John's face twisted into a grimace. 'Rehab.'

I knew the mounting costs of his wife's continual cycle – overdose, emergency room, rehab centre – were killing John. I did his finances. I knew he was fighting to keep his house and pay the bills. It always struck me as odd that he had no money, because he was always in possession of so much of the stuff. But he was stone broke.

I nodded, chewing on my lower lip. 'You think it'll stick this time?'

He didn't answer. He didn't need to. His expression told me everything.

'Thanks for watching Julz,' he said, patting me on the arm. It was meant as a casual gesture, but it almost made me jump it was so unexpected. A thrill coursed down my spine as I turned around and collected the cups of coffee, offering John one.

'Do I smell coffee?' Dornan asked, interrupting our ... I don't even know what it was. It wasn't small talk. It wasn't awkward, exactly, but it was something. John was always asking me questions, innocuous enough – things like *how was your weekend* and *did you get out to see the fireworks at the pier* and *are you going home for the holidays?* I managed to answer vaguely enough, but I knew there would come a day when he got sick of those non-answers and would demand to know the entire truth about me. It was written all over his face every time I was with Dornan. John knew that Dornan and I had a relationship, but he liked to pretend we didn't. Despite his terrible choice of life partner, John Portland still, at least then, believed in the sanctity of marriage, and strongly disapproved of Dornan having both a wife and a mistress. I'd heard them arguing about me once. John had been demanding to know why I wasn't allowed out of the apartment, and that was when Dornan had installed Guillermo as my housemate. Nobody outside of Emilio and Murphy knew the full truth about me, about *us*, even after all this time. But I knew John wanted to know about me, in the way he phrased his questions, always seeking more information. Where did I come from? Why was I still under lock and key and 24-hour guard after almost a decade? I saw the question in his eyes, the bewilderment, and the resentment that, even as president of the Gypsy Brothers, he was powerless to extract the information he so clearly craved from anyone.

'Coffee,' I said, handing Dornan the second cup after he drained his whiskey and set the empty tumbler on the counter. John, who hadn't touched his own cup of coffee, handed it back to me.

'I should take Juliette home,' he said, looking between Dornan and me. 'It's been a long one.'

Dornan nodded in response, not moving from his spot, leaning against the counter and tipping coffee down his throat. He finished the cup in one go and dropped it in the sink.

I opened my mouth to say something, to offer some kind of help or reassurance, but then I closed it again. What was I going to say that could ease the pain of a man with a burden like Caroline Portland?

After they'd left, and the door was securely shut, I shifted my attention to Dornan. 'Somebody should just put her out of her misery,' I said.

Nine years in this life and I was starting to talk like him.

'You're saying what I'm thinking,' Dornan said, passing me as he opened the freezer and dropped a handful of ice cubes into the tumbler he was holding. The coffee had been merely a formality, something to keep us awake after a trying day.

I took the opportunity to drink him in: dark jeans, tight black T-shirt that hugged his hard chest in all the right places, his tattoos peeking out from the sleeves and neckline. The Ross family crest on his neck always bothered me for some reason, maybe because it was inked proof that he belonged to Emilio. The revolver down his left forearm was better. And the Gypsy Brothers tattoo that adorned his back curled up enough in the middle that it edged up above his collar. Dark hair that he'd let grow a little longer recently, peppered with grey, like his permanent three-day stubble.

I'd been waiting for him. I had missed him terribly.

I *hungered* for his touch.

But with everything that had happened with Caroline, what I really needed right now was a stiff drink. I sipped at John's untouched cup, always loath to let good coffee go to waste, and watched Dornan pour whiskey over the ice cubes and take several gulps.

'That bad, huh?' I asked.

'That woman is a fucking train wreck,' he mused, cracking ice cubes between his teeth. He wiped his mouth with the back of his hand, setting his whiskey down and stepping over to me. A small smile tugged at the corner of his mouth as he stood over me, his hips pressing me into the counter as his dark eyes gleamed. The edge of the counter bit painfully into my back, but it didn't matter. I was wholly focused on *him*.

'You have no idea,' he said, threading a hand into my hair and pulling me into him. His stubble was rough but his lips soft, sweet and tangy with the remnants of the whiskey. As his tongue found mine, I melted into his grip, relishing the cold of his mouth from the ice cubes.

'I missed you,' Dornan murmured against my lips. My stomach flipped nervously, anticipation building within me. I wanted him. I needed him.

His kisses grew deeper, more urgent, and I felt the unmistakable line of his rock-hard erection pressing at my waist. I reached down and squeezed his hard length through his jeans, smiling when he knocked my hand away.

'There's plenty of time for that,' he said, taking my wrists and pulling them behind my back. I shivered as his mouth, rapidly losing the coolness of the ice cubes, kissed a rough, wet trail down my neck.

'I missed you so much,' I whispered, tensing as I felt his hands curl around my ass and lift me up. I wrapped my arms around his neck, kissing him long and hard as he carried me through the kitchen and deposited me on the end of the dining table, all without breaking our kiss.

But then he did break it. He pulled away and looked at me, really looked at me, one of those moments when you feel like your soul is laid bare. When you wonder what somebody sees in you. Do they see the lies you've told? The people you've left behind? Or do they just see what they want to see?

He pressed a palm against my chest, pushing me down until I ended up on my back, staring up at the ceiling, my legs bent at the knee and my feet – still clad in the black patent stilettos –braced against the edge of the table. I watched as he went back over to the counter and leaned over, collecting his whiskey and taking a sip.

He didn't speak; neither of us did. I watched him with great interest and barely controlled lust, my chest rising and falling quickly in anticipation. I wanted him. Now.

But he loved to make me wait.

He placed the whiskey between my feet, the ice making a clinking noise as it shifted in the glass. My dress was long, past the knee, and tight. It didn't seem to hinder Dornan's hands, though; he hooked a thumb underneath each side of the skirt and pushed it up, over my knees and up my thighs, until it was bunched around my waist. Just like he'd done several hours ago, but with more patience this time, more control. He took hold of my knees and pulled them apart, the sudden movement making me breathe in sharply.

Touch me. Just touch me. It's been too long. I could already feel wetness building at my core.

I still wasn't wearing panties. Dornan made a small sound of appreciation in his throat as he trailed a hand up my inner thigh and over my bare pussy. He smiled as his fingers slid along my wetness.

'You've been waiting for me,' he murmured, his voice low and gravelly. I nodded, bracing my palms against my thighs.

He leaned in, his head between my legs, so close to me that I could feel his breath on my pussy. It drove me wild, that waiting, that feeling, hoping he was about to dart his tongue out and lick my willing flesh. He stayed there for a moment, just breathing, his fingers digging into the backs of my thighs. *Please do it, just hurry up and do it—*

His tongue found my clit. *Holy mother of God.* It felt good. I arched my hips towards his mouth, greedy for more. I groaned when he took his mouth away and stood straight, picking the whiskey up again and taking another sip.

'What do you want me to do?' he asked, an ice cube still in his mouth, a mischievous glint in his dark eyes.

I looked at the ceiling. I couldn't look him in the eye when he asked me what I wanted him to do.

'You know,' I replied.

In my peripheral vision, I saw him shake his head, a smirk spreading across his face. 'Words. I want words.' He rounded the table so he was at my side, crouching so we were eye to eye.

He leaned in, kissing me deeply. His mouth was cold from the ice cube, refreshing. He tasted so fucking good. His free hand went down to my clit and drew slow, shallow circles that made me moan into his mouth.

He broke the kiss, smiling as he took a chair and placed it at the end of the table. He sat down and dragged it closer, so that he now had unrestricted access to me.

Hands gripped my ass cheeks and pulled me down so I was hovering half-off the table. I heard the clink of ice cubes again and braced myself for the cold.

'Say it,' he ordered.

'Fuck,' I muttered. 'I want your mouth on me. I want you to lick me.'

He raised his head, his smile contagious. 'Lick you where?'

'My pussy,' I begged. 'Please.'

We might have done this only hours earlier, but it had happened so quickly, it was almost as if it hadn't happened at all. And let's face it, I was addicted to this man – too much was never enough.

His head disappeared again. I moaned as Dornan's cold tongue touched against my sensitive nub, pressing the ice against me. I bucked involuntarily, trying to close my legs. The cold was overwhelming. It was too much.

'Don't move,' Dornan hissed, before returning his tongue to my clit. It was slightly warmer now. Sighing, I rested back on my elbows and prayed like hell that he'd finish what he was starting.

More ice. More protesting. The heat and the freezing cold stirred within me, Dornan's hands gripping my ankles like twin vices, the unspoken message perfectly clear: Don't. Move.

'Holy ... Jesus!' I cried, as he dragged an ice cube against my opening. It was freezing cold. It stung, but in a good way.

Then he pushed it inside me, along with a finger.

It burned. The cold cube slowly melted within me, ice turning to water, Dornan's tongue collecting the excess as he licked me. It felt so fucking good, it was almost unbearable. He repeated the action with another ice cube, his fingers sliding down from my pussy to the pucker of my ass.

'You want it here?' he asked, his voice humming against my soaking pussy as he took his thumb and circled the small opening. A thrill shot through me as his finger gently probed at my ass.

Oh God, did I want it there.

'Yes,' I whispered, delighting in the glazed sensation that draped over me, the total submission, the anticipation of what was to come. I tried to relax as he pushed his thumb into my ass, stretching me, opening me up, but I tensed anyway. It was a natural reaction to being entered there.

'Relax,' Dornan growled, pumping slowly as he placed his mouth back over my swollen clit and sucked. Discomfort became pleasure as I got used to his thumb sliding in and out of my ass, and my nerves started to fray.

Under his skilled hands, my ass began to burn.

It was fire and passion and fucking all bound into one ticking time bomb. I didn't want him to stop, didn't want him to leave my ass or my pussy as my legs began to shake and I bucked into his tongue faster.

I thought to reach out and grab his head between my hands, to make sure he finished what he'd started, but he anticipated my move. Before I could thread my hands into his hair and pull him closer into me, he took his finger out, took his mouth away, and stood so fast, the chair behind him flew backwards, crashing onto the tiles.

'Don't stop,' I moaned.

He grabbed my hips roughly, his pants already unbuttoned and his cock standing proudly to attention, the smooth head glistening with pre-come.

'Turn over,' he growled, picking me up and doing the work himself. My hands and knees smacked against the table as I pressed my ass backwards into him, looking back and watching as he pumped his rock-hard cock in his palm.

Ice cubes clinked again, and I gasped as I felt the cold breach my pussy again. A finger pushed one ice cube inside me, then another, until it was all I could do not to scream.

My skin broke out in goosebumps as my teeth began to chatter; it felt like I was simultaneously being frozen and set on fire from within.

I felt the head of his dick trail up and down my pussy, pushing gently, but not enough to gain purchase. I whimpered, pressing back into him, as my hand went to my clit and started circling it. I gasped when he fisted a handful of my hair and pulled.

'You want to come?' he asked, tugging on my hair so he could speak into my ear.

'Yes,' I cried, dropping my hand back onto the table to balance myself.

'The only way you're coming,' he growled, pressing his cock against me, 'is with my dick in your ass.'

Holy fucking Christ, those words were the biggest turn on.

'Do you want me to fuck your ass?' he asked, continuing to press against it.

'Yes,' I moaned, pushing back into him. 'Please.'

I braced myself as Dornan released my hair, his hand going to my hip as he coated the head of his dick with my slickness. Then, wet and swollen, he pushed against my tight hole. It burned a little, but it felt so fucking good.

'Relax,' he urged, one hand coming around to rub my clit. I did, letting myself melt back into him, my ass wanting to resist the breach. I concentrated on stilling that urge to tense, and his dick pushed into my ass.

I moaned loudly, swearing under my breath as he pulled back and sank into me, over and over again. His fingers on my clit, together with his dick in my ass coupled together to form an orgasm that ripped through me like fire and ice.

I screamed. *Dornan.* I'm pretty sure I screamed his name over and over again, even as he continued to fuck me. As I came back down to earth, the aftershocks of my climax made every touch agonising. He didn't stop, though, driving into me relentlessly. I felt his body tense up as he grew even harder, and then he was coming inside me, his chest curled over me as he sank his teeth into the tender flesh of my back.

'Missed you too,' he murmured against my skin, the indents where his teeth had pierced my flesh humming with a pleasant pain.

CHAPTER SEVEN

MARIANA

Afterwards, we showered, holding each other as warm water washed us clean. We didn't speak.

We didn't need to.

He was here. That was all that mattered. And I intended to drink in every single moment of our time together.

When I had dried off and dressed, I poured myself a glass of red wine and headed out to the balcony, wearing one of Dornan's shirts. It was like a dress on me, but I liked the way it wrapped me up in him, even when he wasn't with me. It was late afternoon, and the sun was just reaching that low point in the sky where it shone directly into the apartment. I closed my eyes, basking in the golden rays, warm against my face as I listened to the waves crash onto the shore below.

I sensed him behind me before I saw him. I turned my head and opened my eyes to see him standing there in a pair of jeans, no shirt. Even in his forties, and despite the fact that I'd seen him like this countless times over the years, the man was still fucking irresistible.

He reached a hand behind my ear and then opened his palm in front of my face, a mischievous grin plastered on his face as he held out a coin. 'Penny for your thoughts?' he joked.

I laughed, taking the quarter. 'I was just thinking.'

He stood beside me and I turned back to the ocean, the breeze whipping my hair around my face.

'Thinking happy thoughts?'

'You make me happy,' I said plainly, taking one of his hands between mine and playing with his fingers. They were warm and rough, a working man's hands.

Dornan glanced sideways at me, the breeze picking up his hair and making it dance. 'Are you? Happy?'

I swallowed thickly as he took his hand away, feeling the smile die on my face as I looked out to the water. I wasn't happy and I was. Stolen moments, away from everyone else and their demands. In those, I was happy. Outside of that? The nothingness was a yawning chasm. It hurt. It *ached*.

'I'm happy when I'm with you,' I said finally. I reached out again and took his large hand in mine, squeezing it tightly.

'You did good with the kid,' he said, pulling me under his arm.

It felt safe, here. I felt loved.

'That girl needs a mother, not that fucking thing that pretends to be one,' Dornan added.

I shrugged. 'I didn't do much,' I said softly, enjoying the sting of the salt breeze on my bare arms. 'She wouldn't even talk to me. I don't think children like me, somehow.'

'You'd be a good mother,' Dornan said seriously, drawing me closer.

And I didn't mean to, but I froze. I felt my mouth open a little as I screamed inwardly. The mask slipped, just for a second. And in that moment, the man I loved? I hated him.

'What?' Dornan asked, turning me so we were facing each other, the ocean ebbing and flowing below us, just like it had done for countless years, just like it would keep doing long after we were both bones and ash. In that moment, I felt so inconsequential, so unnecessary, so *deprived*. Because I was somebody's mother. And it wasn't fucking fair.

It wasn't Dornan's fault. He didn't know. And I would never tell him, not unless Emilio was dead and buried and we were free. The problem was I didn't even know if Dornan wanted to be free. There were some things we wouldn't talk about, and his father was one of those things.

'Nothing,' I replied, feeling my chest tighten.

You'd be a good mother. He didn't know the significance of those words, how deep they cut into me, leaving bloodied ribbons of my soul in their wake.

I had been somebody's mother, once upon a time. And now, I was nothing. A piece of property. A mistress. A money launderer. A whore.

'Hey,' he said, taking my chin between his thumb and forefinger and turning my gaze towards his.

I saw the haunted look in his eyes, like a deer in headlights, about to be slammed. 'Don't worry about me,' I said softly, gripping his wrist tightly. 'You worry about your kids, okay? I'll be fine. I'll be right here.'

It wasn't fair of me to ask anything more of him than I already had. He'd already saved my life, kept me alive, kept me safe. All this time.

And he'd saved me from myself on the darkest nights, without even realising it.

'I'll leave her,' Dornan blurted out. 'When they're grown up. When she can't control them. I'll leave her.'

I stiffened. He'd never said anything remotely like that before. I was his mistress, and nothing more. I knew he loved me. It wasn't ideal, but it was all he'd ever had to give me, and I had taken it gratefully. Every time I thought of the alternative, I remembered that, even though I felt trapped and smothered, it could always be worse. So. Much. Worse. Emilio could have sold me at that auction nine years ago. And, as Murphy had so chillingly assured me, nobody made it out of that shit alive. If I'd been bought, and used, and raped, I'd be dead by now.

'You don't have to say that,' I protested, breaking eye contact. 'You don't have to make promises to me, Dornan. I don't expect them.'

I thought more about that, turning his words over in my mind. *When she can't control them.* An admission of vulnerability from a man like Dornan Ross was a shattering revelation. Was he meaning to say that there was someone even more powerful than the all-powerful Gypsy Brothers and Il Sangue Cartel royalty?

I fingered the collar on his shirt. 'Did you love Celia? When you got married?'

Dornan tensed.

'Sorry,' I said quickly. 'You don't have to answer that.'

'It was a business decision,' Dornan said, his tone suddenly clipped. I was losing him. I could feel him shutting down right in front of me.

'I spoke to Anthony the other day,' I said, swiftly changing the subject. Although I despised Dornan's oldest son, Chad, with a passion reserved for people like Emilio, there was something about Anthony, or 'Ant' as everyone called him. I saw his father in him. A tough exterior, but an instinct to protect instead of exploit. Whereas Chad, on the other hand, was just a younger American version of his grandfather, Emilio.

'Yeah?' Dornan's pride was evident.

'He's a good kid.' I tried to think of something to say about the rest of them and drew a blank.

'He's smart.' He smiled proudly, then the smile faded slightly.

'What?' I asked.

Dornan shrugged, tucking loose hair behind my ear and giving it a soft, almost playful tug. 'I wonder what these boys would be like if they had a choice.'

'Everyone has a choice,' I said.

Dornan raised his eyebrows. 'Like you had a choice?'

'I had a choice,' I said boldly. 'I chose you. And you chose me.'

His smile looked pained. 'I'd spend every moment with you if I could, you know that?'

I nodded, smiling sadly. I knew that more than I knew anything. It was a truth that burned inside me, kept me going when the demons in my mind tried to convince me otherwise.

'Do you ever think about the future?' I asked softly.

'Sometimes,' Dornan replied. Any trace of lightness was gone now, replaced by the weary reality of our collective fates.

'And?' I pressed.

He let his hand drop from my face and turned back to the sun, squinting as it slid lower against the orange and blue horizon.

'And it doesn't do any good,' he said gruffly. 'So I think about something else, instead.'

'Oh,' I said softly. I thought about what he'd said about leaving Celia, about how remote that possibility even was. How could I marry him, anyway? Legally, as far as anyone was concerned, I was a dead woman. Dead women couldn't get married.

I didn't want to be a member of the Ross family. I might have loved the son, but I hated the father. No, even if it was ever a possibility, I'd never marry into Emilio's family.

'I have to go,' Dornan said abruptly, wrapping a hand around the back of my neck and pulling me to him. He kissed me on the forehead, his lips lingering for a long time before he pulled away. I didn't move, not wanting him to break away and return me to this unbearable loneliness.

'Don't go,' I murmured against his chest. 'You just got here.'

We played this game far too often, these days.

He kissed the top of my head again, his soft lips leaving a small damp mark against my skin, and then he left. I stared into my empty wine glass, tears forming in my eyes, jolting a little when the front door slammed.

Alone again.

A tear found its way out, dropping into the glass, followed by another, and then another. My chest constricted painfully as my weeping turned to all-out sobs, my eyes blurring as salt water overcame them.

I was happy in brief moments of time, but I was sad the rest of the time.

I lifted my head, blinked away tears. Saw children on the beach across from where I stood, their happy shrieks like blunt knives being driven into my heart. I saw the Ferris wheel on the jetty come to a stop, collect new passengers, and then start turning again. I heard the front door open and Guillermo's sneakers squeaking on the tiles.

You'd be a good mother.

I wondered if my son liked Ferris wheels.

I wondered if he knew that I existed.

I felt someone behind me, but I didn't turn. I didn't want Guillermo to see my tears.

'She die?' he asked, crossing his arms and leaning on the railing beside me.

I shook my head. 'Nope. Still kicking.'

Before he could do any more talking, I turned and pushed past him, walked down the hall and closed the door, shutting myself in my room. I sat on the edge of my bed, pulling Dornan's shirt around me. I was pathetic. I was in love with a man who could never be mine, and I hated myself for that.

***

Later, in the bath, I took a disposable razor and snapped the plastic with my fingers, releasing the sharp blade within. I kept the hot water running and the plug a little loose to make sure the tub was continually refilled with hot water. I laid out underneath a blanket of fluffy bath bubbles until they shifted under the pressure of the running water, revealing the body I worked so hard to keep fit.

Going to the gym was one of the few freedoms I had – not that it was really a freedom with Guillermo in tow, but it was something to break the monotony. Something to focus on as I ran miles and miles on the treadmill, longing for fresh air on my face. They had these fans you could point at your face as you ran, but the air smelled of sweat and socks, not salt and water.

There was a soft knock at the bathroom door, and Guillermo poked his head in.

'You want a drink, girlie?' He made a tipping gesture against his mouth and I allowed a small smile.

'Sure,' I said, placing the razor on the cold tiles that edged the deep tub. I wasn't worried about Guillermo seeing me naked – there were now enough bubbles covering me that the only things visible were my head and the tops of my knees as they stuck out of the water. And I wasn't worried about him trying anything. Over the years, Guillermo had become one of the few people that I could trust to some degree. He'd shared parts of his life with me, stories from his past, and he'd become a constant in my daily life. And, as much as I hated to admit it, I actually felt safer with him around. There were no more random visits from Murphy like there had been in the beginning of my captivity, no worries about coming and going as I pleased. I got my fresh air, and Guillermo was the price I paid.

Guillermo was a murderer. He'd gone to jail for blowing up his house while his wife slept inside with the guy she was cheating on Guillermo with. The cartel had gotten him a light sentence in a plea deal, since Guillermo was one of the power-players with Mexican connections. Even with those connections, he was still in the minor leagues compared to Dornan and John, which was probably why he'd been assigned to me. We had an odd relationship, almost like brother and sister. He reminded me of my own brother in a way, minus the homicidal tendencies, and I wasn't afraid of him trying anything on me.

Guillermo left, returning with two tumblers of what looked like vodka on the rocks. He handed me the one with a slice of lime and took his over to the vanity, leaning against the countertop as he looked at me questioningly.

He nodded his head towards the naked razor on the edge of the tub. 'If you die, I'll kill you,' he said jokingly.

I shrugged, a wry smile touching my lips. 'I'd never die,' I replied, lifting my foot out of the water and watching rivulets of water stream down, back into the tub. 'Who'd make your coffee in the morning?'

He groaned.

'What?' I asked. He was distracting me from the urge to stick my head underwater and drown myself.

'It's just like when I was married,' he said, shaking his head. 'Pretty little wife fucking somebody else in my house, and I have to visit the clubhouse to get any.'

I grinned, staring up at the ceiling. 'This isn't your house. But sounds like a marriage, alright.' I sobered, my grin slipping as I remembered Dornan telling me what Guillermo had done to his cheating wife. Forensics hadn't been able to separate her tissue and bones from that of her lover's without DNA testing every last little piece. I reminded myself to never get on his bad side.

'Don't blow me up, okay?' I drained my vodka and set the glass on the lip of the bath, chewing ice loudly. 'I know exactly how much half and half to put in your coffee. Those bitches at Starbucks have nothing on me.'

He chuckled. 'You're dangerous,' he said in Spanish, closing the door and leaving me alone.

My smile vanished the moment he closed the door. I sat up, my nipples hardening against the cool night air. I drew my knees up out of the water and took hold of the razor blade with one hand, stroking my skin with the other. I hadn't changed. As I pressed the tip of the sharp blade into the wet flesh of my thigh and watched blood rise to the surface, the dull sting that reminded me I was alive brought a smile to my lips once more.

Sometimes the loneliness was too much. Sometimes it broke my soul. When you're all alone for weeks at a stretch, the only touch the one of your enemy and owner, it becomes a daily struggle not to sink into the darkness and be swallowed, whole.

Guillermo was in the apartment, but he hardly qualified as a person I could bare my soul to. I had nobody in the quiet hours of the night. Every secret I shared was a potential weapon that could be turned against me, and I already had enough of those floating around without exposing more.

But I had a sharp razor blade, and a penchant for spilling my own blood, and so I whiled the hours away carving marks into my own skin. The cuts weren't all that noticeable – tiny, deep gouges into the flesh above my knees.

Back when I'd first been taken by Emilio and his men, I had been a cutter. I'd favoured my wrists then, the way I could draw a knife or a piece of glass against my bare flesh and see my blood spring up, something to make me feel. One of the first things Dornan had done for me was tend to my wounds after I'd gouged my wrists, stuck in a windowless room in Emilio's compound and going crazy with claustrophobia and grief.

My nasty little habit had served me well over the years. Kept the demons at bay, the ones that told me to *just call my mother* or *track down Luis in Colombia* or throw myself off the goddamn Sixth Street Bridge.

Because I couldn't do any of those things, not really. If I tried to contact my family, they'd be killed, me along with them. If I tried to track down my son, what good would it do? It would be good for me, to hear his voice, to see his face. But for him? It'd be confusing, dangerous, and we'd both end up in the same predicament. Dead.

The first two options – contacting my family, or committing suicide – weren't all that appealing. The third option, the cutting, was harder to stave off. More difficult to avoid contemplating, because it was the thing that got me through. I loved Dornan, I did. The work I did wasn't particularly hard. I got to spend most of my day listening to music as I did the accounts for Emilio. I even took a sick pleasure in seeing how much money I could launder each day. And I was good at what I did. Despite the fact that I was doing it under duress, I was actually proud of how well I did what I did.

But none of it was real, see? It was all an illusion. I wasn't the accountant. I could lull myself into believing that truth six days out of the week, only to have it cruelly snatched from me under the weight of Emilio's moist palms on my neck, his reptilian eyes. The way he squeezed my nipples so hard it felt like he was going to rip them off, the constant reminder that I was a piece of property that only he controlled. The ever-present threat of Murphy, lurking in the background, licking his lips as he watched me get humiliated.

So I compensated. I cut into my flesh regularly, and it made me feel better. The sight of my own blood made me remember that, despite the world believing I was dead, I was actually very much alive.

CHAPTER EIGHT
DORNAN

They say drowning is a peaceful way to die, but Dornan Ross wasn't so sure about that. He'd been drowning in blood and lies his entire life, since the moment he'd been wrenched from his mother's womb, thrashing and howling in protest.

He'd even been conceived by force, he learned one night when his mother had drank too much and started yelling at his father. She was crying. Her words were stilted, but the meaning was clear: Dornan Ross hadn't been created out of any semblance of love, but out of his father's vicious need for power and dominance over his mother.

He was twelve when he heard that conversation, and nothing had ever been the same for him since. It wasn't sadness for his mother – she'd chosen this life, and she'd married the motherfucker. It wasn't anger at his father – Dornan was too terrified of the man to feel any particular rage towards him.

No, it was the dragging feeling in his gut, the voice inside his head that said *you should never have been born*.

The age of the internet had changed the flesh trade forever – human trafficking operated under Il Sangue's stronghold. They sold anything you desired – women, body parts, children, even newborn babies. There was a demand for everything in this world, and Dornan's father, Emilio Ross, intended to fulfil those needs and make himself a very, very rich man at the same time.

He rarely bothered himself with the details, leaving that delightful job to his son.

And today was fulfilment day.

Dornan walked through the massive warehouse his father owned in San Pedro, on the Port of Los Angeles. Today it was full of packages and deliveries, stacked high to the roof with pallets. They delivered anything and everything. Wine. Furniture. Appliances.

Kidneys. Whores. Newborn babies.

There was a buyer for everything, and the beauty of the internet age meant the cartel could hold auctions every week with prospective bidders attending via their computer screens. Since they'd harnessed the worldwide web for their devious exploits, business had boomed. It meant they seldom had to dress the girls up and auction them live anymore – they just dolled them up in their holding cells, drugged the bitches up, spread their legs wide and took a couple of photos and videos for prospective buyers. Money changed hands seamlessly, was tucked away into offshore accounts, and one of the only people who had to deal with the human face of the entire thing was Dornan himself.

He dreamed about killing his father. About taking a knife and slaughtering him. Emilio had given him life, but he had damned him in the same instance. But Dornan never did it. Too many people relied on his complicity for him to do anything so brash. His sons. His wife. *Mariana* ...

Monday morning. It was the day he always dreaded the most. Sundays were the best, because he got to see Mariana without fail, and fuck the hell out of her. He got to forget for a few precious hours what came the next morning, what horrors would await him. Only last night, they'd barely seen each other at all, and now he was here, and she was not.

He finally reached the back of the warehouse. There was a large machine – an automatic envelope sorter and stamper. It was perpetually broken, and for good reason.

It never got used.

It was a door.

A door down to hell.

Dornan looked around the warehouse, ensuring nobody saw him, then stepped behind the large machine. There were minimal staff working the cover business on a Monday, for this exact reason. They had no fucking idea what happened downstairs in the lead-lined basement.

No idea that their tasks were pointless, their efforts futile, their delivery business barely profitable. Designed, in fact, to run at a loss. They existed purely to deflect attention from everything else. The real business.

The flesh trade downstairs.

Dornan swallowed back bile as he made his way down the three flights of stairs, past the sub-floor and into the depths of a fucking nightmare. The place was a huge, cavernous limestone and concrete bunker dug deep into the earth. It was located close enough to the docks to be convenient for shipping their wares, yet far enough away to avoid undue suspicion.

They weren't exactly FedEx.

There were several large trucks already backed into the massive expanse, an industrial lift bridge responsible for dropping them below the earth and into the real warehouse, where the action was. Dornan took his clipboard from the place it always sat, at the beginning of the rows upon rows of containers, and began his grim routine. The list had forty-three today. A busy day, but not the busiest by any means.

Number one. The code that took up the first line was deceptively simple. It told him, in a matter of letters and numbers, that inside the first container made of plastic and steel and no larger than a single shower cubicle was a cooler, and inside that cooler was a pair of human kidneys on ice. Bad, but at least kidneys didn't have eyes. Dornan reached up and slid a panel of plastic aside to reveal a small viewing pane. The blue cooler sat innocently on the floor. Container number one got a check mark next to it, and the viewing pane was covered again.

Line numbers two and three weren't surprising. Females, bound for new owners who would keep them locked up for their own pleasure. Sometimes they kept them as maids, but as Dornan peered inside containers two and three, he could clearly see that these women weren't going to be cleaning house. They were going to be on their backs, probably screaming, definitely chained up until they learned that escape was futile.

He moved to container number four, his heart sinking into his stomach with a thud. Fuck. These were some of the hardest ones, children notwithstanding. There was much money to be earned from newborn babies – some could fetch in the realm of a hundred grand or more, if the baby's mother was white enough.

You could call them cells, but that would be too generous. You could stand in them. Turn around in them. They were about the size of a portable toilet, minus the toilet itself, and completely soundproof. Air was piped in through a series of one-way vents. The damned things were even air-conditioned for transport, because nobody liked trucking a horde of slaves across the United States, only to open the doors and find they'd all died of heatstroke en route.

That shit used to happen. Not anymore. His father was a clever man, and he'd commissioned an engineer to design the cells a few years ago. The death rate during transfer had gone down almost one hundred percent. There was still the odd girl who'd have a heart attack, literally frightened to death of where she was headed, but apart from that, they did just fine. The buyers appreciated it. They received their goods in working order, on time and discreetly. No longer was it necessary to arrive in the dead of night and herd screaming, crying women out of the back of a truck under the threat of machine-gun fire.

Because, let's face it, they were almost always women.

Now, all they needed at the other end was a forklift. The truck opened, the allocated package was located – all having been stacked in order of drop-off, of course – the forklift took the container, and so it went on, until every single soul had been exorcised from one of the massive trucks they ran weekly from coast to coast.

Sometimes, they even couriered overseas. They were that good.

No longer did Emilio, as kingpin of the entire operation, have to worry about valuable virgins being covertly deflowered en route by his men, or escaping when the doors were opened and sweaty bodies poured forth like an avalanche of sadness and fright.

It wasn't the dirty, crowded shipping container job it had once been.

No, these days it was practically fucking clinical, the way they traded and delivered humans like refrigerators.

Practically fucking civilised. The guys drove the trucks, delivered the goods, and only the buyer had the code to open each large container that housed their human transaction.

The guys never saw the girls they were delivering, and so there was no problem. There was no temptation. Nobody saw a thing.

Except Dornan.

Dornan saw every single soul, stared into every pair of eyes, heard the agonised begging of every single slave they bought and sold. He knew his father did this on purpose, but he'd sold his own soul a very long time ago, and he was indebted to his father for the rest of his life for the favours he had asked and the things he had done.

He hated it. Sometimes he thought about how good it would be to disappear, to slip underneath the surface of the ocean and just swim away.

But it was a briefly indulged fantasy, because he had sons, and *he had Mariana*.

Dornan ticked off the last piece of merchandise on his list. The whole process had taken less than thirty minutes, but it felt like a lifetime. Dornan took the stairs two at a time, not caring that his boots thudded loudly on the metal as he ascended as rapidly as he could. He was a grown man, and the pit – the name he'd given to the basement warehouse of horrors – terrified him.

Lighting a cigarette outside, Dornan wondered briefly if he was turning into his father. He didn't think he was, at least not yet. But his father didn't look into the eyes of the prisoners before he sent them to their hellish fates, and so maybe Dornan was already worse than his father had ever been.

CHAPTER NINE

JOHN

John Portland's morning was fucking splendid. As the president of the Gypsy Brothers MC, there was always something urgent that needed attending on a Monday morning. By 10 a.m. he'd already beaten a guy's front teeth out, sent half his crew on a run, and coordinated the shipping of a new haul of machine guns across to Mexico. His hand was throbbing from where the guy's pointy canine tooth had gouged into his skin, and he had a case full of damp cash to dump at the strip club to be counted and processed.

He stormed into the strip club and was immediately bailed up by Riviera, one of the dancers. Bleached blonde, and with enough fake tan for an episode of *Baywatch*, she thrust her jewel-encrusted tits at him and smiled.

'Hey, John,' she cooed.

'Not now,' John shot back, shouldering her out of his path. His hand was really fucking hurting. Maybe he'd broken something. That guy's face had been like a brick wall. He'd slept in, just had enough time to drop his daughter at the school gates, and then found his fist in someone's face. He hadn't even had a goddamn cup of coffee yet to give him a kicker.

In his good hand, he held a suitcase full of bills. They were supposed to be clean. But when he looked inside, the piles of greenbacks were damp, and some were marked with a fine sheen of blood.

Fucking excellent start to the morning.

He opened the door to the small office on the second floor and dumped the suitcase onto the first of two desks that filled the small, airless room.

The woman behind the desk scooted her seat back and smiled wryly. 'Really, John,' she said. 'You shouldn't have.'

He eyed the suitcase dubiously.

'Please tell me these ones are clean.'

His mood lifted immediately at the sight of Mariana Rodriguez. Pretty, smart and sarcastic as hell, she always managed to distract him from the shit-kicker muscle work he invariably did from day to day. Being Prez might look good on a leather jacket, but in reality it wasn't so fucking special. Plus, being under the thumb of Emilio Ross and his cartel didn't exactly bolster his enthusiasm. Most days, lately, he'd been phoning it in for the sake of keeping the peace. It wasn't like MC President looked great on a resume. The last time he'd held down a legitimate job that wasn't at a front business for Il Sangue was back in high school, fixing bikes at his uncle's garage down in SoCal.

John grimaced. 'I could tell you that, but I'd be lying.'

Mariana stared at the suitcase, resting her chin in her hands. When she leaned forwards like that her dress dipped a little and he could see the outline of her cleavage, and what a welcome sight it was on this particularly shitty morning.

'Do you think if I stare at it long enough, it'll clean itself?'

Her words jolted him out of his breast-worship, and he raked his good hand through his short blonde hair. He'd woken up too late for a shower, and he felt like shit. He must have looked pretty average, too. He'd looked at himself in the rearview before he got off his bike, and his blue eyes were so bloodshot they were practically on fire.

John couldn't help but laugh. 'You know what they say about wishes and horses.'

Mariana frowned. Her American accent was flawless, so he sometimes forgot she wasn't from here. That she didn't always know American sayings.

'Never mind,' he said. 'I picked this up from Enzo. He still owes another payment next week.' He didn't mention how he'd charged extra interest with his fists. Somehow, mentioning that in front of Mariana wouldn't be a good thing, he decided. She might be Dornan's – he wasn't entirely sure – girlfriend? Mistress? Yeah, mistress sounded about right. He didn't really want to think any deeper about where she had come from and why she'd been kicking her own shit in the back office of a seedy dance club for almost a decade, because when he had added things up, they looked very troubling, indeed. He knew Dornan was obsessed with her. He knew that she was Colombian. He knew that she had a baby son, or he'd been a baby once, anyway. He'd seen the photograph.

Aside from that, he didn't know a damn thing about her, except that she was fucking beautiful. Long dark hair that reached past her shoulders and curled ever so slightly at the ends. A tiny waist, high cheekbones and those dark blue eyes – they'd make stunning-looking kids together, with their DNA. He shouldn't even think about that, because he had a wife, and she had Dornan, and they barely even knew each other.

Still. He liked any excuse to come to the burlesque club to see her. Even if it meant fucking his hand up by punching someone whose bone structure was more like a cliff face.

As John was about to explain the contents of the suitcase, Guillermo barrelled into the office.

'I need fifteen grand,' he said, looking at Mariana.

John frowned, reaching over and tugging on Guillermo's leather cut. 'Good morning, Guillermo. Mind telling me why you need fifteen thousand dollars on a Monday morning?'

Guillermo shrugged, stuffing cold pizza into his mouth. 'Oh, hey boss. I don't know,' he said around a mouthful of pizza. 'I just do what Dee tells me to do. And he told me to get fifteen grand for him.'

Mariana looked from Guillermo to John. 'How much is in here?' she asked, patting the suitcase.

John fought back a smirk. 'Ten.'

She smiled, swivelling in her chair and unlocking the safe at her feet. It opened with a *thunk*, and she withdrew a stack of hundreds before closing the safe again and spinning the wheel to lock it.

She unzipped a corner of the suitcase and shoved her stack of bills inside, closing it again and pushing the case across to Guillermo. He wiped his greasy fingers on his jeans and grabbed the suitcase, holding it by his side.

'What's for dinner?' He asked Mariana.

She rolled her dark blue eyes at him. 'I'm not your mother. Order a pizza. *Again.*'

He shook his head. 'I'll get fish tacos from that place you like,' he said, leaving as abruptly as he had arrived.

Mariana turned her attention back to John. 'I swear, he's going to die of a heart attack before he's forty,' she said. 'You got anything else for me to bank today?'

John shrugged. 'Maybe something this afternoon. I just need you to make my regular transfer. Can you put half in this account?' He passed her a piece of paper with a series of numbers and she wrinkled up her nose.

'I need a name,' she said. 'For the banking records.'

'You've never needed a name before.'

She shrugged, picking up a ballpoint pen and twisting it between her fingers. 'It won't work if I don't have an account name to attach to it.'

John stared down at her, his cheery mood gone. 'There is no name,' he snapped. 'Just make it happen. Wire it.'

She threw the piece of paper down on his side of the desk, her smile gone, too. 'New regulations,' she said coolly. 'The bank won't accept the transfer unless I have the name of the bank account.'

John took a deep breath and tried not to lose his shit. It wasn't her fault. She was just doing her job. But how the fuck was he supposed to get money to where it needed to go if he had to use a name? Names were dangerous. Even with the fake alias she was using, they could potentially track her down. Shit.

'Look,' Mariana said, finally meeting his gaze. 'I can wire transfer if the person can collect the cash on the same day. You don't need a bank account for that. You call them and give them a code, and they can go to Western Union and take out the money. They still need to show a driver's licence.'

John nodded, his frayed nerves cooling somewhat. 'Thanks,' he said gruffly, sliding the piece of paper back to her.

He needed to find a better way to get money to Stephanie. He wasn't sure how, but he was going to have to rethink the way he supplemented her before it became impossible.

He thought of Dornan finding out what he'd been doing behind his back, and his stomach knotted. No. He couldn't allow that to happen. Dornan would never forgive him.

'What's wrong with your hand?' Mariana asked, standing up and leaning across the desk to get a better look. Before John could step back, she'd reached out and taken his hand in hers. 'Did somebody bite you?' Her dark blue eyes flashed with concern as she looked from John's injured hand to his eyes.

Jesus, those eyes of hers were dangerous. You could get lost in them. He couldn't afford to get lost in anything that belonged to Dornan. He pulled his hand away. 'It's fine,' he said, brushing off her concern. 'You should see the other guy.'

She shook her head, opening her desk drawer and producing a small first aid kit. 'Let me fix that before it gets infected.'

John shook his head, stepping back towards the door. 'It's fine, really—'

'John!' she said insistently. 'You right handed?'

He nodded.

'How are you going to deliver me money every day without your right hand? Come on. Sit down. Here, have a coffee. Guillermo got an extra one.'

She passed him a Starbucks cup and pointed to the other desk. 'Sit. If I have to look at your hand for much longer, I might puke.'

He laughed, leaning against the second desk, his ankles crossed as he sipped lukewarm coffee. It was sugary and strong, just what he needed. As sugar and caffeine travelled to his brain, he started to relax a little. He wasn't used to anyone taking care of him. His wife was a walking disaster and he'd never expect or want his daughter to take on all the household responsibilities that Caroline ignored, so he did most everything himself. It wasn't so bad – there was worse, he remembered as he looked at Mariana's concentrated expression – but it was nice to have a woman take care of him, for once.

He tensed when she touched a pad of rubbing alcohol to his wound, but didn't pull away or protest. She smiled slightly at his reaction, waiting a moment before she continued cleaning the wound.

He couldn't help it. As covertly as he could, without her noticing, he ran his eyes over every part of her that he could see. She had some sort of make-up on that made her eyes pop, and they looked stunning against her light brown skin and dark silky hair. She was wearing her hair out, and it fell loosely around her face. When she moved, he caught a whiff of her perfume, or maybe it was the shampoo she used. Whatever it was, it smelled of coconut and lime and sex.

He breathed her in deeply, and she looked at him quizzically. 'You feeling okay?'

Oh, he felt better than okay. She smelled so good, he wanted to lean over and take a bite out of her. He smiled. 'Yeah. Better now. Thanks.'

His Monday was looking up.

CHAPTER TEN
MARIANA

Christopher Murphy was a blight on my existence: a man I'd not cared to meet and wished I would never have to endure the misfortune of seeing again.

Sadly, my wish wasn't granted.

I saw him exactly once a week, unless he was away on a job. He needed plenty of money stashed, and I was very, very good at distributing the illegal finances for Il Sangue and its associates. Every Sunday afternoon I was expected to give Murphy and Emilio a rundown on the finances for the week. Safety deposit box numbers, bank accounts, the lot. I memorised everything, didn't write a single thing down that could incriminate anybody. The cartel couldn't afford to be careless, not when they were selling coke and whores and God knows what else. One surprise raid, and it'd all be out in the open. Most of the money was sitting in offshore accounts, numbering into the millions by now, but it was all blood money.

When we'd met, Murphy was a federal air marshal, but he'd since traded that job for a better one, as an agent high up the food chain with the Drug Enforcement Agency. Ironically, he'd scored a position with the drug trafficking unit that was supposed to help stop the cocaine flow across the US border, but his real job, the one Emilio paid him hundreds of thousands of dollars for, was funnelling coke from South America onto North American soil. His connections were spread like tentacles through the law enforcement channels that presided over the illegal drug and human trafficking trades that plagued the gulf; and he was making bank.

He was Emilio's right-hand man.

He'd been the one who had brought me to this godforsaken place.

And now, nine years after I'd returned home one night to find him standing over my father, a gun in his hand and a bored look on his face, Murphy was back in my face. This time he was alone and looking smug as he kicked the front door closed behind him. His gun was on his hip, and he looked smarmy rather than bored. Christopher Murphy was scum dressed in a suit and tie. And he was in my apartment.

'Oh,' I said, feeling my face fall as I watched him from where I was sitting on the couch. 'It's you.'

'Don't look so excited,' he deadpanned.

Guillermo had gone on a run with the club and left me here, a rare event. But sometimes it happened. He'd only left five minutes beforehand. Murphy must have been watching, waiting for him to leave.

I rolled my eyes, feigning disinterest as alarm began to rise within me. It was Monday night. I never saw Murphy outside of our Sunday afternoon meeting, not unless there was a large amount of money to shift. If that were the case, though, we'd do it at the office under Emilio's watchful eye.

Murphy being here in my apartment, alone, could only mean very bad things.

'How'd you get past the alarm?' I asked casually as I calculated the distance between myself and my gun. As luck would have it, it was underneath the couch cushion I was sitting on. I'd still probably get my head blown off before I'd be able to reach it, but it was comforting to know that underneath my ass was a weapon with six bullets in the clip, each with Christopher Murphy written on it.

'I bypassed it,' he said, smiling smugly. 'The perks of working for the DEA. They've got all kinds of things to break through your little locks and codes.'

Great. He now apparently had an all-access pass to the one place I felt safe in the world. I wanted to throw up.

There was a knock at the door. I froze, my eyes darting between Murphy and the door.

'I'd ask you if you brought a friend with you,' I said quietly, 'but I know you don't have any of those.'

I stood, mainly because I didn't want to be a sitting duck. Murphy reached back and opened the front door, while I shifted my balance onto my toes, ready to move quickly if I needed to. I was fucking stupid for not having my gun right at my fingertips! But after nine years you get complacent.

A figure entered through the front door. A woman. She wore black pants and a gun holster that sliced a criss-cross over her white shirt.

'This your partner?' I asked. 'Should have called ahead, Murphy. I would have gotten out the good china.'

The woman, who'd not spoken yet, eyed me. Judgey fucking eyes they were, too. From her appearance, I could see she had some Latina in her, maybe Mexican. She had long, dark brown hair that was swept up into a messy ponytail and caramel-coloured skin, like mine when I went out in the sun. Her almond-shaped eyes were lined with black make-up, and they were narrowed at me.

Yeah. Murphy definitely had a type.

'Mary-anna,' she said, mispronouncing my name on purpose. 'I've heard so much about you.'

'That's funny,' I said, my hands burning to grab the hidden gun. 'I haven't heard a single thing about you.'

She chuckled. 'She's mouthy,' she said to Murphy, but looking at me.

'*She's* right here,' I replied. 'And she's busy, so if we could get to the point …'

Murphy smiled. 'Allie, I'll meet you in the car. Give me a call if that shit-kicker comes back.'

Allie looked put out. 'We'll hear his bike,' she protested, angling herself so that I couldn't hear and placing a hand on Murphy's chest. Only, she was three feet in front of me, and I had excellent hearing.

A wry grin spread across my face as soon as she touched Murphy. Gross.

'Oh, you two are fucking. Sorry, I'm a little slow tonight. I wasn't expecting you to let yourselves into my house, *Allie.*'

She snorted. 'That's Agent Baxter to you, bitch. And this is *your* house?' Allie repeated, turning back to me. 'Really? You own this place?'

I didn't respond.

'How many bedrooms?' she asked, looking around the hallway and lounge room. 'Two? Three? Still holding out hope that they'll let you bring your little bastard to live here?'

My grin vanished. All I saw was red. My fingers tingled impatiently, anxious to wrap them around her throat and squeeze until she begged me to stop.

Seemed I'd absorbed some of Dornan's violent tendencies in the past decade.

As my grin vanished, hers grew.

'You should probably leave,' I said coolly. 'Your boyfriend likes to try and fuck me when we're alone, and I think you're putting him off his game.'

There it was. *Snap.* I could practically see the rage rush through her veins, it was so instantaneous. Her entire demeanour changed, and she lunged for me. Murphy, who'd been silent thus far, reached out and closed his long fingers around the top of her arm, wrenching her back.

'I'm going to kill this bitch,' Allie said, trying to pull her arm from Murphy's grip.

'I could have your ass thrown in jail, and your precious fucking Gypsy Brothers couldn't do a thing about it,' she seethed. 'Who the fuck do you think you are?'

I snorted. 'Someone who looks a lot like you, apparently. Funny that.' Seriously, though. The resemblance was uncanny. We could have been sisters, for Christ's sake. *Eww.*

She lunged again, and Murphy made a growling sound, pulling her roughly towards the front door. 'Go wait in the fucking car,' he fumed. 'I wouldn't touch this filthy whore if you paid me.'

I put a hand to my heart in mock disappointment. 'You're breaking my heart,' I said.

Allie continued to stare at me, trying to kill me with her eyes, and Murphy bundled her out through the front door and slammed it in her face.

'She seems lovely,' I said, my tone sickly sweet. 'Has she met your parents yet?'

'My parents are dead,' Murphy replied stonily.

'What'd you do, kill them for their retirement fund?' I thought it was funny.

Murphy didn't seem overly amused, though. He seemed antsy. I wondered if he was actually worried about what she'd say when he got back to the car. She looked like she'd probably beat him up or something.

'She's fucking crazy,' Murphy replied. 'Lucky she gives good head.'

I expected him to approach me, to do something, but he didn't. He walked *past* the living room, holding a paper bag in one hand, a pair of aviator sunglasses in the other. I reached underneath the couch cushion, quickly locating my gun and flicking the safety off before I hurried into the hallway after him. He strode into the kitchen, dumping the paper bag on the counter as I raised my gun and aimed at him.

I had a gun now. *I was allowed to have a gun*, and it was because of Murphy. It was something Dornan had given me, not long after Murphy had tried to rape me on the dining room floor. Murphy had even brought a syringe full of drugs to make sure I complied. Dornan had beaten him almost to death. The only reason he hadn't was because of John pulling him off Murphy and talking sense into him. Truth be told, I wished that he'd just let Dornan finish the guy off.

Murphy turned and raised his eyebrows in amusement, tossing his sunglasses on the counter. 'Oh, put that away,' he said, pandering, his smile wide but his crazy blue eyes devoid of warmth. He rounded the counter and began opening cupboards and drawers, pulling out cutlery and napkins like he knew the place intimately.

I didn't relax my aim. 'What do you want, Murphy?' I asked impatiently. ''Cause I'm kind of busy right now.'

He looked around. 'Busy doing what?'

I rolled my eyes. 'Staring at the walls.'

He didn't respond.

I cringed as a streak of blood threaded out of one of his nostrils and down over his lip.

'Did the rest of your brain cells just explode?' I asked, gesturing towards his nose.

'I get nosebleeds,' he shrugged, wiping his arm across his face and creating a bright red line of blood on his white shirt. 'It's the heat.' He pressed a napkin to his nose to staunch the bleeding.

I raised my eyebrows. 'Uh, I think it's all the coke you put up there.' Idiot.

He looked unperturbed. Satisfied that the blood had stopped, he threw the napkin in the trash and washed his hands in the kitchen sink.

'What is this?' I gestured to him as the smell of Chinese food hit me.

'Here,' Murphy said, taking several boxes from the bag and placing them on the bench. 'I got your favourite. Egg rolls and lo mein.'

How the fuck did he know what my favourite Chinese takeout was? I was about to issue some witty retort when I swallowed my words. Egg rolls and lo mein *was* my favourite. Sometimes Dornan would surprise me with it.

He hadn't done it in a very long time.

'You brought dinner?' I asked, my tone scathing. 'You want to date me or something, Murphy? While your girlfriend waits in the car?'

He grinned, his tongue sliding across his top teeth as he chuckled. 'I don't think you're exactly *dateable*, honey. Fuckable? Yes. Dateable? Debateable!'

He laughed at his own ridiculous joke, and that made me mad. It made me livid.

Still grasping the gun, I crossed my arms, rooted to the spot in the hallway. Murphy continued to dig through my kitchen drawers, clattering plates and assembling spoons next to each cardboard container.

I won't lie, my mouth was watering. I wanted to shoot that motherfucker dead in my kitchen and step over his bloody corpse, just to eat that takeout.

'Eat,' Murphy commanded.

I stood my ground.

'Tell me why you're here,' I repeated. 'Tell me why your crazy girlfriend knows about my son.'

He took his plate, loaded with steaming hot food, and shovelled a spoonful of lo mein into his mouth. Seemed our Murphy was too retarded to eat with chopsticks. No great surprise there. He started walking towards me, towards the living room. Fuck that. When he was within arm's reach, I raised my gun towards him again.

I pressed the barrel into his forehead, stopping him in his tracks. 'I. Will. Shoot. You.' I said through gritted teeth.

He didn't drop his smile, despite the fact that he had a gun to his head, held by one extremely volatile, pissed-off Colombian woman with a tendency to snap and make bad decisions. No, he licked the grease from his lips and stared me right in the eye, calm as day.

'Don't you want to see your son again, Mariana?'

I'd like to say his words didn't affect me. That they rolled off me, unbidden.

But it would be a lie.

I backed up, felt the sting of tears building in my eyes. Refused to let them out. He didn't deserve my tears.

'Get out,' I demanded. It hurt to talk around the lump in my throat. 'Take your fucking food and get out of my house.'

He moved slowly, our eyes never leaving each other's. I watched, mesmerised, as he pressed his palm towards me in a sign of peace, then ever so slowly reached his right hand inside his suit pocket, balancing his plate in the other.

I watched, my finger ready on the trigger to take down the son of a bitch if he so much as sneezed. He pulled out a piece of paper. A photograph. And held it up to me.

'I can get you what you want,' he said casually, like I wasn't holding a gun to his head.

My heart broke in an instant as I looked at the photo he was holding up.

I swallowed thickly. It was *him*. My baby. Only, he wasn't a baby anymore. This photo was recent. How could I tell it was my Luis and not just some random kid Murphy had plucked off the street and asked to pose? His eyes. They were like mine, dark blue, and inside them I saw my own soul. I knew without a doubt that Murphy was not bluffing. I knew that he had somehow gotten a photograph of my son.

My heart started to beat wildly.

'Where did you get that?' I whispered. *Thudthudthud*. My heart was about ready to beat out of my chest.

'I took it,' Murphy shrugged. 'I'm not exactly a pro at photographing children, but I think I did okay.'

I wanted to take the photo from him. I wanted to shoot him. 'Why?'

'There are plenty more of these,' he said, opening his fingers and letting the piece of paper flutter to the ground. 'Why do you think I took them? I can't very well buy your cooperation with just the one.'

I remained silent; it wasn't easy. My skin was crawling, just from being alone with him. I just wanted to know what the hell Murphy wanted from me, so I could either acquiesce, or shoot him between the eyes.

I kind of hoped I'd get to shoot him. I'd try to aim so that none of his blood would splatter against the photograph that lay on the floor between our feet.

'Ask me,' he said.

'Ask you what?' I sighed.

'Ask me what I need your cooperation with.' He took an egg roll between his fingers and bit into it, hot sauce running down his chin. 'But ask me while I'm sitting down eating. I'm fucking starved.'

***

Ten minutes later, we were sitting at the dining table. Murphy had proceeded to bring a stack of photographs out of his suit pocket and place them face-down on the table beside his hand, but hadn't let me see any more. I'd since collected the one he'd let fall to the ground, and I held it in front of me, my food untouched. I'd also poured myself a vodka, no mixer. No ice, either. After the fucking I'd taken from Dornan on this very dining table, I couldn't think of ice cubes without blushing and getting very, very turned on. Being turned on didn't really match being stuck with Christopher Murphy.

'You're not gonna eat?' Murphy asked around a mouthful of food.

'Just get to the point,' I said.

'Alright.' He stopped eating, looking at me seriously as the snark vanished from his face. I swallowed nervously. Snarky Murphy I could handle. When he got serious, it scared the living shit out of me.

'In approximately—' he paused to check his watch, 'one hour, your father and the rest of your family will be entering the United States government's witness protection program. The DEA are on the ground in Colombia, moving in to take them to a safe house.'

I raised my eyebrows; inside my heart was thundering.

'Why should I believe anything you say?' I replied tersely. *Witness protection? Bullshit.*

He didn't smile, didn't smirk. In fact, this Christopher Murphy was entirely normal, concerned even, and that made him even more terrifying.

'You don't have to,' he said, sitting back and wiping his hands on a napkin. 'But you have two options right now. You run and tell loverboy Dornan and give him the tip-off. Or we make a deal, and you get to see your son again.'

I saw the corner of his mouth twitch, a suppressed smile.

'It's a very good deal.'

I didn't say anything for a moment, my head whirling. I remembered sitting at a similar table in Colombia nine years ago, swallowing packages of what I believed to be cocaine, only to find out later that I'd couriered eighteen pellets of baker's-grade flour across the border as a test.

Was this a test? Were they testing my loyalty after all this time?

'You think you can mention a son I gave up for adoption over eleven years ago and I'll just do whatever you want?'

Murphy eyed me confidently. 'That's exactly what I think.'

Well, I didn't know what to say to that. I pressed my lips together. 'He doesn't even know me,' I said, but my words came out weaker than I'd planned.

'You might think you're covert, and you're clever, but my dear Mariana,' Murphy paused and leaned across the table, smiling smugly, 'you're also *very* fucking predictable.'

'If Emilio heard you talking like this, he would kill you.' I said. 'Slowly. Painfully. I heard what he did to Bella. I'm sure he's done plenty worse since then.'

Murphy's eyes lit up at the mention of her name; the accountant who had been there before me, the girl who had been tortured, piece by piece over the better part of a week, until Dornan shot her and put her out of her misery.

'I *saw* what he did to Bella,' Murphy said. 'Did you know if you drill into the right part of a person's skull, you can see their brain while they're still conscious?' He pretended to drill into his forehead with two fingers, a *zzzz* sound coming from between his teeth.

I was suddenly convinced that he'd played an active part in her grisly demise.

'Anyway,' he said, running his tongue over his teeth, 'your father's actually stopped drinking and gambling. Crazy, right?'

'Unbelievable,' I answered. 'Just like the rest of your story. Why would the DEA help my father go into hiding? It's ludicrous. He's a criminal.'

Murphy waved his fork dismissively. 'He's small fry compared to Emilio and Julian Ross. We're talking about smashing an international drug syndicate here. You think I'd have stuck around for this long if it wasn't worth something huge? My entire career has been devoted to taking these fuckers down.'

I huffed incredulously. 'Murphy, you have a bank account in the Bahamas with hundreds of thousands of dollars in it. Drug money.'

'Drug money,' he smiled. 'That's a cute name for it.'

'It's the truth!' I insisted. 'What the hell are the DEA going to do when they realise you're in on this whole mess?'

He shrugged. 'I'll lay low for a couple of months, then charter myself a plane straight out of Dodge and into early retirement abroad. The government pension isn't exactly enough to pay for all my ... *hobbies*.'

'Emilio will know it was you,' I countered. 'He'll empty your accounts quicker than you can snort a line of coke off your desk.' I'd seen him do it before.

He pursed his lips and stared at me like I was a moron. 'Why do you think I came here?' he responded. 'You're going to make sure that doesn't happen. And in return, I get you your son.'

'What about Dornan?' I asked, dazed.

'What *about* Dornan?' Murphy rebounded.

I searched his face for an indication of how this could go but got nothing. 'I'm not participating in anything that would hurt him. He saved my life.'

Murphy sneered. 'He took you to be his own personal whore. He used – uses – you for his own perverted pleasure. Does he make you say *thank you* after you swallow?'

Wow. That hurt. Even coming from Murphy. *I shouldn't care*, I scolded myself.

'You don't know anything about me,' I answered coldly. 'Or him.'

'I know your son is dying to meet you,' he said, smarmy fuck that he was. 'What else matters? The whole family is in WITSEC, and if you do this one little thing for me, you'll be right there with them.'

'When you say the whole family—'

'He's not included,' Murphy cut me off. 'There's no records of your son even existing. I had the birth certificate and the adoption papers removed from the state office when you started cleaning my money, just in case I ever needed to blackmail you, babe.'

Was he lying? I couldn't tell. The sick thing was, he knew exactly what to say to get me to pay attention, whether it was the truth or not. I wanted to see my son more than I wanted anything in the entire universe.

I'd kill to see him. Die if it meant I could touch his face one more time.

'What do you want me to do?' I asked dully. Dornan's face loomed large in my mind, so distracting I could barely concentrate on what Murphy was saying.

He smiled, and it was like he knew he had me hooked on his bait. Now, to reel me in.

'You're gonna move some money for me, sweetheart,' he said. 'Some of Emilio's money. Don't worry, I'll let you keep a little to get yourself set up. But the bulk of it goes into my personal offshore accounts, are we clear? It costs money to hide.'

I nodded. 'And that's it?'

He nodded, chewing slowly.

'Well, I guess we're done here, then. You need help packing your shit up?' I was acting nonplussed, but inside I was a quivering mess. I needed to be alone so I could figure out what the fuck my next move would be. Some vague feeling in the pit of my stomach told me I had to bring Dornan in on all this, but the urge to investigate a little further myself was too tempting. I still had the burner phone John had gifted me with, and I needed Murphy to leave so I could make some calls.

He threw his fork down, and it made a high-pitched ting against the china as he pushed his plate away. Hurriedly, I closed all of the cardboard boxes and shoved them back into the paper bag, thrusting it at Murphy. He rolled his eyes and removed the lo mein, setting it on the table for me to keep. How thoughtful.

'I can't leave without cracking open the fortune cookies,' he said, standing slowly. 'That would be rude.'

I took a deep breath. 'Open them in the car. With your girlfriend.' I snatched up the two fortune cookies – the romantic motherfucker had brought one for each of us – and stalked towards the front door.

'I'll call you,' Murphy said, knocking his shoulder against mine as he passed me.

'Can't wait,' I threw back, tossing the fortune cookies at him. He caught them easily, a look of amusement on his face. Bastard. I hated him. I hated him almost as much as I hated Emilio.

He pocketed the plastic-wrapped cookies and reached for the door handle but drew back at the last second. 'I almost forgot,' he grinned, looking back at me as he held up the stack of photographs.

I wanted them. But I knew if I showed how much I wanted them, he'd raise the stakes. I held my jaw rigid and slipped the tip of my tongue between my front teeth, biting down until I tasted blood. *Don't react.*

He held the stack out to me, a smirk on his face. 'You want them?'

I reached for them slowly; too slowly. He yanked them back just as my fingers were about to close around them, dropping the paper bag full of leftovers on the floor as his other hand wrapped around my throat. Squeezing tight, he pushed me back into the wall. My head hit the plaster with a dull thunk.

I gave him a sour look, my voice coming out in a rasp as his fingers hovered at my throat. 'I knew there'd be a price. What is it?'

He chewed on his lower lip thoughtfully, watching my mouth with great interest.

'You want to kiss me, Murphy? Is that it?'

He grinned, letting go of my throat and grabbing a chunk of my hair as he pressed me harder against the wall. He pushed his greedy lips against mine, nine years worth of his pent-up frustration crushing against me. It was bad, but not so bad, until he stuck his tongue in my mouth. Gross. I stilled for a few moments, thinking it was a small price to pay in the scheme of things. When his hand started travelling from my waist up towards my chest, I shoved him off me.

'I think I threw up a little in my mouth,' I deadpanned. 'This was fun, we should do it again *never*.' I snatched the photos from his hand, and he made no attempt to stop me this time.

Murphy sniffed, wiping his wet mouth with one finger. Still sampling the goods, no doubt. I knew he was excited about finally laying one on me after all this time, but his pupils were pinpricks. There was something bubbling in his veins, and I was betting on coke.

'You forgot your fortune cookie,' he said, tearing open the packaging and cracking the cookie in half before holding it out to me. 'Read it.'

'No.'

'Then no more photos for you.'

I snatched the broken fortune cookie out of his hand and pulled out the piece of paper, letting the cookie pieces fall to the ground as I read it.

'Fortune favours the brave.' I dropped the piece of paper, and it fell lazily to the ground.

'How brave are you feeling today?' he asked, tucking a stray hair behind my ear. I pulled away sharply. He'd touched me all he was going to touch me today. My skin was already screaming for me to get in the shower and scrub his prints off of me.

I didn't bother answering the brave question. It irritated me.

'Aren't you going to read yours?' I said instead.

He cracked his open and threw the cookie into his mouth, as he unfurled the quote that had been jammed inside. He laughed, handing the piece of paper to me. I took it reluctantly. What I really wanted was for him to fucking leave so I could see the rest of the photos that were clutched in my hand.

'If you would rule the world quietly, you must keep it amused.'

I handed it back to him. 'Looks like you got the right one. I don't want to rule the world.'

Murphy tilted his head to the side. 'Everybody wants to rule the world, Mariana. Which reminds me. If you tell anyone what we spoke about – Dornan included – I will slit your throat ear to ear and hang you off a fucking bridge. And I'll make sure your son sees you die. Got it?'

A chill ran through me. 'Yeah. I got it.'

I opened the door for him, shoving him out and slamming it as hard as I could behind him.

I didn't want to rule the world. I didn't care about power.

I just wanted to be free.

CHAPTER ELEVEN

MARIANA

It was late. Almost midnight, by the time Murphy had left. I spread the photos across my coffee table, drinking them in as his words started to hit home.

I wanted to believe what he was saying. Wanted to believe it wasn't a cruel trick, a test, as Emilio was so fond of subjecting people to. But I'd known Murphy a long time now, knew his subtle little tells, could pretty much always pick when he was lying.

But, faced with the possibility of seeing my son again, my heart overrode my brain until I was so confused, I had no idea if he was lying or telling the truth. My BS meter was completely screwed in the face of the chance to reunite with Luis.

Murphy wanted me to embezzle money for him. A lot of money. It was a probable death sentence. Emilio had people everywhere – hell, he had Murphy, one of the most senior and powerful officers in the DEA.

But it seemed Murphy had grown tired of playing second fiddle to the Il Sangue Cartel. Seemed he wanted it all for himself. Seemed he was cleaning house, and he wanted me to assist him. Maybe it had something to do with Allie. Perhaps it was true love.

I looked at the photos one by one. Luis riding a bicycle. Luis entering a school classroom, a backpack slung over one shoulder. Luis kicking a soccer ball. His hair was long, his skin darker than mine. Lord, he looked exactly like his father. His eyes were the only thing that said he was mine. He looked exactly as I'd imagined he would, and that was a miracle within itself. It was as if I'd dreamed him into existence. He was exquisite. Greedily, as I examined the photographs, I wanted more. I wanted to hear his voice. I wondered if it still had that high, child-like pitch. He was almost twelve. Soon, it'd get deeper, more mature.

I wanted to hear his voice as a child just once before he grew up. Just one time. I wanted to hold him in my arms. I wanted to look into his eyes and see him looking back. I wanted to be his mother.

My hands were shaking.

I weighed up my options. If I told Dornan, Murphy would deny everything. He'd make sure I died, but worst of all, he'd hurt Luis. I'd heard his threat, and I knew he wasn't bluffing.

Fuck.

If Emilio went down, what did that mean for Dornan? For John, even? For Guillermo?

If Emilio went down, what did that mean for me?

The notion that I might one day be free of the Il Sangue Cartel seemed so ludicrous, I couldn't even picture it. I was a survivor, and survivors didn't live on hope and dreams. They lived on blending in and doing what they were fucking told.

Dornan. Luis. It seemed like I was going to have to risk one to protect the other.

Dornan would understand, I reasoned with myself. He was a father. He knew the ferocity of a parent's love.

I'd always loved Luis above all else, even though I'd never known him, even though he'd never remember a single thing about the precious few hours we spent as mother and son before he was taken away. But Dornan against Luis? One or the other? I'd never had to face that ultimatum before.

I thought of how far I'd be willing to go to protect my son. Would I betray Dornan? Could I?

Of course I could. I loved Dornan beyond words, beyond space and time and every shitty thing that stood between us ever finding freedom. But I loved my son more. He was a part of me. He came from me. And I'd tear the fucking world down to lay my eyes on him one more time.

CHAPTER TWELVE
MARIANA

Murphy was long gone, and I'd looked at each photograph at least a dozen times before I sprang into action. I rechecked the front door, making sure it was locked, and jammed a dining chair underneath the door knob for good measure. Once I was certain the place was relatively secure, I retrieved my burner phone from its hiding spot: a canister of flour that sat at the back of the pantry. Shaking the excess powder from the protective ziplock bag, I took the phone out and dialled.

I prayed for an answer.

'What?' the voice on the line said abruptly.

'It's me,' I whispered, my heart thundering in my chest. Nobody was with me, but if Guillermo arrived home from his ride, I didn't want him hearing my conversation.

'We're not due to speak for two weeks,' Este's older brother hissed. 'Is this a safe line?'

Once a month for the past eight-and-a-half years – ever since John gave me the phone – I'd been speaking to Miguel, my dead boyfriend's brother. Checking on my family. Checking on my son. My family still thought I'd died nine years ago, shortly after I was brought to Los Angeles, and I needed to keep it that way. If they ever found out, my father would no doubt do something stupid and reckless and we'd all be dead inside a week.

Miguel was the only person I could think of who I *knew* would keep the secret for me, and, more importantly, keep tabs on the son Este and I had been forced to give up for adoption when we were teenagers. The family who'd adopted Luis were distant relatives of Esteban, and they lived in the same small village that Miguel had settled in after I left. Miguel was the only one in the world who knew where Luis was – but now Murphy had stripped that secret away and turned it into a liability.

'Of course,' I replied. 'This couldn't wait. Something's happened. A man told me my parents have been taken into witness protection. Is that true?' I closed my eyes and leaned against the cool refrigerator door. My legs shook as I waited for Miguel's response.

He let out a long sigh, and I immediately knew something was very wrong. 'Bambina,' he said, 'I am so sorry.'

Oh God. 'What?' I whispered.

I heard the flick of a lighter and a sharp inhale as he smoked.

'Miguel!' I insisted.

'They're dead, bambina.'

I almost choked on my own tongue. 'What?'

Not Luis. Not my baby, please God, not my baby. 'Where is my son?' I asked through gritted teeth, opening my eyes wide and praying like fuck. Not my boy. *Not my boy.*

Miguel coughed. 'Luis is safe, Mariana. He's alive. But your papa. Your mama. Karina and Pablo. They're gone. Dead.'

I covered my mouth with a shaking hand and pressed my palm into my teeth to stifle the scream that was coming from my chest. I couldn't stop it; the rage and the grief threatened to split me open. And the relief. Luis was alive. He mattered the most. He was just a child.

'It's worse. They're looking for Luis. A man was here, a DEA agent. He offered the children at school pesos for his whereabouts. I've got him somewhere safe, but it's only temporary, Ana. There is nothing left for you there. There is no reason for you to stay. *You're collateral for a debt that has been revoked.*'

Even if Emilio did inform me of my family's murder, he'd still never let me go. There are few things in life that are certainties, but this was one of them.

'How?' I asked, feeling like every piece of air had been sucked out of my body. I couldn't breathe. I couldn't think. This had to be some terrible fucking nightmare that I was going to wake up from any minute. I felt my breath coming faster and faster as panic rose in my chest, suffocating me from within.

I heard Miguel clear his throat. 'Julian's men stormed the house, tied them up and poured gasoline on them,' he said quietly.

Julian's men were Emilio's men. Emilio's younger brother oversaw the Colombian operations in his absence, but there was no disputing who the boss of the Il Sangue Cartel was.

'And then?'

A long silence. 'And then they lit a match, Ana.'

I retched once. Dropped the phone onto the kitchen counter and swallowed hard. *Get your shit together.* I took a deep breath, stood straight again. I suddenly had an overwhelming urge to drink something strong, something that would wash away the shock, or at least dull it.

'Mariana!?' Miguel's voice sang up from the cellphone. I picked it up and held it to my ear again, not sure I wanted to hear anything else he had to say. They'd burned. They'd *burned alive.*

'I'm here,' I said, using my free hand to open the freezer and take out a bottle of vodka. I unscrewed the cap and tipped a good amount down my throat, the cold liquid punching my senses awake.

Murphy had been playing a cruel trick on me, and it had almost worked. I thought of my gentle brother and my beautiful sister, and imagined the flesh melting from their faces, their agonised screams, as fire consumed them.

I took another drink. It was making my stomach flip, drinking straight vodka so quickly, but I didn't care. I needed something.

'Luis?' I asked.

'I have him, Ana. But you need to figure something out. You can't come here – they'll kill you both. He's safe. But we need money, passports. You need to help me get him out of Colombia.'

Relief flooded my weary bones, flowing all the way down to my toes along with the last of the vodka in my bloodstream. It was an unfamiliar feeling, to be so terribly sad yet so relieved at the same time. My son was alive. But how long could he survive if the likes of Murphy were looking for him?

I had to do something.

'Are you sure?' I asked. Maybe it was all a misunderstanding. Maybe it was all a bad dream.

He coughed. 'There were witnesses, Ana. People saw. People saw them storm the house, and people saw it burn afterwards. People heard them screaming.'

Oh Jesus. I wished I hadn't asked.

'Keep him safe,' I whispered. 'Please, Miguel, keep him safe for me.'

Miguel's voice cracked. 'He looks like my brother, but he has your eyes, bambina. He asks for you.'

'He knows about me?'

It was almost too much to bear.

'Of course he does, Ana. He has a photo of you – remember your senior dance?'

I did remember. The milk hadn't even stopped leaking from my breasts in the aftermath of Luis' birth and adoption, but Mama had insisted I go to the dance, get back to normal life. Este had borrowed a suit that was too big and presented me with a corsage I knew his mother had stayed up late the night before making. I'd spent the entire night sobbing in the dark outside the dance hall, as Este held me and promised to find a way to get our baby back. I remembered the photo my mother had taken, just as we were leaving the house. My mother had done my make-up for me. I remembered thinking how odd it was that she was acting so normal, especially when my father refused to even look at me, much less engage in a conversation. In fact, he only said one thing to me that night. He appeared as I was getting ready to leave, slapped me across the face hard enough that I tasted blood in my mouth, and told me, 'Keep your legs closed, you little slut.'

I remember holding my cheek, in shock. I wasn't going to have sex. I'd given birth to a *baby* a week earlier. I was barely walking, let alone the rest of it. And my father was calling me a slut. My mother had pulled me outside and snapped a photo of Este and me. He was squinting at the sun and I was still reeling from shock, a reactionary smile plastered across my face. Karina had a Polaroid camera she'd found at a market, and she snapped a photograph, too, let it spit out of the front of the camera, and gave it to me.

It seemed that Polaroid photo had survived and ended up in my son's hands.

'Mariana?'

I snapped back to the present as Miguel's voice cut through blurry memories of days long gone, feeling the flour dust sticking between my clammy fingers. It was hot in the apartment all of a sudden and I desperately needed some fresh air.

'I'll get money. I'll call you again tomorrow,' I said to Miguel in a monotone voice. I ended the call abruptly, switching the phone off and returning it to the ziplock bag and finally back into the canister of flour. After I'd done that, I took the dining chair that I'd wedged beneath the front door knob and carried it back to the dining table, staring at the surface where Dornan and I had fucked. I loved him. I loved him so fucking much, and I didn't want to hurt him. Nausea rolled through me and I swallowed back bile.

Rushing over to the sliding door, I wrenched it open, stepping onto the patio as ocean air hit me. The cold greeted me with a slap that made my skin sting. I breathed deeply, tasting salt on my tongue, wiping floury hands on my skirt. The sea was torrid tonight, churning. It was going to rain. It hardly ever rained in Los Angeles, barren wasteland that it was, but it smelled like the heavens were going to open and dump water any second.

I wondered if anyone had organised a funeral for my family, if there had been anything left to bury. Fire had a nasty way of reducing fully formed people to bones and ash, inconsequential piles of what used to be flesh and blood.

I thought it odd that I wasn't crying. Maybe the relief of knowing Luis had been spared was making the deaths of my parents and siblings less traumatic.

More likely, I was in shock.

Everything Murphy had said to me, about witness protection and getting out of this place? It had all seemed so good, so of course it was a lie. I felt like a fucking idiot for even daring to consider what he'd fed me as truth. He was a shark, and he'd just tried to convince me he wasn't so he could take me by surprise and eat me alive while I wasn't looking. He'd tried to make me trust him.

When something seems too good to be true, it usually is.

I'd never believed that until now.

My parents, my brother, my sister – they weren't going to be saved. They were already dead. And Christopher Murphy had been in Colombia looking for my son.

I was never getting out.

Murphy's deception unleashed something primal inside me. He had poked a sleeping beast that been lying dormant for nine years, curled deep in my belly.

I ran into the bathroom and reached the toilet just in time to throw up the contents of my stomach. Wiping my mouth with the back of my hand, I caught sight of myself in the mirror, and I saw something alight in the recesses of my dark blue eyes.

A thirst for payback. A yearning for vengeance.

My entire body hummed with the desire to inflict suffering upon Emilio Ross and his minions as I washed my mouth out with cold water. For the first time in a very long time, I felt renewed, invincible.

I was hungry for blood.

The front door slammed shut. Sneakers squeaked on tile and I breathed out in relief. Guillermo. I flushed the toilet, washed my hands, and made my way out to the kitchen.

Guillermo was facing away from me, digging in the refrigerator when I saw him pause.

'Did you go out tonight?' he asked, his tone aiming for casual but hitting suspicious.

'No,' I replied honestly. 'I've been here all night.'

He closed the refrigerator, Murphy's Chinese in his hands. 'I didn't know these guys delivered,' he said, slinging the rest of the lo mein into the microwave and hitting start. The thing lit up, heating the food as two eyes stared accusingly at me.

'Murphy dropped it off,' I said. 'He must've heard about the plans for the club ride at your meeting. He was in here five minutes after you left.'

Guillermo nodded. We shared a mutual hatred of Murphy, something that had actually made me relieved in some small way to have Guillermo around, even in the early days.

'What did he want?' Guillermo asked, staring at the microwave as it counted down.

I shrugged. 'What does he ever want?'

Guillermo nodded, taking the lo mein out of the microwave and placing it on the counter. He stood across from me, fork poised in the air above the steaming container.

'He hurt you?'

I shook my head.

Guillermo stabbed his fork into the food. 'We telling Dornan about this?'

I held his gaze. 'Whatever you think.'

'Is there anything I need to deal with?'

I shook my head. 'Just the usual shit. You know what he's like.'

The silence between us was thick, and it smelled like Chinese food.

'If he comes back again, tell me,' Guillermo said. 'He needs to know his fucking place around here.'

I nodded.

'Hey, Guillermo,' I said, watching him eat. 'Can I ask you something?'

He nodded, his dark eyes watching me in anticipation.

'What did it feel like? When you decided to blow up that house?'

He stopped chewing, his eyes darting around the apartment as he swallowed audibly.

'Why do you ask?'

I chewed on the inside of my lip. 'I've wanted to ask you for years. Guess I finally feel like you won't get mad at me if I do.'

He stared at me some more.

'Forget it,' I said, circling the counter and brushing past him to get to the vodka in the freezer. He turned, grabbing my arm and leaning in close to me.

'It felt good,' he said, the ghost of a smile playing on his lips. 'I knew they'd catch me. I knew I'd go to prison. It was still worth it to me, the risk that I'd be in prison until I died.'

His fingers digging into my arm were hurting, but I ignored the pain.

'You don't regret it? Even now?'

He grinned. 'Never.'

'That's what I thought.'

He dropped the smile. 'Is there something I should know, Mariana?'

Now I smiled. 'No. I was just thinking if I kill Murphy one day, maybe I'll call you first.'

He looked uneasy. Very uneasy. 'Don't get involved in shit above your paygrade, cholita. Leave it to the boys. I swear to you, one day Murphy will lose relevance, and on that day your boy Dornan'll be first in line to end that piece of shit.'

'You called me cholita again.'

He dropped my arm and turned back to his food. 'You're talking like a tough girl. Seemed appropriate.'

I stared at the back of his head and smiled.

CHAPTER THIRTEEN
MARIANA

Tuesday morning greeted me with no sign of rain, but with humidity and lazy grey clouds, heavy and swollen with a need for release as they crawled across the Californian sky.

It was a religious holiday. Normally I'd be expected to work anyway, but this particular day was some big deal for Emilio since he was a good, church-going Catholic. The entire Ross family would be there, including the wives and children, which meant I was spared the indignation of having to sit beside Emilio as a priest talked about God and faith and forgiveness. Guillermo had woken me in the night, frantic. His mother was sick, and he needed to get to the hospital in Mexico. Guillermo's absence meant that I had an entire day ahead of me and nothing to do, something that almost never happened.

So when someone knocked at the door, I already had my gun firmly in hand.

'Get your purse,' the man at the door said.

I was sporting sweatpants and unbrushed hair at 3 p.m., with a scowl to match.

'Excuse me?'

John smiled, flashing a mouthful of shiny teeth, his hands jammed into his jeans pockets. Those shiny teeth were at odds with the rest of him – rough stubble, perpetually messed up hair, those bright blue eyes that turned down slightly at the outer corners, giving him the appearance of melancholy even when he was smiling.

And he was smiling right now.

'Get dressed,' he said. 'We're taking you out.' He tilted his head to the side, his grin fading slightly. 'And maybe do something with that bird's nest.'

I raised my eyebrows, but I wasn't offended. Honestly, I was just happy to see another human being that wasn't Murphy.

John shifted slightly and I saw his daughter, Juliette, standing behind him, eyes closed as she nodded her head to music nobody else could hear. The headphones covering her ears looked much too big for her delicate head.

'Come in,' I said, holding the door open and gesturing for them to follow, shoving my gun into my pocket. The photos of Luis were hidden inside a slit in my mattress until I could find a better place for them. It made my stomach twist to think that the safest thing to do was burn them.

John and Juliette followed me inside, the apartment cooler than the muggy heat outside. My mind was still reeling from Murphy's visit the night before, and from the phone call I'd made to Miguel.

I hadn't cried yet. I was definitely still in shock. I'd spent the day sitting on the floor of my living room, staring into space, trying not to throw up.

'What's the occasion?' I asked John as he headed straight for the pot of coffee I'd just brewed. 'You're not Catholic, are you?'

He shrugged, looking pleased with himself. 'Nope. Still get the day off, though. Thank you, Jesus.' He held his mug of steaming black coffee up and clinked it against another imaginary one.

I put my hands on my hips, amused. 'What's going on, John?' And then my smile faded and I felt my entire body go cold.

Was he here to check up on me? Had Murphy sent him? No, that was impossible. He hated Murphy.

'Hey, Earth to Mariana,' John said, stepping forward and clicking his fingers in front of my face. I blinked, pushing my suspicions away as I glanced at Juliette, who was currently sprawled in one of my dining chairs, her blonde hair fanned out around her head on the glass table top.

'She can't hear a damn thing with that iPod in her ears,' John said, taking a swig of coffee. He made a face, set the coffee down, and opened the pantry, searching. 'You got sugar in here?'

He pulled a canister out and set it down on the counter.

The fucking flour canister. Where I hid my phone. I mean, I knew he'd been the one to give me the phone, but did that mean I could trust him? It had been eight-and-a-half years since we'd had that conversation. To be honest, I was very surprised the phone still worked after almost nine years. I guess because I barely used it.

I reached over and grabbed the canister just as he was going to open it. 'That's flour,' I said quickly, holding the canister to my chest. 'The sugar is in the smaller one. And since when do you take sugar?'

He was perceptive. He studied me and the flour canister for a few seconds, before shrugging and returning to the pantry shelf. He grabbed the sugar and dumped several heaped spoonfuls of the stuff into his mug.

'I need the extra energy today. You want some?' he asked, holding the sugar out to me.

I shook my head. 'I'm sweet enough.'

He chuckled, returning the sugar and closing the pantry, the flour seemingly forgotten. 'What does that make me, bitter?'

I smiled. 'Something like that. But seriously ...' I glanced at Juliette again, who seemed to be in a world of her own. I envied the casual way she could be so happily absorbed in the soundtrack on her iPod, the only thing she needed to entertain herself. '... what are you doing here?' I asked.

John downed the rest of his coffee and rinsed his empty mug out, setting it on the drainer. 'Taking you two out. It's a holiday. We should take advantage of it while we can.' He looked beyond me to Juliette. 'And Dornan called me and asked me to.'

'Oh.' I deflated a little. Of course. My knight in shining armour was with his wife and kids and his reprehensible fucking father at Mass. Dornan had just placed a call to his bestie to occupy me so I didn't get up to anything risky while I was left to my own devices for one whole day.

'I take it that's not the response you were looking for?' John enquired.

Damn, he was perceptive. I had practised my poker face to perfection, but there was something about him, something magnetic that made it feel like he could crack my head open and unravel every lie I'd ever told. Maybe it was because I saw him as an actual human being, instead of the monsters I normally encountered. Donning my poker face with Emilio wasn't a choice, it was a matter of survival.

Either way, I could count on one hand the times I'd seen John act so casually. Usually it was within the confines of the tiny office where he'd do money drops, when his mask would occasionally slip and he'd flash me one of those grins. But over the years those smiles had become less and less common. He always seemed like he had the weight of the world on his shoulders these days.

I shrugged. 'No, it's fine. I just wasn't expecting company.'

He nodded, running his tongue over his perfect teeth as he looked me up and down. 'I know.'

'Screw you, asshole,' I joked. 'On my days off, I am the queen of sweatpants and bird's-nest hair.'

He tipped his head back and laughed. The sound was almost startling. It had been years since I'd heard John Portland laugh. It made his eyes sparkle, something about the way the light bounced off his baby blues. There was always some other biker club to worry about, some transaction to officiate, some police heat to deal with. He. Never. Laughed.

I swallowed thickly, my cheeks suddenly pooling with blood. 'I'll go get ready,' I muttered, hightailing it to my bedroom.

I chose something pretty, a blue spaghetti-strap dress – the exact colour of John's eyes – that fell to just above my knees. It was only later that I realised I'd chosen it because of the colour match and that made me feel kind of jittery. I shouldn't be looking at a married man's eyes long enough to notice what colour they were, let alone get lost in them. Because I had Dornan, and he loved me, and he had always done right by me. Dornan adored me. He worshipped me. He'd risked everything to make sure I wasn't sold to the highest bidder as a slave nine years ago. If my heart belonged to anyone, it belonged to Dornan. More importantly, it belonged to my son.

But the heart is a fickle thing, and my heart was lonely. In John Portland's blue eyes I saw something I hadn't seen in a very long time.

Kindness.

CHAPTER FOURTEEN
JOHN

The boardwalk on Santa Monica Beach was teeming with people when they arrived. John parked in a tow zone. He didn't have to worry about things like that. This was his town, and he took what he could get in the way of favours like free parking and generous discounts. He was less keen on the other perks offered to him on a daily basis, like free hookers and every kind of drug under the sun, even the ones the Il Sangue Cartel weren't involved in.

The ice-cream parlour was packed, but it didn't matter. John's booth was always available. It had a permanent 'reserved' sign on it. The irony of having a booth in an ice-cream store didn't escape him, but it sure came in handy when he needed to take his little girl out.

Only his little girl was getting older, and sweet, frozen dairy products and shiny plastic booths had lost some of the lustre they'd once had. Now she remained quiet when he took her out, barely touched her ice cream, and sulked for eighty percent of the visit.

He didn't take it personally. He remembered being fourteen. Fourteen sucked.

Especially today. His only daughter had just had her heart broken by the local stud and it took every tiny bit of self-control John possessed not to ride over to the boy's house and strangle him to death for making his baby hurt. The boy was a senior, and apparently he'd dumped Julz for an older girl, Shailene, whose loose reputation preceded her. John knew of her reputation because he'd had to personally escort Shailene from his clubhouse on several occasions after finding the underage girl drunk and making a play for some young prospect's cock.

It reinforced John's desire to keep Juliette away from his world, but at the same time she was forced into it, because there were only so many places he could keep an eye on her. And entrusting his wife to watch over their daughter was like throwing chum into shark-infested waters and then expecting the sharks to stay away. Caroline always found some way to endanger their daughter, either through sheer neglect, or by doing something completely inappropriate like taking her on a trip to score some blow and making her wait in the car. In the projects. At three in the morning.

Yeah, Caroline didn't get to be in charge of their daughter anymore, and that was probably the only reason she was still relatively young compared to girls like Shailene.

John was glad for today.

'What'll it be?' he asked Mariana and Juliette. Mariana was across from him, a look on her face that said she was still trying to figure out what was going on, and Juliette was beside him, crammed into the middle of the U-shaped booth.

Juliette shrugged, taking her headphones out. 'Whatever.'

Mariana smiled, looking at the menu. 'Surprise me.'

As John approached the counter, he heard Mariana talking to his daughter. Maybe because she wasn't high like Caroline, he thought. No. Today was not about Caroline, or about worrying. Today was a goddamn day off from everything, and unless somebody called to say somebody was dying, they could fuck off until tomorrow.

The woman who owned the place knew his order by heart. 'Add in a …' He surveyed the glass display cabinet, reading each flavour as his eyes passed over the ice cream, 'strawberry, as well.'

He didn't pay for anything here. He'd stopped trying to years ago, after Didi, the owner, had told him his money wasn't welcome. Before John had started frequenting the place, it had been robbed so many times that she was considering boarding the place up and declaring bankruptcy. But John couldn't have that. If they closed, he would have had to take little Juliette to one of those crappy chain stores to buy ice cream, and they sure as shit didn't have a view out to the ocean and the Ferris wheel like this place did.

As Didi bustled off to prepare his order, John couldn't help but listen in to what Mariana and Juliette were talking about. It was quiet in this corner of the store, and the acoustics were excellent. He felt bad for eavesdropping, but he was worried about Julz and her poor broken heart, and he needed to make sure she was okay. She wouldn't speak a word to him about what had happened, and so for her to be chatting up a storm with Mariana made his heart lift.

'Most boys are idiots,' Mariana was saying. 'Especially the popular ones. What was his excuse?'

'He wanted to fuck me,' Juliette said plainly. 'So I dumped him. And he told the whole school he dumped me first.'

John stole a glance at them, his hands balled up into fists, his head about to explode at the casual way his teenage daughter had just mentioned some guy wanting to *fuck* her. John debated getting the club together and cutting the boy's dick off.

Mariana's eyebrows looked like they were about to lift the ceiling off. 'You should get your revenge on this boy,' Mariana said. 'Nothing dangerous, nothing that would lead back to you. But maybe a rumour.'

Juliette leaned in closer. 'What kind of rumour?'

Mariana smiled. 'Oh, you know, something like … he's got herpes or something. Tell people you had to dump him because you caught him kissing his sister.'

Juliette laughed. Mariana looked directly at John and smiled, as if she knew he'd been listening the entire time. John grabbed the ice creams, which had been sitting in the holder for some time already, and took them over to the booth as if he hadn't heard a thing.

'My mama used to make ice cream from fresh cream and strawberries,' Mariana said, taking a bite of her cone. Almost as soon as the words had left her mouth, she seemed to still, her eyes widening slightly, before she composed herself again.

If John had blinked, he would have missed it.

'Do you see her often?' John asked, his tone casual. 'Your mama?'

Mariana froze like a deer in headlights, bracing for the car that was about to plough headfirst into her.

Juliette poked her father. 'Can I play the pinball machine?'

John reached into his pocket, taking a pile of loose change and giving it to her. Immediately, he felt lighter. He hated carrying shrapnel around. 'Stay where I can see you,' he said softly. Juliette rolled her eyes, but she was still smiling. 'Yes, Daddy,' she said, climbing out over the back of the booth and heading for the small bank of pinball machines in the far corner of the ice-cream parlour.

John turned his attention back to Mariana, who was staring out of the window at the water, her ice cream starting to melt in her hand, forgotten.

'You know, in all the time I've known you, I've never heard you talk about your family. I've never really heard you talk about … anything.'

She turned back to meet his gaze; her lips pressed together tightly. 'Yes, I know that.'

John raised his eyebrows slightly. 'How's your ice cream?' Great. She was gonna clam up before he'd even said three words to her.

She smiled, but her eyes remained impassive. 'Cold,' she said, holding it away from her like it was poisoned. 'It's cold.'

John laughed. Mariana remained stony faced and silent.

'Jesus, you really don't get out much, do you?' he said, the humour gone now.

Her lip curled up, an amused smirk. 'It took nine years for you to notice that?'

Nine years. Christ. They'd been working together for nine years, and their conversation had barely gotten past the weather. There had been that one time, when he'd taken the photo from her, and the other time, when he'd given her the burner phone with his number programmed in. He'd wanted to help her, but she hadn't called him once. Not ever.

'You never answered my question. Do you see your mama very much? I know Dornan and Emilio keep you busy in the office.'

'I don't, no. You see your wife very often? I know Dornan and Emilio keep you busy with …' She paused for a moment. '… whatever it is a president does.' She waved her hand at the tattoo on his neck that marked him a Gypsy, before returning her eyes to the water that lapped at the Santa Monica shore.

Wow. Talk about sucker-punching him in the gut with a dig about Caroline. He went to bite back, but then he realised: she was deflecting his questions, diverting his attention. She was like this ghost that was always around. He spent several hours with this woman every week, and beyond her name, he didn't know a damn thing about her. He knew that she was stuck here, but she'd never told him why. And Dornan wasn't one to offer up specifics, even when John pressed him. It seemed that Mariana Rodriguez was off limits in their conversations.

And that was a shame. Because he liked her. She was funny and kind, not to mention fucking beautiful.

Shit. He needed to not think of her like that. She wasn't fucking beautiful. She was nobody. Christ! Under the table, his cock was straining against his pants again at the mere sight of her tongue running lazily across her bottom lip as she stared into space. Those lips looked so soft, he wanted to reach out and brush his finger across them. *Jesus, you're married, and she's taken.* Cold showers. Emilio. Ahhh yes, nothing made his cock go softer than thinking about his psychopathic boss.

'You don't like talking about your family, that's OK. I don't like talking about mine.'

Mariana got up and tossed her cone in the trash. Sitting back down across from him, she started shredding her paper napkin, making a neat pile on the table in front of her. John observed her as he finished his cone, unsure how to rescue the conversation.

'What do you want to talk about?' John asked. 'I'll give you the floor.'

He watched her face, waiting for a reaction, but there was nothing. As she pressed a hand to the window and continued to stare at the sea beyond, it occurred to John that she wasn't ignoring him.

She hadn't even heard him speak.

CHAPTER FIFTEEN
MARIANA

'Can I go on the wheel?' Juliette asked.

The three of us gazed up at the Ferris wheel. John shrugged. 'Sure. You want me to come with you?'

She shook her head. 'I'm not a baby, *Father*.'

Defiant little thing. If I had spoken to my father like that, I would have been smacked upside the head. Then again, if I'd talked to my father at all when I was Juliette's age, he would have smacked me upside the head.

Thinking of him did nothing to lift my black mood. I should be happy, being out here like this, but I was fretting. Why was it suddenly necessary for John to babysit me? Had Dornan somehow figured out Murphy's plan? Was he waiting to see if I shared what I'd learned the previous night with him? Or was this just a happy coincidence, that the very day after Murphy dropped a bomb on me and I then learned the truth – that my entire family had been murdered – that John had decided to take me out?

And John's questions about my family were starting to irritate me. They made me suspicious. Was he baiting me to see if I'd confess knowledge of their deaths, only to punish me for making the forbidden phone call to Este's brother? Has John been listening to the calls I've made through the burner cellphone, the one *he* gave me, this entire time?

So many questions. I didn't know who to trust. Had he brought me out with Juliette so I felt more comfortable, so I let my guard down?

Well, he wasn't getting anything from me. Not one iota. If I was wrong, and this was innocent, I'd apologise later.

Maybe.

Once Juliette was riding the Ferris wheel, John turned his attention to me again. I'd been expecting it. He was as stubborn as me.

'So, you don't like talking about your family,' he said, lighting a cigarette. 'What do you like talking about?'

I shrugged, not meeting his gaze as I squeezed the metal railing that separated us from the wheel. Did he have to pick at me like I was an open wound, begging to be torn open and exposed?

Sighing, he stood closer to me, so that our shoulders touched. I wanted to jerk myself away in protest, but my shoulder burned pleasantly where it touched his. *I am such a loser*, I thought to myself. *Any tiny bit of human contact and I'm fighting to keep my hands to myself.*

I was so deprived of affection, a casual touch of someone's shoulder against mine sent a thrill through me. Not just anyone, though. There was something about John that did it.

I felt heat rise in my cheeks. I couldn't afford to think like that.

'Tell me something about yourself,' John pressed me. 'Tell me anything.' He'd angled his body so it was achingly close to mine, his hips twisted so that his stomach was inches away from my ass. And he was talking directly into my ear, so close I could feel his breath on my neck.

I shook my head resolutely. 'No.'

Out of the corner of my eye, I could see that he looked almost amused. 'Where are you from?' he asked, stepping back a little as we watched Juliette go around and around.

I eyed him warily, shaking my head. His questions made me mad. I would tell him nothing.

John sighed. 'You had a son.'

I wanted to punch him in the face. Was he part of this, then? Was he working with Murphy? Was he trying to find out where Luis was, so he could kill him? I whirled to face John, jabbing my finger into his hard chest as a look of surprise spread across his face.

'Do you really think if I had a son, I would be standing here with you?' I asked, gritting my teeth. How dare he? He had no right to talk about Luis. No right.

He considered that for a moment. Leaned back, putting space between us as he took another drag of his cigarette. He dropped his gaze, staring at the lit end as if he was pondering something, before levelling his eyes at me once more. His stare was intense, but I didn't look away. I wouldn't back down.

'You carry a photo of a baby around, but he's not your son?' John asked dubiously. 'Okay, whatever.' And I could tell he was offended that I wouldn't tell him anything.

He was hurt. And somehow I knew that he was telling the truth. That he wasn't trying to get information from me to hurt me. I had an overwhelming feeling that he was on my side. Call it intuition, call it gut feeling – but suddenly I felt terrible for assuming the worst of him.

I hated to lie – especially to someone who was trying to be nice. But I did. Because he'd been Dornan's best friend forever, and he'd worked for Emilio almost that long, and one more person knowing about my son was one too many. I thought of Murphy, of the way he used Luis as a pawn against me, and how effortlessly it worked. I couldn't handle Emilio Ross doing the same thing. Not to mention Dornan's reaction if he found out that I'd kept the knowledge of my child from him all these years. He'd never forgive me for lying to him about it, even if it was technically only lying by omission.

'He was my baby brother,' I said, skimming the murkiness of the past to extract and craft a suitable lie. 'He died a long time ago. So don't make things up to try and bond with me, John. Do I *look* like somebody's mother to you?'

He looked disappointed. He didn't respond.

'I'm sorry for your loss,' he said finally, dropping his cigarette butt and crushing it under his heel. 'I just assumed, is all.'

'It's fine,' I said, feeling like a fucking bitch for lying to him, nice, dependable John. 'I can see how you'd think that.'

But I clung to my secrets. My son was already in danger, our future together seemingly impossible. They couldn't have his memory, too.

'Like I said, I'm nobody's mother.' I snorted. 'I'd make a lousy mother, anyway.'

John let out a breath, turning to watch as Juliette's chair descended slowly and she was let off the carnival ride.

'You did more motherly things for her in the past hour than her actual mother's done in years,' he said, and my heart broke a little for the both of them.

'John—' I started.

'It's fine,' he said, echoing my previous sentiments. He started towards Juliette. 'Let's go.'

I followed him wordlessly as he walked away from me. He stopped and touched Juliette's shoulder gently when she stopped in front of him, murmured something in her ear. He was a good father.

Soon we were climbing into John's car, the doors making a dull thunk as he closed Juliette's door, then mine. Our eyes caught as he closed my door, and I attempted a small smile. I didn't know what the hell the outing had been for other than a babysitting gig for John, but I still wanted him to know that I was grateful for the brief reprieve from my apartment. He stared down at me through the car window, and something passed between us. I don't know what it was or even how to describe it. It was something, though, because all of a sudden my throat was thick, my stomach was doing flips and the hair on the back of my neck was standing on end. Something inside me lit up, and I had to look away.

I shifted my gaze to the sky, watching the clouds on the horizon as they continued to roll in above us. Everything seemed to get colder almost immediately, and then the sky burst open.

It rained so infrequently in Los Angeles that when it did, it was almost magical. Back home it rained often and the land was lush and green as a result. Here, it seemed to make everything spring to life and sparkle. It washed away the dirt and dust that clung to everything, a byproduct of existing in a desert by the sea.

John swore, shielding his face as he circled the car and got into the driver's seat. I watched him silently as he started the engine and revved it a few times. Maybe he felt my gaze on him, because he glanced up at me sharply. His eyes looked tired. Bloodshot. I wondered when he'd last had a decent night's sleep. I was betting it was the last time Dornan did. Well before I met either of them.

CHAPTER SIXTEEN
MARIANA

It was late. John had dropped me off at my apartment and called me three times to make sure I'd activated the code on the door correctly. Seemed he took his job as protection detail in Dornan's absence seriously.

If only he knew.

I kicked my wet shoes off and walked through the bedroom into the adjoining bathroom, flicking the light on and leaning over the basin, wringing my wet hair out in the sink. I was freezing cold, the water clinging to my skin in tiny droplets that made me shiver.

I caught sight of my eyes in the mirror and cringed. My mother's eyes, my son's eyes. Dark blue. When I'd been born, the doctors had told my mother that they'd eventually turn brown, just like my father's eyes. Because brown was meant to be the dominant gene. But my eyes had only gotten bluer as I got older, bluer and more serious as the innocence of my youth had ebbed away. And now there was nothing in them, nothing but a vast darkness that stretched as far and wide as my empty existence.

I had the sudden urge to call Miguel again and check on Luis. I wrapped my hair up in a towel and padded, barefoot, through my bedroom and into the hallway. I heard rustling and looked for Guillermo, but – wait – Guillermo wasn't here, was he?

Guillermo was in Mexico.

My heart dropped into my stomach as I realised somebody who wasn't Guillermo was in my apartment.

Nothing was out of place. But somebody was here.

I smelled it first.

Oranges. The sharp citrus smell stung my nostrils. I never bought oranges. I hated the way they tasted. Yet I could smell, as plain as day, the overpowering scent of freshly sliced orange.

I took a few tentative steps down the hall, suddenly on high alert.

I didn't have my gun. I'd left it in my handbag, in the bedroom, and now I was here, defenceless, and somebody was in my house. In my fucking kitchen. And then I saw him, hovering in the shadows beside the refrigerator, and as he shifted the streetlight slicing through the blinds cut across his blue eyes.

'I thought you'd never get back,' Murphy said, not moving.

I backed up a little, debating if I had time to run back to the bedroom. My entire body was alight, rage and fear humming in a steady vibration. I couldn't think properly. It was the first time I'd seen Murphy since learning the truth about what had happened to my family.

But he didn't know that I knew. At least, I hoped he didn't know.

He stepped out of the shadows, holding his palms up in a supplicating gesture. 'Did you bring me back a chocolate ice cream?'

I changed my mind. He needed me, and even if he'd somehow intercepted the call I had made to Este's brother, he wouldn't shoot me. He couldn't. I had the keys to the city, as far as he was concerned. I was the co-signatory on every single dirty bank account he'd been stashing money in, in this country and the rest.

'You look more like a vanilla man to me,' I replied coolly, rooted to the spot. 'Boring and weak.'

He laughed, swiping at the drink on the counter. 'You're hilarious. Ever since the first time I stuck my finger inside you, I knew you were fucking hilarious.'

'You're drunk,' I realised, a little surprised.

He was soaking wet, from head to toe. The rain that had begun as we were leaving the ice-cream parlour hadn't eased off, instead it had come down in sheets.

It looked like Murphy hadn't been here long, judging by how soaked through with rain he was. It looked like he'd taken a bath fully clothed. And he was drunk?

Never, in nine years, had I seen him even *slightly* intoxicated. High on cocaine, yes, but not drunk. He was always so controlled, so polished. Now, not so much. Something must have happened. Something to make him lose control.

I mean, apart from him killing my entire family and trying to hunt my illegitimate son to use as collateral against me.

'Have fun with Johnny Boy?' he asked. 'Romantic walks on the beach? Did you share an ice cream before he stuck his dick in you?'

Wait. He was *jealous*?

'His kid was there,' I said, still in disbelief. 'He's my fucking babysitter, Murphy.'

'Sure,' Murphy drawled. 'Babysitters don't fuck you.' He snickered. 'Well, sometimes they do. But they shouldn't, nuh-uh.'

'There's only one person who fucks me,' I replied sharply. 'You'd do well to remember that.'

He laughed again, but there was no joy in the sound. It was a guttural noise that rattled in his chest, full of loathing, full of hate. He hated me,

I realised. He hated me because I had chosen to align with somebody like Dornan, rather than somebody like him.

I didn't move as he reached up and grabbed an unopened bottle of whiskey from the top of the refrigerator and tore the lid off.

I didn't move as he approached, stopping only to throw back a swig straight from the bottle, wiping the excess that dribbled down his chin with his suit sleeve.

I didn't move, and then he was so close to me, I could smell the whiskey on his breath.

'Had to get liquored up before you came over here, huh?'

My mama always said it was my mouth that got me into trouble, and she was right. Even after all this time, I just couldn't help myself when it came to Christopher Fucking Murphy.

He narrowed his ice-blue gaze at me, pushing his black fringe out of his eyes. And then, before I could react, before I could even step back, his hand was wrapped around my face, and I was slammed back into the wall. I saw stars for a second, blinked as I heard something smash against the wall beside me, and then drew in a sharp intake of breath as the jagged teeth of a broken whiskey bottle taunted me. Inches away from my eyes, its sharp edges were still dripping with whiskey.

'Murphy,' I cautioned, 'think about this. You need me. You need me if you want to get your money.'

Fuck!

I struggled to keep my breathing even as I watched his eyes slide from mine, down to my lips, over my chest. A smirk tugged at the corner of his mouth.

'I'm pretty sure there's a way around it, little lady.' The whiskey on his breath burned my nostrils. My mind was whirling. This motherfucker had killed my entire family – or at least been directly responsible for it – and it looked like he was about to kill me, too. I couldn't let that happen. I wouldn't.

You know what he wants, the rational part of my brain screamed. *Give it to him.*

No!

Save yourself.

Jesus.

I reached my hand out, moving slowly in case he thought I was on the attack and he decided to stab me with the broken bottle. I wrapped my hand around the back of his neck and pulled his face closer to mine, pulling even though I wanted to push him away, fighting back the rising panic inside me.

'What do you want, Murphy?' I asked softly. 'Because I'm pretty sure it's not just my cooperation with your little scheme.'

He licked his lips, breathing heavily. He lowered the bottle to his side and seemed to calm down a little, his blue eyes still cold and fucking crazy, but his breathing slower, his urge to stab me apparently in check once again.

'You know what I want,' he breathed. 'I could make your life so fucking sweet,' he brushed a thumb across my bottom lip, 'if you just gave it to me.'

Something violent and dark unleashed itself within me.

'You want to fuck me,' I breathed. 'Fuck me already. I'd be so much better than that little bitch you've been screwing.'

My words were like a green light to someone who's been stuck in a traffic jam for almost a decade. I saw the shift in Murphy's gaze, from predatory but controlled, to completely animalistic. A low growl came from his throat as he fisted a handful of my hair and began dragging me towards my bedroom.

There was a gun in my bedroom. In my purse.

I followed him without fighting. Part of me was screaming inside, trying to convince myself to run, to try and get away, but another part was swiftly concocting a plan.

He threw me towards the bed, where I landed on my side, hard. I rolled onto my back, looking to the left and seeing my purse sitting below the pillow.

I turned my attention back to Murphy, who'd discarded the broken bottle somewhere along the way. His pants were around his ankles and his dick out before I could even blink. I sat up, swallowing back nervous bile that rushed up my throat. I was going to have to fuck him, I realised, my heart sinking at the prospect of him touching any part of me. He palmed his erection, pumping it as he looked down at me.

'You on birth control?' he asked, staring at the space between my legs that was still hidden by my dress.

'No,' I said, almost too quickly. I was, but he didn't need to know that. 'There are condoms in the bathroom. Top drawer.'

He looked pissed, but he pulled his pants back up and held onto the waistband, hurrying into the bathroom. The second he was out of my line of sight, I reached back and into my purse, rummaging around until my fingers touched cold metal. I slid my gun out as inconspicuously as I could, shoving it underneath my pillow with the handle facing me.

The slam of the bathroom drawer made me jump, and then Murphy was in front of me, a foil packet in his hand.

'Put it on,' he demanded.

I looked up at him without taking the packet. 'I think you've got me all wrong,' I deadpanned. 'I don't have a dick.'

His fist slammed into my cheek and I tasted blood. I fell back onto the bed, fighting as he grabbed my wrists.

'You're a very bad girl,' he said, tutting. 'Let's try that again. Put it on *me*. You can suck it first for talking back to me.'

He fisted a handful of my hair and pulled my face closer. I took a deep breath, debating my position. Sure, I could pull the gun out now – assuming I could still reach it – and hold it to his balls, but he could easily just drop down on me and overpower me.

'Open,' he sneered, pushing his erection against my lips. Reluctantly, and out of options, I opened my mouth.

Bitterness coated my tongue as pre-come leaked from his dick and into my mouth. I fought the overpowering urges to throw up and bite down as hard as I could. Death by penis removal – it'd be a fitting end for somebody like him, but I didn't like the idea of potentially being shot in the head as soon as I bit down. Instead, I relaxed my throat, letting him slide in and out of my mouth.

'You like that?' Murphy asked, squeezing my throat painfully with his free hand. His eyes flashed with excitement as he pushed in harder, hitting the back of my throat. I struggled not to gag as he pistoned his hips, driving his dick deep into my mouth again and again.

'Oh, you dirty little whore,' he said, breathing heavily. 'I can feel my cock in your throat. You're my little whore now. I'm taking you with me when we get outta here, you understand?' He squeezed my throat harder when I didn't respond. I nodded, because I couldn't exactly talk with a mouthful of dick.

My fingertips burned, begging me to grab the gun and shoot him. But I couldn't reach, and I couldn't very well just casually lean back, with the way he was holding my head immobile. He sped up, getting rougher as he approached release. Beneath the fear and the rage, I was already getting bored. I'd have a sore jaw after this. It was already screaming in protest.

'Suck harder,' he commanded. 'Suck the come out of me, you dirty whore.'

I didn't change what I was doing. I refused to make it any better for him. At the moment, as it was, it looked like his dirty little long-held fantasy was doing just fine without any enthusiasm on my part.

He let go of my hair all of a sudden, withdrawing from my mouth. I gasped for air as he palmed his wet erection, giving it a couple of tugs. He was close already, and he wanted to draw this out. For fuck's sake.

'I'm about to come all over your face,' he grunted, 'and if you close your eyes, I'll hurt you. You understand?'

I rested back on my elbows and spread my legs open wide, bracing my bare heels on the edge of the bed. 'You're not scared of fucking me, are you, Murphy?'

He sneered, snatching the condom up from beside me. 'Put it on,' he said. 'I wouldn't breed with a dirty little slut like you if you were the last woman on earth.'

Well, the feeling was mutual. I fought the urge to fire off a retort, rage burning in my chest. I needed to get the taste out of my mouth. Now. It was so vile, I was struggling not to puke.

Making my face go blank, I took the foil packet and ripped it open. Dornan didn't wear protection, ever. Murphy didn't know that, though. Thank Christ.

'I don't know how,' I said.

Eyes flashing with frustration and lust, he took the packet from me and rolled the condom onto his erection. Once it was on, he looked at me and grinned.

'Turn over onto your stomach,' he ordered. 'This will hurt, but I promise you'll love it, like the little slut you are.'

Wow, he sure liked the word slut. Wasn't very creative when it came to alternatives.

Again, I thought of the gun. If I laid down on my back, I'd be able to reach it. I wasn't going to flip onto my stomach, not if I could help it. I'd be powerless then. On my stomach, he could capture my wrists, crush me under his weight and I wouldn't even have my arms to fight him off with.

'Don't you want to watch me come?' I pouted. 'That's Dornan's favourite part.'

Mentioning Dornan was exactly what I needed to do to set him off. He launched onto me like a goddamn lion, his lips crashing into mine as he tugged my panties to the side and pushed into me in one hard movement. I wasn't exactly turned on, and my eyes watered at the sudden intrusion.

His skin was cold and damp from the rain. I'd fared better than him, with my umbrella, and so when his freezing cold skin touched mine I jerked back, our kiss broken as he fucked me, rough and fast. He hadn't even undressed me, he was so impatient. I smiled wickedly at him, pushing my hips up to meet his with every thrust.

He closed his eyes, a sigh of appreciation falling from his lips. I kept my own eyes wide open. I thought I'd feel scared at what would come next, but all I felt was the stark relief of knowing I'd soon have one less enemy in the world.

Thrust.

My fingers itched. *Wait.*

Thrust.

Almost.

Thrust.

Now.

I reached up, slid my hand underneath the pillow and curled my fingers around the gun. I located the trigger and kept my index finger on it. Almost.

Thrust.

I rested my free hand on his ass and pulled him deeper. 'Harder,' I murmured.

He liked that. His head fell forward as he used every ounce of energy on making sure he'd bedded himself as deep and as hard as possible with every single thrust. I was mostly numb to it now, too distracted by more devious things.

Thrust.

Wait.

Thrust.

Almost.

Thrust.

Now.

I pulled the gun from its spot under the pillow and pressed the end of the barrel to Murphy's pale forehead. His eyes flew open, ice-blue and full of What-the-Fuck? He stopped everything. Stopped moving, stopped breathing. The only thing that was happening was in his bright eyes.

They were afraid.

'Pull out,' I demanded. He didn't move. 'Now!' I cried, pushing the gun harder against his pale skin. He jerked his hips back, pulling himself out of me, and I almost cried at the immense relief from knowing he wasn't inside me any more.

It was like I'd floated away and was looking on from above. It didn't feel real; none of it did. I was on the bed underneath Murphy, and his eyes started to become wet and glossy. Tears?

'Afraid?' I asked, unable to wipe the grin from my lips. Something had changed inside me through nine years of hate and pain, and that *something* that lurked in the deepest recesses of my dark soul enjoyed Murphy's discomfort entirely too much. Craved it. Wanted more of it.

'Did you kill my family?' I whispered, and the smile I was wearing faded away. Grim realisation spiked in his eyes, and his entire body tensed. A wave of nausea rolled through me. *It's true. He fucking did it.*

He didn't answer, but the answer was clear as day in his eyes; in the way he looked away for a split second before meeting my gaze again, in the stunned look on his face, in the heavy exhale that came from his chest.

I saw the questions in his eyes.

'How?' he asked, his words tumbling out quickly, with urgency. 'You were tracked. You were fucking watched day and night. You don't take a piss without me knowing, so *how*?' Beads of sweat were starting to gather above his eyebrows, and his anxiety made my heart beat faster in excitement.

'Tell me what happened to them,' I demanded. 'Tell me, and I'll let you walk out of here.'

His eyes dipped to the side. I responded by cocking the hammer on the gun, a loud metallic click.

'You really think I didn't check on my family in nine years?' I whispered. 'How stupid are you? How stupid do you think *I* am? Tell me.' My lips quivered as a single tear escaped from my left eye. Damn it. I didn't want him to see what he'd done to me. The pain he'd caused. I didn't want him to have the satisfaction of knowing how I'd suffered thanks to him.

'Your father killed a school kid in a hit-and-run. He was drunk, and when they arrested him, he turned on Emilio,' Murphy spoke slowly, his words careful, measured. 'The feds realised what an opportunity they'd been given and granted your father immunity in exchange for his testimony against the cartel.'

'The feds? Be more specific.'

Murphy scowled. 'The FBI.'

I made a small sound of annoyance in the back of my throat. 'I want a name, asshole. Give me a name. The FBI's a big fucking agency.'

'Why?'

I applied pressure to the trigger and Murphy blanched. 'Lindsay Price. He's investigating Emilio. You tell anybody I told you that and we'll both be dead.'

'And?' I pressed.

Murphy shrugged, his arms beginning to shake as he held himself above the treacherous nozzle of my gun. 'Nobody testifies against Il Sangue, Mariana. Your father was a fool to think he'd even make it to the FBI's safe house.'

'I can only see one fool now,' I said, 'and he's right in front of me.'

Murphy narrowed his eyes, opening his mouth to reply, and I took that as an invitation to jam the barrel of my beautiful gun between Murphy's lips and teeth.

He spoke angry, unintelligible words around the gun in his mouth, his fingers curling around my biceps and squeezing.

I thought of how I'd been stuck here for nine shitty fucking years. I thought of *them*, screaming as they burned and died. And any hesitation that lived inside me was replaced with a cold, numb nothingness.

'Fuck you,' I whispered.

Before I lost my nerve, I pulled the heavy trigger back.

CHAPTER SEVENTEEN
MARIANA

The blast deafened me, the force of the kick throwing Murphy off of me momentarily. What goes up must come down, though, and he landed heavily on my chest a second later, my grip still firmly around the gun in his mouth as his dead weight knocked every ounce of air out of me. His mouth was not what it had been three seconds ago. My eyes had adjusted to the light enough to see his cold, unblinking blue eyes and the gore the bullet had created beyond his shattered teeth.

He was as dead as they come. I'd just killed a man as he hate-fucked me, and I was pretty sure I was going to be murdered brutally for it.

My senses went haywire. My eyes could see better than ever in the dark, every detail soaking into my brain and lying in wait for later, when they'd become my nightmares, no doubt. I drew in a panicked breath as I tried to push Murphy's bleeding corpse off me, but he wouldn't budge. *Jesus.* I was pinned, blood rushing from his mouth onto my stomach and chest and sliding down my right side, pooling underneath me where it quickly grew sticky and cold. I panicked. I started to scream, clapping a hand over my mouth as I shrieked into it, tasting the heavy, metallic blood that coated my lips and palm. Vomit rose in my throat and I swallowed it down.

I forced myself to stop screaming. The immediate threat was gone. Murphy was dead. I'd just successfully avenged the murders of my family in some small way. There was more to do, further to go, but I'd just taken the first brutal, bloody step towards my own redemption.

And it felt fucking scary, but more than that, it felt exhilarating.

But still my primitive brain was freaking the fuck out. I started to wail again.

Focus.

I let go of the gun, let go of my mouth.

Figure it out.

First things first. Get Murphy the fuck off me.

I braced the heels of my palms against his shoulders and pressed my left knee against his leg, leveraging his dead weight enough to haul him, painfully slowly and inch by excruciating inch, until his body sagged onto the bed at my right. But now his weight was pinning my arm, trapping me. I pulled, hard, my tendons stretching painfully as I wrenched my hand free.

I crawled to the edge of the bed and slid onto the floor, backing away on hands and heels. The smell of blood was so thick in the air, it was like I was swimming in the stuff.

Using the wall for support, I stood, my legs trembling violently. I made it three steps to my bathroom and puked in the basin. Adrenalin, maybe. I'd need a new mattress. Would somebody call the cops after hearing that gunshot? I hoped not. I didn't need any attention.

I leaned against the bathroom doorframe and watched as the remainder of Murphy's blood drained out of the dirty hole in the back of his head and onto my Egyptian cotton sheets.

An angry buzz rang in my ears. I couldn't hear a thing. Maybe I'd blown out my own eardrums when I pulled that trigger.

I turned the faucet on to wash the vomit away and noticed blood running down my bare arms for the first time. Dreading what I'd see, I slowly raised my eyes to the large mirror that hung above the basin.

It was as if the devil stared back at me. A pair of dark blue eyes and a shock of long, tangled dark hair were the only things I recognised. The rest was a garish caricature, soaked in blood from head to toe. Was it really possible for one little bullet to do all that harm? Make all that mess? I looked like something out of a slasher movie.

And the blood wasn't the worst part. As I studied my right arm closer, I noticed a fine coating of gritty stuff. Like grains of sand, but bigger.

His skull. My arm, the one that had been trapped underneath him until I'd wrenched it out, was covered in pieces of Murphy's skull.

Luckily I was already in front of the basin, because otherwise the second puke would have gone all over my feet and the floor.

I retched until there was nothing left in my stomach but a hollow ache. I used a towel to wipe the blood from my face, hands and feet as best as I could. I stared longingly at the shower, wanting nothing more than to step underneath the hot water and let it wash every trace of Christopher Murphy from my skin. But I couldn't. I knew I had precious time left to do something.

I crept past Murphy's still form, my eyes returning to his face. His mouth. His broken teeth and the hole in his head.

I reached for my purse, taking my phone quietly as if making a noise would awaken Murphy. He wasn't waking up. Ever.

I was bloody and dirty, and I didn't want to stain the armchair in the corner of my bedroom. I tiptoed backwards, back into the safety of the tiled bathroom, sitting on the floor as I dialled Dornan on my regular phone with shaking fingers. He answered almost immediately.

'Hey.'

I thought hearing his voice might move something inexplicable inside me, make me cry, make me realise the full impact of what had just happened. *I just killed somebody.*

Nothing.

I felt nothing. I missed Dornan. I wanted Dornan here, to help me.

'What are you up to?' I asked, my voice clear, my tone casual. I must be in shock, I thought. That's got to be the only reason I can't feel something right now.

I could hear commotion. He was at home. I heard his boys in the background, his wife. 'Is something wrong?' he asked me.

'Who is that?' I heard his wife say. My heart sank. Doubt flooded through my mind. He was with his wife. He'd go to bed with her tonight, and he'd wake up tomorrow morning with her, and he was never going to leave her for me, so what the hell was I doing, living like a prisoner, lying in wait six days a week only to have him on the seventh for a mere few hours? He'd told me that he didn't sleep with her any more. He told me he didn't love her, that he only stayed because of his boys. And I'd believed him. But was he lying? Did he still touch her? Kiss her?

'It's okay,' I said quickly. 'We can talk tomorrow.'

The ghost of a smile flickered across my mouth as I stared blankly at Murphy's shiny black shoes. They gleamed as the bright bathroom light reflected off them, showing up tiny specks where blood had misted over them. It seemed to have taken forever for the flow of blood from his mouth to slow down.

'Sounds like a plan,' he said coolly, and he hung up on me.

I stared at the screen, chewing on my lip as I glanced up at Murphy.

What the fuck was I going to do with him? He was heavy. I contemplated getting my hands on a chainsaw and dismembering him in my bathtub. Too messy, and maybe a little too gruesome, even for me. Acid? I didn't know what the bath was made out of, or even what type of acid to use. I was completely unprepared for my initiation into the killer club.

I racked my brain. If I could somehow wrap him up in something, then I'd be able to put him in a car and dump the body far, far away. But he was a DEA agent. His DNA was probably everywhere in my apartment, not just from the fact I'd blown a hole in his skull tonight, but from his previous visit where he'd tried to make it like a fucking dinner date. He'd touched everything in my kitchen, in my living room, the dining table ... No, I had to somehow get rid of his body so it would never be found.

I snapped out of my daydreaming and stood, passing Murphy's dead body as I made my way to the kitchen, leaving smudges of blood where I'd not wiped every smidge of blood from the soles of my feet. I was going to have to Lysol the hell out of this apartment, I realised grimly.

But that would have to wait.

I still had the enormous problem of a *body* to get rid of.

I opened the pantry and shifted a few things, finding the flour canister where I always left it. I set it on the counter and reached my hand inside, the blood left on my fingers mingling with the white powder to create globs of garish pink. I swallowed thickly as my fingers located the plastic ziplock bag I was rummaging for. Shaking free the excess flour, I unzipped the plastic bag, tipping the burner phone into my hand. I switched it on and navigated to one of the three numbers it contained.

***

He answered after two rings. 'I thought you'd never call,' John joked, and I could imagine the cocky grin on his face. It was true, I hadn't used the phone to call him once, and he'd given it to me almost a decade ago.

'I need your help.'

He must have heard the seriousness in my voice, because his response was devoid of the jovial tone he'd greeted me with.

'What happened?'

'I shot Murphy. He's dead. He's in my apartment.' Might as well get to the point.

A long pause. Then, 'Fuck, Ana. *Jesus.*'

He never called me Ana. Always addressed me by my full name. I guess murder cut the need for formalities.

'Does anyone know?' John asked quietly. 'Does Dornan know?'

'Nobody knows,' I said, taking a bag of ground coffee from my freezer and kicking it shut again with my bare foot. Another surface I'd need to scrub clean. Great. I flicked the coffee machine on and left it to heat up, taking two mugs from the dish drainer and setting them beside the bag of Colombian roast. The small photo of lush Colombian jungle on the package taunted me, reminding me of where I came from, of where my son was. 'John.'

'Yeah.'

Fuck.

'Will you help me?'

I hated to ask but it was unavoidable. And of all of them, he was the most trustworthy. It still didn't mean he wouldn't betray me, in the end. It just meant he was most likely to keep his mouth shut for longer than anybody else in the Gypsy Brothers.

'I will *always* help you,' he said, some kind of emotion behind his words, and something about the way he said it made me break inside. 'I'm on my way. Don't move. Don't call anybody. Definitely do not answer the door, you hear me?'

'Thank you,' I said, and the line went dead.

I tidied up the flour as the coffee machine hummed to life, dripping the precious stuff into a pot that served two. I kept the burner phone out, in case John decided to call me back. My thoughts wandered as I moved around the kitchen on autopilot, a deep grief punctuated by an eerie calm. Indirectly, and without planning it, I had in some way avenged my family's murders by slaying the person – at least, one of the people – directly responsible. It made my head spin.

And there was one thought louder than the rest, incessant as it sank its barb into me, again and again. I tried to blink it away, even shaking my head from side to side to try and rid myself of the thought, because it was so insignificant it didn't deserve my attention.

The thought wasn't what you'd expect.

It wasn't *I just killed someone*. Not *I'm a murderer*.

No.

The thought that buzzed around my head like a heavy blowfly was: *I'm going to have to buy a new mattress without Dornan noticing.*

I'd just killed a man, and I didn't even care.

Nine years in hell will do that to a person.

CHAPTER EIGHTEEN

MARIANA

I was worried that John might call back and cancel on me. I didn't know where he was, or what he was doing. Shit, he was a busy guy, with a fuck-up for a wife, a teenage daughter who was too pretty to let out of his sight, and a club that needed to be run like a well-oiled machine to keep Emilio happy.

He didn't cancel. He was at my front door six minutes later, dressed in jeans and a leather jacket, a look of grim determination on his face and a five-o'clock shadow to match.

In the six minutes between him hanging up and then arriving at my door, I'd ventured back into the bedroom and located the gun in between all the blood and brain matter on my duvet. I held the gun loosely at my side and waited for the metallic click that signalled the unlocking mechanism at my front door. The door swung open and I raised the gun slowly, almost lazily.

John eyed me warily. 'Is that a gun, or are you excited to see me?'

He entered the apartment and kicked the door shut behind him. Satisfied that he was alone, and that he was here to help, I dropped the gun to my side.

'Is it still raining out there?' I asked. My throat sounded raw. Probably from having Murphy's cock rammed down it. *Well, you should see the other guy*, I thought to myself.

John shrugged. 'A little.' He didn't look wet. Not like Murphy, drenched through with rain and now soaking in all the blood that had once been inside his body.

I padded to the kitchen with John in tow, my stained feet leaving small smudges of blood, and set my gun on the kitchen counter. Taking the two mugs of coffee I'd prepared, I handed one to John, keeping the other for myself.

He took a sip of the coffee and started to choke. He was staring at my chest, I realised. The hallway wasn't lit, but the kitchen was, casting a bright glow over my current state of mess. John slammed the coffee on the counter, his eyes wide. I followed his gaze down to my dress – of course, I was still wearing the baby blue dress that matched John's eyes – and saw again just how much blood I had on me.

'What'd you do?' John coughed. 'Kill him and then roll around on top of him?'

I crossed my arms over my chest, suddenly feeling dizzy. 'Something like that,' I said.

John was quiet for a moment. 'Where is he?' he asked finally.

***

He studied the scene for a few moments without speaking, sipping his coffee every now and then. His head tilted to the side, he was like some kind of rogue detective, taking in every detail. The broken whiskey bottle. The blood-soaked sheets. I stood beside him, not so close that our arms touched, but almost. I copied his head tilt, wanting to see what *he* saw, trying to observe the scene objectively, as if it wasn't me who'd committed the crime.

Murphy wasn't a pretty sight. It was as if his body had softened somehow, melting heavily into the mattress. And his death hadn't been dignified, not one bit. His pants were still around his ankles, his bare legs a pasty white without any blood circulating in them.

The condom still clung to his flaccid penis, the empty end sticking to his thigh. John noticed it instantly, his eyes darting to mine.

'He raped you?'

I shrugged.

'It's a simple question.'

I responded, perhaps a little too sharply. 'You'd think so, wouldn't you?'

John took a step back and turned to me. 'You know, I'm missing some excellent leftover macaroni cheese and a beer for this.' His mouth quirked, as if he were about to laugh.

I snorted behind my coffee cup.

'Seriously, though,' he said. 'What happened here? I need to know. I'm a part of this now.'

I swallowed bitter coffee. 'He was here when you dropped me off.'

He looked up sharply. 'In your apartment?'

I nodded. 'He killed my entire family, and I'm pretty sure he was going to kill me, too.' I hadn't meant to say that, but fuck it, I might as well tell him.

'*What?*'

I was shaking. Why was I shaking? I was cool. I was calm. I was fine. And then suddenly, I was most definitely *not* fine. I started to suck in great lungfuls of air as the room spun around me. *My family is dead.* The people who gave me life, the ones who raised me. And until the very moment those words had left my mouth – *He killed my entire family* – I had been numb to the reality, refusing to accept it was true.

There was no witness protection for me, or them. There never had been. There was only cruel lies. Murphy had disposed of them, and he had been about to do the same to me, once I secured his stash of hidden money for him. It was all so abundantly clear, and I felt like an idiot for even considering that he'd been telling the truth before.

It was the photographs. He'd baited me with promises of seeing my son and I'd thrown logic out the window. It was terrifying how easily he'd manipulated me.

Well, who was the sucker now?

Yeah.

I stumbled, losing my balance as the room continued to spin, and John caught me before I toppled. I hated being weak, but right now, I'd give myself a hall pass.

I started to cry. Deep, wretched sobs.

'Hey,' John said, his face close to mine. 'Ana. You gotta pull yourself together. I can't take care of you and bury this motherfucker at the same time. Ana!'

I heard a loud, high-pitched scream. I think it was coming from me. I was breaking apart.

'Fuck,' I heard John swear. Clamping a hand over my mouth, he hauled me into the bathroom and into the shower recess. A moment later, freezing cold water drenched the both of us and I pushed him back angrily, my screams vanishing as the shock of the cold forced me back to my senses.

'There you are,' he muttered. He reached across me to adjust the water and soon it was warm. I stared at the drain, transfixed, as Murphy's blood washed off me. My dress. I needed to take my dress off and wash the blood from my skin.

I unzipped my dress at the back and unhooked the straps from my shoulders, letting the material fall to the shower floor in a soggy, bloody heap. John's eyes widened slightly as he looked at me, dressed only in a white bra and panties, marked in places with Murphy's blood, the thin cotton steadily turning see-through under the stream of warm water.

Had I imagined it? Had he even looked at me at all?

Yes. He had looked. He was still looking.

It was bad. It was wrong. There was a dead man lying in my bed, killed by my hand, and yet when John's eyes widened and he drew in a sharp breath, it still excited me. I felt pathetic.

'Clean yourself up,' he said gruffly, turning to go. 'I'll make some calls, get this sorted out.'

Calls? Who in the hell was he planning to call?

I caught the sleeve of his leather jacket. He stared at my hand like it was burning him just by resting there.

'Don't go,' I pleaded. 'He's in there and I can't— I just— Please don't leave me here with him.' My voice rose higher with each word until I was begging. Pleading.

I didn't even know what I was trying to say. I started to gasp for air again, panicking.

'Are you going to tell Dornan?' I asked, clawing at the front of his jacket. 'Are you going to tell Emilio?' I couldn't breathe. 'They'll kill me. Jesus, they're going to kill me, aren't they?'

'Hey,' he said firmly. 'Calm. Down.'

He cupped my face with his palm, not afraid to touch me, even though I was a dirty murdering whore with the blood of a dead DEA agent all over her. I could see myself in the mirror beyond John, and I didn't look pretty. I looked like I'd just stepped out of a warzone.

'You have blood on your face,' he said, his tone lower, gentler this time. 'Here, close your eyes.'

With his hands still cupping my face, he guided me back slightly. I closed my eyes as the warm jets of water hit my cheeks, and smelled soap as his fingers rubbed the blood away.

He had to scrub hard in some places, his rough fingertips moving urgently against my skin.

'Sorry,' he apologised.

I didn't move. I was like putty in his hands, ready to fall to the floor the moment he let go of me.

'Okay,' he said finally, pulling me slightly so my face was out of the water.

I was out of the direct stream, but water continued to dribble down my face and into my eyes. I wiped at them with my fingertips, feeling clumps of mascara come away on my skin. John's hands were still around my wrists from where he'd pulled me out of the water, and they tightened when I met his gaze.

His eyes flicked down to my lips, ever so subtly, and then back to my eyes, pinning me in place. One stolen glance at my mouth.

My heart started to race.

A second stolen glance.

The breath in my lungs started to not be enough, and I needed to breathe faster.

I dared a look at his mouth. His teeth bit down into his lip, as though he was causing himself pain to stop himself from doing something.

Mesmerised, almost as if I were in a daze, I reached my hand up and brushed my thumb over the lip he was biting down on.

He tore his head to the side and ripped my hand away, pressing it back to my side. *Wrong move, Ana.* He looked angry. I had read it all wrong. I might have wanted to kiss him, but it was clear by the way he was regarding me that he didn't feel the same way.

'I'm sorry,' I whispered, turning my head to the side.

I felt his eyes on me. They burned into my skin, but I refused to look at him again. I'd just very, very narrowly escaped making a fool of myself. Touching his lip might be forgivable, but if I'd kissed him? Jesus Christ. He'd probably kill me.

'What do you want from me?' he asked finally. I stole a glance at his face, saw the stricken expression of a man who had seen too much suffering in his life.

'Is that a trick question?' I asked quietly. 'Maybe you should tell me what you want, John Portland.'

He tipped his head back and let out a frustrated sigh. Dropping his gaze back to mine, he took a step forward, forcing me back against the cold tiles of the wall. His hands were like cuffs on my wrists, but I wasn't struggling to break free.

He opened his mouth, as if to say something. I could tell he didn't trust me, and I didn't trust him either. I mean, he could be setting me up.

I could be setting him up.

This could all be one giant set-up that went far wider than the two of us.

You never could trust anyone in this Gypsy Brothers world.

He shifted slightly, and my cheeks flushed with blood as I felt hard steel against my hip. *He wants me.* The shock must have been written across my face, plain as day, because he moved back, averted his eyes. He dropped my wrists and went to turn away.

'Stop,' I said, my tone cutting through the tension like sharp glass through flesh. I darted my hand out and grabbed the front of his jacket, yanking so he was forced back around to face me. Poker calm descended upon his expression, and I fixed mine to match.

We stared off.

'You're trying to trick me,' I breathed.

'Why do you immediately assume I'm trying to fuck you over?' he growled.

'You know why,' I snapped. 'You don't get to be a fucking stranger to someone for nine years and then suddenly change your mind after bonding over murder for five minutes.'

His poker face disappeared, morphing into something that looked equal parts lust and rage. His hands found my wrists again, pushed me roughly so my back settled against the tiles once more.

'What do *you* do when you want something you can't have?' he ground out. His blue eyes were bright, a dead giveaway about the state of his mind. When he fired up, they spoke loud and clear. I knew because I'd been looking away from them for years, afraid that if I stared too long I'd get lost in them. And I could absolutely, definitely, categorically, not get lost in John Portland's eyes for even one second.

He. Was. Dornan's. Best. Friend.

'I wait,' I whispered, my own convictions sliding away like melted butter as he rested a hand on my hip, just above my panties, and squeezed.

'And then?'

I thought about the money I'd stockpiled over the years. Emilio's dirty money. My escape plan for a rainy day. And it was pouring with rain right now.

'When nobody's looking, I take it.'

His eyes burned into me.

'Nobody's looking, Ana.'

Something inside me snapped, like an elastic band that had been pulled and pulled until it broke apart. I was starving. Not for food. For affection. For understanding. For the touch of a man who wasn't trying to hurt me.

We came together in a frenzy, lips crashing on lips, hands everywhere. I pulled him close to me, sighing into his mouth as I felt how hard he was against me, only his jeans separating us. Jesus Christ, he tasted exactly like I thought he would, a combination of the coffee we'd just drunk and something sweeter, something undefinable but delicious. I devoured him, unable and unwilling to stop, to come to my senses, until I remembered the reason why he was in my apartment in the first place.

Murphy.

I broke the kiss and pushed a hand against the middle of his chest. I wasn't rough about it, but I was firm. I covered my mouth with a shaking hand, my knees like rubber, my nipples hardened to twin points, clearly visible under my barely there lace bra. I didn't let go of him, though. I held onto him like my very life depended on being in constant physical contact with him, this man who'd pushed me away for nine excruciating years. Because he'd been attracted to me, too? God, the hours upon hours we'd spent together in that tiny office, breathing the same air, working the same jobs, numbers and accounts and with enough sexual tension to make me think of him when I touched myself at night. John Motherfucking Portland, the guy who'd carried a photo of my secret son around with him for months, until it was safe to return it to me. John Motherfucking Portland, who had barely looked into my eyes for nine whole years. The things Emilio did, that he couldn't control.

The dark pleasure Dornan carried and tucked away in an apartment like a dirty secret. A sin. All of those things were what I'd assumed John had thought of me, but now, as I looked at the tight expression on his face, the stricken eyes and the sad, resigned air he wore like a second skin, I realised how utterly wrong I had been.

I opened my mouth, and what I meant to say was, *I thought you didn't really like me.* But that didn't come out. What came out was something else entirely.

'He killed them all,' I said in disbelief, my knees no longer holding me up. John caught me, slowed my fall to the floor. He wrapped his arms around me, getting soaking wet under the shower spray. I closed my eyes, sagging into him as my legs curled around me on the hard tiles.

I cried like I'd never cried in my life. I cried nine years worth of tears, worth of lonely nights, worth of longing. I cried until I couldn't breathe, and then an exhausted calm descended upon me. I was empty. I was broken. The most ironic thing of all was that I had somehow managed to be the only one who'd survived out of all of us.

My mind went to that cool, dark place where it retreated when it couldn't cope any more. The place I'd been when they first took me, the place where I didn't have to be afraid. My tears had soothed me enough to allow me to enter that detached sort of depersonalised state, and I sank into it with relief.

He didn't let go of me, not once. He held me, and he stroked my hair, and he shut off the water when it finally ran cold.

CHAPTER NINETEEN
JOHN

Nine years is a long time to watch somebody from the shadows.

He did it, and he wasn't proud of it. He had a wife and a daughter, and he'd never betrayed them. Not once.

But he'd wanted to.

And now what had he done? Put his hands on another woman. The woman he'd been watching for nine fucking years, picturing in his head as he jerked off in the shower or, less frequently, while he made love to his wife, on the rare night when she was her old self.

'Mariana,' he murmured.

She was falling apart right in front of him, and it scared the shit out of him. He didn't know what to do, so he just held her. She looked so small, so fragile, and so despondent. He was almost certain she'd shatter into a million pieces if he didn't hold her together. He washed her hair with a bottle of shampoo he found in the shower, being careful not to make a face as he picked small pieces of Murphy's skull out of her long tresses.

The water went cold and he shut it off. All the while, his thoughts bounced between two things: the dead body in the bedroom and *that kiss*.

That kiss, the one that set his veins on fire and made him feel like he was losing his fucking mind. Maybe he was going crazy. She was Dornan's woman, and if he ever found out that anyone had so much as touched her, he'd kill them.

Dornan had almost killed Murphy once, for trying to do just that.

Pride swelled in his chest as John thought of Mariana shooting Murphy. He knew he should probably feel dread, but he didn't. Christopher Murphy had been the worst kind of scum, and John couldn't wait to dispose of his body and pretend like he'd never existed. Somebody else would spring up in Murphy's place, some corrupt asshole with their own agenda. Maybe they'd be better than Murphy. Maybe they'd be worse. But Murphy was finally gone.

The body. The pressing task, the thing that needed to be actioned.

'Mariana, hey,' he tried again. He reached for a clean towel and wrapped it around her shoulders. Her teeth were chattering, and her underwear was still specked with the drops of blood that had sunk deep into the fabric, but she was mostly clean apart from that.

Mariana wasn't looking. She was staring into space, not answering him. He shook his head, got up and went back into the bedroom. The smell of death was overpowering, even though Murphy had probably been dead less than two hours. It was the large amount of blood in such a confined space, and he was hardly going to open a window and alert the whole world to the stench.

John found jeans and a black T-shirt for Mariana in the large closet, and then went in search of a change of underwear for her. He hesitated upon opening her dresser drawer and seeing the lace and cotton neatly assembled into sections that seemed to scream 'functional' on one side and 'fuck me' on the other. Shaking his head, he grabbed black panties and a bra from the functional section and took them to her, along with the jeans and shirt.

'I have some clothes for you,' he said. She didn't respond. She was practically catatonic, and that worried John deeply. Fuck! How was he supposed to deal with her mental breakdown *and* find a way to dispose of a fucking DEA agent without a trace at the same time?

Time to stop worrying about being inappropriate and just get on with it.

'Come on,' he said gently, helping her to stand up. 'Come on,' he coaxed her onto the fresh towel he'd put down on the bathroom floor. She stood there wrapped in her own towel, her dark blue eyes fixed to the floor, shivering violently.

She was in shock, John knew that much. He needed to get coffee into her, coffee and sugar and probably some kind of food. He'd never hit a drive-thru on his way to dispose of a body, but there was a first time for everything, right? And he found himself unable to be annoyed with this exotic creature who had broken down in front of him. He was too conscious of who – of *what* – she was, even though she'd never come out and said it to him.

She was one of the ones that had been destined for a basement somewhere, a sex slave for somebody's sick whims. Only for some reason, she'd been spared. Not that you could exactly call this spared, but at least she was still alive. John liked to pretend that that shit didn't go on, but he knew the world he was a part of.

'Come on,' he said. He took the towel from her and started to remove her underwear as discreetly as he could, without looking at the magnificence that lay beneath. He dressed her in clean clothes and then he led her past the grisly reality of the man she'd just killed and down to his car outside.

***

That fucker had been heavy, even with the majority of his blood on the mattress. John contemplated calling a crew to pick up Murphy's body and dispose of it, but once he'd safely wrapped Murphy's lifeless form in the thick comforter and hauled his ass into the back of his pick-up, he'd come to the reluctant conclusion that it would be too risky to involve anyone else. He'd have to come straight back after he ditched Murphy and get someone to help with the mattress disposal.

He picked up McDonald's for Mariana on the way to the county morgue. He ordered her fries, black coffee, lemonade and an apple pie, trying to cover all bases: sugar, salt and fat. She'd perked up a little bit since downing the coffee, the caffeine and fresh air bringing a little colour back into her cheeks.

They got to the morgue soon after Ana had started in on her large serving of fries, John backing the pick-up into the crematorium entrance. She looked up, alarmed, brushing salt off her fingers onto her jeans.

'Where are we?' she asked, looking him in the eye. And just like that, she snapped out of it.

'Stay here,' John said, hopping out of the car. He'd changed from his leather jacket into a black hoodie while they were waiting in the line at the drive-thru, and he flipped the hood over his head before he stepped into the open. 'I've got to speak to somebody. Do not get out of the car. You hear me? Last thing we need is for both of us to show up on the security footage.'

She nodded, and then he was speaking to his buddy, who fetched a steel gurney.

'You want to hang around for the remains?' the attendant asked, as John slipped him an envelope fat with cash. John briefly contemplated taking the ashes home and pissing on them, but decided against it.

'Nah,' he said. 'Just make sure they're gone.'

Less than ten minutes later, Murphy – along with the bloody sheets, towels, Mariana's blue dress and comforter – was roasting nicely in the crematorium furnace. And within the hour, the man who'd caused Ana and everybody else so much grief was nothing more than a pile of ashes and dust.

While John was waiting for Murphy to be pulverised into ash in the furnace, he placed a call to one of his contacts who cleaned crime scenes for a living. He was also a guy who was very fond of cash, and extremely discreet. John gave him the passcode for Mariana's apartment and the guy promised to have the whole place sparkling in two hours. John didn't see how that was possible – she'd tracked blood everywhere – but he didn't argue. If the guy did it that quickly, he'd get a fat tip in his envelope when John dropped off the payment.

When John got back to the car, she was still there. *Thank Fuck.* The last thing he needed was a crazy woman running around with traces of Murphy's blood on her. He'd washed her as well as he could, but there'd still be traces of blood and DNA in her hair, under her fingernails.

'Someone's cleaning your apartment right now,' John said to Mariana. 'He's a pro. He'll wipe every surface, take away every trace of DNA. If the cops come tomorrow, they could turn the place upside down, and the only place they'd find evidence is under your fingernails.'

'Thank you,' Mariana said quietly, looking at him with a sense of wonder.

John shrugged. 'It's kind of what I do. Nothing to be proud of.'

He hated what he did. Despised it.

Still. There were worse things. At least he didn't have to have any part with those poor fucking girls they trucked across the country—

'John,' Ana said, breaking his thoughts.

'Yeah?' he replied gruffly, pulling out of the county morgue parking lot and making a sharp turn onto the service road.

'What happens now?'

He glanced over at her. Her hands were clasped in her lap, and her arms were covered in goosebumps. 'Here,' he said, tossing his leather jacket at her, still a little damp from the shower. 'Put this over yourself. You're shaking.'

She took the jacket wordlessly and draped it across the front of her like a blanket.

'What happens now,' John repeated, watching as headlights whizzed past in an endless succession. Before he knew it, he'd pulled onto the I-5 and they were racing down the freeway.

'What happens now is that we kill some time until they get all that pesky blood out of your apartment.'

'My bed—' Mariana started.

John held up a hand. 'Trust me. When we get back in a few hours, you won't be able to tell the difference.'

She settled back in the seat. John saw the exit he was looking for up ahead, the one that would take them to a secluded spot where he liked to go and sit when he didn't want to be bothered. As he pulled off the road and up a narrow, unpaved track, Mariana tensed beside him.

'Don't worry,' he said, 'I'm not going to kill you.'

CHAPTER TWENTY

MARIANA

John stopped the car in a small clearing of trees and cut the engine. In front of us was a small man-made lake. It was nothing special, and it looked neglected and overgrown, but it was deserted out here, and that was the whole point.

My mind was struggling to catch up after the night's events. What the fuck had just happened? I'd killed Murphy.

Murphy was dead.

I was freaked the fuck out, but I couldn't pretend that I wasn't also feeling victorious in some strange way. He'd committed the ultimate sin when he killed my family, and I'd returned the favour in all its bloody glory. He'd died vulnerable and afraid, and that brought me a small measure of relief, knowing the way my parents and siblings had endured their final moments.

'So,' John said, his hand resting on the steering wheel, 'I think you owe me an explanation.'

It was the least I could give him.

'How do I know I can trust you?' I asked softly.

John laughed. 'I think we're beyond that, don't you?'

I nodded. 'I suppose so. But it's a long story.'

He turned to me and smiled, his perfect teeth glinting in the weak moonlight. 'Honey, I've got all night.'

I licked my lips and rearranged the leather jacket so it was covering every bit of my exposed flesh.

'Have you got a cigarette?' I asked suddenly.

John nodded, pointing at the glove compartment. I opened it, took out a lighter and a pack of cigarettes, and lit up. The smoke burned my chest, and I had to resist the urge to cough. But I liked the feeling. It reminded me that I was alive.

I wound my window down a few inches and blew the smoke out.

'I can't tell you,' I protested, but I was tired and my words lacked conviction.

'Why not?' John pressed. 'What do you think I'm gonna do? Do you think I'm going to use it against you?'

I shrugged. 'Maybe. I have secrets that nobody knows, John. Not Dornan. Not Emilio. Nobody.'

'Like secret sons?' He raised his eyebrows.

I nodded my head in resignation. 'Didn't buy the baby brother story, huh?'

'You don't react like that over a photo of a child that isn't your own,' John said softly. 'I'm a father. I know a mother when I see one. And I swear on my fucking life, I will never tell anyone what you tell me. You can trust me, Ana. I just helped you get rid of the body of a DEA agent. Not any DEA agent, either. The one that happens to work for our boss. I could be killed for that. So let's start hearing some of these secrets so I can understand what the hell I've just gotten myself into.'

He had a point. And I was tired of keeping everything locked up inside. It was lonely and exhausting.

I told him everything. I started with the night Este and I were confronted back in Colombia, how he'd been murdered in front of me on the ground in a dirty alley. How I'd offered myself up in exchange for Emilio letting my family live. How Dornan had saved me from a certain fate as a slave at an auction. How I'd do it all again if it meant my little blue-eyed son would be safe. I told him every last detail, the way my father took Luis from me, how Murphy had killed my family, and now how I'd exacted the ultimate revenge against him, luring him into my bed with promises of a dirty fuck and instead blowing his brains out.

I told him everything, until I was empty, and in the end there wasn't a single word left inside me.

CHAPTER TWENTY-ONE

JOHN

She told him everything, and as soon as she'd finished, all John wanted to do was bundle up every word that she'd uttered and hand it back to her. Because there was power in knowledge, but there was danger, too. And now he was a very real part of it. By helping Ana to dispose of Murphy's body, and now hearing about her family, about her son, he was a pawn in whatever game she was playing at.

He didn't respond. Didn't ask questions. Didn't say anything for a very long time.

'Did you burn the photos?' he asked finally.

She shook her head. 'Not yet.'

'Burn them all.'

'John—'

'Stop. Stop talking for a minute. I need to think. *Fuck*.'

He yanked the car door open and got out, his mind going crazy. So his suspicions about her had been right the entire time. Emilio fucking owned her. Dornan had 'saved' her in some way, but she was still the property of the Il Sangue Cartel, and, to a lesser extent, the Gypsy Brothers. And he'd fucking known that kid was her son! But he guessed she had reasons to distrust him. He was a Gypsy Brother. And he was Dornan's best friend.

He heard Mariana's door open and close, and then she was approaching him, in front of the pick-up. He'd left the headlights on, and they cut a stark line across her midsection.

'John. I just want to go home, okay?'

He twisted his head to look down at her, this beautiful, exotic creature he'd been watching from the wings for the better part of a decade. He remembered the way her mouth had felt, the tight buds of her nipples hardening without him even touching them. His cock stirred painfully at the memory of lusting after a woman who could never be his.

Her dark blue eyes were bloodshot. She looked incredibly tired. And yet she was still exquisite.

'You want to go home?'

She nodded. 'I'm sorry. Maybe I shouldn't have told you all of that.'

He raised his eyebrows. 'It's a little late now, isn't it?'

'Why did you kiss me?'

'What?'

She looked at the ground. 'Never mind.'

He stomped back to the car, not taking his eyes off Mariana as he dragged his door open. She stood immobile for a moment, and then followed, sliding into the passenger seat. He folded himself in behind the steering wheel and jammed the key into the ignition, but didn't turn it.

'Let's just go,' she said softly. Almost like she was pleading.

He pulled the keys out of the ignition and pocketed them, turning on her. He was frustrated. He was pissed.

'You should have told me,' he said finally.

'Told you what?' she asked, but her expression said that she already knew what he was going to say.

'You lied to me. You told me that photo was of your brother. I *knew* I was right. I knew he was your kid. What am I supposed to do with that? What am I meant to do when Dornan finds out? What do you want from me?'

Panic registered in her eyes. She freaked the fuck out and jumped out of the car again. Christ, it was like they were going in circles. Why couldn't she just trust him?

She stood in front of the car again, looking left and right. Was she going to try and run? It seemed absurd, but he'd seen his fair share of runners before. When people panicked, they either froze, or they fled.

And judging by the way Mariana was twitching at the front of his car, she was getting ready to flee.

'Fuck,' John muttered under his breath, jumping out of the car and cutting her off before she could head into the thick trees. He reached for her wrists, found them, and used his body weight to press her against the hood of the pick-up. She was crying. He'd never seen her cry before tonight, not in all the years he'd known her, and now it was like she couldn't stop. Killing someone for the first time would probably do that to you, he surmised grimly. He could barely remember anymore, he'd done it so many times.

'There's nowhere to run,' he murmured in her ear. 'Never has been. You know that, Ana. Don't be stupid.'

She whimpered against him, struggling against his grip before going limp.

'Fuck you, John,' she whispered weakly.

He wrapped his arms around her. 'Shhh,' he said. 'We all go a little crazy the first time we kill somebody. You're gonna be okay. Everything is gonna be okay.'

He didn't believe that, of course, but he'd never tell her that.

CHAPTER TWENTY-TWO
MARIANA

It was almost dawn when we finally got the call to go back to the apartment. I walked tentatively up the stairs, stopping short when I reached the door. John glanced around, checking out the surrounds. Weary, and still sporting mascara-streaked cheeks and puffy eyes from all the crying I'd been doing, I went straight to the scene of the crime, to find it ... sparkling.

Seriously, the place was spotless. Someone had brought in a new mattress, made it with fresh sheets and a duvet I normally kept aside for winter nights. The pillows were plumped, new towels hung over the rail in the bathroom beyond.

They'd even sprayed air freshener – not too much, just enough to mask the cloying smell of congealed blood – and lit a scented candle on my dresser. I stared down at my new mattress, almost expecting to find a chocolate on my pillow or something, but it seemed the service stopped there. My heart lurched when I realised the photos of Luis had been hidden in the mattress. Fuck!

'My photos,' I muttered. 'Shit!' I started opening drawers randomly, praying that whoever had cleaned up had thought to put them somewhere instead of destroying them along with the mattress.

John entered the room, alarmed. 'What's wrong?' he asked.

'You mean apart from the obvious?' I replied, rummaging through sweatpants and pyjama shirts in my bottom drawer.

'What are you looking for?' he asked.

I closed the drawer and straightened, scanning the room as I tried to think of other potential hiding spots. 'Photographs,' I said quietly. 'They were hidden in the mattress.'

John nodded, handing me an A4-sized envelope. I peered inside, breathing a sigh of relief when I saw the photos were all intact. 'Thank you,' I murmured.

'Don't mention it,' John replied, shifting from foot to foot as he glanced into the bathroom. *Oh yeah, the bathroom where we'd just groped each other like horny teenagers while a man lay dead six feet away.* An awkward silence descended upon us, and I wasn't sure where to look. Eventually, my eyes landed back on his lush lips.

'I don't feel anything,' I blurted out, going to sit on the side of my new/old bed. 'Shouldn't I feel something?' I put a hand to my chest and imagined the barren heart that beat beneath my ribcage. The heart of a killer now.

And instead of feeling remorse, I was too busy imagining kissing Dornan's best friend again. My life was a fucking mess.

'I think all the feels happened in the car,' he said, and I didn't know whether to laugh or cry at that.

'Right,' I replied.

'I was kidding,' he added. 'I'm sure if you killed someone you actually cared about, you'd be feeling something. But right now, based on your track record with Murphy, I'd be feeling pretty fucking relieved if I were you.'

I nodded. 'You're right. That must be it.'

Neither of us spoke for a beat.

'What happened to your family?' he asked, and I heard the caution in his voice. Fresh tears sprang to my eyes, and I blotted them away with the sleeve of my T-shirt before they could roll down my cheeks.

'Somebody tied them all up and poured gasoline on them,' I said flatly. 'There was a fire. Nobody made it.'

'And your boy?'

'He's safe.'

'Where is he?' John pressed.

I stared openly at him, keeping my mouth shut. I'd never tell.

'So you let me dispose of a DEA agent for you, but you don't trust me?' He looked affronted.

I shrugged. 'Would you tell me where your daughter was, if the tables were turned?'

John nodded. 'Yeah, okay. I get it. So what are you going to do?'

I looked around. 'What do you mean, what am I going to do? I'm going to do nothing. I'm going to lie low and figure out what the fuck my next move is.'

'You gonna run?' John probed.

'Of course I'm not going to run,' I replied. 'Running means dying. Besides, like you said, there's nowhere to go.'

John nodded again, deep in thought. 'When's Guillermo due back?' he asked finally.

'A few days, I think. I'm not sure. Depends if his mother gets better or goes downhill.'

'I'll sleep on the couch,' he said.

When I raised my eyebrows, he gave me a look that said it was out of my hands.

'It's almost five,' he said. 'I'll crash for a few hours, have some coffee, and leave.'

'Suit yourself,' I said, not moving from my spot.

He left the room, and I lay down on my side, rolling myself into a ball. I didn't mean to fall asleep. I wanted to stay awake, and try to process the last several hours, but before I knew it, I was out like a light.

***

I woke to hear a fist beating on the front door. I jerked awake, sitting straight up in my bed. John appeared, looking tired as fuck. He hadn't slept then. He had a gun in one hand, gesturing for me to stay put.

'Open the fucking door!' a female voice yelled outside.

Allie. That hadn't taken long.

'Murphy's girlfriend,' I whispered.

John's eyebrows shot up as he looked at the front door, apparently undecided.

'Let me answer it,' I said.

John reluctantly moved out of my way, training his gun at the door.

'She's DEA too,' I murmured, pushing his gun gently to his side. 'Let me deal with this.'

I opened the door just a crack, to find a very irate Allie Baxter standing on my front stoop, dressed in jeans and a black Ramones T-shirt. She was off duty. Still packing, though, I could see, judging by the gun holstered on her hip.

'Do I know you?' I asked.

She laughed bitterly. 'You know who I am. Where's Christopher?' she said, barging past me into the apartment. I followed her in, closing the door warily behind me.

'Who the fuck are you?' she asked John, who was sitting at the dining table. He had one hand under the table, and I was ninety-nine percent sure he was aiming a gun at Allie, waiting for her to make one wrong move.

Great. I didn't need another dead DEA agent in my apartment. I'd just gotten rid of the last one.

'I could ask the same of you,' John snapped, resting one palm on the table.

She looked from me to John, disgusted. 'I'm looking for my partner,' she said, scanning the place casually. 'DEA Agent Chris Murphy. Have you seen him?'

I shrugged. 'He was here for maybe ten minutes last night. He needed a favour.'

Her eyes lit up at that. 'Oh, he did, did he?'

'Yeah,' I said slowly. 'And then he left.'

She looked dubious. 'What kind of favour?' she pressed.

I shrugged. 'I can't tell you that. It's confidential.'

She rolled her eyes. 'Oh, come on,' she said. 'You're not even a real accountant.'

'She is, actually,' John interjected. 'Four years at night school. So client confidentiality stands, and it's something we take *very* seriously.'

I looked back at him, surprised. He was pulling this out of his ass. I'd never be allowed to go to something like night school. What point was there in official certification when, on paper, I'd died nine years ago in the Californian desert and been buried for my family to find?

'We? As in the Il Sangue Cartel? I see you're wearing a Gypsy Brothers patch. Maybe I should bring you down to the station for questioning.'

'I'm sure that would be really helpful for your partner,' John replied coolly.

'Allie, we haven't seen him,' I repeated, going back to the front door and holding it open for her. *Get the fuck out of my house, you corrupt bitch.*

She glared at both of us one last time before storming out. Before I could close the door, she stuck her hand out.

'I'll be watching you, Mariana,' she said. 'One false move and your ass is mine.'

I slammed the door in her face so hard it echoed, staring at it for a long while before I made my way back to the dining table. John was looking at me expectantly, waiting for some sort of explanation.

'What was that?' he asked.

I filled him in on her last visit, and on the things Murphy had said to me before I killed him.

John whistled. 'So, they were about to take off together, huh? And take Emilio down in the process?'

'Something like that,' I confirmed. 'He didn't really give me anything specific to go on. Just wanted me to transfer a lot of Emilio's offshore cash into an account for him. And the way they were acting, she was in on it, too.'

John rubbed his hand against the stubble on his chin, seemingly agitated. 'She's a liability,' he mused. 'She'll keep coming back to you until she finds him. And he's in little pieces in the bottom of a crematorium somewhere, so we need to deal with her before she gets the DEA officially sniffing around.'

'Huh,' I said, an idea forming in my mind. 'How hard do you think it'd be to get her bank account details?'

***

We drove in silence to the strip club. In less than twenty-four hours, I'd gone from being a numbers girl to a part of the action. Blood and bullets, all in a day's work.

John had what I needed within an hour. I didn't ask him how. He was the president of the Gypsy Brothers, a motorcycle club controlled by the most powerful drug cartel along the west coast. He could pretty much get whatever he wanted.

'We doing this now?' he asked.

I shrugged. 'Sure.'

The beauty of working for Emilio was that he had all sorts of safeguards already in place when it came to the money laundering business.

For instance, he'd had someone install an IP address blocker in my laptop, so that if any heat ever came down on the finance side of things, it couldn't be tracked from our location inside the club. I didn't understand a lot about the intricacies of it, but I did know that if Emilio thought that it was good enough to hide the staggering amounts of money he was channelling out of the country, then it would surely be good enough for what I planned to do.

'That's a lot of money,' John said, watching over my shoulder as I set up three transfers that equalled more than a hundred thousand dollars, from three of Murphy's bank accounts into Allie's. They'd appear as cash deposits, and with over a hundred grand sitting in her bank account by tomorrow, we might just be able to avoid both her wrath and the DEA's attention. It wasn't the nicest thing to do to somebody, but that bitch had threatened my son, and if she was Team Murphy, then she had to be stopped.

John pulled out a burner phone he'd just purchased, along with a voice-altering device, a small box that he taped to the handset and plugged in using a small cord. He punched in a number and let it ring.

'Yes, hello,' he said to whoever answered. 'This is Timothy at First National Bank, West Hollywood. I'm calling in relation to a large deposit one of your staff has just received. We've had this account flagged as being connected to an international drug cartel run by Emilio Ross.'

The person on the end of the line said something I couldn't hear, and John smiled. 'Of course. Her name is Alexandra Baxter.'

He ended the call and broke open the back of the phone, pulling the SIM card out and snapping it in half.

'You want to get some breakfast with me?' he asked. 'I'm starved.'

I smiled.

CHAPTER TWENTY-THREE

MARIANA

Another Sunday.

I was sitting at the end of a long conference table where the Gypsy Brothers normally held church. This week, however, they were convening in the dining room, and Emilio had commandeered the large boardroom. Across from me, Emilio looked at his watch, and Dornan paced. That was unusual. Dornan was normally in his own meeting with the rest of the Gypsy Brothers, not in here discussing finances with his father, myself and Murphy.

'Are we waiting for Murphy?' I asked finally, looking at the door. He'd been dead less than a week, but neither Dornan nor Emilio seemed to know this.

Emilio unbuttoned his suit jacket and sat back against the large conference table that took up most of the room, so that he was painfully close to me. I wished he'd just sit across from me like any normal person would.

'That's why we're here,' Emilio said, studying me carefully. 'I'd like you to check on something for me. Did you bring that computer?'

I nodded, patting the bag at my feet.

'Get it out,' he said impatiently. 'I don't have all day, girl. Pull up Murphy's bank accounts. The offshore ones.'

So they were missing him already. I was glad we hadn't waited any longer to transfer money from Murphy's accounts into Allie's.

I took a measured breath and reached for the laptop, pulling it from its protective bag. I placed it on the table in front of me and fired it up, navigating to a browser and looking at both of them expectantly.

'Wi-fi password?' I asked. Dornan and Emilio stared at me like I was speaking another language.

'I need an internet connection to log on,' I explained. Seriously, how had these two gotten this far? With people like me to take care of the details, I realised. Great. I loved enabling rich assholes to get richer. My job satisfaction was at an all-time low.

Dornan disappeared, coming back a few moments later with a post-it note. He stuck it to the desk in front of me, making a concerted effort not to touch me at all. He never gave me the silent treatment. I keyed in the wi-fi password, waited for it to connect, and navigated to the website we used for our offshore trade accounts. Within a few moments, I'd pulled up all six bank accounts that I had set up for Murphy in various places in the Caymans and Europe.

I turned the computer to face Emilio, and watched his face with great interest. He sucked a breath in between his teeth, tapping the screen. 'What's this?' He angled the screen so I could see it, pointing to the last transaction on Murphy's account, from only days ago.

I moved closer. 'It's a transfer,' I said. I tilted my head, feigning confusion. 'A few.'

Emilio looked at Dornan, an eyebrow raised. 'Who the fuck is Alexandra Baxter?'

I'd had her pegged as an Allison. Alexandra was much too refined for that woman.

I shrugged.

'Wait,' Dornan said. 'Alexandra. Allie?'

Emilio ran his tongue along his teeth. 'His partner?'

'I'm pretty sure she was more than that.'

Emilio looked pointedly at me. 'Can you find out where she's spending this money?' he asked.

'Not unless I have her online banking details,' I replied. 'I'm not a hacker. I don't even know who we're talking about.'

Emilio waved his hand dismissively. 'We'll go over the figures tomorrow,' he said, turning back to his son. 'You think he's skipped town?'

Dornan lit a cigarette. 'I told you not to trust that motherfucker.'

'Oh, really? You got someone else in the DEA who we can use?'

Emilio glared at me. 'Go.'

I stood and pointed at the laptop, and he placed a hand on it. 'I'll get this back to you,' he said, staring at me until I had the urge to squirm.

I looked at Dornan, but he wouldn't even meet my gaze. Slowly, I turned and left the office, half-expecting one of them to pull out a gun and shoot me in the back.

CHAPTER TWENTY-FOUR
MARIANA

'Your boy left early today,' Guillermo said, as we walked down Santa Monica Boulevard together. I shrugged, worry churning in my stomach. Something was up, and I didn't know if Dornan suspected me of cheating on him with his best friend or murdering his associate. Something was definitely not right and the stress was eating me alive. After the meeting, I'd hung around outside, waiting for Dornan to drive me back to the apartment. It was what we always did on a Sunday. And, sure enough, he had driven me home. He'd pushed me down onto the bed (complete with brand new mattress), fucked me and left without saying more than two sentences to me. I was feeling adrift.

'You miss me while I was gone?' Guillermo asked, teasing me.

'Always,' I replied, smiling. 'Your mom okay?'

'She'll be dead if she doesn't stop eating so much fucking fried shit. I tell her, Mama, you're diabetic, and then I catch her eating cookies and shit behind my back.'

I cleared my throat. 'Who does that remind me of?'

He rolled his eyes. 'Ha ha, very funny. I work out, don't I?' Guillermo pointed to the large gym we were approaching. 'So I can eat whatever I like.'

'I don't think that's how it works,' I replied. 'I'm pretty sure fried chicken every night is going to kill you, regardless.'

'Whatever. I've got arms today,' Guillermo said as we walked into the gym, referring to his workout. I nodded, splitting off into the female changeroom as he entered the male one. I threw my bag in a locker, grabbed my towel and headphones and headed out to the cardio area. I wasn't feeling particularly energetic after the way Dornan had literally come and gone, and so I stepped onto the easiest piece of equipment – the treadmill. The great thing about our gym was the view – like my apartment, it overlooked Santa Monica Beach. The treadmills had prime position, up against the floor-to-ceiling glass windows that framed the beach like a postcard. It was a beautiful day, so I cranked the treadmill up to an easy jog and started running. Back before the gym had opened, Guillermo and I had always run along the path that stretched along the beach, but nowadays he was more concerned with bulking his arms up and talking with his dude friends in the weights section.

I closed my eyes for a moment. I pretended I was running along the beach, instead of on this treadmill. The beach I could always see, but not touch. I imagined there was sand underneath my sneakers, instead of a rubber belt that looped endlessly around and around. I imagined dark blue eyes, a small boy's hands reaching out to me, the warmth of the afternoon sun on my face.

'Excuse me,' a male voice interrupted my daydream.

'Jesus Christ!' I muttered, standing on the sides of the treadmill and holding my chest with one hand, panting, as I stopped the treadmill belt with the other.

I looked to the source of the voice, my eyes landing on a clean-shaven face belonging to a guy with a short crew cut and thick arms that Guillermo would be envious of. *He looks like a cop* was the first thing I thought. Maybe a marine. His hair was the dead giveaway. No one as attractive as this guy would willingly shave their hair that short. He was tall, with striking green eyes that were circled with light brown at the edges of the irises. You'd call them hazel, except that the two colours were completely separate. The green and brown didn't intersect.

'Nope. I'm not Jesus Christ. Sorry if I startled you there.'

My treadmill had slowed to a stop, and I stepped off the edge. Bad idea. I hadn't realised how tall this guy was and now he was towering over me.

'Look,' I said, 'I'm flattered, but I'm kind of busy.' Before he could open his mouth again, I turned and hightailed it over to Guillermo, who'd been oblivious to the entire exchange. Some bodyguard.

He was lying on a bench, sweat pouring from his face as he did chest presses.

'You here to spot me?' he asked through gritted teeth, a vein bulging on his forehead as he lifted again.

'I don't think I'd do it justice,' I said, stealing a glance at Not Jesus Christ. He was talking to the woman at the front counter, flashing his white teeth at her.

'I'm going to shower,' I said, leaving Guillermo to his workout.

I was washing my hair in a shower stall when a voice cut through the silence and almost made me scream.

'Mariana Rodriguez?'

I opened my eyes, which was stupid, because shampoo-laden water flooded them straight away. Fuck! I pulled my head away from the stream of water, my hand searching for my towel.

The hook was empty.

If someone had taken my towel, I'd murder them. I knew how to do that now. I rubbed the water from my stinging eyes and opened them again, gasping when I saw the guy from the treadmill, Not Jesus Christ, leaning against the wall outside the shower, my towel dangling between his thumb and forefinger.

I snatched the towel from his grip, pressing it to my chest.

'Don't worry, I wasn't looking,' he said. The cocky bastard then proceeded to give me a once-over, from head to toe, an amused smile plastered across his face.

'This is the women's changeroom,' I said emphatically, still holding onto the hope that he'd come in here by accident. 'And I think you've got me confused with someone else.'

'You ran away from me,' the guy said. 'We could have done this out there, when you weren't completely naked.' He looked like he was about to dissolve into laughter. 'And I know the name you're going by now, but that's not the name your parents gave you, is it?' As I opened my mouth to argue, he held up a xeroxed copy of my old Colombian driver's licence, complete with my photo.

Shit.

'How do you know my name?' I asked. 'Are you a cop?'

He grinned. 'Maybe. Are you a friend of Christopher Murphy's?'

I wrapped the towel around me. 'No.'

'Do you know him?' The man pressed.

'Maybe.' Fuck. Motherfucking fuck. Was he going to arrest me? Great. I was going to get arrested, and I wasn't even wearing clothes.

'He seems to be missing. You haven't seen him around, have you, Mariana?'

I shook my head. 'Nope.'

He nodded, as if we were sharing a secret or something. He reached into the pocket of his sweatpants and pulled out a business card. 'In case you see him anywhere,' he said, 'or if you want me to take you out to dinner. You eat too many microwave meals with that Mexican schmuck who lives with you.'

How did he know what I ate? Who I lived with?

I took the card, every nerve in my body screaming at me to run as I turned it over.

My eyes just about bugged out of my head when I read the name that was printed on the thick paper.

Agent Lindsay Price, FBI. The name Murphy had given me before I shot him. The same man who was investigating Emilio and the entire cartel.

Jesus Christ.

I looked up from the card, but Agent Lindsay Price was gone.

CHAPTER TWENTY-FIVE

MARIANA

THREE WEEKS LATER

I locked eyes with Dornan, his smirk eliciting a small smile from me as he squeezed his erection, dropping to his knees on the floor in front of me. I saw a bead of pre-come glistening on the head of his cock and my mouth watered at the thought of licking it up. *Later.*

Now it was my turn to receive.

It was difficult to lie on my new mattress, legs spread, a tongue dragging on my clit and not enjoy it. I was a sexual being. I practically lived for these moments. But lying on this bed, all I could think about was Murphy and the look of sheer terror on his face as I shoved a gun between his teeth and pulled the trigger.

Focus. This is your time with Dornan! And it was bonus time, too. It was a Monday night. He never showed up on a Monday night.

An orgasm was building inside me, much slower than normal, not through Dornan's lack of effort. I gasped, squirming as he pushed one finger inside my tight slit, then two. When he added a third finger, I started to moan. The feeling of fullness was overwhelmingly satisfying, and it was enough to send me up over that elusive edge as I fisted the sheets and cried out, my pussy clamping around his fingers as I came.

As I crested down the precipice of my afterglow, a delicious warmth settling in my belly and limbs, Dornan stood over me, thrusting into me in one fast stroke so that I cried out. He didn't last more than a few seconds before he, too, was spilling himself inside me.

I imagined John taking his place for a split second, how his face would look as he came, and blood rose uncomfortably in my cheeks. *Don't think about him. Do not think about him!* What was wrong with me? Suddenly, after nine years with Dornan I was thinking of somebody else just because we'd shared one stupid kiss?

No. I refused to give in to those treacherous feelings that had been gnawing at me ever since I'd kissed John in the shower.

But it raised an interesting question.

If I had a choice, who would I choose?

'Goddamn, that was hot,' Dornan said, pulling out of me and handing me a towel.

I cleaned myself off as well as I could, kissing Dornan's stubbled cheek as I headed for the shower. He responded by grabbing a handful of my ass and squeezing, sending little shooting pains through my body that felt oddly good. I pushed him away playfully, knowing if I wanted to get a shower and some dinner I'd have to avoid another round of our lovemaking.

Standing in the middle of my bathroom, I stared at the empty shower cubicle as the image of John continued to taunt me. What the hell was going on with me? Was I hell-bent on self-destruction? Was I just looking for something to distract me from the memory of Murphy's death stare?

Turning away from the shower, full of self-loathing and arousal, I ran myself a bath instead.

The water pressure was excellent in the building, and it didn't take long for the tub to fill. I dumped a good amount of lavender body wash into the warm water and sank my weary body into the bubbles, sighing in appreciation as my limbs were caressed by liquid heat. It felt divine, and I reminded myself to take more baths.

I grabbed a rolled-up towel from the stack next to my head and nestled it under my neck. I wouldn't be long. I'd have a quick dip, a wash off, and then get dried and join Dornan out in the kitchen, where I could hear him banging and crashing things. I thought of Murphy, of how he'd died here in this very apartment and nobody had even mentioned his absence to me, yet.

I thought of John, closing my eyes as I let my mind drift. I barely ever relaxed, always too tightly wound, but grief and killing had numbed me in some small way. I was too exhausted to be strung out. I was too devastated to be anxious.

It felt good to let go a little. I skimmed my fingertips over fresh self-inflicted wounds on my thighs, the ones I'd been able to hide from Dornan despite what we'd just done. It wasn't too hard. I was good at redirecting his attention to other parts of my body.

The ends of my long hair floated loose around my shoulders, weighed down by the water, as I remembered John's hands on my head, on my face.

I licked my lips and thought of kissing him. I shook my head from side to side, trying to rid myself of thoughts of somebody I'd never be able to touch like that again, and remembered the way he'd cradled me.

I opened my eyes and sat bolt upright in the bath. Fuck! I just wanted to zone out for a while, but all I could think of was John.

CHAPTER TWENTY-SIX

DORNAN

He resisted the urge to join her again in the bath. He'd fuck her all night if it were up to him, but he'd heard her stomach growling. The woman needed sustenance. So instead he lit up a cigarette and went searching in Mariana's kitchen.

He had one go-to dinner recipe: Italian breaded chicken and tomato salad. His mother had made sure to teach him at least one recipe before he'd married his first wife. He'd been such a kid when he left home, but at least he'd been able to cook a meal.

He was looking for breadcrumbs in the pantry when his eyes fell on a tub of flour. That'd work. He could use some egg and flour and smash up some of the stale bread he'd found in the freezer.

He reached for the cream-coloured canister but paused when he saw what looked like spaghetti sauce smeared along the side.

Or blood. Dornan had a way of judging situations. He got gut feelings about things and they almost always turned out to be correct. And his gut wasn't thinking about pasta sauce when he looked at that red smear.

He was thinking about who'd been bleeding in his apartment, and why.

He took the canister out carefully, focusing on the tiny red smear. His senses were in overdrive, his nose conditioned for such macabre things. He scratched his fingernail against the dried red substance and took the cigarette from his mouth as he brought his fingernail up to his nose.

Blood. It was blood. But that wasn't the only thing ringing alarm bells in his head. He shoved the cigarette between his teeth again so both of his hands were free.

Christ, how heavy is this flour? The canister weighed a ton, strange since it was made of plastic. Dornan set it down again, prised the lid off and, on a whim, stuck his clean hand into the white powder.

His fingers hit something solid.

He stopped for a moment, his heart rate increasing in excitement. But it wasn't the kind of excitement that was, well, exciting. It was the buzz of a thousand angry bees, settling in his chest, demanding to know what the fuck was hidden in this container.

No secrets, that was one of his cardinal rules. It was the thing that kept their dysfunctional relationship from completely imploding, from being eaten away by bitter distrust.

He got a grip on the solid thing hidden underneath the flour and pulled it out, sending a plume of white dust around his face.

It was a ziplock bag, wrapped around something about the size and weight of a cheap, disposable cellphone and a charger. He unfolded the layers of plastic, his temples throbbing with the weight of the possibilities.

He glanced towards the bathroom, hearing movement, and tipped the hard rectangular weight into his palm.

Well, what do you know. It was a fucking cellphone.

A rage that presented as cold indifference began to build in his body, the humming of the angry bees only drowned out by the desire for an explanation. But his gut said there was no explanation. She'd deceived him. She'd probably been talking to her family this entire time, risking everything he'd built so carefully. He located the power button and pressed it with a clean thumb, turning the phone on. It immediately demanded a passcode. Dornan jumped as his own phone began to ring, sending the long spike of ash that had been holding on to the end of his half-smoked cigarette onto the ground by his feet. He glanced down at the phone, hearing Mariana as she moved around in the bedroom. He dropped the phone back into the bag, and shoved it back into the flour canister, giving it a good shake to bury it properly. He replaced it in the pantry and swept the small bits of flour that had powdered the counter onto the floor.

Dornan braced against the counter with one hand as he took his cellphone from his jeans just as it stopped ringing. One missed call from Viper. Dornan's stomach dropped as he remembered what had happened earlier in the day.

Another day marked another round at the fulfilment centre, another assortment of women boxed up, sold and ready to be delivered.

Only today had been different.

The cells that contained the prisoners were soundproof, part of their brilliant design. X-rays couldn't pierce the boxes they'd had constructed to herd people like cattle through secure checkpoints and border crossings. But when you moved that little swatch of plastic to the side, sometimes the screams got out.

Today had been one of those days.

Cell four. As soon as he'd looked through the glass, Dornan wanted to die. Because there was a woman, maybe in her late twenties, and she was huddled on the floor, screaming. And she was pregnant. Very pregnant.

Dornan had slammed the viewing pane shut, but it was too late. He could still hear her screams, even though he knew that couldn't be possible. He finished up the other thirty-nine checks, most of them the same as cells two and three. Nobody else had screamed like her. Nobody else had made themselves heard like the woman about to become a mother, who vocalised her doom for nobody except Dornan to hear.

And then they were gone, loaded onto the truck, which rose on its bridge and disappeared into the sub-floor, ready to be driven out to make the scheduled deliveries.

His phone rang again, snapping Dornan out of the garish daydream he kept replaying in his mind. He looked at the screen. It was Viper again. Viper, along with a couple of other Brothers, was running the trucks tonight. It might be a situation. He took the cigarette from his mouth and hit answer. 'Yeah?'

The sound of heavy tyres on asphalt greeted him through the phone. It was loud running trucks back and forth across the zig-zagging roads of the United States.

'We got a situation, boss,' Viper yelled over the steady hum of the road noise. 'I need you to help with a clean-up. I'm pulling in to the rest stop.' He gave an address and Dornan memorised it. A clean-up. That was code. It meant one of the prisoners had died. *Fuck.*

Mariana walked into the loungeroom in a thin bathrobe that left nothing to the imagination, her hair wrapped up in a peach-coloured towel. Dornan fought the urge to tie her up and either interrogate her or fuck her senseless. His cock ruled him when it came to Mariana Rodriguez.

'Which one?' Dornan asked.

'Number four,' Viper replied immediately, and Dornan's suspicions were confirmed.

'Boss, it's fucking bad. Hurry.'

The line went dead.

Mariana hovered at the edge of his vision. 'Everything okay?' she asked.

Dornan raised his fist and slammed it into the counter hard enough that the whole thing shook. The immediate pain calmed him somewhat, but all that rage, all that fight, was still waging a war inside him.

'What happened?'

He raised his gaze to look at her. He drank her in for a good few moments, taking in the curve of her hips, her tiny waist, full breasts and slender neck before his almost-black eyes settled on her dark blue ones. Was she a liar? Had she betrayed him? If she hadn't yet, *would* she?

'Get dressed,' he ordered, thinking about the secret cellphone. He wouldn't let her out of his sight until he got an explanation.

'Why?'

He frowned. 'That's for me to know,' he said, his tone vicious. *Go on, resist me. Argue with me. Do something so I can fucking explode.*

But she didn't. Of course she didn't. Her ability for feeling out situations was just as good as his, if not better. She heard the danger in his voice and decided to obey. She nodded, pulling the robe tighter around her as if it would somehow protect her.

'What should I wear?' she asked softly.

'Something warm,' he said. 'Bring your coat. And your sneakers. We might be digging a hole.' He looked at her pointedly.

Her eyes went big and round, but she didn't protest. She backed away, not letting him out of her sight until she was at her bedroom door.

He hated scaring her. He loved her. But a small part of him, the vengeful, suspicious man inside, was secretly pleased.

CHAPTER TWENTY-SEVEN
DORNAN

FUCK.

It was the single thought that ran through his head.

Fuckfuckfuckfuckfuck.

Viper was opening the back of the large trailer, his face ashen. And there was the muffled, yet unmistakable sound of a woman screaming.

Dornan hadn't spoken a word to Mariana the entire way here. Almost an hour it had taken to arrive, and now she was sitting in the car, probably wondering why the hell she was suddenly privy to cartel activities. Well, until he found out where that fucking phone had come from, and what it was for, she'd be spending a lot of time with him. Fuck what anyone else thought. John might be the boss in name, but Dornan was the leader of this Gypsy pack.

'Why the fuck did you call me out here?' Dornan growled. 'You go in there and you shut them up!'

He was angry. He was angry and so fucking tired of having to deal with this shit day in and day out, so tired of the souls who begged him to let them go – and worse, the ones who didn't beg, the ones who sat in the deepest corners of their cages, defeated, having already given up on life. Yeah, he preferred the fighters. They still had a spark of something in their eyes. Hope.

Not that it ever did them any good.

'I've got a truck full of fucking deliveries,' Viper hissed, his normally tough demeanour dropped completely, replaced with horror. At first Dornan wanted to smash his fist into Viper's face, kick him in the ribs until he bled, and beat the sense back into him. He was a Gypsy Brother, for fuck's sake. What did he expect? Sometimes messed-up shit happened.

But now Dornan was here, and he could hear it too.

Screams that sounded like death cries.

He rushed to the back of the truck, holding his jacket up over his face to keep the rain off. The doors to the container had already been slightly propped open by Viper. The screams grew louder, more insistent, as Dornan walked down the narrow space in between stacks of containers that housed their flesh trades for the day.

He already knew which woman was screaming. Her eyes had been screaming at him inside his mind all goddamn day.

He got to the box, placed his hand on the lock and took a deep breath.

She'd been heavily pregnant. He had known that when he saw her earlier, but it didn't matter. It never mattered. They always took the pregnant ones at least a month before they were due, to make sure they made it to their new owner before they gave birth.

He opened the lock and pulled at the door. His gaze landed on a naked newborn baby, its face a purplish-blue, covered in blood and gunk. Its umbilical cord trailed away between the woman's legs. The woman's face was ashen; she'd lost a lot of blood, more than she should have, judging by the way she was practically bathing in the stuff. She was almost unconscious, her head drooped to one side. She was sipping in little breaths of air, sweat dripping from her forehead. This had never happened before. They'd had women die before, but they'd never had one give birth. This was *not* supposed to happen.

'Holy fuck,' Viper said, over Dornan's shoulder.

'Get outside and keep watch,' Dornan hissed, turning and shoving Viper. He scurried away, seemingly very happy to get away from the woman and her newborn.

'Please,' the woman whimpered. She was so pale, she looked like a corpse, but she was alive and she was still conscious. 'Please help my baby,' she said.

'She needs a doctor,' Mariana said behind him, taking off her coat. 'That baby needs warmth.'

Dornan turned on her, towering over her. 'What the fuck are you doing back here?' he roared. He looked past her to Viper. 'I said to fucking keep watch!'

Viper shrugged, clearly on the cusp of madness. Useless fuck. He'd deal with him later.

Mariana was dressed in just a thin striped tank top and black skirt, her cashmere coat bundled up in her outstretched hands as she glared at Dornan defiantly. 'Are you going to help them? Because if you're not, *move.*'

Speechless, Dornan moved aside so that Mariana could squeeze past him. The space between the containers was narrow, the air thick with horrors best left unseen, and Mariana was here in the middle of it. For so many years, he'd kept a wall up between the reality of what he did with these women and his Mariana, his secret, his dark lover. He'd drawn a line in the sand and made sure she never, ever knew of these things.

Except now she'd seen, and she knew, and would she ever forgive him? A hidden cellphone was nothing compared to this. Dornan knew this.

He watched wordlessly as she knelt down beside the woman and scooped the baby up. The baby wasn't moving. Wasn't crying. It was blue. She stuck her fingers in its mouth and made a scooping motion, then turned it over and hit it lightly on the back a couple of times. The baby started to pink up almost immediately, making a little mewling sound.

'Pocketknife,' Mariana said. 'Sterilise it first.'

Moving on a mixture of autopilot and awe, Dornan unclipped his knife from his belt and clicked it open, taking his lighter and heating the blade for a few seconds to kill any germs. Luckily, he was obsessive about keeping it clean. It had seen its fair share of death and destruction, and you could never be too careful with pesky things like DNA. The knife was clean enough to eat your steak dinner with.

He handed it over to Mariana, pocketing his lighter as he watched her work. She balanced the wrapped baby on her knees and grasped the long, coiled cord that attached baby to mother, cutting through it in one swift motion. Dropping the knife, she stood and turned, thrusting the baby into Dornan's arms. 'Hold him,' she said, and Dornan did. He was struggling to keep up with this. It was a *him*? This was already getting way too fucking personal.

Viper appeared with a large woollen blanket he'd retrieved from the cab of the truck. Mariana made a crude knot in the baby's umbilical cord with bloodied fingers.

'We need to get them to a hospital,' Mariana said, addressing Dornan and Viper.

Viper looked between Dornan and Mariana with a mixture of shock and brutality on his features. 'We ain't taking anyone to a fucking hospital,' he said. 'This is a one-way ticket.'

Mariana ignored him. 'Dornan,' she said, stepping closer to him and peering at the tiny baby, nestled safely in her cashmere coat. 'We have to help this woman. The baby needs to go get checked out, he's cold. He needs warming up.'

Dornan fixed his gaze down at her, frustrated and ready to fucking explode. 'How about I decide?'

Mariana's face twisted into a look of disgust as she reached for the baby and nestled him against her own chest protectively. Dornan was relieved to be free of the baby, who felt like a ticking time bomb in his arms, a burden that was going to be dire no matter which way he played this shitty set of cards he'd been dealt.

'Maybe decide before they both die,' she said pointedly, turning to look at the woman. The mother. The dying woman. Dornan made a mental note to chat to Mariana after he'd sorted this situation. She was getting far too mouthy for his liking. He thought of the hidden phone again and his gut twisted uncomfortably.

The bleeding woman, the product that was holding this entire gig up, was still slumped in the corner. She looked completely fucked. Dornan had to move her, couldn't deal with her in this tiny, confined space. And this truck needed to move, now, before the goddamn highway patrol drove past or something.

'Viper, help me move her into my car.' Mariana looked visibly relieved. Viper opened his mouth to protest and Dornan shook his head emphatically.

'Wait in my truck,' he said, offering his car keys to Mariana. She looked at them for a long moment before taking them. 'Put the heat on,' he added. She didn't answer, just made for the truck's cab and slid into the driver's seat, holding the baby close to her the entire time. A moment later he heard the engine of his truck turn over. Fuck. This was the worst situation he could have imagined.

'Dee, why the fuck are we putting this broad in your truck? She's made us both, and the accountant,' Viper said, pointing towards the truck where Mariana waited. 'And you know Daddy Dearest would never let a live one go, even if we could help the bitch.'

Dornan levelled his gaze at Viper. 'Shut the fuck-up,' he hissed. 'Do not question me. I will handle this. Now. Help me pick this woman up, and for fuck's sake wrap her up first so we don't get blood all over us.'

They got blood all over them anyway, despite the carefully wrapped blanket. Lucky they both wore black almost all the time. It came in handy when you didn't have time to change your clothes in between all the bloodshed and chaos.

A few minutes later Dornan was in the backseat, holding the woman who'd just birthed her baby and who was now dying in his lap in the back of his truck. She'd started to wail as soon as they moved her. It was obvious she was in a lot of pain and her noise was affecting the baby. He was bellowing as well, and it was enough to make Dornan want to eat his own gun just to get some fucking peace and quiet for five seconds.

'You want me to come back there so you can drive?' Mariana asked quietly, twisting in her seat to address him. 'Or I can drive them to the hospital.'

Dornan smiled at her, at his beautiful Mariana. This could be her in his arms, if things had played out differently. He'd saved her, but he'd learned a long time ago that you couldn't save them all. In fact, she was the one and only he'd ever managed to grip tight and raise out of the vicious fate she'd been careening towards, and there had been *thousands*.

He didn't speak. He didn't have to. He saw the recognition on her face as she clutched the baby tighter.

'Dornan,' she whispered. Pleaded. He felt his heart shatter and burst under the pressure of her horrified gaze.

Her horror would have to wait. The woman in his arms was bleeding to death, and she was dying in pain, and he just wanted to take some of her suffering away.

He put a hand to her neck and felt her pulse. It was erratic, all over the place. She cried out again and her back arched off his lap. Her eyes were full of anguish and the shock was starting to wear off. The woman was suffering.

'Will you help my baby?' she asked, looking up at Dornan with eyes that wouldn't be seeing this world for much longer. How did she even have the energy to form words? It was the strength of a mother's love, he reasoned. She wouldn't let go until she was sure her child would be safe.

Dornan nodded, feeling tears prick in his eyes. Goddamn, why did this have to happen now? Why had Viper called him? Why was it always his fucking problem when anything went wrong?

And why had he chosen this night, of all nights, to bring Mariana with him on a run, knowing she might be exposed to something like this, something that had the power to ruin everything between them. She'd never look at him the same way after this, and that realisation broke him inside. He'd done everything to protect her and she was probably going to end up hating him like every other woman he'd ever let in.

The woman's eyes fluttered shut and she relaxed a little. 'Promise me you'll take him some place safe,' she whispered. Dornan wiped a tear from his cheek, and another. He shouldn't be upset. He didn't have the right to be upset and he certainly didn't deserve to get fucking emotional about this woman and her kid.

'I promise,' he said and he wasn't lying. In that moment he made a decision. He didn't know if it was wrong or right, but he did it because nobody deserved to suffer that much. He couldn't take her to a hospital, couldn't get her medical attention, because if she spoke – and they all spoke if they escaped, even the ones who promised they wouldn't – she'd be able to lead the police right to them. She'd seen Dornan's face, and Mariana's and Viper's. She's seen the interior of the truck, knew there were more like her.

No, he couldn't take her to hospital.

'Dornan!' Mariana protested, twisting in her seat.

'It hurts so bad,' the woman whimpered against his chest, opening her eyes again and peering up at him. 'Please, make it stop hurting.'

He nodded, stroking her hair with one hand and reaching for his gun with the other. It had the silencer attached, a small mercy. He pressed the barrel to her chin.

He hugged the woman to his chest one last time, tears forming in his eyes as he looked down into hers.

If she knew what was about to happen, she didn't show it. She didn't panic. She didn't struggle.

'Stop!' Mariana screamed.

A single, muffled shot rang out into the clear, soundless night. It was much too quiet, too controlled a noise to be the bang that ended a life, but it had ended it nonetheless.

She died instantly. Dornan made the sign of the cross above her face and let her sag onto the seat. He'd have to replace it. He'd have to replace the entire interior of the car, but it didn't matter. She was dead and nothing else mattered.

Mariana held the baby to her chest and stared at him with dead, loveless eyes.

'You fucking *monster*,' she said, turning away from him.

The baby began to cry.

CHAPTER TWENTY-EIGHT

MARIANA

'You could have taken her to the hospital.' I'd said the words at least three times, but it was too late.

His eyes glistened. 'She was going to die. Do you understand me? She was never going to make it to a hospital.'

We were parked in front of a 24-hour pharmacy. Dornan had just gone in and bought supplies at my insistence, despite him protesting that we really needed to get 'the kid' to a hospital. Diapers, bottles, a tin of formula and sterilised water were my list of demands and he didn't argue with me for once in our relationship. The baby was suckling on my little finger impatiently as his mother lay dead in the backseat.

Dornan shook a bottle full of powder and water to mix it together.

'How did you know to do all that?' Dornan asked.

I looked down into the baby's face, holding back tears. He'd just killed the baby's mother to save her a long and protracted death. A mercy killing, but why did she have to die at all? It wasn't fair.

Life wasn't fair.

'I watch a lot of television,' I replied wearily, cradling the baby closer as I looked up at the pharmacy sign. My breasts ached as I remembered holding my own little son, feeding him from my body just one time before they took him away. If I could have nursed that baby in the car, I would have without hesitation. He might not have been mine, but the sad fact was, he no longer belonged to anyone. I wondered who his father had been, if he'd even known. If he was a good man, or if the woman had already been a captive when she fell pregnant. Was this baby the result of something pure or something evil?

Not that it mattered. He was a baby and by definition that made him innocent. He was brand new and sacred and exquisite. And he'd been born into the pits of hell.

'You can't keep him,' Dornan said, almost reading my thoughts. 'Don't get too attached.'

I turned my head up to face him as he handed me a small plastic bottle of formula. 'Shut up,' I snapped at him, my mother bear out in full force as I snatched the bottle from his outstretched hand.

'Here, little baby,' I cooed, placing the teat near his mouth. God knows how long he'd been lying on the floor of that horrid little death cell before we'd arrived. It couldn't have been too long, because he hadn't been getting air until I scooped the gunk out of his throat so he could breathe, but it had been long enough that he'd turned cold and blue next to his dying mother.

'I mean it,' he said.

'I know,' I said forcefully. 'But what do you expect me to do? Leave him on the side of the road?'

Dornan scowled. 'We're dropping it off at the hospital.'

'He,' I clarified. 'The baby is a he.'

Dornan started the truck and it roared to life. We drove for a long time. As the trees began to thicken, I looked around outside, the baby now asleep, nestled against my chest. I'd managed to get a few drops of the formula in and to warm him up, at least.

The road we were on looked ... Familiar.

My stomach lurched as I saw where we were pulling into. The county morgue. The same place John and I had come to dispose of Murphy's body. Christ. The Gypsy Brothers and the Il Sangue Cartel were really keeping this place in illegal after-hours business.

I couldn't bear to watch as Dornan dragged the dead woman from the car and onto a waiting steel gurney. He paid the guy a wad of cash and then we were driving again. Pretty soon we were pulling into a dark corner of a run-down hospital parking lot. I could see why Dornan had chosen this place. It looked decrepit, and I doubted it had anything like surveillance cameras to record that we were ever there.

I hugged the baby tight. Was it terrible that I didn't want to let him go? Dornan came around to my side of the truck and opened my door, holding his arms out.

I looked down into the little boy's sweet face. He was still all squashed from having just been born, but his face would spring up soon, his nose would pop out, and he'd be cleaned up. He was going to be breathtaking.

'Ana,' Dornan urged.

With great reluctance, I handed the baby over. I didn't meet Dornan's gaze. I couldn't.

I couldn't bear to look at the man I loved, and see a monster instead.

CHAPTER TWENTY-NINE

MARIANA

An hour later, we were parked at an old warehouse by the wharf. It had started to rain again, gentle drops that pattered against the roof and windows with a soothing rhythm.

Me, I was exhausted. I'd been firing on adrenalin-fuelled cylinders for a couple of hours and I was ready to pass out and sleep for a year. I felt heavy. I felt so unbearably sad.

Plus, Dornan had just dropped a bomb in my lap the size of California. The drugs and guns weren't the only things the Gypsy Brothers and the cartel had been trafficking and selling. In fact, those were just two small parts of the sickening empire Emilio was running, and the third, very large, very lucrative part of his game was people. Women, mostly. Girls. No wonder he'd been so keen to sell me.

It was his fucking specialty, selling girls as slaves.

Not for the first time, I was weirdly appreciative of my unorthodox upbringing, the way I'd had to keep my father's finances afloat by money laundering and shady bookkeeping antics. It was those skills, self-taught and honed to a sharp edge, that had kept me alive all these years. It was those skills, dirty as they were, that had kept me out of the back of a truck on a one-way trip to hell itself.

I demanded answers as soon as we'd steered away from the hospital where he'd run in and deposited the baby on the reception desk. My heart still ached, knowing that little boy needed a mother, knowing he didn't have anyone. At least he was someplace safe. At least now he had some kind of a chance at survival.

'How could you do that?' I asked Dornan as we both stared straight ahead through the front window of the truck. The rain was swiftly growing heavier, and I couldn't help but remember the night I'd killed Murphy.

Dornan took off his shirt and offered it to me. 'Put some water on it. Clean yourself up.'

'Don't you think about them?' I continued, taking the balled-up shirt from his hand. 'Don't they *haunt* you?'

'Never thought about it,' he said quietly. 'Never let myself. Never made eye contact. God gave me sons and I was grateful. I never had to worry about them. I knew they'd be alright. I knew they'd never be a part of that world. At least, not the part that suffers.'

'You mean, the way you don't suffer? Because you're covered in the blood of a woman you just killed, and I'm pretty sure that look on your face is suffering.'

He smiled sadly. I took a section of his shirt and poured bottled water on it, offering it to him first. He had more blood on him than me. I'd only been dirtied by the blood that was on the baby from his birth. Dornan was soaked from head to toe in the blood of a woman he'd cradled in his arms as he shot her in the head. The gun might have been silenced, but a silencer didn't stop the blood spatter. Luckily, he was wearing dark clothes, and being soaked in blood didn't look too different from being soaked from the rain unless you looked closely.

'What made you realise what you were doing was wrong?' I asked.

Dornan flexed his blood-stained hands, took the wet shirt I was holding out and started to rub at his skin. I saw the twitch in his jaw, the way he ground down on his teeth. He was suffering. 'Always knew it was wrong,' he replied quietly, so quietly I almost couldn't hear him above the torrential downpour outside. 'Just never gave it much thought. Never really wanted to think about what happened to them. Where they ended up. If they survived.'

'So what changed?' I asked.

He cleared his throat, then examined one relatively blood-free hand before switching to the other. 'John went to prison. Caroline was pregnant when he was arrested and she just went completely fucking psychotic without him there to watch her every day. I had her committed twice. That bitch charmed the pants off those fucking doctors, convinced them she was on the straight and narrow. They let her out. They always did. By the time the baby was due, I was letting her shoot up on the couch in my office just so I knew she wasn't lying dead in a gutter somewhere with John's baby inside her.'

'Juliette,' I said.

He nodded.

'Caroline had that baby. And then she disappeared. Left the hospital, stole a car and drove away. And guess who was left holding a baby girl?'

My stomach twisted anxiously. 'You.'

He shrugged, dropping the shirt between us. 'Babies are all the same, boys or girls. They cry, they eat, they sleep. But she could've been *my* daughter. That's when shit got hard.'

Something about that made me angry. So, so angry.

'Then why do you do it?' I snapped. 'Because Emilio says you have to? Tell him you can't. Tell him you *won't*.'

'I've got too much to lose,' he replied, squeezing the steering wheel until his knuckles turned white. 'I have *responsibilities*. Much as I'd like to, I can't ever tell him no.'

He stared at me pointedly, maybe the first time he'd looked at me since he'd started recounting his story. His dark eyes glimmered as lightning lit up the car and I felt a lump rise in my throat.

'I do what I do and I get what I get,' he said, reaching across and taking my chin in his hand, brushing his thumb along my lower lip. Something about what he had said – *I get what I get* – stabbed at me painfully, demanding more answers. A creeping suspicion suddenly flooded me and I felt sick.

Me. He was talking about *me*.

I swallowed thickly, my voice momentarily frozen. I opened my mouth to speak and nothing came out. I felt his eyes drilling twin holes into mine.

'Don't tell me you're talking about me,' I said, tears forming in my eyes. 'Please.'

'I've never lied to you,' he said, taking my hand and squeezing it, almost to the point of pain. 'So if you don't want me to tell you ... *don't ask*.'

So it was me. I brought my hand up to my mouth, intending to muffle a sob, but Dornan took hold of it at the last moment. He held it up to the dim light in the truck. There were fine specks of blood. I watched, sobbing openly, as he took my hand and used a clean section of the shirt to gently wipe my skin.

I didn't stop crying. I was so damn emotional all of a sudden, and I didn't know why.

He loves me enough that he'll damn everyone else in the world just to keep me safe. And I hate him for it, but I love him for it more.

I thought of the kiss with John, and shame burned deep inside me. I was a horrible person. How could I be thinking about him while Dornan was shipping people off to their deaths in exchange for my life? I'd called him a monster, and he'd been doing all this for *me*? So that I was safe? So that Emilio didn't make good on his threats to sell me off as a slave, too?

'You should stop,' I whispered.

He took the shirt from my skin and placed it on the dash.

'No, I mean, you should stop ... whatever it is you're doing with these people – and if he gets rid of me, at least you'll be able to sleep at night. I'm not worth all this, Dornan. I'm not worth any of it.'

His head jerked to face me, and then his hands were coming at me, wrapping around my waist, pulling me to him. It was awkward, but the truck was spacious enough that he could drag me onto his lap without me getting jammed between him and the steering wheel. I ended up facing him, one knee on each side of his legs, our noses inches from each other.

I looked up at the roof of the truck. It was grey felt. I attached my gaze to a small tear in the fabric and held it there, trying to stop the tears from flowing down my face even as I felt my teeth chattering.

'Ana.'

I shook my head.

'*Mariana*.'

I tore my eyes from the roof and looked at him, because I knew if I didn't he'd wait all night for me to meet his gaze.

'You want to know what I wished for on my birthday?' I asked him. I couldn't even see anymore, everything warping and bending through the film of my tears.

I felt his warm hand cup my cheek, his thumb brushing away a steady stream of tears as he waited for me to speak.

'I wished that things were different,' I whispered. 'I wished that we could be free.'

He chuckled mirthlessly. 'You'd still love me if we were free?'

I nodded. 'So much,' I replied. 'More than you'll ever know.'

His face softened, almost as if my words had relieved some worry inside him. 'I can't imagine why,' he responded, his voice low and husky, cutting through the continual buzz outside as the rain continued to fall.

I tilted my head. 'You saved my life,' I whispered, shaken by the veracity of my words. 'You didn't even know me and you did that. You're still doing that. I'm sorry I called you a monster. You're not a monster. You're the reason I'm alive.' *And I don't deserve you.*

He moved his thumb along my lips, his gaze shifting between my eyes and my mouth. Something stirred within me and I had the sudden urge to kiss him.

So I did. I placed my hands on either side of his face, his stubble deliciously rough against my cold hands, and leaned down, covering his mouth with mine. He responded immediately, one of his hands fisting my loose hair, the other curling possessively around the back of my neck, pulling me even closer. His tongue met with mine, and a shiver ran down my spine. Our love was electric. Always had been. It was the rest of our lives that was the problem. But right here, right now, in the howling wind, with the metal and glass the only thing between us and the pouring rain, it was almost too easy to pretend that nothing else existed. I melted into him, wanting more, always wanting more. It was like we wanted to devour each other, and maybe one day one of us finally would. But until then, we were here, together, the windows fogging up under the pressure of our heavy breathing and the rain raging on outside. I felt wetness pool between my legs as my heart pounded faster, begging to get closer, to get rid of these annoying layers of fabric that separated us so that we could be together again.

I could feel him beneath me, hard already. Hard for me. And I wanted him. I needed him.

We didn't even need to speak to know what came next. Ours was a dance so finely tuned, we were in perfect sync. We needed each other like we needed air to breathe, and when time forced us apart, it made the world a dull place. Until we met again. And then sparks flew when we collided.

It had been like this for nine years, and I didn't ever want it to stop.

He placed both hands on my hips and lifted me off his lap. I braced myself against the steering wheel as he unzipped his jeans and reached into his boxers, gripping his cock with one hand as he brought his other hand up my thigh, underneath my skirt. I moaned softly as he pushed my panties to the side, his fingers pressing against my wetness. I moaned again, louder this time, when he pushed two fingers inside me.

My noise seemed to be enough to drive him over the edge. He slid his fingers from me, and I ached from the sudden loss. I needed him. I needed him inside of me, around me, possessing me in every way, and I needed it now. His mouth found mine again as he jerked me closer, my legs straddling him, the swollen head of his erection pressing impatiently against my entrance.

His hands went to my hips and his fingers dug into my flesh as he pulled me down onto him. His size made me gasp, all the air leaving my lungs as the noises coming from my throat were drowned by our kiss. With agonising slowness, Dornan pulled me down onto him until I was stretched and full with him, ready to explode.

'Fuck, you're so wet,' he groaned, his voice gravel and smoke, his hips continuing to rock, each thrust driving me wild. His hands moved from my hips, down to my thighs, and I flinched as he pressed against the fresh cuts I'd made just hours ago in the bath. He saw me flinch, connected the dots. His entire body stilled; though I could tell he was desperate to keep slamming up into me, his eyes demanded answers. He pulled the hem of my skirt up to my belly so I was completely exposed to him, scars and all.

'Mariana,' he said in a strangled voice. 'What did you do?'

I closed my eyes, fresh tears pricking at them, demanding release. 'Nothing,' I breathed.

I felt one of his hands wind around my long hair and tug, forcing my face to his.

'Open your eyes,' he murmured.

I did. I opened my eyes to see his own dark eyes staring back, the iris and pupil merging almost seamlessly in the dim light. His eyes looked black, but they were beautiful to me. They were everything.

'Why?' he asked. 'I thought we agreed no more.'

I didn't want to talk about it. I didn't want to think about it. I just wanted to come undone, to shatter apart with him inside me. I just wanted to forget how fleeting our time together always was. But I had made a promise to him not to cut myself years ago, and I had broken that promise.

I put my hands on his shoulders and started to move again, skin against skin, his hand tightening in my hair.

'Mariana,' he demanded. 'Stop.'

He pulled on my hair to the point of pain. I yelped, stilling.

'Look at me.'

I didn't want to look at him. He made me nervous when he spoke like this. I just wanted to fuck and forget. I squeezed my eyes shut.

'Fuck me,' I begged. 'It doesn't matter.'

'No.' He growled, shaking me. 'Tell me what this is. Tell me why. You know how many arteries are here? You could have fucking bled to death.'

You could have fucking bled to death. Yeah. I could. And the saddest thing was, he wouldn't even be the one to find me because he was always somewhere else.

'You're gone so long,' I croaked, opening my eyes again. 'It was my way of keeping track. You're always gone for so fucking long.'

His face fell as he studied the cuts on my thighs, his fingertips hovering over the barely healing flesh. 'That's what this is?' he said, his voice thick. 'You do this until I come back?' He looked closer. 'These are the days?'

My cheeks burned with shame as tears fell on them.

'Baby,' he said sadly. 'You know I want to be there every fucking minute with you. You know I can't live without you. I fucking love you. *Only* you.'

I nodded, still crying. My orgasm hovered inside me, almost there but not quite, and I wanted release. To not have it was painful. I lifted slightly on top of him and pushed down, and he resumed his almost violent lovemaking, leaning back and grabbing my hips again. He thrust deep inside me, and that was all I needed, that single stroke enough to make me cry out as I came around him. A few seconds later he tensed, his fingers digging into my flesh as he slammed home one more time and spilled himself inside me, hot and wet. We sat, unmoving for a few moments, before I disentangled myself from him and returned to the passenger seat, rearranging my clothes as I went.

It was completely fucked up, the way we went from arguing about human lives to screwing each other's brains out, but it seemed our primary method of connecting was physical. Our love demanded to be shown, to be shared. It wasn't good, and it wasn't right, but it was what we had.

Dornan leaned over and kissed me as he was zipping his jeans up. The kiss quickly grew frantic. Dornan grabbed a handful of my hair and tugged me closer to him, and I moaned into his mouth.

I came to my senses. Realised what we'd just done in here, in the same car where he'd shot and killed a woman. I planted a hand on his chest and pushed, breaking the kiss.

'I'd die without you,' he said, releasing his grip on my hair and grasping my chin between his thumb and forefinger.

No, I thought, *I'd die without you*. And it wasn't just about love. It was reality. Without him, I would have been dead a long time ago.

Just as I was opening my mouth to respond, the world exploded.

With a deafening bang, glass flew everywhere. I automatically put my hands to my face, feeling the shock of something devastating vibrating through Dornan's entire body. Cold rain that felt like tiny shards of ice poured into the car, the driver's side window no longer there. When the glass stopped falling and it was just the rain driving sideways into my face, I let my hands fall from my eyes, let them open.

I squinted through the icy sheets of rain that were pouring into the car.

Oh God. Dornan was bleeding. His chest was a mess of blood, the clean bullet hole cut neatly into his shirt bursting forth with dark red blood. Someone had just shot him through the fucking window, and he was literally bleeding out before my eyes.

Another shot rang out and I dove to the side as the front windscreen crashed down around us. Pain blossomed in my arm and I realised I'd been hit. *I'd been shot.* I fought the urge to throw up, gagging as the pain radiated through my shoulder and all the way down to my hand. I refused to look at it, though. If I looked at it I'd probably pass out, and if I passed out I'd probably die. We both would. So I swallowed back vomit and pretended it wasn't happening as I tried to get Dornan to respond. I felt glass cutting my arms and legs, everywhere I moved causing more lacerations.

'Baby,' I whispered, my voice barely audible over the rain.

Nothing. His face was ashen, and he'd slumped to the side a little. I felt sorrow rise inside me as I saw what someone had done to *my* Dornan. His belt was still unbuckled, for Christ's sake. They'd taken him at his most vulnerable moment and shot him from afar, like fucking cowards.

My blood was pumping hot, despite the cold. I could feel the white-hot anger searing a path through my circulatory system, my breath coming out in short, shallow pants.

'Dornan,' I said, a little louder this time.

Through the blistering rain, I heard the dim noise of a car door opening.

Close. Whoever it was, whoever had done this – they were close.

I didn't want to sit up and look, though, because I might get a bullet in the face for being nosey. No, I huddled in the footwell, pulling gently on Dornan's arm so he slid down onto his side, his arm and ribs pressing awkwardly over the glove compartment that separated our seats. It looked uncomfortable, the way he was twisted, but it was better than him being dead.

I snapped out of the haze I'd been in since the first bullet hit, reaching automatically for my purse and, within it, my gun.

Thank you for giving me a gun. Thank you for teaching me how to aim. Thank you for all of it.

Footsteps crunched over loose gravel, and my heart beat furiously.

Don't die, I silently urged Dornan. *Please, don't fucking die on me.*

I'd seen enough death to last me a lifetime.

And then the gravel stopped crunching.

CHAPTER THIRTY

MARIANA

There was a woman at the window and she was aiming a gun at Dornan. Her eyes were fucking wild. Her hair was long and dark, and her black T-shirt was stuck to her. She was soaked to the bone, but that didn't seem to be affecting her aim.

Allie.

Murphy's crooked cop girlfriend, the bitch he was planning to run off with. My stomach lurched painfully at the realisation that she had not, in fact, taken the money I'd transferred into her bank account and run like she should have. I would have run. What an idiot.

She was a cop. She'd just shot Dornan. And now, now she was here to finish the job. To finish me.

'Thanks for the money, cunt,' she spat, glancing at Dornan before shifting her aim to me. Bile crept up my throat and I swallowed forcefully – a side effect of having a gun pointed at your face.

'I'll ask you once,' she said, her teeth grinding each word out with measured rage. 'Where is Christopher?'

'Allie,' I protested. 'Come on. I know you're not that stupid.'

She screamed, frustration written all over her face. 'I don't believe you!' she said, wild with emotion.

'You were in love with him,' I realised all at once. I'd assumed she was just in with Murphy for the money. But the way she said his name – Where is *Christopher*? – the anguish in her words. She had loved him. And now she knew, beyond a shadow of a doubt, that he was dead.

'Allie, he was a bad man,' I said, trying to placate her. 'He killed innocent people. I did what I had to do, and I'm sorry.'

'Oh, you're sorry?' she repeated shrilly. 'You'll be sorry, bitch, when you watch your dirty biker bleed out in front of your eyes.'

My heart sank – she wasn't going to be talked around. She was here to get vengeance.

'Allie,' I said softly. 'Murphy wanted me to go with him when he left. He tried to rape me. He was naked in my bed when he died.'

She scoffed. 'You're a fucking *mexicunt* working at a strip club owned by bikers. You don't get *raped*. You open your mouth and suck and say thank you after you swallow.'

Well, I didn't know what to say to that. 'He asked me to go with him. He was never going to take you. It was all a set-up for you to take the fall.'

'Stop lying. Stop talking!' She shook the gun in front of her for effect.

I took a deep breath and tried to think. *Think!* It was hard to strategise with a gun aimed at you.

'Why Dornan?' I asked. 'He didn't do anything. He wasn't a part of this, Allie.'

'He's never without his fucking whore,' she spat, looking at me. 'Seems only fair that you get to watch him die before I kill you.'

I breathed heavily, my heart thundering in my chest – its low roar filling my ears. My gun, concealed by the darkness, itched in my hand. I had to shoot her. I had to *stop* her.

Allie sneered, letting her aim drop as she looked down into Dornan's lap.

I took my chance. It was the only one I was going to get. As the bitch laughed at Dornan's state of undress, I raised the gun in my hand and squeezed the trigger.

I recoiled as I felt her blood hit my cheek, the deafening roar of my gun something that was becoming far too familiar. Allie hit the dirt before I'd even blinked, the force of the bullet sending her straight onto her back. I rummaged around on the floor in front of my feet, looking for my coat, until I remembered I'd wrapped the baby in it. Desperate, I held a hand to Dornan's red-soaked chest as I tried furiously to slow the tide of his blood. With my other hand, I searched in his pockets for his cellphone. I scrolled through until I found John's number, called it, let it ring.

No answer.

I didn't know who else to call. I couldn't call his wife, could I? I wasn't supposed to exist. And Emilio? No way would I call that bastard.

Jesus Fucking Christ. Who else *could* I call? Not the police. I'd just killed a cop. Again.

John. Answer your fucking phone!

He didn't answer. Again. I looked at Dornan. The blood. There was so much blood.

Above the steady drum of the rain, I heard someone groaning outside. Allie? Jesus. Was she still alive? With a quick glance at Dornan, I opened the door as quietly as I could and slipped out, pressing it shut behind me. The rain was brutal, and I could barely see in front of me. I circled around the back of the pick-up, gun at the ready, my eyes searching for any movement as I rounded the corner of the truck and happened upon Allie. There was blood coming from her mouth, and she had one arm outstretched, reaching clumsily for her gun. In her dying moments, she didn't look like a bitch anymore. She looked like a sad, lost little girl, and I silently cursed Murphy for pulling her into this hellish existence. For the first time, I realised that she was younger than me, just a young woman who fell in love with the wrong man. Don't we all.

She saw me, and her hand reached for the gun more desperately. Before she could grab it and take a shot at me, I placed my foot on her wrist, pinning it to the ground.

She looked up at me, her eyes sad.

'I thought he loved me,' she choked.

I nodded, crouching beside her. 'That's the thing about men like Murphy,' I said softly. 'They're not capable of love, Allie. They only know how to destroy.'

She seemed to soften, her eyes closing momentarily. 'I don't want to die,' she whispered, blinking back tears. 'I didn't know.'

I nodded sympathetically, pushing her hair back from her face.

Before she could do anything, I placed my hand over her mouth and squeezed her nose shut between my thumb and index finger. Shock and realisation lit up in her eyes as she thrashed her head back and forth beneath my grip.

'That's the difference between you and me,' I said to her, as she clawed at my hand and sucked against my palm for air. 'I'm old enough to know better.'

She struggled some more, her face turning a dirty shade of grey as her eyes bulged with effort, then finally dulled and froze open, unseeing.

I took my hand away from her mouth, noticing her blood all over my palm. I wiped it against my side, reasoning that the rain would wash the rest away soon enough. Fuck. I'd just killed somebody with my bare hands. I was turning into someone I didn't even recognise. The terrifying part was the complete detachment I felt. Of course I killed her, I reasoned to myself. She was going to kill me. She shot Dornan.

And that was that. No guilt and long-winded self-searching. No beating myself up about taking another life. No, I took one look around to make sure I wasn't being watched, grabbed Allie's ankles, dragged her over to the side of the wharf and rolled her into the fast-flowing water below.

It sucked her down in a second.

And then she was gone.

***

I vomited beside the car, the act somehow cleansing me. That last vestige of doubt gone. Replaced by numb victory, by indifference. I was exhibiting all the classic symptoms of shock, but I didn't feel shocked. I felt like a fucking lion who'd just protected her cub. Allie had tried to fuck with someone I loved and I had put an end to that.

Dornan.

He was bleeding. He needed help, and quickly. I raced back to my side of the car and yanked the door open, sliding in and assessing how much worse he'd gotten since I'd been gone. He looked bad. His skin was so white he looked like he'd just fade away.

I remembered what he'd said to me. *I do what I do, and I get what I get.*

The knowledge of what he'd done – what he was still doing – slammed home that night. The fact that he was here because of me, that I had somehow caused this just by existing, just by being with him. He had wanted me back then, nine years ago, and he was still paying the price. I saw the souls of every life he'd trafficked in his grief-stricken gaze when he'd told me, and now I might have to live with the fact that we'd never get to say anything to each other again.

The only thing worse than finding out that the man you love has been dealing in innocent lives, buying and selling them and sending them to their deaths, is knowing that he did it for you.

On the floor at my feet, I saw the discarded baby bottle, the tin of infant formula, all covered in a thick sheen of his blood, and I began to shake.

CHAPTER THIRTY-ONE

MARIANA

I struggled to get Dornan out of his seat and into the passenger seat. He was two hundred pounds of solid muscle and rage.

Please don't be dead. You're not dead. You can't die.

You can't die.

I finally got him across the seat, first pulling his upper body across into my seat, and then hoisting his legs over one by one.

I started the ignition. 'Dornan,' I said. I could barely see, with the rain and my tears, but somehow I made it onto the road and towards the hospital where we had dropped the baby off. I prayed that they didn't have cameras. I prayed that they didn't know it was Dornan.

I prayed that this wasn't going to be the end for us.

Ten minutes later, I was back at the hospital, John opening my car door, worry plastered across his features. He'd finally answered his phone, and he must have broken several laws speeding to get to the hospital before me. On the other side of the car, two Gypsy Brothers – Jimmy and some other dude – were pulling Dornan out of the car and onto a gurney. The shock on Jimmy's face was evident as he saw his VP's blood all over the passenger seat. Wait until he got a look at the backseat.

Once Dornan was on the stretcher, some nurses raised the sides and whisked him away. Everything was moving too fast for me, and I felt like I was drowning.

'Get rid of the car,' John roared.

Jimmy moved into action, grabbing my waist and hauling me out of the way. He got into the truck, which was still running, and took off before he'd even closed the door.

I looked down at what was in my hand. My coat, the one that I'd wrapped the baby in. The one that I'd used to try and stem the flow of blood from Dornan's bullet wound.

Life begins, and life ends. So fast. So fleeting.

John grabbed my elbow. 'Hey,' he said gruffly, tugging me into the hospital. Dornan was gone, stretchered away somewhere into the labyrinth of hallways that faced us in the entrance, maybe gone forever.

There was somebody else with us. I couldn't remember his name. Which was bizarre, because I'd seen him enough times at the clubhouse that we were practically acquaintances. But my brain had frozen, stuck on a loop of horror – I heard the baby's pitiful little cry and saw Dornan stroking the mother's hair so tenderly, so softly, before he planted a bullet in her skull.

'Security footage,' John hissed at the guy, who nodded, making a beeline for the building.

'I need to see him,' I said, my tears suddenly stopping, my weeping replaced with an absolute conviction that if I didn't get to Dornan right now, he would die – and if he died, I wouldn't survive. I'd already lost everything else.

Este had been shot, and I didn't cry. I was still in shock. I didn't understand what was happening. But nine years of missing him, his lopsided smile and the way he squeezed my hand tightly to reassure me when I was afraid, the way he held our son and promised me we'd get him back one day? I knew, nine years later, the pain of watching somebody bleed to death in front of you, the regret of not saying goodbye. Because they're just *gone*, and nothing you will ever do for the rest of your existence can turn back time and make those moments appear again, those moments when you just want to say *I love you. I love you.*

John took my elbow again, pulling me along. He stopped short of the emergency doors and yanked me into a room with an empty bed, still messed up like someone had been sleeping there recently, an empty chair beside it. I wondered, briefly, if somebody had just died there. 'They won't let us in,' John said, blocking my attempt to leave the room. His blue eyes were wild, his dark blonde hair all mussed up from his helmet. He hadn't shaved recently, and I had to wonder what hell he had been toiling in. I mean, Dornan got the trafficking, what did John get?

Suddenly I needed to be sick. Very, very sick. I put my hand over my mouth, forcing my throat closed. I retched, but nothing came up.

I needed Dornan, and I needed him now.

'They won't let us in,' John said again. I ignored him, trying to push past him.

'Mariana!' he yelled, taking my shoulders and shaking me. 'Look at me! You can't see him!'

'Screw you!' I said, fighting off his grip. 'His wife will be here in ten minutes, John. His kids. Emilio. Do you think they'll let me see him then? Do you think I'll be allowed to go to his funeral if he fucking *dies*?' I was crying again, great shuddering sobs that hurt as they bubbled up in my chest and left my body. 'Do you think I'll be allowed to live if he fucking dies?'

'He's not going to die,' John said, with conviction. 'He's gonna live. I promise.'

I shook my head. 'Don't make promises you can't keep.'

I looked down at my hands. They were covered in blood, so much that I couldn't even remember who it belonged to anymore. In the space of three hours I'd seen two lives end, one begin, and the person who meant more to me than anything barely holding on.

'Fuck,' I remembered, my hands shaking as I held them up to John. 'I shot somebody. I killed somebody.'

John's eyes narrowed, his eyes searching my face. 'What?'

'It was Allie. She shot Dornan through the window.' I took in a ragged breath, reliving the moment all over again. The deafening blast. The way the light died in his eyes before they closed. So fast. It all happened so goddamn fast.

'Where did she go?' John asked, his tone dangerously calm. Too calm. I knew that tone. It was the eye of the storm.

It was hell about to be unleashed.

My skin hummed, where tiny pieces of glass were still stuck, and my feet were bleeding on the stark white of the hospital floor. My shoulder was pulsating where the bullet had nicked it. But it didn't hurt. I was flooded with adrenalin, with the sharp sense that I had to survive. I was like a deer, eyes wide open, looking for the threat as the bullet whizzes into its body and tears it apart.

'I shot her, but she wasn't dead,' I whispered, looking up at John with a mixture of dread and disbelief. 'I put my hand over her face until she suffocated, and then I rolled her body into the marina.'

John released his grip on me and took a step back, swiping his hand across his stubbled chin.

'You sure she was dead?'

I nodded, taking the gun from my waistband and holding it out to him. He looked around, seemingly shocked, before he shook his head and pressed my hand back to my side.

'Keep it,' he said. 'You might need it.'

I nodded, replacing the gun in the hollow of my back, the metal against my skin oddly comforting as I rearranged my tank top to cover it.

'I need to see him,' I repeated. 'Five minutes, John. I'll shoot *you* if I have to.'

John tipped his head to the side, my threat apparently lost on him as he looked down at me. 'No, you won't,' he said softly.

'Alright, I won't,' I mumbled. Across the hall, I spotted a laundry cart, stacked with fresh sheets and what looked like hospital-issue scrubs.

I raised my arm and pointed. 'Five minutes. That's all I need.'

John turned, saw the scrubs. He sighed, his resolve crumbling before my eyes. 'Wait here.'

He ventured cautiously into the hallway, looking around before darting over and grabbing a stack of folded green clothes. He brought them back into the room and tossed them on the bed.

'Hurry,' he urged, turning around to give me some privacy. I thought about our kiss. It was the wrong thing to be thinking about when my lover was fighting for his life in the ICU.

My heart in my mouth, I stripped my clothes off and wiped myself down as best I could with an extra shirt John had grabbed, before sliding the scrubs on and tucking the gun back into the waistband. I glanced in the small mirror that hung next to the bed. I still looked terrible, my skin caked with dried blood, but I was a damn sight better with fresh clothes.

'Okay,' I said, letting John know I was decent. He turned around and I gave him a tight smile. I was just about to pass him when he grabbed my arm again. I looked up, surprised, to see something else in his face.

Pity? *Affection?*

'Ana,' he said softly, pulling me to him. He wrapped his arms around me and squeezed me, and I melted into his embrace, comforted by the gesture. I felt his hand on my hair as he hugged me tight, as fresh tears started to flow.

'It'll be okay,' he murmured into my hair. 'He's gonna be okay.'

I gave a small nod, hovering there in the space his arms offered, part of me just wanting to stay here in the safe darkness of his embrace. But that was dangerous. Very, very dangerous. He smelled like pine needles and gasoline, and I probably held on to him too tightly. The realisation of what I was doing made me tense. *Dornan is dying in a hospital bed and I'm appreciating the way his best friend smells.*

'I would never let anything happen to you,' John said quietly, and my heart dropped into my stomach with a resounding thud.

Oh *fuck*.

As soon as he'd said that, he released me, but made no move to step back from me, my head barely reaching his chin. 'If he ...' John's face twisted momentarily. 'You'll be okay. Trust me.'

If he dies, you'll be okay.

I nodded again. We stepped out of the room, my bloody clothes discarded and forgotten, and made our way to the critical care ward.

To Dornan.

CHAPTER THIRTY-TWO

MARIANA

Did I ever say it?

I love you.

You saved my life.

Nine years, and I showed him, but did I ever say it?

You are my world.

You are my *everything*.

I didn't know. Standing in a hospital corridor that smelled like bleach, waiting for John to come back and tell me if Dornan was alive or dead, I didn't know if Dornan ever understood that I would have died for him in a heartbeat.

John came back to where I was standing in my green hospital scrubs, a surgical mask in his hand.

'Here,' he said gruffly, handing me the mask. His rough hand brushed against mine when he placed the mask in my outstretched palm, and he let it stay there for a beat too long. I stared at his hand, transfixed and probably in shock.

I wasn't there anymore, though. Maybe it was because I hadn't eaten, or because I was in shock, or because my shoulder had started to bleed through the hospital scrubs I was wearing. Whatever the reason, I was awake one minute, looking at John's mouth intently as he pointed to the blood on my shoulder, thinking *It's weird that I can't hear him all of a sudden.*

Then it was like somebody turned the light out. I didn't even feel it when I hit the floor.

Just ... nothing.

CHAPTER THIRTY-THREE
MARIANA

'You can go,' I said to John, even though I really wanted him to stay. But he had a wife and a daughter and an entire club that was no doubt reacting to the news that their VP had been shot.

He crossed his muscled arms across his chest, covering his Gypsy Brothers patch. His body language said he wasn't going anywhere.

I felt ... relieved. I'd fainted in the corridor on the way to see Dornan, which was both embarrassing and tragic – embarrassing because I wasn't the one who'd been shot in the goddamn chest, and tragic because now Dornan's wife was by his side and I'd missed my chance to see him. My shoulder had been bandaged, just a surface graze, and the bullet had taken a nice chunk of flesh with it. But I was okay.

A nurse bustled in, a clipboard in one hand and the jar I'd just peed in clasped in the other.

'Good news all round,' she said cheerily. 'Everything looks good from the baby's standpoint. Hormones are still high. You just need to eat something. Your blood sugar is low.'

I sat bolt upright in the bed, as John and I baulked in unison. '*What?*'

The nurse's face fell. 'The... pregnancy,' she said, all trace of cheer gone.

'I think there's been some mistake,' I said sharply. 'I'm not pregnant.'

She looked down at the chart in her hand. 'Yes, you are. Your hCG levels are through the roof.'

I laughed maniacally. 'You're crazy.' I looked at John. 'She's crazy!'

She looked at John, then back to me. 'Do you want me to call a psych down so you can talk to someone?' she asked quietly.

'What? No! I want to see my chart. There's been some mix-up. I'm on the pill. There's no way I can be pregnant.'

My stomach was sinking, sinking like quicksand. I tried to remember the last time I'd had a period. Nope. No idea. I thought back over the past several weeks, of how many times I'd puked or felt sick and assumed it was the stress of working for a drug kingpin or murdering a DEA agent that was making me constantly nauseous.

'This is a mistake,' I insisted, snatching my chart from the nurse. She looked affronted. 'Can you give us a minute?' I asked her, motioning to the door.

Before I'd had a chance to read the chart, it was snatched from my hands. John read through the notes as I fumed on the bed. 'Give me that,' I said. 'It's got to be a mistake.'

John's blue eyes looked at me over the clipboard in his hand. 'It's not a mistake. I just watched her test that jar in the next room.'

'Oh God,' I groaned, flopping back on the bed. This was turning into a fucking nightmare.

'Congratulations,' John said, and when I looked at his face, he seemed almost disappointed at the news.

I was pregnant. With Dornan's baby. And Dornan was in the ICU, being operated on, and he might not even live to hear the news.

CHAPTER THIRTY-FOUR

MARIANA

The doctors insisted on keeping me in for observation, which was ridiculous, but I wasn't about to argue with them. The hospital was where Dornan was, and if his wife ever left his bedside, I'd be able to go and see him.

At some point in the night, John woke me to let me know that Dornan had made it through surgery. He was going to be okay, Allie's bullet having narrowly missed his heart. The news made me cry. I suddenly realised why everything had been making me cry lately. Damn pregnancy hormones.

As morning broke, I was itching to see Dornan. John informed me, however, that Dornan's wife had spent the night at his bedside, once he was out of surgery. I was getting antsy in my own hospital room, so on impulse I rode the elevator to the third floor. The maternity floor. I hadn't been able to get the little baby boy from last night's horror show out of my head, and I'd even had nightmares that he was my baby, and I'd been the one who was shot by Dornan.

I tried to tell myself that I was just wandering the halls to keep my mind off Dornan, but it was more than that. I was gravitating towards the nursery, and soon I found myself right there, my hands pressed up against the glass window as I scanned the clear plastic bassinets all lined up inside.

He was there. The last bassinet, tucked into the corner. He was asleep, his little lips suckling away at the air as if he were dreaming of his mother's milk. The name tag on the end of his bassinet was blank.

My heart shattered.

That poor baby. Nobody would ever know who he was. His mother was gone and his future looked bleak.

I wanted to take him home and hold him and feed him and never let him go. I wanted to tell him how sorry I was that there were people like Emilio in the world.

People like Dornan.

Something brushed against the back of my neck and I jumped. I turned my face to see Emilio standing there, smiling indulgently at me. He was smiling like he knew a secret, and that made me fucking terrified.

'How are you feeling, Ana?' he asked, putting an arm around my shoulder. 'You were shot. You shouldn't be out of bed, dear.'

I looked at him for a moment before turning back to the babies. I kept my back rigid, refusing to make it comfortable for Emilio to drape himself around me.

'It was just a flesh wound,' I replied. 'I'm trying to stay out of your family's way until the hospital discharges me.' It was kind of the truth.

'How thoughtful of you,' Emilio said, pulling me closer to his side. 'Always so thoughtful. Tell me, did you decide to drop this little bastard off before his mother died or after?'

Oh God. Sweat started to gather around my temples, and my skin was all itchy. I needed to get away from this man. I didn't say anything.

'I asked you a question, cholita.'

I yelped as bony fingers pressed into my bullet wound. I gagged, the pain so sharp that I almost puked right then and there.

'Ahhhhhhhh,' I cried, doubling over from the pain so my forehead was pressed against the cool glass window that separated us from the babies in the nursery.

Emilio didn't like that. He tugged on a handful of my hair, forcing my head back up, and pulled me along so we were standing directly in front of the *bastard* baby he was talking about.

Emilio grinned, his gold tooth reflecting the harsh fluorescent lights that hung overhead. Even after nine years, I'd never gotten used to that tooth, and it made me jump every goddamn time he opened his mouth.

'Mariana,' he said, his voice like chains being dragged through rocks. His eyes were so much like Dornan's that it scared me. How could you come from a man like Emilio Ross and not turn into him? That thought burrowed into my brain and sat there, dormant, waiting for the time when I'd have to rip it out and answer it.

Somehow, I knew we were heading towards destruction, even as we stood in the calm aftermath of Allie's failed attempt at vengeance.

It wasn't over. It would never be over. Emilio's cold hand squeezed the back of my neck as he directed my gaze towards the smallest baby in the line-up.

'I'm taking this boy home,' he promised, his words turning vicious. 'I'll raise him as my own. And if you ever try and leave your post ...'

I sobbed from the pain of his fingers inside my wound. 'I've given you almost ten years,' I whispered. 'You told me you'd let me go once I repaid the debt.'

He chuckled. 'That was before. This is now. Do you have any idea how fucking marvellous you are at what you do? I was going to shoot you that night but you insisted on coming with me. You've only got yourself to blame, dear.'

I couldn't stop crying. The pain! I just wanted him to get his hands away from me.

'You try and leave, and I'll find you, Ana,' he continued. 'I'll find you and I'll make you watch while I kill that boy in front of you.' He returned his black eyes to me and grinned. 'It's a shame your family is dead. Your sister would be much more fun to kill while you watch than a fucking child.'

My blood ran cold. Even though I knew he was talking about this baby who'd been born in the back of a trafficking truck, all I saw was Luis. And it wasn't just Luis any more. There was another baby, a secret that lived inside me.

I had to get out. I had to find a way to get out of this hell, for both of my children.

CHAPTER THIRTY-FIVE
MARIANA

Dornan woke up.

But nothing was ever the same between us.

Because when I looked into his eyes, I no longer saw the man who had saved me all those years ago.

I saw the man who'd morphed into a monster before my very eyes.

Part of me thought it would have been better if Allie's bullet had killed him, so I wouldn't have to keep living this lie. The bullet didn't kill him, though. It didn't kill him, and he got better, and I still couldn't bring myself to tell him that I was pregnant with his child.

CHAPTER THIRTY-SIX
MARIANA

I still hadn't told him.

This great weight inside me, this thing, this child I carried like a sinful secret. It burdened me and lightened me at the same time. I wanted to tell him, and I didn't. Thirteen weeks now, it had been growing inside me. After I'd found out, I'd dithered and ummed and ahhed and ached. Because I wanted it. And I didn't. I wanted it because it was mine, loved it like I loved the first baby I'd birthed so long ago. Hated it because it was forcing me to choose. Life or death. No matter which one I chose, I was going to regret it. Kill my child, the child Dornan and I had unwittingly created? Or keep it, bring it into this world, only to have it taken from me just like Luis.

I hated myself because I was so selfish. Because if things had been different, if I had been free, I would have been ecstatic to have a baby growing in my womb, even if it was Dornan's.

Especially if it was Dornan's.

I loved him. I loved him even in my darkest moments. Even in his.

But I still couldn't reconcile the man I loved, the father of my child, with the man who had shot that woman in front of me while I held her baby in my arms, begging him to stop.

I still couldn't fathom that the man I loved had been doing this – taking women and selling them as slaves and handing me the money afterwards – and I'd been blissfully unaware.

I knew they were bad people. I knew that. But I'd never known how complicit I was in it all.

And as much as I tried to convince Dornan to stand up to his father, he insisted that he couldn't. That there was a bigger picture to think of. That it wasn't just me he had to worry about.

'You're the kingpin of this operation,' I protested. 'You're the one in charge of all of this.'

'It's not like that.' Dornan replied, stonewalling me.

'It's exactly like that. You let me see something like this and then you pretend that you're doing it for me? Well, don't do it for me. I'd rather die than be the reason for all of this.'

'Shut up,' he growled. 'You don't know what you're talking about, and if he ever hears you—'

'Let him hear me, Dornan,' I cut him off. 'Let him hear everything I say. Because if he thinks he can make you do this for him and use me as a threat? I won't have it. I'll let him sell me as a fucking sex slave before I let you traffic one more soul in my name.'

'Don't you get it?' he yelled. 'This isn't just about you. You're one form of currency, Ana, but I have kids. I have friends. I have a club. How many people do you think had to die before I agreed to do this for my father? I'm no kingpin,' he said bitterly. 'Emilio's the kingpin. I'm the pawn, and so are you.'

'He's your father,' I protested.

'Exactly.'

'Who did he kill, Dornan? Who did he kill to make you go along with this?'

He was silent for a beat.

'That woman I told you about, the first woman I really loved. Her name was Stephanie.'

He'd never told me her name before.

'My father was putting the pressure on for me to join his trafficking operation. Said he needed someone he could trust to run it, and who can you trust more than your own flesh and blood? And I refused. I said no. I said fuck you, do your own dirty work.'

'What happened?'

'She disappeared. I said no, and she fucking vanished into thin air. I already had kids at that point. I didn't love their mother, but I sure as hell didn't hate her enough to risk her. To risk my boys. No. I showed up. I did what I was told to do. I kept my family safe.'

'Your sons – they're his family. That's Emilio's grandsons you're talking about.'

He raised his eyebrows. 'When I say my father's a snake, I'm not fucking kidding around, alright? He'd slit his own mother's throat if it got him where he wanted to go. He'd sell my boys just as soon as he'd sell you.'

'Dornan,' I whispered. 'I don't know if I can live like this anymore.'

I cried. I always cried.

'Really?' he said, and his face twisted with rage. 'And what can you live with? Huh? What's the alternative? You want to leave?'

'I don't want to leave you,' I muttered. 'I want to leave this craziness. This is no place for a—' I'd almost said baby, the word on the tip of my tongue.

'For a what?' he pressed.

'For a life!' I answered.

He just chuckled. 'That's funny,' he said cruelly. 'I thought you understood after all this time. There's only one way out of here, baby, and it's not pretty.'

There has to be a way, I thought to myself. *There has to be something.*

CHAPTER THIRTY-SEVEN

DORNAN

Dornan moved the food around on his plate.

'You don't have to eat it,' Celia said quietly. She took the plate from in front of him and held a cool palm to his throbbing forehead. 'You feeling okay?'

Dornan grunted in response and leaned back so his wife wasn't touching him anymore. Her touch made his skin crawl, made him want to lash out and strike her. But tonight he couldn't even be bothered making a shitty remark about her cooking, so he said nothing. For some reason, ever since he'd been shot, he couldn't stomach eating. The thick steaks Celia had cooked were still bloody in the middle, and that was probably the issue. He'd seen too much blood lately.

Celia – cold, beautiful Celia – shook her head, and then left the kitchen. Dornan didn't care. After this many years of marriage, he was completely disillusioned with the concept. He had thought about divorcing her, but he needed to be close to his kids. He'd been able to get sole custody of his three older sons when he divorced his first wife, Lucia, but her family was nobody special. Celia, on the other hand, had powerful mafia connections on the east coast, their grandfathers very distant relatives somewhere along the line, and she'd probably be able to wrangle shared custody.

Dornan wouldn't have that, and he'd told her exactly that on more than one occasion when she demanded a divorce. The only way she'd be getting away from him was through death. Over the years, their marriage had turned into something of a business alliance. Celia was smart, she was feisty, and she was crucial to getting their east coast relatives to play fair. Their current arrangement worked well enough.

But it wasn't a marriage, and he didn't love her, and he knew every time she looked at him she was probably counting down in her head the minutes until he'd leave again.

He didn't even care anymore. Having Celia – who, he knew for a fact, was fucking somebody else – gave him a measure of protection, a cover story, something to distract people from asking what he was really doing. Sometimes he fantasised about somebody kidnapping Celia, holding her for ransom, and then going to collect her and to pay the kidnappers off, and shooting her in the face instead. Because even though she was his wife, she was also a rather heavy piece of baggage he had to drag around. The thought of getting rid of her tantalised him. Because if she was gone, he'd be able to spend every goddamn night buried balls-deep inside Mariana, fucking her into oblivion and then laying tender kisses on her afterwards.

Dornan wasn't a tender man — in fact, he was the opposite — but Mariana made him want to be a better person. At least she had, until he'd found the fucking cellphone buried in the back of her kitchen cupboard. The question had been on his lips in the truck, just before the deafening bullet had torn apart his chest and his sanity. Who's the phone for, Ana? He'd convinced himself that there was a perfectly legitimate answer for the secret phone. It could be Guillermo's. It could be he'd forgotten about it. Because if it was anything else – if she had betrayed his trust – he couldn't bear to think what would come next. What he'd have to do to her. How he'd have to punish her.

His chest was aching, that phantom bullet still metaphorically jammed up against his heart, its shards spreading through his ribcage, tiny specks of poisoned lead. And it ached for her. He couldn't bear that she might have already betrayed him. He couldn't deal with that shit. It was easier to pretend like he'd never seen the phone, or at least keep the knowledge of its existence in his back pocket, ready to pull out when she was least expecting it. He imagined her eyes widening in fright, because he knew he frightened her. Would she try to lie about it? Or would she confess? Had she been calling somebody without him knowing? The thoughts were like a cancerous rage, swirling inside him. He had to fucking stop thinking about it before it consumed him.

His stomach twisted uneasily again. Maybe he'd caught something. He never got sick, though. Ever. It was something else.

Yeah, come to think of it, he wasn't any better than his father and the rest of the Il Sangue Cartel. He thought of Mariana's face when she'd realised what exactly it was keeping her alive, Dornan's end of the grisly bargain he'd struck with Emilio all those years ago. One life in exchange for many. He tried to forget the horror in her eyes when she'd learned the truth, just before he'd been shot, but it was impossible.

He was snapped back to the present moment by the urge for a cigarette. He could light up, inhale and try to burn the memory of her sad eyes from his brain, one puff at a time. His cigarettes were in the bedroom. He pushed back from the table and made his way to the master bedroom, finding his pack of smokes and lighter in the pocket of his leather jacket.

The light was dim in the cool and quiet bedroom. The kids were always loud, and sometimes this was the only place he could find any peace in this fucking house. As he lit up, he continued to think of Mariana, always alone in her apartment, always lonely. Always begging him to stay.

He thought of the way she'd cried out as he fucked her perfect round ass, the way her light brown skin shimmered as he pulled those tight globes of her ass onto his cock again and again, and the thought made his dick grow hard almost instantly.

He shifted slightly to relieve some of the unbearable pressure of denim on his growing erection, and saw movement out of the corner of his eye.

'Dear husband,' Celia said, leaning against the doorway. 'Care to spare a smoke for your lovely wife?'

Dornan raised an eyebrow and stuck his cigarette between his teeth. 'Knock yourself out,' he said around the stick of tobacco, gesturing to the packet on the bed beside him.

She ignored the packet, instead slinking towards him. Kneeling on the floor in front of his legs, she burrowed her lithe body into the V between his open knees. Her mouth curled up into a smile as she looked towards his lap.

'Happy to see me?' she asked, reaching for his zipper and boldly tugging it down. Dornan watched his wife like one would watch a snake, keeping his eye on her so she didn't suddenly strike. He didn't respond, just watched with detached indifference as she pulled his straining cock out of his jeans and wrapped her lips around the head. It felt good, but knowing it was her made his blood run cold. Didn't make his dick any less stiff, though. He was a man, and what man didn't enjoy a surprise blow job?

She must have wanted something. That was the only explanation for her sudden interest in his dick, after so many years.

He rested back on his hands, cigarette still between his teeth, as he watched his beautiful, cruel wife suck him. She was really getting into it, using both hands. Taking one of his hands off the comforter, he threaded it into her hair and pulled her head back. 'What do you want?' he muttered around the cigarette.

She pouted, her hands still around his erection. 'Nothing. Can't a woman give her husband a blow job anymore?'

He let go of her hair and gestured as if to say, *Don't stop on my account.*

She resumed her sucking, making a small gagging noise as he hit the back of her throat. That amused him more than it should, and he found himself holding back a snicker. His cell vibrated in his pocket and he pulled it out. It was Viper. Christ, what now? Last time Viper had called him, he'd ended the night with a bullet to the chest.

'Yeah?'

It was quiet. Eerily quiet. The only noise on the other end of the phone was steady breathing.

'What?' Dornan asked.

'Boss,' Viper spoke, an urgency in his tone. 'I found her.'

Dornan transferred the phone to his other hand; he could barely hear Viper, he was speaking so quietly. 'Everything all right?'

'Dee,' Viper said.

'What is it?' Dornan asked, impatience growing in his gut.

'Don't freak the fuck out. I found Stephanie.'

Stephanie? *Fuck.* It had been what – sixteen, seventeen years? An anxiousness began to build inside his chest, an annoying, gnawing buzz that ate away at him.

His heart squeezed painfully.

Dead. That's what Viper was going to say, he knew it. Knew it in his bones. The first woman he'd ever truly loved, one he could have imagined leaving this life for. Hell, once he'd even proposed the idea. He would kill everyone in the cartel, and they could leave, go someplace where nobody would ever find them.

She'd laughed.

He'd pretended he was kidding, and they had never mentioned it again. And not long after, she had vanished from the face of the earth, swallowed up no doubt by the same people who had killed Dornan's brother back when they were still weedy teenagers on the verge of becoming men. Gunned down, left in their front yard as a message, and he just knew Stephy had ended up the same way. That knowledge had almost killed him. He'd been a zombie, then become cruel, sadistic, letting her disappearance ruin any good that had existed within him. So he embraced the dark, and he was very, very bad. He killed. He coerced. He traded in lives.

And then he met her.

Mariana.

And she blew his goddamn world to pieces.

She was different from Stephy in every way possible. Mariana was Colombian; Stephy was born-and-bred Texan. Mariana had dark hair and bronze skin; Stephy had strawberry blonde locks, the consistency of fairy floss, and pale skin thanks to her Irish-American ancestry.

Mariana was alive, and Stephy was not.

At least, that's what Dornan had believed for the past sixteen-odd years.

He held the phone so tight, it was a wonder it didn't shatter in his hand.

Viper seemed hesitant. Dornan could've reached through the phone and ripped him a new asshole for not hurrying the fuck-up and spilling what he'd discovered.

'She dead?' Dornan grunted, feigning indifference, but inside, he was ready to explode.

'Dee,' Viper said. 'Where are you right now? I should be telling you this man to man, not on the fucking phone. Where the hell have you been, man?'

'Keep talking,' Dornan said. He struggled to keep his voice steady as he pushed Celia away, and she fell on her pert ass with a thud. 'Tell me.' He tucked his cock back into his pants and started working on the zipper – not easy with one hand.

Celia was on her feet now, staring right at him with dead eyes. She looked positively pissed and like she might want to cut his balls off and shove them down his throat.

Stephy had to be dead. After all this time, it was the only explanation. He knew someone had taken her, probably used her for their own sick pleasure and then murdered her. His chest grew uncomfortably tight as he remembered her hair, those bright eyes, that smile. The one woman he'd truly loved. The woman who'd accepted him with open arms and a laugh, even though he was married, even though he had kids, even though he was a Gypsy Brother with so much baggage it could spell death for them both. She'd started out working in the bar at the clubhouse, but she wasn't a club whore. She was just a university student trying to supplement her income, and when Dornan had found out about Celia's cheating, how she was pregnant and it might be with some other motherfucker's kid, Stephy had been the one who had listened to him. He'd confided everything in her – things about Emilio, about the trafficking, about the government connections. He'd been so smitten with her, and then she'd just … *vanished*.

She'd gone and fucking disappeared on him, so abruptly it was almost as if she'd never existed. He'd gone to her apartment and everything seemed normal. Her purse was still there, all her ID, some cash, her cellphone. It was all normal – too normal. He'd called a crime-scene tech he knew and asked him to check out Stephy's apartment with luminol, and that place had lit up like a fucking Christmas tree in Times Square. There was blood all over the apartment, invisible to the naked eye since someone had painstakingly mopped it all up, but it had been there, and nobody could lose that much blood and still be alive. He hadn't loved another woman for many, many years. Not until Mariana.

They never found Stephanie's body. Dornan had grown older and more bitter, refusing his wife's half-hearted attempts at reconciling, burying himself in his work, waking up at night covered in sweat as he imagined Stephy being brutally murdered.

Imagining it was Emilio who'd been holding the knife. Because she had known too much. Dornan had been too naive, entrusting this girl with cartel information, and so he was certain his father had had a hand in her death. He pictured a bag of bones in a shallow grave, some piece of clothing or a deathbed confession the only way to truly know they were Stephy's remains. It had been so long ago that it would be impossible to identify her. Her flesh would have rotted into the earth a long, long time ago, eaten by greedy worms and insects.

Viper cleared his throat. And he said something that would change the very fabric of Dornan Ross's soul, extinguish the love he felt for the girl he'd long given up for dead, and replace that feeling with a rage so brutal it demanded blood. Simple words was all it took.

'Dee, listen to me. I found her. I found Stephanie. She's alive.'

'Come again?' If the fucker was having a joke at his expense, it would be the last joke he ever made, because Dornan would drive over to his house and kill Viper with his bare hands.

'That's not all,' Viper said.

There was something else? Dornan could hear the reluctance in Viper's tone. *There was something else.*

'Go on,' Dornan ground out.

'She's got a kid, man. A son. He's fifteen. I'm pretty sure he's yours.'

Fifteen.

FIFTEEN.

The kid was fifteen.

He had a son out there, somewhere, and *he hadn't even known.*

It all fit together now, all made total, devastating sense. She hadn't been taken – hadn't been killed.

She had run away. With his baby inside her.

She had stolen something that belonged to him.

Dornan's grip on the phone became even tighter, the plastic starting to buckle under the pressure.

'Boss?' Viper said nervously.

Few things were capable of shocking Dornan Ross these days, jaded and weary as he was, but this was like someone had just dropped an atomic bomb in his lap and asked him to please sit still.

'Where is she?' Dornan asked, feeling almost two decades worth of sadness and guilt collect into a vortex of what could only be described as a black, festering rage.

'Dee—'

'*Where*?' He was so enraged by her apparent betrayal, he couldn't even bear the weight of her name on his lips.

'Colorado,' Viper conceded. 'I'm texting you the address right now.' A brief pause. 'What are you going to do?'

Dornan started to pace, completely ignoring Celia, who was watching his every move. He wondered if she could hear Viper's side of the conversation. Doubtful. Dornan could barely hear him.

'I'm going to go on a little road trip,' Dornan said, ending the call.

He needed to smash something. Now. Celia was in front of him. No. She didn't deserve his wrath, not over this. He tamped down his rage momentarily, as his phone buzzed again with a text message. He glanced at the screen and saw a Colorado address flash up. Took a deep breath.

'Who was that? Everything okay?' Celia asked in a small voice.

No, everything was most certainly not okay. It was the furthest place from okay that was humanly possible.

'Work,' he lied, though he didn't need to explain anything to her. The way she was staring at him was making him itch. The bitch would do well to remember who was in charge in this relationship.

'Dornan,' she said quietly.

He expected her to launch into a tirade – it was her go-to – but instead her eyes filled with tears.

'Fuck,' Dornan muttered. Perhaps a better man would have felt regret over his callousness, over his rough rejection. Not Dornan. All he felt was annoyance. '*Celia*.'

She dissolved into sobs. Dornan hastily did his belt buckle up and glared at his wife. He looked at the screen on his cellphone and back to Celia. Her hands were covering her face now, her shoulders moving up and down as she cried silently.

'Celia, just tell me what you want,' he said gruffly.

'Why don't you touch me anymore?' Celia said, her voice small and lonely. 'Why don't you love me anymore?'

Dornan raised his eyebrows. 'I never loved you,' he spat. 'Not sure where that idea came from.'

Dornan shrugged his leather jacket on, swiped his cigarettes from the bed and shoved them in his pocket. He thought of the deal breaker, the night he'd found her fucking some other guy. *While* she was pregnant with Dornan's fucking kid. With that memory implanted firmly in his brain, any trace of guilt he felt for pushing her away evaporated. He'd punish her until she either left, or died. *Fuck* her.

'I want a divorce!' she screamed.

He laughed. 'You sucked my dick so I'd grant you a divorce? You're crazier than I thought, Celia.'

Mascara streaking down her cheeks, Celia looked like one of the strippers at the club.

'Why won't you just let me go?!'

His chest tightened. He thought of her leaving, their sons in tow. No.

'You know why,' he said.

'They're mine!' she cried. 'They came from me! They grew inside me, and now you want to take them from me? I tried to make you love me, and you just push me away.'

Dornan spread his hands. 'I let you stay here. I let you spend whatever you want. I didn't try and take our sons from you. But I will not forgive what you did, Celia. And I will never let you take my sons from me. Ever. You want to go? There's the goddamn door.'

She pouted, crossing her hands across her chest. 'I fucking hate my life.'

Dornan shrugged as he left. 'Survival of the fittest, baby,' he called over his shoulder. 'We might not like it, but it's better than the alternative.'

'Good luck out there,' Celia snapped sarcastically. 'Don't get shot.'

He had to clench his fists to stop from laying one into her pretty face. He concentrated on the image of Stephanie and what he would do to her when he got to Colorado.

It wouldn't be pretty.

***

He drove all night and into the next day, only stopping when his gas tank ran low. He had just crossed from Utah into Colorado, and to have to stop now was excruciating.

As he was filling the tank of his newly fitted-out truck at a gas station, somewhere near Grand Junction, Dornan's phone rang. It was his lawyer. Jesus, what now? He answered.

Celia had filed for divorce. She'd signed over full custody of their sons. She'd give up her own children, the things she loved most in this world, just to be rid of him.

Dornan didn't know whether to laugh or smash his fists into the hood of his truck and cry.

CHAPTER THIRTY-EIGHT
DORNAN

The house was a modest affair: a single-storey stucco building that sat, squat and neat, between other houses that were exactly the same. Inside it was tidy enough. Chequered tea towels. Kitschy shit that cluttered the mantlepiece above the open fireplace, the coffee table, the windowsill above the sink in the kitchen. Useless possessions irritated him. What was the point of them? They took up space and gathered dust, and then you died and littered the world you left behind with your crap.

There were photographs hanging on the white panelled walls. A baby boy, with Dornan's eyes, his colouring, his DNA. Everything about the kid screamed Dornan. He looked more like him than any of his other sons, for fuck's sake. How was that for irony? He hadn't even known the kid existed, and here he was, his carbon copy, smiling Stephy's lopsided smile, her dimples passed down to *his* son.

His son. Those two words wrapped around him like a vice, pulling tight until he could barely breathe with the injustice of what this bitch had taken from him. He wasn't a good man, had never pretended to be anything remotely in the realm of good, but he loved his children with a ferocity that knew no bounds. He was the father lion, possessive, pride of the pack, poised to strike at and rip the throat from anyone who dared to shatter his carefully constructed world.

Viper had been useful. Giving him the time the bitch was due home, the kid, too. He still didn't know what he was going to say to them, but he was pretty sure it was going to take everything inside him not to smash her face into the kitchen table until she passed out. Sixteen years. And all the time, she'd let him believe she was dead in a shallow fucking grave somewhere.

And *he had a seventh son.*

He found her gun in the second drawer he opened. He knew she'd have one stashed in easy reach, and ironically it was the same one he'd given her. Fucking bitch. He flicked open the chamber, was mildly impressed at the recent cleaning and oiling of the weapon. He emptied the bullets into his pocket and replaced the gun in its spot.

He sat at the kitchen table. It was cheap pine and it looked like someone had traced their initials into it. JP.

His son's name was Jason. He didn't even have Dornan's last name. But he would.

Dornan's hand went into his pocket and he squeezed his fist tight around the bullets he'd just reclaimed.

And then he heard her car in the driveway.

He didn't bother hiding. You couldn't see the kitchen from the front door, so he helped himself to a glass of milk, sat back down at the kitchen table, and he waited.

She took a while. He heard several doors opening and closing, the screech of metal that needed to be greased, the jangle of keys in the door.

And then she was in front of him, her mouth hanging open, the paper shopping bags in her arms falling and crashing to the floor.

Dornan eyed the contents momentarily before returning his gaze to her. He felt beads of milk clinging to the stubble above his lip. He wiped it with the back of his hand and smiled at the bitch who was having conniptions in front of him.

Goddamn, she was still beautiful.

'Hello, Stephy,' he said. 'You got a real nice house here.'

She was frozen. She couldn't form words. Dornan laughed, taking another gulp of milk. He would have preferred beer, but she didn't have any in the refrigerator.

She was so fucking obvious. He saw her eyes dart over to the kitchen drawer where her now-empty revolver was hidden. She rushed over, the shock still sharp on her face, opening the drawer and taking the gun out.

It was stupid, the way his heart hurt when she pointed the gun at him.

'That's not very nice, baby,' he said, his voice low and rough. 'I come all the way here to visit you, and you pull a gun on me?'

She cocked the revolver in trembling hands. She still hadn't said a word to him. Was he really that frightening? She'd loved him, once. She'd let him hold her life in his hands, and now she wanted to end his?

'How's my son?' Dornan asked, his tone shifting rapidly, acerbic and bitter.

She huffed. 'He is not your son.'

So she did speak.

Something broke inside him, something he'd been trying to push down and keep locked away for fifteen years. Longer. Sixteen.

He had loved her, goddamn it! He. Had. Loved. Her.

And she was staring at him like she'd never laid eyes on him in her life. No, it was worse than that. She was staring at him like he was a fucking monster.

'That's funny,' Dornan replied looking at the framed photograph on the wall of a small boy, maybe seven, his dark brown eyes and hair a dead ringer for Dornan's. 'Because I'm pretty fucking sure he is.'

'Get out,' she whispered, her eyes full of tears, her aim steady. 'Get out or I'll shoot you, Dornan, I swear to God.'

Dornan nodded, reaching for his own gun. Terrified, Stephy aimed at his chest and pulled the trigger. And pulled it again. And again.

'It needs bullets to work,' Dornan said calmly. 'Here, have one of mine.'

He aimed at her shin and pulled the trigger on his own Glock, smiling with satisfaction as she went down hard, her lower leg exploding in a mess of blood and bone fragments as she landed between a bunch of bananas and a loaf of bread.

Dornan took a deep breath, the victory of vengeance singing in his veins as he stood up and drank the rest of his milk. He let the empty glass fall to the ground at his feet, where it shattered.

'Stephy,' Dornan teased, stepping between the fallen groceries to get to her.

She cowered in the corner, her hands covering her face, which was turning swiftly pale. She had hurt him, and he was going to hurt her back. He was going to hurt her very, very badly. And the thought filled him with relief.

He holstered his gun. He didn't want this to go too quickly; no, he wanted to draw out her suffering, the way she had drawn out his suffering. His endless fucking pursuit of a shallow grave, of a confession from her killer, of something. And all the time, she had been here, living and smiling and bearing his fucking child.

He knelt beside her, his boots crunching on the broken glass. 'Let's get you cleaned up,' he said, smiling. 'Where's your bathroom?'

She whimpered. She didn't answer. Sighing, he balled his fist up and slammed it into the side of her face. Not too hard, because he didn't want her to pass out. Just hard enough to hurt like a motherfucker.

'Let's try that again. Where's your bathroom?'

She pointed down the hallway. Smiling, Dornan grabbed a fistful of her long blonde hair and started dragging her. She half-crawled, half-limped alongside him, crying out in pain the whole time.

She had a bathtub. Excellent. Dornan rolled his eyes as she started to beg, scooping her up and throwing her hard into the bottom of the tub. She struggled to sit up and he hit her again. His fist throbbed in pain. It felt good. He'd never hit a woman before, not like this.

But she deserved it for what she'd done.

'Here's the deal,' Dornan said, crouching beside the tub and brushing her fringe from her face. 'You tell me when my son is due home, and I promise I won't kill either of you.'

She swallowed thickly. 'School finished at three-thirty,' she said shakily. 'He's usually home by four.'

Dornan nodded, taking a syringe from his pocket, and a vial of morphine he'd made damn sure to bring with him on his long journey. Stephanie stared in horror as he stabbed the syringe into the vial and drew up a colourless liquid. He filled the syringe, and her eyes grew wide as she realised what it was.

'Please,' she begged.

'You remember this, don't you? Just like smack, only better. You liked it the first time. Remember how you used to come underneath me? How I'd give you a hit of the sweet stuff at just the right time? Do you remember that, Stephy?' He wrapped a rubber tourniquet around her arm.

'Dornan!' she cried. 'Please don't do this. My boy needs me, I'm all he has …'

My boy. That made Dornan angry. He pulled the tourniquet tighter and a juicy blue vein popped up against her pale arm.

'You promised,' she said, blood spilling out of her mouth from the spot where he'd punched her. 'You promised!'

Dornan smiled, pushing the plunger down and delivering enough morphine to stop her heart five times over. 'I did promise,' he replied cheerily. He felt crazed. He felt high. He'd loved her, and he'd mourned her, and now he would end her.

'Remember how you promised you'd love me forever? How you'd never leave me? You lied, baby.'

Her eyes started to flutter shut. 'You promised,' she whispered.

He grinned wickedly. 'I know. I lied, too. How does it feel?'

She couldn't answer him, though, because she was dead.

***

A few hours later, the boy came home. *Jason*. His son's name was Jason.

He was exquisite. Dornan could think that without feeling stupid, because he was laying his eyes on his son for the first time, as if he'd just been born, only fifteen years too late.

The boy found the kitchen a mess, and soon after his mother. Dornan confronted him, told him who he was. The boy put up a solid fight, made Dornan proud at the way he punched and kicked, but he had twenty-five years and change on the kid. He knocked him out, injected him with some tranquilliser to keep him subdued, and placed a call to John.

He answered on the second ring.

'Hey, Dee,' John said.

Things had been tense between them of late. Dornan knew the shooting had been stressful for John, and the mystery surrounding Murphy's disappearance hadn't helped matters. He'd also heard through the grapevine that Caroline was up to her usual, so it was no wonder he hardly saw his best friend outside of official club business these days.

'Hey, buddy,' Dornan said, a strange calm descending upon him as he surveyed the damage he'd done to his first love and their son. 'Something's come up. I need you in Colorado, now. Bring Ana.'

While John asked questions, Dornan picked through Stephy's groceries, finding things to fix himself a sandwich. He poured himself a fresh glass of milk and sat at the table, which was covered in Stephanie's blood, and proceeded to eat his first meal of the day as he waited for John and Mariana to arrive.

CHAPTER THIRTY-NINE
JOHN

Dornan had found her.

He'd fucking *found* her. And along with her, his kid.

John hung up the phone and looked around his kitchen, rage and guilt rising inside him. The conversation hadn't gone down well. Dornan had demanded his presence in Colorado, and insisted that he bring Mariana.

Did he know about Murphy? About the kiss? Did he know about the way John had put his hands all over Dornan's woman, about how he wanted to do more and no matter what he tried to do to take his mind off it, he couldn't get her out of his fucking head?

'That's a fifteen-hour drive,' John had protested, as soon as Dornan had made the request. 'I'll grab a flight. Or ride it. I can ride faster than I can drive a car.'

'You're not riding with Mariana on the back of your bike,' Dornan had growled. 'Where are you?'

John glanced at his daughter, lying on the couch as she watched TV. Caroline was in bed, where she'd been for the past three days, only getting up to take more pills. Sometimes she liked uppers, but this week she was systematically knocking herself out for six hours at a stretch. He'd been sleeping on the couch to stay away from her. Their bedroom smelled like unwashed bodies and stale beer, and he wasn't about to go in there and clean it up. At least when she was on a downer, he could keep tabs on where she was.

'I'm at home,' he said. 'Tell me what's going on.'

Dornan cleared his throat. 'I've found Stephanie.'

So it was true. Fuck. Did he know the rest, too? Did he know that John had already known where she was all along?

'Alive?' John asked finally.

'No. Well, yeah. She was alive when I got here.'

Jesus.

John wondered about Jason, Stephanie's son. Dornan's son. He couldn't very well ask about him, though. He wasn't supposed to know Jason existed.

'Okay, you wanna tell me what happened?'

'Not particularly. You'll see soon enough.'

'Give me an address,' John said reluctantly. He didn't write it down. He didn't need to.

He knew exactly where he was going.

CHAPTER FORTY

MARIANA

Somehow knowing that I was pregnant made the nausea worse. It had ramped up significantly since the shooting, and it was taking everything I had to keep it concealed.

Guillermo's mother had improved, and so he'd come back to the apartment. I had hardly seen Dornan in the past few weeks and I'd mostly kept my head down. I'd called Miguel and checked on Luis, desperate for information. My family had been buried in a plot without a funeral. There had been no investigation.

The corrupt fucking police force that was supposed to protect my country was probably being paid by the cartel to do their dirty work. I mean, it made sense. Emilio had Colombia by the balls, and he paid the police commissioner handsomely. I would know. I was the one who organised the cash transfers into his bank account.

It was around eight at night and I was cleaning up the dinner plates after Guillermo had cooked tacos. It was the only thing he knew how to make, and he'd already started before I could protest that my ass was going to get fat from the food he kept bringing home. There was a knock on the door. Guillermo looked at me from his seat at the breakfast bar.

'You expecting company?' he asked, one hand going to the gun at his hip.

I shook my head. 'Nope. You?'

He shook his head, sliding off the stool and approaching the front door. He moved like a freaking cat, he was so stealthy, his feet gliding along the tiles as if they weren't even touching them.

He keyed in the code and the door clicked, whoever was on the other side opening it immediately.

Guillermo aimed at whoever it was, until the person smacked the gun out of his hand and grabbed his arm, twisting it behind his back and slamming him face-first into the wall.

'John?' I asked, watching the gun slide across the tiles.

Guillermo stopped struggling when I said his name.

'Prez?' He frowned, apparently confused.

John let him go with a shove, stepping back and removing the hoodie from his head. 'What the hell was that?' John asked, his face red and his breathing fast. He looked pretty fucking stressed out, and that made my stomach do all sorts of weird things.

'I didn't know it was you,' Guillermo muttered, looking embarrassed.

'What happened?' I asked John.

Guillermo walked back towards the kitchen, massaging his elbow, as John slammed the door shut.

'Pack an overnight bag,' John said tersely. 'Now.'

He never spoke to me like that, and in light of everything that had happened with Murphy, I didn't see the need to ask questions.

'What's going on?' Guillermo asked, looking between John and me.

'Dornan happened,' John said impatiently, looking at me and pointing to my bedroom. I nodded, passing him and entering my room, where I grabbed a duffel bag and started gathering jeans, underwear and make-up. I dumped it all into the bag and zipped it, coming back into the hallway a few moments later.

'You need me to come?' Guillermo asked, an off look on his face. Surely he couldn't tell anything had happened between us just by looking at us, but he had suspicion written all over his face.

'Stay here,' John replied, opening the door and motioning me outside. 'And, call Dornan. He's got about fifteen hours to fill you in while we drive to Colorado.'

Colorado? Where did I know Colorado from? Those post-it notes that John was always giving me, amounts each month to send to a bank account in Colorado. The wire transfer. I wondered if it was related. Probably not, but I made sure to file that mental note away for later.

Once we were on the freeway, I rounded on John. 'What happened?' I asked. 'Guillermo's not here now. You have to tell me. What's in Colorado?'

He stared straight ahead, seemingly in deep thought. Just as I was about to press him again, he started to speak.

'Has Dornan ever mentioned a woman called Stephanie?' he asked, glancing at me before looking back at the road.

My stomach dropped. 'Yeah. His girlfriend? From before we met. Did something happen to her?'

'She disappeared,' John said. 'Sixteen or seventeen years ago, I can't remember exactly when.'

He didn't offer any more.

'Sometimes I'd like to disappear,' I said after a few moments silence.

John's hand shot out. He grabbed hold of my wrist and squeezed tight.

'Ow,' I said, glaring at him. 'You're hurting me.'

'Do you have any idea what we're going to walk into tomorrow?' John hissed. He didn't ease up on the squeezing. I pressed my teeth together in frustration.

'No, I don't know where we're going,' I snapped, finally managing to tug my wrist out of his grip. 'That's what I'm asking you. What happened to this Stephanie woman?'

John's lips pressed together to form a thin line. 'Dornan happened to her,' he said finally.

I thought of the woman from the trafficking operation, the mother who Dornan had shot in the head. I thought of our baby.

'What did he do,' I asked, a lump rising in my throat.

'I'm not entirely sure,' John said. 'Dornan's always thought she was dead, that her body might turn up one day.'

Realisation settled into my bones like an old friend. 'You helped her get away,' I whispered.

John raked a hand through his hair, agitated. 'She was pregnant,' he said. 'She was pregnant and freaking out, and I did the only thing I could think of. I gave her some money and got her out of town.'

I looked back to the road, slumping down in my seat. Shit, it seemed like history was repeating itself.

'Did you – Were you with her?' I asked, jealousy stabbing me in the chest for some unknown reason. I'd kissed him exactly one time, and now I was suddenly jealous of some woman he may or may not have been involved with sixteen years ago? I was losing it. I was really, really losing my fucking mind.

'No,' he said sharply. 'Not at all. Caroline and I, we were good back then. Things were good.'

'Does Dornan know you helped her?' I asked quietly.

John shrugged. 'I don't think so. I don't know.'

Impulsively, I reached for his hand in the dark. He looked down as I laced my fingers in his, as if I'd just given him an electric shock. He didn't pull away, though. He looked at the road, squeezing my hand in his, and I felt tears well up in my eyes. How had things gotten to this? How had we ended up with the terrible burden of Murphy's demise hanging between us like a fatal secret? How had I ended up pregnant with Dornan's baby? How had we ended up in this car, barrelling down the freeway, on our way to Dornan and the woman he had probably killed?

'The baby,' I said suddenly. 'The one she was pregnant with when she left. What happened?'

John looked like the weight of the world was pressing down on his shoulders as he drove.

'He's fifteen years old,' he said wearily, 'and I'm pretty sure his father just murdered his mother.'

I took my hand away, crossing my arms over my stomach, convinced that if I tried to leave I'd be next on my lover's hit list.

Fuck.

We stayed on the road all night and into the morning, checking into a seedy motel that charged by the hour after about ten hours of driving. I'd offered to take the wheel so we could keep going, but John could see how exhausted I was, how nauseous, and he'd insisted we sleep for a couple of hours before we drove the final stretch to Colorado.

The room was like a matchbox, small and threadbare, and when I sat on one of the beds it sagged dramatically. Great. All the trimmings of a five-star establishment. John disappeared for a while, returning with burgers and fries. I inhaled mine, then curled up on the bed furthest from the front door and passed out into a dreamless slumber.

Well, it was dreamless at first, but then I started to have a nightmare. Dornan had his hands around my neck, and he wouldn't let go. He squeezed and squeezed until my neck broke and I died in his hands. I woke up with my own hands at my throat, as I sat bolt upright and gasped for air.

John must have been a light sleeper. As soon as I sat up, he turned on the bedside lamp and jumped out of bed, reaching out for me.

'Are you okay?' he asked, not looking even slightly sleepy. He still looked as wide awake as when we'd arrived, and I guessed that he hadn't slept at all.

'Yeah,' I said, tears streaming down my cheeks. Fucking hormones. John saw my tears, a concerned look on his face as he sat on the edge of my bed and rubbed my bare shoulders. His palms were large and warm, and I wanted to melt into his touch.

Stop! I had to stop reacting to him.

'Bad dream?' he asked, smiling sympathetically.

I nodded.

'You're okay,' he said, reaching up and brushing hair from my face. I leaned into his touch, the move almost an unconscious act, and I saw something shift in his gaze.

I reached for him in the dark like my life depended on it. Without giving myself even a moment to stop and think about what I was doing, I pressed my lips to his, opening my mouth, seeking his tongue. He didn't hesitate, his hands in my hair, at my waist, palming my breasts through the thin material of my tank top. I moaned when he did that, my nipples hardening to stiff peaks when his hand came into contact with them. He pressed into me and I laid back against the pillows, John shifting so his top half was over me. Just as I was losing all sense of reason and reaching for his belt buckle, he pulled back.

'I can't,' he said, pushing me away.

I put a hand over my mouth, scooting up the bed so I was sitting with my back against the headboard. I didn't want to look at him, but I couldn't look away.

'I'm sorry,' I said weakly.

He jumped up and began to pace beside the bed. 'I'm sorry,' he said, his hands balling into fists that looked like they really wanted to smash something. 'You're having his baby. We can't do that ever again, you understand?'

I just watched him pace.

'If I wasn't having his baby, then what?' I asked quietly.

John shook his head, agitated. 'No,' he said, 'no. You're not mine to touch. You're his.'

'Oh, I'm a fucking possession now?' Suddenly I was livid. 'What, I'm Dornan's toy, so you have to find another one?'

He glared at me. 'I don't want another one,' he said. 'But this one's taken. By a man I call my best friend.'

'Huh,' I said. 'Some best friend. You've got a lot of secrets for a best friend, John.'

He scoffed. 'Most of them are yours,' he said angrily. 'Let's not forget that.'

It was like he'd punched me in the face.

'You're right,' I said. 'I shouldn't have called you that night.'

'You should have called Dornan,' John said flatly.

'I did call Dornan,' I snapped. 'He was busy with his wife.'

John eyed me from the end of the bed. 'Do you love him?'

I sighed, frustrated. 'I don't know,' I said, throwing my hands in the air. 'Yes, I do. But he's not the person I met nine years ago. He's scaring me. I don't know how to help him out of this darkness he's sinking into. It's like poison, and I'm scared he's going to pull me in with him.'

'You gonna tell him about the baby?' John asked, gesturing to my stomach.

I took a deep breath and let it out in a long whoosh. 'I don't know,' I said again. 'I don't want to. I'm afraid of what he'll do.' I started to weep. 'I just want my boy back. I just want to leave and never come back. I want to have this baby where no one will ever find her, or me, or Luis, and we can just stop being afraid.'

Oh God, how it felt to finally externalise that awful, aching longing I'd been carrying around for my Luis.

'Her?' John asked.

I nodded. They'd scanned me before I left the hospital after the shooting, and I was already far enough along for them to tell the sex of the baby.

'It's a girl,' I said. 'I can't bring a little girl into this world, John. The things Emilio would do to her.' I shook my head. 'No. I get out or I have a termination. I can't do this if I'm still here. But I don't know if I have it in me to try and run. I don't want to live every day of my life worrying about when a bullet's going to hit me.'

John nodded, coming back to sit beside me and pulling me into his arms.

'I'm glad you called me that night,' he said.

CHAPTER FORTY-ONE

JOHN

Complete and utter carnage.

That was the only way John could describe what he was looking at. Dornan leaned against the basin in the small bathroom, irritation and fatigue competing for real estate on his face.

'You stop in Canada on the way?' Dornan asked.

John ignored the question. Dornan looked wild, still covered in the blood of the dead woman in the bathtub beside them.

'You didn't have time for a shower?' John asked, looking his best friend up and down. Jesus, the smell of old blood in the room was overwhelming, crawling up his nostrils and burrowing in. He wanted to get the fuck out.

'The shower was taken,' Dornan snapped.

Mariana, who'd been explicitly told to stay in the kitchen, appeared in the doorway. Dornan stared at her, and she did the same to him. They didn't speak.

'We need to get her out of here,' John said, positioning his body so that he was blocking Mariana's line of sight to the bathtub.

At his words, Mariana stiffened. 'I'm not going anywhere,' she said, and Dornan chuckled.

'Not you,' he said, studying his knuckle. 'Her.'

Mariana pushed past John and laid eyes on the woman in the bathtub. John scrubbed his hand across his chin, glaring at Dornan.

'What did you do?' Mariana whispered.

'Let me handle this,' John barked, and Mariana's eyes went wide. 'Go and take care of the boy,' he said, gentler this time.

She nodded, disappearing from view.

'You didn't have to do that,' John said.

'Do what?' Dornan asked, grinning.

The bastard was smug. He'd killed the woman he'd been willing to leave the cartel for, and he was fucking smug?

'Let her see ... this,' he said, gesturing to the carnage. 'Was that really necessary?'

Dornan didn't answer. He pushed off the vanity, where he'd been resting one foot, and brushed past John.

CHAPTER FORTY-TWO

MARIANA

I'd never seen Dornan so indifferent in the face of death.

When he'd killed the woman in the backseat of his truck, he had cried. Wept as he pulled the trigger and delivered the bullet that ended her life. I'd seen the anguish in his eyes, seen the devastation that engulfed him.

Now he seemed almost bored with the fact that he'd just killed someone. And not just anyone.

He'd loved her, once. That was the part I found the hardest to accept. He'd loved her, and she'd left, and this was what happened when you left a man like Dornan Ross and never came back. Eventually, he found you, and brutally murdered you.

All of these things raced through my head as I stood in a small bedroom and watched the rise and fall of a young boy's chest.

He might have been fifteen, but in deep sleep he looked younger. He was gorgeous, with olive skin and dark, long eyelashes that covered his closed eyes.

He looked exactly like Dornan. Like a miniature version, though he was almost as tall as him. I held a hand over my mouth as I took him in silently, not wanting to make a noise and risk waking him up. But it seemed like he was knocked out, and that he'd sleep through anything.

I wondered if he'd found his mother. As I was thinking all of this, Dornan entered the room and stood beside me, his hands in his pockets.

'You can stop looking at me like that,' he said, his voice like gravel. He pulled out a cigarette and lit it, sending smoke wafting across the room.

'You shouldn't be smoking in the house,' I said warily, and that made him chuckle. 'Why not?' he replied, tapping ash on the carpet. 'The house is about to burn down.'

I thought of my family. How Emilio had burned them.

How the apple never falls far from the tree.

I looked from Dornan to his unconscious son, a coldness settling into my being. I felt shards of ice travel along my veins and arteries, turning everything frozen and black inside. Everything.

'How could you do this?' I asked him.

Dornan looked at the ground and then back at me, the fury in his eyes unmistakable.

'What would you have done,' he asked darkly, 'if someone had stolen your child away from you?'

I thought of Murphy, the way he had been so heavy in death. Of Allie, her threats against Luis, and how much lighter she had been as I had stolen her breath away and then rolled her body into the water.

I decided that I wasn't one to judge, after all.

CHAPTER FORTY-THREE

DORNAN

They'd cleaned the scene as best they could, and after a lot of convincing on John's part Dornan had agreed not to burn the house down. It was unlikely anyone would trace Stephanie back to Dornan after sixteen years, and he might decide to come back for the boy's things. He was still having trouble referring to Jason as his son. He was like a stranger, this kid who he had to keep sedated to manage, even with his shocking resemblance to Dornan.

They'd buried Stephanie in the woods nearby instead, Dornan insistent on being the one who shovelled dirt onto her bloodied face. He couldn't separate the hate from the love, and the rage, the rage was the worst part of all. At one point, when half her face was still visible, Dornan had started smashing the shovel down onto her head, until John managed to get the shovel away from him.

He wanted to scream and gnash his teeth and bash her fucking head in, but it wouldn't matter because she was already dead. He didn't regret killing her, though. The only thing he regretted was not drawing out her death.

They travelled to a motel, Mariana in the backseat of John's truck, cradling the boy protectively. *At least he'd have her to take care of him*, Dornan mused silently. She'd be a good mother. He'd told her that once, and now she'd have someone to mother. All these thoughts swirling in his brain made perfect sense. He didn't once stop to consider what would happen when the boy woke up. It was a problem that he'd deal with later, and the boy would eventually come around. He'd be mad at first, but he'd understand why his mother was a lying bitch who deserved to die.

They got two rooms at the motel. Dornan dragged the boy in and dumped him on one of two beds in the first room, John and Mariana following on his heels.

'You want to take first shift?' he said, addressing John. 'I know he's tied up, but the little bastard is strong. Like his dad.' Dornan smiled proudly, but neither John nor Mariana smiled back. He was starting to get annoyed by their reactions. Didn't they understand that he'd done this out of love for his son? He was the victim here. He'd just had fifteen years of his child stolen from him, and he intended to make up for lost time just as soon as the boy was awake and calm.

Not now, though. There was no calm space inside Dornan Ross. He was crazed. Drunk on death, on killing. He needed Mariana's softness, needed her around him. Stephanie's blood was on his hands, soaked into the fibres of his clothes. He just wanted to forget.

'I want to talk to you,' he said, tugging Mariana from the room. She looked back at John hesitantly, who seemed to want to say something.

'I'm not gonna kill her,' Dornan said, looking between the pair. Something was off, and he wondered if it was just him, in the aftermath of what had happened, or if there was something he was missing.

John closed his mouth, and Mariana followed Dornan slowly out of the motel room and into the adjoining room. He closed the door behind her. The room was identical to the other one. Two beds. A minibar. A bathroom.

Perfect.

He turned to Mariana, who was hovering at the door, looking everywhere but at him.

'Get on the bed,' he growled, lunging for her. Mariana backed away from him, only stopping when the backs of her knees hit one of the narrow double beds.

'Baby, you're scaring me,' she said, her eyes glassy.

'Why would you be scared of me?' he asked, pressing himself against her so she was forced backwards onto the bed. Her eyes lit up and she pushed her palms against his chest, trying to push him off of her. He didn't like that. It made him mad. Didn't she want to make him feel better? Didn't she want to help him forget?

He grabbed her wrists and forced them over her head, using his weight to press her into the bed. Her eyes grew wide as she struggled against his stronghold.

'Dornan!' she hissed. 'What are you doing?'

He laughed. 'What do you think I'm doing?' he asked, letting go of her wrists and taking hold of the waistband on her pants, tugging hard until the material slid over her hips and down to her knees. She continued to thrash, but he held onto her hips so hard his fingernails drew blood from her flesh.

'You're hurting me!' she cried, pushing at his chest.

He didn't stop. Couldn't stop. All he saw was red.

'Dornan!' More forceful this time.

'Shut up!' he snarled, taking hold of her hips and flipping her onto her stomach. He unzipped his jeans, letting out a breath as he pressed his cock between her ass cheeks.

'It's not too late,' Mariana whispered, her voice shaky. 'You can stop. I don't want to do this. You're not giving me a choice.'

He thought about that *choice* as he spat on his hand and rubbed between her legs. 'No,' he said finally, 'I'm not.'

He thrust into her, and she yelled, her sounds muffled by Dornan pushing her face into the pillow.

He pressed his other hand into the small of her back, needing release, needing calm before he snapped again and hurt her. He'd stop soon enough. Just a few minutes, and then he'd stop. She was upset because of Stephanie, but she'd understand. She loved him. She'd want to take his pain away.

She started to really struggle against his hands, turning her head to the side to look at him, and that made him fucking angry. Couldn't she see, after everything, that he needed her? After everything he'd done for her, after he'd changed his entire existence for her, couldn't she just shut her mouth and let him give her some of his rage, some of the ache inside him?

He laid over her, his large body enveloping her small one. She softened immediately, as if she were relieved. That made his gut twist, made his veins sizzle. Was she a liar, too? Was she just waiting for the moment when she could stab him in the back and run? He collected her small wrists in one hand and pressed them above her head until she whimpered and pressed her eyes tightly shut.

He barely even heard her gasps. There was only need, thick and present and requiring satiety.

He dragged a hand through her thick, silky hair, stopping at the ends and tugging hard. Mariana didn't resist his insolent tug, following the movement like a good little kitty so her neck was outstretched, exposed. He imagined biting into her throat like some kind of lovesick pseudo-vampire, but instead he wrapped his hand around her pretty throat and squeezed.

Her dark blue eyes came alive once more, still wet, but this time tears started to streak across her skin, mixing in with clumped mascara so it looked like she was weeping blackness. It didn't make sense. Their fucking was like fighting most of the time, animals in heat, pain and blood and submission the things that got both of them off. A small part of him knew this was different – that this wasn't good for her, that she had said no, that she was crying as if he were *raping* her – but he pushed that aside, because it didn't matter what she needed in that moment. It only mattered that he get rid of this feeling inside, that he get rid of the image of Stephanie lying in the tub begging for her fucking life, and replace it with something else.

Mariana struggled underneath him, her nails digging into his hand that was clasped at her throat. She took in tiny sips of air, her eyes streaming with tears, the fear inside them both comforting and nauseating at the same time. The only sound was skin slapping against skin, the small choking sounds coming from her throat, and the bed banging against the thin stucco wall with every brutal thrust into her pliant flesh.

CHAPTER FORTY-FOUR

MARIANA

It felt like my wrists were about to snap in two. My throat, though, was where most of the pain blossomed from. I could take in shallow breaths, but Dornan's weight crushed me into the lumpy motel mattress, and my lungs burned, begging to be filled with oxygen. The room started to spin. There were tears in my eyes. *He's supposed to love me.* And I guess the most fucked-up part of all was that he did love me. Even as he held me down, he loved me in the only way he knew how. With violence. With anger. With pain.

I'd become hardened over the years but I'd never, ever felt this torn beneath him. I'd wanted to tell him about the baby for a split second there, but after what I'd seen – how he'd butchered his ex-girlfriend – everything inside me said to shut my mouth, to give nothing away.

And my heart. My heart was hurting, because it was breaking in two. I still loved him, deep down in the dark places inside me. But I was afraid of him. I hated him. I was terrified of this man.

And John. I wanted John. He was safe. He was gentle. He didn't look at me like a possession. He didn't lock me up and have me followed and hurt me. He didn't murder women – not that I knew of anyway. He was tender. He was loving.

Love. I choked tears back, clinging onto consciousness by a tattered thread, as Dornan finished with one final thrust and collapsed on top of me.

I sucked in a breath the moment his hold on me loosened, coughing and choking as fresh air burned my lungs.

In the shock that came after, I imagined stepping onto a plane with Dornan's baby nestled inside my belly, safe and hidden. I imagined the utter relief as the plane took off. And then he would be there, dragging me from my seat, shoving me inside a toilet stall and killing me with his bare hands while his dark eyes burned with *Why?*

I lay on the edge of the bed, not daring to move, until the last of the sticky liquid had seeped from inside me and turned cold beneath my thighs. I waited until Dornan was sleeping, his breath coming in slow increments, his form still. Rolling my legs off the side of the bed, I moved slowly and silently, heading for the bathroom. Once I was in there, I locked the door and stepped into the shower, turning on the hot water.

I'd never been raped before. Is that what it was like? It had been less traumatic letting Murphy fuck me than it had been begging Dornan not to. I was shaking and I couldn't stop.

I held my wrists up to the weak light the bare bulb was throwing off overhead. I saw fresh bruises blossoming across my skin, and marvelled at how close love and death could become. Dirty, messy, inexplicably intertwined. I didn't cry. I was numb. My heart beat in a steady rhythm, and I imagined the second tiny heart within me. Pressing a hand against my flat stomach, I said a silent prayer for the life inside me.

I remembered the piece of paper the ultrasound technician had handed to me, the one I'd been supposed to give my doctor.

The baby inside me was a girl.

She was a girl, and I wanted her more than anything, but at the same time my heart told me it was utterly selfish to bring a little girl into this world I was imprisoned in. Would she be corrupted? Would she be sold? Would her father end up destroying her?

Weary but warm under the generous hot water, I said a silent *sorry* to my daughter, whatever her fate might be. I pleaded for her forgiveness – for my carelessness, for my selfishness, that I wasn't even sure if I had the strength to be her mother. Because she might be inside me, but I'd never stared into her eyes, never held her in my arms and begged to keep her as she was ripped away from me. No, at the moment she was nothing more than a blurry picture and a plus sign on a pregnancy test.

It wasn't too late for an abortion. I still had time. But that time was fast running out, and if I decided to terminate I'd have to make plans. Get help. *John.* It would always come back to John.

I could terminate the pregnancy, but I'd heard her strong little heartbeat thundering along in my ears. I'd seen her move. She had arms, and legs, and a heart. She'd already survived Murphy, and Allie shooting me. She was a fighter. She deserved a chance.

On the other hand, she had a father who was a murderer. A grandfather who was a monster. A family wrapped up in lies and death and torturous pain. She'd either become one of them or be imprisoned by them, and I didn't know which one was worse.

Whatever happened, if she even survived long enough to be born, her life wasn't going to be easy.

The merciful path would be to make the choice for her, to lie down on a hard hospital bed, spread my legs and let a stranger vacuum her from me. To let her fade away before anyone ever knew of her existence.

But I knew I couldn't do that.

I couldn't bear to destroy the one good thing Dornan and I had left.

CHAPTER FORTY-FIVE

MARIANA

Dornan rolled over and kissed me on the mouth, tasting like stale whiskey and lies, before closing himself in the bathroom. The motel would have to burn the sheets, streaked with blood from where he'd slept.

While he was showering I dressed and headed outside, making sure to wrap a scarf around my neck to hide the bruises Dornan had left. I couldn't bear to spend another moment with him, but I was ashamed that I'd been so fucking weak. I could have yelled for John. But I hadn't, because being forced was preferable to watching John and Dornan kill each other if I'd cried out for help.

I just wanted to be alone for five minutes, so of course as soon as I opened the front door I ran smack bang into John.

He looked shattered, and I realised he hadn't slept for days. I gave him a sympathetic look, affronted when he returned it with a tight-lipped stare.

'Bad night?' I guessed.

He sneered, looking past me. 'Not as good as yours,' he said cruelly, flicking his gaze up and down me. 'You get off on Dornan killing people?'

Furious, I yanked my scarf down and tipped my head back so he could see the bruising across my neck. 'Go fuck yourself,' I said, swallowing back tears as his face fell.

'Are you alright?' he asked, reaching out a hand to touch my neck. I pulled away sharply, narrowing my eyes at him.

'I'm fine,' I snapped. 'Don't you worry about me, John. I'm just fine.'

CHAPTER FORTY-SIX
MARIANA

It was a tense drive home. I sat in the back of the truck with Jason, who Dornan had drugged yet again. I was starting to seriously worry about him killing his new son, who I'd still not actually seen awake in almost twenty-four hours, with an overdose. The kid had wet himself in his comatose state, and we drove home with the smell of piss filling the car.

When we finally arrived back in Los Angeles, John drove to my apartment. When we pulled up, I didn't move. After a few moments, Dornan turned around, looking at me expectantly. 'You can get out,' he said.

I didn't budge. 'Where are you taking him?' I asked, pushing the boy's fringe off his face.

'To the clubhouse,' Dornan replied. 'Don't worry, I'll take good care of him. I'll let him wake up and give him something to eat, introduce him to his brothers. He'll be fine.'

I felt my mouth open in shock. 'You just fucking murdered his mother,' I hissed. 'You can't just feed him and expect him to be okay.'

Dornan's mouth twisted into a grimace. He got out of the car, yanking my door open and gesturing for me to get out. I hesitated for a moment, and he took hold of my arm, pulling me to my feet.

I looked down at John, who was watching with a detached expression on his face. I knew there was nothing he could reasonably do, but it still pissed me off that he was just going along with everything without questioning Dornan's sanity.

'I'll be back in a sec,' Dornan said to John, placing his hand in the small of my back and taking my duffel bag from me. I cringed against his touch as he escorted me up the stairs, remembering how he had forced himself into me, while I'd been begging him to stop. As soon as we were at the front door to my apartment, I took the bag from him, unlocking the door and letting myself in.

The apartment was empty, Guillermo nowhere in sight. As soon as we stepped into the kitchen I turned on Dornan.

'You need to bring Jason up here,' I said. 'I'll take care of him. He doesn't belong at the club.'

Dornan raised his eyebrows. 'And what are you gonna do with him, huh? You're not his family. You're not anybody. What makes you think he'd be better off here with a stranger?'

I laughed in disbelief. 'A stranger?' I echoed. 'You're a stranger! He doesn't even know you. The only thing he knows is that you murdered his mother!'

Dornan stepped forward and slapped me across the face, so hard I tasted blood. I brought my hand up to my cheek, shocked by his sudden outburst, but not surprised.

'You're losing it,' I said coldly. 'You're really fucking losing your mind.'

'I thought you, of all people, would understand,' he said, and for a moment he sounded like a lost little boy, completely at odds with the way he'd been acting.

'I don't understand,' I said. 'What happened to you? So she left you. Why would she stay here and bring a baby into this fucking mess?'

'Shut up,' he said through gritted teeth.

'No,' I replied. 'No, I won't. You tell me, Dornan. Tell me why she should have stayed with you – while you were married, by the way – and had a baby in this fucking life? She deserved better. Your son deserved better than this.'

'Shut up!' he roared, pushing me hard against the wall. He charged at me, and before I could get out of his way, I felt a hand around my throat and a fist in my stomach. I doubled over in pain, gasping silently for air that wasn't there, but he didn't release his grip. I saw stars, then brilliant bursts of white that spread across my vision and merged into one, and still he wouldn't let go.

CHAPTER FORTY-SEVEN
MARIANA

The bleeding didn't start right away.

I was out for a while. How long, I'm not sure. All I remember is that the sun, bright and unrelenting, started to bother my eyes and finally I had to open them.

The ache was dull, low in my abdomen. It wasn't so bad at first, just like I was having a period.

For a while, I forgot I was pregnant. Must've been from when I knocked my head against the tiles.

Then I started to notice a dampness between my legs, like I'd just peed my pants.

And then the pain, sharp knives stabbing into my womb, one after another. I gasped at the intensity as I struggled to sit up, wetness flooding between my thighs. I winced, one hand to my stomach as I came to a sitting position, and it was only then that I saw the blood streaking my thighs and pooling onto the floor beneath me. And I knew.

I expected to feel sadness, grief at losing the baby that had gone undetected by anyone else so long inside me. I knew immediately that there was no hope for the tiny creature who'd been a part of me for three short months. I watched, nauseated, as she bled from me and onto the stark white tiles.

He did this, I thought to myself. *He killed his own child. For nothing.*

Dornan would be back at the clubhouse by now, now that he'd kidnapped his secret son and dragged him back to Los Angeles, a son who would no doubt hate his father for ripping him from the only life he'd ever known. And in doing so, inadvertently, Dornan had killed something that hadn't even lived.

There was a knocking at the door. Three sharp raps at first, then a yell.

Was he back already? God, no. Not now. Not like this. Another yell.

Relief flooded through me.

John.

I heard the lock hiss and the front door open.

'Jesus,' John said, falling to his knees beside me. He pulled my head into his lap, taking out his phone. His voice calling for an ambulance sounded so far away, it was like I was listening to someone in another universe.

'Mariana!' I heard him yelling. The sound was so faint. I opened my mouth and tried to respond, but the pain was too much, and the sound came out as a whimper.

I blacked out again.

CHAPTER FORTY-EIGHT

MARIANA

I was awake for bits and pieces of the ambulance trip. The emergency line operator had tried to convince John to drive me to the hospital, telling him that a miscarriage wasn't life-threatening, but he'd been insistent. And with good reason. I wasn't just having a miscarriage, I was haemorrhaging, and the bleeding wouldn't stop. I came to in an operating theatre, my legs in stirrups and a kind-faced nurse stroking my cheek as I closed my eyes again.

Later, when I woke up, I was in a regular hospital bed. I tried to sit up, but the pain was excruciating. Even though no one had told me, even though I had no real way of telling, I knew the baby was gone.

John was dozing in the seat beside my bed, and when I tried to move he woke up, his bloodshot eyes finding mine. He reached for my hand, and I let him because I couldn't bear not to touch him any longer.

'Don't sit up,' he whispered. 'You've just come out of surgery. You lost a lot of blood. Here, I'll move the bed.'

He took a remote in his other hand and pressed a button, slowly inclining my head. The change in pressure made me dizzy, and I closed my eyes to stop the room from spinning.

'Where's Dornan?' I asked immediately, and John's face fell.

'Not here,' he said, his mouth twisting. 'Not yet, anyway.'

I nodded, squeezing his hand.

'What did he do before I found you?' John asked. 'He says he hit you, but not hard enough to hurt you.'

I laughed mirthlessly. 'It was hard enough,' I said.

'You lost the baby,' John blurted out.

I nodded again. I looked at the ceiling for a moment. When I looked back to John, I saw angry tears in his eyes.

'I'm okay,' I said, 'really.'

He shook his head, standing and pressing his lips to my forehead. It felt good. It felt wonderful.

'What do you want to do?' he asked me.

I looked at the door, making sure we were still alone. 'I want to take these kids. I want us to get Juliette, and Jason, and I want us to leave, before it gets any worse.'

John swallowed thickly, nodding. 'I have to get Juliette from school,' he said, placing my hand back on the bed and stepping back. 'I'll come back to check on you. You want me to call Guillermo to come sit with you?'

I shook my head. I wasn't afraid of Dornan showing up. I had nothing left to lose.

John just stood there, his leather jacket over one arm. He didn't want to go. I could see that it was killing him to leave me.

'Go,' I said. 'I'll be here when you get back.'

Eventually he left, trudging down the hallway until I couldn't hear his boots any more.

It was strange that I wasn't bawling my eyes out. But I was eerily calm. Maybe even grateful, in some small way. My love for Dornan had been the thing that was keeping me stuck, stopping me from taking any real action in my life. I had a son waiting for me in Colombia and access to millions of dollars in cartel money, and yet I'd been sitting on my hands waiting for something I could react to.

But now I could see my future, and it was as stark as it was brutal. If I stayed, I was going to end up like Stephanie and Murphy and Allie and everyone else who had ever been touched by the cartel – dead or, worse, like Dornan. I'd already killed two people. How long would it take for me to kill five? Ten? How long would it be before I started to accept what they did to those girls, before I grew totally complacent?

I was thinking about all of this when Dornan arrived. His helmet in one hand, tears on his cheeks as he stared at me with those midnight eyes. He looked positively grief-stricken, and his indulgence in such a display of emotion at something he had caused made me turn cold and dead inside.

He made a beeline towards me, dropping his helmet on the floor and gathering me in his arms. I didn't return the embrace, freezing until he finally pulled away.

'Did you know?' he whispered, his low voice vibrating in my chest.

I nodded. 'I was going to tell you, but then Colorado happened.'

'Fuck,' he said, falling into the chair by my side, covering his face with his hands. 'I'm sorry,' he said, taking my hand and pressing his lips against my fingers. His kiss was cold. He must have ridden with his visor open, the wind chilling his skin.

I didn't reply.

He leaned over and pressed his cheek against my stomach. 'I'm so fucking sorry,' he said, his deep voice breaking.

I should have felt something. Pity. Anger. Hatred. But I didn't. I felt nothing for the man who had once been my entire universe.

'You didn't mean it,' I said blankly, threading my fingers through his hair. In my head, I was already planning how to get away from him because he'd destroyed our love so swiftly, so brutally, I barely remembered what it was that had tethered us together for so many years.

CHAPTER FORTY-NINE
JOHN

'Daddy?' Juliette said, her big green eyes welling up with tears as she craned her neck to look at him. 'Daddy, what happened?'

She darted a hand towards his cheek, touching the bloody skin before he could catch her wrist. As his hand grasped her small arm, her eyes went wider, her skin paled and she flinched, as though he was going to hurt her.

'Shhh,' he ground out, trying to sound comforting as he released her wrist. 'It's okay. Everything is okay.'

He clamped his teeth down on the inside of his lip, hard, so he wouldn't argue with her.

'Who did this to you?' she whispered, drawing her hand back to her side.

John couldn't help but stare at her hand, transfixed, as though she might become infected now that she'd seen and touched the horror that he was trying to keep away from her.

'It's not my blood. It's Mariana's. She ... She fell. She was hurt, badly. It's her blood.'

That was the moment something broke inside him; first strung tight, like a bowstring, a delicate cord that snapped under the weight of her words.

Who did this to you?

He was ashamed that he didn't have a good answer, that nobody had done anything to him, that he had done nothing to stop this from happening, and that Mariana had almost died because he'd let Dornan walk her inside without following.

Part of him wished that Dornan had just knocked him out when he'd had the chance.

But another part of him, a part that sounded extremely familiar, like a beautiful young seductress, had the loudest voice of them all. *We have to take these kids, and we have to leave.*

CHAPTER FIFTY

MARIANA

SIX WEEKS LATER

Nine years is a long time, and it isn't.

Nine summers.

Nine falls.

Nine winters.

Nine springs.

Nine anniversaries that marked the night Este bled to death, a bullet in his chest, his only crime the fact that he was with me.

I thought I knew how my life would end. In fact, I'd fantasised about it enough times to know the details intimately. I'd drive my car off a bridge and let myself drown. Or I'd cut into the soft flesh at my wrists until I hit an artery, letting my life force pour from me until I was a bloodless husk, floating in water that would grow cold. Or, more realistically, I wouldn't have to end my own life at all: it'd be snuffed out by Emilio, or Murphy, or even by Dornan himself. I imagined a smooth silver bullet, puncturing my skull at point-blank range, tearing through bone as it bedded into my brain and exploded.

I'd resigned myself for so long to the fact my life was in somebody else's control, that I assumed my death would be as well.

But that was before, when I was selfish, when I only thought about myself. That was back when I was in love with the man who'd saved me, instead of just afraid of him. And I was afraid of Dornan. Afraid of what he was. Afraid of what he was becoming. There was a darkness within him – there always had been – but it was growing, threatening to swallow up everything else in its wake.

I was terrified.

***

I held John's hand in the dark. Nobody knew he was here with me. He'd come in like a ghost and he'd leave the same way. We were lying on the floor in my bedroom, the door locked in case Guillermo got back to the apartment and came knocking. We were on our backs, side by side, and we'd just done something very, very wrong.

But it had felt so good.

I rolled onto him again, feeling his bare skin underneath mine. I straddled him, splaying my palms over his warm chest as he grew hard underneath me once more.

We didn't speak. Didn't make any noise. I lowered myself onto him, stretching around him until I felt like I could barely breathe. Slowly, gently, I rocked against him as we tried to devour each other with our mouths.

He was everything Dornan was not. He wasn't a fucker. He was a lovemaker. I didn't even know what I felt for John, but when he moved inside me it felt like he was loving me, even if only for a fleeting moment.

But it wasn't just some kind of love that drew us together, at least not in the typical way.

It was desperation.

He kissed me, his lips soft, his stubble deliciously rough, lifting my hips up and pressing me into his lap as he thrust into me. We came at almost the same time, so, so quietly, and that made it feel even more illicit, more exciting. Even when Guillermo wasn't around, after I'd relayed news of Agent Lindsay Price bailing me up in the gym showers, we'd convinced ourselves that we were being watched. And who knows? Maybe we were, even then.

John supported himself on his hands, covering my body with his as he withdrew from me and went in search of his clothes.

I heard the shower start, decided I might as well join him. We didn't turn any lights on. I'd already lit candles everywhere, and they illuminated the bathroom enough that we could see.

Somehow, it felt safer in the dark. Part of me couldn't believe how brazen we were being – carrying on while Guillermo could come back to the apartment at any moment.

I slipped into the shower and found John, pulling him towards me. He held me tight, pressing his lips to the top of my head. I didn't even know how this had happened, but it had.

'What's going on in that head of yours?' John asked, cupping my chin and bringing it up to meet his eyes. They shone bright blue, even in the dim flicker of candlelight.

'Hawaii,' I said, smiling tiredly.

He grinned. 'Hawaii?'

'Yeah,' I said, leaning my head against his chest as he held me tightly. 'We could do it. Take these kids and get the hell out of here.'

'If they found us, they would kill us,' John said soberly. 'Remember Colorado?'

'Of course,' I said, pulling away so I could see his eyes. 'Of course I remember. That's why, if we did leave, we'd have to kill them first.'

PART 3
EMPIRE

I loved you at your darkest.

ROMANS 5:8

PROLOGUE
MARIANA

People aren't born monsters.

They're made that way.

After all, how do you fight the darkness when you're thrust into it?

Same goes for vengeful beasts. They aren't born. They're created, fuelled by one singular moment in time when the universe wrongs them and their existence shatters.

I'd been with Dornan Ross for almost a decade. Slept in his bed, sewn up his wounds, tasted his blood, seen inside his soul.

I was the mistress of a monstrous man. Dornan Ross, vice-president of one of the most feared biker gangs in the United States.

Son of the most powerful drug kingpin along the West Coast.

A man whose entire being was predicated on violence, blood and death.

But even I wasn't prepared for what he did.

He killed our child. He put his boot into my stomach and *kicked our baby to death*.

He killed the love I had for him.

And he took away the only family his son had ever known. Left his mother in a bathtub full of blood and a hotshot still hanging from her arm, for a sixteen-year-old boy to find.

I'd been foolish enough to question the brutality he'd delivered to his son's mother, and lost my own child as punishment.

I should have known it would always come down to this, from the very moment I laid eyes on him in that motel.

I should have known his salvation was too good to be true.

Because it's all gone now, the dark secret love I had for him bleeding away in the darkness that came afterwards.

Now, there's only hate.

Now, I just want to escape.

Even if it means I have to kill him to be free.

***

I loved Dornan Ross once. I loved him so much that he became a part of me. I loved him despite his darkness, despite the impossibility of us ever being able to have a real life together.

I fucking *worshipped* the man. But false Gods always betray your devotion eventually. They peel off their mask, and you stare at a stranger. They are the shark and you are the prey, and you wonder how you ever thought you could trust them not to devour you on sight.

CHAPTER ONE

MARIANA

You might've walked past us and wondered why a woman like me – twenty-eight years old, no tattoos, modestly dressed – was with *him*.

The president of the most lethal biker club in California, the Gypsy Brothers MC – John Portland. Covered in tattoos, smoking, the crest of his brotherhood inked on the flesh above his heart. That tattoo was hidden from public view as we stood side by side on the Santa Monica Pier and watched his daughter and my kind-of-not-really stepson ride the Ferris wheel, two teenagers clearly experiencing the first stages of love. Fifteen and sixteen. When I was their age I'd already given birth to my only child and had him taken from me. I'd already been tainted by life.

My not-stepson had found his mother dead, murdered by his father – my lover – a few months earlier, and it was safe to say he'd been tainted by life, too.

John's daughter had been too, to a lesser extent. Junkie mother. A father who presided over criminals and murderers. Despite her beginnings, she still had traces of the naivety that summer love and an overprotective daddy provided. She still slept soundly at night, from what I could gather.

Sadly, it wouldn't always be that way, but on that pier, in the sunshine, none of us had any way of knowing the horror that lay ahead, its gaping maw ready to scoop us up when we least expected.

'We'll have to watch out for him,' I teased, tilting my head towards Dornan's youngest son, Jason, as he rode the Ferris wheel with John's daughter, Juliette.

Beside me, leaning against the railing that flanked the pier, the man I was secretly in love with shook his head. 'Don't even,' he murmured, rubbing his stubbled chin with his palm.

I started to laugh, until I saw John wasn't laughing. Or smiling at all. I gestured to the two teenagers as they rode in a carriage high atop the Santa Monica coastline. 'They're kids. You can't seriously be worried about him.'

John's eyes cut through me, making me wonder if I should be worried.

'John,' I tried again, 'he's a kid. He's sixteen years old.'

John's knuckles turned white as he gripped the railing feverishly. 'He's not a kid. He's Dornan's kid.'

I rolled my eyes. 'He didn't even know Dornan until a few months ago.'

'Yeah, but he's still Dornan's blood. Still Emilio's blood.'

I shrugged. 'She's not that much younger than I was when Emilio came for my family.' And left with me as a consolation prize.

John appeared pained. 'Jesus Christ, Ana,' he said, his words like bullets, forceful and cold, metallic. This was our eternal impasse, our universal hesitation. We were in love. We wanted to run away, to flee Los Angeles and the eventual death it promised us.

But he wouldn't leave with Dornan's son, Jason.

I wouldn't leave without him.

And so we were stuck.

'Will you miss him?' John asked me.

My heart squeezed painfully. 'I'm not leaving Jason, John.'

He shook his head, his eyes glued to his daughter as she laughed and pointed out things to her crush. 'Not Jason. Dornan.'

Oh.

Dornan Ross, the man who'd been my lover for almost ten years, since the day he collected me from a dirty motel in San Diego and claimed me as his own. From the instant he'd stopped his drug kingpin father from selling me as a sex slave to cover my father's impossible debt.

John Portland had been Dornan's best friend for longer than I'd known either of them – twenty years or more, I'd guess. I knew they'd met as teenagers, formed a fast friendship, a friendship that soon became a brotherhood of bikers called the Gypsy Brothers, a club that John had presided over since its inception.

I smoothed down my tank top, painfully aware that we were out in the open, an afternoon ice-cream date with his daughter and the stray I'd taken in. Dornan's son Jason, the one he'd been unaware of for sixteen years, emerged from the fairground ride with Juliette, stepping back onto the pier, two teenagers in love, even if they didn't know it yet. It was a rare day for any of us to be out, but the weather was so beautiful, John had collected us all in his beat-up car and brought us out into the sunshine for some fudge sundaes and a chance to dip our toes in the cold water.

It wasn't a typical outing, to say the least. On a day like today, I'd normally be working for my boss, Emilio, cooking his books and making sure his hefty cartel profits were funnelled into all the right places. Or, if I got a day off – rare for a Saturday – I'd inevitably be on my back, or my knees, or my stomach, with Dornan. But today was Emilio's birthday, and he insisted on a great big family celebration – one that none of us were invited to. I was surprised Dornan hadn't insisted on taking Jason to the family event, but I think he worried about how unstable Jason might be in a large gathering of the people who'd inadvertently caused his mother to die.

Yes, I was sleeping with two men. I was in love with one of them, and I was terrified of the other. When I first arrived in California ten years ago I'd loved Dornan, but now I loathed him. I was ready to leave him, or kill him, or both. Anything to get away.

But the world kept spinning, and the cartel kept trading, and I kept my feet on the ground, too scared to make a run for freedom lest a bullet find its way between my shoulder blades.

'Can we go feel the water?' Juliette asked her father.

'Sure,' John shrugged, his face lighting up for his daughter like she was the sun. And she was, to him. That made me fall for him even more than I already had, to see the love he had for his daughter. Without thinking, I reached out and placed my hand on Jason's shoulder. He was only sixteen, but already well taller than me, and the picture of his father – all olive skin and deep brown eyes, a product of their Italian heritage.

Jase flinched when I touched him; I pulled my hand away and smiled instead. I didn't want to apologise and bring attention to how jumpy he was, so I left it. Juliette grabbed his hand – the contrast between them night and day, what with her bamboo green eyes and straw blonde hair – and pulled him towards the beach. He didn't flinch when she touched him, and that's how I knew it was already love in bloom.

I realised I'd been daydreaming and turned my attention back to John. He was just as stunning as the day I'd met him, but age had weathered him in a way that only made him more attractive to me. He was barely forty, but the lines around his eyes told a story of far more trauma than a man his age should have seen.

I loved his hands. Rough palms from the mechanical work he did, but smooth on top. Rough fingers that spread me open and worshipped me, not missing an inch of my flesh; smooth on top, for those times when he'd brush a knuckle along my cheek or put my hand on his as I travelled on the back of his motorcycle.

Dornan's hands didn't have an ounce of smoothness; they were rough and big and good for holding over my mouth while he fucked me until I screamed. I won't pretend that I didn't like it. I lived for his brutal touch. I was addicted to it.

But the addiction had become too dangerous. It was a nasty habit that was going to kill me one day, a day that would come very soon if I didn't figure my life out and get out of Los Angeles.

I was entirely certain that if I didn't make a bold move soon – run, or hand myself over to the police, or just plain kill my dark lover while he slept beside me – I'd be the one who'd end up dead, dumped on the side of the road in a ditch somewhere, or maybe cut into little pieces and fed to the sharks. Because Dornan Ross had changed. He'd grown cruel. He used to use violence in the most delicious of ways – a hand over my face to stifle the noise that accompanied the mind-blowing orgasm he was giving me with his other hand; a subtle choke that made me see stars as my heart sped up in anticipation; a finger forced into my mouth so I could suck on it, tease him, pretend it was his cock I had my lips wrapped around. A violence that would have me smashed up against the nearest wall, fingers that bruised me with their passion as he wrenched my thighs apart and entered me so hard that I ached for days afterward.

That violent love was the thing that made us. When we met I was only nineteen years old and his father's property, thanks to a deal I'd brokered to repay a debt my own father had racked up, and to keep my family from being slaughtered. One set of parents. One sister. One brother. I had given my servitude for their lives.

Emilio had killed them eventually, anyway. Loose ends and all that.

That violent love reached its peak when I saw the blood on my lover's hands and the body of the woman he'd killed for daring to flee from him. Her face had been so badly beaten she was unrecognisable.

I still saw her when I closed my eyes at night. *Stephanie.* He'd killed her for concealing a pregnancy and leaving him seventeen years earlier, and he had punished her by beating her until she was almost dead, and then giving her a hotshot of heroin to finish off the job.

That this was the man I'd fallen fiercely in love with as a young woman was impossible to me. This was a man who'd risked everything for me, a lowly Colombian slave on her way to auction. He'd defied his father, and in doing so, had taken my heart and my loyalty. He'd done it out of some goodness that existed inside of him, something that couldn't bear to see me come to harm.

'He's struggling,' I said, nodding my head towards Jason. 'He has nightmares. He barely talks. He barely eats, and teenage boys are supposed to eat everything in sight. I'm worried about him.'

John side-eyed me. 'And your son? Luis? How's he doing?'

I immediately baulked at his line of questioning. He was inferring that I cared more about a boy who wasn't my son than the boy who was waiting for me in Colombia, my beautiful son, Luis. He was thirteen. I hadn't laid eyes on him since the day he was taken from me by my father – the day he was born.

'He's safe,' I said, my throat itching. 'He's with family. And that's where we should be going. All four of us.'

John pulled a face. 'You really want to take Dornan's son after you saw what he did to the woman who kept him secret his entire life?'

I didn't want to think about that. About how Dornan had become the monster he'd been trying to save me from all those years ago.

About how a lover could become your captor.

I didn't want to think about how a lover, in a rage over your incessant questions and your disbelief that they could murder somebody in cold blood, could beat you until the baby inside you, the one that was still a secret, died.

Didn't want to remember how a lover, in a post-murder-fuelled high, could pin you down and rape you, while still covered in the blood of the woman he murdered hours beforehand.

Didn't want to reconcile all the ways a lover could become the person you hated the most in the world.

Especially because, if you were like me, black-hearted and completely corrupted, you already had *another* lover.

John Portland. Of course he had to be Dornan's best friend, just to dial shit right up to eleven on the crazy scale.

It was complicated.

It was wrong.

I didn't care.

I was in love with a man who was not my lover, and soon we would leave this place.

Together. I'd convince him that Jason needed to come with us. That he needed protecting from Dornan, the man who would surely mould him into a beast if given half a chance.

We were leaving.

And we were *never* coming back.

***

'Hey,' John said, snapping a finger in front of my face. God, he was fucking beautiful, with his dirty blond hair, tanned skin and those brilliant blue eyes that looked just like the ocean we were standing before. With his tight black T-shirt and dark denim jeans, he looked casual. Add the steel-toed boots and the biker tattoos that covered his arms and neck, and he looked lethal. *Casually lethal.* That was my John.

'Will you miss Dornan?' John repeated. His question wasn't born from jealousy, or insecurity. He seemed genuinely ... curious.

'I miss him already,' I said, shrugging. It was so bright, and I could already feel my skin start to prickle under the Californian sun. I'd spent so long indoors over the years as the cartel's captive that my skin didn't know what to do when I was allowed out into direct sun. 'I miss the person he used to be. Don't you?'

John nodded, running his tongue along his teeth, seemingly deep in thought himself.

'Will you miss Caroline?' I asked softly, my stomach squeezing painfully at the mention of John's crazy wife.

Yes, I was fucking not one, but two *married* men, one by choice, the other through necessity. I was not a good person. I was just trying to survive, stay one step ahead, and I was so fucking tired of it all.

John shook his head. 'Caroline was already an addict when I met her. I never got to know her well enough away from the drugs to be able to miss her.' He paused for a moment, the lines around his eyes creasing as he frowned. 'My wife and I are basically strangers who share a child.'

I thought back to the countless times I'd seen John's wife stumbling down the hallways of the Gypsy Brothers clubhouse, high as a kite, sometimes with a thin trail of blood still fresh on her arm from where she'd injected the heroin. I'd seen her in all kinds of trouble – a couple of overdoses, plenty of times when she'd plain forget that she was naked from the waist down as she wandered around.

I'd seen the shame in John's eyes every time she did something to embarrass herself. I knew the shame wasn't for him, it was for their daughter, Juliette.

I hated Caroline bitterly, not because I was in love with her husband, but because she had everything I'd ever wanted and yet she spent her life cruising about in a drug-addled haze, because she couldn't cope with the fact that she was somebody's mother, or wife. She'd been a nurse, once, and I'm pretty sure she'd started on pain pills before she graduated to smack.

When we left and made a run for it we were taking John's daughter, but we were categorically *not* taking his wife. A part of me selfishly hoped Dornan would kill her once we left. She deserved it more than Stephanie had.

I swallowed thickly, a sense of impending doom settling upon me like a plague of ants crawling over every inch of my skin. I glanced at John, and we both knew what I was thinking.

'We can't take him,' John said firmly. 'They will hunt us to the ends of the earth if we take their blood.'

We both watched Jason, down on the sand, as he spoke to Juliette beside him. They were sitting now, him hugging his knees and her cross-legged, her eyes only for him. Something squeezed painfully in my chest as I watched Jase and Juliette, knowing the destruction that lay ahead. Because even if we pulled this off, even if we managed to get away and make a run from the Gypsy Brothers, we'd be running forever. For the rest of our lives, we would be looking over our shoulders and sleeping in shifts to make sure we didn't all wake up dead, courtesy of Dornan and his family.

I chewed on the inside of my cheek, tasting blood. 'We have to take him,' I countered. 'Or I will never forgive myself. Or you.'

'You're going to be the death of me, woman,' John sighed, pulling a packet of cigarettes from his pocket and offering one to me. I took it, because I needed something to do with my hands, and since we were in public I couldn't be using those hands to unbutton his jeans and squeeze his cock.

Even though that was what I'd really, really prefer to be doing. If we didn't have these kids with us, I wouldn't have been able to stop myself from dragging John into a back alley, dropping to my knees, and sucking his cock until he came down my throat. John might have been the tender lover, the man who took his time, but it seemed we didn't have an abundance of time as of late. It was hard to be gentle when you didn't know if somebody was waiting around the corner to blow your brains out at any given moment. It was impossible to slow down and enjoy each other when we were both trapped in a constant vortex of crushing reality – that we might die very horrifically, very soon. And, despite the impending doom that floated around us like a choking fog, we both still found it impossible to keep our hands off each other. Which was kind of hard, in a crowd of tourists and locals alike, all getting their fix on a sunny day while we tried not to give in to carnal desire and go screw in the backseat of John's car.

Lucky we had these kids with us then, because if anyone we knew ever saw me do that with John, we'd both end up with our heads sawn off and hung over a freeway overpass as punishment.

I happened to like my head very much. John's, too. So we never let ourselves be tempted anywhere remotely public.

'Those jeans look good on you,' I said, glancing at him. Something to break the malaise, because otherwise we'd talk in circles and never come to a decision one way or the other.

'Your skirt, too,' he replied, looking straight ahead as he lit his cigarette. 'It'd look better off, though. You wearing underwear?'

I felt my nipples stiffen to hard peaks as I took the lighter from his outstretched fingers and held the flame to my own cigarette, wishing he was doing it for me. Along with my tank top, I was wearing a loose black skirt that sat just above my knees. 'Not today,' I murmured.

John shook his head, turning away so he could readjust his jeans as subtly as possible. 'Goddamn it,' he swore, holding his smoke between his teeth as he used two hands to fumble with the waistband of his jeans.

'I'm so wet right now,' I said casually, just loud enough for John to hear. 'If I sit down in your car, I'm going to mess your seat up.'

'Fuck you. I'm going to get coffee,' he muttered. 'Make sure that little shit doesn't touch my daughter.' He walked away without looking back at me. I snickered, wondering how obvious my nipples were underneath my black tank top.

I didn't mess John's car seat up, but we did ditch the kids pretty soon after that. Dropped them back at my apartment and made sure they were securely inside before we drove to a deserted football field and fucked until we were raw and panting.

We were getting careless.

Looking back, it was a miracle nobody found out about us sooner. But I couldn't focus on that then, naked and spread open along the backseat of John's car as he pounded me into the leather. Both of us slick with sweat, my head slamming against the car door with every thrust, his hands pressing my knees so wide it felt like I'd break in two. We fucked like two people about to be murdered, two death row prisoners tied together, devouring each other, one last meal while we waited for the executioner to come and blow a bullet through each of us.

We fucked like we were starved, like dirty, raw copulation was the only thing that could feed us, the only act that could make us whole again.

We loved each other so much, it was a wonder we didn't just burst into flames from the strength of our desperation right then and there.

We'd burn eventually.

I think we both understood that.

We just didn't know when the Reaper was coming to collect our corrupted souls.

CHAPTER TWO

MARIANA

I was cutting into a red bell pepper a few days later when my phone buzzed. I still remember the moment like it was yesterday – the way the sun was perched high on the horizon, ready to swallow up the shadow of my apartment building that overlooked Santa Monica Beach; the Ferris wheel on the pier, a giant silhouette against the bright blue sky. I can taste the pepper in my mouth, sharp and cold from the refrigerator; I can hear the waves as they crash onto the shore beneath my apartment. I can still remember opening the window, a cool breeze hitting my face as I marvelled at how the sky and John's eyes could be exactly the same colour.

Peace was always fleeting in my world.

My twenty-ninth birthday and I was still here. Still with Dornan. Still with John. Trapped between three men: one that I loved, one that I used to love, and one that I despised with every fibre of my being.

And number three, lucky last, was calling me. *Emilio* flashed up on my cellphone, and I was so startled I almost chopped my fingers clean off.

Emilio never called me. I wasn't even sure he had my number until that moment. Why would he call me? Maybe Dornan was dead. The thought briefly occurred to me, and then it was gone, a wisp of smoke on a summer breeze. *Maybe Dornan is dead.*

I set my knife down and hit the green answer button, bring the phone to my ear.

'Happy birthday, Mariana,' Emilio drawled. I heard loud noise, traffic in the background. I remembered Dornan telling me his father had travelled to Bogota for a meeting with his brother, Julian. Perhaps that explained the noise.

They were still searching for Christopher Murphy, shady DEA agent and Emilio's right-hand man. They'd never find him, though – this I knew for certain.

They didn't know, though. They were still searching for answers to his disappearance. *If only Emilio knew what I'd done*, I thought to myself, a sick feeling in the pit of my stomach as I remembered how Murphy's blood had tasted, how my ears had buzzed for a week after I'd shot him in the face at point-blank range.

'Did you kill my family?' *I whispered. Realisation spiked in his eyes, and his entire body tensed. A wave of nausea rolled through me.*

He didn't respond, but the answer was clear as day in his eyes; in the way he looked away for a split second before meeting my gaze again, in the stunned expression on his face, in the heavy exhale that came from his chest. His mouth around the gun was revolting, the metallic knock of tooth on polished steel enough to make me cringe.

I saw the questions in his eyes. How? How did I know? How had I found out what he'd done?

'You really think I didn't check on my family in nine years?' *I whispered.* 'How stupid are you? How stupid do you think I am?'

And then, before I lost my nerve, I pulled the heavy trigger back. I'd just killed a man as he hate-fucked me, and I was pretty sure I was going to be murdered brutally for it.

I was the murderess who had finally put Christopher Murphy in the ground – or, more accurately, in a crematorium – and Emilio could *never* know.

'Thank you,' I said, pressing my fingers against my eyelids. Emilio Ross wasn't the kind of man to wish me a happy birthday. He was the kind of man who thought I took up too much air just by breathing in the same room as him.

'I got you something,' he added, and I stiffened. Swallowing thickly, I tried not to panic. *It's probably nothing.*

But it was never nothing with Emilio.

'You didn't have to do that,' I breathed, clutching the phone harder.

'I did,' he replied, his tone betraying nothing. 'I got you something ... appropriate.'

My stomach twisted violently. *Appropriate?*

'Go to the front door,' Emilio instructed.

I bristled, looking towards the entryway of my apartment.

'Are you going to shoot me?' I asked. *Shit.* I hadn't meant to say that. The words had come out of their own volition.

Emilio snorted. 'And cut short your valuable working life with me? I think not,' he said, and he sounded amused. 'Go. Now.'

With knees made of rubber, I shuffled towards the front door of my apartment. It was no longer a secret that I was free to the outside world; Emilio knew. He'd never said a word about it. And in my head, I'd figured it was because, after almost ten years, he'd finally started to trust me. Or because I had Guillermo, a Gypsy Brother and key cartel shitkicker, as my permanent roomie. My round-the-clock bodyguard.

Maybe I was wrong, though. Maybe Emilio didn't trust me at all.

Maybe he'd found out my secrets. There were *so many* secrets. Killing Murphy. Killing Murphy's girlfriend and DEA partner, and screwing John all over this goddamn apartment whenever Dornan and Guillermo were elsewhere. *My son.* Yeah, I had plenty of secrets for Emilio to unearth.

I keyed in the code to disarm the front door and let it open a crack. I peered around the corner, spotting a slick black SUV downstairs.

So Emilio wasn't in Colombia then.

'Open it all the way,' he commanded, and I did.

On the front stoop, there was a large plain cardboard box, big enough to fit a carry-on suitcase, or maybe a new computer. Maybe that was it, I thought numbly, trying to shake the crawling feeling that pervaded every inch of my skin. Yeah, I decided. I'd told Emilio about my work computer getting slower and how it'd be a good idea to replace it soon. *He was giving me a computer.*

It sounded so unrealistic, but I clung to the benign possibility that it was something normal at my doorstep, because I couldn't begin to fathom what it would be if it were not.

'Going somewhere?' Guillermo asked, from his spot on the couch. Sprawled out in front of an old episode of *SVU*, he was eating a slice of Papa John's pizza and swilling Budweiser. I tucked the phone between my ear and shoulder, squatting in front of the package.

No, I turned and mouthed at him as I picked up the box – it was heavy – and carried it to the dining table. It was rarely used for dining, and most often used for fucking, with its convenient height and width.

The box was sealed with thick duct tape. I placed it in the middle of the table and took a few steps to the kitchen to grab a pair of scissors.

'Is it open yet?' Emilio asked, and I remembered that he couldn't see what I was doing in the safety of my own apartment.

'I'm cutting through the tape,' I answered, trying not to sound too impatient.

'Good, *cholita*,' he replied. 'You enjoy. Happy birthday.'

He ended the call. I took the phone away from my ear, staring at the screen for a moment before placing the phone on the table beside the mystery box.

I didn't want to open the package – something screamed at me to just get rid of it – but I knew Emilio was outside waiting on me, and my curiosity won over my suspicion.

Like a bandaid, I ripped the box open as quickly as I could. The cardboard packaging fell away to reveal an innocuous-looking pink suitcase, one of those hard-shell ones with four wheels that glides like a dream when you're pushing it through a crowded airport. Not that I'd remember. I hadn't been on a plane since Murphy had brought me to America almost a decade ago and released me into Dornan's clutches.

Dornan. I wondered, briefly, if he'd remember what day it was. Probably not, unless John reminded him.

John had already called to wish me a happy birthday, because he was a stand-up fucking guy with things like that. He had the capacity to think about people outside of himself. It was one of the reasons I'd fallen in love with him.

Yeah. Crazy, isn't it? Being in love with two men at the same time, knowing one is poison and one is safety but not being able to do a damn thing about either of them.

The suitcase. It sat on my table, prompting a thousand questions. Was Emilio sending me away somewhere? Was the suitcase even the point, or was there something inside?

I stepped back for a moment, closing my eyes, letting the drone of the TV and the breeze from the kitchen window centre me. My heart was hammering in my chest, and more than anything, I did not want to open the goddamn suitcase.

Shit.

I stepped forward again, unsteady fingers clasping the metal zipper. In slow motion, I pulled, undoing one short side, then the long edge, then the final side of the suitcase.

Taking a deep breath, I peeled back the lid of the suitcase. There was ... a toy?

A child's stuffed animal. It was a bunny rabbit. A soft blue, with a Quickstop tag still attached. Five dollars and ninety-nine cents, somebody had paid for this toy. It rested upon a thick knitted blanket that was made up of squares in every colour of the rainbow.

I'd seen this toy before.

Guillermo sauntered in, a fresh slice of pizza in his hand. 'You get a package?' he asked, around a mouthful of cheese and dough.

Something about the way the blanket was resting started to make me uneasy, but I pushed the feeling away.

'Emilio delivered this,' I said, pointing at the open case.

Guillermo stopped chewing, but didn't appear alarmed. 'He gave you a suitcase? What, you going somewhere for the boss?'

'I hope not,' I murmured, staring down at the stuffed toy. Maybe it had something sewn into it. Maybe he *was* sending me on a trip. A drug run? I'd done one of those for him before. Christ, I could still taste the thick olive oil that coated the plastic pellets of white powder he'd forced me to swallow, at the very beginning of my complicated relationship with the Il Sangue Cartel.

Guillermo stood beside me, picking up the toy and shaking it. He turned it over, inspecting the stitching. Nothing seemed amiss.

I looked back at the baby blanket. Emilio knew about my miscarriage – there had been no hiding it from him – and the thought that he was taunting me about it suddenly sprang to mind. I swallowed a lump in my throat as I remembered bleeding out on this very floor, at the hands of my lover.

Was that it? Was he reminding me of all I'd lost? Was he that cruel?

If only it had been that. A dig. A taunt. Anything would have been better than what was actually beneath the blanket.

'What's in there?' Guillermo asked. I glanced at him, picking up the edge of the woollen blanket and peeling it back.

I screamed.

'Fucking Christ!' Guillermo yelled, dropping his pizza and backing away. I dry-heaved, sinking to my knees, the reality of my *gift* so horrific, I could barely believe what my eyes were telling me.

I was still screaming.

'Where the fuck – *stop screaming.*'

I kept screaming, only the noise coming from me had turned into more of a low wail. My eyes were blurred from too many tears, hot as they ran down my cheeks and dripped onto the floor. I felt like I was losing my grip on reality, but it was the opposite, really: I'd been thrust violently back into reality. My reality. The one where I was nothing more than a pawn in Emilio's quest for total control over his son.

'Shut the fuck up!' Guillermo hissed, hushing me. He dropped to his knees in front of me, pulling me into his chest, his eyes darting around the room as he clamped a hand over my mouth. I fought for a second, wild with horror and disbelief, clawing at his arms, but he was patient. He was strong. The man bench-pressed more than my weight every day at the gym, and he had no trouble keeping a hold around me.

'Shhhhhh,' he said, low and long. Shhhhhh. Like waves retracting out from the shore. *Shhhhhh.*

I sagged, eventually, and Guillermo raised his eyebrows in question. He was asking me if he could take his hand away. I nodded, and he pulled his palm away from my mouth, ever so slowly.

'Where did it come from?' he asked quietly, his tone deadly serious. I choked, deciding whether to throw up. Nope. I kept my lunch down for the moment as I racked my brain for an answer.

'Emilio,' I croaked, finally. 'It came from Emilio.'

'Why?'

I thought back to the night Dornan had been shot. How he'd almost bled to death in the car beside me, only hours after we'd taken an orphan baby boy to the hospital and dropped him off at the counter, wrapped in a bloody coat.

Emilio's cold hand squeezed the back of my neck as he directed my gaze towards the smallest baby in the line-up.

'I'm taking this boy home,' he promised, his words turning vicious. 'I'll raise him as my own. And if you ever try and leave your post ...'

I sobbed from the pain of his fingers inside my wound. 'I've given you almost ten years,' I whispered. 'You told me you'd let me go once I repaid the debt.'

He chuckled. 'That was before. This is now. Do you have any idea how fucking marvellous you are at what you do? I was going to shoot you that night, and you insisted on coming with me. You've only got yourself to blame, dear.'

I couldn't stop crying. The pain! I just wanted him to get his hands away from me.

'You try and leave, and I'll find you, Ana,' he continued. 'I'll find you and I'll make you watch while I kill that boy in front of you.' He returned his black eyes to me and grinned.

It wasn't over. It would never be over.

Solemnly, Guillermo and I stood over the suitcase; over the dead infant lying on his side in a swathe of blankets, dressed in a pale yellow jumpsuit, already cold, his skin waxy and pale in death, face frozen in an eternal sleep, on his side, as if someone tucked him up in his bed and left him to die.

Only, I know he hadn't just been left to die. He'd been killed. Smothered, probably. And I knew who was responsible.

Somewhere in the background, a phone started to ring. It was mine. In slow motion, I reached for it.

I pressed answer and switched the phone to speaker mode, holding it in front of me so that Guillermo could hear. I didn't speak. I couldn't speak.

'I take it by your screams that you opened your gift,' Emilio said, the only things filling the room his voice, and death.

'Why?' I asked, my voice anguished beyond recognition.

'Your gift, Mariana. A lesson.'

'What lesson?' I cried. 'What lesson!?'

'An important lesson. Are you ready?'

I didn't answer. I was reeling.

'Don't ever try to tempt fate,' Emilio said coldly. His words barely broke the surface of my reality. Because there was a fucking suitcase on my kitchen table with a dead baby inside it.

I dropped the phone, and the screen cracked, turning black. Guillermo's fingers were on my arm, I realised, digging in painfully. I looked down at his hand as if I were moving in slow motion, feeling the way he trembled violently against my flesh.

'I didn't sign up for this,' he said hoarsely. 'Nah, man, no fucking way. I didn't sign up for this.'

I tilted my head to the side, getting a better look at the baby boy.

Button nose.

Dark hair.

Rosebud lips.

Dead.

I reached my hand out to touch his cheek, knowing it'd be cold but unable to stop myself. I was a mother, after all. My instinct said to nurture, to protect, even if this child was too far gone. Guillermo tugged my arm back forcefully before I could make contact.

'What?' I asked dumbly. That ringing in my ears – the buzzing noise that wouldn't go away for weeks after Murphy – it was back. It filled my head with a reverberating whine that was as excruciating as it was bleak.

A car revved loudly outside, and Guillermo left the suitcase long enough to peer out of the window next to the front door.

'He's gone,' he said.

Emilio had gotten what he came for. My horror. My screams. Now he could continue his day, having ticked the box *Fuck with Mariana's head*.

Guillermo slowly folded the suitcase lid shut, the tiny body disappearing from view.

'Wait,' I said weakly. 'We have to call the police.' An image of Lindsay Price floated somewhere in my racing thoughts, the FBI agent who'd accosted me in the women's showers at my gym. I had to call him.

Guillermo glared at me with bloodshot eyes. 'The fuck did you just say?'

'The police. The FBI. We have to call someone. Guillermo, it's a baby!'

He eyed me wearily. 'You want to get killed?' he asked, abandoning the suitcase midway through zipping it up. *There was a baby in there.* Fuck. The room was starting to spin and I wanted to be sick.

'Please don't close it,' I whispered.

'What the fuck is wrong with you?' Guillermo snapped. 'You want to get him out and read him a fuckin' bedtime story before we put him in the ground? He's DEAD.'

I knew it was illogical, but … 'If you zip it, he won't be able to get any air.'

'Get in the car,' Guillermo hissed. 'Now. Kid's cold. He's been dead for hours. Days, even. He ain't ever gonna need fucking *air.*'

'Wait,' I stalled, desperate. 'Why are we going in the car? Where are we going?'

Guillermo looked like he was about to rip my head off. 'We gotta get rid of this, Ana. Your DNA's all over it. Mine, too. If this is a set-up, then they set us up good. No cleaner purification than fire.'

'We're going to set him on fire?'

Guillermo made the sign of the cross and murmured some silent prayer to the ceiling. 'Crematorium.'

Oh.

'Why would they set us up?' I asked, bile rising in my throat. I put a hand to my chest and made a gagging sound. 'Guillermo, why would they set us up?'

He glared at me as he keyed in the combination for the front door lock. 'Maybe they think we've been disloyal.'

I couldn't be certain, but I was pretty sure the tone in his voice was *accusation*.

I thought about that as Guillermo yanked the front door open with his right hand, the suitcase in his left. I thought about all of the ways I'd been disloyal to the cartel, and there were plenty. A carefully constructed web of deceit. I thought of the blood on my own hands, the blood on John's, the sins we'd indulged in, both collectively and apart.

I followed Guillermo from the apartment, unable to speak, unable to rip the image of the poor child from my mind.

CHAPTER THREE

LINDSAY

Agent Lindsay Price was eyeing a plate of mystery meat when a call came through on his cellphone. He was at the FBI's training facility in Quantico giving a lecture on interrogation techniques, and briefly considered going back into the cafeteria kitchen and interrogating the chef until they told him what he'd be puking up in about three hours.

In the end, he was relieved that he'd gotten the call, for two reasons.

One, because even airplane food was better than this shit, and he'd be calling his day short to high-tail it back to Los Angeles.

Two, because of the reason he was being summoned back to LA.

A body had washed up on the banks of the Los Angeles River – the part that was actually flowing, way up near Long Beach – badly decomposed and virtually unidentifiable.

Except they'd already run a preliminary swab of DNA sample through CODIS and come up with a match.

A DEA agent by the name of Alexandra Baxter.

***

Eight gruelling hours of cabs, turbulence, shitty plane food and LA traffic later, and with a Venti Americano in hand from the Starbucks inside LAX, Lindsay was standing on the edge of the Los Angeles River, watching as police divers searched the bay for anything that might provide clues as to how this woman had come to her end. It was already night back on the East Coast and Lindsay was tired, but giddy, at the same time. He'd been tracking Baxter and her crooked partner, Christopher Murphy, for over a year, their roles in a wider web of corruption and compliance with the Il Sangue drug cartel something he was determined to crack. The problem was, the further he dug into the case, the wider the hole got, filled with tip-offs and trafficked women and missing persons that stretched across the globe. It was a case that saw him come up against brick walls every single day, and so this body was like someone finally taking a sledgehammer through one of those walls and saying, *'Here, step on into this crazy shit.'*

There'd been no leads, save for that one woman. Mariana Rodriguez. She was definitely involved in the bigger picture somehow. Lindsay had spent countless hours combing through her life, her history. Had it not been for the frequent visits Christopher Murphy made to her apartment in the weeks before his death, Lindsay wouldn't have even known she existed.

But she did exist.

And her father had once worked for the cartel, many years ago, before he and the rest of his family turned up dead in a house fire, their hands and feet still bound in death, despite the flames demolishing everything else. Even the walls of their small house in Villanueva hadn't survived the fire, but the bindings on their hands and feet had. A painful way to die.

Drowning was meant to be much more peaceful, but the after-effects on a corpse could be horrific. Lindsay scanned the river's edge, locating a white tent that was no doubt shrouding the body in question.

He made his way over to the tent, the afternoon sun warming his face. Despite being November, it was like a spring day in Los Angeles, much different to chilly Virginia, where he'd been hours earlier. He didn't walk too quickly as he approached the plastic tent the medical examiner had erected. Nobody needed to see what he was about to see a moment sooner than was absolutely necessary.

He was already on good terms with Kathryn Donovan, the city's Chief Medical Examiner, having worked many cases together over the years he'd served with the FBI's organised crime division in LA. Squatting beside the body, she greeted him with a raise of her eyebrows, the rest of her pale face obscured by the surgical mask tied tightly to her head.

'I figured you'd be at the morgue by now,' Lindsay said by way of greeting.

Dr Donovan tilted her head, stripping her gloves and mask off and dropping them into a makeshift trash can as she stood. 'That for me?' she asked, practically prising the lukewarm coffee from Lindsay's hand and pouring a slug into her mouth. Lindsay watched, amused, as she made a face and let the liquid pour back out of her pursed lips and into the cup.

'That's terrible,' she said, handing the now useless brew back to Lindsay as she motioned an assistant for fresh gloves. She snapped hers on before handing a pair to Lindsay. *No face mask?* he wanted to ask her, but didn't dare. He tossed his beloved Starbucks cup in the trash and pulled his own set of gloves on, finally looking head-on at the long-lost body of Alexandra Baxter.

It wasn't a pretty sight.

'Guess she's not been sunning herself in the Virgin Islands like we thought,' Lindsay mused, standing near enough to Kathryn that their shoulders almost touched. It was close quarters in a small tent like this.

'Nope,' Kathryn said beside him. 'And by the way, the only reason we're not back at the morgue already is because we've been waiting on you. So thank you. I now get to spend all day *and* all night with this delightfully perplexing young woman.'

Lindsay was grateful for the small talk. It distracted from the grisly image at his feet.

Allie had been a pretty girl in life, but death had stripped that beauty away. Her long red hair was missing large chunks, and her face looked as if it had melted like a candle left in the midday sun. Features flattened, merging into one another, lips pulled back over teeth that looked entirely inhuman from the damage the water and elements had done. The clothes that still clung to her body had fused with her skin, and one of her feet was gone. Somebody might've removed it prior to her death, but more likely the fish or some sudden impact would have taken it clean off underwater.

Lindsay had seen bodies pulled from the water before. They often looked intact until you touched them and flesh started to come away in your gloved hands. Water and dead bodies didn't mix well, and nobody ever wanted to attend them. Fishing suicides out of the LA River was something they made rookies do.

But this wasn't suicide.

This was a cop.

A cop who had mysteriously come into possession of tens of thousands of dollars six months ago, and promptly disappeared.

'Sorry,' Lindsay said. 'You know the drill. Federal case, they make me walk the crime scene before the body's allowed to leave.'

Kathryn nodded, crouching again beside the body and motioning for Lindsay to do the same. Reluctantly, he squatted on his haunches, feeling the burn in his thighs from his weight training that morning. 6 a.m. now seemed like it had been years ago.

'You okay there?' Kathryn said, side-eyeing the way Lindsay's legs were trembling.

He nodded. 'Thanks for sticking around, Katie. I owe you hot coffee on the way back to the office.'

'Huh,' she said. 'You owe me dinner at the Roosevelt and a night of mind-blowing sex, at the very least.'

Lindsay stifled the urge to laugh, only for the fact that there was a dead body about five inches from his leather shoe. He'd never slept with Kathryn. She was as dry-witted as they came, as inappropriate as a foul-mouthed teenage girl looking to get a reaction out of her parents. She possessed no filter. The thing about her job, though, was that she didn't need one. It wasn't as if the dead could take offence, much less speak back.

Luckily, she was damned good at her job. Lindsay had long since suspected that her sarcastic, inappropriate comments were a way of trying to lighten the heavy film of death that covered her existence.

Kathryn launched into a long spiel of clinical observations and hypotheses about the body. She lifted one of Allie's arms – gently, so it didn't detach from her bloated corpse – and showed Lindsay just how advanced decomposition was.

Allie had been submerged, or floating along currents, for what looked like several months. It was a miracle she'd remained intact, what with the water and the weather, not to mention the sea creatures that were all looking for a free meal. As if on cue, a tiny crab crawled out of a neat hole in Allie's chest and darted along her collarbone before disappearing underneath her ragged red hair.

Lindsay's stomach turned at the thought the crab had just been eating whatever was left inside her.

After they'd examined the body, Kathryn and Lindsay walked the scene in a grid, starting on the shore and ending up barefoot and wading out into the shallows.

There was nothing, of course. Nothing to signal what had happened, or where. Allie could have been dumped in the water hundreds of miles away, or a few hundred feet. If this had been Florida, Lindsay's last port of call, gators would have found Allie long before any human did. The sneaky fuckers found bodies and stashed them deep underwater, in small caves or under logs, macabre keepsakes until their hunger stirred again and they decided to eat their catch.

But they weren't in Florida, and Allie Baxter had not been made into swamp feed, and now it was up to Lindsay to figure out how this young fellow officer had found her watery grave.

CHAPTER FOUR
MARIANA

'Guillermo,' I said.

He didn't answer.

'*Guillermo.*'

He white-knuckled the steering wheel. 'What?'

We drove along the freeway, windows down, my hair flying around my face wildly in the breeze. It was the weekend and the I-5 was relatively clear, a small mercy.

'I'm going in,' I declared boldly.

Guillermo ripped his eyes from the road and stared at me until I was squirming in my seat, wishing he'd pay attention to where he was driving.

'To Emilio?'

I shook my head. 'With the ... *baby.*'

'To the crematorium? No fucking way.' He slapped his hand against the wheel, agitated. 'My life was never this complicated until you turned up. You got a way of pissing people off, you know?'

I might have grown a skin of steel, but his words found chinks in my armour and sliced deep. I sagged back in my seat, deflated, feeling the last bits of my strength bleed out through the cracks.

I squinted against the bright sun, a sun that sat bloated and accusing in the sky. I'd forgotten my sunglasses. The sunlight hurt. Everything hurt.

I rested my elbow on the sill of my open window, feeling warm air as it whipped past us. Any other day and this might be an enjoyable outing. Sunday was normally the one day when I could do something outside of the cartel. Go to the beach. Swim. Or, more frequently, lie on my bathroom floor and stare up at the exhaust fan as it turned lazily in the ceiling, for hours, as I recounted every single moment of Murphy's death. The moment he took his last breath, exhaled it, and breathed into me the reality that I was a killer. As the tiles chilled my skin, I'd think about how much blood he'd had inside him, the way it had soaked into my sheets and the carpet on my bedroom floor, his life force, gone, because of me. About how it would look to be slid into an oven, a bloodless corpse, and now I was about to see just what it looked like.

'How could anyone do that to a child?' I whispered.

'He didn't just do it to no child,' Guillermo said. 'He did it to *you.*'

I leaned forward in my seat, pressing my palms against my eyes until it hurt. The physical pain was a welcome relief from the way my heart was shattering into a million bloody pieces inside my ribcage.

'You know,' Guillermo said, 'maybe it's better this way. That kid, he'd be put to work in a fucking kiddie porn house, or worse.'

I took my hands away from my eyes and sat up, facing Guillermo. 'There's worse?'

He fixed me with a stare. 'There's always worse.'

I sagged in my seat, wiping more tears from my cheeks. My pores hurt where the saltwater had seeped in. I'd only been awake a few hours, but I was exhausted. One look at Guillermo told me that he looked how I felt.

***

It took too long to get to where we were going. I counted three police cruisers on our journey and wondered each time if we'd be pulled over. Guillermo's car was nondescript, a late-model Nissan that looked more like a soccer-mom vehicle, but the window tint wasn't quite dark enough to hide the gang tattoos that had been etched across his neck and all over his arms for the world to see and judge. He was like a magnet for attention, and so each time I saw a police car I cringed and waited for the flash of lights to tell us to pull over.

But of course, nothing happened. Nothing ever did when you were expecting it to. It was only when you were caught off-guard that the nightmarish realities happened.

I thought about calling John. Realised that would mean Guillermo would hear. Decided that was too risky.

Shit.

Guillermo pulled into the back of the funeral home and cut the engine, neither of us saying anything for a moment. I kept having paranoid thoughts that I could smell the death that sat on the backseat, encased in a plastic sarcophagus, but it was just my mind playing tricks on me. I think.

'Wait here,' Guillermo said finally, opening his car door and slamming it again.

Like hell. I got out, getting exactly three steps before Guillermo had rounded the car and backed me against it, effectively pinning me in place.

'Am I speaking Chinese? Wait. *Here.*' He stepped back enough for me to open my door again, but I didn't. Emboldened by grief and rage, I reached into my purse and pulled out the handgun I always carried.

'I'm going in,' I said grimly. 'So grab the suitcase and let's go, *ese*.'

Guillermo stepped back, shaking his head as he eyed the gun I was pointing at him. 'Gotta say, my feelings are kinda hurt,' he said, patting his chest with his palm. 'I ever point a gun at your head?'

'I do what you tell me to do,' I said calmly, the gun heavy but also oddly soothing. A mechanism by which I could be heard for once. A tool for controlling a situation that would ordinarily be out of my control.

'So do it now,' Guillermo hissed, looking around to make sure nobody could see our little Mexican/Colombian standoff in the back lot of Budget Funerals. 'Do what I'm telling you. Put that fucking thing away and get in the car before you accidentally shoot me, you silly bitch.'

I shook my head. 'I saved that baby,' I said, my throat burning as a lump grew and grew within it. 'I saved him, and he died because our fucking boss wanted to teach me a lesson. I started this, and I'm going to finish it, Guillermo.'

'Pointing a gun at me ain't gonna bring that kid back,' he ground out. 'Watching him burn ain't gonna do anything except fill your head with more black shit, so black you won't be able to close your eyes at night without seeing it. You really want that?'

I shrugged. 'I can't close my eyes anyway, so it doesn't matter.'

Guillermo made a low noise in the back of his throat. Not a growl, but almost. 'You see some freaky blue eyes when you close yours?'

I swallowed thickly, my pulse pounding in my temples. My grip on the gun wavered. 'What?'

'I'm not an idiot,' he said, his dark eyes shining in the stark sunlight. It was too hot. Too bright. Too loud. Everything was too goddamn loud.

I looked around the lot nervously.

'I know my place,' Guillermo said, his expression tight as he shoved his hands in his jean pockets. 'I'm the thug. I'm the stupid Mexican who does the grunt work.'

'You're not stupid,' I said.

One corner of his mouth tugged up for a second, and then it was gone again. 'No. I'm not. You know who was stupid?'

I wasn't sure I liked where he was going with this. 'Who?' I asked reluctantly.

'That damn DEA agent,' he said, and in that moment, all doubt was gone. Guillermo knew I'd killed Murphy. He knew.

'Guillermo,' I whispered.

'You move the money, too?' he cut in.

I chewed on the inside of my cheek, my arms heavy and tired from pointing the gun at him for so long. I wondered how long I could aim it at him before I'd have to lower it. How long before one of the employees at Budget Funerals came out for a cigarette break and found me bailing up a biker at gunpoint in their parking lot.

'You trust me?' Guillermo asked, his eyes wild as he fixed them on me. It was an excellent question. Did I trust him? Did I trust anyone?

'I killed Murphy,' I said, the gun getting warm in my sweaty hand. 'I killed his girlfriend, too.'

'I knew it,' Guillermo muttered, shaking his head. 'Of course it was you. Look at you. Waving a gun around. Creeping around with the prez like I'm stupid. Of course I know. You've changed, Ana. You finally grew some fucking *cajones*.' He grabbed his crotch for effect. 'If I didn't know better, I'd say your balls are made of brass, *cholita*.'

That saying – my blood ran cold – it's such a cliche. But I swear, in that moment, I felt all of the thick red blood in my veins turn into freezing sludge and sharp icicles that cut me from the inside.

I sagged against the car, all the fight draining out of me. I wanted to cry. *Creeping around with the prez.* Jesus Christ. It was all going to come undone.

'You love him?' Guillermo asked.

'Who, Murphy?' I asked incredulously.

Guillermo rolled his eyes. 'John. You love John.' It was a statement more than a question. It was true.

Yes. A thousand million times, yes.

'Shut up!' I said, launching myself at him.

He stepped back, my show of brute force apparently unperturbing to him, and raked his eyes up and down me. I imagined how crazy I must have looked. Messy hair, cheeks raw from crying and waving a loaded gun around like I was some kind of gangster.

'You got it bad for him, don't you?'

Was I really that easy to read?

'You don't know anything,' I protested. The gun was so fucking heavy.

'Dornan will find out, you know,' Guillermo said.

'Shut up!' I replied. 'I will fucking shoot you, Guillermo!'

I saw the impatience on his face. I felt the trepidation. Any minute now, somebody was going to see us: one woman, holding a gun at one man, as they stood beside one car that housed the body of one infant who'd been inexplicably caught up in a war that was fought with blood and innocents.

'You're not gonna shoot me,' Guillermo said, the self-assured prick that he was.

'Give me this one thing,' I urged.

He glared at me. Neither of us spoke for several long, excruciating moments. Guillermo sighed audibly.

'Put that fucking thing away,' he said finally. 'Don't talk. Don't tell them your name. *Definitely* don't tell them your name.'

I nodded.

'Wait here.'

He shook his head again, apparently very disappointed in my sudden raging psychosis, and disappeared into the service door, carrying the pink suitcase in his arms like it was fragile cargo. For all his bravado, Guillermo was one of the good guys. Well, one of the better guys, at least. I felt guilt at the way I'd just treated him, but I'd been desperate.

Then again, once upon a time I'd believed that Dornan was one of the good guys, and look where we were now. He was a baby trafficker and a fucking murderer.

I waited beside the car, staring at the fire escape door where Guillermo had disappeared. Just when I thought he'd been lying to me, that he'd taken the boy's body and gone on with the plan without me, the door opened a crack.

'Hurry up,' he murmured.

I entered, jumping a little as the thick steel door closed behind me. My eyes took a moment to adjust to the dim inside, as I followed Guillermo blindly through a series of scuffed linoleum hallways. I started to catch the signs as we walked past. There was a viewing room. Then another. A records room full of boxes and files. The further we got into the belly of this place, the more uneasy I became. The staff stared openly, and I guess I couldn't blame them. I didn't belong there. I was dressed for a day on the sofa, watching re-runs on TV, my hair in a messy bun and flip-flops on my feet. I wasn't exactly dressed for a funeral.

'In here,' Guillermo said tersely, ushering me through a door. The smell hit me right away. The stench of scorched bones settled into my nostrils and I wanted to gag, but it hardly seemed appropriate. There was a guy, probably in his early twenties, wearing a white plastic apron and white plastic boots that belonged in mud and dirt, not in a place like this. I studied the boots for a moment. It looked like somebody had tried to scrub blood flecks off them and failed. The apron was the same. Dull brown patches that told a harrowing tale.

I looked from the apron to the boy's eyes and was shocked to realise he was younger than I'd first thought. His light brown eyes looked dulled by life – no wonder, when he was spending his living hours with the dead.

'Hey.' I turned my head to Guillermo's voice, having forgotten him for a moment there. He stared down at something in front of him, pointedly, and my eyes followed his path.

Baby Doe was on a small metal table, lying on his side, just as he'd been in the suitcase. His eyes were closed – a small mercy – and Guillermo was arranging a blanket over him.

I crossed myself, thinking that it had been years since I'd been inside the walls of a church, let alone made the sign of the cross upon myself.

I try to believe that the next part didn't happen, but it did.

I looked away as his bones burned.

I waited while those bones were ground into dust.

It was so *loud*. I hadn't imagined it would be so loud.

***

I carried him away with me in a box.

It was so small. Too small to house the remains of what had once been a living, breathing, innocent human being.

I threw up in the parking lot, feeling the grit of bone dust on my skin, in my hair, and realising that Guillermo had been right – I should never have gone inside.

But nobody, least of all a child, should have to burn alone, forgotten, in a place called Budget *fucking* Funerals.

I wiped my mouth with the back of my hand and got back into the car, staring straight ahead.

'You still with me?' Guillermo asked, putting a hand on my shoulder.

I nodded. The sorrow inside me splintered, became two halves of something that birthed something new.

Rage. The sort of quiet rage that turns men into monsters. I felt it crack apart the grief in my chest and travel like vine tendrils, down my veins, until my fingertips and my toes and my cheeks hummed with a hot fury that felt like a fever.

I vowed to kill Emilio Ross if it was the last thing I ever did.

CHAPTER FIVE

MARIANA

'Where are we going?' I asked Guillermo as we drove.

'Home,' he replied firmly.

Home. I'd had a home, once upon a time.

The small cardboard box on my lap weighed barely a pound, but its weight on my existence was unbearable. This child would never have a home, unless you counted the ground where I would finally bury his remains.

Guillermo handled the car silently and with purpose, occasionally turning his head ever so slightly to look at me. To check on me? I didn't return his gaze; I couldn't. I couldn't do anything except think about the dead baby who had now been reduced to ash and dust and poured into a small box as if he had never existed.

The freeway traffic was heavy, and it took us a long time to go across town to Santa Monica. By the time I'd walked into my apartment I was seething. I was rage personified.

'Hey, we gotta talk about this shit. We're due to see the big man. Where do you think you're going?'

I didn't bother to stop to acknowledge his question. I was on a mission. I stormed into my room, hot tears threatening to roll down my cheeks. I hadn't let myself think about Emilio while I watched the baby burn, because it had seemed disrespectful to be considering my problems when a child was decomposing into ash in front of my very eyes.

Guillermo followed me into my bedroom, and that pissed me off. I couldn't even indulge my rage in private, it seemed. I turned on him, pushing my palms against his broad shoulders.

'Give me five fucking minutes, Guillermo,' I muttered, pointing to the door. He didn't move.

'Get out!' I yelled. 'Just go.' I was going to cry. I was going to cry, and once I started, I wasn't sure if or when I could stop. It was like there was a tidal wave of fear and rage and sorrow that had been building up inside me for ten years, and it had reached tsunami proportions. I was about to lose my shit, and I was about to lose it in a massive way.

But Guillermo didn't *just go*. I pushed him again, hard, and he grabbed my wrists, shaking me. 'What the fuck are you doing?' he breathed, his eyes narrowed to slits.

I couldn't see his face anymore. All I could see was rage. And in my rage, I saw Emilio in my mind's eye, dead on the ground, blood leaking from the hole in his head, the hole that I was about to put there.

'I'm going to kill that motherfucker,' I raged, the answer to all of my problems so simple, yet so profound, it was almost like an epiphany. Guillermo's face fell, his grip around my wrists lessened, and I pulled myself from him, running into the bathroom. I slammed the door behind me, locking it loudly for effect. It had been six months or more, and every time I was alone in this bathroom all I could think of were two things: Christopher Murphy's blood circling down my shower drain, and John Portland's feverish hands as he cupped my face and guided his lips to mine.

I looked at myself in the mirror as Guillermo pounded his fist on the door. I looked fucking terrible. I'd done my make-up extra special this morning, being that it was my birthday and all. But now, my mascara was plastered over my cheeks, my normally bronze skin was pale and blotchy, and the whites of my eyes were so fucking bloodshot, it was like someone had taken a scouring pad to them.

'Mariana,' Guillermo called, 'you're not killing anybody today.'

I ignored him, turning on the cold faucet and splashing my face with water to try and snap myself out of my stupor. That image, that singular image of Emilio with blood pumping out of his head, just the same way Murphy's blood had pumped out of his head, filled me with some kind of renewed hope. I had always wanted to kill him, but I had never really believed that I could.

Now, I knew that it was the only possible thing left for me to do.

The cold water didn't work. It didn't dissipate my rage; indeed, it only grew. Maybe it was because now I was actually a killer. I'd racked up two kills to my name, and ending Emilio would solve every problem that I had in my life. If he was dead, I would be free. If he was dead, I could have my son back.

If he was dead, I could finally get out of this fucking place.

I dried my face with a towel, taking one last look at myself in the mirror. I didn't bother reapplying my make-up. I didn't give a shit what I would look like, because either way, Emilio Ross was going down. It was hardly a fucking fashion parade, shooting somebody square in the face.

I opened the bathroom door, fully expecting to see Guillermo standing outside, waiting for me. But he wasn't there. I heard a soft beeping noise, and suspicion grew in the pit of my stomach. I stormed through my bedroom, the closest room to the front door, to see him tapping something into the security keypad on the wall. He looked up as I approached, guilt written all over his face, as if I had caught him in the middle of something he didn't want me to know about.

My handbag was sitting on the hall table. Inside was my gun. I snatched up the bag, rummaging through it, almost sighing in bitter relief when my fingers touched cold metal. I drew my piece and aimed it at his head.

'Tell me you didn't just change the fucking security code to try and keep me in here,' I said.

Guillermo stood his ground.

'Since when do you think it's okay to keep aiming a motherfucking gun at me?' he mocked. 'I just risked my fucking *dick* by taking you to the crematorium. Pulled it out of my pants and rested it on the fucking chopping block. And this is how you say thank you?'

I could hear the blood pumping in my veins, hot and thick and syrupy. That blood, it needed reparation. It demanded it.

'I don't care about your dick,' I said, deathly calm.

He rolled his eyes, bracing himself against the front door. 'And I don't care about your little revenge vendetta,' he snapped back. 'You stupid girl, you really think you're going to achieve anything by going down to see the boss man, guns blazing? No. He'll take you back to San Diego and shove you in that dungeon of his so fast, you won't even know what's happening until he slams the door shut on your pretty Colombian face.'

Well. I didn't know what to say to that.

'Think about it,' Guillermo drawled, pointing at his temple. 'He wanted you to react, Ana. He's trying to make you crack.'

I dropped the gun to my side, curiosity winning against the rage, at least temporarily.

'Why,' I asked. 'Why would he do this now?'

Guillermo raised his eyebrows. 'He's trying to get into everyone's heads, isn't he? His right-hand man still hasn't shown up, alive or dead, and Emilio wants to know what the fuck happened to his supposedly loyal prick of a business associate.'

Murphy. He was talking about Murphy.

Guillermo raked his eyes over me. 'Girl, he knows Murphy visited you. He knows ain't nobody seen the man after he left you.'

I swallowed thickly. 'What are you trying to say?'

Guillermo took a step forward. 'Nothing. I ain't trying to say *nothing*. I don't know what happened, and I don't want to know, because knowing anything like that puts me in the firing line, you hear me?'

'You know he's dead. You know I killed him.'

'I know you can be fucking stupid, Ana.'

My anger kicked up a beat. I wanted to kill Emilio. I wanted to feel his blood on my hands. I wanted it to soak into my skin. I wanted his death to become a part of who I was. If that was stupid? So be it.

'Open the door,' I said, my voice hard.

He didn't budge.

'Now, Guillermo.'

He shook his head. Fucking prick. I responded by taking aim at the door, just to the left of his head, and squeezing down three pounds on a six-pound trigger. If I sneezed, Guillermo would be as good as dead.

He just stared at me.

'Open. The. Door.'

'No. Fucking. Way.'

There was a hard rap on the door outside, and it was lucky I didn't blow Guillermo's head off. He stepped to the side and ducked, as I stared at the door, panting heavily. I took my finger off the trigger.

Guillermo glared at me, motioning for me to lower the gun. 'Jesus fucking Christ, I'm on your side, bitch. Settle down.'

I was seething. 'Who did you call?' I demanded. Guillermo ignored my question, tapping a code into the security pad that I didn't quite catch, and opened the door with a heavy thunk.

I gripped my gun tightly at my side, ready to aim at whoever the fuck was daring to come into my house when I was reeling from the events that had happened today. My finger itched against the hard metal trigger, begging for release. I hoped that it was Emilio. In that moment, I didn't even care if he shot me as well. As long as I got a bullet in him first. He needed to bleed for what he had done. For everything that he had done.

But it wasn't Emilio. It wasn't Dornan.

It was John.

Of all the people I had expected to see on my doorstep, John had been the last one. I loved him. And up until that moment, I had truly believed that he and I were the only two that were aware of that fact. Tears pricking at my eyes, I stared at Guillermo.

Could I really trust him?

Was this a test?
Was Guillermo in with Emilio?
I couldn't begin to imagine what he was thinking or who he was allied with, so I turned my attention back to John. He entered my apartment, closing the door behind him and standing silently in front of me. He was a sight to behold – ripped jeans and a tight black shirt that showed off his muscles to fine definition. He looked hot, not just in the sexual sense, but because sweat was beading on his forehead, his shirt sticking to his chest.

'Did you run here?' I asked. *Did you run here?* What kind of stupid-ass question was that?

His expression was grave as he looked at the gun I gripped tightly by my side. 'Heard you weren't doing too well. You know me. I can't help myself.'

I didn't know whether to laugh or scream.

CHAPTER SIX

JOHN

He'd been smoking on the back porch when the message came through from Guillermo.

Get here now. M is going fucking crazy.

John had peered into the house to see Juliette talking on the phone, like she always did these days. Caroline had bailed a couple of days earlier, and John was beyond taking to the streets of LA to look for his drug-addled wife. His stolen moments with Mariana had made him realise that the only person who could really help Caroline was Caroline herself.

Plus, a very tiny part of him – the part that he liked to pretend didn't exist – imagined a day when the police would turn up and inform him that his wife had finally taken too much heroin, or crossed the wrong dealer, and ended up dead in a ditch.

One could always dream, right?

'Julie!' John hollered at his daughter through the screen door, making sure to hold his cigarette away from the mesh so that smoke didn't seep into the house. 'I'm going out for a little while. You okay here?'

'Yeah, Daddy,' Juliette's voice filtered back to him. 'I'm on the phone!'

John rolled his eyes. She was on the phone to that kid again. Long-lost son of Dornan. The kid who'd had to discover his own mother dead in a bathroom covered in her blood, before meeting his father – her murderer – for the very first time. A terrible feeling swept over John as he locked the door. They lived on a quiet street, safe enough, but you could never be too careful when you were the president of the Gypsy Brothers MC.

Truth be told, that sinking feeling he lived with these days wasn't because he was worried about the neighbourhood he lived in. It was the constant recall of the casual manner Dornan had displayed in the wake of murdering Stephanie, the woman he'd once loved above everything else.

It was the abject terror that Dornan would find out that John was fucking Mariana. That John loved Mariana.

It was the way his imagination presented Mariana's death to him in countless grisly ways.

John checked the locks three times before he felt confident enough to leave his daughter alone.

***

Ten minutes later, Guillermo was letting him into Mariana's apartment in Santa Monica.

'He told me you weren't yourself,' John said, hoping those words were benign enough to appease her.

'Not myself,' Mariana snapped, her eyes flashing with what looked like rage. Oh, shit. He'd never, not in ten years, seen her like *this*. Mariana Rodriguez was poised, she was controlled, she was almost annoyingly detached unless you pressed her in just the right way. Usually up against a wall, with three fingers and a tongue. That was the thing that inevitably made her icy exterior melt away, the thing that made her turn to butter under John's touch.

But he could hardly fuck the rage out of his little spitfire in front of Dornan's lackey. Guillermo didn't know about their relationship, and John very much wanted to keep it that way. Keeping his head attached to his body was high on his priority list, and if Guillermo ratted him out to Dornan, he'd likely cut John's head off and have it mounted on the wall at the clubhouse as a trophy. Disturbingly, he and Mariana had spoken at length – more than once – about how Dornan would choose to kill them if he ever found out about them. Decapitation always seemed to be at the forefront of their predictions.

Shaking that image from his mind, John focused on the woman he loved. She was shaking, pacing, tapping a gun against her leg. In some terrifying way, she reminded him very much of Dornan.

She looked like she'd finally lost her mind.

Maybe she had.

'Will somebody please tell me what the fuck is going on?' John asked, making sure to use his pleasant voice. Unlike Dornan, who liked to ask questions with his fists, John always opted for tact and friendliness as a first resort. Sometimes it worked. Sometimes it just bought an extra five minutes before shit got crazy and fists became essential.

'A dead baby,' Mariana was muttering as she paced. 'He killed a baby!'

John glanced at Guillermo, remembering the day just months ago when he'd come back to the apartment to check on Mariana and found her in a pool of blood, miscarrying Dornan's baby, thanks to those very same fists Dornan used to fight his way through life. Seemed Mariana had argued with Dornan about how unhinged he'd become, and earned herself a beating and a brush with death as thanks for her concern.

Was that what she was talking about now? Her dead baby?

John saw that Mariana's finger had crept back onto the trigger of her gun, and that was dangerous. He'd seen grown men blow holes clean through their feet by accident before, just because they'd been too itchy with a trigger as they bounced about.

'Hey,' John said, his voice sharper this time as he tried to snap Mariana out of her trance. 'Ana. What's happening?'

Mariana glared at Guillermo, who, for once, wasn't cracking jokes. And that was deeply troubling to John.

'Guillermo?' John said. 'Want to fill me in?'

Guillermo's eyes darted about the apartment, first to John, then Mariana, then to a cardboard package sitting on the kitchen countertop.

'That something I need to be worried about?' John asked, suddenly alarmed. He'd seen his fair share of suspicious packages. Severed fingers. Dirty bombs. You never knew what the new day was going to bring when you were a Gypsy Brother.

'I need to get out of here,' Mariana said, that damned gun still in her hand. She wielded it like it was a lifeline.

'Guillermo!' John yelled. 'Fucking *talk*!'

Guillermo cleared his throat. 'Boss man sent a package today. For her birthday.'

John used the distraction to step nearer to Mariana, closing his hand over hers and squeezing tightly. 'Gun, please,' he said, feeling her bones crunch under his grip. He didn't want to hurt her, not one little hair on her head, but more than that, he didn't want her to shoot him by accident. Mariana might have been small – five two to his six one – but she was strong. It took some serious force for her to concede, dropping her grip on the gun so that it fell neatly into John's other hand.

She stared at him with what looked like bitter rage. Funnily enough, it didn't make her look any less beautiful. Her dark blue eyes were like twin storms on the horizon, threatening to destroy everything in their path.

John rolled his eyes, emptying the bullets from her gun and pocketing them. The gun went in the back of his jeans, where it rested in the small of his back.

'This better not be a bomb,' he said, shoving past Guillermo and Mariana to pick up the box on the counter. He shook it gently, surprised at the sound it made. It was like someone had filled it with gravel.

He wasn't entirely surprised when Mariana snatched the box from his hands.

'Don't,' she said.

'Tell me what it is, and I won't have to,' he countered.

They stared off for a moment until Guillermo's voice broke through the tense silence.

'They're ashes. Emilio delivered a body this morning. A fucking kid.'

John stepped back as if he'd just touched a live wire. He immediately felt regret at having shaken the box so casually. His palms burned accusingly, glowering hot with shame.

'What? Whose kid?'

Mariana slid the box back onto the counter, the mention of a dead child apparently having snapped her out of whatever psychotic break she'd been experiencing.

'Remember the woman I told you about? She was meant to be delivered to a buyer,' Mariana said, 'but she was pregnant. She gave birth in the truck. It was the night Dornan was shot. We took the baby to the hospital, the same hospital where Dornan ended up after – well, you know.'

John remembered all too well. The night Dornan had been shot by a cop, a vengeance shooting after Mariana had killed the cop's partner, Murphy. The guy had been dead for months and he was still causing fucking problems.

John nodded, feeling his teeth grinding in his mouth. It was as if a dark cloud had settled over the room, and everyone was stuck in its shadow. Something was very, very fucked up, and John wasn't sure if he wanted the whole story now that he'd heard the teaser reel.

'Emilio knew what we'd done, how we'd saved the baby and taken him to the ER. He found me at the hospital, watching the baby through the nursery window. He threatened me. Said if I ever betrayed the family in any way, he'd take the baby and ...' She trailed off, her eyes lingering on the cardboard box.

John's stomach squeezed painfully, and all the air went out of his lungs as if somebody had hit him with a baseball bat. He glanced at Guillermo in horror, and then back at Mariana.

'Do they think you've betrayed them?' John asked, choosing his words carefully. He kept giving Guillermo surreptitious glances, wondering if the guy was even remotely trustworthy.

'Don't look at me, man,' Guillermo said, shaking his head. 'I ain't no baby killer.'

'I didn't say you were,' John snapped.

Mariana's eyes darted towards John, and in that moment, he saw the uncertainty that *maybe somebody knew about them.* The moment passed between them silently, swiftly, until John blinked and it was gone.

'I haven't done anything,' Mariana whispered.

'Apart from take out Emilio's best inside man.'

John and Mariana both snapped their attention to Guillermo, who held his palms up in a sign of submission. 'Hey, whoa, you all think I'm some dumb fuck, but I live with her.' He pointed at Mariana. 'I was ninety per cent sure one of you had something to do with it. Can't say I'm disappointed. It's been peaceful these past months, without that Murphy motherfucker following you around all the time.'

John clenched his knuckles until they made several faint popping sounds. Guillermo shifted on his feet uneasily, glancing down at John's balled hands.

'You can trust me, Prez,' Guillermo said. 'Six months that asshole's been missing, and I ain't said a word to nobody. This situation?' Guillermo gestured to Mariana, to the apartment they were standing in. 'It suits me. This girl?' He put his hand on Mariana's shoulder. 'I like this girl. Not like that. She's like a sister to me. Like a daughter.'

'The same way Dornan's a brother? The same way I'm your brother?'

Guillermo chuckled, but there was no joy in the sound he made. 'Man, you know my deal. I'm a hired fucking thug. I wear the patch, I look out for my boys, but I would shoot any one of them, you included, if she needed me to.'

John felt his eyebrows practically hit the roof. He hadn't known that Guillermo could speak that many consecutive sentences, let alone have an opinion on something that didn't involve free pussy or cheap beer.

'How'd the ... package get here, anyway?'

'Emilio called me this morning,' Mariana said quietly. She was as removed now as she had been fiery, not five minutes earlier. 'He told me there was something waiting outside the front door for me, and I knew he was outside watching. I had this weird feeling that he was going to shoot me or something. But instead, I found this big box.' She was gesturing with her hands the size of the box. 'I brought it inside and locked the door again, and I opened it. It was a suitcase. And inside ...' Her chin wobbled, tears welling in her eyes. 'When I saw the box sitting outside, I thought ... I thought it was a computer. To replace my old one. I didn't think–' She made a little gasping sound, holding her chest with her hand. She looked so young when she was terrified. She looked like the girl Dornan had first ushered into his office ten years ago, instead of the steely woman she'd been forced to become.

John stood there helplessly. All he wanted to do was kill somebody. Rip them apart, limb by limb, until this pressure in his chest went away. This throb in his skull. This desperation that sat in his stomach like lead. He'd always known what kind of men he worked for – was controlled by – but this? This was something else. In that moment, John's thoughts flashed to his own death, and part of him knew there was almost no chance they were going to escape with their lives. It was just that cut and dried, that fucking sure. He loved this woman more than he'd ever loved anyone, and as she wept in front of him he could already see how the blood would look when it seeped from her nose and her mouth, the way she would cry as her life bled away. As she *died*. John ground his teeth together hopelessly. He just wanted to be with her. More than that, he just wanted her to be free. He just wanted her to be able to see the son she'd had ripped from her as a teenager, the son she hadn't seen since he was hours old, the son who was waiting for her in Colombia until it was safe enough for them all to leave Los Angeles.

An unbearable sadness fell upon John. He didn't want to die. Didn't want Ana to die. Didn't want to leave Juliette with the likes of Caroline to guide her through life.

We could just get in the car now, John thought. Knock Guillermo out – hell, shoot him dead – get the car, get Juliette, and drive across that border. It was only three hours from LA to the Mexican crossing. They'd get over there, get some fake IDs and disappear. Shit, they didn't even need to go to Mexico. LAX was a thirty-minute drive away if the traffic was favourable. They could ask for the first flight to England, or Australia, or fucking Antarctica.

She wouldn't do it. She wouldn't leave without Jason. And John wouldn't leave without her. So they were all stuck.

'Show her some fucking comfort, man,' Guillermo said, his words cutting through John's vortex of thoughts as he gestured to a sobbing Mariana.

'You're the one who lives with her,' John said gruffly.

'You're the one who's in love with her,' Guillermo shot back.

Well, he didn't know what the fuck to say to that, but he did briefly regret emptying Mariana's gun of bullets. He'd very much have liked to empty the thing into Guillermo's face right now.

'What the fuck did you just say?' John asked.

'You think I can't hear you sneaking around in here?' Guillermo shot back.

That was it. Prick was practically begging for it. John launched at Guillermo, one hand grabbing his T-shirt in a fist, the other reared back and ready to slam into the fucker's meaty face.

How was Guillermo still *smiling*?

'Hey!' Mariana said sharply, her fist closing over the one John was about to eviscerate this motherfucker with, punch by bloody punch.

John turned his head to where Mariana stood. 'Let. Go,' he growled.

She didn't.

'He's not our enemy,' Mariana whispered, her long nails digging into his arm. 'He's our friend. And right now, we can use all the friends we can get.'

John took a ragged breath. Let go of Guillermo. Took a step back, running a hand over his head.

'Does Dornan know about what happened today?' he asked finally.

Mariana just stared at him.

'Nope.' Guillermo glanced at Mariana before returning his attention to John. 'He's not in a good place, man. Not after Colorado. If he sees her like this …'

So Guillermo knew about Stephanie.

'No shit,' John replied.

'I'm right here,' Mariana muttered.

'And you're hardly giving me straight answers,' John snapped at her, looking back to Guillermo. 'Anything else I should know?'

He shrugged. 'Nothing that comes to mind right now.'

Jesus, fuck. Things were unravelling faster than John had anticipated. He felt hollow. Tired. Fucking worn out. Like someone had taken an ice-cream scoop and carved out his insides.

He closed his eyes for a moment, pressing the fingers of one hand against his eyelids for a brief reprieve. Dead babies and boxes of ash were more than he'd been wanting to deal with today. Any day.

It was in that moment that he realised, with absolute fucking clarity, that despite everything he'd promised Mariana, this life was almost certainly going to kill them all. If Guillermo knew about his relationship with Mariana, then who else knew? Granted, it was almost impossible for John not to openly stare at Mariana whenever they happened to be within shooting distance of each other. He knew that Dornan knew something was up. He'd been banking on the fact that Dornan probably thought John's hostility was because of the way he had brutally slain Stephanie back in Colorado and then asked John to do the clean-up, just months beforehand.

Did Dornan know?

Was this child's death some kind of message?

Were he and Mariana deluding themselves that they could run from these people?

'It's almost twelve,' Guillermo said, pointing at the small digital clock on the microwave. 'We're gonna be late for church if we don't hustle.'

Just like that, his words seemed to close the conversation. Church, just another word for the weekly meet at the Gypsy Brothers clubhouse, was something none of them could miss, unless they were dead. John stared at Mariana pointedly as he slipped the empty gun back into her handbag and held it out in front of her. She took it, looking a little calmer than she had when he'd arrived.

'I gotta change this fuckin' shirt,' Guillermo said. 'I smell like barbecue.'

Mariana flinched, and John glared at Guillermo's back as he disappeared into the second bedroom he'd claimed as his own. Even alone, he daren't put his hands on Mariana. She looked like she might scream if anyone touched her.

'I should change, too,' Mariana said quietly. She disappeared, returning a few moments later in a plain black dress and heels. She looked ready for a funeral.

'We going?' she asked.

John could feel grit on his skin, like fine beach sand, and though it was likely psychological and not from the box of some kid's ashes he'd just inadvertently manhandled, he still wanted to wash his hands with some boiling water. 'Let me just use the bathroom,' he said, heading for Mariana's bedroom at the front of the apartment, and the ensuite that was attached. As he went to pass her, she grabbed onto his forearm. 'Can I have my ammunition, please?'

John stopped, raising his eyebrows as he stared down at the woman he loved more than he loved almost anything. Something in her eyes unsettled him deeply. 'Can I trust you to keep your finger off the goddamn trigger?'

She rolled her eyes. 'Yes, John. I'm angry. I'm not an idiot.'

'You sure about that?' John asked. 'Because you look like you're about to murder somebody.'

'I'm fine,' Mariana said, waving her hand dismissively. 'Just change the code back so we can go to the clubhouse together.' Guillermo re-entered the kitchen, looking exactly the same as he had before he went to change his clothes. 'It's zero-six-six-six,' he interjected.

Mariana stilled briefly, car keys in her hand as she stood by the front door. 'The devil's number. How appropriate.'

'Wait. I need to talk to you,' John said, taking Ana's elbow and leading her into her bedroom. She followed him without a fight, and closed the door behind her.

'I'll just wait here then, shall I?' Guillermo hollered, rummaging around in the kitchen.

John rolled his eyes. He still didn't trust the guy. Had never had the greatest feeling about him. Maybe because of the way Guillermo had dealt with his own wife and the guy she'd been fucking in secret, blowing their house to smithereens and reducing two humans to pieces of charred flesh that had to be scraped off what remained of the walls. Technically John was a cheater, and he wondered what Guillermo would do to him.

'Ana. Look at me.'

After a few seconds, she made eye contact. Her dark blue eyes were clouded, and she looked like she might cry again. He hated it when she cried. Made him feel fucking powerless.

'We're leaving,' John said resolutely.

'What?' Mariana said. 'What are you talking about?'

'You wanna bring the kid, we'll bring him. The four of us. Me, you, Juliette, Jason. I'll organise new papers for all of us. Passports. Birth certificates. We are not hanging around here until we find ourselves in the firing line.'

'John–' Mariana started.

'Don't *John* me,' he cut her off. 'I know why you're packing that gun. You're going to try and kill Emilio? You know that's exactly what he's expecting of you today, right? Jesus Christ, it's like he's chumming the waters with blood and you're swimming up, thinking you're about to get your teeth into something.'

Mariana looked at the ceiling pointedly.

'Promise me you won't do anything stupid.'

She narrowed her gaze on him. 'I won't do anything stupid.'

She went to pass him, heading for the door. Without thinking, John's hand shot out, pulling her back to him. He took her shoulders and turned her so that she was up against the door, squeezing her chin so hard he was probably hurting her.

'We're getting out of here,' he murmured against her lips. 'I promise you.'

'I don't need a man to save me,' she whispered, her eyes wet.

John kissed her, long and hard, pressing his body against hers until he was practically grinding her into the bedroom door.

'Good,' he said. 'Because I need you to save me.'

And he did need her to save him from this.

There was a rap of knuckles on the door.

'We rolling?' Guillermo hollered.

With great reluctance, John peeled himself from Mariana's slight form, swiping a thumb across her face to erase the smear of red lipstick he'd just kissed halfway across her cheek.

'Gimme five,' John yelled back, finally letting Mariana go. 'I'll meet you out there.'

She nodded, straightening her clothes before she opened the door and stepped out into the hallway.

John felt strangely out of place as he wandered through Mariana's bedroom – a place where he'd fucked her countless times behind the security a locked door afforded – and into her bathroom. He had an eerie feeling of deja vu that he couldn't quite place. That sinking feeling again. That inescapable reality.

He went into the bathroom, and by the time he heard Guillermo yelling and bashing his fists against the front door not thirty seconds later, Mariana was long gone.

John burst out of the bathroom, almost bowling Guillermo over. The Mexican's face was red, his fists white as he clenched them tight, raining down blows on the locked front door.

'She changed the fucking code again!' Guillermo said.

John looked up at the ceiling, taking a deep breath, hoping Guillermo was just clumsy-fingered. 'Here, let me try,' he said, shoving him aside and entering the code. Zero-six-six-six-hash.

Nope. Nothing.

More alarmingly, he knew that if they entered the wrong code more than five times, an alarm would be triggered remotely and the security company would call Dornan. Not a great idea to have him turn up with armed guards to find his girlfriend missing and John and Guillermo standing sheepishly in her foyer.

'I'll try her birthday,' Guillermo said, reaching his hand out to hit the keypad next to the door. John caught his hand mid-air. 'Don't do that.'

Guillermo looked surprised. 'Huh?'

'If you do that enough times, the alarm gets triggered. Dornan gets a call. How the hell are we supposed to explain us being stuck in here?'

Guillermo sagged against the door. 'Well, how the fuck are we supposed to get out? We don't turn up to church, Boss is gonna notice that, too, send out a fucking search party to cut our nuts off.'

John was already dialling Mariana's cell. She answered on the second ring, and he heard the noise of the highway in the background.

'What the hell do you think you're doing?' John asked, trying to keep his voice as steady as possible. He didn't need her hanging up on him.

'I'm meeting with Emilio,' she said, her voice sounding far away. He imagined the way she'd balance the cellphone on her knees while she drove, her hair blowing around her face as she cruised down the freeway. She always drove with the windows down, no matter what the weather was like outside. Said it made her feel alive.

Well, she wouldn't be alive much longer if she was going to pull shit like this.

Guillermo leaned over towards John and yelled, 'You'd better let us out of this fucking place, now!'

John narrowed his eyes at Guillermo, as if to say, *what the fuck?* He purposefully took three steps away from him, staring at the tiled floor as he pinched the bridge of his nose.

'Just tell me what you're doing,' John said wearily. 'Tell me why you've got a gun and six bullets and don't want us to come with you to your meeting with Emilio.'

'She took the box,' Guillermo said. At first John was confused, until he looked to where Guillermo was pointing at the kitchen counter, where a box of human ashes had sat just minutes ago.

'And a box of ashes,' John added, a feeling of utter dread forming in the pit of his stomach and travelling like icy tentacles to every part of his body, until he was consumed by the feeling. His heart beat faster as he imagined the countless horrible fates that would befall the woman he loved, should she try anything so stupid as to murder Emilio Ross in his own building, surrounded by security and family and no doubt his own fucking son across the desk.

Mariana's voice came through clearly. 'Emilio needs to die. Then we can all be free.'

She ended the call. John looked at the screen in disbelief.

'Call Dornan,' John said to Guillermo, as he pocketed the phone and picked up a heavy brass vase that sat in the foyer.

'And tell him that Mariana's on her way to kill Emilio?' Guillermo asked in disbelief.

John looked at the floor-to-ceiling window that butted up against the front door and prayed it wasn't bulletproof. 'No,' he said, gripping the neck of the vase with two hands and rearing it back like a baseball bat. 'Tell him you got clumsy again and broke the fucking window.'

Guillermo looked up from his phone. 'Huh?'

John swung.

CHAPTER SEVEN

MARIANA

I'd put on my best calm voice on the phone, but as soon as I'd ended John's call, a mile from the Gypsy Brothers clubhouse, I had started to shake. I drove down Abbot Kinney and turned onto Venice Boulevard, passing tourists and moms pushing strollers with one hand, Starbucks firmly gripped in the other. People liked to think of Venice as a hip, grungy place, but if they knew what happened inside the nondescript warehouse I was pulling up to, they'd drop their pumpkin spiced lattes onto the pavement and run.

I parked in front of the clubhouse and gripped my steering wheel, trying to catch a breath. Dark desires stirred within me, ones that had lain dormant for years, the spark of the girl I had been when I was first thrust into this life. The girl I had been forced to be when I killed first Murphy, then his partner, Allie.

Breathe in.

I was probably going to die in the next thirty minutes.

Breathe out.

I was going to die because my shock had worn off, and in its place, a violent rage had taken hold of me. I was its willing hostage, its dutiful foot soldier, its vengeful lover.

Breathe in.

It spread through my veins like poison, an elaborate network of arteries and organs that ached for reprisal. My pale shocked cheeks were now flushed with anger as I placed a palm on the office door and pushed, not bothering to knock.

***

Emilio Ross sat behind the great wooden desk in an office he occupied for two hours every week. He didn't need anything so elaborate, but he insisted for the other 166 hours a week, that this room was off-limits. Normally, I knocked and waited for his gruff invitation to enter.

This time though I walked right in, shoulders squared, eyes steeled, every ounce of me screaming with silent rage.

I didn't even glance at Dornan, who'd replaced Murphy in these financial meetings we had every Sunday. No, in that moment, he didn't even exist. I went straight for Emilio, who didn't look at all surprised that he'd finally hit a nerve in me that I couldn't ignore.

'Mariana,' Emilio greeted me, amusement written all over his face. 'You're late.'

I smiled thinly, the box in my hands far heavier than its actual weight. 'I am. I had a very busy morning.'

In my peripheral vision, I could see Dornan staring at me, and I knew he was probably dying inside that he wasn't in on whatever Emilio and I were discussing.

'I suppose I should be lenient, since it's your birthday,' Emilio said sweetly, his sugar-laden words failing to cover the poisonous barbs that lurked beneath. 'I trust you got my gift, darling?'

Darling? He'd never called me *darling* in ten years. The word sounded like cursing coming from his mouth.

I dropped my smile, but didn't turn my gaze away. To be able to out-stare a powerful man is a very rare gift, and I intended to use that gift. I stared at Emilio Ross until my eyes were burning, begging for me to blink, or look away, but I refused.

I'd assumed that I would place the box neatly in front of him and step away, but in that moment, the way his cold eyes surveyed me with an almost amused look, that shock I'd been experiencing subsided. In its wake, a tsunami of rage swelled through me, unbidden, uncontainable.

'I got your gift,' I replied, opening the cardboard box. 'I'm returning it.'

I said a silent prayer, an apology for the child whose remains I was about to use to prove a point. He shouldn't have had to bear the weight of my anger, but it was too late. I'd tried to save his little life once, had held his newborn flesh against mine and warmed his body as his mother lay dead in the car seat behind us. He'd survived being born in a tiny cell in the back of a truck, he'd survived the cold and the dark as his mother bled to death beside him, and he'd survived the precarious months since then. But he had not survived ultimately. He was dead, and Emilio had killed him. His death could not be in vain. An innocent child didn't deserve this ending, not after he was already dead. He didn't deserve to be disrespected. But in what I did next, I hoped that I would be standing up to his killer, to make sure his death didn't mean nothing. *I'm so sorry*, I offered up to his poor tiny soul, as I did what I did next.

I tipped the box upside down over Emilio's ridiculous fucking desk, sending pieces of ash and bone in a pile that gave off grey dust, enough to choke a person. Emilio closed his mouth as soon as he realised what it was I'd just deposited in front of him. Something about the look in his eyes tantalised me – he was surprised. Not angry. Just shocked.

'I'm impressed,' Emilio said, pursing his thin lips together as he looked down at the ashes in front of him. 'I didn't think you had this in you.'

'Neither did I,' I replied.

Beside me, I heard Dornan clear his throat. 'Will somebody please tell me what the fuck is going on?'

Emilio's eyes were on the ashes in front of him, and it was then I realised I'd won. I'd out-stared him. Out-manoeuvred him. Question was, how was he going to punish me for it?

I turned my cold gaze to Dornan. It was almost comical how much he looked like his father – the Italian features, the dark eyes, their identical cheekbone structure. I marvelled momentarily at how I could have fallen so hard, so fast, for a man who looked eerily like the person I hated most in this world.

'Your father delivered a package to me this morning,' I said, my voice monotone. 'He even called me to make sure I personally unwrapped it.'

Dornan shifted uneasily in his seat, looking between me and his father. Emilio wore a smirk as he looked between the mess on his desk and me. It was almost as if he were pleased that I'd done this. Maybe he was.

'And?' Dornan pressed. 'What was in the package? What is that?'

'A dead baby,' I said flatly.

Dornan raised his eyebrows. '*What!*'

'The baby we took to the hospital the night you were shot. We tempted fate.' I looked back at Emilio, who couldn't wipe the smile off his smug fucking face. 'Luckily, your dear father was here to restore the balance in the world. Make sure nobody got away unaccounted for.' My words were dripping with sarcasm, and it was a wonder Emilio didn't stand up and slap me from across the table. He was oddly removed, and I realised how much he was enjoying this – watching my reaction unfold.

I would give him nothing. Not a single outcry, not a single tear. I could be a blank slate, a monster, just like the two men I was currently sharing oxygen with inside this stuffy room.

I heard footsteps in the hallway come closer, rapidly, as if someone were running. I had two guesses as to who they belonged to. Sure enough, the door burst open to reveal Guillermo, his round face shiny with sweat as he held on to the door handle, panting heavily.

'Get out,' I said to him. 'We're not finished yet.'

Guillermo looked like I'd shot him, he was so surprised. Glancing at Emilio, who tipped his chin in a gesture that said he agreed with my sentiments, Guillermo closed the door again.

I could feel Dornan's presence beside me. He was bewildered. He was angry. Most of all, he was afraid. I didn't even need to look at him to know that he was terrified for me. Because if his father could kill an innocent baby, what would he do to me?

'Pop, tell me she's wrong.'

I side-eyed Dornan, a little surprised that he'd found his voice. He was a man who could intimidate anybody except his own father.

Emilio leaned back in his chair. 'She's not wrong,' Emilio countered. 'You two left quite the mess for me to clean up. You should be thanking me for tying up your loose ends.'

I laughed mirthlessly. 'Are you fucking kidding me?' I exclaimed. 'Seriously. We should thank you.'

Emilio didn't respond. His smile started to shrink a little. His amusement, it would seem, was turning to displeasure.

'How did you do it?' I asked, smacking my palms down on the desk as I stood over the man I'd once feared too much to even look in the eye. 'Did you even do it yourself? Or did you make somebody else, you fucking coward!' I picked up the closest thing to my right hand – ironically, a framed photograph of Emilio with several of his grandchildren, Dornan's sons – and drew my arm back, aiming right for Emilio's face. I was going to smash that framed photograph into his face so hard he'd see stars. He'd need stitches from where the glass shattered and cut his face. He'd probably kill me for my transgression.

I no longer had the capacity to care if I lived or died.

But somebody else did. Out of nowhere, Dornan was behind me, his hand around my wrist, twisting painfully so that my grip on the photo frame faltered. With an angry cry, my fingers loosened and the photo fell to the floor, bouncing harmlessly.

Dornan pulled my arm, hard enough that I was forced to face him. 'Hey!' he said. 'Look at me. What do you think you're doing?' His fingers were squeezing my upper arms so hard, it ached. I struggled in his grip, my eyes only for Emilio.

'Look at me!' he roared. It was like time stood still for that moment, our tragic tableau representative of our entire lives – Emilio, smirking as he crossed his leather shoes on the edge of the desk where a dead child's ashes lay scattered; Dornan, hurting me, always hurting me. And me. Useless.

Pathetic. Emilio had killed a baby. He was a human trafficker. He dealt in women and children like it was nothing. I'd known the depths of his depravity for almost a year now, ever since that night when Dornan had been shot, when he'd revealed to me the cost of keeping me alive was to do his father's bidding – transporting human beings across state lines, across countries, stealing people and selling them. Selling them! And I'd sat on my hands and blamed my need to protect Luis and done nothing.

In some ways, I was just as bad as them. Worse. Because I couldn't help feeling – knowing – that if I'd done things differently, the nameless baby Emilio had killed would be alive right now. Maybe even his mother, if we'd taken her to a hospital instead of Dornan shooting her in the back of his truck to relieve her suffering as she slowly bled out after giving birth. I could have done something, anything, and I'd been sitting on my hands for a year, hell, for ten fucking years, and I had nobody to blame but myself.

'Look at me, goddamn it,' Dornan muttered. I did. I raised my eyes. I could only imagine what they looked like. Wild. Empty. I was empty inside. Dornan's dark eyes widened a little when he saw my gaze. I think I must have repulsed him, then. With my face twisted into a mask of rage and grief, my eyes blank and hollow, it was a wonder he recognised me at all.

'It was easy, really,' Emilio said. I didn't look away from Dornan as Emilio continued to speak. 'I used a pillow. Didn't take more than a few minutes. He struggled, a bit, but then he stopped. He looked so peaceful, Mariana. It made me wonder what your child would have looked like if it hadn't died inside of you.'

I saw the light die in Dornan's eyes as his father spoke so casually about murdering an infant. The subtle way his broad shoulders curved inward, the way his whole body seemed to deflate. He took his hands off me, let them hang at his sides.

'Go home,' Dornan bit out, his eyes pained. He put his hands on his hips, shaking his head as he finally broke our gaze.

'We still have our meeting,' I replied, feeling like my insides had been hollowed out with a melon scoop. Like someone had taken out every bit of energy and life inside me, and left a vacuous nothingness in its wake.

'The meeting is cancelled,' Dornan said, the first trace of decisiveness I think I'd ever seen him display around his father. Dead kids brought out the rebel in him.

'Good,' I replied. 'It's my birthday. I'm taking the day off.'

Without looking back at Emilio, I slung my bag over my shoulder and brushed past Dornan without giving him eye contact.

My hand was on the door handle when Emilio chuckled. It was a noise that made me want to go on a murderous rampage. I felt the weight of the gun in my handbag and briefly contemplated if I could get off a couple of bullets before Dornan could stop me. He was, after all, blocking my aim.

I swallowed down the need for immediate violence and turned on my heel, my eyes landing directly on the man I most hated. 'Do I amuse you?' I asked softly.

Emilio grinned, wiping some of the ashes off the desk and onto the floor as he held my gaze. 'I've finally driven you mad,' he whispered, the delight – the wonder – clear in his raspy voice.

I stilled. Was he right? 'I was mad when I met you,' I said bitterly, opening the door. 'No sane person would have agreed to *this*.'

CHAPTER EIGHT

DORNAN

Mariana slammed the door so hard, it was a wonder the fucking thing didn't fall off the hinges. He listened to the click of her high heels as they disappeared down the hallway, away from them.

And then he turned and faced his father, and whatever the fuck it was that was on the desk in front of him.

'I should follow her,' Dornan said, his eyes lingering on the closed door.

Emilio slapped the desk, making little pieces of bone bounce in the shockwave of his gesture.

'Sit. Your goon will watch her. If he can move his fat ass fast enough to catch her.'

Dornan sat in the chair across from his father, his fingers itching for a cigarette. Fuck it. Why had he quit smoking again? It was something he'd done just recently, after Mariana had lost the baby. If he wanted to get her pregnant again, he couldn't be going around smoking all the damn time and snorting flake off strippers' tits. He needed to take care of himself so they didn't lose another pregnancy. Somehow, in his mind, this self-enforced penance made it easier to believe that she'd forgive him one day, that they'd have a family of their own. In the wake of his divorce from Celia, marrying Mariana was something he was determined to do.

Fuck it. 'You got any cigarettes?'

Emilio watched his son wordlessly, dragging a packet of expensive-looking Italian cigarettes from his top pocket and sliding them through grimy ash towards his son. Dornan picked up the packet gingerly, shaking off ash before he opened it and withdrew a smoke. Placing it between his teeth, he took the lighter from inside the packet and lit up.

It tasted good. So good. Emilio raised his eyebrows as if to say *What about me?* and Dornan slid the packet back, making sure to avoid the mess Mariana had made on the table.

'She didn't call you,' Emilio said, lighting up his own cigarette. 'I'm surprised. If not you – who?'

Dornan had to think about that for a moment. Who had Mariana called when she'd received a dead child on her doorstep? The thought of her in that moment was horrifying to Dornan. He loved her more than almost anything. He loved her so fiercely, sometimes it scared him. And she hadn't called him when something so monumental had happened.

Dornan knew what his father was doing. Trying to drive a wedge between them, to make him distrust Ana. And even though he knew this on an intellectual level, it was still impossible not to let that question burrow into his head like a fat worm and sit there, in the middle of his brain, burning him. Who had she called?

'Guillermo was already there,' Dornan said dismissively. 'That's what I pay him for. To be with her. Always.'

'Where you'd like to be, no doubt,' Emilio mused. 'Ana's a very beautiful woman, son. Beautiful women have needs. Do you really think it's a wise idea to have a thug like Guillermo living with her? On her couch. In her kitchen. Maybe even in her bed, who knows? You think he's licking that Colombian kitty of hers while you're hard at work, earning the money for your family?'

It took every ounce of self-control that Dornan possessed to keep from flying across the desk and smashing his fists into his father's face, but that self-control unfortunately didn't extend to the visual image Emilio had just implanted into Dornan's mind. Guillermo's fat fucking bald head perched between Mariana's thighs as she moaned and writhed on the bed. Whether it was true or not was completely irrelevant. Just the act of imagining the scene was enough to make Dornan want to go to Ana's apartment and put a bullet between Guillermo's eyes.

He needed to talk about something else before he killed somebody, right now.

They observed each other for a little while, Dornan smoking angrily, Emilio puffing away leisurely, as if the remains of a dead kid weren't right in front of him.

It was Emilio who finally broke the silence.

'You broke procedure when you took this kid to the hospital.' He gestured at the ashes for effect, then tapped his own cigarette ash on the top of the kid's remains, making Dornan's stomach turn violently. It just kept getting worse.

'We should never have been transporting somebody that pregnant in the first place,' Dornan replied, unable to tear his gaze from the spot where Emilio's light-grey cigarette ash had crumbled on top of the darker, sandier remains. He sucked desperately at his own cigarette, knowing that wasn't what he needed, but utterly bereft at the thought of what he did need. He needed some fucking peace. He needed to not be doing this shit anymore. He needed his father to either stop what he was doing, or die, neither of which was likely to happen any time soon. The old bastard would outlive all of them. Of that, he had no doubt.

'That's not your concern,' Emilio replied, waving his hand dismissively. 'Your concern is to get the package from A to B. Your concern is to do what you're told so I don't have the fucking FBI breathing down my neck.'

Dornan baulked. 'The FBI aren't after you because I let some kid live after I shot his mother. The FBI are after you because your fucking business partner double-crossed you to go sun himself in the fucking Bahamas with his new piece of ass and a bunch of our money.'

Emilio's smile had dropped completely. 'Are you quite finished?'

'The mother was dead,' Dornan continued. 'The kid was still worth something. I did what I thought best at the time. Dump the kid, let the hospital do their thing, and then go in and get the kid back once we knew it was viable.' It was a lie, but one he'd had plenty of time to construct. 'I didn't know I was about to get fuckin' shot, did I?'

'The kid would have been fine,' Emilio replied. 'You should have called me.'

Dornan itched to get up and leave, get away from the oppressive stare his father was beaming down on his face like twin fucking laser beams that were burning holes in his skin.

'The kid didn't look right. He would have died. I made an executive decision. That *kid* was worth a lot of money.'

Emilio brushed some of the ash away from where he'd been resting his clasped hands. 'Come on, son. We both know you didn't take pity on that child because of money.'

Dornan didn't respond. Of course he hadn't. He'd taken the kid to a hospital because he wasn't about to kill an innocent fucking baby that had just been born.

At least, not purposely. An image swam in his vision – Mariana's pale face as she sat on a hospital stretcher, her accusing eyes, the blood that still stained her thighs. He'd accidentally killed his own unborn baby, so why not somebody else's?

Emilio let his previous words hang in the air for an excruciating moment before he cleared his throat, pressing on again. 'Here's what I think happened,' he said. 'I think your pretty little whore batted her eyelashes at you – and, son, they're powerful fucking eyelashes, I get it – and you handed her your dick, and you let her wrap her fingers right around the shaft and *lead you astray*.'

'You're wrong,' Dornan snapped. 'That bullet fucked things up.'

Emilio raised his eyebrows at the sudden rise in Dornan's voice. 'Speaking of that bullet. Any ideas on who fired it?'

'No,' Dornan said warily, 'but I'm betting you have some.'

Emilio opened the drawer in his desk, pulled out a specimen jar, and slid it across the dark mahogany surface to his son.

'Somebody wanted you dead, my boy.'

My boy. His father hadn't said that since Dornan had been an actual little boy. When his brother had still been around. Before he was gunned down in front of their house and Dornan had been left all alone with an unhinged mother and a megalomaniac for a father.

Something about those two words hurt more than that damn bullet had.

Dornan picked up the small jar, marvelling at the piece of twisted metal within. It no longer resembled a bullet. It had punctured his chest cavity and exploded inside him, blooming fatal shards of metal that shredded his insides like ribbons. It was ironic that something that started out smooth and oval-shaped spread into something that looked eerily flower-like when it pierced flesh. This had been *inside* him. Dornan's chest ached as he remembered the shot, out of nowhere. He'd been so confused, the pain not beginning right away. It had felt more like somebody had punched him square in the middle of his chest, like some kind of pressure had exploded inside him. He remembered the broken glass all around his face, in slow motion. The rain, as it battered them inside the car.

He remembered Mariana, her small hands pressing over his bloody chest as she tried to stop the bleeding. He remembered voices, even after he'd lost the ability to keep his eyes open and he'd tasted his own blood bubbling up in his mouth, drowning him from the inside. He'd been too far away to understand what the voices were saying.

He remembered a second gunshot. Mariana had shot somebody, or at least, she'd shot at somebody. The memory jerked him out of his daydream with a violence that was as unsettling as it was fierce. Fuck. Mariana had shot at somebody? He'd never remembered that before.

Did she know who had tried to kill him?

No, it couldn't be possible. She'd told him, in the hospital, that she had driven him to the hospital as soon as she'd managed to move him out of the driver's seat of his truck. That John and Viper and some of the other brothers had met them there, taken care of the surveillance footage.

He had almost died – half an inch to the right and the bullet would have hit his heart – but he hadn't died, and *did she know who had shot him*?

'I want you to take care of that little bitch for me.' Emilio's words roused Dornan from his macabre reliving of his near-death experience. He pushed those thoughts away, struggling to focus.

'You want me to kill her?' Dornan asked, confused. 'The best money launderer we've ever had? Because she didn't like that you delivered a dead baby to her doorstep?'

Emilio laughed, grinding his cigarette butt into the pile of ash on the desk in such a casual manner, it made Dornan cringe.

'I don't want you to kill her,' Emilio replied. 'She's far too valuable to me. She may be fiery, but she's a good girl with my money. Such a good girl.' Emilio's smile bared his teeth in a way that was entirely unsettling to Dornan. He'd always been afraid of his father, especially when Mariana was involved.

'Well?' Dornan pressed.

'I want you to marry that little bitch,' Emilio said, staring at Dornan until he wanted to squirm. 'Fuck her. All day and all night, you fuck her. Get her pregnant again. I want that cunt barefoot and compliant, you hear me? The FBI is breathing down my fucking neck, and the last thing I need is for them to cherry-pick your little whore out of our organisation and turn her against us.'

Dornan got lost somewhere between the words 'barefoot' and 'whore', but he got the general gist of what his father intended. It was shocking. It was oddly exciting. Still, Dornan didn't want to just act like he was excited at the prospect of trapping the woman he loved so that she could truly, irrevocably, never leave, by sealing their fate together with a child he could use as leverage. That would be wrong.

It sounded like a great fucking idea, though. Now that Celia was gone, he'd fuck Mariana until his dick was raw, come inside her until he was empty, and have so many babies with her she'd never even think to leave his side.

Dornan cleared his throat, shooting for an expression of amusement.

'You think sticking a ring on her finger and knocking her up will make her less likely to turn on us? It's been ten years. If she were a traitor, she would have gone by now.'

Emilio steepled his fingers in front of him. 'Are you saying you don't want to *finally* marry the woman you've been pining over like a pathetic fucking dog for the better part of the last decade?'

'No–'

'You're saying you don't want to kick that Mexican schmuck out of that apartment – your apartment, don't forget – and move in there with her? Don't you want to control her, son?'

'I do control her,' Dornan replied, perhaps a little too defensively. 'I know where she goes. I know her every move. Marrying her wouldn't change that.'

'You know her every move, huh? You know where she got a cremation, last-minute this morning?' Emilio picked up a handful of the ashes and let them spill through his open fingers, back onto the desk. 'Because I'm pretty fucking sure she didn't just burn this kid in a fireplace.'

Dornan's heart sank at that thought. Why hadn't she called him this morning? He would have helped her take care of the kid. But maybe that was the whole point. His father had done it, so indirectly it was Dornan's fault, because he refused to forsake Emilio. And by cutting Dornan out of the equation completely, Mariana was making sure he knew that she would not tolerate Il Sangue's bullshit forever. She had never been totally complicit, one of the many reasons Dornan loved her so much, but she had never been this defiant. Reckless, even.

'She was in my car when I dropped off the mother's body that night,' Dornan said. He sounded a hell of a lot more self-assured than he felt. 'Before this fucking bullet happened.'

Emilio seemed curious. 'She ride along with you a lot?'

Dornan knew what he was really asking. Emilio was asking how much Mariana had witnessed. How much the FBI could potentially get out of her.

'Never. This was different.'

'How so?'

'Nothing. It was … Nothing. I took her with me. It was a mistake. It won't happen again.'

Emilio rattled off some more instructions, but all Dornan could think about was that fucking cellphone he'd found hidden in Mariana's kitchen all those months ago, and whether she'd betrayed him already. He stared at the tiny, blossomed bullet that had once lived inside him for a brief spell, and a wave of pain touched his chest sharply, suspicion and regret all wound up in one imaginary stab to the heart.

'Son,' Emilio said sharply. Dornan raised his eyes from the bullet to meet his father's gaze – cold, almost reptilian. He'd always been terrified of the man. Dornan Ross loved his mother, but *love* was not an emotion he'd ever associated with the man who gave him life.

'Has she said or done anything to make you believe she could be involved with Agent Murphy's disappearance? Think, son. Cast your mind back. It's been a long time since that girl made her way to us. And Christopher always had a certain obsession with our Mariana, didn't he?'

Dornan nodded. 'Yeah. You could say that.'

Emilio brushed his palms off. 'Think. And think some more. You can love somebody and still find the weak spots in their armour. You understand?'

'Yeah.'

Emilio slammed his open palm on the table, making Dornan blink. 'You're not getting it, boy.' It was funny being called a boy at forty-odd years of age, but damn if it didn't make him feel like he was seven again.

'I'm not asking you if you want her to be a part of this. I know you don't. I don't, either. Because if your little girlfriend is in on this – if she's planning something with my fucking money – I go to prison.' He pointed at himself, jabbing a finger into his own chest as his face flushed with anger. 'You go to prison,' a jab at the air in front of Dornan, 'and the house of cards burns to the ground. You'll last a day in prison before Sinaloa, or Medellin, or hell, the fucking FBI kill you to shut you up. Think of your *sons*. Think of your *club*. Do not think of her and how well she sucks your cock. Am. I. Clear.'

Dornan nodded. 'Crystal.'

'Right,' Emilio said, apparently satisfied. 'Let me ask you again. Do you think there is *any* chance Mariana is in on Murphy's disappearance? Do you think she's been talking to the FBI behind our backs? I will not act until I have proof, out of respect for you and only because of you.'

Dornan laughed. 'You expect me to believe that?'

Emilio ran his tongue over his teeth, fiddling with his deep crimson tie. 'You are my only son. I'm not getting any younger. All of this will be yours soon, and you'll have to decide who you can trust to love your sons.'

A flash of Jason and Juliette came to him then. The girl he'd helped raise as if she were his own, and the boy who really was his own, but he'd never known existed. Of all his children, he thought of them, his son and John's daughter, falling in love, and the thought gave him a small amount of comfort. At least out of the seven sons he had, he could trust one of their girlfriends. Even with the way he and John had grown distant over the years, he still thought of Juliette as one of his own.

'You didn't trust Celia,' Dornan said wryly, referring to his ex-wife, freshly divorced and back in New York now with her family on an extended 'trip'.

'You didn't love Celia,' Emilio replied. 'You love Mariana. Love is the thing that messes everything else up. Love makes us blind. Love makes us foolish.'

You got that right, Dornan thought.

'One last time. Do you think Mariana has been compromised?'

Everything inside Dornan wanted to scream no. But he remembered the cellphone he'd found hidden in a bag of flour in Mariana's kitchen cupboard, smeared with blood. How enraged he'd been at the fact she'd hidden it from him. Who had she been calling? Why didn't she want him to know? He'd been in such denial that she could betray him, he'd never looked at the spot in her kitchen again to see if the phone was still hidden in there. He'd never checked the outgoing calls. Never tried to trace the phone back to a supplier, or a call list, or even asked her about it.

Because the moment he'd been about to ask her was the moment he'd instead lashed out with his fists, beat her until she was knocked out on the floor, and then he'd gotten the call that she'd lost their baby.

The secret phone had been relegated to an uncertain fate. He hadn't wanted to deal with it. If it were bad? He'd kill her. He'd wrap his hands around her neck and fucking kill her. He'd watch the life drain out of her face, squeeze harder as she choked and begged silently for him to stop.

It was a fact that if she'd betrayed him by fucking somebody else, or by feeding information to the FBI, or by funnelling money to Murphy – he would destroy her.

But if Dornan destroyed Mariana, then he'd be all alone. So he didn't ask about the phone.

Now, though, now it was time to get some fucking answers.

'I don't think she's been compromised, no,' Dornan said to his father, choosing his words carefully.

Emilio nodded. 'Thinking is one thing. I want you to know one hundred and ten per cent, son. Will you do that for me?'

'Yes,' Dornan replied, his chest feeling like someone had parked a truck on top of it.

'Tell me if you can't,' Emilio persisted. 'Right now. There's no shame in honesty, my boy. If you can't do this – beat the answers out of her, if you have to, violence goes a long way in drawing out the truth from a woman – then I'll step in and I'll be the bad person.'

'No,' Dornan said quickly, imagining all of the horrible torture devices he'd seen his father employ in the past. He'd once seen Emilio hammer nails into a woman's forehead while she was fully conscious, in an effort to torture the truth out of her. No. Emilio could not have his twisted way with Mariana.

'Give me a couple of days,' Dornan said, standing quickly. 'I'll prove she's not a threat.'

'How's the sex?' Emilio asked suddenly.

'What?'

'The sex. She still a little whore for you in the bedroom? Because if she's not, she's getting it from somewhere else. Question is – is she getting it from our friend Murphy?'

Dornan just blinked at that question. He imagined Murphy's stupid grin as Mariana bobbed in his lap. No. He'd kill them. He'd slaughter the pair of them.

'She has never betrayed this family,' Dornan said defiantly. 'She's loyal. Always has been.'

But the phone, his mind urged. *Why does she need a secret burner phone? Is it to call Murphy? Is it?*

Is she in with the FBI?

Has she been tainted?

Is Mariana a fucking snitch?

'Loyalty doesn't always last, son,' Emilio added, on a more serious note. 'They might be loyal at the beginning, but it doesn't mean they'll be loyal until the end. Beat a dog and that dog will bite you, given the chance.'

He took the vial containing the bullet between his thumb and forefinger and held it up for Dornan. 'Beat a woman like Mariana, kill her unborn child, and who knows what she'll do to make you pay?'

Emilio grinned, flesh pulled back over pointed teeth as he shook the bullet in the vial for effect. *He's a sadistic fuck*, Dornan mused to himself. And then he thought, *but so am I.*

CHAPTER NINE

LINDSAY

Somewhere close by, another man was studying another bullet. But the body that had held this bullet hadn't survived the impact. Allie Baxter's cold, dead corpse lay naked on a metal gurney, the flesh around her hairline slipping from her scalp as the medical examiner sawed off the top of her skull.

After dropping his suitcase back at his apartment in Silver Lake, changing into a fresh shirt and making the obligatory pre-autopsy stop for coffee, Lindsay had walked into the deserted LA County Department of Medical Examiner-Coroner. For such a long name, the place was depressingly simple – it was the place where dead people kicked around, for a brief period of time, where they were sliced and sawed and sewn back together, before they were either reduced to ash or interred in the ground, or sometimes both.

From the outside, the building itself was quite beautiful – old, rendered with limestones and reds, not quite Spanish architecture, but close. It annoyed him that he couldn't place the name for such a building. Lindsay Price liked to think he knew a little of everything.

It was after hours, and he'd had to be buzzed in. A guy dressed in janitorial garb led him through a maze of corridors, down a tiny elevator, and into the partially submerged basement that housed the city's morgue.

Not all bodies came here, of course. Just the suspicious deaths. There were already too many suspect deaths for the building to accommodate, and large refrigerated shipping containers sat in the parking lot out back, housing the overflow in neatly stacked shelves. Lindsay had spent a lot of time in these walls over his career, and he was always glad to leave.

It was going to be a long night.

The janitor guy pointed to a small room and Lindsay grimaced internally. He'd been in this room only once before – a shady guy, small-time drug-dealing type, had died in his apartment and nobody had noticed the stench of decay for months. It was only when the neighbours started hearing strange noises – what turned out to be swarms of blowflies battering the windows, trapped – that the police knocked his door down and discovered the guy face down at the dinner table, gun still beside his head, as his flesh broke away from his face and started to puddle on the table in front of him, like rancid candle wax. This particular room had been installed with a sophisticated ventilation system meant to draw out gases and odours, but some deaths just insisted on overpowering all your senses, no matter how well the fans extracted the rotten air.

Lindsay had never been able to forget that guy, but he had a feeling this was going to be much worse.

As if on cue, the door opened an inch and a gloved hand came out.

'Detective,' a female voice called out. 'You want to see this?'

Not really, Lindsay thought, steeling himself as he entered the small autopsy suite. He almost gagged when the taste of rotten flesh stuck to his tongue like glue. A smell so bad you could actually taste it in the air. Lindsay mentally calculated how many years until he could retire.

'Here,' Kathryn said, handing him a surgical mask. It was lined with scented cotton, unlike regular masks, the eucalyptus smell masking about three per cent of the stench that filled the room like poison. Kathryn was good about things like that. Some other medical examiners were known for their penchant for making cops throw up.

'Coffee's outside,' Lindsay volunteered. 'Extra hot, extra cream.'

Kathryn nodded, not wasting any time as she began cutting a Y-shaped incision into Allie's bare chest. The image of the crab came into Lindsay's mind again, and he wondered if it was still burrowed into her hair.

'Any idea on cause of death?' Lindsay asked. Kathryn nodded, lifting her scalpel long enough to gesture to a small vial on the counter behind Lindsay. He turned, grateful to put space between himself and the body, and picked up the small evidence jar carefully.

'Somebody shot her?' Lindsay asked.

'At that angle, she didn't shoot herself,' Kathryn replied, resuming her incisions. 'The decomp's too advanced for me to tell if she was still alive when she was put in the river, but the bullet was in one of her lungs. So either she drowned in her own blood from being shot, or she drowned shortly afterwards in the water.'

Lindsay nodded. 'You mind if I call one of my guys in ballistics, get an early report on this bullet?'

Kathryn nodded. 'Go for it. Miss Baxter and I need some girl time to bond, see if I can't get any more secrets out of her.'

Kathryn powered up a Stryker saw and brought it down to Allie's skull. Lindsay's shock was still fresh. Whenever he'd imagined that skull over the past months, he'd always imagined it lying on a beach somewhere tropical, its owner grinning smugly as she sipped from a cocktail and leaned back on her hand. He'd seen the money in her bank account, watched as withdrawals were made over and over again. He'd genuinely believed that she was alive and sticking the middle finger to every law enforcement agency that existed as she lived on her drug cartel money with her equally corrupt partner.

Lindsay swallowed thickly, adjusting his plastic goggles as bits of skin and skull made a sheen of dust in front of Kathryn's intensely focused face.

This part was always the *worst*.

He had to wait, staring at the wall, as Kathryn cut the top of Allie's skull clean off. How somebody could do that to another human being – even a dead one – was beyond him. Lindsay could reach into a person's past, into the darkest recesses of their mind, and figure out what they'd done. But he couldn't reach inside their bodies and figure out how they'd met their maker.

After what seemed like an eternity, the loud whining noise stopped. Kathryn placed the saw on the bench beside her and used two hands to gently wiggle the top of Allie's skull free. That was the moment Lindsay decided he had about three minutes in him before he needed to puke.

Lindsay made a face under his mask, pocketing the vial that held his precious bullet of evidence. He stripped his gloves off, trying not to look directly at the hideously decomposed brain Kathryn was lifting out of Allie's open skull. *Now. Got to leave, right the fuck now.* The worst part of leaving this room was knowing his clothes would still smell like death long after he'd left the building. He should have thought ahead and changed into a less expensive suit.

'Next time, don't wear your Armani,' Kathryn said, apparently reading his mind.

'I'll call you from the lab,' Lindsay replied, swallowing back coffee and stomach acid. 'Have fun.'

Kathryn snickered.

Lindsay was about to high-tail it when he noticed the two cups of coffee sitting on a filing cabinet in the hallway, probably stone cold by now.

'Your coffee's going cold out here,' he called through the remaining crack in the door.

'It always does,' Kathryn replied. 'You enjoy yours.'

He wouldn't; he left it where it sat, a sacrificial lamb left on a filing cabinet altar. He rushed outside, taking the stairs two at a time, and just made it to the bottom and outside before he heaved his stomach up, all over a rose bush that was thriving despite the dry Los Angeles climate.

***

Back at the Bureau's main office downtown, Lindsay lucked out. It was late, but a ballistics tech was still kicking around the lab, blasting some pop shit at a volume that made Lindsay want to jump out of a window, or smash the computer it was coming from, all distorted and tinny. Nobody appreciated quality these days. They didn't even buy their music, just downloaded it from torrent websites, and they were the fucking FBI.

Nothing was the way it used to be. Lindsay was only forty, but he felt old. Worn out. Twenty years in the force kind of had that effect.

'Hey,' Lindsay called from the doorway of the laboratory. He didn't want to walk in unheard and spook the lab tech – this was a room full of guns and bullets, for Christ's sake – but the dude working at his computer was totally oblivious.

Lindsay rolled his eyes, marched in and slammed the specimen jar on the desk so hard the whole thing rattled.

The guy jumped so high, Lindsay was surprised his head didn't hit the fucking ceiling.

Lindsay blinked, his patience fraying, as the lab tech scrambled for the mute button.

'I need a bullet run.'

The guy started typing, barely glancing at Lindsay. 'I'm off the clock in five,' he said. 'I've got a booking at Romera's. Leave it with me and I'll add it to the pile.'

Lindsay ran his tongue over his teeth, tasting the faint remnants of coffee and vomit. No. He would not add it to the pile.

'A cop was killed. She washed up in Long Beach this morning. This bullet's the only thing we have. I guess Romera's is gonna have to wait.'

The tech paled, his eyes meeting Lindsay's as he held out his palm. Lindsay smiled congenially, smacking the jar into his hand.

'Give me thirty minutes,' the tech said.

Lindsay nodded. 'I'll be back in ten.'

Time enough to get coffee from the Starbucks down on Westwood and drive around in the peace that one could only enjoy in downtown LA in the quiet of the night. He drove as he sipped his Americano, all the while theorising how Alexandra Baxter had met her death. He was betting on a certain DEA agent called Christopher Murphy, who hadn't been seen or heard from in the same time that Allie had been missing. Had he killed her? Dumped her body and fled, keeping their shared steals to himself?

Or was it just a matter of time before his body washed up, a matching bullet hole for a crab to burrow into and make a home?

***

Fifteen minutes later, Lindsay was carrying two cups of coffee back to the lab. He'd decided to be nicer to the lab tech, in hopes that it'd speed up the process. At first, when he walked in, the lab was empty, and Lindsay almost threw his second cup of coffee at the fucking wall. That bastard had left? Gone to keep his dinner reservation?

No. He hurried back into the lab a few moments after Lindsay, skittish and almost excited. He was waving around a printout that looked like a series of lines and going on about striations and barrels.

'Here,' Lindsay interrupted, handing him coffee.

'Is it black?' the guy asked breathlessly. 'I'm vegan.'

He frowned. 'Romera's is a steakhouse.'

The guy tore the lid off the coffee – which was black and steaming hot, luckily for him, the *vegan steakhouse frequenter* – and started pouring sugar packets into the brew. 'My girlfriend likes to eat dead animals. I see enough dead people to never eat meat again.'

Lindsay thought of Allie's skull. 'Fair call.'

The lab tech handed Lindsay a piece of paper with those irregular lines again.

'You want the good news or the bad news?'

'Just start talking.' *Before I throttle you.*

'See these striations? They're rare.'

Lindsay's ears pricked up. 'How rare?'

The guy grinned. 'Only four hundred and twenty of this model were ever made with the extended barrel.'

It was like fucking Christmas.

Lindsay almost forgot to ask. 'What's the bad news?'

'They're made in Italy. There's only ever been a few recorded in the United States. Course, doesn't mean it didn't come here illegally.'

Like Christmas and a blowjob all at once. He knew a man who favoured Italian weaponry. His name was Emilio Ross. Could it really be that easy?

Il Sangue. *Of course.* The very people who'd no doubt been depositing money into Allie's bank account.

A quiet sense of excitement began to build in Lindsay's chest; the thrill of the chase in these cases was addictive. It was what he lived on. It was the thing that kept him going through the long nights and the harsh realities and the midnight autopsies.

Having someone to chase.

'What does the gun look like?' he asked, almost breathless.

The tech clicked around a few more pages and pulled up a picture that made Lindsay's dick want to go hard.

The bullet striations. A rare handgun with a wooden inlaid grip. The Il Sangue Cartel.

Lindsay Price knew exactly where he'd seen a gun like that before. In a gym locker in Santa Monica.

Seemed a visit to Mariana Rodriguez was long overdue.

CHAPTER TEN
MARIANA

'You ever think about leaving?' I asked Guillermo, as we sped down the freeway some twenty minutes later, headed back to the apartment minus a box of ashes, a funeral procession without a body.

Guillermo reached a hand out without warning, grabbing my upper arm. Not rough, but insistent. *Stop.* I felt his fingers dig into my skin as I squinted against the harsh sunlight, trying to make out his expression.

'These are dangerous times, Ana,' Guillermo said, his expression grave as he watched the road in front of him. 'Dangerous times. He's testing you, don't forget. He wants you to fail. He wants you to run, so he can aim at your back and pull the trigger.'

I nodded, crossing my arms against my chest as I remembered the box of bones and ash. It was sad, how little remained after you burned an infant child to cinders. It was barely enough to fill a box the size of a coffee mug.

'Where's John?' I asked.

'Being the fucking prez, now that he knows you're okay. I had to stop him from coming in and getting himself killed by your beloved.'

I snorted. 'Who, Dornan? He's hardly my beloved anymore. Not after everything he's done.'

He must have heard the violent reality behind my words. 'It was bad, huh? In Colorado?'

I opened my mouth to answer him and a sob came out. Just one. An overflow of emotion, and then I caught it and shoved it back down where it needed to stay. 'He's not the man he used to be,' I said, staring out of the window as Los Angeles passed by in a blur of asphalt, overpasses, and randomly spaced palm trees. 'There's killing someone and there's murdering someone. You know?'

Guillermo nodded, and I suddenly remembered what he had gone to prison for. Killing his wife for betraying him. 'I didn't mean–'

'It's okay,' he said, cutting me off. 'Don't worry about it. I don't.'

'Did you know Stephanie?' I asked him. I thought of her, the woman I had never known except in myth, as the woman Dornan had first loved, and then in death, as I greeted her bloody corpse in a bathtub in Colorado.

I'd never seen Dornan so indifferent in the face of death. When he'd killed the woman in the backseat of his truck, he had cried. Wept as he pulled the trigger and delivered the bullet that ended her life. I'd seen the anguish in his eyes, seen the devastation that engulfed him. Now he seemed almost bored with the fact that he'd just killed someone. And not just anyone. He'd loved her, once. That was the part I found the hardest to accept. He'd loved her, and she'd left, and this was what happened when you left a man like Dornan Ross and never came back.

Eventually, he found you, and then he slaughtered you.

Guillermo nodded. 'I did know her.'

'Do you think she deserved to die?'

He frowned. 'I didn't even know she was alive.'

I thought back to my ill-fated pregnancy. How I'd given myself two choices – get an abortion, or run. I'd wanted that baby. A daughter. I wasn't going to erase her. I was going to *run*. And then, before I could, he killed her while she was still in my womb.

'He killed Stephanie because she took his son. He killed her because she wanted a better life for her child. He beat her until her face was ...' I couldn't even think of an adequate way to describe it. Pulp, maybe. 'Until it was *gone*. It was just a mess. You couldn't even tell who she'd been.'

'She was a pretty girl when I knew her.'

I'm sure she was,' I replied. I remembered Dornan's hands on me after he'd murdered her, the way he held me down and forced himself inside me. It hurt. But him – he *liked* it. He was turned on by my begging. The way I fought him off excited him. That was not the man I'd fallen in love with.

'So you're not going to run, are you?'

Guillermo's eyebrows were raised, the prison tattoos on his neck slick with sweat despite the AC blasting in our faces. His sudden question snapped me out of my macabre rerun of that night in the motel room, when Dornan began his systematic destruction of anything good I'd ever seen in him. The night he'd turned into my nightmare. The night I started to be more afraid of him than I was of his father.

The night my lover became my nightmare.

'No,' I said softly, tucking my long hair behind my ears. As Guillermo drove, I rested my head against the window, my throat thick, my eyes burning behind my dark sunglasses, my black clothes like magnets attracting heat. I felt like I was burning up, but inside I was so cold.

I opened my mouth, my breath hitching in my throat. Closed it again. I didn't want to breathe in the tiny particles of bone dust that had somehow attached themselves to my shirt, to the seat I was sitting on. There was already enough death inside me without swallowing more.

'Don't ever pull a fucking stunt like that again, you hear me?' Guillermo said. 'Don't ever change that code on me.'

'Don't ever change it on *me*,' I shot back. 'You know how long I was stuck in that goddamn apartment before you came along. I refuse to be trapped in there for one more minute of my life.'

Something in my words appeared to get through to him. He sagged a little in his seat. 'Sorry.'

I don't think he'd ever apologised to me in all these years. Suddenly I felt shame at the way I'd effectively trapped him and John inside the apartment.

'Me too,' I muttered.

We drove in silence for a bit. The sun was filtered by the traffic haze that always seemed to hang in Los Angeles. On the freeway at this time of day it was brutal. We sat in a crawling procession of cars, everyone poisoning the air together as we fought each other to get where we needed to be. I'd grown to hate this place. The place that had represented freedom to me as a child growing up in Colombia had inadvertently become my prison cell. I couldn't wait to put my bare feet in the dark soil of the jungle in some lush locale in South America, or maybe it'd be white sand in some tropical paradise. Whatever, it didn't matter, because it would be somewhere other than here.

I dared to consider John's words from earlier. At the time I'd still been too focused on Emilio and the baby to think about what he'd been saying, but now I couldn't stop thinking about it.

'Can we stop at the beach on the way back?' I asked quietly, my throat aching at the sudden exertion. Guillermo looked at me oddly, but he didn't argue. 'Sure,' he grunted. 'Why the fuck not.'

***

It was hot and crowded at the beach, but I found a small stretch of sand that wasn't taken over by towels and kids. I didn't even undress. I kicked off my shoes and walked into the water fully clothed, painfully aware that the remains of an infant child were now on Emilio's desk.

I waded into the water quickly, deeper into the waves, letting my arms float away from my body, fingers outstretched. The waves helped me, dragging me deeper as they pulled back from shore. I cried. I cried for that baby. I cried for my son. I cried for Dornan. Why couldn't he be good for me? Why couldn't he take me away from this? Why, in saving me from Emilio's plans to sell me all those years ago, had he brought me here, to *this*?

I felt like I was losing my mind. I wondered, briefly, how hard it would be to drown myself without Guillermo saving me.

I let myself sink into the water. It felt delicious, like a balm against my skin that burned in the Californian sunshine. My Colombian skin wasn't used to the sun anymore, and though it was still milky brown, it didn't like being outside. A decade of closed rooms and no windows will do that to a person.

The water rushed around me, my long dark hair floating wildly in the waves. I lifted my feet from the sandy ocean floor and let myself float.

Let myself sink.

It was quiet down here. Peaceful. As peaceful as you could get when you'd just waited while a child's body burned to cinders.

I opened my mouth and screamed silently against the safety of the waves. As loud as I could, knowing nobody would ever hear how much sorrow tore at my throat as saltwater rushed into my mouth. It made my eyes sting, but I didn't care. In the silence and the cold, I felt so ... *free*. I imagined opening my lungs and taking in a mouthful of saltwater. Just breathing it in like it was air, until it filled me up. It would hurt, no doubt. My body would try to fight it. My survival instinct would kick in.

Luis. I could never kill myself, knowing my son was alive and waiting for me to come to him in Colombia. Never.

I kicked towards the surface with great reluctance.

I felt Guillermo beside me, and then his strong arm was hooked around my chest and under my own arm, pulling me close. I glanced over, seeing that he'd walked into the water, jeans and all. At least he'd taken his shoes off.

'They say drowning is a peaceful way to go,' he said, a knowing smile on his face as he dragged me closer to shore, his kick strong. I felt like I was a wet blanket. I wasn't even strong enough to pull away and slip beneath the water's surface. I was too much of a coward to even figure out how to drown.

'Sorry, baby,' he said, treading water in front of me, holding my head above the surface by cupping his hand below my chin. 'Today's not your day.'

I nodded dully, looking at a couple of surfers who were paddling past us, giving me strange glances. I suppose I did look a sight, fully dressed and crying my eyes out while I half-heartedly tried to drown myself in Santa Monica Bay.

Guillermo's grip eased, and he stood next to me, the water up to his shoulders. He was pretty much the same height as me, and I let my feet drop to the sandy ocean floor.

'You love him?'

I refocused my gaze on Guillermo as his words pierced my fog. 'Who?'

'Prez. John. You never answered me before. Too busy with your pretty little gun. So tell me. You love him?'

I nodded, shivering. I don't think I'd let myself believe it until that moment. But I did. Oh, how I loved that man. I didn't want to be here, metaphorically and almost literally drowning. I wanted to be with him. I wanted to be tucked underneath his chin as he told me everything was going to be okay. I wanted to be in a car with him, flying down the freeway, breaking the speed limit as we left every single Gypsy Brother and the Il Sangue Cartel for dust, never to be seen again.

'You got shitty luck with men, honey,' Guillermo said, trying to make me smile. 'Shitty, shitty luck. Remind me never to get involved with you, yeah?'

I smiled a watery smile that matched our surroundings.

'I'm tired, Guillermo.'

'I know. Me too.'

I saw the Ferris wheel in the distance, and behind it, my apartment. 'I miss my family.' *I miss my boy.*

We stood in the water, as it gently rocked us from side to side.

'Come on,' Guillermo said, putting a hand on my shoulder. 'We got things to do.'

I nodded, wading to shore with him.

'You gonna call John?' Guillermo asked, as we walked along the sand, headed for the car.

I stopped in my tracks. 'Yes. No. I don't know.'

'He'll pull the trigger, Mariana. *Think*. He'll do something drastic. Kids are sacred to him. Kids are the one thing you don't mess with.'

I swallowed thickly.

'Just make sure you got your shit in a row before you start plotting with him, girl, because he's going to snap, and you'll be the one in the firing line when Emilio comes looking for penance.'

'Hard to keep track of all the lies, isn't it?' He gave me a knowing smile.

I nodded.

CHAPTER ELEVEN

JOHN

John Portland hated lap dances. Despised strip clubs.

It was an odd fact for a man like him. A biker. A president. A criminal. A murderer. And, ironically, a man who ran a strip club. It was funny, he could stare into the eyes of his victim and pull the trigger, cold as ice, but when a woman lowered her ass into his lap, he suddenly burned up like he had a fever. He didn't want hands touching him, clammy hands that had touched everybody else. He didn't even like his wife's hands when they reached out to him.

He liked Mariana's hands, though, and that was a problem. A big fucking problem.

She'd almost gotten herself killed today, and only escaped by some survival instinct she possessed, the thing that had carried her through a decade with the cartel. She should have died a hundred times by now, but she wasn't dead. She was alive. She was beautiful. She was somebody else's.

Dornan Ross was not like John. Dornan very much enjoyed the attention of women, and their clammy hands. He had a decidedly different way of looking at the world, a more fluid appreciation of relationships and monogamy. He could touch a stripper or a whore, stick his dick inside them, snort flake off their tits, and it didn't *mean* anything aside from a good time. If anyone looked at his women sideways, though, he would kill them.

He never used to be like that. John used to like him, trust him. Christ, Dornan was the only one John had trusted with his own baby daughter, fifteen years ago, when he was in prison and Caroline ran away from the screaming newborn who was already a tiny little addict.

Time had worn them both down, two brothers in arms, complete strangers. Now John despised Dornan.

Sometimes, when he was screwing Mariana, he'd fantasise about a world where Dornan Ross did not exist.

His lines had been clearly drawn. But the years and the bodies and the lies wore everyone down in different ways. They were no longer the brothers in arms they'd been as teenagers, setting off on the open road, criss-crossing the country with abandon. They were prisoners of fate now, soldiers of a fortune that they could never have foretold.

Or, perhaps they could have foretold it.

Perhaps they should have.

John had never wanted to be a biker. Fuck! He'd never wanted to kill a man with his bare hands. Had never wanted to be involved in the shit that came with being indebted to a cartel like Il Sangue, carved and sculpted from the ruins of Dornan's father's enemies. John was a simple man and he'd wanted simple things. But once you were in with a man like Emilio Ross – just one time, one job, one task, one loan, one favour – before you'd even finished striking the deal with him, he'd already sucked your soul out of your body and put it in his cabinet with the rest of his trophies. Sometimes he did it literally – displaying a photograph of you with your family, with anyone you loved, under the guise of affection and concern; and sometimes he just told you that he owned your ass from now until the day you died. By his hand, if you fucked up.

And now John did want to die. There was a stripper grinding on him, trying to push one of her fat nipples between his lips. He kept turning his head, trying not to offend her, but in the end he had to stand up and grab her by her shoulders. 'How much do I have to pay you to go away?' he asked, fishing a twenty out of his wallet. The blonde didn't smile, but she plucked the money out of his hand and tottered away on her six-inch stilettos.

John turned his attention to Dornan, who was sitting on a low armchair to his left, seemingly fascinated as another stripper shook a line of white powder onto his cock and then snorted it right off. Dornan caught him looking and it seemed to amuse him. He fisted a hand in the woman's hair and squeezed her cheeks with his other hand. 'You gonna pay for that?' he asked, guiding her mouth to his erection. Dornan stared at John as the woman made a gagging noise.

John wanted a fucking drink. Beer wouldn't cut it, he needed something stronger – like maybe bleach, so he could pour it into his eyes and pretend he'd never seen what he'd just accidentally glimpsed.

'I can see the cogs turning in your head, Johnny boy,' Dornan chuckled. His teeth gleamed in the oscillating light, his grin too big and bold to be anything but artificial. He looked like he wanted to lean over and start eating the girl who was gagging painfully on him, and not in a good way. He looked like a wolf. He looked like his father.

'You celebrating your divorce?' John asked, his fingers itching for a drink. Whiskey, vodka ... anything, Christ. He was the president of the Gypsy Brothers and why wasn't somebody bringing him a fucking drink already?

'Hey!' John barked over his shoulder, towards the bar. 'Two whiskeys. On the rocks.'

He held up two fingers briefly before turning his attention back to Dornan. He focused on his face, not on what was going on in his lap. Because Jesus Christ, *could he not get a room?*

'You must be happy,' John said, choosing his words carefully. 'To be away from Celia.'

Dornan shrugged, accepting the whiskey that a waitress was holding out to him. John did the same, closing his eyes briefly and tipping the amber liquid down his throat, enjoying the delicious burn that took the edge off his frustration, his terror. 'Sure. Yeah. I don't want to talk about Celia right now.'

'What do you want to talk about, brother?'

That word. *Brother*. It sparked something in Dornan's eyes. Something wounded. He stared down at the stripper on his cock and then pushed her away with force. She landed on her ass, hard, but she was too high to be offended. 'Go,' Dornan barked, zipping his jeans as he turned his full attention to John.

'I figured you'd be celebrating with Mariana,' John said, and didn't the shit hit the fucking fan right then.

'Did you have anything to do with the shit she pulled this morning?' Dornan asked.

Get straight to the point, why don't you?

John clenched his teeth, suddenly itching for a cigarette. 'No.'

Dornan held his eyes for a few moments before he seemed satisfied.

'What the fuck is going on, Dee? Kids? A *baby?*'

Dornan took a swig of whiskey and slammed the glass down on a table beside him. 'It wasn't fucking me, okay? You think I'd do something like that?'

John apparently took too long to answer, because Dornan's entire demeanour changed. 'Fuck,' Dornan muttered, looking to the ceiling. He was like a tightly wound coil, about to snap. About to explode.

'You need to do something about your father,' John said in a measured, controlled voice that belied his utter rage. 'Now.'

Dornan gave John a withering stare. 'You might be the prez, big boy, but don't ever think you get to tell me what to do.'

'I'm not telling you as the prez, you fuck, I'm telling you as your friend. Your father murdered a KID.'

Dornan pounded the table with his fist. 'Don't you ever fucking say that. Not here, not anywhere. You hear me? Don't talk about my family.'

'For fuck's sake, how many of these things does Mariana have to deal with before you do something about him?'

Dornan went very still, his eyes far away for a brief second. And for a moment, the aura of anger that surrounded him was gone, replaced by an unsteady silence. 'I'm going to make things right with Ana,' he murmured, spinning his empty glass with two fingers. 'We'll have another baby. I'll marry her. Things will be made right again.'

John felt like he'd been punched in the fucking heart. He would kill Dornan before that happened. Even if it meant he died with him. If anyone was marrying Mariana, it was John.

You have a daughter, John. Calm your shit. Get it together.

It wasn't easy to be calm around a storm like Dornan Ross. He made you see the worst in yourself, like a mirror, held up to expose your dirtiest truths. He was like poison.

'You really think that's gonna fix what's done? You think that'll make up for the shit you've done to her? You think she'll ever forget that the only reason she isn't fat and pregnant right now is because you beat that baby out of her?'

John couldn't take any more. The club suddenly felt too small, like the walls were closing in, squeezing the air out of him. He stood, and that would have been fine, except that Dornan stood too, his face in John's.

'This conversation isn't fucking finished,' Dornan seethed. 'Sit your ass down.'

John held his ground. He even laughed, because it was really this absurd right now. 'You know who you're acting like right now, don't you? I mean, I don't even need to say it.'

They were starting to attract attention from other Gypsy Brothers. Viper, sitting a few feet away with a topless brunette, watched the scene unfold as he pushed the woman away. There was a thick tension in the air.

John didn't need a sixth sense to tell him that something bad was about to happen.

'You should say it,' Dornan said, throwing his empty tumbler at the floor so that it exploded in a mess of glass shards.

'You're acting like your father, Dee. You're acting like you've lost your fucking mind.'

John had been anticipating the swing, yet it still came as a surprise. In twenty-odd years they'd never come to blows. Not once. But as Dornan's fist came at him, John knew with a certainty that lived in his bones that one day very soon, one of them was going to kill the other. It was the only way.

John jerked his head back in time to lessen the blow, but not avoid it completely. Dornan's fist connected with his jaw, and he felt his teeth move in his mouth. It was like poking a sleeping snake. John attacked, a hand on each of Dornan's shoulders as he smashed the hard part of his forehead into his nose. It hurt, but it'd hurt Dornan more. Sure enough, Dee stepped back, blood exploding from his nose as he held a hand to his broken face.

And then Dornan pulled a fucking gun on him.

'Put that away, shithead,' John said, suddenly aware that Dornan was unhinged enough to actually shoot him right now. Goddamn it, why'd he have to open his mouth?

Dornan grinned, blood seeping from his nose and down his chin, staining his teeth a ghoulish red. It gave him the appearance of a vampire, one who'd just been feeding on some poor victim.

Dornan didn't put it away. He stepped into John's space, so their noses were almost touching, and he rammed the barrel of the gun underneath John's chin. It was hard to breathe with a metal gun barrel pressing against your windpipe, but it wouldn't exactly be the first time John had been at gunpoint. It was, however, the first time he'd experienced it at the hands of one of his own men.

John was aware of the crowd gathering around them. Nobody spoke. Over Dornan's shoulder, John saw Viper, an original Gypsy Brother, circling behind as if to offer assistance. John gave him a sharp look that stopped him in his tracks. He didn't need assistance. He would beat down this motherfucker for his transgression all by himself.

'You've lost your fucking mind,' John said to his oldest friend, his voice barely above a whisper. Dornan stared at him, his pupils and irises the same black in the low light of the club. He looked possessed. Demonic. John suspected both were true.

'You gonna shoot me?' John asked, bringing his hand up and tightening it around Dornan's wrist. 'Your oldest friend. The one who would do anything for you. If you shoot me, who would ever have your back?'

'I don't need anyone to have my back,' Dornan seethed. 'I got my back.'

John smacked the gun away, taking Dornan by surprise as he grabbed his throat. He had always been an excellent hand at poker. Maybe he should have played more, gotten a nice stash of cash happening so he could get out of this fucking place.

Hindsight's a cruel bitch.

John tightened his grip around Dornan's neck and drove him into the wall, hard. He heard his skull hit the brick wall with a loud *thwack*, and took the opportunity to bend Dornan's arm until it was almost at breaking point. The gun dropped out of his grip, and John kicked it away, using both hands to grab hold of Dornan's shirt.

'Don't you EVER pull a fucking gun on me!' he roared. Dornan shoved him away, throwing him off balance. He was heavier than John, higher than John, crazier than John. Insanity seemed to breed a strength that normal men could not possess. Dornan kept coming at John, who'd now lost the element of surprise. He charged John, tackling him around his waist as they both slammed to the floor. Dornan straddled John, bloodthirst in his eyes, as he rained blows down on his face.

Nobody was stepping in to stop this, and John understood why. For a club that had always prided itself on being a singular organism, two factions had slowly started to emerge. Without voicing it, people were starting to bleed towards one side or the other. Towards John, or Dornan.

Their club was falling apart at the seams.

Dornan was still hitting John, but the blows were less forceful now that he had him pinned. Almost like Dornan thought John had given up.

'Apologise,' Dornan ground out, his bloody face hovering above John's. 'Now.'

Something old and forgotten was unleashed in John. The part of him he tried to hide. The part that enjoyed blood and violence as much as Dornan did. John lived by a different set of morals than Dornan Ross, but that didn't mean he didn't take great delight in beating down somebody who had it coming. And Dornan had it coming.

This was overdue.

John's adrenaline spiked, and he flipped Dornan easily. The tables were suddenly turned, but John wasn't going to settle for a few punches. No, he wrapped both hands around his best friend's throat and squeezed hard enough that Dornan was actually scared. He heard Dornan's breath get stuck in his throat as he struggled beneath him. Whatever Dornan had been snorting off that stripper's skin might've made him feel invincible for a short sprint, but John was filled with enough rage and contempt for a fucking marathon.

'I will never apologise for telling you the truth,' John said, his teeth about to shatter they were clenched so tight. 'You killed Stephanie. The woman you've been looking for for fifteen fuckin' years! Because you were still in love with her! And you killed her, Dee. Why?

'You tie your own kid up and drug him and dump him in your trunk and leave him there so he pisses himself. He didn't do anything to you. He didn't even know you.'

'Shut up!' Dornan managed, his words barely audible. He started to prise John's fingers from his throat, but John wasn't finished yet. He picked up Dornan's head with very little effort, slamming it back into the ground. Once. Twice. Three times. Dornan stopped fighting.

'You beat the woman you say you love until your baby was dead. You say Juliette's the daughter you never had, but that's not true, is it? You had a daughter. She was alive. And you beat her mother until you killed the baby inside her.'

Dornan snapped. Perhaps he had seen himself in the mirror John was holding up and decided he didn't like what he saw. Whatever it was, he managed to break free of John's grip and then they were on their feet somehow, throwing punch after punch.

John still hadn't gone for his own gun, but it was only a matter of time. Something had to put an end to this shit. As Dornan punched John in the jaw, he staggered back, the fight clearly wearing on him.

'Don't ever fucking talk about Stephanie again,' Dornan said. 'About any of it. Do you understand?'

John used the segue to get down low, to kick his leg out and sweep Dornan's feet from underneath him. He went down hard, making a sound as the air knocked out of him again.

The time for games was over.

John pulled his gun, cocking it as he stepped over Dornan. He planted one foot on either side of Dornan's torso, aiming the gun right between his fucking eyes, and everything in him screamed at him to pull the fucking trigger and end this. Kill the motherfucker, save the girl, and everyone could live happily ever after. Only, it was never going to be that easy. John knew only too well how surrounded he was by people who were firmly in Dornan's allegiance, people who were probably aiming their guns at him right now. Instead of unloading a round of bullets in Dornan like he wanted to, John changed his grip on the gun and brought the butt down straight into his forehead. Dornan's eyes rolled back in his head momentarily, before they refocused on John, the fight completely gone.

'I buried Stephanie!' John roared, spittle landing on Dornan's cheek. 'I will talk about whoever, whenever, because I dug her grave with my bare hands and I fucking buried that poor bitch myself!'

The place was as quiet as the dirt grave John had lowered Stephanie into, back in Colorado. Nobody moved a muscle. Jaws were on the floor and somebody had turned the music off completely. Even the girls who were supposed to be dancing onstage were motionless, their eyes bugging out as they took in the scene unfolding.

Anarchy like this had never existed within the Gypsy Brothers before. The brotherhood was bleeding away in front of everyone, replaced by mistrust and greed. And in Dornan's case, by a darkness so black he couldn't even see his way back to the light.

Selfishly, John wanted to reach through and pull him back. To go back to a time when things were simpler. To know who was a friend and who was an enemy.

But it was too late. He'd seen too much. The blood. The death. It was all just too fucking much.

'Let me tell you what happens if you stay on this road, brother.' John's eyes burned, his throat thick. Dornan had been his only true friend. What had gone so colossally wrong? When? Where? Before Mariana, before any of it, where had their paths diverged so violently?

And then, John understood. An epiphany that lay beneath him, beaten and still. Dornan had been born on this road. Naked, bloody, screaming, a pawn in a game much bigger than him. A chess piece that belonged to Emilio Ross, in blood and in name.

John could run.

Mariana could run.

But Dornan would never be able to run from the thing he came from. The thing that created him. The darkness didn't just exist within him.

He *was* the fucking darkness.

CHAPTER TWELVE

DORNAN

It was quiet as John left. He didn't go without leaving his mark – in this case, spitting his own blood on the floor of the strip club before he smashed the doors open and disappeared.

Dornan stared at the ceiling for a minute. A fleeting moment of peace after he'd just had the shit beaten out of him. He didn't know whether to feel embarrassed that John had at times overpowered him, or victorious that he was still here while John had walked away. As he was lying there, catching his breath, a female face appeared in his vision. The stripper who'd been grinding on him just a few minutes ago was now ashen, her eyes big and alarmed, her tits still shiny from where he'd sucked on them.

How quickly things could go from good to terrible.

'Are you okay, baby?' the stripper asked, reaching a hand down to him as if she were going to pull him up. A waifish thing, all skin and bone and tits, and she was offering to help him up. Dornan would have laughed had the situation not been so dire. As it was, he got to his feet and smacked her hand away. 'Scram,' he said, and she did.

A lot of the club members were in this place. A lot of customers, too, and they'd seen the entire thing. Dornan looked around at the tight faces, the stares, and he laughed.

'Hasn't anyone ever seen a scuffle before? Get back to your fucking drinks!'

And just like that, the place thawed. The music was turned back up, the girls onstage grabbed at the nearest pole and started grinding, and most of the onlookers dispersed to other tables. A few customers left, casting worried glances behind them. They were probably tourists. Regulars didn't usually get their panties in a knot when things got ugly.

Viper approached Dornan carefully, a look of unease on his face. He was a tall skinny thing, with a deadly bite if you messed with him – hence, the name Viper. He was also called Viper because he liked to bite the women he fucked, all over their bodies, but that was an aside.

'What was that?' Viper asked, cool concern masking the worry Dornan could see in his eyes, clear as day. Dornan wiped blood from his nose, leaving a sticky trail of the red stuff up his arm.

'That was John signing his ticket out,' Dornan said, placing his fingers between his lips and whistling, short and shrill. The rest of the Gypsy Brothers who'd witnessed the fight drifted over to him, drinks and women forgotten. There were over a dozen core club members present, and they formed a loose circle around Dornan and Viper.

Dornan looked at each of them, right in the eyes, before he delivered his proclamation.

'He's done.'

The music was loud in the club, the flashing lights bright, but their focus on Dornan was so absolute, he could have whispered and everyone would have understood.

'We have to make it official,' Viper said beside him. 'A vote.'

Dornan nodded. 'We do.'

He let the silence stretch on until it became uncomfortable. He grinned, his teeth still bloody, and for that he was glad. It made him look more commanding to be covered in battle blood.

'I look forward to your votes,' Dornan said finally, again making eye contact with each of the Gypsy Brothers in front of him.

He left before anyone started asking questions. Took himself off to his motorcycle and tried to call Mariana. He was going to need stitches in some of these cuts on his face, a hot shower, and then he was going to need to have his dick sucked.

He called her three times. She didn't answer. Santa Monica was only ten minutes by car at this time of night, faster on a motorcycle, but if she wasn't there Dornan would be pissed.

He tried her one more time. It rang out. Dornan smiled as he thought about who else lived nearby. Somebody who could tend his wounds. Somebody who John loved above all else.

He shoved his cellphone into his jeans pocket and pulled on his helmet, gunning the engine before he roared down Venice Boulevard.

CHAPTER THIRTEEN
JOHN

He drove around in circles after smashing his fists into Dornan's face; windows down, radio blasting. Anything to drown out the blood that roared and pulsed at his temples, in the tips of his fingers, that steady smash of blood around his heart as rage pumped through him, alive and bright red. Red stoplights and red road signs and red gas station signs, Dornan's red blood splashed across John's torn knuckles, the world a haze of John's anger and Dornan's violence. The old Dornan never would have killed Stephanie. The old Dornan would have thrown himself off a roof sooner than laid a hand on a woman, his pregnant mistress at that.

He had changed. Embraced his darkness, gone full circle. He'd pulled away from his father in the early days, resisted his vacuous demands for bloodshed and absolute loyalty – loyalty he had given, bloodshed he had kept to a minimum – but now it seemed Dornan Ross relished the hunt of bloodletting as much as his soulless father.

After driving aimlessly for what seemed like an hour, John pulled in to Redondo Beach and parked on the shoulder of the road. Hands shaking, he took out his cellphone and called home.

He called twice, each time getting the red 'busy' symbol flashing up on the screen. More red.

His daughter was probably still on the phone to that fucking kid, the one she and Mariana seemed obsessed with. Dornan, too, for that matter. Everyone was so concerned for this kid who'd found his poor mother dead in a bathtub full of blood, but nobody seemed to care that John had had to dig her goddamn grave in the dirt behind her house. Nobody seemed to care that he'd had to spend hours wiping down every surface for prints and possible DNA, especially when he was a mechanic and most definitely not a crime scene cleaner.

Then he felt like shit, because of course poor kid. John felt bad for him. He was so young, and he'd just been stolen from the only life he'd ever known. Of course John's sweet daughter was going to try to help him. She was a little naïve when it came to club matters, his Juliette, and he had to wonder if protecting her from the worst of his role as president of the MC had unwittingly sheltered her from being safe in the midst of monsters and killers. The body count around a Sunday church meeting at the Gypsy Brothers clubhouse was in the hundreds. Thousands if you counted all the deaths from the drugs they'd sold over the years. From two guys – himself and Dornan – making some shit up on a road trip on their motorcycles, John could never have imagined that this would end up their fate.

The red tinge started to dissipate a little from John's view of the world, and with that he pulled back onto the road and pointed his car home. He'd have to sneak in, get his face sorted and wash off the bulk of all this blood before Juliette saw and freaked out.

About thirty minutes later, he turned into his driveway, uneasiness pooling in his gut, thick and anxious, as he observed his dark, quiet house. Julz always left a light on for him.

The engine had barely stopped when John was out of the car, his legs burning as he scaled the stairs up to the front door two at a time. He burst into the unlocked door to absolute silence.

'Juliette!' he yelled, checking the kitchen. Empty. Living room – empty. Every room was empty.

Fuck.

She was fifteen. Sometimes she did things like ride her bike to the gas station a couple of blocks away for milk or candy, but she always left a note.

A note. Yes. It'd been dark in the kitchen – had he missed a note from her? John left his daughter's bedroom, sensing movement as he passed his own. He stopped, pivoting and gripping the two sides of the doorframe.

A familiar sight, but one that never ceased to terrify him.

His wife, Caroline, was in the throes of a heroin high. It wasn't hard to tell. She was on her back in the middle of their bed – a bed he hadn't shared with her in months, opting instead to crash on the couch with a gun beside him – and she was laughing. There was something invisible on the ceiling, and it was fucking hilarious.

'Caroline,' he hissed. She didn't flinch. John took a step into the room he'd long since abandoned and was immediately hit by the smell of junkie. It was a unique smell – body odour, but mixed with some kind of sweet scent, sickly, like rotting oranges. Maybe it was Caroline's perfume. He'd never lived with another junkie to compare.

'Hey,' John said, more forcefully this time. He reached out to touch her arm and recoiled when he saw the fresh needle still hanging from the crook of her elbow. Fucking hell. John had no idea where she'd gotten the money for a hit. He didn't want to know. He didn't want to have to imagine his wife doing all manner of terrible things – fucking, stealing, bribing – to get the white powder she so viciously craved. He didn't have to worry about other Gypsy Brothers, who all respected John and had far more desirable options to choose from on the female menu at the clubhouse. But there were plenty of men in Los Angeles who owed John no respect, or Caroline, for that matter. Men who would pay good money to disrespect her. All of these things crossed John's mind as he watched Caroline laugh, her eyes rolling back in her head every so often.

He'd liked to have thought that his next move was unconscious, but it was a very deliberate one. He reached behind his back to the gun tucked snugly into his waistband and pulled it out, resting it against Caroline's forehead. If she felt it, or even knew he was there, she didn't show it. She was too busy focusing on something over his shoulder, something that only existed in her opiate-soaked haze.

He looked at the fit still around her arm, the needle that hadn't quite been emptied still resting in her vein. If he pressed down, would she die? Would it be too much? Or what if he shot her in the head and made it look like she'd shot herself?

The woman whose only service to John Portland in their entire time together had been the child she bore him chose that exact moment to start a high-pitched giggle. It was loud. Frenzied, even. But her eyes weren't laughing. They were vacant. Haunted. He didn't need to put a bullet in her to send her to hell. She was already there.

Taking a deep breath, John put his gun back into his waistband. 'Caroline,' he barked, flicking his wife's forehead with his thumb and middle finger. 'Hey! Where's Juliette?'

Caroline finally seemed to hear him. 'School,' she muttered.

John ground his back teeth in frustration. 'It's fucking night time, Caroline,' he said. 'She's not at fucking school. Did she come see you before she left?'

Of course she would have. She was a good girl. She'd always check with whichever parent was home before she went anywhere.

Caroline sat bolt upright in bed, reaching for John's belt buckle. 'Twenty,' she said. 'Twenty.'

John had the sudden urge to smash his fist into her head so hard she'd be decapitated, but he suppressed that urge, because he wasn't Dornan and he didn't hurt women, even when he thought they well deserved it.

'Dornan,' Caroline said, and the hairs on John's arms stood up.

'Dornan *what*?' John ground out. *Dornan's been giving you twenty dollars to suck his dick?* John highly doubted it, but then he'd also doubted Dornan was capable of cold-blooded murder of a woman he'd once professed to love.

Caroline flopped onto her back again. 'Julie's at Dornan's,' she whispered, and then she passed out cold.

Fuck. Double fuck. Of all the places in the world, the one he least wanted to find his daughter was anywhere near Dornan Ross. John sped the whole short drive to his house. It was only a couple of blocks, but it felt like an eternity.

Take my cunt wife, he mused as he walked up to Dornan's front door and knocked sharply, three sharp raps that shook the door. *Burn my house to the ground. You can have everything of mine, but you cannot have my daughter.*

Or my Mariana, he realised a moment later.

Dornan's oldest son, Chad, answered the door. He opened it without a word, and John noticed his knuckles were raw and bloody. He nodded in greeting, walking past Chad and down the long hallway that demarcated the rooms in Dornan's Spanish-style abode. So many rooms for so many sons – six there had been, and it seemed once you had six, you got one for free. At least that was the way it had gone, with Dornan stumbling upon his unknown son, his seventh progeny, the secret John had kept for sixteen years as he broke his ass sending Stephanie money to keep them from starving and losing their goddamn house, far away from Dornan's lethal lifestyle.

John wondered how long it would be before Dornan figured out that he'd known of this seventh son all along, from the moment he'd personally purchased the pregnancy test and made Stephanie take it in a McDonald's bathroom in West Hollywood. He couldn't remember what the fuck he'd been doing all the way up in Wankville that day – no doubt something to do with drugs or cash or beating somebody up for payments owed – but he did remember how pale Stephanie's face had turned when she handed him the piss stick with two lines in it. And he *did* remember shelling out three hundred bucks in twenties, a greyhound ticket to Colorado purchased with a fake ID, and a promise that he'd help her if she decided not to come back.

Dornan had blamed Stephanie for stealing his son away all those years ago, but if he found out his best friend was the instigator of the entire 'Get the fuck away from the Ross Family' plan, John knew he'd retaliate. Painfully. And Dornan knew Juliette was John's entire existence. He'd give anything, kill anyone, for his only child.

His only child, who right now was applying an ice pack to Dornan's nose as he sat and smoked and drank whiskey at his dining table. He grinned when he saw John, but it wasn't a friendly gesture so much as a warning.

'Juliette,' John said, aiming for casual yet loving father, but ending up sounding strangled. She turned sharply, her face drawn, concern etched in her features.

'Hey, Dad. I'm just helping Uncle Dornan.'

John nodded, circling the pair as he moved closer. No sudden moves. What to say? He could blame their need for a hasty departure on Caroline.

'Sweetheart, that's nice of you, but we have to go,' John said, his eyes never leaving Dornan's.

Dornan smirked, putting his hand on the ice pack and pulling his head back slightly. 'It's okay, darlin',' he said, motioning towards John with a tilt of his chin, 'your daddy seems upset.'

John ignored him. 'Your mother's not good,' he said. 'She's sick. I need to get back to her.'

He noticed, for the first time, the kid sitting on the other side of the room. The refrigerator had been obscuring his presence, and since he hadn't moved a muscle since John had walked in he'd attracted zero attention.

'You been there the whole time?' he asked Jason, who nodded. 'Jesus. This kid here's like a goddamn ninja.'

Juliette glanced at Jase as she dabbed antiseptic ointment onto a piece of gauze and continued to tend to the wounds John had inflicted on Dornan's face. A cut right above his nose looked red and angry; purple shadows were starting to appear under his eyes. It wasn't a pretty sight, but it didn't seem to worry his psychotic brother in arms, who sat still like a kid waiting for their lollipop at the fucking doctor's surgery, getting their shots.

'That's my boy,' Dornan said evenly, glancing at Jase and then back at John. 'Stealthy, like his brothers.' He smiled at Juliette, and it was the first gesture John had seen that seemed genuine. 'You didn't have to do this, sweetheart. You're a good girl. Good to our family.'

Sweetheart. Please.

'Juliette,' John said. Forceful, this time. He'd rather she hated him, as long as she still listened to him. There was no time to play soft cop right now, not when Dornan could reach out and pluck out her eyeballs before John could so much as clear the space between them. Not that Dornan would hurt Juliette. She was like a daughter to him. Had been his daughter, really, for the first few months of her life, until John had been released from prison and was able to get back to the new family he'd unwittingly created when he screwed Caroline in a haze of weed and booze. He didn't really drink anymore, because he sure as shit didn't want to end up making that mistake twice. Having one daughter – one beautiful, smart, perfect daughter – to keep tabs on in a vicious underworld where the things you loved became your weaknesses, was hard enough without adding more to the mix.

'Did I ever tell you the story about when you were born?' Dornan asked Juliette, his eyes all for John.

Juliette looked kind of confused, but she could stay confused. She didn't need to know this asshole was responsible for her survival in her first six months while her mother sold herself for blow and slept in gutters.

'We're going,' John said, stepping forward and tugging Juliette's elbow.

'Dad!' she protested, stumbling a little as she followed him. John turned towards the hallway and the exit it promised, but suddenly he was blocked.

By Jason.

Little bastard.

'Did he hurt you?' Jason asked Juliette, alarm in his eyes.

Juliette shrugged John's hand off, wrapping her arms around herself. 'What?' she asked. 'No. I'm fine. I'll call you later.'

Mercifully, she headed for the front door.

'Move,' he growled, but Jason stayed put. John's eyebrows practically hit the roof. 'Really, kid?' he asked without thinking. 'You don't think that maybe you're barking up the wrong tree if you're worried about violence against women?'

Jason sagged immediately, letting him pass. John felt shitty for delivering such a low blow – the poor kid – but desperate times and all that. By the time he got outside, Juliette was already sitting in the passenger seat, her arms folded tightly across her chest and her eyes shiny with tears. She always got upset if she saw John hurt. It frightened her, and rightly so. She shouldn't have to worry about her parents not making it home. Shouldn't have to be tricked into leaving the house with Dornan, an obvious and cruel move to fuck with John. His heart was torn up at how Juliette was worrying in the seat beside him, yet wouldn't say a word.

John made the quick decision not to go straight home – in his fantasy, Caroline might have more time to miraculously die before they arrived to find her – and instead drove towards Hermosa Beach. It was a little over thirty minutes to get there with no traffic, and thankfully there was none this late at night.

He could tell that Juliette was too cut up to ask where they were going. John said nothing. Eventually, after about fifteen minutes of silence, she cleared her throat.

'Where are we going?' she asked quietly.

'For a father–daughter drive,' John replied. 'Humour your old man.'

'You're not even that old,' Julz said, fiddling with her jacket sleeve. 'I don't know why you always say that.'

He snorted. 'It's all about how old you feel. I feel like I'm about a hundred right now.'

Juliette seemed to digest that. 'It's because you never get any sleep, Daddy,' she said quietly. 'You're always busy worrying about everybody else.'

She was a smart girl. It broke his black heart that she noticed so much.

'Don't worry about me,' John said, making the turn that would take them to Hermosa. It was utterly desolate on the streets of LA tonight. He hadn't seen it this quiet in forever.

'You hungry, kiddo?' he asked. He hadn't taken her shopping for groceries in a week or so, and they were down to pop tarts and long-life milk. Juliette never complained, and John barely remembered to eat these days.

'Starving,' Juliette replied. 'Your face, though.'

John waved his hand dismissively. 'We'll get a booth in back.'

He cleaned his face up as best he could with some water and napkins before he headed into the diner. It was one of those old mom and pop style diners, covered in a layer of grease, and with management who had seen John come in bloody and hungry more than once. He led Julz straight to one of the booths in back – dark, away from the windows.

They ordered quickly: a steak for John, who was still feeling off after the whole fight and only picked at his food, and apple pie with ice cream for Julz. As she was shovelling pie, John set his knife and fork down and tried to formulate a question that wouldn't make her shut down.

'Did you hit Uncle Dornan?' she asked around a mouthful of pie, before he'd even decided what to ask her.

His mouth opened, but no words came out. He wasn't quite sure what to say to that. 'Yeah,' he said, finally. 'I did.'

Juliette nodded. 'He must have deserved it,' she said, taking another bite. 'You only hurt people if they deserve it.'

John scrubbed his palm across his mouth, his brain screaming for words that would divert the attention from what he was. A lowlife fucking criminal.

'Was it because of what happened in Colorado?' she asked softly, not looking him in the eye this time. 'With Jase and his mom?'

John's stomach knotted painfully. 'What do you know about that?' he asked. 'You shouldn't know anything about that.'

Juliette placed her fork on her empty plate and straightened in her side of the booth. 'Jason told me,' she said. 'He needed to tell somebody, Dad.'

She was right. The poor kid did need somebody to confide in. But why did it have to be *his* daughter? Why couldn't it be anyone else?

'You'd think he would be talking to his brothers,' John said tightly, gripping his steak knife so hard he had to set it down. Juliette went quiet.

'What?' John prompted.

'The boys aren't nice to him,' she said to the table.

Jesus. Open a can of worms and watch them wriggle out. 'What do you mean?' John asked tiredly. He couldn't believe he'd disassociated himself from the boy's plight so brutally, but he was just trying to survive here. Dornan's youngest son was a liability. John might've funded his survival for the better part of sixteen years, even as he grew in his mother's womb, but he was terrified at the thought of taking the boy when they left LA. Almost like Dornan would be able to seek out his own blood, his DNA, easier and more swiftly than if the boy was not an issue.

'The boys have always been good to me,' Julz said softly, referring collectively to Dornan's six other sons, who ranged in age from seventeen to twenty-four. 'But they're really scary, Dad. They hung Jason off a bridge by his feet and he says he almost fell.'

'What kind of bridge?' John asked.

'The I-5,' Juliette replied.

'Shit!' John said. 'They hung him over the fu– the goddamn freeway by his feet?'

'Yeah. He could've died, Dad. I wish he could come live with us.'

John made a growling sound under his breath. 'No daughter of mine will ever be living with one of Dornan's sons.'

Juliette settled back in her seat, a wry smile on her lips. 'You won't say that when I marry him,' she said, and John didn't know what to say to that.

CHAPTER FOURTEEN
MARIANA

Dornan had tried to call three times.

Each time, I'd let it go to voicemail, but then I realised that if I didn't call him back and talk to him, he'd damn well show up at the apartment.

I couldn't bear for him to be in the apartment with me. He was still living between two houses, spending most nights with his sons in the house he'd shared with his wife, and even though she'd moved out, I had definitely not moved in. With all of his kids there – he had seven, all boys, a number that still made me cringe – I refused to move into a mad house filled with teenagers and testosterone. And so far, he'd acquiesced. Hadn't packed my stuff up and told me I didn't have a choice. I think, after Stephanie's death, Dornan Ross had decided that walking on eggshells was going to be the way to win me back.

It wasn't, because nothing was going to win me back, but he didn't need to know that.

It was late. Almost midnight. I wasn't even going to attempt to sleep after the day we'd had. Instead, I was sitting on a stool, tucked into the kitchen counter as I smoked cigarette after cigarette, lighting one off another. Beside my hand was a tumbler of vodka and melted ice, a half-empty bottle reminding me it was time to replenish my stocks. It had been full when I'd started a couple of hours earlier. I preferred wine, but wine led to a messy kind of drunk. Vodka was the perfect thing to dull the ache in my skull, while letting me stay in control of myself. The last thing I needed was to start mouthing off to Emilio, or worse. Guillermo and John had both been right. I should have listened to them.

I was going to be severely punished for my reckless show of defiance in Emilio's office. And although I didn't regret doing it, I was so annoyed at myself for having acted so impulsively after almost a decade of careful, measured steps. Things were starting to unravel, fast, and I needed more time. Before we made a run for it. Before I got my boy back. *Luis. Baby. Mama's coming for you.*

With much reluctance, I called Dornan's number. He picked up after the first ring.

'Thought you might be dead,' he said, his annoyance coming loud and clear over the line. It was noisy in the background, music and voices clamouring to be heard.

'The night's still young,' I said, not liking the way my words slurred ever so slightly at the ends. I stared into the bottom of my glass of vodka and had the unbearable urge to scream.

'What's that supposed to mean?' Dornan said sharply. 'Are you okay?'

'I'm fine,' I said, taking a gulp of vodka and enjoying the way it burned on the way down. 'Don't worry. I'm not about to slit my wrists just yet.'

'Don't joke,' Dornan said. 'Why the fuck didn't you call me this morning? I had to find out in a meeting with my father?'

I heard the hurt in his voice and chose to push it aside. He didn't get my sympathy anymore. 'I'm sorry,' I snapped back, pouring more vodka into my glass. 'I wasn't really thinking about your feelings when I was trying to deal with a dead kid delivery in my fucking *kitchen*.'

I heard a female voice, the titter of laughter, a squeal. 'Where are you?' I asked. 'Are you at the clubhouse?'

'Where else would I be?'

His voice sounded ... strange. 'Are you *high*?'

'Are you drunk?' he shot back, the cruelty clear in his deep voice.

'Absolutely,' I answered, unashamed. 'If you can't get drunk on your own birthday, when can you?'

That floated in the air between us for a moment. I heard Dornan make a sound in the back of his throat. 'Fuck. I'm sorry.'

'Don't be,' I replied, watching the untouched cigarette in my hand as it burned down to the filter. 'I'm not in the mood for company right now.'

'Right,' Dornan said. 'Well, I'll see you later.'

He ended the call before I could make a bitchy remark. I knew exactly where he was, and it wasn't the clubhouse. They didn't play stripper music at the Gypsy Brothers HQ. They played death metal and old eighties classics that made me cringe. I'd distinctly heard sexy music in the background, and I knew exactly what it was from. My office was in the back of the club, for Christ's sake. I knew the music playlist by heart.

I wondered if he was cheating on me. If he had his dick in somebody else right this minute.

I decided I didn't care. I was cheating on him, after all. And if some stripper could buy me a few days without having to fuck the man who'd decided raping me and beating our unborn baby to death was the right way to love me? I'd pay her myself.

It was only when I'd set the phone down that I realised it was technically still my birthday. At least for another seven minutes. I texted Guillermo. *Where are you? Bring birthday cake / vodka.* He replied almost immediately. *Sorry, got a situation. Be back in the morning.*

I slumped over the counter, burying my face in my arms. I closed my eyes for a second, my fingers still around the bottom of the vodka bottle. I just needed to rest, just for a few minutes, and then I'd resume my pity party for one.

***

'Ana,' a voice murmured in my ear. I sat bolt upright, one side of my face cold and squished from where it had lain on the countertop.

'Huh?' I said, my voice still thick from sleep and all the vodka I'd just downed. My eyes felt gritty, like I'd just taken a face full of sand.

'John? What are you doing here?'

I looked at him again. In the bright light of the kitchen, he was an apparition. He had a swollen lip, and had he split his forehead open? 'What happened to you?'

He raised his eyebrows. 'More like who.'

My heart sank. 'What happened?'

John shrugged. 'I don't even know,' he said, running his hand through his dirty blond hair. 'Dornan and I ... Ana, we can't save him. He's too far gone.'

'I know that.'

'So what the fuck are we waiting for? Waiting around to die?'

'I don't know, you tell me.'

He looked at the floor. 'When I got home, Juliette was gone. He'd picked her up and taken her back to his place to fix him up. But really, to get at me.'

My stomach roiled at that knowledge. Dornan had taken John's teenage daughter, at night, without asking him, as a warning?

'Is she okay?'

John waved his hand dismissively, but there was hurt in his eyes. Anger. 'I picked her up, took her for a drive. She's at home now, hopefully asleep.'

I exhaled a sigh of relief.

'Come with me,' he said. 'Hawaii. Miami … Fuck, Australia. I know people. Good people who'll help us.'

I looked around my empty apartment. 'Where were you when you were fighting?'

John looked at the floor again.

'I called him,' I said, eyeing off the vodka again. My head felt like it was going to split in half, and my mouth was unbearably dry. 'Dornan told me he was at the clubhouse, but last time I checked, you don't play stripping music there.'

'He was at the strip club,' John confirmed. 'We were supposed to be having a meeting.' He gestured to his face. 'I don't think he liked what I had to say.'

'Was he high? He sounded high.'

John nodded. 'He's developing quite the taste for his daddy's product.'

I scrunched my face up. 'That sounds disgusting.'

John laughed. 'You should have seen him snorting it. It *was* disgusting. That stuff'll make your nose bleed like a goddamn faucet.'

'Like your head?' As if on cue, the split on his forehead was open again, blood streaming down his face. 'Shit,' he muttered, and before I could think to get up and get a towel, he'd taken his T-shirt off and had balled it up, pressing it to his bleeding forehead. I swallowed, my eyes drifting down his chest, past chiselled abs and a smooth, tattooed chest. His jeans were slung low around his narrow waist, and I found myself staring at the top button of his fly, almost like I could use the force to unbutton it from three feet away.

He gave me an odd look, and I tore my gaze away from the clothing I would have liked him to remove, motioning for him to move the T-shirt from his forehead. The cut continued to bleed heavily.

'Let me help you,' I said, hearing my words as they came out a little thicker than normal, muffled by exhaustion and too much alcohol. I was dying for a drink of water, but I needed some steri-strips first. 'Wait there,' I said. 'I've got a first aid kit somewhere around here.'

I rummaged in a few kitchen cabinets, finally finding the kit under the sink. I grabbed it and turned back to John, noticing where his eyes had been – squarely on my ass. It was nice to feel wanted without any strings attached. Nice to feel desired. I tried to push that away, my nipples hard enough to cut glass as I thought of the last time John and I had been together. The way he'd made me cry out beneath him.

Jesus, woman. Get a grip. He'll have bled to death from this cut by the time you get your shit together.

'Sit down,' I said, patting the stool. 'So I can reach better.'

He did, and I got to work, washing my hands with alcohol sanitiser, before setting up my tools – gauze, steri-strips, cotton balls and alcohol solution. The strip club was dirty. If you shone one of those luma-lights down there, it'd light up like a fucking Christmas tree in Times Square, all body fluids and blood from old fights.

'I'm not used to people helping me,' John said, keeping perfectly still as I dabbed the alcohol solution around his cut.

'This is deep, John,' I said, trying to focus but suddenly aware that if I was just a tiny bit closer, I could rub one of my nipples against his lips. Stop. Fix him first, and then figure out a way to screw him without getting killed.

'That's what she said.' That glint in his eye, and I couldn't help but laugh.

'I'm serious. You need stitches.' *I'm serious. Deep sounds exactly like what I'll say when you ask me how I want it.*

'No time for stitches,' he said, waving a hand dismissively. 'Unless you've got a needle and thread?'

'A needle and thread,' I repeated, taking a steri-strip and closing his wound as best I could. 'You'll have a scar on your head the size of Tennessee. I mean, I'll love you anyway, even if you're horribly disfigured.'

'What?' He sucked in a breath, and my chest tightened.

'I was kidding,' I said, pressing another steri-strip to his cut. 'You won't be disfigured. It'll be a little line.'

His hand shot out, fingers wrapping around my wrist and squeezing. 'That's not what I meant.'

Oh.

'You ... love me?' He said the words like they were in another language and he wasn't quite sure how they fit together in a sentence.

I stopped what I was doing, meeting his gaze. 'Of course I love you, you idiot,' I replied. 'You think I'd risk my head for somebody I just kind of thought was okay?'

He smiled, teeth and all, and it was like the sun was beaming directly onto my face. I felt blood rise in my cheeks as we digested that reality together. Had I really never told him that I loved him? Had he never told me? It was just something that I knew, at a cellular level, something that I didn't ever have to question, not after that first night we'd spent together. I loved him as ferociously as I had ever loved anyone.

'You hungry?'

I nodded. I wasn't offended that he hadn't said it back. I wasn't a teenage girl with stars in her eyes. John loved me, whether he said it or not. He'd risked everything for me, more than once. The way he stared at me when he thought I wasn't looking was not the stare of casual affection. He loved me so much, I was afraid when we had to associate with each other in front of other human beings, because couldn't they see how bright we burned for each other?

'Come on. I'm taking you out. He can hardly be suspicious if I take you out for the birthday he forgot.'

I glanced at the clock. It was almost 2 a.m. 'It isn't my birthday anymore.'
John shrugged. 'And?'
'Okay,' I said. 'Give me a minute.'

I changed into a tank top and a skirt that hung loose over my hips. You know, just in case we stopped off on the way. It's not like we were going to fuck in a restaurant.

We went to Denny's, over in Burbank, where nobody would spot us. I was already experiencing the hangover from hell, and I ordered the biggest cup of coffee they had. Strong. Black. When it arrived I dumped my body weight in sugar into it, gave it a stir and mainlined it as quickly as I could.

I had waffles and bacon. John had eggs. 'Next time I'll take you somewhere a little more upmarket,' he said, drinking his coffee.

I shrugged. 'I love diners,' I said, stabbing a piece of waffle with my fork and drizzling maple syrup all over it.

John laughed, his eyebrows raised in that adorable way. 'You love *diners*,' he repeated dubiously.

I winced as I saw the gauze on his forehead redden. 'Don't smile,' I said, gesturing to his wound with my fork. 'In fact, no facial expressions from now on, okay? Or I will take you to the hospital and make you get stitches.'

He arranged his face into a perfect blank stare. 'Yes, ma'am,' he said, dissolving into laughter. I made a disapproving sound in my throat. 'You're opening your wound again, silly. You're gonna bleed all over the place.'

The gauze was steadily getting redder. 'Jesus, he really got you good,' I said. After the words had left my mouth, I winced, realising how stupid they sounded. He'd just brawled with his best friend, my lover, and from the sounds of it, he'd been lucky to walk away.

He didn't take offence, though. He smirked, and that fucking dimple in his cheek was enough to make a woman orgasm just by looking at it. He had that playful twinkle back in his bright blue eyes, almost like the fight with Dornan had woken him up or something. Given him some motivation to make a move.

'You think this is bad?' he said, spinning his coffee cup around and around. 'You should see the other guy.'

I sat back in my side of the booth, raised one eyebrow. 'Oh, yeah?'

'I'm pretty sure his nose is broken,' he said.

I smiled wryly, thinking about how it was about time somebody knocked some sense into Dornan, even as my chest tightened at the thought of him being hurt. Old habits died hard. He'd hurt me so much, I should've been numb to his suffering. And yet I found myself hoping that he was all right. *Did he need me?*

On a practical level, I was also thinking about whether he was at my apartment right now, wondering where I was, waiting for me to patch him up. Then again, he was impatient. If he arrived and I wasn't there, he'd call me. My phone had lain on the table beside my breakfast the entire time, silent.

'You must have been mad,' I said, 'to break his nose.'

John's playful expression dropped away.

'What?' I asked.

'He pulled a gun on me,' he said, making his hand into the shape of a gun and wedging it beneath his chin, his fingertips – the make-believe barrel – pressed into his throat.

'He pulled a gun on you?' I echoed. Suddenly, I wasn't envisioning a testosterone-fuelled fracas, but a full-on vicious cage fight to the death.

'He didn't like some of the things I called him out on,' John said, pressing his fingers to his forehead. They came away red, the gauze pad taped to his skin completely soaked through. A waitress came over, barely glancing at John's wound. For all she knew, he was an extra from one of the nearby studio lots. We were in television city, make-believe land, and our oddness made us blend in, in a way.

John paid the waitress and she took my waffles to box up. I'd barely touched them, too busy talking, but I might want them after a couple of hours' sleep.

'You got a bathroom?' John asked her. The woman looked at him like he was an idiot. She didn't even respond with words, just pointed to a door in the back.

'I'm gonna go get this cleaned up,' he said.

I held up my purse. 'I'll come with you. I brought extra gauze. Since you insist on not getting stitches.'

Luckily there was a staff bathroom and changeroom that nobody seemed to be using. John held the door open for me and then locked it, testing it to make sure it couldn't open. We were good. He leaned down while I took off the old gauze and tried my best to clean the wound again. It was deep, and looked nasty.

'Does it hurt?' I asked him.

He shrugged. 'I've had things hurt a lot more.'

'Like what?'

He licked his lips, put his hands on my waist. 'Like my cock right now.'

Lust dragged through my belly like wildfire and I swear, I *felt* my pupils dilate.

'Oh, yeah? Your cock needs medical attention, too?'

He smirked, pulling me close with a forceful jerk. I could feel his hardness against my belly, and I wanted it all to myself. An empty ache throbbed between my thighs, demanding to be filled.

He brought a finger to my chin, tilting my face up to his. One kiss. That was all it took for my lamb to become a lion.

'Take your fucking panties off before I rip them off.' His eyes burned with desire and I felt my heart skip a beat.

Shit. I was about ready to come just from his words.

I hitched my skirt up, making it a show for him as I hooked my thumbs into the edges of my panties and slid them down my thighs. I was wearing white panties, and there was a clear wet patch on the inside. John saw it as I stepped out of the panties and he made a growling noise in the back of his throat, snatching them from me.

He fell to his knees before me, prising my thighs apart. I had to shuffle my feet wider apart to accommodate him. His tongue touched me, ever so gently, and it took everything inside me not to scream.

'John,' I begged. I wasn't even sure what I was begging for. I just knew that I needed him, desperately. He slid a finger inside me and I tightened around it, involuntary, pulsing with need. A finger wasn't going to be enough. I needed him. Inside me. Now. I squeezed his head, my hands fisted in his hair. Every time his tongue touched me, it was like a fucking inferno lit up inside me. Every time he pulled away, I pressed my hips forward, seeking that wet caress that was threatening to bring me undone in a Denny's bathroom stall. Of all places.

Guess I'd been wrong. Seemed we really were going to fuck in a restaurant bathroom.

When he pulled his face away, I just about crumpled over on myself. I caught a look at myself in the mirror – clumped mascara from the nap I'd taken on the kitchen counter earlier; my cheeks flushed.

'Somebody might catch us,' John said, that teasing glint in his eye.

I held onto his arms, my legs still shaking from the way he'd cruelly taunted me until I was almost coming. 'Let's shoot everyone on that bridge when we come to it,' I said, pulling my tank top down to expose a nipple. I pulled his hair, and he went with it, bringing his mouth to my pebbled nipple and sucking hard enough that pleasure hummed dangerously close to pain.

He pulled his mouth away and picked me up effortlessly, his hands cupping my ass cheeks. 'Wrap your legs around me,' he murmured. I did, breathless with anticipation as he walked me backward to the sink. He dropped me onto the edge, and luckily the thing was built solid enough, because he hitched my skirt up and slammed into me so hard, my head went back into the mirror and left a little crack in the glass. Not enough to draw blood. Not even enough to see stars. But enough that I hoped I'd be driving past this Denny's with Dornan one time, and have to stop off, and come in here to relive this moment, one crack in the mirror and John's hand over my mouth as he made me come so hard, I drew blood along his arm with my fingernails. Especially when he pulled back and with every insistent thrust inside me, he told me he loved me.

I love you. Fuck. *I love you.* Fuck! At one point, I thought his love was going to send me through the wall and into the next room. With my free hand I gripped the edge of the basin, as hot, wet kisses trailed up my neck, one thumb on my clit, making me come so hard I bit down on his shoulder without thinking, and John shuddered forcefully as he came inside me.

I felt bruised inside. I'd be sore for days after that. Some very sick part of me wondered if I'd still feel like this, raw and tender, the next time Dornan put his fingers or his mouth or his cock near me.

I hoped so.

I know, it's not right. I never said I was a good person, did I? Part of me was already looking forward to the bruised places Dornan would touch inside me, the map John had made when he'd fucked the shit out of me, to put it plainly, and that Dornan would never know I was feeling John's touch when he was inside me.

It made me want to fuck again just to feel that rush of illicit love.

***

The drive home took time. John took the scenic route, which meant he drove all around LA. Trying to avoid having to drop me off. I got inspired halfway home and opened the container that held my leftover waffles, dipping my finger into some of the syrup and smearing it all over his cock. I licked it all off as he tried not to crash. I think he liked that. Sure sounded like it, and by the way he was pressing his hips up, his cock bottoming out at the back of my throat, I think I was doing just fine.

'I meant what I said,' I murmured, just as we were rounding the corner to my apartment block, John's maple-syrup-covered dick securely back in his pants and my own panties back on under my skirt. The clock on the dashboard said 3:48 a.m. I was into my first full day of being twenty-nine. So far, it wasn't so bad.

I'd already kissed John goodbye in the parking lot of the diner. This close to home, it'd be foolish to do something so obvious. Emilio haunted these streets. Dornan lived here half the time. And while Guillermo might in theory be accepting of some relationship between me and John, I still didn't want to give him, or anyone else, a reason to tear us apart before we'd even had our chance to get away from them all.

CHAPTER FIFTEEN
MARIANA

I was in the shower when I had my near-death experience. I mean, I almost had a goddamn heart attack. Washing shampoo from my hair, I closed my eyes for the briefest of moments, letting the suds wash down my face until the water ran clear.

When I closed my eyes, I *swear* he wasn't there. But when I opened them again, I jerked back in shock, my ass and palms hitting the cold wall tiles behind me as Dornan stood in my bathroom, watching me like a fucking creeper.

He seemed slightly amused by my *Psycho* victim rendition. All that was missing was the shower curtain to wrap around myself while Norman Bates went to town. My bathroom was all tile and glass, but besides that, I hoped Dornan wasn't in here to murder me.

'Sorry,' he said, a faint smile playing on his lips.

Jesus, John hadn't been wrong. Dornan looked like someone had run him over, thrown the car in reverse, and driven over him again, paying particular attention to his head.

I shut the water off, taking the towel Dornan offered me.

'What the hell happened to you?' I asked, feeling genuine worry for Dornan in the sea of bitterness that was getting higher and more treacherous to navigate with every passing day.

'John happened to me.' He paused for a beat. 'Did you speak to him?'

Well, damn. It wasn't worth lying. I'd only be found out, wouldn't I? And lying about John was going to arouse a whole lot of suspicion. I wondered, briefly, if Dornan could see the cogs turning in my mind the way I sometimes saw them in his.

'He came around asking for a first aid kit,' I replied. 'His head wouldn't stop bleeding.' I drew a line down the middle of my forehead with my index finger. Fucking fuck fuck, it was harder to lie when you hadn't come up with the lie in the first place. Could he tell? Dornan was as sharp as they come, but as I studied his bloodshot eyes, it was pretty clear that there was enough of something bubbling away in his veins to dull his ability to read me.

Dornan watched as I wrapped the towel around my torso, tucking it in tightly. Normally this was the part where he'd rip the towel from me and fuck me up against the wall, but tonight he made no such move. I knew my suspicions had been right. He was getting it somewhere else. So was I, so I didn't exactly judge him, but it was one more nail in our coffin.

My hair hung around my face, soaking wet and straight. I stepped out of the shower, taking the hand that Dornan offered me. It was an odd gesture, almost gentlemanly. And my Dornan was anything but a gentleman.

'And?'

'And ... he said you guys got into an argument,' I continued. Jesus, the circles under my eyes were getting darker. Too much stress. Not enough sleep. The bottle of vodka probably hadn't helped, either. 'He didn't really seem in the mood to talk.'

'And?' Dornan pressed.

Shit, shit, shit!

'I asked him to take me to pick up waffles,' I said. 'I don't feel safe by myself at night, and Guillermo said he was busy. And I wanted birthday waffles.' *And I'm so fucking sick of having to explain my every move to you.* What had once been concern and an overprotective instinct had morphed into an absolute need to control and micro-manage every facet of my life under the guise of making sure nothing bad happened to me. When the plain truth was, Dornan and his father WERE the bad that happened to me.

Dornan went to open his mouth again and without thinking, I pressed a finger to his lips. 'Please,' I said quietly, 'do not say *and* again. It's been a long day. Days. It's a new day now, right? And I'm going to finish my birthday waffles.' The birthday guilt trip was effective, at least. I walked past him, looking back as he stood mute. 'You coming?'

He nodded, his dark eyes hooded, drawn. 'Give me a minute.'

He closed the bathroom door until just a sliver of light could be seen at the sides, and I heard water running. I used the alone time to lose the towel and throw on the first nightgown I could find – something long, beige, and definitely not sexy. It was like a potato sack, only softer. I scooped up my wet hair, piling it into a messy bun on top of my head and using hairpins to keep it there. I padded into the kitchen, barefoot, and what I saw took my breath away, replacing it with something between a hiccup and a sob.

There were candles everywhere. Dozens of them. They smelled like vanilla, the entire kitchen and dining area smothered in candlelight. I felt my chest crack open as I saw the way he'd arranged them. There were flowers in the middle of the table, white lilies. Something turned uneasily inside my stomach – they were death lilies. They were for funerals, not birthdays.

'I'm sorry I wasn't here,' Dornan said at my back, his voice like gravel, even more hoarse than normal. I glanced at his throat, seeing red marks, wondering if they were from John's hands. Funny how hands were so versatile. They could take you to the brink of death, or the brink of orgasm, just with the way you used them. He stepped closer, wrapping his arms around me, and a hard rock rose in my throat, refusing to budge.

I looked up, tears burning my eyes and blurring the room into a garish caricature of candles and stucco ceiling.

He kissed the top of my head, one palm smoothing down the hair at the crown of my skull. Just like my mother used to do when I was a girl, but I wasn't a girl anymore, and my mother was dead. The hard lump in my throat turned into a moan; the threat of tears spilling over became twin tidal waves pouring down my face. It had been less than twenty-four hours since the suitcase baby had been delivered. It played on a loop in my mind, no matter how hard I tried to switch it off. I couldn't even replace the image of the little boy with one of Murphy's face after I'd shot him. It wouldn't go away.

'Hey,' Dornan murmured, one hand coming around to my chin and tilting it so I was looking at him over my shoulder. 'Talk to me. You never talk to me anymore.'

I turned in his arms, resting my face against his chest for a second. His heart thrummed along slowly, evenly. In my mind, I'd already said goodbye to him a long time ago, checked out of the relationship the moment I woke up in the hospital, my pregnancy over, my baby scraped away. I'd gotten used to the idea that Dornan Ross was no longer the great love of my life, but the heart is a fickle thing. My heart still remembered his concerned eyes, his insistent touch, the way he'd always kept me safe. My heart was a goddamn traitor.

What about John? It's possible to love two men at once, you know. I wouldn't be the first woman torn between obligation and desire.

I wanted to take him by the shoulders and shake him. I'd managed to push everything away for months now, to forget the man he used to be, but suddenly I was overcome by the memory of the first time I ever saw him. Sadness engulfed me and my eyes started to fill with fresh tears. I wouldn't blink, didn't want to let them fall down my cheeks and give them to him. They fell, anyway. Gravity is strange like that.

'What happened to us?' I whispered against his neck, just loud enough for him to hear. 'We used to be different.'

A different question. *What have we done to each other? What have I done to you?*

He tucked a stray strand of hair up on top of my head, winding it around a hairpin so it stayed put. 'It's not too late,' he murmured, his hands on my neck, firm, but gentle. 'We can start over. I'll get us a new place. A real house. We can have a baby.'

I turned my head away, covering my mouth with my palm so I didn't cry out. 'We had a baby,' I whispered, my teeth gritted as grief was replaced by rage, my tears falling of their own volition. 'You never hurt me in ten years,' I seethed. 'Why'd you have to hurt me like that when I was carrying our *baby*?' I stepped back and shoved him as hard as I could, barely moving the solid mountain of muscle.

'I'm sorry,' he said, digging his fingers into my hips as he knelt in front of me. He lifted my nightgown, and I tried to push him away, until I realised he wasn't trying anything sexual. He rested his stubbled cheek against the bare flesh beneath my belly button, moving his head back and forth ever so slightly, rubbing against my skin. His fingers dug into the backs of my thighs as he pulled me as close as possible, and I had to steady myself on his shoulders so that I didn't fall.

'Why are you doing this?' I whispered. 'Why now?'

And no, I wasn't perfect, and no, I hadn't even been sure about keeping the baby Dornan and I had conceived unknowingly. But in the end, by his act of violence, he'd taken that choice away. He'd ended a life that was yet to begin. And although he'd said the words, he had yet to show me that he was ever truly sorry. Mostly, I think, he just wanted to forget about it and move on. A dark few days in the evolution of him, of us. In the space of three days, he murdered his son's mother, raped me while her blood was still all over him, and then punched me so hard for questioning him about said murder that our baby died.

Before then, I would have said there was hope for him. For us. We'd walked a dark road, Dornan and I, months and years of violence and suffering and compromise, thanks to our fathers and the choices they'd made.

'Why am I doing what?' he asked me slowly. And truth be told, I didn't even know what I was trying to quantify. What was he doing? Begging for my forgiveness, on his knees, the both of us surrounded with enough flickering candles to wipe out half the apartment building.

He straightened, my thighs aching from where his fingers had been as he towered over me once more. He bent his head down to mine and kissed me, taking me by surprise. He tasted like whiskey and cigarettes. His kiss was soft, almost hesitant. He kissed me like a boy would kiss a girl on prom night, one hand at my waist and the other cupping my chin. It was the sweetest gesture he'd ever made, and something in my chest expanded painfully, a supernova that stretched insistently, ready to shatter me.

How could I feel anything for him?

He broke the kiss, another anomaly, and pulled his head back so we were eye to eye. 'I wish I could take it all back,' he said, his eyes glassy.

Damn him to fucking hell. I had to hate him. I couldn't love him.

My heart was a fickle bitch.

He picked me up like I was weightless, gripping me so tight it was almost painful. I wrapped my legs around his waist, my head burrowed into the space between his shoulder and ear, almost like a child, my breath and his neck creating a warm pocket of air that I stared into vacantly.

He laid me down on my bed, and softness enveloped me. It felt blissful, to sink into downy blankets as hands stroked my face. I was shivering despite the heat, burning up with a fever that no medicine could fix.

Heartsick and confused, as the man who professed to love me the most, for once, touched me with loving hands.

'You remind me of her,' he whispered, his thumb tracing my bottom lip. 'Stephanie. She had a fire inside her, like you. You would have liked her.'

I stared at the ceiling, remembering *Stephanie*, who I'd met only in death. The memory was anything but pleasant.

'You can't say that,' I choked. 'You murdered her. You can't *say* that.'

Dornan's palm wiped the tears away from my cheeks, but more streaked down to take their place. 'Shhhh,' he said. 'It's okay. It's okay.'

I shook my head. 'It's not okay.'

He kissed me. His mouth silenced me, drowned me out. He ground his hardness against my thigh and I remember wondering if I'd go to hell for fucking two men in the space of a few hours. A whore. That's what I'd been labelled as. Might as well enjoy the benefits.

I felt guilt, thick and swirling in my belly, as I pictured John's face. If he saw this, he would kill Dornan. But he was the other man, and he knew it. He had no say, and for that matter, neither did I.

Dornan hitched my nightgown up over my knees, bunching the material around my hips. The air on my stomach and thighs was cold, despite the night heat. I think it was being exposed like this, a gentle caress, a loving touch. Two hands, one on each of my knees, and then I was open, my hips protesting at how wide he'd parted them, his cock heavy as it rested against my pussy. My nipples were hard pearls beneath my thin nightgown, the material deliciously rough as it rubbed against them. I throbbed with desire – I still possessed desire for this man, somehow – and shame blanketed me like fog.

It was so much easier to detach when you were thrown onto a bed and fucked without any tenderness. When you weren't given a chance to say yes or no. When it was mechanical, going through the motions.

Love made things ... complicated.

What would he do if I said I didn't want this?

'Stop,' I said, pushing his hands away. He gave me an odd look, his cock in his palm, the blunt tip glistening with pre-come. We regarded each other silently, my hips arching of their own accord as he slid his free hand up the inside of my thigh and slipped a finger inside me.

'That doesn't feel like stop to me,' he murmured hoarsely, lowering himself, my eyes glued to the bruises blossoming on his neck. John's hands had made fine work of Dornan's flesh, before they'd made fine work of mine.

'Fuck,' Dornan groaned, pushing inside me so tenderly, it was as if he were another person. He'd never been gentle with me, not once in ten years, and I hadn't asked him to be. But something had possessed him. He rocked his hips against mine, slow and soft, his cock stretching the bruised parts of me that John had been anything but *gentle* with when he fucked me against a bathroom sink in a diner not three hours earlier. I cried out when he touched the spaces inside me that John had already punished. It hurt. I liked that it hurt. Above me, moving faster, it was clear that Dornan liked my pain, too.

We'd been together ten years, Dornan and I, and I can safely say that this was the first – and last – time we'd ever made love.

It was tragic. He was trying to start anew, a fresh beginning, and I was opening, yielding my flesh to him one last time to say goodbye to the man who saved me all those years ago.

And neither of us was brave enough to admit what we were doing.

CHAPTER SIXTEEN

DORNAN

The ring had been burning a hole in his pocket since he'd gone home to get it that afternoon. At the same time, one singular thought had burned in his head.

Had the woman he loved turned her loyalties against him?

It had gone something like this: His father had given his macabre version of a blessing to a Dornan-Mariana marriage, as well as a warning about where her allegiances might lie; Dornan had walked out of the meeting, and straight out onto Venice Boulevard. He didn't pass go. He didn't collect two hundred dollars. All he did was get on his motorcycle, speed home and find the ring his grandmother had left to him when she died.

He'd considered asking her properly if she'd marry him, but *what if she said no?*

She hated him for what he'd done. For everything. And he couldn't even blame her, because she was right to hate him. To fear him.

None of that mattered, though. She was his. She would always be his. Since the moment he'd laid eyes on her in that motel room in San Diego, he'd known.

Ten years. She'd be fine. She'd be happy again.

Was she fucking somebody else?

'Pack a bag,' Dornan called into the bedroom.

Mariana appeared in the doorway, wearing nothing except panties and a confused look on her face. Her hair was wild, from where he'd ground her into the bed, and her nipples still glistened from where his mouth had just been.

Dornan groaned, pressing his palms into his eyes. His dick hurt at the thought of fucking her again, yet, of its own accord, it stirred to life once more. She was the only woman in the world capable of killing him via sex. She'd literally suck the life out of him if he wasn't careful. He could fuck her all day, every day, and still the itch would not be scratched away.

'Where are we going?' she asked.

'Can you please put some fucking clothes on,' Dornan asked, squeezing his cock through his jeans. His clothes were already in the trunk of the car that waited for them downstairs – one small bag and a pair of shoes, enough for a quick jaunt out of LA.

Mariana raised one eyebrow, her lips tugging upward in the closest thing he'd seen to a smile in a while. 'I don't think you've ever said that to me before,' she said, leaning against the doorframe that led to the bedroom.

In the hallway, Dornan slipped his boots on, then his leather jacket. His fingers smelled like sex, and that was okay with him. There would be a lot more sex where they were headed.

Was she fucking somebody else?

'Where are we going?' Mariana called from the bedroom. 'I'm kind of tired. Can we just stay here?'

No. They could not just stay here. *Fuck.*

Dornan strode back into the bedroom to see Mariana on her back in the centre of the bed, again, with nothing on except those damn lace panties that left nothing to the imagination. Her legs were parted enough that he could see her pussy through the fine material.

Who else had seen her like this?

Without thinking, he yanked the edge of the comforter up and threw it over her, so she was sandwiched like a burrito.

The post-coital calm disappeared from her face and she sat up on the bed, alarmed. 'What's going on?' she asked. 'Is it bad? Are you taking me to Emilio? He's going to kill me, isn't he? *Motherfucker.*'

The motherfucker didn't seem to be directed at his father specifically; rather, it sounded like Mariana chastising herself, her voice ringing with disbelief.

'Hey.' He touched her thigh; she was shaking. 'Stop.'

'Fuck!' Mariana yelled, hitting the bed with her fists.

Something about her anger made him feel calmer. Almost like a transference. She was terrified, staring down at the comforter like it might offer up an answer to her problems, and he felt soothed by her desperation. Probably because the more desperate she was, the more she had to rely on him to survive.

'I'm just taking you somewhere because I fucked up your birthday.

Okay? Don't ruin the surprise.' He softened his words for her, slowed them right down. Like soothing a child.

Her eyes lifted to meet his. 'Your father sent me a surprise for my birthday. I don't want a fucking surprise.'

Well, shit. 'We're going to Vegas. The Wynn. Room service and champagne. You'll like it.'

Her shoulders fell; she exhaled a breath that she'd been holding in for a while. 'What did Emilio say?' she asked breathlessly.

'About Vegas? Nothing. I didn't tell him.' It was true. Pop could hold the fort down for twenty-four goddamn hours.

'Not about *Vegas*, Dornan. What did he say about what I did?'

He licked his lips. 'Nothing much. I think he's more impressed than mad. But I get the impression if you ever pull that shit again, he'll shoot you in your fucking face. So maybe call me next time you decide to stage a coup.'

Her eyes were like fucking laser beams slicing him to bloody ribbons. 'Maybe tell him the same thing,' she said, and just like that, their connection was broken. She got up off the bed and started opening and slamming cupboards, her tits bouncing as she stomped around the room in her little panties and nothing else.

Who else has seen her like this?

Dornan thought it wise to shut up. He waited patiently until she had ventured into the bathroom, probably to pack make-up or something, and then he took the opportunity to rummage through her closet as quietly as possible. He knew what he was looking for. And when he found it, he smirked. He pulled the dress out, slipped it from its hanger, and rolled it up into a ball, shoving it into her bag underneath the rest of the clothes she'd packed.

'Let's go,' he called into the bathroom.

They were already going to hit traffic, at this rate.

CHAPTER SEVENTEEN
MARIANA

Ten years in America and I'd never set foot in Nevada. Sure, I'd seen it in movies, read about the place, but driving into Sin City in the back of a pimped-out limousine was something entirely different to experience. The place was alive and dying all at once – the towering hotels, the decaying storefronts, the shells of high-rise buildings long since abandoned and waiting for their date with the demolition crew.

It was a place of extremes, more so than Los Angeles could ever be. It made me realise how out of my comfort zone I felt in this foreign city. It was only a five-hour drive, even with the traffic we'd hit on the highway, but it was another universe. The sun had risen while we were driving, or rather, while we were being driven. Dornan spent the majority of the drive on the phone to various club members. Viper called about a shipment of weapons, then Chad called his father to let him know about a deal going down with another club. I caught snippets of each conversation but tried to ignore it for the most part, thankful for the distraction that business afforded Dornan.

And then there was John. He called a few times before Dornan answered. Their conversation was brief and to the point; from the sounds of it, they were going to deal with things like adults and pretend nothing had ever happened. Fucking males and their inability to figure shit out. Not that I particularly cared. After the sex I'd just experienced underneath Dornan's greedy hands, I was feeling exposed. Vulnerable. Memories of the good times had started flooding back to me. I'd never forgive him for the things he did, for the death and destruction he'd brought upon us, but I was starting to feel an aching void inside me that was the space he used to occupy. The darkest recess inside my treacherous heart muscle called out for Dornan Ross to put me back together again, to hold me close, to cradle me safely in his strong arms.

He hadn't been that man in a long time, but then, I hadn't been that girl in years, either.

Driving down the main street in Vegas was ... interesting. I wondered why Dornan had chosen this place, of all places. When I asked him, he shrugged, a hint of something in his eyes. *Don't ruin the surprise*, he kept telling me, and I just prayed that the surprise wasn't my own violent death in a Vegas motel room at eight in the morning.

If I died here, I'd be so fucking pissed, I'd haunt Dornan and his father until their last breath. I made that vow, just as we pulled up in front of a swanky building, its gold mirrored windows reflecting the desert and surrounding buildings with a brilliant sheen.

I found myself marvelling at the change in Dornan; the rough biker carried himself like a businessman going to a high-powered meeting where he would call the shots. He was dressed up more than normal, even though he was still sporting his uniform. But the leather jacket bore no insignia, his hair was neat instead of mussed up by the wind and his helmet, and his black T-shirt looked like it came from an expensive store, hugging his broad chest in all the right places. His dark denim jeans were a slimmer cut than usual, his boots were new, and goddamn it, my lover looked like he'd just entered the WITSEC program for former bikers and drug cartel members. He looked like sex on a stick, his stubble neatly trimmed and sculpted around his chin, his dark eyes flanked by thick eyelashes that most females would be envious of, and the salt-and-pepper at his temples softened his dark brown mop of hair. The one tell-tale sign that he was a criminal was the slight bulge at the spot where the waistband of his jeans gripped his lower back, a gun neatly stashed against his skin, should we encounter any trouble. Oh, and the fact that he had two black eyes and a broken nose. *Thanks, John.*

We didn't need to check in, a private butler whisking us straight from the limo to our room. It was a penthouse suite overlooking Vegas. The city was a mess of contradictions – who the fuck thought it was a good idea to put a city in the middle of a desert, anyway? So many buildings. So many billboards, each screaming about a two-for-one seafood buffet, or a shooting range, when they weren't loudly advertising their respective casino floors. It was overwhelming, suddenly being thrust into the artifice of it all. I hadn't had any time to prep. I didn't even know what the hell I'd packed in my bag, though I suspected it was mostly summer dresses and flip-flops. This was something entirely different. This was about Dornan and Mariana and nobody else.

And yet, when I locked myself in the bathroom to freshen up, I stared at the edge of the basin and remembered John.

This was my first time in Vegas, and it was likely also my last, because I was either about to be killed, or, if I survived this 'surprise trip' and John and I managed to get away, we'd be going a little further afield than the next state over.

When I was done, the image of that Denny's bathroom still visceral and unrelenting in my mind, I headed back out to the suite. It was bigger than my apartment, and looked like something out of a *Vogue Living* magazine. Dornan was standing at the window, his hands folded across his chest as he watched the city stir into action below. For a city that was switched on twenty-four seven, it sure seemed sluggish on a Monday morning. Probably everyone was hungover, or broke, or both.

'What are we really doing here?' I asked, joining him at the full-length window.

He turned to me, his face impossible to read. 'Brunch. You should wear the white dress.'

Oh.

Shit.

How fucking stupid was I? I caught my reaction before my face conveyed it, tamped it down quickly and trapped it.

The *white* dress.

The trip to Vegas.

The last-minute plans.

'Why are we here?' I repeated, my chest a carved-out hollow because I already knew the answer. Dornan didn't answer. He opened my overnight bag and pulled out the white dress, handing it to me with an air of finality.

The dress in one hand, I stared down at Las Vegas Boulevard and wondered, if I ran at the glass hard enough, would it break and let me fall to my bloody death fifty floors below? I handed it back. Dornan laid the dress out on the bed instead, smoothing out the creases.

'Your father would never allow this,' I said, staring at the dress Dornan had arranged. I didn't have my burner phone with me. I couldn't call John. Fuck! I needed to call John.

Right.

Now.

Dornan smirked, standing before me and tugging the hem of my dress. I resisted, holding on to that hem with everything I had. Dornan raised his eyebrows and took hold of my wrists, squeezing them just enough to show his strength.

'Allow what?'

I rolled my eyes, trying to shake his grip off, but he was having none of it. He tightened his fingers around my wrists, and they throbbed in protest.

'A trip to Vegas. A white dress. Look at what you're wearing!'

He shrugged. 'Maybe we're going to have a nice dinner.'

'It's the middle of the morning,' I shot back. My wrists were on fire. There'd be marks on them tonight.

'Maybe we're going to have a nice *brunch*,' Dornan said, his jaw tensed, his demeanour no longer amused. Now he just looked fed up.

'I'm not marrying you,' I said, the words out of my mouth before I could think twice.

He slapped me across the face so hard I tasted blood. My wrists were free, though, and purely on instinct I punched him in the face, as hard as I could.

Right in the nose.

The nose that John had broken the night before. *Teamwork.*

Blood exploded from his face and he stepped back, cupping his hands over his nose. All I could see were his eyes – black, cold, determined. The pain of my blow hadn't angered him, or so it seemed. No, it seemed that the violence had only strengthened his resolve.

He took his hands away and blood dripped onto his shirt, a chilling grin spreading across his face. His nose was bent slightly, and red.

Oh, Jesus. I was going to pay for that.

He came at me like a fucking CIA operative: blunt, fast, effective. He grabbed my hair and yanked, spinning me until I was in his arms. Before I could break free, he had his arms locked around my neck, squeezing against my carotid artery, and within a matter of seconds, the room went black.

**

I woke up on the plush carpeted floor of the limousine we'd travelled in to Vegas. I had no idea how I'd gotten there, or how long I'd been there. I had some drool on my cheek. I wiped it away, craning my head to take in the dimly lit interior of the car.

Dornan sat on the seat above me, his knees wide, his face clean. He held an ice pack against the bridge of his nose, but the damn thing was swelling anyway. There were dark circles under his eyes, and cuts on his skin from the fight with John. He looked terrible.

'It's lucky I brought an extra shirt,' he said, taking the ice pack away from his nose. 'Though we're gonna have to retouch the photos.'

I sat up on my elbows, noticing the white dress now on me. The air-conditioning was cold between my thighs. I felt with one hand – no panties. *Figured*.

'How kind of you to dress me,' I said, dragging myself to my knees and sliding up onto the seat opposite. I was four feet away from Dornan, but if I'd been able to jump out of the limousine, I would have. We weren't moving. I looked out of the window to see a large, garish sign in the shape of an arrow, pointing down at a chapel that was adorned with Elvis.

Could life get any worse? I looked around the car for something sharp that I could use to kill myself. There was nothing sharp, unless you counted Dornan's eyes. I had the sudden urge to crawl over to him and rip those eyes out of their sockets.

Dornan tossed my purse at me. It hit my arm and fell onto the seat beside me.

'Put some fucking make-up on,' he said. 'You look like shit.'

He tossed something else at me. Panties. Black lacy ones. I rolled my eyes, hooking them over my shoes and sliding them up my thighs and over my ass. *Better*. That felt better.

'Why do I need make-up?' I asked, rummaging through my bag. I still had my gun. I pulled it out and pointed it at Dornan's head. I smiled, amused.

'I thought you would have taken this out,' I said, marvelling at the way it felt in my hand. It felt like power.

He grinned, holding out his open hand. Nestled in his palm, six shiny bullets.

I stuffed the useless gun back into my purse and yanked out my make-up bag. I took my sweet time applying foundation and blush.

***

'Why'd you want me to wear make-up, anyway?' I asked Dornan as we approached the counter inside the chapel. 'It's not like anyone's going to see this.'

He smiled a plastic smile, one hand pressed into the small of my back as he drove me towards the tired-looking woman behind the counter that screamed CHEAP WEDDING CEREMONIES.

'Our children will ask to see the photos one day,' he said, his voice steeled, his expression a mask of self-preservation. 'You should look beautiful for them.'

My knees actually buckled when he said that. They just plain stopped working, and the ground rushed up at me. Dornan's big hands were there to keep me steady, of course. He leaned me into him, tucked me into his side so I was pressed against him.

'I'm going to throw up,' I said, scanning the foyer for a bathroom.

'Oh, good,' Dornan replied, half-dragging me towards the sign marked BATHROOMS. 'Maybe you're knocked up again already.'

Fucking bastard. His casual indifference stung. He pushed me into the women's toilets and into the first stall, gathering my long hair up off my face as I dry-retched over the bowl.

'I'm more used to holding your hair when my dick's in your mouth,' he said, and I would have cringed had there not been a steady stream of vomit coming out of my mouth. My stomach roiled again, once, twice. False alarms. I flushed, jerking back from Dornan's grip as I pushed past him and out of the cubicle.

A woman was washing her hands, wearing a wedding dress so enormous it took up most of the square footage in the small area. She looked at Dornan in the mirror, and he stared back until she cast her gaze to the ground.

'You feeling better, honey?' he asked, rubbing my back in mock concern.

I could tell he was mocking me because of the pissy look on his face. I looked at his nose and wanted to punch it again. He glared at the woman and she scurried out of the bathroom, her dress bunching up as she got stuck in the door before she popped out onto the other side like a champagne cork being let free. The door swung shut again and we were alone.

'I'm not marrying you,' I said.

Dornan didn't say anything, just looked at the ceiling. I glanced at his fists. Yeah. He was about to fucking rage.

'Give me one of those bullets,' I said, gesturing to his pants pocket. 'I'll put it right in my head. You won't have to worry about me causing problems anymore.'

I'd put the bullet in him first, but he didn't need to know that, did he?

'That sweet act back at the apartment, what was that?' I was hurting. I felt like he'd stabbed me right in the chest. He'd been soft and tender and I had fallen for it, so desperate to believe that there was still some good in him. I'd been betraying him for months. I was in love with another man. But the way he had been with me – tender – it tore my soul to shreds. He had tricked me. I had fallen for it.

'Do you know where Murphy is?' he asked me, his tone deathly calm. Too calm.

Oh, God. My stomach lurched again as I remembered the taste of Murphy's blood in my mouth, the way he'd bled everywhere. All over me, all over my bed, all over the floor.

Dominoes. We'd piled them up, he and I, and they were starting to fall. One by one, the lies would set us free, even if that freedom meant certain death.

'No,' I replied. 'No, I don't.'

And the truth was, I didn't know. John had handled the burning of his body. And, I assumed, the disposal of whatever had been left over. Gravel and ash. Hell, maybe he was still at the same crematorium where Guillermo and I had taken the baby only yesterday. As far as I was concerned, the whereabouts of Christopher Murphy – what was left of him – was a mystery to me.

I would have to ask John what he did with Murphy's remains, assuming I made it out of Vegas alive.

'The FBI are looking for him,' Dornan said, taking my hand again and squeezing my wrist.

I didn't bother pulling away, the image of Agent Lindsay Price clear in my mind – the FBI agent who'd cornered me in the locker room at the gym Guillermo and I frequented, stolen my towel, and asked me where Murphy was. I'd never told Dornan. I couldn't. I no longer trusted the man who, once upon a time, would have laid down his life to protect me.

'The FBI are looking for him,' Dornan repeated, 'and they're getting closer.'

'Great,' I replied. 'Maybe when they find him, they can ask him where he stashed hundreds of thousands of dollars of your father's money.'

Dornan turned and smashed his fist into the mirror. Shards exploded in a rain of cold glass, sharp and tacky.

'They're going to call you as a witness, you stupid bitch,' he said, ignoring his bleeding knuckles as they dripped all over the floor.

Something reached into my chest and squeezed violently, the part of me that screamed MURDERER. *I* killed Murphy. The blood was on *my* hands, in *my* apartment, in the grout between *my* bathroom tiles. And even though John had it swept clean by a specialist crew, I'd watched enough TV to know that it'd only take a single missed speck of blood to put me away for the rest of my natural life.

And I couldn't be in prison. I could plot and thieve and run from the Gypsy Brothers and Il Sangue, but I couldn't break out of a federal penitentiary. That was beyond my particular set of skills. I couldn't ever, *ever* be caught for the terrible things I had done in the name of survival. Two police officers – Murphy, and his squeeze and DEA partner, Allie Baxter – were both dead by my hand.

Dornan must have seen something on my face. 'You know where he is, don't you?'

I shook my head vehemently. 'No.'

'Then why do you look like you're about to pee all over the fucking floor?' he growled.

'They'll arrest me for money laundering,' I said quietly, my eyes wide, my breathing laboured. I wasn't putting on an act. They really would arrest me for that. And ironically, the sentences for white-collar crimes like funnelling money – profits of drug supply and human trafficking at that – to every known tax haven in the world were probably harsher than if I'd just stepped out onto the strip with a machete and started hacking gamble-happy tourists to pieces.

America, the land of the free, really fucking liked collecting taxes. It didn't like it when you tried to hide money. Especially when you got that money for doing very bad things.

'Why do you think we're here?' Dornan asked, his anger subsiding for the moment. I glanced at the broken mirror, the remaining shards casting a haunting image of us, shattered and warped a thousand times over as our reflections existed in tiny slices of glass.

'Because you don't have to testify against your spouse in court,' I said vacantly, rubbing my wrist as faint bruises began to appear. I mean, I'd been a little slow to catch on, but I wasn't an idiot.

'Bingo,' Dornan said. He wrapped his hand in paper towels to stem the bleeding. Then, as I continued to stand there like a waste of space, he put his hands on my hips and guided me over to the unbroken mirror that hung over the neighbouring basin. He started to fuss with my hair, moving strands to where they belonged and smoothing down the knots he'd created when he fisted clumps of my hair and pulled. There were flowers woven into my hair, my messy topknot.

'Did you put these in my hair?' I asked slowly, horrified at the way he'd dressed me and arranged me as if I were his doll.

'I did,' Dornan replied, tucking a small pink rose back into my hair. 'You can thank me later.'

Somehow the act of decorating my hair was more disturbing than almost anything he'd ever done. It was his way of communicating that he could do whatever he wanted with me – and if I didn't like it, he'd force it anyway, just to get things the way he wanted.

I watched him silently in the mirror's reflection, weighing my options. They were feather-light. *They didn't exist.*

'You good?' he asked. It was like the fight had bled out of him. Maybe it had. I nodded.

'Then let's go get fucking married,' he said, pulling the bloody napkin from his knuckles. 'Don't worry. If you still hate me this much in a year, we'll just get fucking divorced.'

His casual words belied the intent in his eyes. I knew that look. We would be married, but we would not ever be getting divorced. The only way I would ever be undoing what was about to happen would be if one of us died and the other was widowed.

John was going to want to murder Dornan when he found out about this.

'Does your father know about this?' I asked again, my heart hollow as the answer knocked around it like a frenzied moth in the dark. Because I already knew the answer.

'Of course,' Dornan replied, ushering me out of the bathroom. I glanced back at the shattered glass one last time, a sense of doom crushing down on me.

'Esteban and I were going to get married,' I said softly, letting him lead me to the altar, his reluctant bride. 'But your father had him killed before we could do it.'

'Lucky me,' Dornan said, as Elvis started singing 'Suspicious Minds' at top volume over the speaker system. *Oh, the irony.* 'Now I get the honour of calling you wife while he's napping in the dirt.'

I made a choking sound in the back of my throat as his words slammed into me.

'You motherfucker,' I shot, anger blossoming in my chest like noxious fumes.

He took something from his pocket and held it out to me, seemingly unaffected by my reaction. 'Have some gum. You need it.'

If looks were knives, he'd have been sliced clean in half. 'How thoughtful,' I said, snatching the packet from him.

I unwrapped a stick of gum and stuck it between my teeth. Mint flooded my mouth, sharp and tangy, and from that moment on I'd always associate white dresses and Elvis with sticky-sweet mint and broken bones.

CHAPTER EIGHTEEN
DORNAN

The ceremony was short. It wasn't, however, remotely sweet. When it was time for them to kiss, Dornan could have sworn Mariana flinched.

He'd have to punish her for that.

And he had just the punishment to fit her crime. The crime of not loving him anymore. The crime of checking out. She was physically here with him, but her mind was just gone.

But her body would be his. He would mark her so that any man who touched her knew she belonged to him. He would dig into her flesh until her eyes burned from the pain.

He'd seen the threads of them unravelling, but by the time he understood how serious it was, she was already somewhere else.

And he couldn't figure out where.

The phone, the incriminating evidence against her, was like a ticking time bomb in Dornan's existence. He'd almost asked her about it so many times, but he had never actually spoken the words aloud, because he didn't want to know the answer. She was all he had, the only person who loved him that wasn't required to by virtue of sharing his DNA, and he couldn't bear the thought that she might have betrayed him.

That fucking phone, though. It was prepaid, a flimsy piece of shit that led nowhere. No details, no call history that he could find when he scrolled through the phone's basic functions – nothing. Murphy was the one who could get things like call logs easily and discreetly, and that motherfucker was either ghosting all of them, or dead. Dornan had packed the phone for this trip specifically, taking the opportunity to steal it from its hiding spot while Mariana was packing. Because he was tired of waiting around for answers, and it was time to get them himself.

The phone was in Dornan's suitcase now, locked inside his gun case with his Beretta – his other piece, the one he wasn't currently hiding in the waistband of his jeans. He had a smaller handgun for everyday concealed carry. A Beretta was too fucking heavy to carry around all day, and it made him itch.

The phone. The phone. The *phone*.

Now, if fucking Murphy hadn't disappeared, he could have checked the official call records for it, subpoenaed information, gotten answers. But Murphy was nowhere to be found, and perhaps that was because he was the one she was calling from this goddamn phone in the first place.

Dornan's other investigative contacts didn't have FBI clearance, so they had to do some shady shit to get answers. Shady shit took time.

Fucking Murphy.

If he was still alive when they found him, Dornan was going to murder him.

If she was going to double-cross the cartel, it made sense that Ana would work with Murphy. He was a DEA agent. He was shady as fuck. And Dornan hated him.

But Ana hated Murphy, too. So if the phone had come from him, then he was either blackmailing her somehow, or giving her something she wanted.

But what?

Her family? The people who thought she was long dead?

What was he missing?

Was it somehow tied to Guillermo, the man Dornan had entrusted with Mariana's security detail? He'd been loyal to Dornan always, but everybody had a weakness. He'd put the hot-headed Mexican in Mariana's apartment for protection, but was he sticking his dick in Dornan's girlfriend – wait, his *wife* – behind his back? If that was the case, he'd chop the fucking thing off and barbecue it, and force Guillermo to eat it.

'Nice ring,' Mariana said, peering at the rock on her hand. 'Who'd you steal it from?'

Dornan grinned, but inside he felt cold. This wasn't the future he'd imagined for them. This wasn't how he'd pictured their wedding.

He hadn't even asked her to marry him, he'd forced her.

If she's betrayed us, I will fucking kill her. I will rip her fucking head off, and Murphy's too.

'It was my grandmother's,' he said, a hollow ache inside his chest. He'd had that ring since his mother's mother died and he was a young man, unwed and sowing his wild oats. He'd intended to give it to Stephanie, but then she left him. He'd never felt Celia was worthy of it. And somewhere in the depths of his black soul, he imagined Mariana would be buried in the ground wearing it, very soon.

'Oh,' Mariana said quietly.

Dornan got the driver to take a detour on the way back to the hotel: Franco's ink shop, right on Freemont. He knew Franco well. He'd been tattooing Gypsies for years, until he moved out to Nevada and started making bank by tattooing tramp stamps on drunken brides instead.

Mariana glanced at the store's sign warily as Dornan pressed his hand into the small of her back, directing her into the front of Franco's studio. Needles whirred noisily, the air-conditioning so cold it was like being in the fucking Arctic.

Better than sweating, Dornan thought. He pulled Mariana right up to the counter and knocked his fist against the glass display case once, twice, three times. A young punk girl wandered out, and Dornan couldn't help but stare at the stretcher earrings that had turned her earlobes into giant holes.

'Can I help you?' she asked, clearly unimpressed by him. That's right, he wasn't in LA. Nobody knew him here, at least not by sight, and definitely not when he was in civilian clothing, nary a Gypsy Brothers patch to be seen.

He looked the punk bitch up and down. 'Tell Franco that Dornan Ross is here,' he said, the smile he flashed her more like a wolf baring teeth. The girl's eyes went wide and she nodded, scurrying away.

'Wow,' Mariana said, leaning back against the glass counter. 'The place where everybody knows your name.'

He raised his eyebrows. 'They got *Cheers* on TV in Colombia, wife?' He liked the sound of that word when he said it. She was his wife. And she'd come around to embrace her new position. Eventually. Probably.

She didn't really have a choice.

She frowned. 'I haven't been in Colombia in ten years, *husband*.'

She said the word like she was talking about stepping in dog shit. It brought that rage out of him, that cloying, violent need for blood.

'Where'd you watch *Cheers*?' he asked, not really caring, but needing to fill the silence until Franco got his ass out here.

'In the apartment,' she replied. 'Guillermo and I watch reruns.'

'He rub your back and fix you tea, too?' Dornan asked. That fucker better not have laid a hand on her.

'Sometimes,' she said, catching his eye. She was fucking with him, and he hated it, but it didn't matter, because he was about to fuck with her.

Franco, a short, rotund man with a white beard and a shiny bald head, barged out of the back of the shop, making a beeline for Dornan. They exchanged pleasantries, Dornan slapping the man on the back hard enough that he thought he might break him, and then the three of them went into a back booth.

'Alrighty,' Franco said, peering up at them from his five foot nothing stance. 'What's the big bad biker getting today?'

Dornan smiled. Gotcha. He gestured to Mariana, draping an arm over her bare shoulders. 'My wife would like a more lasting reminder of our union. Apparently a ring isn't good enough these days.'

Mariana's head snapped around like the kid in the fucking *Exorcist* movie. She tried to pull away, but Dornan was strong. He held her to his side, squeezing her shoulders under his broad arm.

'What the fuck?' she hissed. Franco looked between the two of them, apparently not in a hurry at all. 'Do you want a moment to talk amongst yourselves while I get the needles?' he offered.

Dornan nodded. 'Sounds like a plan, Franco.'

Franco wandered out back and Dornan released Mariana. She backed up, away from him, but it didn't matter. He had her cornered, and she knew it.

'What are you doing?' she snapped. 'Are you out of your fucking mind? You want to brand me like I'm an animal?'

He grabbed her wrist, not bothering to be gentle, thinking she fucking deserved it rough after the performance she'd put on. He'd done everything for her, and she was freezing him out at every turn.

'It's tradition,' Dornan said. 'All the wives of Gypsies get a tattoo. It's part of your role. Or would you prefer to be marked with cum and lines of coke like all the club whores? Like I said, we can get a fucking divorce. But I need me a wife, babe. If it's not you, I'll have to donate you to the fine members of my club.'

'Fuck you,' Mariana said, shoving him in the chest. Of course he didn't move. 'As if you'd share me.'

Dornan chuckled. 'I might not like it, but, darlin', I'd do just about anything to prove a point.'

Mariana's smirk dropped, replaced by unadulterated horror.

'No,' she said. 'Don't do this. You don't have to do this.'

Dornan guided her to the chair and sat her down, marvelling at how beautiful his trapped little bird was, now.

'Yes, I do,' he said, nodding to the ring on her finger. 'Take that off and put it on the other hand. It'll be a few days until the swelling goes down.'

CHAPTER NINETEEN

MARIANA

I slammed the door in Dornan's face, closed the lid of the toilet seat, and sat. I looked at my ring finger, swollen, hurting so fucking brutally I wanted to rip the whole finger off. I wondered if the needle and the tattooing equipment had even been sterile.

I didn't want this fucking abomination on my finger. A skull. He'd had them tattoo a skull on my finger, and a matching faux band so that it represented a ring. Because a piece of paper legally binding us together and a diamond the size of my pinkie fingernail wasn't enough to seal the deal. I was surprised he hadn't just tattooed PROPERTY OF DORNAN ROSS over my face for everyone to see.

I didn't want this marriage.

I didn't want to be holed up in a fucking bathroom in Las Vegas while Dornan raged outside the door, ravenous for the release that only my body could give him. He had wed me, and now it was pretty clear that he wanted to fuck me. Consummation of a commitment ten years in the making.

Fuck that.

I didn't want him on me. In me. Near me.

I wanted John.

But John wasn't here. He was somewhere else, and I was here, and nothing else mattered.

'What the fuck are you doing in there?' Dornan asked. 'You can't stay in there forever.'

'Fuck you!' I yelled back, wrapping my arms around myself and resting my forehead on my knees. I knocked my finger against my leg and cried out. Goddamn it. It hurt.

I caught sight of myself in the mirror across from me. Pale. Not the actual colour of my skin – I was Colombian, after all – but the pallor. It screamed misery. So did my eyes. Red and bloodshot. My hair was messed up. My stomach was screaming for food and my hands shook from stress and lack of sugar.

I'm married to the man who is going to kill me if I don't get away from him.

I was a mess.

More than that – I was fucking doomed.

I rested my face in my hands and cried.

CHAPTER TWENTY
DORNAN

Mariana hadn't said a word while Franco was tattooing the ring onto her finger. It was tradition, but neither of his other wives had gotten them, and Dornan hadn't pressed the issue. But his Mariana ... she was something to be coveted. She was something to be marked.

And marking her was exactly what he wanted to do right now. He wanted to rip the fucking bathroom door off its hinges, pick her up, throw her onto the bathroom vanity and fuck her until she screamed and he had to gag her. He wanted to kiss those soft, dewy lips, get them wet and swollen, and then push her onto her knees so that he could slide his dick right into her wet mouth. He wanted to come all over her face, her beautiful tits, her ass. He'd been waiting for the day when he could have her freely, when his father would finally allow their union to be official ... But there was one problem.

She was locked in the bathroom.

Had been for the better part of an hour.

She wasn't coming out.

He smashed his fist against the bathroom door.

Inside, he waged a war. Against her. Against himself. Against every shitty thing he had ever done.

He lifted his fist to smash the door again, even though his knuckles were already a bloody mess, even though he didn't deserve her forgiveness. He craved it. He'd stood in the sunshine of her love once, and now on the other side, it was midnight, and he was cold.

Fist in the air, he almost hit her in the goddamn face when she yanked the door open abruptly and stood there, wearing her pretty strapless white dress, her tattoo angry and red-black around her ring finger.

'What?' she snapped.

He felt the angry wall inside of him collapse, if only for a moment. He was just *tired*.

'I want to go back to that first time in your apartment,' Dornan said gruffly, flexing the fist he'd just about driven into her face by accident. He reached out a hand, cupped her face tenderly with his rough skin.

'Why?' she asked tightly.

He sighed. 'I want to do better. You deserve better.'

Her eyelashes fluttered as she looked at him briefly, and then back at the ground. She was fucking beautiful. She was his wife, and he couldn't quite believe it. She smiled wryly, and for a moment he thought she might have been going to drop this shit.

The words that came out of her mouth, though, were like a cold pickaxe she was jamming into his heart.

'I want to go back to that night your father came for me,' she muttered, 'so that I could shoot him in the fucking face, and never have to meet you.'

Mariana smacked his hand away from her face like it was fire, and he was burning her skin. He saw red. He saw Mariana on the floor of her apartment, as he laid his fists into her for daring to defy him, and he saw the puddle of blood that had greeted him afterward, when she was already in the hospital, their baby long dead. The sting of her rejection was acute; it was utterly unbearable.

'When are you going to stop punishing me?' Dornan roared, slamming his palm against the wall beside her head.

CHAPTER TWENTY-ONE
MARIANA

I saw red.

'You think I'm punishing you?' I screamed, pushing him. 'I can't even fucking look at you without feeling like you're beating me against a wall!'

And maybe I was goading him. Maybe I wanted him to force me, so then at least I could say it wasn't my fault. That he wouldn't take no for an answer. Because I could already tell, from that psychotic glimmer in his dark brown eyes, that he wasn't taking no for an answer tonight. He'd claimed me on paper, and now he wanted to claim my body with his.

'I'm sorry, I'm SORRY!' he raged. He started to pace in front of me.

I watched, not daring to leave the safety of the bathroom doorway. If he came at me, if he tried to grab me, at least I had a chance at shutting him out and going back to my safe room.

But he didn't grab me, or try to kiss me, and that surprised me. If anything, the pacing seemed to calm him.

At least, I thought he was calming down, until he spoke.

'You've been avoiding me for months,' he said coldly, levelling his black gaze at me.

'What?' I tried not to squirm under the spotlight of his words.

He just raised his eyebrows. 'I know you, Mariana Rodriguez. Mariana *Ross*. You are a woman who demands to be fucked. You used to be addicted to my cock. So if you haven't been fucking *me*, who *have* you been fucking?'

My stomach dropped. 'What?'

'Who. Huh? Guillermo? I'll slit his dirty throat and screw you beside him, in a puddle of his blood.'

I grimaced at the visual. I didn't doubt him for a second. 'No, I haven't been fucking *Guillermo*,' I replied. *As if.* 'I'd rather sew my vagina shut than fuck him.'

'Who, then? Someone from the club?'

Getting warmer. He was pacing and pacing and this was so very bad. He'd never been suspicious before. Ever.

He stopped dead in his tracks, lifting his eyes from the shitty red and yellow checkered carpet. 'Did my father touch you?'

I thought of all the times Emilio had *touched* me – pinched nipples, pulled hair, slapped cheeks. He'd been rough. Threatening. But in all these years, Emilio Ross had never once tried to have sex with me.

'No,' I snapped. 'There's nobody. You're being paranoid, Dornan.'

He chuckled, the gesture devoid of any joy. He was in pain, I realised. He was crying out for me to love him in the way I showed him love – with pain, and sex, and blood.

'I know what you want,' I whispered through gritted teeth. 'And you're not going to get it from me. You don't deserve it.'

'WHO ARE YOU FUCKING?' he roared, raising his hand as if he were about to hit me.

'Nobody,' I replied calmly, refusing to cower under his physical threat. I would show no weakness, even though inside my alarm bells were screaming, *Get out! Get out!*

There was nowhere to go. *There was never anywhere to go.*

I stood my ground against my dark lover, glaring at him as emotion rose thick in my throat. And then, in an act of entirely false bravado, I slipped underneath his arm, still braced against the doorframe, and headed for the minibar.

The hotel we were staying in wasn't amazing, but the minibar was. They'd laid out a selection of spirits that made my mouth water, and I ran my fingers along the lids, selecting a small bottle of vodka. Opening it, I poured half the bottle over my tattooed finger, squeezing my eyes shut as they teared up. I gasped, blinking away the hot moisture that had gathered at the corners of my eyelashes, as I slammed a mouthful of vodka and felt it burn all the way down inside of me. All the while, I felt Dornan's eyes drilling into me, his questions, his suspicion.

He came to stand beside me at the minibar, running a hand through my long hair. I still had the damned flower wreath in it, and as soon as I'd finished the vodka, I was going to rip it out and throw it into the trash. I didn't want to look pretty. I wanted to be left alone to scream into my pillow and sob until the sun came up again.

The fingers in my hair turned into a fist, the gentle caress turning into a tight tug as he wound strands around his fingers and pulled, hard. I didn't resist, letting my head go with the swift motion. I didn't fancy losing any hair today.

'You're telling me you've been fucking yourself? Getting yourself off?' he asked, his breath hot on my cheek.

I nodded as much as I could with the way he was holding my head back. What else could I say without placing John under suspicion?

'I don't fucking believe you,' he growled.

I turned my gaze to him, an open challenge in my eyes. 'I'll show you.'

He appeared to think about it for a moment, his eyes lighting up with what looked like lust. He let go of my hair, dropped his hand to his side. 'You'd better,' he replied, reaching for the vodka bottle in my hand and pointing to the couch. 'Now.'

We stared off for a moment. *Oh, this is actually going to happen*, I realised. Well. Whatever. I'd give him a show he wouldn't soon forget. I'd make his cock ache until it was painful instead of pleasant.

I snatched the vodka back, took a long slug, and slammed the bottle down on the counter, wiping my mouth with the back of my hand. I stalked over to the couch, standing in front of it, facing away from Dornan as I hitched my dress up to my hips. I hooked my fingers into my white panties and tugged them down, bending at the waist until they reached my ankles. Then, without kicking off my patent heels, I turned, sat my ass down on the couch, and spread my legs, bracing my feet against the edge of the cushions.

Surprisingly, Dornan hadn't moved from the minibar. I'd half expected him to grab me while I was bent and removing my panties, but it seemed my *husband* possessed restraint I wasn't aware of. He'd left the vodka where it was, and selected a bottle of bourbon instead.

'You have a very pretty cunt,' he growled, squeezing his dick through his pants. His jaw was so tight, it looked like it might shatter if he clenched it any harder.

'I know,' I said, reaching down and spreading myself open for him to see. He let out a small growl in the back of his throat, his erection bulging through his pants, the black material stretched thin.

Something inside me broke mournfully apart as I realised the only way I'd be able to keep up this pretence would be to keep fucking Dornan until the very last minute. I didn't know how I'd be able to do that, not after what he'd done and what he'd put me through, but I knew it was the only way to evade suspicion. To avoid being caught out.

I slipped one finger inside myself, sliding it back and forth in my wet heat.

'You fuck yourself like that?'

I nodded, never breaking our gaze. In my peripheral vision, I saw him squeeze his cock, moving closer to me, the neck of the bourbon bottle still clutched tightly in his hand. I sank two fingers inside myself, letting out a small moan, surprised at how wet I was. How fucking aroused I was.

It wasn't about sex, I realised. This was about power. Being the one in power was getting me off. Having Dornan in front of me, knowing all he wanted to do was throw himself on top of me and push into me until I broke in half, that was power. The fact that he hadn't touched me yet, but continued to watch my bizarre little show, *that* was power.

'You want a front row seat?' I offered boldly. Kicking the edge of the coffee table in front of me to make room for his bulky frame, I pointed with my free hand. Dornan smirked, dropping the bottle onto the carpet with a heavy thud.

Taking three steps, he didn't stop until he was standing above me.

He sank to his knees in front of me, his eyes greedily taking in my wet pussy, my swollen clit, my nipples that peeked out of my plunging dress.

Grinning, Dornan stuck two fingers into his mouth, wetting them as he watched me fuck myself. He took hold of my wrist with one hand, pulling my own fingers away from myself, his own fingers braced to enter me.

'Hey.'

He stopped, his fingers millimetres from my entrance. He looked dazed, as if the lust inside him was consuming him like a virus in his blood.

I took his wrists and guided his hands to my ankles. He wrapped his fingers around my flesh and squeezed.

'Keep them there,' I said, gazing into his dark eyes, shocked at how complicit he was being. 'Don't interrupt me, or I'll never do this again.'

He squeezed my ankles in response, breathing heavily.

'You're so wet,' he murmured. 'I want to be inside you.'

He licked his lips as he stared at my slick pussy, and I could tell this was killing him. He was dying to press me into the couch and fuck me into oblivion.

Wasn't going to happen.

I continued to massage my swollen bud with my fingers, using my free hand to reach down and tilt his chin, forcing him to meet my gaze.

'Look at me,' I breathed. 'I have some things I want to say to you.'

He didn't look away. I was impressed by his restraint. I took a deep breath, preparing to relive the horrors of the recent past.

'You put life inside me,' I whispered, continuing to rub myself. I squirmed under my own touch, so close to coming. He nodded, slow-blinking.

'You made me feel the worst pain imaginable,' I breathed. I felt my words leak out of me, a confession of sorts, and settle upon him. They entered him, soaking into his soul. He wasn't trying to make me stop talking. He was hanging on my every word, my every hitched gasp, my every touch as I brought myself to the brink of orgasm in front of him.

'You put life inside me,' I said, lifting my hips slightly as I slowed my fingers. If I didn't settle down, I was going to come before he'd paid his penance at all. 'You put life inside of me, and you turned it into death.'

'I'm so sorry,' he whispered, his expression so fucking anguished, so fucking bereft, that it took everything inside myself not to stop and pull him onto me, into me, to sate his sadness and his regret with my body, the same dance we had danced for a decade.

'What do you want?' I breathed, writhing as I continued to slowly finger-fuck myself. 'You want to fuck me? You want to come inside me?'

He nodded, his eyes hooded with lust as he stared, mesmerised, at what I was doing to myself. He took one hand away from my ankle and used it to pull his dick out of his pants, squeezing it until his knuckles turned red.

'Too bad,' I whispered, withdrawing my fingers from my pussy and pressing them into his mouth. He sucked them until it hurt, getting every single drop of me from my skin. 'You want to fuck me? You *earn* it.'

He was panting, hard, on his knees in front of me, and I saw the way he kept glancing at my bare pussy as he stroked his cock in his fist.

'You taste so fucking good,' he murmured around my fingers. 'So fucking good.'

I stopped abruptly, and Dornan's eyes widened, as if I'd broken the spell. *Bullshit*, I thought. I slid my hand into his short hair and pulled, bringing his face right up to mine.

But I didn't kiss him.

'Make me come with your tongue,' I demanded. '*Only* your tongue. You want me to forgive you? You'd better start by making me feel good.'

My voice was suddenly thick with emotion. Why? Why now?

Maybe because, after ten years, I was finally starting to take some goddamn responsibility for my own fate. In the beginning I'd needed Dornan's brutality, I'd needed his domination, but now I needed his submission, his reparation. I needed his desire to soothe me, to beg my forgiveness.

With my hand in his hair, I pushed his head down between my thighs.

His eyes gleamed up at me, full of lust, inexplicably calm. It was as if, by taking charge of the dynamic we shared, he was momentarily relieved.

'I might be yours on paper, but this pussy belongs to me now, you understand?'

CHAPTER TWENTY-TWO

DORNAN

Her dark blue eyes gleamed with conviction, simmered with anger as she stared down at him. In her rage, she was absolutely *stunning*.

'This body is mine,' she whispered to him. 'It was yours, Dornan, and you did what you did, and it's not yours anymore. If you want it back? You earn it. You earn my love. You earn your place inside my cunt. *You earn my fucking mouth around your cock.*'

He nodded, breaking their stare, his eyes sliding down her beautiful tits, her stomach, before coming to rest upon her sweet cunt. He stilled for a moment, breathing in the scent of her.

He licked his lips, pressing the flat of his tongue against her swollen bundle of nerves.

'Fuck!' she exclaimed, her fingers pulling his hair to the point of pain. He didn't care. He liked pain, especially with sex. The two belonged together. Pain and fucking. But, as he licked her he was gentle. She'd suffered too much because of him, felt too much pain, and it was time for him to reel it the fuck in and crawl his way back to her side. She was his now, legally, but she was broken. His bird was broken. And it was up to him to fix her.

'You worship me,' she moaned, as he sucked her clit into his mouth. 'You make me believe in you again. You— Oh!' She ground herself against his mouth desperately. 'You make me remember why I fucking *love* you so much, Dornan. You're the fucking kingpin in of all this— *oh, fuck!* And you just made me your … *queen*. You just tattooed my status on my skin. It's time to start treating me like a fucking queen.'

And this time, when she came against his tongue, he didn't try to cover her mouth or muffle her noises. There was no reason to silence his queen. No, as she cried out and writhed under his tongue, he revelled in the sweet noise of her unsuppressed joy, her exhilaration, as he sucked in a final breath and squeezed his cock, coming violently against his thigh.

***

The next morning, Viper called him. His LAPD contact had done some digging and found the call logs for Mariana's secret cellphone. The contents of which were very interesting indeed.

She was still sleeping peacefully, out cold, when Dornan took the call in the hallway and then came back into the room. Seemed he and his new wife had some talking to do.

That was, if he didn't kill her first.

CHAPTER TWENTY-THREE

MARIANA

My hand hurt.

The pain had extended beyond my ring finger and my entire hand was just throbbing now. It pounded with the rhythm of my heart, relentless, nauseating. It wasn't physically that painful, per se, but it was knowing it was there, wanting to rip it off with my fingernails but knowing I couldn't. Laser removal was in my future, assuming I survived being the wife of California's most notorious biker and the daughter-in-law of the most lethal drug kingpin of the entire Gulf.

I saw a dirt grave in my future, too.

I'd fallen asleep in my dress, my make-up still caked on. My eyes itched from the clumped mascara, and concealer streaked my pillow. I was beyond caring. Try washing blood out of a pillowcase and then come talk to me about a few smears of liquid make-up.

I sat up in the bed – the large, downy, luxurious bed – and immediately lay down again as the room began to circle me viciously. The vodka. The lack of food. The reminder that Dornan and I were married.

If I'd had anything left in my stomach I would have surely thrown it up. Instead, I curled back into the foetal position and pulled the sheets over my face.

The other side of the bed was empty; I wondered where Dornan was. Reluctantly, I sat up again, scanning the room for him.

He was sitting on the end of the bed, staring at me intently, something in his hand.

'Hello, Mrs Ross,' he said, his voice sticky-sweet with fake enthusiasm, his teeth bared in a large grin that didn't reach his dark eyes. Oh God, what had I done now?

'Morning,' I said, crossing my legs in a yoga pose and arranging the blankets around me like a protective shroud. It had to be a hundred degrees out, the sun blazing a path straight to my eyeballs, but the room was as cold as ice. I rubbed my hands down my arms as goosebumps sprang up on my skin.

'You okay?' I asked Dornan. Something was up. Better to get it over and done with. Rip the bandaid. It was always about making the pain as quick as possible. No point extending our misery.

Dornan dropped the grin, his eyes on mine. He ran his tongue over his teeth and looked at whatever he was holding. I let my eyes follow his, but his big hands were mostly obscuring the object.

'Can I trust you?' he asked me.

I raised my eyebrows. 'What kind of question is that? Can you trust *me*? Can I trust *you*?'

I didn't even see the blow that hit me. Something in his hand, hard and blunt, smashed into the side of my head, just above my left ear, and I went down faster than an old Vegas casino with a wrecking ball and some explosives. That is to say, I flew off the bed and onto the floor, the the carpet cushioning my fall.

'Wrong answer,' Dornan said coldly, standing above me. I rolled onto my back, taking in his expression: serious, distant.

Shit.

I opened my mouth to speak as he held up a cellphone. My cellphone. The burner cellphone John had given to me.

'You hit me with a fucking cellphone?' I asked, getting up on my elbows as the side of my head throbbed painfully. 'What if I was pregnant, you fucking idiot?'

He kicked me in the stomach for that. I made an oomph sound as he crouched beside me, his hand stroking my hair. 'If you were pregnant,' he mused, 'you drank enough last night to destroy any baby's brain cells. Besides, you just finished your period three days ago. You couldn't be pregnant, unless we made a baby in the apartment before we left yesterday.'

My mouth hung open in shock as he rubbed circles on my stomach with the tip of his finger. 'It could be happening right now,' he said, tracing a path from my pelvis right up to my belly button and jabbing his finger in hard enough to make me wince. 'What do you think?' he asked. 'Would it be my baby, Mariana? Or would it be someone else's? Because if there's even the slightest chance it isn't mine ... I'll stick my hand inside you and rip your fucking womb out.' He made his free hand into the shape of a claw and made a pulling motion in the air.

If I thought I'd known fear before, I didn't. Not until that moment.

I swallowed, incredulous, that image in my mind completely fucking disturbing. 'What is wrong with you?' I exclaimed. 'Seriously, what the fuck is wrong with you? You bring me here and marry me and then *this*?'

I was stunned, but he had the phone. *He had the phone!* He was going to kill me. I would die here, now, in a hotel room in the middle of the fucking desert, and it would be a fitting end to our union.

'I'm going to ask you one more time,' he said, standing and holding a hand out to me.

With great reluctance, outweighed only by self-preservation and the desire not to be kicked again, I accepted. He hauled me to my feet and took me by my arms, backing me into the kitchenette. Brazenly, I reached for a bottle of anything to hit him with, but he was faster. He grabbed my wrist and bent it so hard I thought it would snap.

'Fuck!' I yelled.

He responded by hitting me again with the phone, the plastic smacking into my cheekbone. I gasped for air, my head flying back, my body pinned by his hips.

'Fuck you,' he said. 'You see this?'

He held the phone in front of my eyes and I squinted, trying to focus.

'What?' I half-asked, half-begged. '*What?*'

'Blood,' Dornan said. I saw the dried red blood on the phone and my entire body stilled. A tiny speck of red. It looked innocent enough. Innocuous. Dazed, I felt my cheek for broken skin. My scalp. None. I wasn't bleeding.

I knew it wasn't my blood.

'Whose blood?' I asked. 'Yours?'

He cocked his head to the side, eyes raging like a wildfire burned inside his skull. And it probably did – my psychotic husband. I stumbled over the word. *Husband.* Seven letters, my death sentence.

'How stupid do you think I am?' he said.

I held his gaze. 'Stop. Stop! Just ask me. Just tell me what's going on, because I don't understand!' My voice got louder as I spoke, rising to a feverish pitch by the end of my sentence. I didn't know if I was yelling or begging at that point. All I knew was, he had that hand on me, the one he'd just threatened to disembowel me with, and I couldn't stop shaking, *and he had the phone.*

'Is. This. Your. Phone?'

'Yes!' I screamed.

His eyes lit up like wildfire. Oh God. *OhGodOhGodOhGod.*

His face gave away nothing. I wondered if it would be the last thing I would ever see.

I tried not to struggle as Dornan traced a finger underneath each of my eyes, in the hollow part, the socket, and it took every ounce of self-restraint not to flinch. I was half-convinced he was going to poke my eyes out, but his finger travelled down to my mouth. He pushed it between my lips and I let him, because more than anything, I really did not want him to hit me with that fucking phone again.

Had he found phone records? I deleted John's number every time I called him. Still, a lot had changed in ten years. It was 2008, and you could find almost anything you wanted information-wise if you looked in the right places.

'It's not what you think,' I said around his finger, needing to break the unbearable silence that stretched between us.

'I don't believe you,' Dornan whispered. I couldn't respond, because his finger was halfway down my throat, but I shook my head anyway.

He dropped the phone onto the counter that he had me pinned against and brought his free hand to my throat, squeezing.

Idiot. He had a finger in my mouth. I bit down as hard as I could, and suddenly I was flying through the air again.

'You fucking cunt!' Dornan yelled, as I crashed into the bathroom door.

Dazed, and with blood in my mouth – his, not mine – I scrambled to my knees, crawling away from him.

I wasn't fast enough, and the only escape in this room was the goddamn door anyway. He was between me and that precious exit, so I had nowhere to go.

There was never anywhere to go.

How many times had I repeated that thought to myself lately?

Too many.

Hands found my hair and yanked me up. I decided I was going to shave my head so he couldn't use my hair as a weapon against me anymore. For now, wanting to keep my scalp, I followed his momentum as he tossed me onto the bed.

'This finger is very fucking important,' he said, holding up his bloodied index finger. 'I use it to shoot people. I use it when I ride. I use it when I fuck you.' He leaned down so that his nose was touching mine, his breath hot on my mouth. 'If you've damaged it, I'll cut yours off. I'll cut all of them off.'

'*Don'tbesuchababy*,' I said, my words slurring together. He slapped me across the face, but I barely felt it. Something had dulled in my head when it hit the bathroom door. My thoughts were slow. My pain receptors slower.

A hand wrapped around my throat and squeezed, Dornan's expression resigned as he stared down at me. 'Whose fucking blood is it?'

Tears were streaming out of my eyes of their own accord, an entirely reflexive response. I felt like I was about to die.

'Mine,' I said. 'The blood is mine.'

He shook me. 'You're LYING!'

Jesus, fuck, he was going to kill me.

'I cut myself!' I gasped, fighting for breath, for the ability to speak. 'You know I cut myself. It's my blood. I swear.'

Dornan appeared torn. 'You promised me you didn't do that anymore.'

'I started doing it again,' I lied.

He loosened his fingers a little and I tried to get up, but he wasn't having that. Staring twin bullet holes into my head, he straddled me, one knee on either side of my chest. I tried to push him off, but he was too heavy. Too strong. His knees squeezed my ribcage until I thought my lungs would burst.

'Keep talking,' he ground out. 'Why? Why should I believe you? Why would you start hurting yourself again?'

'I found out my whole family was dead.'

Shock registered on Dornan's face. 'What?'

The truth, now. My eyes filled with tears and spilled over.

'Your father had them killed,' I whispered.

I could barely make out the expression on Dornan's face anymore. My eyes weren't focusing, and I wanted to pass out.

His fingers tightened. *This is it. This is where I die*. Tears leaked from the corners of my eyes as I ached for my son. For John. They'd never even know what had become of me. They'd never know that I didn't want to be married to Dornan, or that I'd fought to get back to them. They'd just never know, and I'd be gone. I wondered, in those moments, my fingernails scratching against Dornan's hands, if he'd burn me or bury me. Would I sink into the earth? Would he bury me in the desert? Would he just leave me here, in this room, for the maid to find when she came to make the beds and restock the minibar?

Please, I mouthed. Dornan was killing me, and he wasn't even watching as I died. I could feel the life ebbing from me as I starved for oxygen, my brain screaming for a single breath of air, my chest locked and shuddering. He seemed momentarily distracted, his fingers loosening a little, and I took the opportunity to twist my head to the side and bite his hand.

He pulled his hands away, giving me an annoyed glance and a smack on the cheek, but nothing compared to what he'd been doing earlier.

I choked and gasped for air, prompting Dornan to reach for a bottle of Evian that sat on the bedside table, courtesy of the hotel. A five-dollar bottle of water, but I would have paid a million dollars for it. He unscrewed it and handed it to me, watching silently as I chugged it down. I drank it too fast and I coughed, getting water down the front of my dress in the process.

'You done trying to kill me?' I asked.

Dornan got off me.

I couldn't stop coughing. My throat was on fire.

'What do you need?' Dornan asked, as if some water or some fucking food could fix the fact that he'd beaten me ten shades of black and blue and then almost strangled me to death.

'Who did you think I'd be calling?' I asked him. I put on my best wounded face, which wasn't a stretch. 'Because I know you wouldn't react like that if you thought I was calling my family in Colombia.'

He stared at the wall. 'I don't know,' he said. 'I just ... you get further away from me, every day. Every single day. You used to melt when I touched you. Now you recoil like I'm a monster.'

Apt words from the man himself. He understood what he was, even then.

'You know why I recoil,' I said, my voice throaty and rough. I coughed, drank some more water. 'I don't trust you.'

Dornan growled. 'I've done everything for you! Everything, you understand?'

I nodded. 'Yeah. Still doesn't change what you did to me. To our baby. To Stephanie. To your *son*.'

'That's it?' he said. 'That's why you're acting like this?'

'*That's it?*' I repeated, dumbfounded. 'Yeah. How many more innocent lives do you snuff out because what they do is inconvenient to you?'

He didn't respond.

'Don't you want to know how he killed them?' I whispered. 'How your father wiped out my entire family?'

He levelled his glassy eyes at me, and I took that as an invitation to continue.

'Your father had his men go to Villanueva and burn their house to the ground. But first they tied them up, so they burned too.'

'Who told you that?' Dornan asked. He seemed shocked. Like his father had never told him.

'It doesn't matter who told me,' I said. 'All that matters is that it's true. Your father nullified his bargain with me when he killed my family. Me in exchange for their lives, that was the deal. And he killed them anyway.'

'I'm sorry,' he said.

He opened his mouth to say something else but I cut him off with a sharp flick of my hand. 'I can't, okay? I just ... can't.'

Dornan didn't argue. He went to my suitcase at the end of the bed and unzipped it, my skin crawling as I remembered the baby suitcase. I shook my head to try and get rid of the memory, my neck screaming in protest. I watched as Dornan lifted a grey knee-length dress and a blue scarf from the bag, bringing them over to me.

Dornan basically dressed me in the new dress, as if I were a child. He sat beside me and watched silently as I applied heavy foundation to my bruised neck before working on my face. I was red and blue from my wrists to my head, and although I tried my best, when I was done I still looked like shit. I needed a shower and about three weeks at home, where nobody could see me.

John. What was he going to say when he saw this?

'You should have told me about your family,' Dornan said, shame burning in his eyes.

I shook my head, resisting the overwhelming urge to roll my eyes. 'How long are we staying in Vegas?' I asked him.

He shrugged, standing up so that he was in front of me. 'How long do you *want* to stay?'

Oh, yeah, almost get killed, and now I get to decide how long we were staying.

Suddenly I felt like a little girl. Not a happy one. I felt powerless. Scared. Exhausted. 'I want a shower and some food and I want to go home,' I whispered. 'Can we please just go home?'

Dornan stared down at me for a long moment before nodding. 'Yeah,' he said, and I wondered what was going through his head at that moment. The phone was seemingly forgotten, the urge to murder me on hiatus for the time being. He looked remorseful. I didn't care.

He picked up the room service menu and handed it to me. 'Whatever you want,' he said.

How generous of you, I wanted to snap, but I bit my tongue, taking the menu silently. 'I think I'll shower first,' I said, putting the menu to the side and sliding off the bed, the room spinning as I straightened on my feet. Dornan put his hands out to steady me, and I looked at them like they were cockroaches on me. I pushed him off, making my way into the bathroom with him hot on my heels. Guess he didn't want me to lock myself in here again.

Without speaking – I was still coughing – I turned around, motioning to the zipper in the back of my dress. The room spun around me like a vortex of patterned tile and dark green wallpaper. And him.

Dornan unzipped me and I let the stupid dress fall to the floor, vowing to burn the fucking thing as soon as we were back home. I didn't want any lasting reminders of this trip. I'd have to find a way to lose the ring, too. Maybe I'd cut my finger off in a 'freak' accident in the kitchen. I could live just fine with nine fingers, right?

I wrapped my arms around myself and waited, staring at the wall, as Dornan turned on the shower and adjusted the temperature. He held out a hand to help me in, but I side-stepped it, practically hugging the tiled wall as I inched under the hot water. Avoiding any eye contact, I shuffled to the far corner of the shower, as far away from him as I could get, and slid down the wall, sitting underneath the high-pressure shower head with my knees drawn up to my chest. I covered my face with my hands, parting my fingers slowly so I knew where Dornan was. Because, more than the fact that I couldn't trust him, I could also no longer even try to predict what he was about to do next.

I peered at him through a river of mascara and my webbed fingers and saw his erection clearly bulging from his jeans. I wondered how it could be that a man could find such erotic thoughts while looking at the woman he'd almost just killed, as she sat naked in the bottom of a shower and wept.

CHAPTER TWENTY-FOUR

MARIANA

I didn't even know what time it was. I'd showered, wrapped myself in a fluffy robe, and come back out to the bed, where I now sat. My stomach was empty and growling for food.

'I'll order us some food,' Dornan said. To go from such violence to total normality in such a short span of time was frightening, but a relief all the same. I'd almost died just now by Dornan's hand – literally, his hand around my throat, cutting off my oxygen – and it was time to form some kind of escape plan.

An immediate one.

First, though, I had to survive the here and now. My stomach grumbled insistently, so loud that Dornan heard it. 'You want eggs?' he asked. What a fucking gentleman, this guy. A whirlwind (forced) wedding in Vegas, almost murdering me, and now he was offering to get me eggs.

'I'll be fine,' I said, waving my hand dismissively. 'You go shower. I'll order for us. What do you want?'

'Surprise me,' he said, and I cringed. Surprises were bad. I didn't ever want another surprise in my life again.

I waited until the shower was running and grabbed the room service menu. I did briefly contemplate the idea of running while Dornan showered, but it would've been for nothing. I had no money, no ID, I was an illegal immigrant, and I didn't know Vegas. I could call John, sure, once I found a pay phone somewhere, but he'd get caught. We both would. The grip of the cartel was just too powerful.

I decided to stay in the room and avoid having to think about any of this for at least another twenty-four hours. I settled on what I wanted to order – eggs and bacon for me, eggs and steak for Dornan – and was about to pick up the phone when the fucking thing rang so loudly, I almost fell on the floor. I answered the phone as Dornan poked his head out of the bathroom door, a towel around his waist and dripping water everywhere.

'Who is it?' he asked.

'It's room service,' a familiar male voice on the other end said.

'It's room service,' I parroted back to Dornan. Oh, shit. I knew that voice. Velvet-smooth and cunning. Somebody who was looking for Murphy.

'Act normally,' said FBI Agent Lindsay Price. 'You're going to meet me downstairs in one hour, do you understand? Say yes so Dornan hears.'

'Yes,' I replied, well aware that Dornan was still watching intently.

'You're going to come unarmed. Say "scrambled eggs".'

This was ridiculous. I didn't want to meet Lindsay downstairs. He was probably here to fucking arrest me. I couldn't leave Los Angeles with John and the kids if I was being arrested. *I couldn't get back to my son if I was being arrested.*

'No, that's wrong,' I said. 'That's not what I said.'

I rolled my eyes at Dornan and said something into the phone in Spanish. 'This guy's English is terrible,' I whispered, my hand over the receiver. 'Go finish your shower.'

'Don't forget coffee,' Dornan called, closing the bathroom door. I heard the shower start up again and returned my attention to the phone. 'What the hell are you doing?' I hissed. 'Are you trying to get me killed?'

'I was about three seconds from busting into your room this morning. How's your neck?'

I felt like someone had knocked the wind out of me. Again.

'You're listening to us?' I whispered.

'Mostly watching,' Lindsay replied.

Oh, for the love of all that is holy. Cameras!? A scarlet blush crept up my body and settled in my cheeks as I thought about what I'd been doing the night before. Putting on a porn show for an audience of one.

I hadn't realised there was an audience of more than one. I felt like I'd been punched in the face. I mean, I had basically been punched in the face by Dornan – but this felt even worse than that.

'Your boyfriend's pretty violent. Seems like even he thinks you've got something to do with Agent Murphy disappearing into thin air.'

Boyfriend. He hadn't said husband. So obviously they hadn't been watching everything. He hadn't picked up on the fact that Ms Rodriguez was now a reluctant Mrs, complete with a black and red wedding band tattoo that had started to scab over. How disgustingly delightful.

'Watching *how*?' I exclaimed, looking around the room.

'The FBI is blessed with a generous technology budget. Trust me. We got plenty of angles.' He seemed to hesitate for a moment. 'Are you okay?'

'I'm not okay,' I seethed, watching the bathroom door intently. 'Isn't that against the law? Filming someone without their permission?'

'It's called a warrant,' Lindsay said.

A warrant? *Fuck me.* I was ready to hang up, but something about his tone, and the mention of a motherfucking warrant, kept the phone glued to my ear.

'He almost killed you, you know that, right?'

I wanted to throw the phone out of the window. 'I guess I'm just lucky the FBI were watching out for me,' I replied, my words dripping with sarcasm. 'Thank you.'

Lindsay sighed. 'We were in the hallway. Another few seconds and we would have been busting your door down.'

I didn't respond. I could barely hear above the screaming in my head.

'I'm on your side,' he added. I snorted. 'Mariana, I know how violent Dornan is. I understand the danger you're in. I can help you. I might be the only one who can help you at this point. Let me help you.'

The words I'd uttered to John came back to haunt me: *I don't need a man to save me.* Maybe I was wrong. Maybe I did.

'Here's what's going to happen,' Lindsay said, shifting gears. 'I'm going to send two cups of coffee up with your food. One will be drugged for your dear boyfriend. He needs to take a nap so we can talk. The drugs will last at least an hour, but I only need five minutes.'

'What if I don't want to talk?' I asked. 'What if I'd rather you just went away?'

I heard him shuffling papers. 'You don't have to talk,' he said. 'But I'd strongly suggest that you at least give me five minutes of your time, Ms Rodriguez. Do you really think you'll be able to make it back to your son and protect him without the FBI's help?'

'Okay,' I said, cutting him off before he could make any more mention of my *son*. 'But,' I added, switching the receiver from my left ear to my right, 'Dornan's a big guy – he needs a horse tranquilliser to knock him down. A Percocet isn't going to cut it.'

'I'll keep that in mind,' he replied. 'The black coffee's for him. Don't drink it. We want him asleep, not you dead.'

'Whatever,' I snapped, my ears buzzing, the line already dead.

Somehow the FBI had tracked us to Vegas. Shit. Shit. SHIT!

***

I thought I'd throw up waiting for the knock on the door and for 'room service' to appear. When a guy in his mid-thirties appeared at the door, wearing an ill-fitting hotel uniform and wheeling a tray bursting with breakfast foods, I glared at him so intently I'm surprised he didn't catch on fire from my death rays. Sure enough, two cups of coffee sat in the middle of the tray, steam billowing from them. That right there was the biggest giveaway. I'd never had room service coffee delivered at any temperature but lukewarm. They were obviously camped out in a room nearby, watching us and preparing poisoned coffee to send to our room.

Fuckers.

I debated telling Dornan about Lindsay's call and the spiked coffee, but I decided against it, sipping at my latte as I watched Dornan down his black coffee in about three gulps.

The coffee worked quickly. I'd already anticipated Dornan's suspicion at suddenly feeling woozy and drugged, so I figured I'd lessen it a little if possible. While he drank his coffee I gave him the quickest blowjob in the history of blowjobs, hating myself the entire time, and now armed with the knowledge that Lindsay could see everything I was doing. *Great.* As I swallowed, Dornan's hand on my head, I made a mental note to thank Lindsay for saving my life when I was being choked out.

Seriously. They couldn't have knocked and pretended to be cleaners or something?

Instead, they'd watched as I fought for my life. More embarrassingly, they'd watched while I had, quote, 'fucked myself', and given Dornan a peep show to rival all others. I'd made myself come in front of him, and probably half of Lindsay's unit.

I started to panic as I contemplated where else they might've had cameras. In my apartment, the place where I'd killed Murphy? That didn't make sense, though. If they'd had cameras hidden in my apartment, I'd already be sitting in a cell, serving my life sentence without parole.

That was the punishment for killing a federal officer of the law, last time I checked.

Add money laundering, drug running and (unknowingly) balancing the books for an entire human trafficking operation for the better part of ten years, and it was easy to watch the consecutive life sentences stack on top of one another like Tetris bricks.

Dornan was snoring soon after he finished his coffee and I'd finished him. He didn't even make it to the bed, sprawled out on the couch in the sitting area. I prodded him a couple of times, then, relatively comfortable with the fact that he was deep asleep, I got dressed, brushed my teeth, grabbed my purse and headed downstairs.

A black Escalade was parked at the front entrance to the Wynn, the door already open for me. I picked the guy holding the door straight away – black suit, short hair, one of those little earpieces in his ear with a cord that ran down under his suit jacket. He held out a hand to help me step up into the SUV, but I ignored it, preferring to use the handle inside the doorframe to pull myself up and onto the black leather seat that flanked the rear of the interior. I winced as the door closed and the central locking clicked with a sound of permanence.

FBI Agent Lindsay Price sat beside me in the dim cabin, the dark tint on the windows saving us from the worst of the unrelenting Nevada sun. He was still the same as I remembered – green eyes and dark hair cut close to his skull, military style – but he looked a little rougher around the edges than the first time we'd met. He looked like he'd missed a day of the impeccable shaving routine he obviously adhered to. His chin bore a five o'clock shadow and his eyes were lined with fatigue, despite it being only nine in the morning.

'Your bag, please?' Lindsay asked.

'Well hello to you, too.' I clutched my bag tightly, glaring at him.

Lindsay raised his eyebrows. 'Look,' he sighed. 'We can do this the hard way. I can take out my gun,' he patted his hip holster, 'and I can threaten you, maybe throw some cuffs on you. But I don't want to. I'm not going to.'

I didn't say anything.

'Just give me the bag,' he said, holding out his hand. 'Please.'

I don't know what it was. Maybe it was the fact that I was so tired. Worn out, frayed. It seemed I'd momentarily lost the ability to resist. Without breaking eye contact, I placed the bag on the seat between us and he scooped it up, rummaging around until he found my gun and pulled it out.

'That's mine,' I said, reaching for it.

Lindsay opened the chamber, presumably to check for bullets. 'A woman carrying an unloaded gun, and there are no bullets in her bag. Did your boyfriend take them?'

I didn't bother correcting the term boyfriend to husband. He'd find out soon enough, no doubt.

'What, were you filming us on the car trip, too?' I asked.

'Educated guess,' Lindsay shrugged.

'How'd you know I'd bring a gun?' I asked.

He smiled. Not in an arrogant, cocky way. Just a smile. 'Because I told you not to.'

'You think you know everything about me?' I asked.

'Twelve years in the FBI profiling unit, there's a good chance I know more about you than you know about yourself.'

'Oh yeah?'

'Yeah. I know you're planning something. I know the only thing stopping you from running is one John Portland.'

I sat back, stunned. I don't know why I was stunned. I mean, if they'd been watching me, then they'd probably know about John.

'I know you're still hoping you can get out of this without anyone getting hurt,' Lindsay added, his voice softening.

'And let me guess,' I said evenly. 'You're here to tell me I can't. Right?'

'I'm here to implore you to do the right thing.' He patted the gun on his lap – *my* fucking gun, the one I'd used to kill Murphy and Allie.

Panic began to rise in my throat. 'Why do you need my gun?' I asked.

'Insurance.' He paused for effect. *Insurance for what?* 'That's all. Go see your little boyfriend. Stay out of trouble.'

With great irritation, I flashed him the skull tattoo on my ring finger. 'You mean my husband.'

Lindsay snatched up my hand and studied the tattoo. 'What is this? You guys got matching promise rings?'

I rolled my eyes, holding up my right hand, where my actual wedding band sat. 'I can't wear it until the tattoo heals. Apparently gold just doesn't seal the deal like ink these days.'

Lindsay's mouth practically hit the floor of the SUV. 'You're legally married?'

'Yeah,' I replied. 'Dornan finally decided that he wanted to marry me. I found out when I got to the altar. Aren't I lucky?'

His expression was grave. 'You don't understand what this means for you and me.'

'Oh come on, Agent Price,' I said, pursing my lips mockingly. 'You can't be jealous, surely.'

His green eyes were ablaze. 'You do know why he did this, don't you?'

I shrugged. 'Entrapment. Control. Paranoia. Or maybe he just really, really loves me.'

Lindsay wet his lips with his tongue, at the same time shaking his head. 'He married you so you wouldn't have to testify against him. The FBI is building a case against his father's cartel. A case that very much hinges on your testimony against these men, Ms Rodriguez. Sorry, *Mrs Ross*.'

I felt my stomach sinking. 'Who says I was going to testify?'

'Your kid,' Lindsay said pointedly.

He had me, and we both knew it. I'd do anything to protect Luis. I already had, indirectly, when I'd killed Murphy and Allie.

Speaking of.

'I need to deliver Agent Murphy's subpoena,' Lindsay said quietly. 'Any idea where he might be?'

I narrowed my eyes. 'No.' *Not unless you count the fact that little pieces of him were probably left over in that crematorium I'd visited again the other day.*

Nobody spoke for a long, uncomfortable moment. I watched as cars pulled up to the front entrance of the Wynn and people got out. Regular people, excited to gamble and take in a show and eat way too much at the seafood buffet. People who were oblivious to the seedy underbelly of the world, their masks still firmly over their eyes as reality painted a very different picture.

'I haven't had a lot of sleep lately,' Lindsay said, changing tack. 'Do you know why?'

I feigned boredom. 'No, but I bet you're going to tell me anyway.'

'I've been investigating a murder.' *Great.* 'A young woman.' *Awesome.* 'A fellow federal officer, actually.'

Fuck.

My heart skipped inside my chest. The dominos. They kept falling.

No, the fucking sky was falling.

'She was a DEA agent,' Lindsay said, his eyes drilling into me so intensely I itched. 'Somebody shot her.'

No shit. I wanted to look away, but to look away would be admitting guilt.

'And?' I challenged. I tried to recall whether looking up or looking down signalled a lie. In the end, I couldn't remember at all, so I kept my gaze glued to Lindsay's eyes.

'I think you killed her,' Lindsay said softly.

There it was. The real reason he wanted to see me so desperately. My head swam – drowned – in what might happen next. I saw walls and prison bars, and a cell door slamming shut in my face.

'Fuck you.'

Lindsay didn't answer.

'What do you need from me?' I asked slowly, a crushing feeling of defeat pressing down on me.

'I need to know what they did to you,' Lindsay said. 'And what they made you do for them.'

'How? When?'

'Soon. Very soon.'

I swallowed thickly. 'How am I supposed to trust you?' I asked. 'What if you're just like everybody else?' And suddenly I wanted to cry. Because he didn't seem like everybody else. Lindsay Price seemed like a real stand-up guy. Maybe he wasn't. He could have been an axe murderer, for all I knew. Could have been working for Emilio.

'I'm not like the men you're used to,' Lindsay said. He put his hand on my arm in a comforting gesture, and surprisingly, I didn't shrug it off. It was warm.

'What are you like, then?' I whispered. My eyes burned with unshed tears as a lump grew in my throat.

'I believe in justice,' he said, handing me the gun back. 'But I also believe in survival. I believe that sometimes, the law doesn't understand what a person can endure before they break.'

I stared at the gun in my hands in disbelief. 'I thought–'

'A gesture of goodwill,' he interrupted. 'That gun is my only piece of evidence linking you to Alexandra Baxter's murder. I know you killed her, Mariana. I don't need to take your gun to know that. I only need to take your gun to *prove* that.'

'If Emilio finds out I've spoken to you, he'll kill me,' I said, my hands shaking as they cupped the gun.

Lindsay nodded. 'Don't tell anyone. Don't write it down, don't even think about our conversation until the next time we meet. Understood?'

I nodded.

'I know what they did to your family,' he added. 'For what it's worth … I'm sorry.'

In the edges of my mind, I saw them screaming as they burned. I didn't want to see that. I looked out of my window. 'How long does that sedative last?' I asked him, changing the subject as I stared at the gold-tinted stack of glass that made up the Wynn.

Lindsay tapped a button in his armrest and a screen unfolded from the ceiling. He aimed a small remote and it flashed to life, a black and white image of a hotel room becoming visible. He pointed to the middle of the screen. 'Long enough.'

I peered closer, picking Dornan's still frame on the couch in the centre of the suite. I glanced at Lindsay as something unsettling occurred to me. 'What happens next?' I asked quietly.

'That depends,' Lindsay replied. 'The situation isn't as clear-cut as it was. You're now not compelled to testify. You'll have to choose. We can't force you to give evidence against your husband.' He said the word 'husband' like he was talking about having to wipe dog shit off his shoe. I got the feeling he really didn't like Dornan.

Neither did I, anymore, so we had that in common.

'No shit,' I replied. 'Could've gotten here a day earlier, saved me the pain.' I flashed my tattooed finger at him.

'I think you like the pain,' Lindsay murmured, his tone almost sad. 'I think you don't remember how to survive without pain. You're always either running at it, or away from it, but what you can't see is that you're going to drown in it. Either that, or your husband will kill you. At this rate, I'd put my money on him.'

Ouch.

Neither of us said anything for a moment. I glanced at the screen in front of us again. Dornan hadn't moved. Maybe he was dead. That would solve some of my problems.

'I'm tired of the pain,' I answered finally. 'I don't want it anymore.'

I was only too aware that Dornan would stir if I was gone much longer.

'You testify against Emilio, against Dornan, and the rest of his club, and you get immunity. You get your son back.'

Fuck him for using my son as blackmail material. 'I'm not saying one word for you unless you can guarantee John's safety. We both get immunity.'

Lindsay lifted his eyebrows. 'No can do. He goes down with his club.'

'I love him,' I said quietly. 'I can't let him go down with them.'

'You loved Dornan once, too. And see how that turned out?'

I closed my eyes and tried not to have a total meltdown. I had to agree to whatever Lindsay was saying or he'd never let me out of his sight again. I couldn't very well slip away into the night if I was being tracked by the FBI.

'You say you're tired of the pain,' Lindsay added. 'Let me help you. Let me take it away. All you have to do is say yes.'

I rested my forehead on the back of the seat in front of me. Everything, it seemed, hinged on the next thing that came out of my mouth. Three letters or two.

'Yes,' I lied. Without Lindsay agreeing to give John immunity, I wasn't testifying. I was running. We were running. I just had to get back to John and formulate a get the fuck out of town plan. I sucked in a breath as a wave of dizziness slammed into me. I had to get out of the car before I passed out. I stuffed the gun back into my bag, searching for the door handle. I heard a click as the doors unlocked and I opened the door, gulping in the hot Nevada air as the same dude on the outside of the car held out a hand to help me down.

I slid out of the SUV, turning back to face him as my feet hit the ground. The last image I had of Lindsay Price was his serious expression as he watched me silently. He almost seemed ... relieved.

I slammed the door so hard, I swear the car moved. My wrist throbbed from the sudden exertion, and I rushed back into the hotel lobby, parting a sea of tourists with the force of my heels against the polished floor.

Soon. Something was going to happen soon.

How was I going to tell John?

We had to leave Vegas *now*.

I rode the lift back to the hotel suite with one hand against the mirrored wall. I was tired.

I was so fucking tired of this life.

CHAPTER TWENTY-FIVE

JOHN

Two days.

Two whole days and he hadn't been able to contact Mariana. Something was amiss, but he had no fucking idea what it was or how to find out.

Oh, and they were driving to San fucking Diego, on Emilio's orders. Caroline, who for once was straight and sober, was driving down with Juliette, for some event Emilio had insisted the entire club attend. And John was riding his motorcycle with the rest of the Gypsy Brothers, because presidential duties demanded he lead the pack. For the moment, at least. After the shit that went down at the strip club with Dornan, he was fairly sure he wouldn't be presiding over his club much longer. An invested man would have cared. A man who wanted to pull the trigger and run had no time to care about such things.

John had been at home when he'd received a call about an urgent club meet. 'Stay away from that boy, you hear me?' he had said to his daughter, as he grabbed his leather jacket and the keys to his motorcycle.

Juliette rolled her eyes at him, barely looking away from the television. 'Daddy, I don't even like him. I just feel sorry for him.' Stretching her long legs out on the sofa, she finally turned her gaze to John. Her expression grew troubled. 'His brothers are so horrible. They're always hurting him.'

John shrugged. 'Boys can be rough, baby. Especially those boys.' He thought of Dornan's sons, pack of wildlings that they were. They'd never had a sister to soften them, to teach them that sometimes you had to be gentle. They were loud and brash and they communicated with their fists. Dornan's oldest sons were in their twenties now, patch-wearing Gypsy Brothers with little kids of their own, and they were still animals.

'Why did Uncle Dornan do that to Jase's mom?' Juliette asked quietly. 'He's part of our family. He's always been good, Dad.'

John rubbed his hand across his stubbled chin, contemplating how to answer that question. His daughter was his only child, his world, and how was he supposed to explain to her what his best friend had done to his own son? How was he supposed to explain to his teenage daughter that dear Uncle Dornan had murdered his son's mother in cold blood and left her in a bathtub full of blood for him to find?

He couldn't. He refused to put that mental image inside Juliette's precious mind. He prayed that the young boy had been vague on the details of the visceral horror he had endured upon seeing his slain mother.

John sat on the arm of the sofa, wondering what the fuck he could say. He bit the inside of his cheek, the memory of Stephanie's bloody corpse at the forefront of his mind.

'It's not for you to worry about,' he said. 'I can't talk about it anymore.'

Juliette's face fell. 'Okay,' she said, looking back to the TV. It was clear she was hurt, but she didn't say anything. She was a good girl. Always had been. Sometimes too good.

'Sweetie,' John said, cursing the Gypsy Brothers' existence as he reached out a hand to his daughter. She looked at it like it was a piece of shit and pulled away, out of his reach.

'Did you help him kill her?' Juliette asked suddenly. There it was. Her attitude. He was almost relieved to hear it. It was better than her fear.

'No,' he replied. 'I didn't help him kill her. I would never hurt a woman. A mother.'

'But you do hurt people. Don't you?' She looked at his messed-up knuckles, and John found himself shoving his hands in his pockets, ashamed.

'Your Uncle Dornan was out of line,' John said tightly.

She blinked her big green eyes up at him. 'It was because Dornan found them, wasn't it? Jason said he knew–'

John's expression must have changed, because she stopped mid-sentence. 'Never mind,' Juliette said, looking at the floor.

'You can tell me, Julie,' John said. He felt sweat gather on the back of his neck. Too many secrets. Too many lies. *Don't shut down on me now, Julie.*

'Jason said he knew you before,' she said. 'That you sent them money. Is that why we never have any money?'

John looked around the cramped living room, acutely aware of how well Caroline could hear things, even when she was high. 'Where's your mother?'

Juliette shrugged. John looked around again, feeling deeply unsettled. 'We can talk about this later,' he said, taking a twenty out of his beat-up wallet and passing it to Juliette. 'Order pizza if you get hungry. And don't tell anyone about what you and Jason discussed, okay?' He lowered his voice to a barely audible level. 'If your mother hears talk about sending money off, she will lose her goddamn mind. Understand?'

She nodded.

'Don't go to his house,' John added. They both knew who he was referring to.

Juliette frowned. 'Don't tell me I can't see him, Dad,' she said. 'If I don't go see him, he's all alone.'

He could hardly argue with that. Instead, he kissed the top of her head before shrugging into his leather jacket. The thing seemed to get heavier with time, and it was true, the burden of who he was and who he had to be was a weight he bore alone, a weight he couldn't bear to hold for another moment but which stayed with him, unrelenting, pressing down on his shoulders with every step he took. He glimpsed himself in the hallway mirror on his way out. He looked worn out, used up. He looked like somebody who should've gotten out of this game a long time ago.

Before he could go anywhere, though, he got the phone call from Viper. Club business in San Diego. Dornan had demanded John's presence immediately. And Caroline's. And *Juliette's*.

Not just club business, though. A celebration. Seemed the woman he would have laid down his life for, the woman he loved more than anything, had been unreachable for two days because she was busy marrying Dornan.

CHAPTER TWENTY-SIX
MARIANA

Dornan's father lived on a compound that belonged in a Hollywood movie. It was ridiculous: a massive parcel of land, the main part of which was surrounded by a six-foot solid brick fence. A fence topped with razor wire and broken glass. Basically, unless Emilio wanted you to enter or leave, you were fucked.

Which was why it seemed such an odd place to hold a party. Yeah, you could jazz the place up, get out some tables and break out the crystal wine glasses, but at the end of the day the place resembled a prison more than the palatial homestead it was obviously trying to convey. Perhaps I was just biased; I'd started my days as a captive in this very place, locked underground in a tiny cell, stripped and humiliated and prepared for an auction where Emilio had planned to sell me as a slave.

Dornan had been the only reason I hadn't ended up living in a dog cage at the end of some psychopath's bed, naked and wearing a chain around my neck. Maybe. Probably.

But now I was one of the *familia*, welcomed with open arms. It was surreal, like a nightmare that you can't quite wake up from but that you know is about to give you a heart attack if you stay in it for a moment longer.

After Dornan had finally woken from his drugged slumber around noon, we left Vegas. We'd stopped off in LA briefly on our way back, for showers, extra clothes and Dornan's motorcycle. I'd voted to stay in the limo, but Dornan rejected that. He hadn't told me anything about where we'd be going on the motorcycle, other than that we were celebrating our quickie nuptials with his family. Something I was just thrilled about. He also hadn't seemed suspicious about the way he'd passed out for several hours after drinking the drugged coffee Lindsay had sent up to our hotel room, which was a small mercy.

At Emilio's compound, four hours later, I had to fight to keep my jaw off the pavement as I surveyed no less than fifty Harley-Davidson motorcycles parked up inside the compound, flanking the long driveway that culminated in a large circle in front of the main house. There were dozens of cars too. I spied John's, and wondered where he was. How he'd been told about what had happened in Vegas, and by who.

If he thought I'd betrayed him.

A deep sorrow spread through me. My finger was still throbbing. How had it come to this? Marrying a man by force, letting him flaunt our union in front of everyone he knew? In front of the man I actually loved? Lying to everyone, conducting secret meetings with the FBI after allowing them to drug said husband ... Things were spiralling completely out of control.

And in the middle of the raging storm was the image of my son. He was waiting for me. He was safe, but for how long?

I pushed him out of my mind as Dornan pulled me from his motorcycle, placed his hand into the small of my back and propelled me along the path that led to the front door of Emilio's mansion. It wouldn't do me any good, thinking about Luis when I was about to enter the lion's den. I needed strength, not weakness.

I needed cunning, not despair.

'Are you ready?' Dornan asked me, and I plastered on my fake smile. I let the mask fall into place and steeled myself for the biggest act of my life. The lie. *I love you.* When really, I wanted to burn this place to the ground with Dornan and his father inside. Lindsay's words played on repeat in my head, a soothing chant, a reassurance that this was all going to be blown up *soon*.

'I'm ready,' I murmured, leaning into him.

He liked that. It seemed to make him proud as he looked me up and down, from my throbbing finger marked with his brand, to my eyes, covered expertly with layers of heavy make-up to hide the marks. The scarf around my neck, to conceal the bruises he'd raged upon my skin. I was beaten and broken, but in that moment, all I felt was impatience. I wasn't afraid. I was just waiting. The FBI was coming for us. Lindsay Price was going to make sure Emilio and Dornan were punished for their sins.

I just had to get to John and let him know what had transpired before he was punished, too.

***

It was a lavish party, to say the least. Every Gypsy Brother seemed to be in attendance, as well as at least half of the children fathered by the club members. I caught John's eye as Dornan and I walked into the room to applause and cheers, but he looked away. It didn't matter; what could I communicate to him in a crowd of Gypsy Brothers and cartel members who would murder us if they knew the truth? I had to find a way to get to him. But I had to be patient. Get Dornan hammered, break away and hope John came looking for me. I knew he'd be dying to get me alone, if only to demand an explanation as to why the fuck Dornan and I were now married.

The minutes dragged on. It was almost like an out-of-body experience – I was there, but I wasn't. Somebody had made a wedding cake, but instead of a bride and groom on top, there were two tacky motorcycle helmets. I tried not to throw up in my mouth when I saw that. I spoke to so many people I'd never even met, and it was strange, going from being the girl hidden away and not talked about, to the girl Dornan suddenly wanted to parade around like a prized head of cattle. He kept worrying, too. Kept taking me aside and touching my neck and asking if I was all right, until I snapped at him and told him to relax and quit reminding me of what he'd done. He largely ignored me after that, which was a blessed relief.

John, I screamed inside my head. *I need you. Where are you?* I had to warn him before Lindsay and the FBI moved in, and closed off our only hope of getting out of this alive.

CHAPTER TWENTY-SEVEN

DORNAN

Dornan left Mariana with Jase and Juliette and approached John. He'd been planning this moment since John's fist had connected with his face a few nights earlier. When he'd dared to question Dornan in front of their club. You didn't question a brother. Ever.

John needed to be displaced.

'Congratulations,' John said, looking anything but congratulatory.

Dornan could empathise. He'd just gotten rid of his own ball-and-chain in the form of divorcing Celia, and John was still stuck with that whore Caroline, who was currently harassing a poor young waitress for more champagne.

'Thanks, Johnny Boy,' Dornan said, slapping John on the arm. He hadn't used that name for his best friend in a long time. He didn't pause before he delivered his next line.

'Boys are waiting in the garage,' he said. 'We're voting. Now.'

John's eyes seemed to cloud over momentarily when he heard the words. *We're voting.* John didn't ask what they were voting on. Something told Dornan he already knew.

John quickly regained his composure, passing Dornan as he made his way to the large garage at the other end of the house. Dornan followed, watching the large, red and black Gypsy Brothers patch that sat in the middle of John's back. Everyone else had black and white patches. Only the president got red.

They'd have to get someone to unravel all that thread. Dornan might be taking the patch, but he'd never take the jacket off a brother's back.

CHAPTER TWENTY-EIGHT
JOHN

The vote for prez went in Dornan's favour. Overwhelmingly.

John understood. It was like a chain reaction. He stared at the faces of his brothers in arms as they sat around a makeshift table and cast their votes for the Gypsy Brothers presidency, men he would have laid down his life for – many that he actually had risked his life to protect. Yet, one by one, they voted against him. They were afraid, John realised, about halfway through the proceedings. Not Dornan's sons, of course – the board was half made up of people somehow related to Dornan by marriage or blood, so it wasn't surprising that his coup was so successful.

What was surprising was that John didn't care. He just couldn't muster a single fuck about what was happening. No, instead a nervous buzz began in the pit of his stomach and spread through his body. At first he didn't understand what it was, and then he could have laughed when he figured it out.

He was excited. He was thrilled. He was getting out.

Then he remembered that Dornan and Mariana were married, and his brief elation was tempered by rage.

John sat back and watched as Dornan was sworn in as president. That buzz became an angry scream in his ears, as he imagined Mariana having to say the words 'I do' to this motherfucker. That was the sole reason for his violent need to kill Dornan in that moment. If it were just a matter of being usurped by the Gypsy Brothers, he would have gotten up on the table and done the fucking moonwalk.

After they voted Dornan in, it was time to decide on a new VP. Not surprisingly, almost half the men voted for John. Perhaps that was their way of trying to make amends for essentially betraying their president by overthrowing him and installing a madman as leader. But despite the votes, one person got more – Dornan's oldest son Chad, who was possibly the least intelligent person John had ever encountered. Jacked up on a daily cocktail of roids and speed, Chad was a surprising choice.

It just showed how far things had gone.

It was only when Dornan was passing his VP patch to Chad that John realised he needed to give his patches to Dornan. He'd lived in this jacket for years, ever since the last one had been shredded by knife slashes when he'd been in a fight with a rival cartel member. The patches were originals, having survived the past several decades unmarred. Stained with engine oil and probably blood, but always with him.

John slid off his jacket, realising for the first time how heavy the thick leather was. The thing weighed a ton. No wonder his shoulders always felt like they bore the weight of the world on them. Was this how it felt to be free? To be a normal person? Just a thin shirt on your back, no traces of a club patch that acted as a homing beacon for violence?

John turned the jacket over, but before he started to tug at the thread holding the club insignia to the beat-up leather, he stopped. He held the jacket out to Dornan, who didn't move.

'I'm not taking your jacket, John,' he said, and for a moment John could have sworn he saw shame flicker in Dornan's eyes.

Undeterred, John dropped the jacket onto the table in front of Dornan. 'I want you to have it,' he said, stepping back. 'I'll get a new one.' *I'll trade you my fucking jacket for your wife.*

Dornan regarded him gravely. 'We gonna have trouble, brother?'

John smiled, reaching out and slapping Dornan on the shoulder. 'No trouble, brother. My loyalty is to the club, whether I'm president or not.'

An awkward silence fell over the room. John let his eyes roam around once more, and then he turned and left the only friends he'd ever known.

CHAPTER TWENTY-NINE
MARIANA

'Are you okay?' I asked Jason.

He nodded, looking jumpy as always. His eyes travelled around the large sitting room that had been dressed up and filled with party guests. I opened my mouth to ask him why he had a black eye and a cut on his lip when I felt a cold hand on the back of my neck. I jumped, expecting to see Dornan. Instead, when I turned around Emilio stared back at me with his beady black eyes, bringing one hand to my cheek.

'You look so pretty, Mariana,' he said, using a single finger to pull my scarf down enough to expose the bruises on my throat. The sight of them made him smile, a grotesque expression that made him look like he was about to eat me.

'Thank you,' I replied, swallowing my discomfort as best I could.

'It looks like my son got a little excited,' he said, dropping his eyes to my throat again. 'He gets that from me, you know.'

'I can only imagine,' I said.

'You ever pull a stunt like that again,' he said quietly, tucking a stray hair behind my ear, 'and I'll take you down to Budget Funerals and put you in the oven myself. Alive. Do you understand?'

Budget Funerals. He'd mentioned the place by name. Had it been on the box of ashes that I'd dumped on his desk? I couldn't remember. The hairs on the back of my neck started to prickle uncomfortably as my heart raced to a gallop.

Out of the corner of my eye, I could see that Jason and Juliette were taking this entire conversation in, their eyes like saucers, their mouths slack with shock. I moved ever so slightly, making sure they weren't in Emilio's line of sight, and nodded. 'I understand.'

'Nobody is irreplaceable, darling,' he said with a grin. He still had his hand on the side of my head, just above my ear. I wanted him to stop touching me, but what was I going to do? I was in a room full of his family and his people. He could literally have murdered me where I stood and nobody would have dared to stop him. Well, except John, but he was MIA, along with Dornan and half the Gypsy Brothers.

'You might think you've got power now that you're married to my son, but he's been married before. You replaced Celia. I won't have a problem finding somebody to replace you.'

I nodded, trying to stay outwardly calm. I wanted to lean over and throw up all over Emilio's expensive Italian loafers, but he'd probably make me lick them clean as punishment. Instead I stood there, frozen, until a warm hand snaked around my waist and squeezed. Jase flinched as he made eye contact with whoever it was hugging me to their side.

I smelled John, but that couldn't be right. I whipped my head to the left, confused. Dornan was beside me, but he was wearing John's jacket. My heart rate rose to fever pitch as I stepped back, almost ending up in Juliette's lap as I tried to understand what was going on.

'What are you wearing?' I asked Dornan, frowning in confusion as I re-read the patch above his heart that clearly said PRESIDENT. 'Why are you wearing John's jacket?' *Did you kill John?* I mean, why else would he have his jacket?

Dornan grinned. 'We just voted. You're looking at the new president of the Gypsy Brothers.'

I opened my mouth to ask where John was, but then I saw him in the corner, talking to Viper but casting glances our way. He was okay. He was not the president anymore, but he was okay. Thank God.

I looked back to Jason, and my heart broke. He'd flinched when he saw his father, I realised. He was that terrified of Dornan that he couldn't even be near him. I heard Lindsay's words replay in my mind. Soon. I'd get away sooner. Me and John and Juliette and Jason. I would insist, and John would do it because he loved me. Because it was the right thing to do.

I heard the sound of cutlery clinking on glass. Emilio had disappeared, making his way to the centre of the large room.

'A toast to the lovely bride and groom,' he called out, a hush settling over the crowd as Dornan took hold of my arm and dragged me towards his father. His fingers hurt as they dug into my arm. There'd be more bruises tomorrow to add to my collection.

'My dear friends and family,' Emilio said, 'let's give a warm welcome to my son's new wife, and my new daughter. I give you Mariana Ross.'

There were claps and cheers, and hugs from Emilio. First he embraced his son, something I'd never seen him do in ten years, and then he hugged me, almost crushing me in his arms. He might've been old, but the man was strong. Just as I thought he was letting go, he leaned in and gave me a wet kiss, right on my mouth. I almost jerked my head back, stopping myself just in time. If I made him angry he'd kill me, and then there wouldn't be any escaping for a new life and a chance to finally be reunited with Luis.

'We're a very affectionate family,' Emilio whispered in my ear. 'We share ... *everything*.'

I gritted my teeth and kept my fake smile plastered on. Beside me, Dornan was oblivious, his friends and fellow club members congratulating him in a steady procession. Me, I was just there to look good. None of them gave me so much as a sideways glance. Then again, maybe they were too scared of Dornan yanking their eyeballs out for daring to look at his property.

As Emilio was finally disentangling himself from me, there was a scuffle and yelling from the edge of the room. A female voice. *Juliette*. I batted Emilio's hands out of my path, rushing to where I'd been standing in front of Jason and Juliette only moments earlier. Jason was on the ground, curled into the foetal position, his older brothers standing around him but nobody paying him any regard. Only Juliette was helping him, on her knees beside Jason, her hands pulling his shirt up to look at the damage.

John appeared by my right side, and Dornan soon joined him on my left. Oh, the irony of being flanked by your husband and your lover as you look at the son one of them hid away from the other.

'What happened?' I asked, acutely aware that the entire room seemed to have eyeballs on us. Juliette looked up, her eyes wet with tears, and that's when I noticed the blood on her hands.

I fell to my knees next to Juliette, searching for the source of the blood. Juliette lifted Jase's shirt, and I saw a long red line across his stomach, one that was seeping blood at an alarming rate.

'What happened?' Dornan asked, his voice deathly calm.

The boys started to fidget. I mean, they were hardly boys. All six of Dornan's older sons were patch-wearing Gypsy Brothers, ranging in age from Chad, the oldest at twenty-four, to Ant, the youngest at seventeen. Ant was only a few months older than Jase, but the difference in the two boys was stark. Ant was already a tattooed, drinking, drug-taking little smart ass, whereas Jason – apart from the tattoos he'd been forced to have inked upon his flesh – was relatively unmarked by the life.

Except now he had a dirty big slice in his belly, and his blood was all over the floor.

'It's just a flesh wound,' Jase muttered, his ghostly pale face telling me otherwise.

John yanked Juliette to her feet and tucked her under his arm, apparently not worried about the blood on her hands making a mess of his clothes. He'd likely seen a lot more blood in his time, and while it was true that Jason didn't exactly seem to be bleeding to death before everyone's eyes, he'd still been gouged deep enough to make him hurt.

'Dornan,' I snapped. 'Do something.'

He looked vaguely irritated by my directness. Well, fuck him. His son was bleeding on the floor at the hand of one of his other sons and he was standing there looking almost bored.

'Which one of you shitheads did this?' Dornan asked. There was much snickering and pushing between the brothers before Ant cleared his throat. Little fuck. I should've known it would be him. He followed Juliette around like a sick puppy, even though she told him constantly that he was like a brother to her, and no she would not date him. The kid was a date rape waiting to happen.

'It was an accident,' Ant shrugged, mirroring the way his father often acted when confronted with the truth. Deny, deny, deny.

'How do you accidentally stab somebody?' I interjected. 'No, really, I want to know.'

Ant sneered at me. I wanted to punch his head in, but I was well aware that we had a rather large audience.

'Ant, take your shirt off,' Dornan ordered, snapping his fingers. 'Now.'

With seemingly great reluctance, Ant took his shirt off and slapped it into his father's open palm. Dornan fixed him with a hard stare before turning to me. 'Here,' he said, handing me the shirt. 'For the blood.'

I took the shirt and pressed it to Jase's wound. The blood had already slowed to a trickle, but that wasn't the point. Who would do that? Hurt their own brother so brutally, so casually?

Little fucking savages.

'Get the fuck out of here,' Dornan said, and his older sons dispersed like rats in torchlight. 'You'll toughen up soon enough,' he said to Jason, and then he walked away. I stared at him as he left, incredulous.

'Let's get you to one of the bedrooms,' John said to Jason, kneeling beside me. 'Clean you up.'

Jason nodded, and together we managed to help him into a guest room on the ground floor without making his wound bleed too much. By the time Jason was lying on the bed, Juliette sitting by his side, I was ready to find a knife of my own and slit Ant's throat.

John located a first aid kit and I made quick work of the long cut. It looked like Ant had simply walked past Jason and dragged the tip of a knife along his stomach until it split open. I wanted to kill that kid.

Once Jason was bandaged, I left him to find some painkillers. I was barely two steps down the hall when an arm shot out of a doorway and yanked me inside. John. Before I could even open my mouth, he had the door locked and my hand held up to the light, examining the skull tattoo on my ring finger.

Our eyes met and I fought back tears. 'I didn't know where you were,' he breathed, dropping my hand and putting his fingers up to my mouth. He leaned in and kissed me, so softly that I could hardly believe it was the same man who'd picked me up and fucked me against a bathroom basin less than a week ago.

'I'm sorry,' I said, swallowing the rock in my throat. 'I didn't want to – I had to go along with it or I don't know what he would've done.'

John shook his head. 'Doesn't matter. We're getting out. We're taking those kids with us.'

I breathed a sigh of relief. Those kids. I nodded. 'Yeah, we are,' I agreed. 'And we have to do it now. This week. The FBI thinks I'm going to testify against Dornan and Emilio in exchange for immunity.'

'What?' John said.

I told him about how Lindsay had drugged Dornan and insisted I meet with him in Vegas. How they were planning to move on the cartel and the Gypsy Brothers very soon. John listened intently, his forehead lined deep with worry.

'We need cash,' he said.

I nodded excitedly. My insurance policy was about to pay off. 'I've got cash,' I replied. 'Lots and lots of cash. Think you can gather it up for us?'

John smiled, shaking his head. 'I knew it,' he said. 'I'm impressed.'

I rested my head on his shoulder for a brief moment, terrified at the prospect of having to go back out there and interact with Dornan and Emilio.

'I play the long game,' I said quietly.

John chuckled. 'That's good,' he said. 'Because I've got twenty-seven dollars to my name. Shit, I don't even own a leather jacket anymore.'

I looked up sharply as the puzzle pieces slammed together in my brain. 'That's your jacket Dornan's wearing? In front of you? Parading around like you're not even here?'

John nodded, cupping my chin with his hand and pulling my face to his. 'That would be the one,' he murmured against my lips, kissing me again. 'So we'll have to go somewhere warm, okay?'

'Okay,' I agreed, grabbing onto his wrists for dear life as he held my face in his palms.

'Now,' he said, grinning, 'tell me where I need to find this money.'

I couldn't help but grin back. I'd always been a planner. A saver of options for rainy days and escape plans. Thank Christ. Life on the run was going to be so much easier when we were millionaires.

CHAPTER THIRTY

MARIANA

We rode back to LA, a motley procession of motorcycles and the occasional car. I wasn't lucky enough to be a passenger in air-conditioned comfort, unless you counted the air blasting past my skull at a hundred miles an hour. No, I got the same four-hour ride on the back of Dornan's motorcycle that I'd endured on the way to San Diego, my entire body numb from the waist down by the time we rattled into Santa Monica.

Dornan deposited me at the gate to my apartment complex. 'Pack your shit,' he said, his sunglasses showing me my own reflection. I didn't look good. I looked sick with stress and anxiety.

'Pack my shit?' I echoed. 'What do you mean?'

He looked at me like I was an idiot. 'Pack your shit because I'm coming back tonight with my pickup and we're taking your stuff to my house.'

I snorted. 'I'm not living with those fucking savages.'

'Yes, you are,' Dornan snapped. 'They're not savages.'

'Honey,' I said, placing my hand on Dornan's shoulder as I spoke in the sweetest, most sickly sarcastic voice I could muster, 'your sons told me last night that they'd like to feed you sleeping tablets and then, quote, take me "for a spin". I don't think they were talking about taking me for a motorcycle ride.'

Dornan didn't say anything.

'That's what I thought,' I said, turning on my heel and walking towards my apartment.

'We got a meeting tomorrow,' Dornan called to me. I stopped in my tracks and turned back to face him. 'Tomorrow? What for?'

Dornan shrugged. 'Something about Sunday being a holiday in Italy,' he shrugged. 'My father's going away on business, so we're meeting tomorrow.'

Shit.

'And the club's meeting as well?'

Dornan peered at me with what seemed like suspicion. 'Yeah. Why?'

I rolled my eyes. 'So I can mentally prepare myself to see those boys of yours again. You should teach them how to treat a lady with respect.'

Dornan revved his engine loudly. 'If I have spare time, I'm going to use it disrespecting you in that bedroom up there, not teaching them shit.'

What a stand-up father. I fought the urge to respond with something sharp and condescending. Instead, I stood and watched as Dornan took off down Santa Monica Boulevard, not taking my eyes off him until he'd disappeared.

As I was turning to head upstairs to my apartment, something made me look back to the road.

A black Escalade was parked on the corner. No big deal, right? Common car, especially in LA. Except the window was down, and the guy at the wheel was staring right at me. He was wearing dark tinted sunglasses, and had one of those earpieces attached to a cord that disappeared under his shirt collar. He was FBI, plain as day, and he wasn't even trying to hide it. *They're watching me*, I realised, sickened. *Lindsay's making sure I don't slip away.* Maybe he did know me better than I thought. I turned and took the stairs two at a time, bursting into my apartment and slamming the door behind me.

Guillermo was at the breakfast bar, shovelling Cheerios into his mouth. I ignored the drips of milk all over the counter and walked right up to him, my hand outstretched.

'I need your phone,' I said, breathless and insistent as my eyes bored into his.

He lowered his spoon slowly, licking milk from his lips. 'Why do you need my phone?' he asked slowly, pushing the cereal bowl away as he held my gaze. I didn't respond. I just looked at him, and sure enough, he reached into his pocket and withdrew his cellphone, placing it in the centre of my palm.

'You've got five minutes,' he said, his face unreadable. I watched as he walked past me to the front door, opened it, and then closed it silently behind him.

I dialled John's number. He answered after two rings. 'Yeah?'

'It's Ana,' I said. 'There's FBI sitting outside my apartment.'

'Shit,' John muttered. 'Watching you?'

'I don't think they're watching Mrs Mayflower downstairs,' I said, referring to my geriatric neighbour who was both legally blind and almost deaf.

'What's your feeling?' John asked.

'My feeling is bad,' I said, looking around the apartment nervously. Was this place bugged like the hotel room had been? Shit, I hadn't even considered that possibility. 'Wait a minute.' I switched on the small radio that sat on my kitchen windowsill. Placebo blasted out of the tiny speakers, and I turned that fucker up as loud as it would go without drawing suspicion. Then, I stepped out onto the balcony and closed the glass door behind me. If the balcony was bugged, I was shit out of luck, but I felt like it was the safest option.

'Okay,' I continued. 'Dornan says the Sunday meeting's been moved to tomorrow at noon. I say we leave right after. Any longer and the FBI will make it impossible. Any sooner and they'll notice we're gone before we even make it through downtown LA traffic.'

'Yeah. My thoughts exactly.'

Something else occurred to me. It was useless to leave if we didn't have a means to fund our escape.

'Did you find it?' I asked.

He knew what I meant by *it*. 'All of it,' he said, and it sounded like he was smiling.

'Good,' I said, sagging back against the balcony wall as relief flooded my limbs. 'That's really good.'

CHAPTER THIRTY-ONE

LINDSAY

'Morgan,' Lindsay barked across the packed briefing room.

Lindsay's colleague and fellow FBI officer, Peter Morgan, stood up at the desk he was occupying and made his way to the front of the room. Standing next to Lindsay, he addressed the twenty-odd federal agents who were assembled, ready to jump into action as soon as they were given the command.

Another officer handed out clipboards with photos and vital information while Morgan elaborated. 'There's a shipment of young girls coming from Mexico,' he said, his expression grave. 'There are babies, people. We have to take these bastards down before we end up with a shipping container full of dead Mexican children.'

The room was deathly quiet. Mentioning children and trafficking tended to have that effect.

Their raid had been scheduled for Sunday, but intel suggested that the Gypsy Brothers members and their overlord, Emilio Ross, had brought the meeting forward to Friday – and today was Friday. Lindsay had scrambled to grab as many bodies as he could to help pull off such a raid, and so long as the LAPD sent over a couple of officers for manpower if things got ugly, they'd be fine. He could have waited until the following Sunday, but something in his gut told Lindsay not to give Mariana Rodriguez a week to rethink her agreement to testify, or for Emilio Ross to be tipped off by someone inside the Bureau and hightail it to Colombia.

Morgan finished his briefing and Lindsay took charge once again, detailing floor plans of the Gypsy Brothers clubhouse and the surrounding areas. No exit left uncovered. No stone left unturned. No member of the Ross family left uncuffed.

And then, after he'd finished talking, it was just a matter of waiting the morning out. This was always the hardest part. Sitting on your hands and waiting for the bad guys to be in the right place at the right time, when all you wanted to do was go in, guns blazing, and drag them out of whatever hole they were currently hiding in.

'This'll be good,' Morgan remarked after the briefing had ended.

Lindsay smiled. 'Like shooting fish in a barrel.'

CHAPTER THIRTY-TWO
DORNAN

It was 11:43. Church was due to start in seventeen minutes, and Viper wanted to talk?

'It'd better be fucking urgent,' Dornan muttered, showing Viper into the office where his father was already sitting, flicking through the newspaper. He didn't even look up to acknowledge Viper's presence.

'It can't wait,' Viper said, and something about his expression made Dornan baulk.

'Shit, did somebody die?'

'Yeah,' Viper said. 'Somebody did die. We'll get to that.'

Emilio looked mildly interested.

Viper pulled several folded pieces of paper from inside his leather jacket and placed them on the desk. Dornan went to reach for them, but Emilio was faster. 'The fuck am I looking at here?' he asked impatiently.

'If I'm right,' Viper said, 'you're looking at sixteen years' worth of money being wired from John to Stephanie.'

Dornan felt like he'd been punched in the heart. 'Come again?'

Viper looked deeply troubled. He was implicating the man who, until this week, had been his club president, the man he'd sworn loyalty to.

'John knew where Stephanie was the whole time. He sent her money every single month. Plus extras. Doctors' bills from her pregnancy. From Jason's birth. School fees.'

Dornan snatched the papers from his father, who scowled but didn't say anything. Heart racing, fire in his veins, Dornan swept his eyes down the columns that didn't really mean anything – until he started to focus on the titles of each column. There were dates and times and ... Holy shit, John had really kept Stephanie from him for the better part of two decades. John had kept his son's existence from him.

Dornan made a growling sound in the back of his throat, charging for the door. Viper cut him off. 'Move or I will rip your head off,' he strained.

'There's more,' Viper said, blocking Dornan's path. 'It's about your wife.'

CHAPTER THIRTY-THREE
MARIANA

It was weird going to our weekly meeting on a Friday instead of a Sunday. Sunday was 'church', after all, even if the Gypsy Brothers' church had nothing to do with God or religion. It was a tradition, one they never broke. I was betting that the new president was keen to get his hands dirty, and he sure as shit didn't want to wait until Sunday to start throwing his weight around.

John and I had a plan: as soon as the meeting finished we were going to head back to the strip club, grab the money he'd hidden there, collect Juliette and Jason from John's house, and get the hell out of town. John assured me he'd organised a car for us, a Chevy Tahoe. He'd arranged for it to be parked outside the clubhouse, down the block a few hundred metres, the key to be taped behind the licence plate.

Once we got out of town, there was a car switch, several states to pass through, and then a private jet that would take us the last part of our journey. Colombia beckoned with open arms and the promise of my Luis. And once we had my son safely in our custody … we could literally go anywhere in the world.

All we had to do was get through our respective meetings – John with his fellow club members, and me with Emilio and Dornan. We did this every week. We could do it one more time. Right?

I was on edge. Jittery. My stomach was tied in knots and I kept feeling like I might throw up. But I could act. I could poker-face my way through anything. I'd been acting my way through the last ten years of my life without ever getting caught.

We were going to make it.

Only we were screwed before we even got a chance to head into our meetings.

We arrived at the clubhouse early, as was custom. I arrived with Dornan, as usual, and John strolled in at 11:47 a.m. Thirteen excruciating minutes until we could get this over and done with and then disappear into the wind. Our new life taunted me relentlessly. I wanted it more than I'd ever wanted anything in my life.

Dornan had already peeled off somewhere, and Emilio was nowhere to be seen. John was talking to another Gypsy Brother, and I leaned against the wall and tried not to attract any attention – easier said than done when you were the only woman in a club full of men. It didn't matter at any rate, because while I was trying to remain inconspicuous, the doors to the club burst open, and FBI officers started streaming in. I saw Lindsay across the room, before he could see me. I acted on autopilot. I locked eyes with John, gestured to the fire escape at the back of the club, and we ran.

CHAPTER THIRTY-FOUR

DORNAN

Dornan backed up and let Viper speak.

'After I found these transactions, I decided to take a look at John's house ...' he trailed off.

'Don't get shy now,' Emilio said. He seemed intrigued, but it wasn't his money. It was John taking pity on some girl and sending her some of his cash. Dornan could tell that his father thought this was no big deal.

Viper placed a cellphone on the desk. He looked like he was about to have a damned heart attack.

'Whose is it?' Dornan asked. His head was throbbing. He almost didn't want to know. He definitely didn't want to be blindsided while his father was standing beside him.

'I found this phone in John's garden shed,' Viper said. 'It was hidden thoroughly. When I unearthed it and turned it on, guess which number was first on the call list?'

Dornan closed his eyes briefly, pinching the bridge of his nose. He already knew the answer. The phone in front of him was a cheap burner phone. He'd seen one exactly the same.

'He's been calling your wife,' Viper said, his eyes darting around as if he didn't know where to look. 'Or rather, they've been calling each other.'

Dornan's resolve shattered. It made perfect sense. Of course! He knew she'd been seeing somebody else, even when she tried to deny it. Of course it would be John – the man who was everything Dornan had never quite been able to emulate. The good one. The kind one. The one who didn't beat you until you miscarried. Or, for that matter, the one who didn't beat you at all, because he was just a fucking stand-up guy.

'There's more,' Viper said.

Emilio was openly entertained now, apparently having forgotten the time and their impending meeting. Seemed this juicy news was reason enough to be late.

'Please, by all means, go on,' Emilio said, steepling his fingers and leaning his chin on them. 'You're really very good at setting the scene. Very thorough.'

Viper glanced at Dornan. 'Once I figured out they'd been talking, I decided it was worth looking into something that's been bothering me ever since you told me about it, Mr Ross. The ashes you mentioned to me. You asked me to track down where she had the kid cremated at such short notice and I found it – Budget Funerals. We've already talked about this, but after I told you I decided to do some more digging. I asked the guy if I could look at his security tapes from the week Agent Murphy went missing.'

Emilio drew a sharp breath. There was nothing playful about his attention now.

'John took a body to be disposed of the same day Murphy disappeared,' Viper said. 'I asked the guy about it, convinced him that John had sent me to make sure any personal effects had been destroyed along with the body.'

He dug into his pocket and pulled out an ID badge, with Murphy's face staring out next to the letters DEA.

He slid it across the table for Emilio to see. 'I rechecked the tapes. Mariana was waiting in the car while John loaded Murphy's body for burning.'

Emilio stood, pounding his fist on the desk. 'That fucking cunt!' he roared, his eyes so big Dornan thought they might explode out of his head and roll along the floor. Dornan didn't know what to do. His wife was a traitor. His wife wasn't loyal to him. She was loyal to John. She was in love with John.

And they were both standing five feet away, separated only by the soundproof walls this office boasted; thank God for small miracles in a sea of shitty news.

'I'll kill them both,' Dornan decided out loud, reaching for his gun.

'Stop,' Viper said. 'There's more. I checked the accounts after I found all of this. She's been skimming your money. I didn't have time to put it all together, but the amount so far is over seven figures.'

Emilio looked like he was about to cut Viper's skull open and rip out his brain, just to see if he could get the answers faster than Viper was relaying them.

'But seven figures is–'

'Millions,' Viper confirmed.

Dornan and Emilio both moved for the door at the same time.

But they never reached it. It exploded open, a stream of FBI agents yelling commands at the three of them, and then Dornan was on the floor, hands behind his back and his face pressed into the rough carpet as the bony knee of an FBI agent dug into the small of his back.

Emilio was cursing in Italian, the same sentence, over and over again.

'*I will cut her fucking head off. I will saw their fucking heads off!*'

No, he wouldn't. Dornan would beat him to it. And he wouldn't need a blade. No. Dornan would rip his pretty wife's head from her body simply with the force of his rage, and then he would do the same to his best friend, the man he'd trusted more than anyone else in his entire life.

CHAPTER THIRTY-FIVE
MARIANA

I'd like to say we escaped, that our plan was brilliant, but our plan was hasty and panicked. John went first, sliding down the fire escape to the back alley below, hidden from street view. This was even better, I surmised, as I felt John's hand on my ankle, guiding me down so I didn't fall and break my neck in these ridiculous high heels Dornan insisted I wear to meetings. We could make a clean break while the others languished in police cells. We'd be in Colombia before some of them even made bail.

But that's where the illusion shattered. Because I looked down, and the man holding my ankle wasn't John. It was Lindsay.

'Mariana.' He smiled, pulling me down to the ground and then pushing me up against the wall, cold handcuffs wrapping around my wrists and clicking shut. 'How nice of you to join us.'

In my peripheral vision I saw John, handcuffed and gagged, as he was dragged away. He hadn't even been able to yell out to warn me of the danger below. Lindsay wrenched me away from the wall and pushed me forward. I moved awkwardly in my heels as he propelled me around to the front of the clubhouse, following in John's footsteps, where at least fifteen police cars sat waiting to be filled. I looked on in horror as I saw John being wrestled into one car, Dornan into another, and Emilio into a third. Cuffs firmly in place, Lindsay spun me around to face him. He smiled again, and Christ almighty if he didn't look like some Hollywood movie star who'd been plucked off the street and handed a gun and a badge. His bright white teeth were dazzling, and he looked clean. Too clean. Even his navy blue suit jacket looked freshly pressed.

We, on the other hand, we were all dirty, even if we didn't look it on the surface. Emilio's dirt was the poison that ran through his veins, the beady look in his dark eyes, the bit of phlegm that always seemed to be trapped in his chest, that rumbled when he spoke and made me want to scream at him to clear his damn throat every time he opened his mouth.

Dornan and John were dirty anyway, with their beard scruff, the tattoos that covered their skin in various stages of bright and dull colouring, the leather vests they never, ever washed, their palms stained with engine oil and probably blood.

We were all dirty, dishevelled, less than.

Lindsay, though, was resplendent. He had us now, and he knew it.

And he beamed.

CHAPTER THIRTY-SIX
LINDSAY

Divide and conquer – that was the key to getting people to turn on each other. Lindsay was well versed in this technique, and it was perfect for today's situation: a group of highly paranoid criminals with shady moral codes who would just as soon rat on someone as take a bullet for them. It was the law of averages. Eventually, one of them would turn on the rest.

Speaking of. In front of him sat Mariana Rodrig– no, it was Ross now, wasn't it? Mariana Ross. Didn't roll off the tongue as nicely as Rodriguez, but Lindsay suspected that she'd roll off his tongue nicely no matter what her name was. He tried not to think about how beautiful she was, though. It had already made him go softer on her than he should have, when he gave her the gun back in Vegas. It was a dumb move. He knew the second she got out of that car that she wasn't going to testify for him.

He'd been questioning her for at least thirty minutes but the woman was like a vault. She wasn't saying anything, and she looked bereft. Lindsay suspected he'd interrupted her escape plans. Well, he had literally interrupted her shimmying down the fire escape in heels and a pencil skirt, but he suspected she'd planned to be on her way to some exotic locale by now, instead of sitting chained to an interrogation table inside the LAPD's downtown station. As much as Lindsay loathed this place, the FBI headquarters simply couldn't handle this volume of arrests at one time.

'This is your last chance at getting immunity,' he reminded her. 'I mean it. Just because I feel sorry for you doesn't mean I can make the murder charge go away.' He slid a piece of paper over to her side of the table. 'We know you killed Allie Baxter. You're going away, for twenty-five to life. Not that you'll survive that long. The cartels run the prisons. You'll be dead before you get to dinner on your first day.'

It was only then that she started to communicate.

'You'll never get immunity approved for a cop killer,' Mariana said to him. 'Why would you offer such a thing?'

Lindsay smiled. 'Killing a dirty cop isn't quite the same as killing, say, a cop like me.'

Mariana raised one eyebrow. 'A cop like you?'

'Exemplary. Unblemished record. Solid cases. You definitely don't want to get caught for killing a cop like me.'

She didn't look convinced.

'Your testimony could bring an entire cartel to its knees,' Lindsay said. 'It could dismantle their drug operations. Their arms deals. Their human trafficking.' He saw her flinch. 'You want to help the women and children Emilio is selling, don't you? The babies? The babies he sells while they're still in their mothers' wombs? Mariana, don't you want to stop those children from being sold to porn rings and paedophiles?'

'Stop,' she said, covering her ears. 'Please stop.'

'Do you think anyone stops when those children beg them to stop?'

Mariana glared at him. 'John and I are a package deal,' she said. 'We both get immunity, then I testify.'

Lindsay laughed. 'What? You're kidding, right? Immunity for the president of the club who was running the trafficking in the first place? I don't think so.'

'He didn't have anything to do with it,' she said forcefully.

'Guess you can tell that to your buddies in your prison cell.'

'Do you really think I'm afraid of prison,' she shot back, 'after the life I've lived? Prison would be a walk in the park compared to that. You can either give us both immunity, or you can process me, because I'm not saying another word without John.'

Lindsay realised that she didn't care what happened to her. She was in love with this guy, and she was never going to cooperate unless he was part of the deal.

Mariana sat back in her metal chair and smiled at Lindsay smugly. 'You should see the things I could get for you,' she teased. 'I think the word "damning" ought to cover it.'

Lindsay was finding it harder to smile at her. She was asking him to do the impossible.

'Wait here,' he said.

***

Fifteen minutes later, Lindsay marched John Portland into Mariana's interrogation room. Her eyes practically popped out of her skull, she looked so surprised. She covered her reaction quickly, though, with a smile. 'See, that wasn't so hard,' she said to Lindsay.

He just made a noise at the back of his throat. He could technically lose his job for this, but if an entire cartel was taken down through his efforts, then all would be forgiven. Probably.

Lindsay left them alone for a moment under the pretence of getting John a chair, but when he peered at them through the one-way glass window, they remained silent. They were smart. They'd almost been smart enough to get out before Lindsay had scooped them up. Almost.

After a few moments of watching them exchange silent glances, he headed back in, a chair in one hand, coffee in the other. The coffee was for him. Criminals didn't get coffee until they gave him something. If these two delivered, he'd buy them a lifetime supply of Starbucks to go with their immunity.

John sat in the chair. Lindsay leaned against the table and sipped coffee. They all looked at each other silently. And then Mariana Rodriguez began to talk.

***

Mariana had insisted on going to the clubhouse to collect the financial evidence herself. She'd also insisted on taking John with her. Said she wouldn't do a thing if he was out of her sight for a single second. John hadn't said a damn thing.

After much toing and froing, Lindsay sent them both with Agent Morgan to recover the evidence Mariana was so adamant about – the financial records that could prove a link between Emilio Ross, the Il Sangue Cartel, and the human trafficking ring. He watched them leave, relieved that he was able to cut a deal that would see Mariana kept safe. He'd only met the woman twice, but he'd watched her for hours upon hours over the last few months. There was something about her that endeared her to him, even if he couldn't quite articulate what it was.

His coffee long since cold, Lindsay gathered his files and dumped them on his desk, and then headed down to the lock-up to see who he could rattle next. Yeah, he had Mariana's testimony, but it didn't mean he couldn't make his case even more bulletproof with additional testimony. He was looking forward to interrogating Emilio and Dornan Ross. He was practically giddy about the prospect of waving their life sentences in their faces, because that's what they'd get for the things they'd done. He intended to impress upon them that his case against them would bury them so deep, they'd never see the light of day again.

He was feeling pretty chipper as he approached the police officer on duty and held out his badge for verification. 'I'm ready for Dornan and Emilio Ross to be brought upstairs for questioning,' he said, scanning the lock-up for the father and son.

The officer shrugged. 'They're gone.'

Lindsay just about died on the spot. 'I'm sorry, what?'

A senior officer who was sitting at a nearby desk chimed in. 'Yeah. Apparently they had some hotshot lawyer down here, demanding to know what they were under arrest for. He got them out, like, three hours ago.'

'We'll have all the evidence we need to convict those two sorry sons of bitches. It's being collected right now.'

'Well, you needed it three hours ago,' the senior officer replied. 'We had no choice but to let them go.'

Lindsay was incredulous. 'It's an FBI case. It's called a twenty-four hour hold, for Christ's sake.'

The duty officer opened his mouth to speak but Lindsay cut him off as a fresh wave of panic slammed him. 'Wait, did you say they've been gone for three hours? *Fuck!*'=

CHAPTER THIRTY-SEVEN

MARIANA

We were completely and utterly screwed. Emilio had somehow skipped his holding cell and beaten us to the strip club, pouncing the moment we'd entered the place with Agent Morgan.

The same Agent Morgan who was now bleeding to death at my feet, courtesy of a bullet to his chest. Two of Dornan's sons held my arms behind my back. Viper and two other Gypsy Brothers were holding John. It had taken three men to restrain him.

Behind the desk John usually sat at, in the office we shared, Emilio paced.

He'd already filled us in on the information Viper had pieced together. We were fucked. Emilio knew everything. He knew I'd killed Murphy. He knew John and I were together. He knew I'd been skimming cartel money for years. And he knew John had been responsible for Stephanie's disappearance.

This was it. Our final moments. I'd always wondered what would happen if the house of cards came crashing down, and now I knew. This. Death.

Turns out, I didn't much like waiting to die.

'You're going to kill us,' I spat at Emilio. 'What are you waiting for?'

He didn't stop pacing as he locked those cold, dead eyes on me. 'A call.

I'm waiting for a call from my son. He went to your house, John, assuming that's the first place you'd hit. Such a family man, we all thought you'd go back for your daughter before stopping here. Who knew?'

John growled, straining against the stronghold his three club brothers had on him.

'I wonder what they'll do with your precious daughter,' Emilio mused.

'I'll fucking kill you if you touch her!' John roared, lunging over the desk.

Emilio smiled. 'I won't touch her,' he said, smirking. 'But I will watch.'

***

They locked me in a room by myself and left me there. It was more of a broom closet really, full of cleaning supplies and towels. There was nothing sharp. No windows. The best hope I had was to try to set something on fire. I'd probably die very quickly, though. So I refrained.

I paced the tiny room, once my eyes had adjusted to the darkness. At least I paced until I heard the screams coming from downstairs. Once I heard those screams I started screaming. It didn't matter, though. Nobody came to let me out.

CHAPTER THIRTY-EIGHT

DORNAN

Dornan didn't quite know what he was doing. It was as if his need for vengeance had overtaken his mind. He'd gone to John's house in search of John, with a bag of smack as a bribe to get Caroline to tell him where John had gone if he wasn't there.

Caroline didn't tell Dornan anything. But it didn't matter. He'd handed over the heroin willingly. He'd taken her child as payment.

Juliette. The baby he'd taken in after Caroline abandoned her in the hospital in search of her next fix. The baby who John hadn't been able to meet until she was already months old and staring into Dornan's eyes like he was her daddy. The only parent she'd known from birth. They'd always had a special bond, he and Julie.

And now he had taken her from her home, and he was going to hurt her. The darkness inside him clamoured for her blood, even though part of him was distraught at the prospect of what he was about to do. He was about to take that girl he'd once thought of as his own, the girl who meant more to John Portland than breathing, more than air, more than living ... and Dornan was going to destroy her.

An eye for an eye, a tooth for a tooth. A life for a life. John had taken everything from Dornan. He'd taken Stephanie. He'd taken Jason. He'd taken Mariana.

And so Dornan would take Juliette from John. Break her into little pieces so that she could never be put back together again. It was a fitting revenge for such a systematic betrayal.

'Please,' Juliette begged, tied to a chair on the empty stage of the strip club. Before her stood a video camera on a tripod, a flashing red light indicating that it was recording. He would hurt her. He would break her, and then he would force John to watch the highlights reel.

'Dornan!' she implored. 'You don't have to do this!'

But he did have to do this. Because in that moment, he didn't even see Juliette, the girl he'd treated like one of his own. He didn't see his father, watching silently from the floor below.

He only saw Stephanie, crying as he beat her half to death. The woman who'd taken his heart, and his son, and his hope that he could ever be something better than what he was.

He saw John. The man who he'd trusted above all else, the man who'd now taken not one, but two women he loved, and made them despise him. Yes, in the girl's green eyes he saw treachery and betrayal, but most of all, he saw her fear, and *he liked it*.

John had taken Stephanie. Sent her away. John had taken his son in the process, and now Jase hated him. His own father. John had taken his youngest son once, and now he was planning to take him again? Yes, as if the betrayal was not cutting enough, John and Mariana had been planning to take Jason when they fled town.

John had stolen Mariana from Dornan. And she had gone to him, like a moth to a flame, like none of the shit they'd been through in the past ten years had ever happened. Dornan had risked his life for her, taken a bullet for her, left his wife and married her! He would have fucking died for her, and none of it mattered, because she wanted John.

He'd always vowed to protect this girl, Juliette. But he didn't protect her. He took a knife and cut her clothes from her body, and when she was naked and sobbing he told his sons to destroy her.

And they had tried. All of them. All except Jason, who'd been found and brought to the strip club, kicking and screaming blue murder, who was now unconscious at Dornan's feet because he'd been so distraught at the sight of Chad laying his body upon Juliette's and violating her. All six of his older sons had done as Dornan had told them to. Some more willingly than others. They'd all walked away after committing different variations of the same heinous act upon the defenceless girl, and she was still here. She was still breathing.

She was a fighter, like her daddy. It was going to take more to break her.

It was going to take Dornan to break her.

It was just the two of them now, on the stage; them, and a camera and a small table where Dornan was laying his clothes in a neat pile as he pulled them from his body.

As she continued to protest.

'You're supposed to be my family!' Juliette screamed, bleeding all over the fucking place.

He stared at the girl in front of him, and something inside him said *stop*. It was a whimper, not a scream, that voice of dissent that said *It's not too late to let her go*. But something else, something much louder and more powerful drowned that protest out. The beast inside him demanded vengeance, demanded destruction. And the beast needed to be fed.

Dornan swallowed. Took a deep breath, took a step towards her, his belt in his hands.

And he became the monster he was born to be.

CHAPTER THIRTY-NINE

DORNAN

'Get up.'

Jason was at his feet, his face bloody and swollen from being beaten unconscious.

'Where is she?' he begged. 'Please, where is she?'

Dornan reached down and grabbed the back of his son's neck. His anger gave him brute strength, and it was the easiest thing in the world to drag the insolent little fucker away from the stage where a naked Juliette lay, unconscious and bleeding from what Dornan had done to her. In one hand he gripped his son. In the other, the remnants of Juliette's clothing – a macabre souvenir of the dignity he'd stolen from her.

He entered the small office where John was being held, still dragging Jase. As soon as they were both safely in the room and the door locked, he shoved Jase away. He fell to the floor and scrambled into the corner, getting as far away from his father as he could.

'Where's Ana?' Dornan asked, scanning the faces around him. Viper and Jimmy and … oh yes. John. Tied to a chair, his face much like Jase's – bloody and swollen and bruised.

'She's down the hall,' Jimmy replied. 'Want me to get her?'

Dornan shook his head. 'Not yet.'

He circled John's chair once before stopping in front of him.

'Johnny Boy,' he said.

John refused to look at his oldest friend. Dornan thought that was odd. Shouldn't he be begging Dornan to let Juliette go?

But then he remembered, John didn't know about Juliette.

Dornan steeled himself, the sticky bunch of fabric in his hand. He dropped the bloodied clothing on John's lap, piece by piece. John looked at the material, either disinterested or confused, Dornan couldn't tell which.

And then he dropped the last piece. The piece of T-shirt with the little rainbow icon that, just two hours ago, had sat above Juliette's heart as she wore her regular clothes and lived her regular life.

John's eyes widened when he saw the rainbow, his head whipping up so that he could look at Dornan.

'No,' he said hoarsely.

Dornan smirked.

'No!' John screamed, bucking against his ropes. 'No! No! *No!*'

Dornan, who'd started pacing in front of his bound, traitorous friend, stopped on his heel and turned in front of John. He stood so close, their legs touching, that had John been able to pry his hands free from their bindings, he'd have been able to swing at him.

'Sixteen years you kept Stephanie from me.'

John looked down at the bloody ribbons of clothing in his lap, horrified. Transfixed. 'What did you do?' he breathed.

'Sixteen years, I could have had my son.'

'WHAT DID YOU DO?' John roared, his face bright red, his knuckles white as he tried to twist them away from the chair.

'How long were you fucking my wife?' Dornan asked. It suddenly occurred to him that it was the last time he'd likely refer to Mariana as his wife.

'If you hurt Julie–'

Dornan tutted. 'I already hurt Julie. Jesus, John, didn't you hear her screaming? That was your daughter and my sons, but she was the only one who screamed.'

John made a guttural noise in the back of his throat, pulling against the ropes that bound him to the chair. He was going to either make himself bleed or snap the rope soon enough.

Dornan drew his gun and pressed it against John's lips, against his teeth. 'We're talking about my wife first, John. She suck your cock, *John*? Did my wife suck good cock?'

John's eyes flashed with anger. Dornan drew the gun away and used it to pistol-whip him across the face. Blood flew from John's mouth and through the air, landing on the ground with a sickening splat.

'What else, huh? You steal my wife, you steal my money, you steal my FUCKING SON?'

'Why is there blood on her clothes?' John panted. 'Why are her clothes cut up?'

Dornan grabbed a second chair and planted it right in front of John's, straddling it. He rested his elbows on the top of the backrest, watching John as an eerie calm descended upon him. Little by little, the angry buzz was starting to recede. *This is what it feels like*, he realised. To switch it all off and walk away from ever caring about anything else again. *This is what it feels like to be my father.*

It felt ... oddly freeing. No more worry. No more pain. Just the self-assured conviction that the man in front of him – the man he'd trusted with his own life, his own *wife*, his own fucking kids – that this man would suffer for his betrayal.

John levelled his gaze at Dornan. 'Why are her clothes cut up?' he repeated. 'ANSWER ME!'

Dornan responded by taking his gun, pressing it down into John's groin, and pulling the trigger. The blast was deafening; John's howl of pain even more so. His pain rocked him to the side and he crashed to the ground, still tied to the chair at an awkward angle. Dornan could only imagine the pain John must have been feeling. A bullet in the cock. There were major arteries down there. The steady stream of blood pouring from John's lap made sense then. His skin went pasty-white and he started to hyperventilate, gasping for air.

'Now bring her in,' Dornan said to Jimmy, who obliged, scuttling away and coming back not thirty seconds later with Mariana in tow.

'Oh God,' she cried, running towards John.

Dornan stopped her, a hand around her throat as he drove her against the wall. 'Nuh-uh,' he said, grinning at her. 'No touching.' He pressed his hips against Mariana, effectively pinning her to the wall. 'Jimmy!' he barked. 'Get out your gun. Take all the bullets out. Leave one in the chamber and give it to Jason.'

Everyone looked at Dornan as if he were mad. 'What if the little fuck shoots you?' Jimmy asked. 'Or me?'

Dornan glared at him. 'He won't shoot you. Just fucking do it.'

With great reluctance, Jimmy handed the gun to Jason. He immediately pointed it at Dornan.

'If you want to redeem yourself,' he said to his youngest son, 'you'll put John here out of his misery. He's in pain. You don't want him to be in pain, do you, son?'

Dornan motioned for everyone to leave the room. Soon it was just Jase and John, Dornan and Mariana. She was saying John's name, over and over. Dornan didn't like that. 'Stop, bitch,' he ground out. She didn't stop.

'I said STOP, BITCH!' He pulled her head forward and then slammed it back into the wall, watching in fascination as her eyes rolled back in her head. He dragged her out of the room and closed the door, and waited for the gunshot. Either Jason would kill John to ease his pain, or he'd turn the gun on himself and blow his brains out. There really was no telling which way it would go. But one thing he did know, he couldn't stay and watch.

In the hallway, Mariana continued to struggle, and Dornan continued to brace her against the wall. She was fading fast; pretty soon she'd be still. Jimmy and Viper leaned against the opposite wall and said nothing. Dornan wondered where Guillermo was. Whose side he was on. He made a mental note to find out. But first, he had to wait for that blast.

What he didn't expect was that Chad would wander up the hallway, looking almost rueful, his hands covered in blood.

'Pop,' Chad said, holding out his blood-soaked hands. 'Whatever you did to Julz – I can't wake her. I think she's dying.'

Mariana found a second wind and started struggling again. 'What did you do?' she wailed. 'Oh God. Oh *God*. What did you do to her?'

Dornan opened his mouth to speak as a deafening gunshot rang out. He felt his breath hitch for a moment as he wondered who was dead in the office just a few feet away – his best friend, or his son.

'Hold her,' Dornan snapped, throwing Mariana at Viper. He opened the office door, and saw his son on the floor, the gun to his temple, desperately pulling the trigger over and over again to a series of empty clicks.

Dornan watched him do this for a few moments, unable to look down at John. And then he forced himself to look.

John was dead. Gone.

A moment of horrified shame lurked at the back of Dornan's pitch-black mind. He pushed it down, though, with the rest of the terrible things that he'd done. He didn't have time to ruminate now. His best friend was dead at his feet, and his son was now smashing the barrel of his gun into his face.

'Chad!' Dornan snapped. 'Get him out of here.'

Chad obliged, hooking his bloodied wet hands under Jason's arms and dragging him from the room. As they passed, Dornan snatched his gun from Jase and jammed it into the back of his jeans again.

Emilio entered the small office, coming to a standstill beside Dornan. He put his hand on his son's shoulder, and it sat there, like a dead roach that Dornan desperately wanted to throw off.

'We always hurt the ones we love,' Emilio said, squeezing his shoulder. 'Remember when you begged me to keep her? I told you, son, this day would come.'

He let his hand drop.

Dornan continued to stare down at the body in front of him as Emilio cleared his throat.

'We have to go,' Emilio said, his tone becoming urgent. His tone was never urgent, which meant the situation was dire. 'We have to get out. The Feds are going to find one of their own dead here, and we need to be gone before then. Clean up crew will sort this, but only if we move. Kill her and let's get the fuck out of here. Unless you want me to do it?'

Dornan started to pace. He tugged at his hair.

'I'll do it,' Emilio snapped, drawing his gun.

'Don't fucking touch her!' Dornan yelled at his father. 'I'm about to shoot my fucking wife,' he choked out. 'Give me a goddamn minute, will you?'

Emilio fixed his son with a hard glare. 'You've got five minutes,' he said through gritted teeth. 'Then you're on your own.'

CHAPTER FORTY

DORNAN

Emilio was gone. John was dead. The boys had all cleared out, taking an unconscious Juliette and a crazed Jason with them. It was just Dornan and Mariana, locked in a room together. They were ending exactly as they'd begun, only this time there was a dead man lying on the floor between them, a man they'd both loved dearly at one time in their lives. A man who Mariana had just spent the past few moments trying to save.

But there were some things that were beyond repair. A bullet in the brain, for example. John was dead. He'd been dead since the moment Jason planted a bullet in his skull. Now Mariana was standing again, only this time she was covered in John's blood.

'Hurry up,' Mariana said, her eyes full of tears, her entire body shaking violently. 'Just do it. Just kill me!'

Dornan was crying now, too. The shock was starting to dissipate, and the rage along with it. Now he just felt a hollow ache inside, that familiar emptiness that defined his existence. He'd killed John. Juliette was almost dead. And his wife stood in front of him, begging him to kill her, and he couldn't bear to end her life like this.

He still loved her. Despite the treachery, the betrayal, the lies, he loved her. He would always love her.

'I don't want to kill you,' he rasped. 'I want to save you. I want you to run.'

'No,' she protested. 'No, Dornan.'

'You have five minutes,' he said to her, his hand coming to rest on her cheek. His fingers burned where their skin met.

She was sobbing. Hysterical. 'What if I don't run?'

He shrugged, his own eyes burning with regret. 'Then I take you back to Emilio, and he can do whatever he wants to you.'

Her sobs stilled. She looked up at him, her eyes wide, hands thick with John's blood. The sight made him bitterly jealous, for no good reason. John was dead; he was gone. But blood had been their thing, the thing that bound Dornan and Mariana together, from the very first time he'd bandaged her wounds all those years ago.

'Did you ever really love me?'

She slapped him across the face, hard. Enough so that he tasted blood. How did somebody as small as his Mariana slap him so he bled? The taste of his own blood set off something primal, and he growled, grabbing her wrist and twisting it until she cried out.

She ripped her hand away and stepped back. 'Of course I fucking loved you. I loved you so much I thought I would die. Don't you know the things I did for you? For us?'

All he saw was her with John. It consumed him until he thought he might go totally insane.

He narrowed his eyes. 'Enlighten me.'

She shook her head, laughing mirthlessly. 'You stupid bastard,' she said. 'I loved you until the end. I loved you even after I saw what you did to Stephanie. What you did to your own son. I still loved you.'

He nodded, his throat tight. 'So what was it, then? The thing that destroyed us?'

She straightened, took a step back. 'You *know*.'

And it was true, he did know. He'd killed their child. Hurt her so much, it had died and bled away.

This was his fault.

'It was always going to end like this,' she whispered, tears dripping onto her dirty cheeks. Her words stunned him, physically, to the point that he had to step back to keep his balance.

'Like what?' he asked.

'With blood. We started with blood, and that's how we ended.'

'Is this what this is?' he asked sadly. 'The end?' He'd been so fucking happy when he married her. It was the first day he'd truly been able to say that she was his and not his father's. But now, looking at the weeping mess in front of him, the traitor, the seductress who'd been lying to him all this time, Dornan Ross had to wonder – had she ever been his at all?

'Yes,' she said, looking down at John. His eyes were still frozen open, unseeing. It wasn't fair.

Mariana knelt beside John, reaching her hand out. With love. She reached for him with so much tenderness, so much despair, that it took everything inside Dornan to stop himself from putting the gun in his own mouth and pulling the trigger. Had she ever looked at him like that?

'Don't fucking touch him,' Dornan said, jealousy surging through him as he aimed the gun at the woman he'd loved.

She swallowed thickly, guiding the gun up to her forehead. 'Do it,' she urged, tears streaming down her face. 'DO IT!'

He grabbed her, pulled her back to her feet. He wanted to kill her. He wanted to save her. He wanted to take it all back.

'I'm sorry,' he said hoarsely. 'For everything.'

She was sobbing, staring at John.

'Ana. He's not waking up.' Dornan just needed to ask her one question. 'Ana?'

She waited for his next words, searching his face.

'The way you … looked at him. Did you ever feel like that about me? Or was it love because you needed me? Because the alternative was too much to bear?'

Her eyes flashed with emotion as she stepped back to him, taking his face in her bloody hands. He heard her chest rattle when she breathed and sobbed all at once.

'I looked at you like that,' she implored, her gaze the truest thing he'd ever seen. 'I looked at you all the time.'

'I didn't see it,' he said, his resolve faltering, his gun dropping to his side.

She shook him, and he let her. 'You were too busy looking at everyone else!' she cried. 'All I ever wanted was you, don't you understand, Dornan? All I ever wanted was the man who saved me. He was my everything.'

He wanted to hold her to his chest and never let her go. He wanted to give her fat babies and a house she could feel safe in, and most of all, her freedom. Her own name. He'd always wanted those things for her, but right now, more than ever before, he saw the life they could have had, he saw the baby he'd killed as if it had survived and been born happy, he saw every single thing that would have happened if he'd played a different hand.

He wanted to make it right.

It would never be right.

He staggered back, pushing her away. 'Go,' he said hoarsely.

'Dornan,' she protested, reaching out.

'Go!' He gritted his teeth. 'If you touch me again, Ana, I will grab onto you, and I will never, ever let you leave me. We'll end in blood when I decide, and we'll end together. It won't be pretty. I'll take everything from you, whether you give it to me or not.'

She shrank away like he was fire and she'd burn if she touched him. 'If you loved me, you wouldn't.'

'I loved Juliette!' he roared, and for the first time he let the weight of what he'd done to John's daughter sink into his bones. Fifteen years ago, he'd watched her be born. He'd taken care of her. Today, he'd tortured and raped her and left her for dead. The girl who'd been like a daughter to him. The girl who'd been punished for her father's sins.

Why can't we ever turn back the fucking clock?

Still, Mariana didn't move.

'GO!' he repeated.

And then, just as he'd decided to reach out for her, she turned on bare feet and fled.

Don't chase her. Don't fucking chase her.

Dornan turned slowly away. Every bone in his body screamed to go after her, until he saw John. Fuck. He crumpled to his knees beside his friend, the floor slick with blood, and shook his friend.

'John,' he whispered. 'Johnny Boy.'

Dornan let out a guttural sound, the sound an animal makes when its child has been killed. With much difficulty, he shifted John's dead weight onto his lap, his tears falling down onto his friend's still face, a face now marred with a perfect round bullet hole, smack in the middle of his forehead.

'John,' he whispered. 'Brother. *I'm sorry.*'

He thought of Juliette, then. Of Mariana.

He looked at the gun and thought about blowing his brains out.

It was tempting.

CHAPTER FORTY-ONE

MARIANA

My chest screamed in agony as I tried to draw another ragged breath. Stones and old bits of glass bit into my bare feet as I ran blindly in the night, without any idea of where I was going, if anyone was following me, or what I would do if I ran into Emilio. In the distance, the busy streetlights beckoned through a fog of haze that blanketed my vision.

John. Juliette. He'd killed them. I sobbed as I ran away, every step a jolt that said *turn around*.

Every step reminding me that I was a terrible human being.

Jason was still alive. I'd told him that I would protect him. That I would take him away from all of this, to the safety of a life that would now only ever be an idle thought, a daydream, an ill-placed fantasy.

I was a terrible person, because he'd trusted me, and because I was never, ever going back. I was getting the fuck out of here. My brain had been reduced to the most basic of operations, and it said: RUN.

So I did. Achingly aware that I was out in the open, that if the wrong person cast a glance my way I'd be shot in the back and left to bleed out on the ground, I kept running.

Headlights loomed in the distance.

Fuck! They'd found me. Dornan had changed his mind. Emilio had put his men on the scent. Something. All I knew was, I'd been found, and my brief taste of freedom was coming to a close.

'Mariana,' a self-assured voice called out.

I froze.

'I know you can hear me.'

'Go away,' I said, wincing as the soles of my feet bled.

'Come on,' Lindsay said, holding out his hand as he drove alongside me.

I shook my head, sticking to the pavement. No. I wouldn't go with him. I couldn't trust anyone. All people ever did was lie and cheat and spill blood like it was nothing. But it wasn't nothing. How much more blood would be taken from me before I'd be empty? How many more wrong moves?

'I'm not going with you,' I said, his eyes and the headlights appearing in double as the world started to spin around me. I stumbled and fell to my knees, and suddenly there were warm hands on my shoulders.

'Come on,' Lindsay said, draping his suit jacket around me as he led me to his car. 'I'll keep you safe. I promise.'

'Where?' I argued, too weak to fight him. 'In prison?'

He opened the back door of his Escalade and bundled me in, laying me across the backseat. 'I'm not taking you in, Mariana,' he said softly. He closed the door, and a moment later he was jumping into the driver's seat.

It took me a moment to register the words. 'Then where *are* you taking me?'

He pulled away from the kerb, and I lay on my back across the leather seats, the car accelerating so fast it was like we were flying.

'To a safehouse,' Lindsay murmured as he navigated traffic. 'There's someone waiting for you there, and I promise you, you're going to want to meet him.'

CHAPTER FORTY-TWO

LUIS

I met my mother for the first time when I was born. Briefly, and then I waited another fourteen years to meet her a second time, inside the walls of an FBI safehouse.

She was younger than I'd imagined, but when she raised her eyes to mine, I saw all those lost years in her stricken expression. Her bare feet were cut and bleeding. Her dress was torn and she was covered in blood.

They say you can never remember the first moments of your life. That it's impossible for the brain to be able to store that kind of information. But there are some things that transcend the realm of possibility, some algorithms too complex for us to explain away with just science. The nights I had spent looking at my mother's faded photograph paled in comparison to this moment, this flesh and blood, and *blood-covered* woman who sat before me, as if she'd just fought a battle and barely made it out alive. Maybe she hadn't made it out entirely. Her eyes were sad. They said she'd lost something very dear to her. That she'd left something behind.

'Mariana,' the FBI agent said, grasping one of her hands and placing his other palm on my shoulder. 'This is Luis. He's been waiting a long time to meet you.'

My mother started to cry, and it hurt inside my chest that she was so upset. What had happened to her? Had she been trapped somewhere? Had she just escaped?

'Don't cry, Mama,' I said, my throat tight. I was fourteen years old, and I didn't cry. I wouldn't cry. But in front of my mother? I wanted to crawl into her lap and cling to her and never let her go.

Her eyebrows rose in disbelief when I said *Mama*.

'Luis?'

There are some things that cannot be explained. A child can't remember his mother's voice from the day he was born. And yet ... 'Your voice,' I said. 'I remember your voice.'

That made her cry harder. I chewed on the inside of my cheek. I didn't want her to cry. I wanted her to speak so that I could hear her voice again.

We sat in stunned silence, observing each other.

'You look exactly like your father,' my mother said to me.

I nodded. It was true, I did. I'd seen the photographs. I was his spitting image.

'But I have your eyes,' I said to her.

She blinked fat tears, tears that wound a line through the dried blood and the dirt on her cheeks. It was incredible. Like the warrior I'd always envisaged her to be, here she was, risen from ashes, this mythical person who, until this moment, had only existed in hope and a faded photograph I carried around with me like it was my saving grace.

Agent Price nudged me, pointing at the empty seat next to this woman he called Mariana. I stepped over and sat down so that I was next to her.

My mother dropped the agent's hand and turned to face me, stretching her fingers towards me ever so slowly, almost as if I might disappear if she moved too fast, like smoke on the wind.

'Can I?' she asked hesitantly, her eyes darting to my hands.

I nodded, offering them to her. She took them in her hands, drawing a deep, almost choking breath when our skin met. I hated to be touched, hated to be hugged by my aunt or my cousins, hated to have any affection. My whole life, I'd always felt like a weird kid, the outcast, because I'd just wanted people to leave me alone.

But when my mother studied the ridges on my palms, when she turned them over to look at each finger, at my wrists, when she let my hands gently go and pressed her fingertips against my cheeks, it was like someone had poured a balm onto my skin. I didn't want to shrink away.

'You're real,' she whispered, cupping my chin in her hand.

I nodded, squeezing her wrist with my hand.

'I'm so sorry,' she said, 'that I ever let you out of my sight.'

She wrapped her arms around me and squeezed, and we stayed that way for a very long time. It was nothing like I imagined it would be. It was so much better.

After a long time, the agent cleared his throat. 'I'm sorry,' he said. 'It's time for me to take you both, now.'

'Where are we going?' my mother whispered.

I saw him glance at me before his gaze settled on my mother.

'Home. You're going home.'

CHAPTER FORTY-THREE
DORNAN

There was a hollow feeling in Dornan Ross's chest that he just couldn't seem to shake. He'd tried to fill it with so many things over the years, with fucking and money, and little lines of flake that made his brain spark and bubble but left him with a hideous comedown afterward. He tried to fill it with children, and wives, and control.

He tried to fill it with everything he fucking could, but it was like a black hole, and it demanded to be fed, and it never, ever fucking closed up. It was never full. It was never sated. It just got bigger, and greedier, until one day, it swallowed him whole.

All these things occurred to him as he watched six Gypsy Brothers lower John Portland's coffin into the earth. The day was brilliant, the normally hazy Los Angeles sky clear and blue. Sweat gathered around Dornan's collar as he tugged at his tie. It seemed like far too nice a day to bury the best friend you'd murdered. He glanced across to the second slightly smaller coffin that contained John's daughter's remains. Yes, the sky was much too blue to be burying the girl he'd once thought of as his own.

CHAPTER FORTY-FOUR
MARIANA

COLOMBIA, 2014

'Lindsay,' I said, smiling broadly as two machine-gun toting guards flanked me – one male, one female. You could never be too careful when the world believed you were dead. Especially when you alone controlled an eighty-something per cent stake in the South and Central American cocaine trade. 'It's been a long time.'

Lindsay smirked back at me, raising his arms as Guillermo patted him down for weapons or wires. I might have been happy to see my old FBI handler, but that didn't mean I trusted him. Men – especially extremely attractive men – were not to be trusted.

After finding nothing, Guillermo slapped him hard on the back and Lindsay lowered his arms to his sides.

My two guards, a black-belt badass by the name of Maria, and a hulk-sized Colombian called Alejandro, followed Guillermo out of my sitting room, the door closing behind them.

Lindsay shoved his hands in his suit pockets and paced the length of the large room where I spent most of my time. It's not that I was afraid to go outdoors, but it was summer in Colombia, and as soon as I went outside my flesh turned an angry red. For a native Colombian, it was annoying that I could no longer tolerate the sun in my own country, but ten years spent largely indoors had made my skin and my eyes incredibly sensitive.

'You haven't been here in months,' I said.

Lindsay threw his hands up in mock frustration. 'You won't let me see you.'

'I let you today.'

He laughed.

'You look beautiful in that dress,' he said in Spanish. He spoke the language almost as well as I did, a girl who was born and raised speaking the mother tongue.

'Thank you,' I replied, in English, smoothing down the black dress I wore. I would only address him in English, which annoyed him greatly, since he'd learned the language purely to impress me. I didn't need his silver tongue or his sweet Spanish adorations turning me soft. I knew he wanted me; I wanted him, too, and it had been a very long time between lovers. The last man I had slept with was Dornan. But I couldn't trust anyone, and so I was alone.

It was easier that way. Men only broke your heart. Burrowed in and settled, and then shattered you from within.

My heart was mine alone. It belonged to my children. No man would ever breach its solid walls again.

'Uncle!' Adelita cried, her long, messy hair flying behind her as she ran into the room and barrelled straight into Lindsay.

His eyes lit up, a smile he only smiled for her. They were not related to each other in any way, and they didn't see each other for months or years at a time, but Adelita loved Lindsay as if he were her family.

My darling Adelita. Almost six years old now, and beautiful, a female version of her father.

The blue eyes. The wide cheeks and angular cheekbones. The dirty blonde hair, thick and impossible to untangle. They have the same toes, the same fingers. Until the day I gave birth to her, I did not know who her father was. Whether I'd carried a part of Dornan or a part of John for nine dangerous months, as I fled and hid and swelled with a baby I was terrified to bring into my chaotic existence, where we'd be forced to live in the shadows until fate caught up with us.

I loved her anyway, my baby girl. I didn't care who her father was. I didn't hope one way or the other, because despite everything, despite the blood and the lies and the betrayal, Dornan had let me run. *He had let me go.* Even as I hated him bitterly for everything he'd done – for murdering John, and Juliette, for beating me so badly that I'd miscarried the baby that was his – I still loved him, deep down, somewhere where the light could never quite get in, in the dark. I loved him because he let me go free.

But when I'd given birth in a makeshift hospital room inside an FBI safehouse, Lindsay by my side, Luis pacing anxiously in the hallway, I'd known. My Adelita had cried, and before they'd even placed her wet, howling little body on my bare chest, I saw a tuft of her blonde hair sticking up, and I knew she was John's daughter.

'Lindsay, are you staying for dinner?' Adelita asked.

He shrugged his shoulders, looking to me. I nodded. 'Of course I am!' he said, wrapping her up in another hug, her little face pressed up against his neck. For a moment I imagined Lindsay was John and my throat ached.

'Why don't you go play, *bebe*,' I said to Adelita. 'We need to talk for just a minute. Can you find Lindsay some of that cake you baked the other day?'

Adelita agreed, skipping off to the kitchen in search of cake. That would keep her busy for at least a few minutes, and I could figure out what Lindsay was here for. Once she was gone, I gestured to the couch. 'Sit. You want a drink?'

'Please,' he replied, sitting down.

I went to the large oak cabinet that ran along one wall, and selected a bottle of whiskey. I grabbed two tumblers and poured us each a double, because from the look on Lindsay's face, we were going to need it. I handed one to Lindsay and sat beside him, waiting for him to speak.

'You look pale, Ana,' Lindsay said finally, his smile shrinking. 'You look tired.'

I smiled, despite myself. 'Your eyes look heavy,' I said quietly. 'Like they're weighed down with a terrible secret.'

He looked at the floor, a self-deprecating smile reappearing on his lips. 'You always did know how to read me,' he said.

'What is it, Lindsay? What is so important that you had to come to Colombia to tell me?'

He lifted his head and met my eyes again. 'We raided the Gypsy Brothers' clubhouse. We found a fingerprint in Dornan's room. Juliette Portland's fingerprint.'

I stared at him in horror, disbelief settling into my chest like an old friend. There was a chance that John's daughter – Adelita's half-sister – was still alive?

'It's old. It has to be,' I breathed.

'It's a fresh fingerprint, Mariana. We have reason to believe that, *somehow*, Juliette is alive. And she is with the Gypsy Brothers.'

EPILOGUE

MARIANA

When I was a girl, I'd dream about marrying my king.

When I met Esteban, I knew. I knew he was the one for me. Something about the way he looked at me seeped into my bones and settled there. Warm. Familiar. I loved him so much, there was this constant ache in my chest.

I was nineteen when I felt him take his last breath, in my arms in a dirty alley. My life was over. I thought I'd die, too.

I didn't. That heart of mine kept beating and aching, missing my lover, missing our son.

When I was a girl, I'd dream about marrying my king.

I never thought Dornan Ross would end up my king. But he did. He made me his queen.

I didn't want it.

He didn't care.

Our wedding night was spent in a hotel room in Vegas, with me locked in the bathroom, staring at the wall as he threatened to smash the door down and then beat my head in.

He'd already killed our child. I wasn't going to let him get inside me again. Wasn't going to let him poison me.

I wasn't going to let him corrupt me ever again.

It didn't matter. He broke the door down eventually.

He got inside me again.

And that's where he stayed, until the bitter end.

Because of all the things in life, love is the most confusing. The most all-consuming. The reason we breathe, the light in our darkness.

At sixteen, love devastated me, his perfect button nose and sweet baby smell overwhelming as my father took him from my arms and into the night.

At nineteen, love saved me, a dangerous man with a heart that was determined to own mine.

At twenty-nine love almost freed me ... but in the end, love broke me.

I wish I could tell you that things ended differently – but I'd be lying. I don't know if he regrets what he did, or if he's happy, but it doesn't matter, really.

It doesn't change the fact that the man who loved me ended up being the same man who would destroy me.

ACKNOWLEDGEMENTS

So many people have been instrumental in making this series come to life. Firstly, thank you to my family. I love you to the moon and back. You always inspire me to keep going when the going gets tough.

To Anna and Gem at Harpercollins. Thank you for picking up *Seven Sons*, reading it and 'getting' what I was trying to do. For understanding my style of storytelling, and for not running the other way when you began to read of Dornan and Mariana and the Gypsy Brothers. You've helped me bring to life an entire backstory that began as a throwaway comment and which, when finished, will span sixteen years of storyline and over two hundred thousand words of story.

To Kathy, Anna and Deonie, my editing dream team at HarperCollins: Thank you for your exhaustive, detailed edits. Thank you for pushing me to do my best work. Thank you for forcing me out of my comfort zone. My writing is so much stronger because of you all.

To my dear friends, for always being there for me. You know who you are.

To every single person who reads the stories I write — thank you, a million times, thank you. You allow me to project my stories onto the cinema screen inside your mind, and there is no better feeling for a writer than hearing how a story affected a reader. Without you, I'd be lost.

DISCOVER THE WORLD OF
LILI ST. GERMAIN

For exclusive content, articles and updates, sign up to Lili's newsletter here:
www.lilisaintgermain.com/newsletter

www.lilisaintgermain.com
@lili_stgermain
lilisaintgermain